THE FOLLY BEACH
MYSTERY COLLECTION

Folly Beach Mysteries

Folly

The Pier

Washout

The Edge

The Marsh

Ghosts

Missing

Final Cut

First Light

Boneyard Beach

Silent Night

Dead Center

Discord

THE FOLLY BEACH
MYSTERY COLLECTION

BILL NOEL

ISBN: 978-1-942212-97-3

Enigma House Press
Goshen, Kentucky 40026
www.enigmahousepress.com

BONEYARD BEACH

PROLOGUE

"Beauty is in the eyes of the beer holder!" rang out one more time on the boat crammed with eleven of my fellow college students. I clasped my hands against my ears. How many more times would I have to hear it before my brain exploded? How had I let Cleveland talk me into going on the euphemistically-named "moonlight marsh educational activity" when everyone knew that it was an excuse to get away from the pressures of tests, studying, and boring professors? More importantly, it was an excuse to get smashed.

If I had any doubt about the intent, it was clarified when the guys lugged three large maroon and white coolers down the pier and hefted them onto the twenty-five foot long Carolina Skiff with letters on the hull announcing to all but observers with severe cataracts that it was *MAD MEL'S MAGICAL MARSH MACHINE*. This was my last chance to let reason prevail and scamper off the pier and hitch a ride back to the college library to study for Dr. Hansel's test. I'd turned to go when Cleveland came up behind me, put his arms around my shoulders and said, "Drew, ready to party?"

He didn't wait for my answer as he led, nearly shoved, me toward the boat, stepped around an old bald-headed guy, dressed in camo gear, who I would have guessed from a mile away was Mad Mel, and then deserted me to grab a beer. I didn't drink, but didn't dare ask if they thought to bring anything non-alcoholic on the "educational activity."

Thirty minutes, or about twenty renditions later of the obnoxious 'beauty is…" chant, on a boat now cluttered with two- dozen empty beer cans, the captain slammed the bow of the skiff onto the beach.

"Holy crap!" a classmate yelled. "We've landed on the moon."

He was 239,000 miles off—see, I do pay attention in class—but I understood what he'd meant. The sand was dotted with large, white, windswept trees, straggly vegetation, and other than the nonsensical sounds and laughter from the boat, dead silence. The sun was on its descent behind the trees and their eerie shadows reached out to the boat like a witch's talons drawing us in.

We had reached our destination and half the group bounded over the side to the wet sand. One of the coeds landed in water that lapped over her feet. "Shit!" she yelled and high stepped it out of the surf. The student behind her laughed, not the sympathetic response the tennis-shoe-soaked coed had hoped for.

Six guys lugged the coolers over the side and staggered, more from beverages consumed on the journey than from the weight of the coolers, up the small incline to where the sand met native vegetation. The rest of us—yes, even I—followed the coolers like ants following the lead ant dragging a cake crumb.

"Halt!" Mad Mel bellowed. "Before you go farting around and doing whatever worthless college students do, this craft is departing at twenty-two hundred. Be here! If you don't have a moon beam, stay with someone who does. It'll be dark in ninety minutes."

Charming, I thought, and wondered how he'd managed to book any tours. Two guys were mumbling something about when twenty-two hundred was and two gals were giggling about finding the nearest porta potty. And, Timothy, standing beside me, asked what a moon beam was.

I said, "A flashlight."

"Why didn't Rambo say so?"

I didn't have an answer and it didn't matter because Timothy had already beelined it to the cooler. Once again, I wondered why I had come.

I'm not naïve to the ways of my fellow College of Charleston students; after all, I'm a junior and live in a dorm, but I'm also a loner by nature, and have never been one to get caught up in the partying that is as normal in colleges as student loans and all-nighters. I stepped away from the crowd and realized that I only knew four of the eleven students and would consider none of them friends. I knew the names of four guys because I'd met them while attending Gay-Straight Alliance meetings. Yes, I'm gay. It's no big deal and I don't flaunt it. I don't march in gay pride parades; I don't have any interest in crusading for gay rights or protesting intolerance. Most people who know me casually don't know anything about my sexual persuasion. For that matter, they don't know my religion, my political affiliation, or whether I prefer hamburgers to hot dogs. I'm a loner who happens to be gay.

I'm also an observer and would rather listen to a conversation than participate in it. That's why I'd chosen to move to the edge of the vegetation, sit on one of the horizontal branches of a sun and sand whitewashed oak and observe: observe my fellow students attack the beer cooler, observe the historic Morris Island lighthouse off shore as only the top third benefited from the setting sun, and observe the seagulls as they circled the exposed sandbar in front of the lighthouse.

I also observed two guys as they walked away from the others, stepped over two of the downed trees, and disappeared down a path toward the marsh. They were backlit by the sun, but I could tell that they had been strolling hand-in-hand.

A little later, I was in the same spot, a hundred yards from the coolers, and the sky had gone from bright orange, to a muted blue-orange with darkness soon to follow. There were three people gathered around the coolers like they were afraid that a band of marauding pirates would sneak ashore and steal the beer. The boat hadn't moved and I saw Mad Mel's silhouette as he leaned against his Magical Marsh Machine. I couldn't see anyone else, but the sounds of laughter and an occasional whoop in the distance let me know that there wouldn't be beer left for pirates to commandeer.

I had finally stopped rehearsing my answers for tomorrow's test and had begun relaxing. Participating in this educational activity wouldn't have been on my to-do list, but it wasn't as bad as it could have been.

That was until I heard a rustling sound behind me. I turned in time to see a three-foot long, thick piece of a whitewashed oak branch coming at me. I felt nothing as it slammed my head.

Drew Casey never heard the laughter as his fellow students climbed on board *Mad Mel's Magical Marsh Machine*. He never heard the captain shout, "Everybody here?" Nor did he hear the slurred voices of a few of the students say, "Yes." And he missed hearing their drunken voices chant seven times on the return trip to the dock, "Beauty is in the eyes of the beer holder."

CHAPTER ONE

The pulsating roar of an engine from a retro-styled Chevrolet Camaro, unencumbered by a traditional, sound-deflecting muffler, reached me seconds before someone pounded on my door. My keen perception told me that my peaceful morning enjoying a cup of freshly-brewed coffee while I regaled in not having to be anywhere was about to end.

I had retired to South Carolina eight years ago. Since then, someone in a pick-up truck and another person in a car had tried to run me down; someone else tried to shorten my life with the sharp end of a pair of shears; I've had a gun pointed in my face more than once; another person had tried to drown me, and a malcontent with a torch attempted to turn me into a crispy critter.

While pondering retirement for several years before I took the plunge, I had devoured nearly every book and magazine article about how, when, and where to retire, and regaled in stories of happy retirees living out their dreams as they rode off into the sunset on a golf cart. As shocking as it may seem, not a single publication had mentioned how many different ways a retiree could be murdered. I should consider writing that book, and I would if I enjoyed reading and writing. I don't.

If I'd spent my life working in law enforcement, what I had experienced may not have been unusual, but give me a break. I was in my mid-sixties, lived on a small barrier island, and owned Landrum Gallery, a tiny photo gallery named after yours truly in an egocentric moment. How dangerous should that be? The closest

I'd ever come to a law enforcement career was during a brief stint as a school crossing guard when I was in the sixth grade.

Now what? I thought as I exhaled and headed to the door to welcome one of my more outlandish friends, and owner of the Camaro.

"Hey Chris, got a question," Mel Evans shoved past me as I opened the door. He rushed to the kitchen and Mr. Coffee.

The new arrival grabbed a mug, poured a cup, and looked around the kitchen like he was looking for Frisch's breakfast bar. My kitchen was the most underused room in my small cottage and he should have been thrilled that I had coffee.

"What's there to eat?" asked the six-foot-one, sixty-year old with a salt-and-pepper, Brillo-pad haircut. He wore woodland camo field pants sheared off at the knee and a leather bomber jacket with the sleeves cut off at the shoulder and a frown that appeared surgically implanted.

"Is that the question you barged in and disturbed my peaceful morning for?" I asked and refreshed my coffee.

Mel's unlikely friend Jim "Dude" Sloan, an aging hippie and owner of the island's largest surf shop, had introduced us. Mel ran a marsh tour business that catered to young adults who wanted to get away from the judgmental crowd and party on the small islands or low-tide sandbars that surrounded my home on Folly Beach, or its better known big brother, Charleston, a stone's throw away.

"No, smart ass, that's not it, but I can't get to it until I've had something to eat."

"Then you knocked on the wrong door unless you want corn flakes sans milk, or M&Ms, or Cheetos."

Mel returned to the living room and I followed. "Considering your culinary options, I long for the good old days back in seventy-three when I joined the Marines. They dropped us from a chopper in the swamp on a five-day training mission and we had to catch and eat bugs, cute critters, and snakes that didn't taste like chicken no matter what they say."

I pointed toward the kitchen and said, "There's been a mouse sneaking in. Have at it."

"Damned rodent'll starve to death in there. Where're the Cheetos?"

Instead of casing the kitchen for Mickey, five minutes later Mel had finished a half bag of Cheetos, gulped down a can of Budweiser Light that he managed to find tucked-in behind a box- wine in the refrigerator, plopped down in one of the kitchen chairs, and belched.

Mel looked at the empty beer can and then around the room like he expected someone to be hiding in the corner, or maybe he's looking for the mouse for dessert. I sat and waited.

"Now the question," he said. "About time."

He waved my comment away. "Let's say hypothetically someone took a dozen kids for a moonlight ride and docked at Boneyard Beach."

Mel hesitated. Boneyard Beach was a desolate area at the north end of Folly Beach that overlooked the historic Morris Island lighthouse.

"Okay," I said and waited.

"The next day," Mel shook his head, "the guy who hypothetically booked the trip calls and says that only eleven of them made it back." He held out both hands and his frown deepened.

I suspected that Mr. Hypothetical had been feasting on my Cheetos and beer. "Did the hypothetical someone stay with the boat or was he on the beach with the group?"

Mel shook his head and then nodded, an incongruous visual message if there ever was one.

"Sort of both," he said.

I again waited, anticipating an interesting explanation.

"He left them on shore and stayed with the craft, except when he hypothetically had to piss. He didn't think that needed to be a group activity, so he went the opposite direction from the sorry-ass students."

I didn't believe that needed a response so I nodded. "Did the hypothetical captain take a head count before he headed back?"

Mel brow furled and he stared at me. "Umm, he sort of yelled, 'Everybody here?'"

"And?" I prompted after Mel's long hesitation.

"Heard some slurred yeses," he said, not more than a whisper. "Then shoved off."

"Anybody say no or act concerned about someone missing when they got to the dock?"

"Not a hypothetical peep."

"Anyone sober?"

"Only the hypothetical captain," Mel came close to grinning, but couldn't get his facial muscles to cooperate. "He didn't want to be a bad influence on today's spoiled, sniveling, rudderless brats."

I hesitated, shook my head, and wanted to ask what kind of influence a marsh boat operator who hypothetically specialized in ferrying groups of *spoiled, sniveling, rudderless brats* to isolated beach parties would have by staying sober.

I resisted and asked, "What did the caller want?"

This time Mel did grin. "Wanted to know if the hypothetical captain found any leftover bodies on the boat this morning."

"No, I assume."

"Affirmative."

"Affirmative to finding a body, or to no?"

"Affirmative to no."

"So," I said, still confused, "What's your question?"

"Think the hypothetical captain might be in trouble?"

"Affirmative."

After my no-brainer answer to Mel's long-coming question, he stared into his coffee mug, and then at his empty beer can. "Got any whiskey?"

"Coffee, white wine, beer," I said.

He shook his head. "This sure as hell ain't a well-stocked advice center."

"There's no shortage of advice, but you'll have to go somewhere else if you want a wider drink selection."

"I'll stick with coffee." He walked over to Mr. Coffee and refilled his mug. "I've got to stop the hypothetical crap. It's too big a word for this old, broken-down jarhead to throw around. It all happened to me."

I made a half-hearted attempt to act surprised. I had met Mel a few years back when a body had turned up in the marsh and a friend of mine had been accused of putting it there. Mel took a couple of us to the site where the body had been found and later helped us catch the killer. The former Marine was gruff, and more profane than I preferred, but I was fascinated with his near- twenty year friendship with Dude Sloan, the sentence-challenged hippie. Dude was as opposite from Mel as two people could be. Mel had mustered out of the Marine Corp after twenty years of serving "your damned country and you'd better not forget it," as he was prone to say. He had moved to Charleston and hitchhiked to Folly on weekends to surf and fell in love with the area. "You think I could be in trouble?"

"What did the kid say after you said that you didn't find a body?"

Mel stood and walked to the window. His white adidas tennis shoes looking as out of place with the rest of his attire as LeBron James at a KKK rally. "The twerp mumbled something about hell to pay, cops, lawyers, lawsuits, and maybe firing squad. By that point, my ears were burning and my focus screwed."

He returned to the chair and put both elbows on the table. "So what do you think?"

By now I had no idea what to think, but did have more questions.

"When did you take the group out?"

He glanced down at his black, stainless-steel Fossil watch with more dials and buttons than a Boeing 747, and then back at me.

"Eighteen-hundred, two hours before sunset."

"And returned?"

He looked back down at his watch like the answers were engraved on the bezel.

"Twenty-two-hundred. Was black as a witch's ... umm, witch's hat."

"What kind of group was it?"

"College students."

The phrase *pulling teeth* came to mind as I tried to drag information out of my friend.

"Why do you think that?"

"They were that age and acted stupid like college students."

"Stupid how?"

"Half were plastered before we left the dock. The whole way to Boneyard Beach they kept chanting, 'Beauty is in the eyes of the beer holder.' They did it over and over, and over and over." Mel gritted his teeth. "I was about ready to say, beauty in my eyes is throwing you twerps overboard."

Mel's career path after leaving the military had taken a rather strange direction for someone who had been accustomed, "brainwashed" according to Dude, to the rigors and inflexibility of the life of a Marine. He went from working for a septic tank cleaning company to buying a struggling marsh tour business from an old-timer who had actually cared about the ecology. Mel piloted the business into a lucrative niche market where none of the customers cared a whit about anything other than having a good time. I smiled when I thought of Mel and college students in the same sentence.

I needed to hear more about the group before offering advice.

"Were they couples?" I asked.

"Good question. Let me think, umm, don't think so. Didn't notice hugging, smooching, or pawing each other. But, I wasn't surveilling them closely and could be wrong. Remember, I wasn't with them on the beach."

"Did you get their names?"

"No need. Only got the name of the guy who booked the trip and paid with a credit card. He was the one who called today. Damned kid's name's Cleveland F. Whitstone." Mel scowled at his coffee mug. "Have you ever heard a snootier name? *F*'s probably for Farnsworth."

I agreed.

"If you're not going to feed me any better and aren't offering better liquoring, think you could get around to dispensing advice?"

Mel wasn't the type to ask for help, and I wasn't sure what he wanted, but it was time to give it my best shot.

"If I were in your adidas, I'd go to the police and tell them the whole thing. It'd be best if they heard it from you than before hearing it from someone else. You don't know what happened, but from what you said, there's a good possibility something did. Something bad."

"You're probably right."

"I'll go with you to tell Chief LaMond."

Chief Cindy LaMond was the head of Folly Beach's Department of Public Safety which included the island's police and fire department. She was also a close friend.

Mel leaned back in the chair. "I can damned well take care of it myself." He folded his arms like, *and that's final!*

I was surprised by his reaction, but shouldn't have been.

Mel was self-sufficient, stubborn, and goal-directed.

"Tell you what you can do," he said after a pause. "I want to go back and see if there's anything to be found."

Like a body, I thought. "Want to go?"

Why not? Mel had never asked for anything and I'd always enjoyed rides through the marsh and its ever-changing look and personality. Besides, he had me curious.

I gave him my best morning smile. "Sure, when?"

"Now."

He stood and looked around the kitchen. "Any grub to go?"

"Not after you inhaled the Cheetos."

"Then grab your gear and let's haul ass."

CHAPTER TWO

Fifteen minutes after I had grabbed my camera and canvas Tilley hat we pulled up to the hand-painted, wooden sign nailed to a sawed-off telephone pole stanchion, announcing *Folly View Marina, Private Property*. The marina was less than a mile off- island and just past the Mariner's Cay condo complex and marina. Folly View had been dubbed the working-man's marina with its weather-worn dock and two dozen deep-water boat slips. Mel undid the rusty chain that blocked the entrance and pulled the growling V8 into the small, tire-rutted parking lot, slammed on the brakes, and skidded to a halt on the crushed shell, gravel, dirt, and weed-covered pavement. We would've made it sooner, but before leaving the island, Mel stopped at the Circle K combination gas station, convenience store, and Subway for three packs of Hostess Twinkies, two packs of Monster Size Slim Jims, and a six-pack of Budweiser.

"Breakfast, the most important meal of the day," Mel mumbled as he used his teeth to rip open the Slim Jims package as we crossed the lot and stepped on the floating dock. The smell of decaying fish thwarted my appetite.

Nine-inch high, black letters reading *MAD MEL'S MAGICAL MARSH MACHINE* on the side of a Carolina Skiff left no doubt about which craft was Mel's. Subtle was not a word I'd heard used to describe him. The boat was docked next to an older, smaller version of his skiff.

Mel nodded to a man working on the neighboring boat's engine. "Morning, Nemo."

"Back to you, Double M," replied the thirty-something, chubby gentlemen about my height at five-foot ten, with a black, Charleston RiverDogs ball cap pulled down touching his ears. He turned from looking at us to the sky. "Don't get wet out there."

A wall of black clouds had gathered in the West. Mel followed the other man's gaze. "They're heading inland. Ain't coming our way."

Minutes later, Mel was navigating the narrow five-mile- long waterway that snaked its way through the marsh behind Folly Beach and opened onto Lighthouse Inlet, the body of water that separated Folly from Morris Island to the north. Mel took a right at the inlet; the iconic, and unfortunately deteriorating, Morris Island Light-house was surrounded by water on our left and the Boneyard Beach to the right.

I leaned closer to Mel and yelled over the roar of the engine. "Who was that at the dock?"

Mel turned his head in my direction and yelled, "What?" I repeated the question.

"Goes by Captain Nemo," Mel yelled. "Real name's Nathan something. He's a competitor. Runs a tiny-assed marsh tour and fishing business. All he does is work on his boat. It's broken down more than it works. Nemo's okay but doesn't say much. Hang on!" Mel yelled over the roar of the boat's huge Evinrude.

Before I could grip the rail, Mel plowed the craft onto the beach.

The bow jerked up as it skidded on shore. My Nikon was strapped around my neck which was the only thing that saved it from leaving the boat ahead of me. Instead, it clanked against the seat and my elbow hit the bulkhead.

Mel heard the camera hit, looked back at me, and smiled. "Told you to hang on."

I looked at my camera; there wasn't any apparent damage, and then glared at Mel. "How about more notice next time?"

Two pelicans had been perched on a log half-in the water and watched our abrupt entrance to their serene environment. One looked at the other and they lumbered off to find a less human-infested resting spot.

Mel ignored my question. "These are the coordinates where we hit land last night." He pointed to his left. "Or it was a little more that way."

I didn't see evidence that anything had been here within the past twenty-four hours. Mel said that it had been low tide so overnight's incoming tide would have obliterated footprints. The beach was thirty yards wide and then patches of sea oats and various marsh weeds began taking over. There was a handful of dead oak trees rising from the sand that reminded me of a horror movie where zombie arms or some Hollywood monster rose out of the earth and grabbed the ankle of an unsuspecting teen. There were more of the twisted, bare, sun, wind, and salt-air bleached oaks closer to the vegetation line. Life had been suffocated out of the trees when the inlet had begun migrating inland over the last 150 years. Life-sustaining freshwater which fed the large trees' roots was replaced by saltwater as the beachfront eroded. From appearances, we could have been on a deserted island. It took little imagination to see how the area had acquired its nickname.

"You going to follow me or stare at those damned trees?" Mel screamed.

He had walked about forty yards from where he had nearly

hurled me out of the Magical Marsh Machine and reached down to pick up two empty beer cans.

"I tried to get the twerps to police the area but it was as dark as the witch's hat I told you about earlier," Mel said as I mushed through the sand to where he was standing. "Let's see if there's more trash." He turned and walked away from the water, hesitated, and turned toward me. "Holler if you find a dead body."

I said that he could count on it and I walked away from him but still toward the thickening vegetation. A rumble of thunder broke the silence and I glanced up. Ominous black clouds were rolling toward us and the short, windswept-shaped trees began to sway with the increasing wind. The distinct smell of rain filled the air.

"Should we head back?" I yelled.

Mel was twenty yards to my left and looking over the lip of a concrete foundation that was one of the remaining remnants of the Folly Beach Coast Guard LORAN station that inhabited the island's north end until 1980. Graffiti artists had adopted the military adage that if it moves, salute it; if it doesn't move, paint it. The military would have gone apoplectic at what was painted on their deserted foundations, but couldn't argue that it'd lacked creativity. Mel didn't find litter from last night's escapade or a body within the foundation's walls and walked to a narrow path that led to the edge of the marsh. He ignored my question; a talent that he had come close to perfecting.

I kept glancing at the darkening sky and at Mel as he walked deeper into the area nearest the marsh. He was focused on something out of my line of sight. I was more focused on the increasing movement of the charcoal-black clouds and thunder that sounded like it was just on the other side of the dune; the clouds that Mel had proclaimed were going inland.

"Damn!" Mel screamed.

During my first week on Folly, I was within a two hundred yards of where I now stood. I had been minding my own business and photographing the sunrise behind the lighthouse when I heard a gunshot and moments later stumbled on the body of a seriously-dead Charleston developer. My dreams of a peaceful retirement were shattered and for the next few weeks my life was turned upside down, not to mention that I was almost killed in the process.

Thoughts of that morning washed over me as I rushed to Mel, a few yards away. Instead of a corpse, I found Mel hopping on one foot and swatting at an army of ants climbing up his leg, chewing flesh as they went. He had trampled on their colony.

I swallowed a smile as he continued to curse and swat the small but painful insects. I also watched where I stepped.

Mel had hopped back to the beach when the storm clouds unleashed a torrent of rain on Boneyard Beach, Mel, the Magical Marsh Machine, and the person who had asked Mel if we should head back.

It took a couple of minutes to dislodge the boat from the rain-drenched sand and back into water deep enough for Mel to start the engine. He spewed a multitude of profanities that he had acquired from twenty years in the military as he navigated through the curvy stream on the return trip to the Folly View Marina. He had pulled his camouflaged fatigue cap down as far as he could on his head to help block the windswept, pelting rain from his eyes. I sat behind him and was glad that my Tilley provided much more protection from the elements. I couldn't help but smile as he continued to elevate his left leg and smack real and imaginary ants.

Other than profanely telling me not to drip on his precious seats, Mel said little on our return ride from the marina to my house. I asked if he had learned anything from the soaking trip to Boneyard Beach.

"Two things," he said as we crossed the new bridge to Folly twenty miles per hour over the posted limit. "Learned that we didn't do a good job policing the area last night, and that the damned rain clouds didn't go where they were supposed to."

I didn't think missing two empty beer cans was a poor policing job, but did think Captain Nemo's weather forecast was more accurate than Mel's. I chose not to mention it to my chauffeur. What I did do was remind him to tell Chief LaMond about the call he had received and what he had remembered about the possibly ill-fated excursion.

"I heard you the first time," he barked.

CHAPTER THREE

I had spent the majority of my working life in the human resources department of a large health care company in Kentucky. Many of the issues I dealt with were contentious, repetitive, and occasionally rewarding; but overall, the corporate environment with multiple layers of bureaucracy was, to put it kindly, tedious. Excitement, adventure, close friendships, and an overwhelming desire to get out of bed and go to the office each day were in short supply. On the other hand, it paid well, had regular hours, and if one didn't mind a rigid, rules-driven environment, it was a pleasant place to work.

And then along came retirement, Folly Beach, and Charles Fowler. Charles was two years my junior, twenty-five pounds lighter, two inches shorter, and had thirty years seniority over me on the quirky island and in retirement. He had moved to Folly from Detroit at the ripe young age of thirty-four and hadn't held a steady job since.

In addition to stumbling on a dead body my first week on Folly, I had met Charles, the man whom I would have bet my life savings on that I would never, yes, never, have become friends with. Thankfully, no one had offered me that bet. For reasons known only to the deities who rule the universe, Charles had become the closest thing I ever had to a brother, confidant, and close friend. Over the years, I had taught him photography; he had taught me how to goof off. I had taught him … well, I can't think of anything else I had taught him; but he had given me countless lessons on not taking things seriously, how to see the good in everyone, regardless of their station in life or degree of obnoxiousness, and how to overcome my lifetime of rigidity.

Charles and I had lived through encounters with murderers, threats and attempts on our lives, and be it through skill or pure luck, we had helped the police put a few evil folks behind bars and in one instance, helped send a murderer to hell.

"So it's final," Charles said. I nodded.

We were sitting in two rickety chairs in the small storeroom, break room, and all-purpose gathering area, behind the showroom at Landrum Gallery.

"September first?" Charles said as he ran his hand through his thinning hair.

"Yes."

"Three and a half months?" he said. One more nod.

Charles leaned back in the chair and I stared at the large, blue, *UTD* on his long-sleeve T-shirt. He looked down at the shirt.

"Like it?" he asked. "University of Texas at Dallas. They're the comets; mascot's called Temoc, that's comet spelled backwards."

Charles owned as many T-shirts—most college and university logoed, and all long sleeved—as he did books and he had as many books as the Library of Congress. I had quit asking him about the shirts years ago, but that had never stopped him from offering tidbits about them.

I lied. "Interesting."

"Positive?"

I figured he wasn't making sure that I thought his shirt was interesting and was verifying that the gallery would be closing in September. Charles was good at many things; at awkward transitions, he was exceptional.

"Yes," I said. "We've been over this many times and you know I can't continue to lose money. It's time."

"And we're only going to open Saturday and Sunday until then?"

We had also had this discussion more than once. Charles figured that if he said it enough times, I'd change my mind. When I opened the gallery seven years ago, he assumed the position of sales manager. I say assumed, because I had never asked him to work here nor had I paid him a dime for the work he'd done. He'd said he preferred it that way so he wouldn't have to deal with the "Feds" which meant the Internal Revenue Service. A while back he promoted himself to executive sales manager. From what I was paying him, I was in no position to object.

"Yes," I said to the Saturday and Sunday question.

He closed his eyes and lowered his head. "Okay," he whispered.

I felt like a heel.

My cell phone rang and yanked me out of my misery. "Morning, Cindy," I said, after seeing *Cindy LaMond* on the screen.

"Don't think I agree," Chief LaMond said. "I'm sitting in my car at the end of the road on the old Coast Guard property. Sweat's running down my face, the danged sun's in my eyes, my polished shoes are all mucked up with wet sand and my socks are speckled with sandspurs." She took a deep breath. "And, oh yeah, I just got finished ogling a stinky corpse. And you want to be cheery?"

This was not the way I wanted to be distracted from Charles's distress over the gallery's closing. I knew precisely where Cindy was. A locked gate at the end of East Ashley Avenue stopped public vehicles from accessing the former Coast Guard property, but police and fire officials could unlock it and proceed to the end of the paved road and the beach. She was also no more than three hundred yards from where Mel and I had stepped ashore yesterday.

"A drowning?" I asked as calmly as I could muster. Charles looked up from the table and stared at the phone.

"Let me think," Cindy said. "Body's fifty yards back from the high-tide line; it's up a path from the beach to the marsh; in the middle of some straggly old trees. It's half covered with a bunch of palmetto leaves; and, oh yeah, his head's smashed in. Drowning, don't think so, but hey, I'm only the lowly police chief. COD will come from folks with a higher pay grade and medical-school learnin'."

"You said *his head*, so it's a guy," I said.

Charles leaned close to the phone and struggled to hear Cindy's side of the conversation.

"Can't slip anything by you," she said.

I tapped *Speaker* on the phone so Charles wouldn't fall out of the chair listening.

"How long's he been there?" I asked. "Know who he is?"

"The ME's here now and thinks not more than a couple of days, but will have a better idea later. Don't know who he is, no ID on the body."

"Age?" I asked and gave a silent prayer that he was an old man.

"Early 20s. Listen, Chris, I've got to go. I knew you'd want to know since you're such a Nosy Nellie."

"Quick question," I said. "Has Mel Evans contacted you?"

"No, why?"

"Just wondering," I said, knowing she wouldn't believe me. I heard the muffled sounds of someone talking to Cindy.

"On my way," she said to the other voice.

"Don't forget the party tonight, Chris," she said and was gone.

I won't, I thought, but it wasn't the party I was thinking about.

CHAPTER FOUR

easons—excuses—to have parties on Folly Beach have been footloose and plentiful. St. Patrick's Day, Fourth of July, local events like the Sea and Sand Festival, Folly Gras, or special events like "I saw a dolphin, let's celebrate," or "Clint's got a case of beer, party's on," can gather a crowd. So I wasn't surprised when Cindy's shorter-half, Larry, had called to invite me to a *zero party*. I didn't ask what it meant, I'd asked when and where.

Three days before the event I had run into Cindy at Mr. John's Beach Store and she told me that the *zero party* was to celebrate two memorable birthdays that ended in zero and which fell within two weeks of each other: Cindy's 50th and Larry's 60th. They had decided to host the party since they figured no one else would appreciate the calendar-unique event as much as they would. I told her that it wasn't true, but we both knew that she was right, and besides, she had the nicest yard for parties of anyone I knew.

The evening was cool for May so I walked six blocks to the LaMonds's home on East Indian Avenue. Cindy and Larry moved into the attractive, elevated, house five years ago when they got married. Behind it was their private, narrow wooden walkway that traversed a section of the marsh and ended at the Folly River. The house would have cost much more than the local hardware store owner and a public servant could afford but Larry had inherited the property from Randolph Hall, who had owned Pewter Hardware until he left it to Larry fourteen years ago. If Hall had lived anywhere other than on Folly, he would have been considered eccentric. In addition to owning the hardware store, Hall had inherited a fortune, had no living relatives and left the store and house to Larry and the balance of his estate to area animal shelters. Larry had tried to turn down the more-than-generous inheritance, but Hall had crafted his will so Larry couldn't disclaim the store, nor could he sell it for ten years. Larry had hidden it well, but he was embarrassed by the windfall and felt that he hadn't deserved it. I heard voices coming from behind the house and walked around to the backyard instead of going to the front door.

Several people were gathered on the large, crushed-shell patio. White smoke poured out of a high-end, stainless-steel gas grill at the far corner of the yard. Larry waved smoke out of his face and was swinging around tongs that were as long as his arm. He wore an apron with *Hell if I know if it's done!* in red script on the front. Larry was five-foot-one in elevator sneakers and had often been asked if he'd been a jockey. He hated horses and had learned over the years to smile and say no, rather than spew insults. The apron ended at his white socks. He looked flustered but by holding the tongs showed that he knew more about cooking than I did. I wasn't inclined to offer assistance.

Cindy leaned against the wooden rail on the pier and was talking to Brandon, Larry's only full-time employee, and to a tall, trim couple I didn't know. Cindy saw me at the corner of the house and waved me over. I shook Brandon's hand and Cindy introduced me to her next-door-neighbors, the Muenstermans. I suspected that they had passed the zero milestones that the party was celebrating.

"I see Larry has things under control," I said with a grin.

Cindy laughed. "I gave him one rule before he started the grill. It had to be at least twenty feet from the house. I didn't want my fire department showing up."

"New grill?"

She looked at the smoke billowing from the appliance. "It's debut, special order. He got a humongous discount because he buys a bunch of cheaper models from the company. In my government world, it's called a bribe. In addition to bellowing boss smoke signals, that one's supposed to do everything including getting cable TV and all thirty-seven ESPN channels." She shook her head.

"Hope it can cook burgers," I said.

Cindy continued to watch the smoke. "It's no accident that I have Woody's Pizza on speed dial."

Brandon excused himself and left to help Larry, and the Muenstermans drifted toward the bar.

"Where's Karen?" Cindy asked.

Karen Lawson was a detective in the Charleston County Sheriff's office and the woman I'd been dating for four years. She was also the daughter of Folly's former police chief and current mayor, Brian Newman, a fact that occasionally made my life interesting.

"She left this morning for a two-week training session in Charlotte. Something about making her a better detective."

"I doubt that's possible. She's already the best the sheriff has."

Cindy's Folly Beach Department of Public Safety provided police services for the town but the county sheriff's office investigated the more serious crimes on the island. Karen had handled all the major crimes on Folly until about two years ago, when politics and petty disputes raised their ugly heads and in his infinite stupidity, the sheriff decided she shouldn't work cases where her father was chief and now mayor.

"Speaking of detectives," I said, "know more about the body?"

"Not . . ." she looked over my shoulder toward the corner of the house and interrupted herself. "Holy crapola, he came."

I turned, followed her gaze, and echoed, "Holy crapola!"

"Come with me," Cindy said as she pushed herself away from the wooden railing.

"What's he doing here?"

"In a moment of monumental foolhardiness, I invited him," Cindy said and smiled in the direction of her newest arrival, Brad Burton, and his wife, Hazel.

Brad had retired from the sheriff's office six months ago and moved to Folly. In what must have had the irony-gods giggling, the Burtons became my next door neighbors. I had had one brief conversation with Brad since they moved, but had never spoken to Hazel. She had spent most of her time preparing their house in Charleston to be sold. During Burton's last few years as a detective, our paths had crossed several times, none positive. He had been Detective Lawson's partner and investigated the murder that I had stumbled across eight years ago. He pegged me as the murderer and had never forgotten that he was wrong. I had stuck my nose in his business on few occasions since and he had treated me with disdain. From my perspective, he had been a terrible detective; he was lazy, rude, and all-around incompetent. To reach the rank that he had achieved, he had to be better than I'd speculated, but it seemed that the closer he'd come to retirement, the closer he had come to worthless.

Cindy reached to shake his hand. "Welcome Detect …Brad."

"Thanks for the invitation, Chief," he said as he shook her hand. "Meet my wife, Hazel."

"Nice to meet you, Hazel. Please call me Cindy."

I stood a few feet behind Cindy and watched her exude more charm, smiles, and slobber than I had ever seen from her. I got a sugar high from watching.

Brad noticed me standing behind Cindy and offered a weak smile. Hazel walked over. "Hi, Chris, I'm Hazel. I've seen you in the yard but haven't had a chance to talk. Brad's told me a lot about you."

I followed Cindy's lead and smiled. "I bet he has."

We spent a few seconds talking about the weather before Cindy pointed the Burton's toward the bar and told them to help themselves.

Cindy took my elbow. "Let's check on Chef Emeril LaLarry. Looks like a forest fire over there." She led me toward the grill. "Honest, I only invited Burton because he was new here and had been a cop."

A cop who had no use for the Folly Beach force, I thought.

"Who would've thought he would come?" Cindy continued before we reached the grill and Larry who waved smoke out of his face and coughed.

"How can you tell when these little buggers are done?" Larry asked as Cindy joined him in waving the smoke away.

I hadn't realized how prophetic his apron was.

Cindy took the mitt from the alleged chef and lifted the top of the oversized grill. More smoke bellowed out and twenty-five former beef patties appeared through the smoke. They were about thirty seconds from cremation. I'd seen juicier charcoal briquettes.

"Dear," Cindy said, and gritted her teeth, "I believe these were done five months ago." She turned the grill off and turned to me. "What'd I tell you about Woody's?"

Larry shook his head. "The freakin' sales rep didn't tell me that this thing'd get hot enough to start a nuclear reaction."

Larry and Cindy conferred and she called Woody's to order half-dozen pizzas and then announced that the smoke-signal exhibition was over and that everyone should grab another drink and that food would arrive shortly.

I left the hosts discussing how the grilling had gone astray and walked over to Cal Ballew, a former country music "star" who owned one of Folly's more popular bars, officially titled Cal's Country Bar and Burgers. He had an uncanny resemblance to Hank Williams Sr., wore a sweat-stained Stetson that had travelled thousands of miles with the six-foot three inch crooner, during his forty-plus years touring bars, nightclubs, and anywhere else that would allow him to perform. His lone hit record was on the charts in 1962. In the spirit of Folly-fashion, Cal's Stetson was complimented by a faded-black golf shirt, shamrock-green short shorts, and cowboy boots. I counted Cal as a good friend.

"Where's your guitar?" I asked as he dangled his arm over my shoulder.

Cal was known to start singing country classics wherever two or more people were gathered.

"Arthritis in my strummin' fingers. Old age is travelling by jet; used to come by train. Way too fast, way too fast. I moseyed past another big *zero* birthday last year."

"Seven?"

He nodded and bowed.

Cal leaned closer and asked if the latest arrival was Detective Burton. I told him yes and that it was now Brad Burton. Cal said thank God and looked toward the river. "What do you know about the body they found?"

I cringed and told him not much. That would change for the worse.

Charles, usually the first to arrive at an event and thirty minutes before the announced time, appeared next. He looked around and spotted me and was at my side before I could wave him over.

"What'd you learn about the murder?" he asked.

Words like *hello* and *hi* were nearly extinct on the barrier island and I had begun to feel disoriented whenever I heard a conversation starting with one of them. It had been weeks since I had experienced that feeling.

"Nothing you don't know."

He waved a homemade, wooden cane around the yard; a cane with no apparent purpose other than to be his constant companion. "You're telling me that you've been right here in the chief's yard and haven't cornered her with a passel of questions?"

Somewhere in Charles's vivid, and often disconcerting, imagination, he believed he was a private detective, more accurately, the owner, president, and sole full-time employee of CDA—Charles's Detective Agency. What's more frightening, he thought that I was a part-time employee of his imaginary business.

I took a sip of wine and shook my head while in the back of it I was conflicted by what Mel had told me. I knew if I shared it with Charles, he would have us going off half-cocked and in warp speed trying to solve a murder that was none of our business. I also knew that if Charles learned that I knew something related to the death of the young man, I would need an emotional suit of armor to deflect his wrath. The party was becoming less festive.

"Come on." Charles headed toward Cindy and waved for me to follow.

Cindy was talking to Dude who had arrived while Charles was complaining that I wasn't doing my job and leaving valuable information about the murder on the table. Dude, an expert on all things celestial, both astronomy and astrology, was telling Cindy about her astrological sign and what fate had in store for her. I didn't hear all of her response, but it sounded like she didn't give an "ass's ass" unless it involved losing thirty pounds.

Dude's head moved like a bobble-head doll. "Nope, Chieftress."

Charles squeezed between the aging hippie and in her mind the thirty pound overweight police chief. "Don't mean to interrupt."

"Did too," Dude said. "Me be jawin' with Chieftress. You be steppin' on my words." He folded his arms over his glow-in- the-dark florescent tie-dyed T-shirt. "Word book say that be meaning of interruption."

Charles looked at Dude. "Sorry, you're right." He then turned to Cindy who had stepped back to see the outcome of Dude versus Charles. "Chris wanted me to ask what you know about the murder."

I looked at Charles out of the corner of my eye and shrugged in Cindy's direction.

The chief rolled her eyes. "Listen good, Charles. This is all I'm going to say." She hesitated and waited for him to acknowledge her statement. He gave a slight nod. "The ME says that the victim was killed between seven p.m. and midnight the night before he was found. Death caused by BFT, blunt-force trauma, weapon unknown. The end." She smiled. "Now, party hardy."

Charles tapped the cane on the patio. "Who was he?"

Cindy took a sip of the beer that she had been liberally consuming. "What itty-bitty part of *the end* did you not grast— grasp?"

"Me got it," Dude said even though he wasn't the intended recipient of Cindy's question.

Cindy held out her hand, palm out, in Dude's direction. "See?"

"Yeah, so who was he?" Charles asked, unfazed by Cindy's comment.

"Okay Charles, you win," the chief said. "Here's the skinny. If you tell anyone, I'll deny saying it." Charles leaned closer to Cindy. "I have absolutely, positively no idea who he was. There, you dragged it out of me." She took another swig of beer.

Dude turned from Cindy to Charles and then back to Cindy. "Enough dead-speak. Where be MM?"

Cindy got a puzzled look on her face. "MM?"

"Mad Mel, Mel Evans," I said and was pleased since it was one of the few times that I could translate for Dude. I was usually the recipient of Dude-speak translations.

"Oh," Cindy said. "Guess he's not here because I didn't invite him. Why?"

Dude said, "Gregorian calendar say he be member of zero club. We be partying for zero honorees."

I looked at him with new respect. First because he knew what the Gregorian calendar was and second because it was one of the longest statements I'd heard him make.

"We don't know Mr. Evans that well and didn't know about his birthday," Cindy said. "Sorry. How old is he?"

"MM be the big 780 full moons last week," the surf shop owner said.

I glanced at Charles who said, "Sixty."

"Oh," Cindy said. "If we'd known we would have invited him. Again, sorry."

"Chieftress forgiven," Dude said. "Put MM B-day on calendar on wall to invite to next zero party."

"Good idea," Cindy said.

It was a good answer since Cindy hadn't been around Dude as much as Charles and I had so she didn't know if he was serious, and I doubted that she had a Gregorian calendar on her wall that went out another decade, 130 full moons to Dude.

The aging hippie seemed pleased that he had accomplished his mission, excused himself, and headed across the patio to Larry who was looking toward the road, probably waiting for pizzas.

Cindy watched Dude go and shook her head, a common reaction to my surfing buddy.

"I'm bar bound, want to amble with me?" she asked. Instead of waiting for an answer, she put her arms around Charles and me and led us to the bar.

"Cindy," Charles said as he took a beer out of a tin garbage pail filled with ice and cans of Budweiser, Bud Light, and Coors. "Didn't Brian Newman turn 70 this year?"

She took a gulp of Bud Light and looked at Charles. "That would be a big yes siree."

Charles looked around the patio. "Couldn't he make it?"

"Don't know. He *be* in the same group as Mel: uninvited."

"Why?" Charles asked before I could.

"I didn't invite anyone I work with. I couldn't see an upside of having any of them around in the unlikely, highly unlikely, event that I have some sort of out-of-body experience and do something stupid tonight. Catch my drift?"

Charles raised his can of Budweiser in the air; I did the same with my white wine; and Cindy followed with her Bud Light. We toasted her wise decision.

With fresh drinks in hand, the Eagles singing "One of These Nights" from the outdoor speakers, the *zero* party in full swing, minus Mel and Brian, and with the increasing anticipation of food arriving, it was turning out to be a good night.

That was until Cindy said, "Speaking of Mel, why did you want to know if he'd talked to me?"

Charles's head jerked in my direction. "Yeah, why?"

I ignored him and said to Cindy, "Nothing. He said he wanted to talk to you and I wondered if he had.

"Nope," she said and looked at Larry who was paying the pizza delivery man.

Charles tapped his cane on my foot and glared at me. He knew there was more to my question; after all, he was a faux- detective.

I whispered, "Later."

He stabbed the cane into my foot as the sounds of the Rolling Stones mumbling "Brown Sugar" filled the air. "Count on it."

Arrival of the pizzas made Charles forget Mel and why I wanted to know if he had talked to the chief. Cal, Cindy, Larry, Charles, and I had gathered around one of the never-used, expensive patio tables that Larry had conned another vendor out of so we could feast on hockey-puck, cremated hamburger replacement pizzas. Good fortune, and a lack of chairs at our table, had sent Brad and Hazel Burton to the other table to break pizza bread with Brandon, the Muenstermans, and Dude. I'd be surprised if that combination wouldn't inspire the Muenstermans to put their house on the market.

"Prince, or his name de jour, was singing "Purple Rain," a slight breeze was keeping the temperature comfortable, and Woody's pizza was ten times better than whatever Larry could have produced from the grill.

"Ya'll hear about the .5 club?" Cal asked after we'd refreshed our drinks.

"The what club?" Larry asked and then sipped his martini. I thought it was an excellent question.

"Point 5," Cal said as if it was self-explanatory. "You know, point like a dot and five like the number on the other side of four and shy of six."

"So what the chicken turd does it mean?" Cindy asked, crudely speaking for all of us.

Cal leaned back in the chair and tilted his Stetson up and away from his eyes. "Walkin' group."

I was beginning to think that he was taking anti-verbosity lessons from Dude.

"What about it?" I asked.

"You know old man Carr, don't you?" Cal asked. "Chester Carr?" I said.

"That's the one."

Chester Carr was a friend who was a Folly Beach native. I talked with him a few times when he had worked at Bert's Market, the beach's iconic grocery that never closed, and then we got better acquainted when he befriended Melinda Beale, Charles's aunt who had moved to Folly two years ago, bringing with her unbridled spirit, a refreshing sense of humor, a thrust adventure, and terminal cancer. She left us a year ago and I'm certain that she's now spreading her unique sense of joy to her fellow heavenly residents.

"Walking group," Cindy said. "Chester Carr. Isn't he like 137 years old?"

"Not ninety yet," Cal said. "Besides the group is a bunch of seasoned citizens Chester's herded together. They ain't going to push his speed to heart attack miles per hour."

"What about the group?" I repeated.

Cal looked at each of us. "Thought since some of y'all are aging a bit, you might want to take a gander at joining."

Cindy jabbed Larry in the ribs. "That means you dear. You could use some good exercise besides lifting boxes of nails and hardware-do-hickey things."

"Two questions," Charles said. "Who's in the group?" He held his thumb in the air. "And," he added his index finger to his raised thumb, "what in decimal-world does .5 mean?"

Cal removed his Stetson and set it on the table, wiped sweat off his forehead, and said, "For one, I'm in the group. Then there's Theodore Stoll, Harriet Grindstone, then there's Chris's bud William Hansel, and a new guy named Potsticker or something like that, and four or five others whose names these beers have removed from my memory." He tilted his Coors in my direction.

I had known William Hansel since my second week on Folly when he had been my neighbor until a peeved murderer torched my rental house with me in it. William was one of the few African Americans who called Folly Beach home and earned a paycheck as a professor at the College of Charleston. I wasn't familiar with the others Cal had mentioned.

Cindy chuckled. "Theo Stoll?"

Cal nodded.

"What's so funny?" Charles asked.

Cindy said, "If Theo's in the walking group, .5 means they walk .5 inches a week. A lump of coal'd turn to a diamond quicker than he can cross Center Street. Sure it's the same Theodore Stoll?"

I wondered how many Theodore Stolls there could be on the island.

"Plum sure," Cal said.

Larry had his elbows on the table. "You said some guy named Pot something."

"Yeah," Cal said. "Potstick or Potting soil or something."

"What's his first name?" Larry asked. He had given up on Cal remembering the last name. "Abe, I think. Why?"

"Just curious," Larry said. "More drinks, anyone?"

Charles raised his hand and Larry pointed to the bar. What a great host, I thought.

We spent the next five minutes speculating about the origin of the group's name before Cindy stuffed the last bite of pizza in her mouth and muttered that she'd better check on her other guests. She said that she needed to see if Dude had confused them into a stupor or if Brad Burton was telling them how awful all of us at our table were. Charles said he'd go with her in case she needed an extra set of hands to strangle Burton.

And Larry leaned over and asked if I could stop by his store in the morning. He said he had a problem and may need my help.

If that didn't pique my interest, nothing would.

CHAPTER FIVE

Pewter Hardware was in a seashell-pink, concrete block building with four parking spaces in its tiny lot. The building, located next to the post office, would fit in the lighting section of Home Depot, but if you were thin, and didn't have to pass anyone in the aisle, you could get to most anything there you could need.

I was more than curious why Larry wanted to talk to me, so I was at the store as soon as it opened. Scattered storms were predicted so I drove. That's the excuse I used; the truth was that I was too lazy to hoof it. Brandon greeted me before I'd had a chance to look around and shared that he had a great time at the party but that his head felt like "fifty pounds of cement in a forty pound sack."

I didn't have any hardware store analogies, so I said that I understood and asked where Larry was.

"The boy called as I was unlocking the door. He'll be here shortly." Brandon smiled. "Get it? Larry, shortly."

Larry's diminutive size not only would have been perfect for a jockey but had been perfect for climbing up gutter downspouts and trellises and entering second-story windows. His previous career had been as a cat burglar but he'd given it up at the urging of the Georgia Department of Corrections when as incentive they'd given him free room and board for eight years. That world was behind Larry, but his lack of altitude hadn't changed and provided fodder for jokes—attempts at jokes—from Brandon and others.

I frowned but Brandon had already turned and started straightening water hoses on the endcap near the entry.

I heard Larry before I saw him. That wasn't a short joke. He had opened the door but hadn't stepped in. "Thanks for coming to the party last night," he said and peeked inside and yelled to Brandon, "Can you handle the crowd for a few minutes?"

I was the crowd.

Brandon was in back and yelled that he thought he could. Larry jerked his head in the direction of a small, Folly River Park across the street. "Let's check out the view."

Larry's house backed up to the river and he had plenty of time to check the view, so I assumed it was his way of getting out of earshot of Brandon or the crowd that might descend any moment. We walked up the slight incline into the park and Larry said, "Did you see a semi run over me last night?"

I said no and that I would have noticed and he said that he felt like something gigantic had traversed his head. From my extensive study of this morning's condition of last night's attendees, I think I can conclude that beer retailers had a serious spike in sales the last twenty-four hours.

Larry plopped down on the closest seat at the picnic table. I sat across from him and remained silent. This was his story and I didn't want to clutter his alcohol-jumbled brain with extraneous chatter. He closed his eyes and squeezed the bridge of his nose.

"Have you run across someone named Abraham Pottinger?"

Larry asked as he slowly opened his eyes. "He's been here about three months."

"Don't believe so. Who's he?"

"Blast from the past."

My head didn't hurt as much as Brandon's or Larry's, but that was a bit too cryptic. "Explain."

"I met him in Atlanta in the eighties." Larry stared at the river and seemingly into his past. "I was between careers." He hesitated and then smiled. "Giving up my job at the chop shop after three police raids and transitioning to burglary."

I was one of only a handful of people on Folly who knew about his left-of-legal past before his stint in prison and his move here. To his credit, the first person he told when he had arrived was then chief of police, Brian Newman. He'd said he wanted Newman to know so if anything bad happened on Folly the chief would suspect and want to talk to Larry and that the newcomer would understand and cooperate. At that moment, Newman gained respect far beyond Larry's size and they'd become friends.

I said, "That was a long time ago."

Larry nodded. "I ran into Abe at a scuzzy diner that catered to some of the city's lowest lowlifes. He always wore the latest fashions and talked like an English professor."

Larry paused again and continued to gaze into the past. "What brought you together?" I asked.

"Money."

"Explain," I said a second time.

"Abe's a con man, a damned good one. He could con the tats off Kid Rock. I'd seen him a couple of times in the diner and one day he stopped at my table, said that he needed a partner in a business deal he was working on. I asked him why he was talking to me and he said that he needed someone who appeared to be unsavory and little." Larry smiled. "Half of that, the little part, rubbed me wrong and I told him so. He went in sweet-talk mode and before he was done had me convinced that my size was the next best thing to penicillin. Told you he was good."

"Business deal?"

"He had business cards that said *Abraham R. Pottinger and Associates, Theft Risk Consultants*. He'd approach mid-sized businesses, the ones with some money but not big enough to afford full-time security like mom-and-pop jewelry stores, high-end appliance stores. He'd tell them 'for a one-time, affordable fee' he would conduct a thorough analysis of the business and provide the owner with a foolproof, written plan to prevent theft from outside and from employees."

"Why'd he need you?"

Larry smiled but the lines around his eyes didn't cooperate. "He told me that he was doing okay, but wanted to be able to introduce me to the store owners as one of his associates. He'd point to me and tell them I was a reformed burglar and would be able to bring my expertise to Abe's *thorough analysis*."

"What happened?"

"It sounded good. Hell, I even started believing it. The man could con the Pope into becoming Muslim. Anyway, Abe's affordable fee was up in the thousands and may have been worth it if the service was legit. We sold the proposal to a dozen businesses. Exactly zero of them received a plan."

"I suppose for their fee the businesses learned not to buy a security analysis," I said.

"Good point. Some of the businesses reported the scam to the police and Abe disappeared from my life as quickly as he entered it." Larry rubbed the bridge of his nose again and looked me in the eyes. "Until last week."

"What happened?"

Larry pointed toward his store. "He walked through the door sporting a big, con-artist grin, bent down and gave me a hug, and said how great it was to see me. I nearly threw up; my past stomped on me like a combat boot on a cricket."

"What did he want?"

Larry pounded his fist on the table and took a deep breath. "He said he'd heard that I was here and wanted to stop in and see his *old friend*. He said that he'd turned his life around and was now as straight as a laser. Said he'd moved to the beach and bought a house and planned to spend the rest of his life enjoying the simple things."

"You didn't believe him."

"Not for a nanosecond," Larry said without hesitating. "Once a con man, always a con man."

I didn't remind Larry that he'd turned his life around and wondered if Abe could've done the same.

"Have you seen him since then?"

"No, thank God. He said we needed to get together sometime over a drink and talk about old times. I thought right, *when hell freezes over*."

"What do you want my help with?" I asked, remembering what Larry had said last night.

Larry looked at the table, toward his store, and then back at me. "Remember last night when Cal was talking about the walking group?"

I said that I did.

"Remember when Cal was saying who was in the group? He said that some guy named *Potsticker or something like that* was in it."

I remembered.

"That's mighty close to Pottinger. If it's him, it means nothing but trouble. Trust me."

I'd known Larry for a long time. If he said it meant trouble, it did. "What do you want me to do?"

"Don't know, thinking this up on the fly. Maybe you could join the group and figure out what Abe's up to."

I nearly laughed when he said that I could join a walking group, but realized that if the group was headed by Chester Carr, there couldn't be much walking involved.

"Why me?"

"I trust you Chris. You're good at sniffing out bad stuff and don't jump off the pier until you see it's safe below. If you need to, you can take Charles with you. Will you help?"

No, no way, please no, I thought.

"Of course."

CHAPTER SIX

A knock on the door distracted me from thinking about Larry, his nefarious history, and a guy named *Potsticker or something like that* who could be Larry's past coming to haunt him. The disruption was okay with me since I had no idea what to do about Larry's situation. It was okay until I opened the door.

"Are you Christopher Landrum?" asked a tall gentleman, in his mid-thirties, sporting a buzz cut, a starched-white shirt, slacks with a sharp crease, spit-polished shoes, what appeared to be a new navy blazer, and a frown.

No one outside the Department of Motor Vehicles had called calling me Christopher in the last fifty years, but I said yes.

He handed me a card that indicated that he was Detective Kenneth Adair with the Charleston County Sheriff's Office. "May I come in?"

I figured it would have been rude, and rather unproductive, to have followed my urge and slammed the door in his face. I stepped aside, waved him in, and asked if he wanted anything to drink. He declined, and I asked what I could do for him.

"I have a few questions, Mr. Landrum. Purely routine."

Unlikely, I thought as I suggested that we would be more comfortable in the kitchen, and offered him a seat at the table.

"Do you know Mel Evans?" he asked.

As I looked in the detective's penetrating stare, I decided that it was time to adhere to Dude-mode. "Yes."

Being an astute detective that I suspected him to be, he realized after a few seconds of silence that I was finished.

"Were you with Mr. Evans last Thursday on his boat, the …" Adair took a notebook out of his blazer's inside pocket, flipped through a few pages, and continued, "*Mad Mel's Magical Marsh Machine*?"

"I was."

"What was the nature of your excursion?"

"Mel had taken a group on a, umm, picnic, the night before and it got too dark to see what they may have left on the beach, so he asked if I could help him make sure the site was cleaned up."

I was following the old television detective show line: "The truth, the whole truth, nothing but the truth." Yes, I was skipping *the whole truth* part. I also realized that he was looking at me like he didn't believe a word I was saying.

"Where was this so-called picnic?"

"Out at the end of Folly, an area often referred to as Boneyard Beach."

He leaned forward. "Did you find anything unusual when you got there?"

Like a dead body, I wondered. "Only a few empty beer cans."

He wrote something in his notebook, although I doubted that he would have forgotten *few empty beer cans*. I asked again if he wanted something to drink, and again he declined. I was failing to win him over with kindness.

"How long were you there?"

I smiled. "Until the sky opened up and a torrential downpour soaked us."

His scowl indicated that he didn't see the humor in us standing in the rain. "So how long were you there before the rain?"

"No more than fifteen, twenty minutes."

"And then you returned to the marina?"

"Correct."

"Did Mr. Evans indicate that anything unusual happened during the picnic?"

I was now back *to the truth, nothing but the truth.* "No." Mel had told me that nothing unusual had happened *during* the picnic. "Why?"

He returned the notebook to his pocket and leaned back. "You've been dating one of our detectives."

I didn't hear a question so I sat silently.

His frown broke, but his expression was still professional and didn't disclose anything. "I don't know her well," he said, "but I hear that Detective Lawson thinks highly of you, and that over the years, you've been tangentially involved in some investigations."

I still didn't hear a question, but nodded anyway.

"I wouldn't give this much information to someone I was questioning, but because of your, umm, relationship with Lawson, I'll share that our office has received a missing-person's report about someone who participated in Mr. Evan's excursion."

"Did the person go missing during the trip?"

Detective Adair shook his head. "That's where it gets vague. The person filing the report knows that the alleged missing person, a male, college student, was on the trip but thinks that he wasn't on the boat when it returned to the dock."

"Did anyone else notice him missing?"

"No. I believe that as a result of alcohol consumption, the others wouldn't have noticed even the strangest occurrence."

Adair would have already known about the body on the beach, so he was playing games with me. I wanted to ask if the body had been identified as the student but that would have opened a door that I thought needed to remain closed.

"Who told you that I was with Mel?"

Adair's frown returned. "Sorry, I can't say." He stood. "I believe that's all the questions," he hesitated and then added, "for now."

"Have you talked with Mel?"

"Yes," he said in a tone that indicated that it was all he was going to say. I walked him to the door and he thanked me for taking time to talk and said for me to say hi to Detective Lawson and to call him if I thought of anything else.

Until recently, I had to leave the house to find myself in trouble. It now seemed that trouble came knocking. I was on the phone to Chief LaMond before the detective was out of the drive.

"What now, Chris?" she said.

I hated caller ID. "Wondering if you know the name of the murder victim?"

"Drew Casey. Bye."

"Whoa. Anything else?"

"Oh, thought you asked his name."

"You know better, Chief LaMond."

She giggled. "Sorry, you're just too easy to fiddle with."

I heard her sigh and then she said, "He was a junior at the College of Charleston. Lived by himself in an apartment off-campus. His family's out west somewhere but they've been estranged since he graduated from high school. Reason unknown and no one knows how to contact them. Mr. Casey must have money since he paid cash for his tuition and didn't give the college information on his parents when he enrolled. The name and number he gave for the person to contact in case of an emergency came up a dead end. There was no such number and only about a zillion people in the country with the common name. Seems strange, doesn't it?"

"Yes."

"So, that's it. I'm getting this third hand. As usual, the high-and-mighty sheriff's office is shutting out us little-ole-town, dumb-fuzz folks."

With roughly twenty-five employees, the Folly Beach Department of Public Safety wasn't tiny, but was charged with providing police, fire, medical, and rescue services to the island that can swell to sixty thousand people during peak season; a daunting task that often overwhelms the department's ability to meet its varied obligations. Nevertheless, considering the challenges, Cindy's department performed admirably. There is not always an amiable working relationship between her department and the sheriff's office and information was seldom effectively communicated, causing more conflict.

I thanked her for what information she did have and asked if she could let me know if she found out anything else.

"Chris, you know I live to share confidential public-safety information with you," she said, in her East Tennessee sarcastic tone.

"That's why you're my favorite law enforcement officer on Folly Beach," I said.

"Moose manure." She hung up.

Who told the police that I had been with Mel on his boat? Did the police believe Mel killed the student? Did they suspect that I was part of it?

What have I gotten into?

I was less successful with my next call. Mel's answering machine informed me that he was unavailable and that if I left a number and a brief message that he *might* get back with me. I left him a Dude-like message saying, "Chris here, so was detective. Call," and hoped that would have been enticing enough to get his attention.

I called Charles and was less successful than with my call to Mel. Charles, to add to his list of idiosyncrasies, didn't own an answering machine or cell phone. I listened to his phone ring a half dozen times and gave up.

My stomach began to growl; skirting questions from a detective and two unsuccessful phone calls made me hungry. My cupboard was in its usual state of bare, so I headed to the Lost Dog Café for a late breakfast. The Dog was a few blocks from the house and I could have walked but instead rationalized several reasons why I should drive instead of admitting that laziness trumped them all.

The Dog was a block off Center Street and the most popular breakfast spot on Folly Beach. I expected a long wait after driving around the block twice trying to find an empty parking place. I lucked into a space two blocks from the restaurant and realized that I wasn't much closer than if I'd left the car at home. The Dog was located in a former Laundromat, but you would never have known that the colorful restaurant had ever been anything but the place to get good food, stimulating conversation, and gossip galore. My luck changed when I saw Charles seated on the front deck.

He reached down, picked up his cane and pointed it at the seat on the other side of the small table. He scooted his coffee mug, *Folly Current* newspaper, and Tilley hat over to his side of the table to make room for me.

I said, "Good morning," like most normal people I had known before moving to Folly would have done—remember, remarks like *good morning*, *hi* or *hello*, appeared to be borderline rude.

He said, "Mel, what's the deal? Larry, what'd he want?

Dead guy, what do you know?"

I rest my case. I delayed having to answer the master inquisitor when Brittany, one of the Dog's more cheerful waitresses, noticed me and asked if I was ready to order. I looked at Charles's half-eaten French toast, and said the same. She gave me one of her high-powered smiles, said she'd take care of it for one of her "more handsome" customers, and delivered the check to the table behind us.

"Enough foodie talk," Charles said before Brittany had time to put in my order. "What's up with Mel?"

"Why do you thing something's up?"

"You asked Cindy if he'd talked to her and when I asked you about it you said you'd tell me later." He looked at his wrist where most normal people would wear a watch. Charles, not a full- time resident in the world of normal, didn't own a timepiece but didn't hesitate to imagine one like he imagined so many other things. He pointed his fork at me. "Later just arrived."

Charles was like darkness chasing sunset. At times it took longer to catch it, but it always did. There was no reason not to tell him everything; and perhaps he could shed light on what had happened. I began with Mel arriving at my door and our trip to Boneyard Beach. Charles gave me dirty looks twice and interrupted to castigate me for not calling him and taking him with us. I overlooked his whiny criticism. I proceeded to tell him about the visit by Detective Adair and how I limited my answers to the specific questions he had asked and even then being as brief as possible.

Charles looked around the patio and then back at me. "Thomas Jefferson said, 'The most valuable of all talents is that of never using two words when one will do.'"

Another of Charles's quirks was quoting United States presidents. I had never known if the quotes were real, never cared enough to check, but did know that with the quantity of books he had in his apartment and his proclamation that he had read them all except the cookbooks, that his presidential utterances could be accurate—or not.

I finished describing Detective Adair's demeanor and how I skirted *the whole truth* in telling the detective why Mel wanted to return to Boneyard Beach, when Brittany arrived with my breakfast.

I managed a couple of bites before Charles started with the questions.

"Learn anything about the body?"

I shared what Cindy had told me about Drew Casey.

Charles huffed and leaned toward me. "And when were you going to tell me this?"

My inpatient friend thought that I should tell him about anything that I ever learned that he didn't already know within seconds, or less, of learning it.

"Just did. And, for the record, I called you as soon as I got off the phone with the chief. Guess who didn't answer?"

A large construction truck drove past and the sound of its engine wiped out most of his words. I heard, "Excuses, excuses ... forgive you this time."

I let him mumble as I watched a group of vacationers waiting in front of the restaurant for a table. I avoided eye contact with three different couples who kept looking our direction and wondering if we were ever going to vacate the valuable piece of real estate. Brittany returned with coffee for Charles. The fragrance of freshly brewed coffee filled the air around the table and I continued to avoid eye contact with the antsy diner wannabes.

"So what did Larry want to talk about?" Charles asked, finished for now with Mel's story.

"Seems an acquaintance from his past has come to Folly," I shared what Larry had told me about Abraham Pottinger.

"Is he about Larry's age, wears fancy duds, and looks a little like George Clooney will when he's sixty?"

"Could be. All I know is that he's about the same age as Larry and wore good clothes back when Larry knew him. Why?"

"Seen a stranger around town a few times. The fellow's out of place. Who here wears pressed khaki shorts?"

"Could be," I told Charles that Larry didn't trust Pottinger regardless what he had professed about changing from his life of crime.

"Larry doesn't think leopard-Abe can change his spots?"

"You got it."

"Does Larry remember that he changed his?"

Charles was one of the few on Folly who knew about Larry's past and his life-altering transition to a well-respected business owner.

"Sure, but Larry can spot a problem a mile away. If he has a bad feeling about Pottinger, there's something there."

"Then," Charles tilted his head and nodded, "what does Larry want us to do?"

Us, I thought, but didn't say it because it would have been a waste of a word.

"Cal told me that one of the members of the .5 group's name was something like 'Potsticker.' Larry thinks it's Pottinger." I took a sip of coffee and continued, "If it is, Larry is convinced that he's not in the group for exercise. He's out to con members out of their false teeth, as Larry put it."

"And we're supposed to do what about it?"

"Larry asked me to join the walking group to try to figure out what Pottinger's up to."

Charles chuckled. "You in a walking group. Didn't know Larry was that funny."

I smiled and told Charles that if the group was headed by Chester, I wouldn't have to worry about too much walking.

"Sounds like what the group needs is someone to do some detectin'. When do *we* start?"

CHAPTER SEVEN

The .5 group gathered at the crack of dawn every other day at the Folly Pier. Their dedication impressed me until Chester confessed that "crack of dawn" was nine-o'clock, or two and a half hours after sunrise. Today would be the group's next walk so Charles and I decided to stroll by Chester's house around the time they should be finishing.

My crack of dawn arrived hours earlier than Chester's, and I had time to kill and used my culinary skills and fixed a bowl of Cheerios, and wondered what Charles and I were getting into. What were we supposed to do if the newcomer in the group was Abraham Pottinger? I could picture Charles sidling up to him and saying, "Abe, good buddy, how're you planning to rip off these geezers?"

Charles may not be that direct, but he wouldn't burn too much daylight before finding a way to interrogate Abe. If he was as good at the con as Larry had said, Pottinger would see through Charles's questions and if he had a less than legitimate motive for being here, he wouldn't have to search far to learn that we were friends with Larry. The weather forecast called for scattered showers, so maybe I would luck out and it would rain on Chester's parade and I wouldn't have to face the alleged con artist.

The rain gods had forsaken me. The sky was clear and the temperature mild as the walkers' *crack of dawn* had come and gone. Chester lived on West Ashley Avenue, a block off Center Street, the location of most of the small island's retail establishments, restaurants, and bars. I met Charles in front of St. James Gate, one of Folly's newest restaurants, where today he wore an orange University of Texas San Antonio long-sleeve T- shirt with something that looked like a bird's head on it, blue shorts with ravels on the legs, florescent-red tennis shoes, Tilley hat, and his cane. I was attired in my Folly summer uniform of a faded golf shirt, shorts, canvas Crocs, and a Tilley similar to the one that I had given Charles a few years back.

He pointed to the logo on his shirt. "Get it?"

"Get what? That bird's head?"

"Chris, oh Chris," He leaned against his cane. "I figured that since you're a college graduate you'd know that it's a roadrunner." He smiled. "Walking group. Roadrunner."

I nodded, not because I cared, but to get him to shut up. I changed the subject. "I figure they've had time to get to Chester's. Ready to stroll by?"

"See if I get the plan." He pointed his cane toward our destination. "We're going to say, 'Hey group, you look like you've been out for a walk. Can we stop and jabber a while. Oh, hi stranger, you look like the crook Larry said was over here swindling the life savings out of old folks. We're here to make sure you get locked up for the rest of your dirty, rotten, lying, stealing life."

I bit my lip and tried to keep a straight face. "You've got it."

"Then lead on."

Moments later, Charles and I were strolling by Chester's house when Charles glanced looked over at the screened-in porch where several people were gathered.

He turned to me and in a stage whisper said, "Look, there's Chester." He then turned toward the porch. "Hey, Chester, how're you doing?"

Not inconspicuous, but better than yelling, "Hey, Chester, who's that crook with you?"

"Yo, Charles, Chris. Come join us."

So far our well-thought-out, highly-detailed plan was on track.

Chester opened the screen door and waved us in. He was five-foot-six, mostly bald, chunky, his shape complemented by Coke-bottle-thick glasses, and in the words of Charles's late aunt, "a spittin' image of Mr. Magoo."

"Say hi to our little group of walkers," Chester took a deep breath and gestured toward the five others. Sweat rolled down his face.

"Wobbly Walkers," said a short, attractive lady in a wooden rocking chair nearest the door.

"Silly girl," said a man leaning on the back of the woman's rocker. "We're senior strollers." He leaned his head back, the bill of his black USS Yorktown ball cap pointed toward the ceiling. His way-off-white, sleeveless T-shirt slid off one shoulder as he tried to act insulted by the wobbly walker remark.

"That's ET," Chester said by way of introduction as he pointed to the man who looked about 117, but was no older than 85.

ET shuffled over and shook our hands. "Name's Theodore Stoll, Theo to my friends."

"ET to everyone here," interrupted the rocking-chair lady. Theo looked at her and said, "Huh?"

She smiled at him and repeated what she had said. When he turned back toward us, the lady cupped her hand around her ear and nodded. Got it, Theo's hard of hearing.

Theo nodded and continued. "A term of endearment, after the loveable movie alien." He pulled up his black, knee-high support stockings that now reached his shiny, green jogging shorts.

The lady held her hand in front of her face and giggled. Theo pointed to the rocking chair. "That's Connie DeWalt.

Cute as a button, ain't she?"

Connie was in her mid-sixties but still had the figure of a fifty year old. She nodded in our direction, said "it's a pleasure," and winked at Theo.

"Excuse our condition," Chester said. "We just finished our longest walk ever."

"Where'd you go?" Charles asked.

Chester wiped sweat off his left arm. "Started at the foot of the pier. Too many steps to start on the pier. Walked all the way up to city hall and back here."

It was a distance that could better be described in yards rather than in miles.

"Come meet the rest of the group," Chester said. He stepped around the rocking chair and led us to the wicker chair leaned against the window frame. "Meet David Darnell. He's new to Folly. Moved here and opened an insurance agency."

David unfolded himself from the chair, towered over us with his six-foot-five or so frame, gave each of us a firm, insurance-salesman handshake, and told us that he and Alice, his wife of forty years, had moved to Folly to get away from the rat race and frigid winters in Boston.

"So what do you two do?" he asked.

Charles told him that he was retired, and that I owned the island's best and only photo gallery, but that it was open two days a week, and that quicker than a blink of the eye I was going to close it and deprive the photo-buying public of getting any more pictures. It wasn't how I would have introduced myself but Charles didn't give me time to answer.

I saw a head peak around the talkative insurance agent.

"A couple more to meet," Chester said. "Harriet Grindstone,

these are my friends Chris and Charles," as if she hadn't already heard our names three times in the last five minutes.

Harriet managed to slip past David and firmly shake our hands. She was thin but had a strong grip for someone whom I judged to be around 70. I suspected that her walking clothes doubled her weight.

"The weather's terrible today, isn't it?" she said as way of introduction.

I thought the weather was perfect but I agreed. Charles, the chameleon, also agreed with her, Chester shrugged, and David who was standing behind her rolled his eyes.

"Your friends William Hansel and Cal Bellew are usually with us along with two more irregulars. Life must have gotten in their way today," Chester said, and led us to the other person on the porch we hadn't met."

"Fellows, meet our newest member, Abraham Pottinger." Bingo.

"Pleased to meet you gentlemen. Call me Abe, like Honest Abe," Pottinger said, and rushed to shake our hands.

At five-foot-seven, he was three inches shorter than me, not fat, not thin, had a full head of dyed black hair, and Charles was right, he had a strong resemblance to an older George Clooney.

"Believe I've seen you around town," Charles said.

I didn't tell Pottinger that Charles had remembered him because of his non-Folly attire, which today included Tide-white Nike tennis shoes, pressed khaki shorts, and a white, Brooks Brothers' polo shirt. He looked as out of place as a Maserati at a moped rally.

Abe turned to me. "Thought you looked familiar. Walked by your gallery a few times. I'll stop in the next time I'm that way."

"That's all of us," Chester said, and scooted closer to Abe, Charles, and me. "Want some Kool-Aid? It's our drink of choice. Got Fig Newtons too." He leaned closer and whispered, "Prevents constipation, you know." He pointed to a small round table between the door into the house and a rocking chairs.

"Think I'll have some," Charles said. "Abe, can I get you more

Kool-Aid or cookies?"

Charles was already on the hunt.

Abe declined and Charles made his way to the refreshment table. Chester reached for four chairs that were folded and leaning against the wall, unfolded two of them and said for us to take a load off.

Abe's chair was closest and Charles asked him how long he'd been on Folly. He said a couple of months, and then Charles asked, in a way only he could, "Why?"

"Good question, my friend," Abe said, clasped his hands behind his head, and leaned back. "I was in the theft-risk consulting business out west. Sure, I made plenty of money working with businesses helping them prevent theft from employees and outsiders, but it got old. Before that I was in financial planning and wealth management. Still dabble in it." He paused and looked toward the ocean. "Found out that I had a friend or two in the Charleston area and decided to shred my business cards and move here to soak in the fresh salt air, sunshine, and fine people like the walking group here." He waved his hand around the porch.

Harriet and Connie were talking but kept glancing at Abe. If they missed anything he said, it wasn't much. Theo and David were in a stimulating conversation about their leg problems, swelling and aching, and the best brand of support socks.

Chester moved his chair closer to Charles but didn't interrupt Abe as he told us more than we could understand about how the price of silver futures in India affected gold in the United States. Charles attention drifted and I was surprised that it was more than he, the ultimate trivia collector, wanted to know.

Charles turned to Chester. "So tell us about your group?"

"Charles, I owe it all to your dear aunt. When that sweet and sexy, if I might add, Melinda came into my life last year, I was about ready to check out." He shook his head. "I was in the final stretch of time in this world. My wife, Rosie, God rest her soul, was already with our maker. We were childless, and if I was honest with myself, I hadn't contributed one little kidney bean to society. I was ready to go."

Charles leaned over and patted Chester's knee. "Now Chester, don't be—"

"Hold on, Charles, I haven't finished."

Charles sat back and pointed his palm at Chester. "Sorry."

Chester looked at me and then at Charles. Abe was still leaned back in his chair, taking everything in. "As I was saying, your aunt barreled into my life full of energy, humor, and despite her terminal disease, more hope and positive outlook than anyone I'd ever known. To use a word that was popular before most people were born, I was smitten."

Charles hesitated and then said, "Aunt M. sure liked you."

Chester's face turned red. "Shouldn't tell you this seeing that you're her nephew, but if I'd been a few years younger, I think she and I would have had more fun on the Serta than sleeping, if you know what I mean."

I didn't think there could be any doubt, and neither did Charles who said, "I understand."

"Eww!" Harriet said.

I didn't think that she and Connie had missed much. Chester coughed and leaned closer to Charles. "Anyway, Melinda recharged my batteries. She convinced me that I wasn't nearing the end, but was only beginning to enjoy my twilight years, and that I needed to get in shape and smell the roses." He chuckled. "And smell the rose, the wine kind, if you get my drift."

"So," I said before Charles did, "the walking group is to help you get in shape?"

He reached down and patted his calf. "She said with a little work, I'd once again be a chick magnet and sexier than ever."

"Eww!" Connie and Harriet said concurrently.

They scooted their chairs closer to Chester. Our   conversation   was more interesting than whatever they had been talking about.

"Tell them your silly-ass rules," Harriet said. She had no trouble finding things to complain about.

Chester frowned at her. "They're not silly, they're thorough." He turned back to us. "I started the group as a New Year's resolution and promise to Melinda, well, to her spirit since by that time she was already up there charming God." He pointed to the ceiling, but I suspected he meant to heaven rather than Melinda and God hanging out on the roof. "Members must be at least sixty to join; don't want any of those young whippersnappers horning in and trying to make us marathon runners."

I glanced around the room. There wasn't a gnat's chance in a bat cave of that happening.

"I lied about my age to get in," Connie said. She had scooted her chair even closer.

"No she didn't," Chester said. "That's why I made up a two page application and had each applicant show proof of age. Even her." He pointed at Connie.

"Yeah," Theo said. He moved closer to the expanding group around Charles and me. "At first he said a driver's license would do and then anal Chester said it was too easy to forge so he made us show a passport or an original birth certificate. Know how hard it is for folks our age to come up with an original birth certificate?"

"You know that's not the reason, Theo," Chester said. "Two of you don't have driver's licenses any more, and one of you, whom I will not identify, had your license yanked by the police after you ran down three stop signs and the next day drove your car down the boat ramp into the river."

"Whatever," Harriet said. "The point is, why in the hell do we need to go to all that trouble to walk around Folly Beach? You wouldn't find any of these silly-ass rules back in Montana where I grew up," she groused. "We didn't need rules and silly- ass papers to fill out. Yep, I remember back when this was a free country."

Theo showed more energy than I had noticed when he pointed outside. "And then foreigners came and stole it from the Indians."

"You would know," Harriet said. She winked at Theo. "You were there."

"I want to make sure our group stays within the defined parameters," Chester said.

Harriet raised her hand and was acknowledged by Chester. "Tell the boys about the last statement on your silly-ass application."

Chester shook his head. "All it says is, 'The .5 Club will not be liable for members who fall and break a part of their body or drop dead during any group-organized walk."

"Wise addition," Abe said. "Good risk management."

Harriet exhaled. "Legal gobbledygook, bull-hockey if you ask me."

Chester leaned forward and glared at her. "I didn't ask you."

How could I not want to be a part of this fun group, I wondered.

"So where'd the groups' name come from?" Charles asked. Chester shook his head. "Sorry Charles, that's a secret.

Only official members of the group are privy to knowing."

Harriet mumbled, "That's the next to last statement on the silly-ass application."

Chester ignored her, or perhaps didn't hear her. "I've got an idea," he said, snapped his fingers, and looked at Charles and then at me. "You two boys might be old enough. Why don't you join us?"

"Only if you can find your original birth certificate or passport," Harriet said. "Martians and illegal aliens don't need to waste time applying."

"Wow, that's a great idea," Charles said.

Great, since that was the reason for walking by Chester's house. I also suspected that Charles was enthused because he would learn what .5 meant.

CHAPTER EIGHT

The next morning, I was sitting at my kitchen table, sipping coffee and filling out Chester's two-page application chock-full of questions and "silly-ass" rules. I wondered why he needed my shoe size, but if I wanted to be a member of the .5 group, whatever that meant, I had to play by his rules. I was also thinking how positive an impact Charles' aunt had on Chester. Even after her death, she'd touched many lives.

I refilled my coffee and questioned what I could learn about Larry's nemesis by strolling around Folly. Abe seemed like a nice enough guy. He asked more questions than I was comfortable with, but appeared interested in the others, and wasn't asking anything too personal. If he had an ulterior motive, it wasn't apparent; then again, that's what defined a good con artist.

Someone pounding on the door interrupted my peaceful morning; something that was happening way too often. Mel was on the screened-in porch, looking like he did the last time that he'd disrupted my morning, except today he wore a camouflaged fatigue cap with *Semper Fi* on the crown.

"Don't take this old Marine more than once to know where there ain't food," he said, and shoved a box from Dunkin' Donuts at me and squeezed past me into the room. "You're not out of coffee, are you?"

He was already in the kitchen and looking for a mug. "Speaking of food," he said, although I didn't recall talking about the subject, "why the hell wasn't I invited to the big shindig the other night? I turned the big 6-0 this year."

"Don't know. I didn't make the guest list."

"Oh well," Mel said, "it's water over the damn dam. Probably had something to do with me hardly knowing that little- squirt, hardware store guy."

I nodded like I thought that that minor detail might have been the reason he wasn't invited.

"Don't think it's because I'm queer, do you?"

"No. Most likely it was because Larry and Cindy don't know you well enough to appreciate your charming, warm, and friendly personality."

Mel stared at me; his often-displayed frown deepened. "You making fun of me?"

"Yep." I opened the box and offered him the first donut.

"Thought so," he mumbled because his mouth was already full of the bigger portion of a chocolate glazed goodies. He smiled and a crumb slipped out of his mouth.

"I don't suppose you're here to feed me and let me make fun of you," I said and took a bite of a sugar-coated cholesterol builder.

He finished the first donut with one more bite and grabbed another.

"Cop came to talk to me again last night."

"Have you talked to Chief LaMond?"

"Umm, no."

There went that advantage, I thought. "Who was it?"

Mel snarled. "Detective Asshole."

"Adair?"

"That's what I said."

"What'd he want?"

"Asked if I knew someone named Drew Casey. I asked him if that was the body they found. He said something like 'I'm asking the questions,' I refrained from smacking the crap out of him, and told him that I didn't think I knew anyone with that name."

I shared that Casey was the dead student.

His frown deepened. "Chris, I'm afraid this Casey person may be gay. It's starting to hit a little close to my crib."

"Did Adair say Casey was gay?"

"No, but he asked me if I'd ever been to LeBar." Mel sat back in the chair and appeared to lose interest in the donuts.

"Where's that?"

"Downtown Charleston, half block off North King."

"Never heard of it."

"No surprise. It's a hole-in-the-wall neighborhood gay bar. You straight folks lead such a sheltered life, never get out, never experience the joys of the world."

And he said all that with his patented frown. "What'd you tell him?"

"Told him that I'd been there a few times. Maybe twice with Caldwell; a couple of times by myself. I wasn't a regular."

Caldwell Ramsey and Mel had been together for several years and lived in a small house on the outskirts of Charleston. Caldwell, at six-foot-five, towered over Mel, had played basketball at Clemson in the mid-eighties, had a quick smile, something that his partner had never mastered, and was African American.

"Did Adair ask if you were gay?"

"Shit no." He reached for another donut. His appetite had returned.

"Did you tell him you were?"

"Negatory. No ask, no tell. Didn't figure it was any of his

freakin' business." He paused, looked at the depleting collection of donuts, and then back at me. "I don't hide my sexual preference; at least not since I was mustered out of the not-so-gay-friendly United States Marine Corp." He held his arms out to the side. "As you can tell from my non-pastel wardrobe, I don't flaunt it either. It's a part of me the same as my cheerful disposition." He winked, a glimmer of humor showing through. "I don't give it much thought."

"Did you get the impression that the detective was implying that Drew Casey was gay?"

"No doubt. I gave it a lot of thought last night, couldn't sleep, and Caldwell's in Nashville this week so I couldn't talk to him about it. I don't have gaydar, can't tell if a fellow's gay just by looking at him, but the more I thought about it, several of the kids on the excursion just might have been of my persuasion."

"Why?"

"Most of my college groups are opposite-gender attached—guy-gal, gal-guy, couldn't pry them apart with a crowbar. This group was different, but I didn't think about it until after asshole detective left last night. The group was all-friendly like but didn't seem hitched-up M-F. It could also have been my imagination running wild after the kind of questions assho—Adair kept asking."

"How did Adair leave it?"

"He ran out of questions. He asked me some things about others in the group and I told him that I didn't know anything more than what I told him the first time." Mel paused and looked at the ceiling and started to reach for another donut, but pulled his hand back. "He said we might need to talk further."

"That's it?"

"He told me not to leave town."

I'd watched enough television to know that it's seldom a good sign when the cop tells you not to leave town. I pointed that out to Mel and he agreed that it was not the ending for their conversation he would have desired. It took me fifteen minutes to convince him that contacting an attorney would be in his best interest; three more minutes for him to decide that he didn't know any attorneys; and, another minute for me to remind him that he did know one, an attorney who owed him a big favor.

Sean Aker was one of Folly's four practicing lawyers and had been a friend for as long as I had lived on the island. Sean had been half of the law firm of Aker & Long until Long was murdered and the police had fingered Sean as the prime suspect. During those traumatic few days, Dude had introduced me to Mel and with the captain's help and his Magical Marsh Machine, we were able to find the killer and come within a hair of losing our lives in the process.

The weather was still nice so Mel and I walked three blocks to Sean's second floor office on Center Street two doors from City Hall.

"Morning, Marlene," I said to the receptionist as Mel and I entered the office of Sean Aker, Attorney at Law.

Marlene had been holding her pet Shih Tzu on her lap and sat her canine companion on the floor and looked at her watch. "Chris, what brings you out so early?"

It was ten, but that was early for anyone to be visiting the law office that handled mainly DUIs, criminal defense, family practice law and estate law and more mundane wills. Many of Sean's clients didn't get out of bed, or meet bail, until afternoon. I asked if she remembered Mel and she smiled and said "of course," and then I asked if the boss was in.

Marlene smiled and looked at Sean's closed door. "He's here, been on a call, off the phone now and asleep if you ask me. Let me check." She dialed his extension. Sean answered and she told him who was here and he said he'd be right out.

Sean opened the door with a hand-painted parachute over it,

reflecting one of his hobbies—skydiving, not painting. He glanced at me and moved to Mel and gave him an exaggerated hug which clearly made the former Marine uncomfortable. Sean was in his mid-forties, about my height but weighed a zillion pounds less, and had short, curly hair. His white, Ben Silver polo shirt, khakis, and deck shoes on sockless feet were in strong contrast to Mel's battle-field attire.

Sean stood back from Mel and looked at me. "What trouble are you two bringing me this morning?"

He signaled us into his office. "Marlene, hold all my calls."

She giggled. "As if you're going to get any this early." She picked her dog up and placed it where it had been when we had entered.

The office had a schizophrenic feel to it. There was an orange surfboard leaned against the wall in the far corner and a packed-parachute in the other corner. Then there was a foot-high bronze statue of Lady Justice on his desk. One side of her scales held paperclips; the other red jellybeans. The candy had been there so long that I suspected that it would be as chewy as the paperclips. Three law books were piled beside the statue and a dozen legal folders were stacked on top of the legal tomes.

This was Mel's first visit to the skydiving, surfing, scuba- diving attorney's office. Mel filled one of the side chairs in front of Sean's desk. He looked around the office and focused on the parachute, which I admit, was not a normal law office accessory.

"Planning on jumping out the window?" Mel asked.

Sean turned toward where Mel was looking and chuckled. "Considering some of my clients, I've thought about it a few times, but that's not why it's here. Some buddies and I are going skydiving this afternoon. I didn't want to leave it on the motorcycle."

"I jumped a few times when I was in the service," Mel said. "Gotten smarter in my old age, wouldn't do it again if a damned Sauroposeidon was chasing me off a cliff."

"A what?" Sean asked before I could show my ignorance.

"Big-assed dinosaur. Enough about you. Chris here," he hesitated and pointed his thumb at me, "thinks I need a good attorney. I didn't know any good ones, so we came to see you."

Sean leaned back in his chair and winked at Mel. "Not the way to start; showing how stupid I am by embarrassing me in front of Chris by talking about a *sopodun*, or whatever you called that dino-thing, and then saying that I'm not a good attorney."

"See," Mel said. "There you go again, all about you. Can you use your law school learnin' and help me?"

Sean pulled a yellow legal pad out of his top drawer and grabbed a pen from under today's Charleston *Post and Courier*. He put on his lawyer's face. "Okay, what's up?"

"This poker-up-his-ass detective from Charleston hinted that I killed some stupid college kid. He didn't arrest me but came back again and—"

"Whoa," Sean interrupted. He glanced over at me, and tilted his head, as if to say, "What have you brought me now?" He turned back to Mel. "Start from the beginning."

Mel and I started tag-teaming Sean with everything we knew about the death of Drew Casey, Mel's fateful excursion to Boneyard Beach, the call Mel had received about a missing member of the group, a detailed description of Detective Adair's two visits to Mel's house, our visit to the spot on the beach where the party took place, and the detective's visit to my house and his questions.

During our recitation, Sean jotted notes that looked like a cross between the lost art of shorthand and a two-year-old writing the Gettysburg Address. Mel and I had gotten to the point where I suggested that he contact an attorney, when Sean dropped the pen and said, "Duh!"

Mel looked at me and turned to Sean. He leaned forward and put his ample elbows on Sean's desk. "Sean, Chris, I didn't kill anybody, especially not some college squirt. I didn't do anything wrong except take a bunch of drunk college kids to the beach and let them party and let off steam."

Sean leaned toward Mel. "Mel, I don't doubt you, but does the word irrelevant mean anything to you?"

"Sure, so what?"

"It means that it doesn't matter one atom, or one whatever- is-smaller than an atom, if you killed that kid. If the police believe that you did, you're in, and here's a legal phrase for you, deep Dalmatian dung."

Mel shook his head. "What do I do?" he asked in a low voice.

"First," Sean said, "give me a buck, and I'm your lawyer." Mel reached for his wallet. "Didn't know lawyers came that cheap."

"We don't. That's the retainer. The comma and extra zeros come later."

Mel looked down at the desk. "All I've got is a boat and a Camaro, both upside down. Sean, I can't pay—"

Sean held his hand, palm toward Mel. "Mel, I owe you my life. We're okay for now. If you're charged with murder, I'll need to bring in someone who handles that level of defense and we'll have to figure something out."

"I didn't do it, Sean."

"Remember irrelevant?"

Mel shook his head, flipped a dollar bill on the desk, and said, "What now?"

"If the cops contact you, do three things." Sean pulled open a desk drawer, took out a card, and handed it to Mel. "First, say these six words, 'I need to call my lawyer,' second, dial my cell phone, and third, don't say another word until I get there. I mean it, Mel, not a word."

Mel looked at Sean, over at me, than at the parachute in the corner. "Crap, maybe I could go with you this afternoon and jump without one of those things."

It wasn't a bad idea.

CHAPTER NINE

On the walk to Mel's car I tried to reassure him that he had nothing to worry about; a poor attempt at best. From what the tour guide had told me, combined with the type of questions that Detective Adair had asked, Mel was more than a blip on police radar.

Instead of going in the house and worrying, I drove off- island to the Harris Teeter to do some irregular grocery shopping. My grocery list was short and I could walk next door from the house to Bert's and pick up what I needed, but I had realized that my cupboard was one bag of Cheetos from bare and I needed a major grocery trip.

"Ah, Mr. Landrum," came the deep voice of William Hansel from behind me. "I see you've found it necessary to increase your stock of canned goods and cleaning supplies."

Only William, a tenured professor of hospitality and tourism, could describe a grocery cart holding two cans of sliced peaches and a can of Comet Cleanser in a way that could sound like a master's thesis on American consumerism. Regardless of his professorial way with words, he was one of my favorite people and I had spent many summer days sitting beside his garden enjoying ice tea that he had insisted on delivering on a silver platter and discussing the various issues of the day and his frustrations with the staid world of academia.

"And you as well," I said and peeked in his cart containing three boxes of tea, and four ears of corn.

"Did you hear about the college student who tragically lost his life on the far end of our island?" he asked.

I pulled my cart out of the center of the aisle. "Drew Casey," I remembered that he was a student at William's college. "Did you know him?"

William moved his cart behind mine and out of the traffic pattern. He was my height, lighter in weight, much darker in color, and as usual, well-dressed. William shook his head. "Not only was I aware of who he was, Mr. Casey was a student in two of my classes. His demise was tragic."

"Do you know much about him?"

He sighed. "Unlike many of my colleagues who feel that they must befriend their charges to effectively communicate classroom material, I espouse a more detached pedagogical paradigm. I present the prescribed material, explain and repeat where necessary, and trust it to the students to assimilate the information. I choose to not share laughs, libations, or personal histories as means of inculcating classroom information into the brains of my impressionable charges."

No would have sufficed, but that would have been too Dude like. I would have been wrong.

William continued, "But I must say, Mr. Casey provided a different construct."

"What's that mean?"

"You have been well-enough acquainted with me over the years to know that I harbor no biases or prejudices against anyone based on physical or mental differences."

That was true. He had never spoken negatively about anyone since I had known him. Being African American, he had a ringside seat to racial tensions; he had experienced an emotional breakdown four years ago; and on a less-serious level, I had watched him stuffily navigate the more laid-back vocabulary of many Lowcountry residents. He could have been called the master of differences.

"I agree."

He looked around the aisle to see if anyone was close enough to hear. No one was. "Mr. Casey was a homosexual. I, you understand, am not making judgments. Some of the finest and most creative people throughout history were reported to have shared that proclivity: Lord Byron, Oscar Wilde, Walt Whitman, Leonard Bernstein, Michelangelo, my heavens, even Leonardo Da Vinci. You do understand I am sharing what Mr. Casey had shared with me."

I nodded and thought that *he was gay* should have covered it; but again, William was William.

He tapped the handles on his cart. "Mr. Casey chose not to wear his sexual inclination on his sleeve. Even though I had given no signs of being interested in his life outside my classroom, he had a way of pulling one in. I must confess that while I had no interest in his lifestyle choices, he, in a quiet and endearing manner, shared with me his estrangement from his family. He kept to himself and didn't appear to take up friendships with his classmates. He seemed to be a kind and gentle young man."

"Did he say why he was estranged from his family?"

"He never shared that fact or supposition."

"Did he have enemies?"

"I was not able to detect anyone who would have harbored ill will toward him. Then again, I wasn't able to observe any of his interactions outside the lecture hall or my office."

"Do you think his murder had anything to do with him being gay?" I was reaching for straws.

"I would have no way of knowing, but if I was forced to speculate, I would have to believe it could have been a contributing factor."

"Did you know the other students on the outing?"

"I have not seen a list of the participants, so it is possible, but no one has said anything about being with the group." He shrugged, "I have no further knowledge of the situation."

"Changing the subject," I said, after realizing that William couldn't shed additional light on Drew Casey, "I hear you're in Chester's walking group."

William smiled. "That would be accurate. My teaching is continuing to keep my mental faculties clear, and buoyantly sharp. But since I surpassed the three score mark three years ago, my physical limitations are escalating."

I assumed he meant that he was getting old and out of shape and said, "Me too, although my mental faculties have never been as clear as yours."

He chuckled. "Ah, you underestimate yourself. Nevertheless, I felt that joining Chester's group would provide me with the incentive to work on improving my physical condition without resorting to joining a physical improvement facility or embracing yoga class." He chuckled again at what I guessed was the thought of a sixty-three year old, male college professor twisting his body in the shape of a pretzel in front of a room full of trim, youthful soccer moms.

"Isn't Abe Pottinger in the group?"

"That would be correct. Why?"

"Nothing really," I said—more accurately, lied. "I met him at Chester's yesterday and heard he was new here. Just curious about your take on him."

"He and I have only walked three or four times together. I had a doctor's appointment and missed yesterday's stroll."

"What's your first impression?"

"Mr. Pottinger appears nice enough. He comes with a sales background. He is curious and asks questions about each of the members. He hadn't attempted to sell me anything, but I wouldn't be surprised if that changed at some point."

"What does he sell?"

"I have no idea." William gave me a sideways glance. "I am curious about your line of questioning. Please don't get angry for me saying this, but your interest appears on a deeper level than mere curiosity."

"Not really," I lied again. "I believe he's someone Larry LaMond knew years ago in Atlanta and was wondering why he was here. I'll ask the next time I see him."

"I would think that would be an expedient way of soothing your curiosity."

Not really.

CHAPTER TEN

It had been months since I had opened the gallery on weekdays, but I still stopped by a couple of times during the week to make sure the ancient air conditioner was still working and that no one had broken in and stolen anything. Deep down I believed that my photos had exceptional worth and a thief with good taste and an eye for outstanding art would find it hard to pass up stealing them. I also believed that one day I'd get a metal detector and find a zillion dollars' worth of doubloons in front of the Tides Hotel. We all have fantasies, or so I told myself.

It was a couple of hours after my visit with William when the bell over the front door jingled and Charles yelled, "You open to handle the rush?"

I was in the back room and realized that I wasn't the only one with fantasies.

"Dream on," I said and waited for him to come around the corner.

He tapped his cane on the wood floor in rhythm with his steps as he came through the gallery and into the back room. He wore a long-sleeve, orange Buffalo State College T-shirt, ratty cargo pants that he wore nearly as often as the sun had come up, his Tilley, and a larger-than-usual smile.

"Why so cheerful?" I asked as he walked to the small refrigerator and grabbed a Diet Pepsi.

"I'm meeting Heather at the Surf Bar at seven."

Heather Lee and Charles had dated for four years and had been engaged for a short time last year. Everyone who knew them was convinced that they were destined for each other, but Charles had confided that he doubted that he was the "marrying kind." He was probably right. The reason that he had proposed was to honor the dying wish of his aunt. Though Heather and Charles had not been joined in holy matrimony, they were joined in similar interests, potent feeling for each other, and quirkiness.

It was a little after five so I didn't think he answered my question, but knew that if he did it would be on his terms and time frame.

Charles looked at his bare wrist. "Got two hours before I'm meeting Heather, want to go over with me? I'll let you buy me a beer, or two."

How could I refuse such a generous offer? The Surf Bar was less than a block off Center Street and across the street from the Folly Beach Department of Public Safety. It was also fewer than a hundred yards from the gallery so we walked. Two surf boards, one red, the other yellow, were attached to the fascia over the door of the faded blue bar. The inside dining area was packed with a smattering of what appeared to be college students bemoaning how hot it had been on the beach; two tables of construction workers were in mismatched chairs at the mismatched tables who could have told the college students what it was really like to be hot; and five vacationers were taking in the ambiance of the surf memorabilia that dotted the walls, ceiling, and bar.

It was loud so I pointed toward the patio and Charles followed me outside where there were three tables that hadn't been invaded by diners and drinkers. We grabbed one in the corner as far away from the noise as possible. A large-screen television adorned one wall and was playing a video of surfers maneuvering waves of a size that had never been seen at Folly. Luckily, the sound was muted.

A harried bartender rushed over and took our order while telling us that two waitresses were late and if we needed anything else to come inside and yell. He left and I asked Charles if there was anything special about tonight since it was rare for him to take Heather out. She was a massage therapist and plied her trade at

Millie's, a popular Folly Beach salon. About the only time Charles and Heather frequented eating establishments was when she attended open-mic night at Cal's Country Bar and Grill and occasionally charmed her way into the weekly gathering of the Folly Beach Bluegrass Society. In addition to her paying gig as a massage therapist, Heather prided herself as being a psychic and a rising, country-music star. Her psychic skills were questionable, but there was no question about her singing ability—she had none. That had never stopped her. If she hadn't doted over Charles and brought such joy to his life, and if she hadn't been fun to be around, I would have strangled her long ago, in the middle of her nearly-unrecognizable rendition of "Crazy."

The bartender brought our drinks and set them down so hard that chardonnay sloshed out of the Ball jar and Charles's beer nearly tipped over. It appeared that the waitresses still hadn't arrived. Our silence came to a halt when four men arrived and grabbed the table nearest us. Mel was one of the four and saw me, smiled, as much as Mel ever smiled, and moved around to take the chair closest to our table. The other three chairs filled and the occupants started looking for a server.

I leaned back and told Mel that they were short on help and if they wanted drinks before sunrise, someone would need to go inside. He passed the information along to the man sitting to his right, who jumped up and headed to the bar. The two men on the other side of the table were in deep conversation about pollutants in the marsh and something about wanting to find a lawyer to sue someone. Mel ignored them and put his hand to his mouth and whispered, "Marsh tour captains. I'll introduce you when Robbie gets back with the real reason we're here. Beer. Oh yeah, we're also celebrating Timothy's announcement that he's tying the damn knot with his better, much-better, half."

Charles nearly fell out of his chair leaning to hear what Mel had said. I nodded to Mel and shared with Charles who the group was and why they were here.

Robbie returned with his hands wrapped around four bottles of Miller High Life and set them on the center of the table.

The others grabbed the bottles as if they were winning lottery tickets.

Each captain took a quick sip and then Mel stood and pointed to our table. "Guys, want you to meet my friends." He pointed at Charles. "The one with the stupid shirt's Charles Fowler." He turned to me. "The boring looking one's Chris Landrum, he owns that photo store on Center Street. Don't know what the hell Charles does except get in trouble."

I was disappointed that none of Mel's colleagues asked what kind of trouble; I'd have been interested in hearing Mel's version. They didn't pretend to be interested in who or what we were.

Mel continued, "Chris, Charles, this here's Folly's leading, and damned near all of its, marsh tour boat captains." Mel hesitated and looked around the patio. "We get together every month to talk about how cheap vacationers are, bitch about government regulations, talk about stupid things that happen on our charters, share what we've scheduled, and to fix prices. Today we're celebrating Timothy's announcement that he's committing single suicide, ending his forty-three years of freedom, happiness, and all that other crap that goes with being unhitched." Mel took a sip and pointed to the chunky, long-stringy-haired man who looked like the stereotypical boat captain.

Timothy chuckled, and held his bottle in the air. "At least I'm marrying a woman."

Mel frowned and I thought he was going to leap across the table and grab Timothy's throat but instead he faked a smile. "Right. Anyway, he's marrying above his raisin'. Y'all might know her, Samantha, she waits tables at Loggerheads."

The name wasn't familiar so I smiled at Timothy and said, "Congratulations."

"Robbie's the ugly cuss stuck sitting next to Timothy," Mel said. "He owns the company that has those god-awful, glow-in- the-dark kayaks you see flitting around the river like water bugs. He's got a shiny-new boat like mine, and's big in that ecological bullshit people talk about in the marsh."

Robbie stood, all six foot two of him, with his shaved head covered with a FB ball cap, and held his bottle up to Charles and me. "Pleased to meet you," he said. "If you ever want the *best* tour of the marsh or to rent a kayak, I'm your man."

Mel waved his hand in front of Robbie's face. "Down Robbie. This ain't no damned marketing meetin'."

Robbie smiled and sat.

Mel put his hand on the shoulder of the person sitting next to him. "Little twerp's Nathan."

I remembered him from Mel's dock the day we went to Bone-yard Beach.

"Friends call me Nemo," the little twerp said as he looked up from his bottle and managed a hint of a smile. He had on a *Hard Rock Café, Toronto* T-shirt, and his long, black hair was pulled in a ponytail and held with a child's, multi-colored rubber band with a plastic blue butterfly attached.

"Nathan," Mel said, establishing that he wasn't a friend, "has an old beat up fishing boat and cons people into hiring him to take them on e-co-logical, natural, environmental, blah-blah-blah trips to the hinterlands. Throws out all sort of highfalutin' words to prove that he earned his PhD in eco-crap. Impresses the hell out of librarians and AARP wobblies."

Nathan smiled and pointed his bottle at Mel. "Jealousy rears its ugly head, again."

Note to self, I thought. *Don't invite myself to any of these happy, cheerful meetings.*

Before I could figure out something to say, Timothy snapped his fingers. "Now I remember. You two caught that killer a while back; the one who had something to do with the beach church."

Robbie piped in, "Yeah. Mel said he may be in a bind with the cops about a kid getting himself killed last week. Said you're helping him."

I looked at Mel. He shrugged.

Robbie continued, "Think you'll catch the killer like you did the church guy?"

Charles sat back in his chair.

I flinched.

A college-aged waitress bounced up to the table and announced that she was "Randi with an *I*," and took a second round of drink order from the captains and a second beer for Charles and chardonnay for me.

"If the boss man comes around, y'all be sure and tell him how good a job I'm doing," she said and winked at Mel. "He's already chewed my ass for being late."

Her wink was wasted on Mel, but he fended a smile from his underused smile muscles and Randi, with an *I*, headed inside.

Mel turned to Robbie. "I don't need no damned help. Didn't do anything wrong and don't know nothing about that dead kid."

Robbie looked at Nemo and then at Timothy before turning back to Mel. "You said the cops talked to you and asked if you'd been to that queer bar in Charleston. Mel, you know we've got your back, but you're gay and it sounds like the dead guy was too. It's your business, not mine, but it sounds like you need all the help you can get."

Charles cleared his throat. "Ronald Reagan said, 'We can't help everyone, but everyone can help someone.'"

The captains turned to my friend. Robbie nodded; Timothy tilted his head and looked at Charles like he was a warthog; and, Nemo's face mutated into a snarl.

Mel pounded his hand on the table knocking over an empty bottle in front of him. "Told you I don't need any damned help. Period!"

"Doesn't sound that way to me," Nemo said.

"It's none of our business," Robbie said. "Mel will do what he has to do."

Timothy leaned against the table. "It sure as heck is our business. If someone gets killed on one of our charters, it'll hurt us all." He paused and looked around the table. "Whether you admit it or not, business sucks. There's too many of us doing the same thing. I don't know about you, but Samantha and I need all the money we can pull together to get off to a good life."

Nemo said, "I agree with Timothy. No offense Mel, but with you running college students out in the middle of nowhere to get drunk, that sure as hell don't bode well for the environmental tours the rest of us are doing."

I would hate to hear what it would sound like if Nemo meant to offend Mel. I gripped the edge of the table and waited for Mel to explode.

Randi returned before Mel could use his military training and break every bone in Nemo's body. She set the drinks on the table, told us how delighted she was to be waiting on us, and was oblivious to the increasing tension between Mel and Nemo.

Randi left to spread her charm to other customers and Robbie said, "Come on, Nemo, there's enough room for all of us. The economy's in a lull but I hear it's picking up. We need to support our friend. We know Mel didn't have anything to do with the kid's death."

"Do we?" Nemo said.

Mel took a deep breath, flung a five dollar bill on the table, stood and stormed off the patio. I hated to see him go, but considering the alternatives, his departure could have saved him from being arrested for assaulting a marsh tour captain, or two, or three.

Charles watched Mel leave and stared at three hand-painted wooden signs near the exit. Each had an arrow and one said, *Hawaii 5,550 miles*, another read, *Baja, California 1,854 miles*, and the third, *Folly Beach 2 blocks*.

"Think that's as a crow flies or as a car drives?" he said.

Over the years, Charles had been accused of being a nut, a fruitcake with too much whiskey in it, and as flaky as a croissant. Granted, these were accurate, but he was a master at saying or doing something outlandish to diffuse a difficult situation.

"Hell if I know," Nemo said.

Robbie said, "Better be a crow. You'd have a hard time driving to Hawaii."

Timothy shrugged and took a long draw on his beer.

And I silently repeated what Nemo had said when Robbie proclaimed that we knew that Mel hadn't killed the college student. "Do we?"

CHAPTER ELEVEN

Heather passed Timothy, Nemo, and Robbie as they left through the same outdoor exit that Mel had huffed and puffed through. Timothy whispered something to her and patted her shoulder as they passed in the doorway; the other captains ignored Charles's girlfriend.

Charles glanced at his watch-less wrist as Heather arrived at the table.

"Don't give me that I'm-late-if-I'm-not-early look, Chucky," Heather said as she gave him a peck on the cheek and shook her head at the same time. Charles detested being called anything but Charles. Only Heather could get away with calling him Chucky; further proof that love was blind, or deaf. She pulled out a chair and moving one of his empty beer bottles to his side of the table and looked at me. "What's up with you two and Timothy?"

"Why?" I asked.

Heather pointed to where she and Timothy had spoken. "He said something about y'all wading in deep trouble." She frowned. "Said if Chucky here drowns, Timothy'd have a shoulder for me to cry on." She held her nose. "Ewe!"

Charles asked, "Do you know Timothy?"

Can't slip anything by my friend, I thought.

"Not really," she said. "Know Samantha better. She's his fiancé, you know."

We didn't an hour ago, but Charles sat back and said with much confidence. "Sure, we knew that. How do you know them?"

"Samantha's a regular at Millie's, comes in each week." Heather rolled her eyes. "She spends every penny she makes waitressing on her locks, her fingernails, her toenails, and for me, massages. Yeah! Timothy's been in a few times to fetch her after her remodeling. Not sure about him."

Randi, with an *I*, noticed the addition to our table and came to get Heather's order. "Better lay menu's on us," Heather said. "I'm starved. You joining us, Chris?"

I glanced over at Charles and he shrugged, so I said, "Sure."

Heather held three fingers in the air. "Three menus, and I suppose these boys'll want more giggle-juice."

"On the way," Randi said without asking for a translation. Charles watched the waitress walk away and turned to

Heather. "Why aren't you sure about Timothy?"

I knew he wouldn't forget. Charles is a dry sponge for rumors; he'll suck up more of them than the nearest two competitors combined.

"Samantha's having second thoughts about tying the knot."

"Why?" Charles repeated.

"She didn't say, but I think it has something to do with him being closed-minded."

"About what?" I asked.

Randi returned with Heather's Budweiser and three menus. Heather asked her to come back in a few minutes so she could catch up with our drinking. She took a gulp and turned to me.

"Think maybe her fella's a bit shy on tolerance for those who're different," Heather said. She then took another drink.

"For example?" I asked and figured if I asked the same question as many ways as possible, we'd get an answer.

Heather looked around. The table the captains had occupied was empty and no one was within fifteen feet. "I didn't want to say it out loud, but Samantha told me that Timothy said he couldn't stand fags, A-rabs, and blacks, but he didn't say blacks, you know."

I suspected that we did. "Samantha had trouble with that?" I asked.

Heather continued to look around. "One of her best friends from high school is black and she was planning to invite her to the wedding but was afraid Timothy would say something that'd cause a ruckus."

"Sounds like he's more than a bit intolerant," I said. "Think she'll call off the wedding?"

"Probably not, but she's also worried about money. Said Timothy's business ain't quite paying the bills and he's always complaining about it. Said there're too many boats chasing too few customers, or something like that. Said the bank's ready to come a callin'."

"She say anything else?" Charles asked.

"Gee, Chucky, do I look like a psycho-chiatrist or a reporter?"

Randi returned and asked if we were ready to order. Heather said she didn't know about the "two old men" but she was. Fish sandwiches all around plus an extra order of fries, and more beer and wine, seemed to satisfy Randi's quest.

"Who's the bald one?" Heather asked before Charles tried to pump more information about Samantha. "He looks familiar."

Charles acted like he'd known him forever. "Robbie."

"Has he got an older sister?" Heather asked.

"Don't know. We just met him. Why?"

Heather closed her eyes and wiggled her freckled nose. It was like she was conjuring up an image. "He looks like a younger, taller, and balder version of one of Millie's clients. Her name's Connie DeWalt. Thought that may be why he looked familiar. Connie's always bragging about her brother, how he's a self-made, successful entrepreneur, but I don't recall her saying what he did to be so successful. I'm often working in another room and don't hear everything Millie's clients say."

"Is she attractive, in her mid-sixties but looks younger?" I asked.

"Sounds like her."

"We met her at Chester Carr's house," I said. "She's in his walking group."

Heather nodded. "Think I heard her say something about being around a bunch of geezers."

Charles leaned forward in his chair and pointed his finger at Heather. "You're looking at two of those geezers, so watch what you're saying."

"It's a walking group that Chester started," I said. "He credits Melinda for getting him started down the road to health, and Charles and I think it would be good for us. Besides, it would support Chester."

Heather turned to Charles and grinned. "Now Chucky, don't get yourself hurt out jogging."

"Walking, Heather."

"Whatever, just don't get hurt." She pointed at the table that had been occupied by the captains. "Who else was in that group?"

"Mel was, but left before the others," I said.

"Rumor around the salon is that the dead college student was on Mel's boat and that a cop was talking to him about it— talking to Mel, not the dead college student. Could he have something to do with it?"

Charles and I both said no.

"And the other guy?" Heather asked.

She was falling under Charles's nosy spell. "Nemo," Charles said.

Heather grinned. "The missing clownfish in that old movie?"

"Don't believe it's the same one," said Charles, as if Heather would have confused the two. "Nemo's Latin for *nobody* or *no one*, you know."

Now that one I didn't know, and wondered why Charles did.

Heather said, "Oh."

CHAPTER TWELVE

Free parking near the pier was always at a premium, so most of the group parked at Chester's and then he drove them the whopping two blocks to the foot of the pier where the walks began. I said we would meet them there. The "early morning" trips began at nine o'clock so Charles, of course, expected me to be there at eight thirty. I had the completed two-page application and had slipped my passport in my pocket in case Chester was serious about seeing proof that I had been around more than sixty years.

It was a cool day with a low cloud cover. Charles greeted me in the pier's parking lot wearing tan shorts, a green and gold long-sleeve T-shirt with a large T and Arkansas Tech in smaller print underneath.

He pointed his cane toward Charleston. "Ready to stroll to the Battery?"

Charleston's historic Battery was eleven miles away and the longest walk that Chester had mentioned was about the length of seven football fields so I assumed my hyperbole-prone friend was teasing.

"If you are, I am," I said and sat on the bottom step to await the arrival of the group.

A half hour later, Chester rolled into the lot and seven people rolled-out of his thirty-year-old, baby blue Mercury Grand Marquis land yacht. Chester maneuvered himself around the group, flailed his arms, and herded everyone over to Charles and me. He would have made a sheep dog proud.

"A near-record crowd today," Chester said with a big smile on his face. He was proud of his creation.

The near-record group included Theo, William, Harriet, David, Honest Abe Pottinger, Connie DeWalt, the group leader Chester, and the two soon-to-be newest members, Charles and me.

Chester held out one hand at me and the other at Charles. "Applications?"

Charles had folded his application to the size of a postcard and handed it to Chester while I unfolded mine and handed it over. Chester read our responses and asked for proof of age—honest, he did.

Harriet was standing behind Chester and mumbled, "Oh Christ-on-a-stick, Chester. Can't you see they're way over sixty?"

I wasn't happy about her description, and it did nothing to speed up Chester's review of the documents. He scanned my passport and Charles's original birth certificate, looked at me— probably to see if my face was the one on the document—and said, "Can't be too careful."

A terrorist crossing the border from Mexico carrying an AK-47 would have received less scrutiny, but this was Chester's club and rules.

"Can we got on with it?" Harriet asked.

David asked, "Where to today?"

Chester looked at each member of the group. "Thought we'd head up Arctic then over to Bert's before heading to the house."

"How about down Arctic?" David said.

"Think we need to go up Center Street; maybe make all the way to Woody's," Harriet added.

Chester rolled his eyes, a magnified sight behind the bottle-thick glasses. He leaned close to me. "This is a debate we have only every other day."

Chester raised his hand above his head and pointed up Arctic Avenue. "It's my group. That way."

"Dictator," Harriet mumbled.

David said, "You win."

Chester moved a foot from Theo's ear and screamed the destination.

"That far?" Theo yelled as if Chester couldn't hear any better than he could.

Chester's proposed route was no more than five long blocks and I figured even Theo could make it.

"Guess the Battery's safe from this group today," Charles whispered, even though a whisper wasn't necessary.

Chester gave another herding motion and we slowly, I emphasize slowly, headed east on Arctic Avenue.

After thirty yards, Abe was already ten paces ahead of the rest of us, revealing that he was not accustomed to being in a walking group. He looked at a street address on one of the small condo buildings on the ocean side of the road and said, "How come it's called Arctic Avenue? Shouldn't that be in iceberg country?"

It was a fair question and one that I had naively asked my first week on the island. I gave him the same answer I had been given. "Heck if I know?"

Abe looked at Charles who shrugged. And, he was the one who had known what nemo meant in Latin. The rest of the group was struggling to make the "exhausting" walk, as Harriet bemoaned, and hadn't heard the question.

We were half way up the block when Theo yelled from the back of the pack, "Where are we going, Chester?"

Chester was fifteen or so strides in front of Theo and stopped and walked back to the man bringing up the rear. Chester put his arm around him, leaned close to his ear, and repeated our flight plan. Harriet had also slowed to let Theo catch up with her. She smiled and gave him a kiss on the cheek and said something like she was glad he was with us.

Chester moved beside Charles and me. "Theo's getting worse."

"Memory?" Charles asked.

"Afraid the guy's losing his mind, like really losing his mind," Chester said. "Alzheimer's I suspect but he won't see a doc about it."

Charles looked back to Harriet and Theo. "What's his story?"

"Sad one," Chester said. "He invented a replacement-window system that uses a highfalutin gas between the glass panes that keeps cold air out in the winter, scorching heat out in the summer, and noise out all the time. Started his own company and sold it three years ago to that humongous window company that I can never remember the name of. He pocketed several million dollars. He and his wife moved here and she up and died six months after moving into their dream house on the marsh. They'd been married fifty-two years. Sad."

I looked back at Theo and Harriet. "Looks like she's taken him under her wing."

"She really has," Chester said. "Some of the others make fun of him behind his back because he's so slow. He thinks they call him ET as a compliment. It means Energizer Turtle. He keeps on going, going, going, but at a speed that would take time-lapse photography to detect movement." Chester looked toward Abe leading the group and said that he'd better catch up with the leaders so they didn't miss the turn to Bert's.

Charles looked at the frontrunners—walkers—and then back at the rest of the group. "This bunch is almost as much fun as the boat captains."

Chester had caught up with the leaders and turned them in the direction of Bert's. I turned and watched Theo laughing at something that Harriet had said, and wondered about Larry's request and how I had planned to get the slightest idea about what, if anything, Abe was planning to do to rip people off.

I sighed, stretched out my arms, and turned to Charles. "True, but look how much exercise we're getting."

I wondered if that was all we'd get by following Larry's hunches.

"Well, well," exclaimed Eric, Bert's Market's amiable clerk and man with the most-recognizable beard on Folly Beach. "What brings such a distinguished group in this morning?"

Calling us distinguished said a lot about other customers who frequented Bert's at all hours of the day and night, but I let Chester answer. He moved to the front of the group, pulled his shoulders back, and said with great pride "Eric, this is our walking group. We start at the pier and head out in different directions a few times a week."

"Welcome," Eric said. "What can I get for you after such a long excursion, Chester? Water, candy, oxygen?"

Eric had known Chester since the group's leader had worked part-time in the store and felt comfortable teasing him. Besides, I agreed with Eric about oxygen since Chester now leaned against the counter and was trying to catch his breath. David and Abraham appeared full of energy and antsy to continue, but Harriet and William had followed Chester's lead and leaned on the nearest horizontal surface.

"Funny," Chester said and wiped sweat off his forehead. "We needed to cool off; we're about at the mid-point of our longest walk yet. After the group jabbers a bit and cools down, I'm going to buy each one an ice-cream sandwich."

I moved away from Chester and Eric and spotted Abe in the back corner of the store huddled with Connie and Harriet. Their body language screamed something more intense than talking about the walk, so I moved over one aisle and as close as possible without appearing to eavesdrop. I picked up a jar of pickles and studied the label like it contained a map to the fountain of youth.

Abe had an arm around Connie but was talking to Harriet. "Incredible deal for us more mature adults." He lowered his voice and all I could make out was, "…simple as that … few papers and the money starts rolling in … turn your house into cash today …"

Harriet glanced over at me but must have figured that I wasn't close enough to hear or didn't care if I overheard. She turned to Abe. "It's called a reverse mortgage?"

"Sure is," Abe said. "All the smart people in California, Florida, and New York are jumping on the bandwagon. You get to stay in your house as long as you want, and the company pays you a lot of money each month for as long as you live."

He said something about how much they would get after their house was appraised, but I didn't catch the details.

"And you're the exclusive agent for the company in the Charleston area?" Connie asked.

"Sure am." Abe noticed me and my fascination with the pickle jar. He smiled at me and motioned for the ladies to move closer to him.

Harriet asked, "Are other companies selling it?"

"Oh yes. It's the hottest thing in wealth management."

"So why should I go with your company?" she asked. *Excellent question*, I thought.

"Excellent question," Abe not only thought but said. "Here's the best part. My company has a huge international conglomerate behind it. It's so hush-hush that I'm not even at liberty to divulge the name, but rest assured, you've heard of it. They're wanting to corner the reverse mortgage market. They've got deep pockets and don't mind paying more, much more I might add, for the houses now so they can flush competitors out." He mumbled something else I couldn't hear and then said, "For the next forty-five days, they're paying a twenty percent premium to people who take advantage of their already great deal. I put my house in the program and am getting way more than anyone else offered and lifetime security."

Connie looked at the floor and back at Abe. "Interesting."

They moved farther down the aisle and would have known that I was listening if I followed. I heard Abe say something about getting together with the ladies later when Chester interrupted and asked us to gather around the ice-cream freezer.

That was when I learned that Theo could move faster than a glacier. He was the first to the freezer and the others followed. Chester said that since this was the longest hike to date, he was buying everyone a treat. No one applauded, but they were pleased.

The distance to the ending point of the excursion from Bert's was a long block and a half along the second busiest street on the island, so Chester's treat provided not only a cool refreshment but enough sugar to keep the group energized. We were in the home-stretch, albeit a long one, walking single file since there were no sidewalks and we occasionally had to step on the busy street. Charles was in front of me tapping his way with his cane on the gravel berm and William was a step to my rear. Abe walked in front of Charles and had his left arm around Connie. Between the sounds of cars roaring by, I caught Abe sharing more about the miracle product, reverse mortgages. Harriet was behind Connie and seemed more intent on complaining about us walking too fast, the dust we were stirring up along the way, and the nerve of Chester making the group walk so far.

On a more pleasant note, William walked behind me and was humming "What A Wonderful World." From anyone else, it may have been a pleasant sound; from one of the best singers that I'd ever heard, it was a delight.

The mood turned less pleasant when William tapped me on the

shoulder and asked if I had learned anything more about the murder. He said that after our conversation, he'd heard that several of his students had known the dead man and were "bummed." I told him that he knew as much as I did, and he said that he hoped that the authorities had a better understanding than the two of us. I agreed.

"Chris, allow me to ask you another question." He continued before I agreed to allow him to ask. "Are you familiar with a financial product known as a reverse mortgage?"

I had received a brochure in the mail a year or so ago from a finance company in Columbia touting the benefits to the elderly of getting one. I was not in a financial bind and deposited the colorful brochure in the trash with other junk mail. I had made the mistake of asking Bob Howard about the product, something that I had only learned about through the brochure. He began one of his Bob Howard patented rants about how reverse mortgages are the worst thing since mosquitos and Twitter and how they took advantage of the elderly and something about the downfall of the global economy. I had asked him what was wrong with them and all I got, or could understand, was that they were high-interest loans against the house and that the fees were, in his words, "damned astronomical," the heirs may not get the house, and all the house expenses still fell to the person getting the reverse mortgage. Bob conceded, in a whisper as I recall, that for some people they could be a good thing. He didn't say the same for mosquitos and Twitter.

"William, I'm no expert, but from what I've heard, they need to be looked at closely before going down that road. Why?"

William pointed to the front of the group. "Abe called last night to talk to me about them. It seems he represents a company getting into the business of selling the product and was touting the advantages. I, as you are well aware, am quite conservative and look askance at anything new, particularly when it comes to my economic wellbeing."

"Wise," I said.

"I told Abe that I would contemplate the opportunity. I wish I'd replied in the negative. He told me that he was also a financial advisor and that if I wished to look at investment opportunities that far exceeded the index funds, he would be glad to review my portfolio."

"What'd you say?"

William chuckled. "I informed him that I was a college professor and that to me a portfolio was something that I had my students prepare to showcase their work and that I would never be financially 'loaded,' as my students say, enough to need a financial advisor. He shook his head and said 'you never know,' and for me to keep him in mind if I ever needed assistance with my wealth-management plan."

From comments that he had made over the years, I knew that William was more financially secure than he would let on, but was relieved that he didn't let Abraham know it.

"Did he say anything else?" I asked.

"Not much. He did indicate that he was working with Theo and since everyone in the group knew that Mr. Stoll was well off, that should tell me something about Abe's financial-management savvy."

Knowing Larry's history with Abe and his concerns about Abe's arrival on Folly, I was afraid that it told me too much.

CHAPTER THIRTEEN

The group walked, crawled, up three steps to Chester's screened-in porch on his faded-yellow cottage. We looked more like we had traversed Pennsylvania barefoot rather than the five-block-long walk with an ice cream break in the middle. Harriet complained about having to move one of Chester's plastic chairs off the walk; Connie said that she may have pulled a muscle in her calf while crossing Center Street and sat in the lawn chair that Harriet had griped about having to move and rubbed her leg. Theo yelled "What?" at Connie, and went on to say that he may be suffering sunstroke; and, David didn't say anything because he was gasping for breath. Charles and I followed David's lead and didn't say anything, not because we couldn't breathe but because we had nothing to say. Abe put his arm around Theo and said, "Refreshing!"

William smiled and said something pedantic that meant that it was fun, and Chester said, "Lemonade anyone?"

That got everyone's attention except Connie who was sitting in front of the house when a rusting, silver Nissan Maxima skidded to a stop in the gravel along the side of the road. I was on the porch and saw Connie rise from the chair, warily put weight on her leg, and limp to the passenger side of the car. The windows were tinted and the passenger window was partially down so I couldn't get a clear look at the driver but he looked vaguely familiar. Abe was helping Chester with the plastic cups he was filling from a sailing-flag covered, glass pitcher that he brought from the kitchen. Harriet remained true to her complaining self when she said, "It's about time." To Abe's credit, he smiled and thanked her for being patient. Con artist or consummate salesman?

The Nissan was thirty feet away and I couldn't hear what was being said, but Connie was flailing her arm around and had the windowsill in a death grip with her other hand. Saying that she was agitated would be mild. She pushed away from the car and it spun its wheels in the gravel as it pulled back on the street. Connie turned and stormed toward the porch; her calf injury having miraculously recuperated. She yanked on Chester's screen door so hard that I was afraid that it would pull off its hinges, took a deep breath, and grabbed the last cup of lemonade. The rest of us pretended that nothing had happened and even Abe didn't try to comfort her.

Chester cleared his throat, and failing to get everyone's attention, clapped his hands. All but Theo stopped talking and looked at the host. Harriet tapped Theo on the arm and pointed at Chester.

Chester increased his volume and said, "Folks, our humble walking group added two new members today."

Everyone but Charles and I clapped, feebly, but an effort nonetheless. I attributed the lack of enthusiasm to the exhausting excursion.

After the non-thunderous applause died down, Chester said, "Now that Charles and Chris are full-fledged members, we can tell them the genesis of our name." He nodded and looked outside, probably to make sure that no television crew or international spy ring was eavesdropping on the soon-to-be revealed secret. "The lofty goal of our group is to walk from where the old Coast Guard station began at the end of East Ashley Avenue to the end of the island where we can have a view of the glorious Morris Island Lighthouse."

Harriet interrupted. "It'll never happen."

Chester ignored her. "The distance from the stanchions at East Ashley to the end of the island is a quarter of a mile, and the return trip an equal distance."

Harriet, oozing sarcasm, said, "Who knew he was a mathematician?"

Chester shook his head. "Anyway, the full walk will equal a half mile. Now, you know all those oval stickers you see on young people's cars that say 13.1 or 26.2?"

Chester stared at me until I nodded. "Well, that's the number of miles that those young, fit folks run, in a mini-marathon or a marathon."

I wondered if Chester thought Charles and I didn't know that, but I decided to remain silent and nodded, again.

"So, in case you haven't figured it out, the .5 stands for a half mile, the distance to the lighthouse view and back. There you go, now you know the secret. Cool, huh?"

"Stupid," Harriet said.

Charles said, "Cool."

And Connie remained quiet on the other side of the room. She stared out at the road and rubbed her forehead. Charles was talking to Chester about where he could get a .5 sticker to put on his bicycle, so I took the opportunity to get more lemonade and moved to the vacant chair beside Connie.

"You okay?" I asked.

She continued to stare out the screen window but said, "Yeah, he drives me crazy."

"Who?"

"My brother," She tilted her head toward the road. "That was

Robbie out there while you all were pretending you didn't see us arguing."

"Does he run marsh tours?"

Connie finally looked up at me. "Yeah. You know him?"

"Not really. I met him last night at the Surf Bar. He was with some of the other captains."

"That's probably where the trouble started."

"Trouble?" I asked.

"Yeah, his buddy Timothy's getting married to a nice gal who works at Loggerhead's."

I told her that was what I'd heard.

"Seems that Timothy's long on ignorance and short on cash and asked Robbie if he could *borrow* two thousand dollars to help get through the wedding expenses. Robbie's got two thousand bucks like this is my natural hair color hair and I have all my teeth. You can guess what my stupid brother pulled up to ask for."

"Money."

"He had the audacity to ask me if I'd lend Timothy two thousand dollars. Can you believe that?"

I said I thought that was unreasonable.

"You bet your cute tush it was," she said and shook her head. "Now don't get me wrong, I want Timothy and Samantha to be happy. Sam seems like a nice gal, but I don't know what she sees in Timothy. He's a moocher, always griping about how bad business is and thinks there are too many captains doing the same thing out there and Folly'd be better off if one or more of them disappeared." She paused and shook her head again. "Oh well, love beats all. If I had it, I'd lend the money to Sam but never to Timothy. Don't matter anyway, I don't have it to give, excuse me, to lend."

I asked if I could get her more lemonade and she said that would be nice. Charles, Chester, and now David were in deep conversation about the stickers; William had excused himself and headed home; and, Abe was in the corner whispering with Harriet.

I returned with Connie's drink. She took a sip and then said, "Looks like Timothy might get his wish about getting rid of one of the captains."

I asked what she meant.

"Rumor is that a guy named Mel killed one of his passengers, some college kid."

"Why do they think he did it?"

Connie looked around and leaned closer. "Now this is rumor, you understand."

I motioned for her to continue.

"Robbie likes Mel, even though Mel's gay; says he lives with a man, and get this, the man he lives with is black." Connie looked at the ground and shook her head. "What's the world coming to? Anyway, rumor has it that the dead college kid was gay and that Mel made a pass at him and the college kid who was decades younger than the captain rebuked him."

I waited for more, but Connie seemed to be at the end of her story. "They think that Mel killed the young man because of that?"

Knowing Mel, it's farfetched, but I also knew that nothing spreads faster than a rumor, regardless how valid or ridiculous it may be. It hurt to think this kind of thing was being said about a friend. I had no idea what had happened the night of the party, but knew that Mel would not have killed the kid for that reason.

"Connie, I've known Mel Evans for years. I would trust him with my life, in fact I did trust him with it a year or so ago. I can't believe he killed the student."

"I'm just telling you what's going around. Somebody killed him, Mel was responsible for the group, and I hear the police have interrogated him."

"That may be so, but that doesn't mean he had anything to do with it."

"Tell you what." She looked at the street, and back at me. "I'll take your word about Mel and if anybody asks my opinion, I'll say I don't know anything. Fair enough?"

I told her that it was, but I still had a sour feeling in my stomach. Regardless how I had defended him, Mel was responsible for the group and opened himself up to suspicion because he did a poor job of accounting for members of the group when they left Boneyard Beach.

CHAPTER FOURTEEN

Chester had run out of lemonade and everyone but Charles and I had drifted away, most likely to ice sore legs and feet, and to take an afternoon nap to recuperate from their longest walk yet.

Chester watched David as he walked to his car. "Fellows, could you spare a few more minutes? Got something to bounce off you."

Put like that, I knew that Chester wouldn't have been able to get rid of Charles if he'd pointed a loaded copperhead at him. "Think so," Charles said. He then glanced at me.

"Of course," I said.

Chester said, "Let's go in where it's cooler."

Chester's front door opened to a small living room with two oversized, dark-green, velour recliners facing a large-screen television that was the size of bank vault. Chester hadn't entered the world of flat-screen televisions, but also hadn't deprived himself of the largest screen I'd ever seen in a floor-model set. Two lamps provided the room's illumination and everything was neat and uncluttered. A window air conditioner was loud, but the cool air felt good.

"How about something a bit stronger to sip on?" he said as he weaved his way around the recliners and television and stood in the kitchen doorway. "Got whiskey, wine, and beer. No dancing girls or peanuts."

I said wine and Charles said, "Beer. Sure there're no dancing girls?"

Chester laughed and went to get our drinks.

Charles pointed to a photo beside an old-fashioned, clunky, black telephone, perched on a small table under the window. In stark contrast to the phone, there was a high-tech digital answering machine. The photo was sepia and from the clothing, I would guess it had been taken in the 1940s. Chester returned with our drinks and caught me looking at the picture.

"Wedding day, June 3, 1944," he said and handed me a glass of white wine. "That's my blushing bride Rosie. An angel, a true angel."

Charles took the Budweiser from Chester. "You were quite a fetching couple."

I wouldn't have been that generous. Chester's glasses in the photograph were smaller than those he wore today, and he had more hair, but I can say that his appearance has improved with age. Rosie's nose was pinched and out of proportion to her face; and if she had a chin, it was well hidden. They had big grins and appeared happy, and that's what mattered.

"Thanks. She's been gone eleven years and until your aunt came along, I had never thought of another woman. Charles, I do miss Melinda."

Charles was seldom at a loss for words, but this was one of those moments. He smiled. I suspected that a trip down memory lane wasn't the reason for Chester asking us to stay.

"What's up, Chester?" I asked.

He had lowered himself on the vacant recliner and took a sip of beer. "This is kind of hard for me to talk about. I don't know anything for sure. I'm guessing. Gee, I don't know, maybe …"

Charles interrupted. "Spit it out."

Chester looked down at his bottle and then up at Charles. "Since you're a detective, I thought I'd talk to you about this."

I started to debunk Chester's assumption about Charles being a detective, but had come to realize that it would be useless. Charles thought he was, some others actually believed him, and truth be known, he and I had solved some crimes, enough to lend a touch of credence to Charles's claim.

The impatient, alleged detective, said, "About what?"

"It's about Abraham Pottinger, you know, from .5."

We had just walked roughly .2 with him and spent an hour on Chester's porch talking to him, so I was pretty certain I knew which Abraham Pottinger Chester was referring to.

"There's something fishy about him," Chester continued. "He sort of drifted into the group. Hadn't been here long."

I asked, "Who brought him in?"

"That's the funny thing. I was in Mr. John's Beach Store talking to Paul, the owner, you know? I wanted to get one of the new Folly Beach T-shirts with the big red FB on the front, think they're cool looking. Anyway, he came up and introduced himself, said he was new to the beach and had heard about my group. He said he needed some exercise and wondered how he could join. He was dressed all formal like and looked out of place."

Chester paused. A mistake around Charles. William had once said that Charles had *horror vacui*. I had no idea what it meant so I used Charles trivia-collecting technique and asked. William said it was Latin for fear of empty spaces; said it usually referred to visual space, but could also describe Charles's inordinate need for words to fill silence. I had said, "Whatever."

"What happened?" Charles asked.

"First, he didn't look like he met our stringent age requirement, so I asked to see his drivers' license. Low and behold, he was over sixty, sixty-one in fact. I gave him an application, always carry a few extras around with me, and told him where and when we meet. He showed up the next day with his completed application in hand and joined us for our walk up Center Street."

"What's fishy about him?" I asked.

"Now I could be one-hundred percent wrong, so don't take this as gospel, but I'm beginning to think his motives are not pure and he's not that interested in exercise."

"Why?" Charles asked.

"The way he's latched onto the gals in the group. Don't think it's a hanky-panky thing, although they're mighty attractive.

Anyway, my hearing's not the best, but I am able to catch smidgens of his conversations and he's always talking about ways they can make oodles of money."

"Reverse mortgages?" Charles said.

Chester smiled. "See, I knew you'd figure it out. Did you catch all that today?"

Charles reached over his shoulder and patted himself on the back. "Sure did."

I asked, "What do you think's wrong with him talking to them about reverse mortgages?"

Chester looked back down at his bottle and then nodded. "I know there's such a thing, but he's always talking about how he can offer such a better deal than other companies. How's that possible? Just seems fishy."

"What do you want us to do?" Charles asked. A great question, I thought.

"Hold on, Charles," Chester said. "There's more."

"And?" Charles asked.

"It's about my buddy Theo." Chester shook his head. "Don't know if you noticed, but he's, how shall I say it, he's in declining mental health. Probably Alzheimer's, he's forgetting things. The other day he forgot where he lived."

I was beginning to wonder about Chester's "mental health" since he'd told us the same thing about Theo the other day, but I let him continue.

"I'm afraid Theo is low-hanging fruit for scam artists. We old folks are more susceptible for that kind of thing. I read in a magazine where there's something in the brain that gets a bit scrambled as we get older. It's not only folks with Alzheimer's, but all of us. I think it said we believe more of the scams than we would've when we were younger. Scary. Want more to drink?"

We declined.

"Think Abe is running a scam on Theo?" I asked.

"Don't know. That's what I want you to figure out." Charles said, "Why do you think he might be?"

"Theo's old, Theo's rich, Theo's losing his mind. And, oh yeah, Abe's been huddling up with him more each walk and before you got here today, Abe asked Theo to lunch tomorrow. Fishy."

And so it seems, particularly after what Larry had told me. Chester said that was all he had, so I asked him if he wanted us to walk with him to the pier so he could get his car. He said no, that he'd get it after a nap.

"Why didn't you tell Chester about Abe and Larry?" Charles asked after we had left the cottage. Charles had to make a delivery for the surf shop and I told him that I'd walk there with him.

"I couldn't think how to tell him without divulging more than he knows about Larry's past. Plus, I didn't want Chester's feelings of 'fishy' to be clouded by Larry's suspicions."

"Good point." We'd reached Folly's only stop light. "What's your take on what Chester said?"

"I didn't hear all of it at Bert's, but Abe was pushing his reverse mortgage idea on Connie and Harriet. Theo's wealthy so he wouldn't have interest in it."

Traffic stopped and we headed across Center Street. "Theo'd be a lot bigger fish to fry if Larry's suspicions are accurate," Charles said as we reached the sidewalk.

"You can say that again," I said. We were now at the steps in front of the surf shop.

Charles paused on the first step. "So what are we going to do . . ."

My cell phone interrupted the rest of his rather predictable question. The screen read *Mad Mel*. "Morning Mel," I said.

"Damned caller ID!"

I agreed.

"What are you doing for lunch tomorrow?" he asked.

Mel's normal voice was about as loud as a drill instructor so Charles didn't have to lean close to hear.

Abe hadn't invited me to his lunch with Theo, so I said, "Nothing, why?"

"Meet me at the Crab House, eleven hundred hours."

Charles moved a step back and pointed his index finger at his chest.

"Can Charles come?"

"Could I stop him?"

"Probably not," I said.

"Then why in the hell did you ask?"

"Being polite."

"You failed!" Mel blurted.

"We'll be there."

"On time?"

With Charles, there's no other way, so I said, "You bet." The line went dead.

Charles seemed to forget his trip to the surf shop and ushered me to a patch of shade around the side of the building. "What's that about?"

"Don't know. You heard as much as I did."

Charles leaned against his cane. "Mel doesn't invite people to lunch unless he's got a powerful reason. And why drive to the Crab House when it would've been easier to meet us on Folly."

"He's embarrassed to be seen with you," I said.

"Funny. He said Crab House before you asked him if I could come."

"We'll have to wait and find out. Speaking of waiting, isn't Dude waiting for you to deliver a package?"

Charles nodded and pointed his cane at the surf shop. "United Parcel Charles to the rescue." He waved bye as he scampered up the steps.

Despite the comment by one of the walkers that he was having a sunstroke, the temperature was mild for May, so I decided to walk to the end of the pier instead of heading home. Folly's iconic pier was more than a thousand feet long and stuck out into the Atlantic and served as the figurative center of the island's coastline. I often ventured to the far end of the structure when I needed to think, or when I wanted to have a good view of the beach, or if I wanted to take a nap in the shade under the diamond- shaped, elevated second deck. This would be a good time for all three.

A dozen or so fishermen were spread out along the rail, a flock of seagulls circled overhead, and the smell of filleted fish filled the air. The vacation season wasn't in full swing so the beach wasn't as crowded as it would be in a few more weeks, and the end of the pier was deserted so I had my choice of benches.

Instead of falling asleep, my mind wandered and tried to assimilate everything that'd been happening the last few days. The death of the college student was tragic, and even though he'd been on Mel's charter, it was difficult to believe that he had anything to do with it. So, why had the rumors of his involvement been spread so quickly? Granted, Mel was gay and apparently so was the student. But so are many others, here on Folly and elsewhere. Was the bias against gays so strong that people automatically jumped to conclusions? And then there's Abe Pottinger. Was Larry right about Abe's less-than-stellar reason for being here? Or, since Larry knew Abe and his sordid past, was my friend biased against him? How did that differ from how people viewed Mel?

Chester didn't know anything about Abe and Larry's relationship, and yet he thought something was fishy about the newcomer. How much credence could I put into Chester's suspicions?

And now both Larry and Chester want Charles and me to see what we can learn about Abe. How are we supposed to do that? Add to all that, Mel wants to meet me—and of course Charles—for lunch. Something told me that he didn't just crave our company.

And then I fell asleep.

CHAPTER FIFTEEN

The Charleston Crab House was eight miles from home and on Wappoo Creek, a waterway that branches off the Ashley River on the west side of the city. We arrived on-time by Charles's Standard Time, or thirty minutes before Mel had said, and were ushered to a table on the outdoor patio overlooking the scenic waterway. While we waited for Mel we were treated to a float-by from two small sailboats and three dolphins frolicking near the dock. So far, the day was perfect.

Mel headed our way and I doubted that the day would stay perfect. His normal sour expression seemed festive compared to the look on his face, and I suspected that a storm was nearing. The former Marine didn't disappoint.

"They're out to get me," Mel groused as he yanked the chair out from under the table and plopped down.

Charles glanced toward the door; probably to see if he meant it literally.

"Who?" I asked, assuming that the time for civil greetings had passed.

Mel glared at Charles and then at me. "Damned if I know."

It was time for me to keep my mouth shut and let Mel tell us whatever it was.

Charles, to no surprise, didn't adhere to that philosophy. "How do you know?"

Mel took a deep breath. "I've taken fire in combat. I've been in more bar fights than I can count. And, I'm pretty good at catching people bad mouthing me behind my back. I can damned sure tell when someone's got me in their scope."

"Humor us and say why you think you've been targeted," I said.

"Yeah," Charles said. "I haven't been shot at, I know I haven't been in many—okay, no—bar fights and would bet money that Chris hasn't either. We're not as good as you at knowing when someone's out to get us."

Mel stared at Charles and then waved for the waitress who had been talking to three customers at the next table. She looked over and Mel shouted for her to bring him the "strongest brew in there." He pointed toward the bar so she'd know where they kept the brews.

Mel glanced at a passing sailboat and turned to me. "That detective called yesterday."

"Adair?" I asked.

"Yeah. Said he had some 'routine' follow-up questions, and all casual-like said, 'Remind me how often you visited LeBar.' Well, I reminded him that I'd said a couple of times with Caldwell and maybe a couple of times by myself."

Charles rubbed his three-day-old beard stubble. "So?"

Mel picked at his paper napkin and leaned back in his chair when the waitress brought his drink and asked us what we wanted. Charles said a beer and that he didn't care how strong it was, and I ordered wine. The waitress left and Mel leaned forward and put his elbows on the table.

"I sort of underestimated the number."

"Sort of?" Charles said.

"Yeah, more like a dozen times by myself. Never counted because I didn't see any damned reason to. Who knew somebody'd be keeping score."

"And you didn't tell Adair anything different than you did the first time?" I asked.

"No. Stupid not to, but no."

I would agree it was stupid to not tell the detective the number of visits, but I was having a hard time seeing why that made Mel think someone was out to get him. Again, I waited to let Mel's story unfold at his pace.

The waitress returned with Charles and my drink and, to his credit, Charles sipped his beer and didn't ask Mel what he'd meant.

"It gets worse," Mel mumbled. "Adair asked me if I was sure that I didn't know the dead kid. I said no, I didn't remember him."

"But?" Charles said.

Mel glared at him. "A few times I was there I may have gotten a bit snookered. LeBar's small and often it's ass-to-ass, steppin'-on-toes packed. Every once in a while, a lost straight person stumbled in, but it's rare. The regulars have the queer factor in common, but they're varied after that: tall, short, bi, trans, black, white, old, and young, like college students."

A light was coming through the cracks in Mel's story. "College students like Drew Casey?"

"Adair asked if I met Drew Casey in LeBar." I wanted to scream, "Did you?" but waited.

"I told him no, but to be honest, I could have."

Charles said, "Could have?"

"I was a few generations older than some of the folks in there, and with my handsome looks and charming smile, several of them recognized me." Mel grinned to let us know he was kidding about the looks and smile. "Anyway, I was a conversation piece, maybe even some kind of challenge to a few of them, and they sort of flirted."

I prayed that I was wrong about where this seemed to be headed, but asked anyway. "Was Casey one of the college students?"

"I don't know, I really don't." Mel shook his head and looked down at the table. "There was always a bunch of them, it's dark, and I seldom had a shortage of beers. Guys, he could have been."

"What about the kid who rented the boat and who blew the whistle on you?" Charles asked.

"Charles, did you miss the part where I said I was pickled, in the dark, and packed in like sand in concrete? I don't freakin' know!"

"Did you leave the bar with any of them?" asked fearless Charles.

"Shit no!" Mel slammed his fist down on the metal table. "Why would you even ask that? Caldwell and I are committed to each other, have been for years, always will be. You know that!"

Charles held up both hands, palms facing Mel. "Didn't mean to insult you. You know cops'll come at you with that."

"Have you told Sean any of this?" I asked.

"I've got a meeting with him this afternoon. Wanted to see what you thought before spilling my guts to an attorney."

I shook my head. "I don't know what the police have or if someone's trying to frame you, but from Adair's questions, he thinks you're more involved than taking the group to the beach."

Charles picked his cane off the deck and pointed it at Mel. "Don't know what Sean will say, but my unprofessional, untrained legal advice would be for you to keep your trap shut and let your lawyer do the talking."

Food arrived and we ate in silence with a few bursts of frustration, anger, and whether he'd admit it, fear from Mel mixed in. I reinforced what Charles had suggested about Mel keeping his mouth closed and letting his attorney do the talking. Mel said that he would, but his personality and direct approach to a problem would make it hard. He had looked at his watch a couple of times and finally said that he needed to get to his meeting with Sean. He thanked us for listening to his ramblings and said he'd get lunch. That was a new experience for me but I managed to handle it without reaching for the check. Charles, as usual, managed to sit on both hands during the awkward check-grabbing portion of the meal. Mel stood, saluted us, started for the exit, then turned and said that we could get the cumshaw. Charles saw the confused look in my eyes and whispered, "Marine-speak for tip."

Mel was gone, I had enjoyed a nice meal, prayed that he would follow our, and Sean's advice, added another word to my vocabulary, and listened to Charles say that we needed another drink. I succumbed.

"What do you make of it?" he asked after the waitress delivered our drinks.

I took a leap and decided that he was talking about Mel's situation. "He's playing with fire lying to the police. Asking Mel a second time about his trips to the bar, tells me that Detective Adair knows that it's more than two visits without Caldwell."

"You betcha."

"But, nothing I know about Mel tells me that he would pick-up, or be picked-up at a bar by a college student."

Charles tilted his head to the left. "Even if he was snookered."

"I doubt it. Trouble is, if Adair must have a witness who claims that Mel was there with Drew Casey, and Mel's already on record lying about the number of times he was there and denying that he knew Casey, he's twisted himself into a knot. That's a knot that'll take more than Sean to untie."

Charles rolled up his napkin and tried to tie it in a knot. "That macho-Marine could be in a minefield of trouble."

We sipped our drinks and Charles scooted his chair around so he had a better view of the creek.

"Umm," he said and shook his head. "What?"

"Nothing."

I'd spent countless hours with him over the years. If I'd learned anything, it was that *nothing* was never nothing. I lowered my head and looked at him with my upturned eyes. He caved.

"Okay, okay," he muttered. "Speaking of knots, think Heather and I should tie one?"

That wouldn't have been on my top twenty list of what "nothing" had meant. Before she left us with only memories, Charles's Aunt Melinda had made a deathbed wish that Charles would get married. Melinda had lived in a small apartment across the hall from Heather and they had talked about how much Heather wanted to become Mrs. Fowler. At an impromptu memorial for his aunt, Charles proposed, but in the months since then, he'd told Heather that he couldn't go through with it. He told her he had proposed more because of Melinda. Heather had been hurt, angry, and had felt rejected. But they had continued to date.

I wondered why he had brought it up again. "Do you want to?"

Charles stared at the creek like he thought a mermaid was about to leap out of the water and say yea or nay.

"Remember when we first met," he said, and continued to stare at the water.

"Sure."

"I told you that people thought I was gay because I'd never had a girlfriend."

I smiled, which was wasted on him since he continued to look at the water. "You said you weren't gay but that you couldn't afford yourself much less a girlfriend."

"Good memory. Did you know people are saying that again?"

"Why?"

"Umm," he hesitated but never wavered from watching the fascinating creek. "Umm, they're saying that since I hang around with you so much, we must be lovers."

That threw me. "Think I should tell Karen?" I used humor, or attempts at humor, as my main defense against things that made me uncomfortable or when I didn't know what to say.

Charles turned away from the creek, shook his head, and looked at me. "Suspect she already knows you're not gay." He shook his head again. "Chris, you know I'm not gay, and most of the time it doesn't bother me about what people think, but it got me to start thinking again about getting married."

"Any conclusions?"

"Most people my age have settled down, married—some two or three times—and have a passel of kids, and mortgages, and IRAs, and, patios and patio furniture, and, well, bunches of stuff. Seems like I should be settling down before it's too late." He sighed. "I know Heather wants to and Lord knows, I couldn't find anyone better. It was about the last thing Melinda said to me." He paused and then turned back to wait for the mermaid.

That's what Melinda wanted and what Heather wants. "What does Charles want?"

He fiddled with his glass and folded his napkin into the shape of a sail. I didn't think he was going to answer, but he said, "I've lived alone my entire life. I eat what I want to eat when I want to eat, go where I want when I want, do what I want when I want, wash my underwear once a month whether it needs it or not. Chris, I don't know if I could change." He paused. "Don't know if I want to."

That was more than I wanted to know, but it was good he was talking about it.

"What's your gut tell you?"

"Most of the time I start pondering this, my guts too busy with heartburn to tell me anything."

That should tell him something. "You need to listen to your heart, head, and your gut and if they all say yes, that's your answer. It should come down to what you want, and only what you want."

"Easier said than done."

I nodded. "Yes."

"Okay, now that we have my future figured out, how about you? When are you and Karen getting hitched?"

It was my turn to stare at the mesmerizing creek. "Good question, my friend; good question."

CHAPTER SIXTEEN

I dropped Charles at his place after eight miles of talking around his question about my matrimonial plans. It wasn't that I was avoiding answering; it was having to answer the same question that I posed to him at the Crab Shack. Avoidance was another one of my defense mechanisms that I had perfected over the decades, so instead of further pondering the question that I had no answer to, I turned my attention to Mel.

I was pulling into the drive when I remembered that William had the murder victim in two classes. I backed out of the drive and drove five blocks to the professor's small, well- kept house. William was in the garden when I pulled in behind his car. He looked up from tilling the soil, or whatever you do to work garden-growing magic. He smiled and leaned the hoe against the oak tree that shaded the back half of the garden.

He waved me to two shaded chairs. "You've come to give me a temporary respite from this laborious task."

I smiled. "And to give you a break from hoeing."

"Shall I fetch ice tea?" he asked.

"Sounds good, can I help?"

"Unnecessary, I'll return momentarily," He took off his sweat and dirt-stained gardening gloves and headed to the house.

I had spent several summer days under this tree during my first year on Folly. Gardening was William's passion and he had said that it was his way of escaping the demands of his students, his idealistic yet unrealistic administrators, and the petty bickering that takes place in most work environments. I had spent many years working in a large, bureaucratic company and had shared similar stories with him. I'm not certain that misery loves company, but it made for interesting conversations.

William returned with a silver platter holding two large glasses of tea and a silver ice bucket. I thanked him and he said that it was the break that he needed. Of course he used more multi- syllable words to say it.

"While I appreciate your appearance," he said, "I suspect that this visit is for more than providing me with a chance to catch my breath."

"Guilty as suspected," I took a sip of tea. "I was wondering if you remembered anything else about Drew Casey or his classmates that could help me figure out what's going on."

William took another sip and nodded in the direction of the house that I had lived in when I first moved to Folly; more accurately, the house that replaced my house, since mine had been torched with me in it by a murderer who thought that I was getting too close to learning his identity. "Am I detecting that you're having more than a passing interest in the tragic death of my student? Have we, meaning you singularly, forgotten the fatal result one can face from becoming ensnarled in police business?"

"You're right, of course. I know what I'm doing can be dangerous, but as you have figured, I don't take kindly to people accusing my friends of things they didn't do. I've known Mel Evans for going on two years. I've trusted him with my life, and I've never seen anything to indicate that he could have harmed that kid. For that reason—"

William raised both hands. "Chris, no need to continue. I can only hope that I have as good a friend as you if I find myself in such a difficult situation."

"You do, and you're looking at him."

"I'm humbled. In return, allow me to respond to your initial query. As I said the last time you broached this topic, I make it a practice not to become involved in my students' lives outside the classroom. But I knew that you had an interest in Mr. Casey's death, so I put my classroom-only practice on hiatus and paid particular attention to what students were saying about the young man's demise."

"Learn anything?"

"I did, but I don't know what to make of it. Perhaps it will provide you with some enlightenment. And to be honest, I had heard some of this long before Mr. Casey's death, but I was hesitant to talk about such matters."

I motioned for him to continue.

"A month ago, I asked him how he was doing. It was a benign enquiry and I often ask students the same thing. Their typical responses center on classes and majors." He hesitated and tilted his head. "Mr. Casey's answer was outside those parameters. He shared that he had been teased relentlessly by some classmates."

"About what?"

"His sexual orientation," William said, almost in a whisper. "He wasn't one to hide his homosexuality and was paying the price for his openness."

"Did he say who was teasing him?"

"He didn't share names, and I didn't ask. He said he didn't want to make a case out of it and dropped it thereafter."

William may have thought that was critical information, but I didn't hear anything that could be helpful. "Was that it?"

"That's only a prelude to what I shall now disclose."

He stopped making eye contact, and was uncomfortable with the topic. I again asked him to continue.

"The day before yesterday, I overheard two students who had been on the fateful excursion. One of them, Dawn Henderson by name, said to Peter Mellon that she was glad that, and this is her quote, 'the queer' got what he had coming to him. I've had the impression that Ms. Henderson was, how shall I say it, pre- judgmental when it came to African Americans. I suppose those feelings could also apply to homosexuals, but I'm not certain. She went on to say that she knew that the 'queer boat driver' had killed him."

"She said she knew?"

"Those were her words, but here's the part that I believe to be most significant. Mr. Mellon chided his classmate when he told her that she didn't know that the, umm, homosexual boat captain killed Mr. Casey. Mr. Mellon said that all she knew was that Mr. Casey, along with more than one other gay individual, landed on Boneyard Beach with the group, but she did not recall seeing him get off the boat when it returned to the dock."

"Why not?"

"Because, according to Mr. Mellon, he and his fellow adventurers were so inebriated that they wouldn't have known if Santa Claus and his reindeer had exited the boat upon return to its mooring."

"What did she say to that?"

William chuckled. "She gave him a look that I was pleased that she had not directed at me, and said that she 'knew what she knew,' whatever that meant."

"What did her classmate say?"

"They walked away and I felt it unwise to follow."

"One more question. My understanding is that one person booked the excursion and that Mel didn't get the names of the others, so I doubt any of them knew Mel or anything about him before they had met on the dock."

"Appears logical."

"Then how did Dawn Henderson know Mel was gay? That would have been the last impression I would have had when I met him for the first time. He looks and acts every bit the ex-Marine that he is; he dresses macho, rants-and-raves macho, and unless pushed, never says anything about his personal life."

"That would be my assessment."

"Do you recall anything that either of the students said that indicated they knew?"

"No."

William kept glancing at the hoe and at the garden. I had pushed him out of his comfort zone, both by talking about Mel's sexual orientation and his sharing that he had been eavesdropping. It was time to change the subject, so I asked him what he had planted for the growing season. He smiled, exhaled, and went into a monologue about the various vegetables that were planted, what he would be planting next, when they would be ready to harvest, what kind of salads he made with some of them, and how he prepared the meat that he featured with each veggie. He said a lot more, but with my total lack of interest in gardening and cooking, I tuned out somewhere around how the zucchini would be ready in the next couple of weeks, but he would have to wait until the fall for the parsnip, or maybe it was catnip.

I thanked him for the tea and conversation. He thanked me for stopping by and allowing him to take a break. I told him that it was my pleasure, and he told me not to get myself killed.

I agreed that that would be a good idea and left him with a smile on his face. I wasn't as cheery.

CHAPTER SEVENTEEN

I pulled in the drive and Chief Cindy LaMond pulled in behind
me in her unmarked Crown Vic.

I met her in the yard between the two cars. "What'd I do
wrong now, Chief?"

"Several things, I'm sure." She shook her head. "But, that's not
why I stopped."

I started to make a smart comment, but waited.

"I'll stop playing police chief around seven; can you stop by the
house after that? I promise Larry won't try to fix supper."

"Having a zero-plus-a-few-days party?"

She frowned. "Nope. You're the only guest, unless you want to
bring your new-best friend Brad Burton."

"Right. What's up?"

"Later."

"I'll be there, sans Burton."

I had a couple of hours to ponder Cindy's invitation. It only took
me five minutes to realize that I had no idea what it was about, so I
took the remaining time to take a nap, and prepare a healthy supper

of peanut butter on Ritz crackers; okay, not healthy, but my refrigerator was plum out of zucchini and parsnip.

Charles wasn't with me, so I was able to arrive at the LaMonds at seven rather than early. Cindy greeted me and said that Larry was on the patio. We stopped in the kitchen on the way, she grabbed a can of Budweiser and poured me a glass of Chardonnay, and I followed her.

Three patio chairs had been pulled in a tight triangle on the crushed-shell surface and Larry occupied the one facing the marsh. A small glass-topped table beside his chair held an opened pizza box from Woody's, two beer cans, and Larry's Pewter Hardware ball cap. He heard the door open and jumped up, turned, and greeted me with a smile. His Pewter Hardware logoed white polo shirt had a dirt stain on the shoulder and was pulled out of his khaki slacks. He wore tennis shoes but they were untied. It looked like he had spent the day wrestling uncooperative sheets of plywood.

He shook my hand; his smile was intact but seemed forced. "Have a seat. I'll be back." He headed into the house.

Cindy pointed to the pizza box and asked if I wanted a slice, glanced at the door, and whispered, "Larry wanted to fire up the grill and fix burgers. You and the fire department should be thankful that I talked him out of it."

I told her that I had already eaten and thanked her for the offer. Larry returned and flopped down in his chair. The plywood must have won the battle. Cindy took the remaining chair and asked if I was certain that I didn't want pizza. I again said I was certain, and she said, "Good, more for me."

Larry took a long draw on his beer, glanced at Cindy, and back at me. "Guess you're wondering why we asked you over."

I didn't want to appear too shocked at the invitation seeing that we're friends, but I'd only been at their house a few times and they were more spontaneous for gatherings like the zero party.

"Had me wondering."

"It's about Abe Pottinger. Have you met him?"

"Yes, in fact Charles and I are now official members of the .5 club. It would have been easier if we tried to drop in on the president at the White House than getting past Chester's membership requirements."

Cindy smiled and Larry shook his head.

"Anyway," I continued, "we took our first walk with the group the other day and spent some time talking to Abe. I think you're right, Larry, he's up to something. He was pushing reverse mortgages to a few members. I'm no expert, but he was touting a much higher monthly payment to his 'clients' than other companies offer. I don't know if he's gotten any of them to sign up, but I wouldn't be surprised if he wasn't close."

"No surprise," Larry said. "That's Abe."

"Do either of you know Theodore Stoll, goes by Theo?" I asked.

"By sight only," Cindy said.

Larry nodded. "Yeah, he lives up the street; big house facing the marsh."

Cindy looked at Larry. "How do you know where he lives?"

"He's been in the store a few times. Nice gent, but forgetful. He bought WD-40 for a squeaky door. Came in a week later to buy WD-40; said he had a squeaky door. He told me all about his house." Larry shook his head. "Not that I didn't want to sell another can of the stuff, but I asked him if it was the same door he'd been in earlier to get something for. He said yes, and that he must have forgotten that he already bought a can. How do you forget something like that?"

"Why'd you want to know if we knew him?" Cindy asked.

I told them about how some in the group were worried about his "forgetfulness" and how Abe had been talking to him about his finances. They were afraid that Theo may be vulnerable and since no one knows much about Pottinger, they were worried.

"Good reason to be," Larry said. "But that's not, umm, not the reason we asked you over."

Cindy said, "Let me get you a refill." She popped out of her chair and headed toward the door. From the way they were acting, I thought she was right about me needing more wine.

Larry mumbled something about the weather and how bad today's traffic had been, evidently stalling until Cindy returned.

Cindy handed me my glass. "Where are we, Larry?"

"Waiting for you."

Cindy took her seat and looked at her husband. "Tell him."

"Well, umm," Larry began, hesitated, and continued. "Abe came in the store yesterday. He asked me if I could spare a few minutes. There weren't any customers and Brandon was there if any came in. I said yes and escorted him to the side yard." He took another gulp of beer.

"Get on with it sweetie. Chris doesn't have all night." I wanted to hug her, but instead focused on Larry.

"Abe started talking to me all friendly. Said he'd heard that my wife was the police chief. Said that he was proud of me for owning Pewter Hardware. And since it was the only hardware store on Folly, it must be a goldmine."

Cindy interrupted. "Little does he know."

Larry continued, "He slobbered on about how he was so glad that I'd made a legitimate living and life for myself. If I didn't know him like I do, I'd have felt good about what he was saying. I kept waiting for the other shoe to drop. He blabbered some more goody-goody stuff and then he got around to why he was there. Need more wine? I'm getting another beer."

I said no and he headed to the kitchen.

Cindy watched him go inside and turned to me. "This is rough on him, please be patient. He'll get to the end of his story. Before daylight."

Larry returned and looked at Cindy and she motioned for him to continue.

"Then Abe threw some shit at the fan and it smacked me in the face."

Figuratively, I hoped.

"The damned crook leaned against the side of the building and said something like, 'Wouldn't it be terrible if the citizens of your quaint island learned that you're a thief, and here you are married to the police chief.' He then said, and I think these are his exact words, 'Her career would be in the crapper, and you'd be run out of town on a rail quicker than you can say cat burglar.'"

Larry's whole torso shook, his hands clutched into fists, and he glared at his beer can.

Cindy leaned over and patted his arm. "It's okay hon, we'll get through it. Why don't you tell Chris what Pottinger wants?"

Larry looked up from the can. "Abe looked at me and said, 'You're a good friend, Larry. I've always liked you. I can make this problem go away.'"

"The problem that Abe had just created," I said.

Larry nodded. "He said that he'd driven by our house and could tell that I made a good living and with a wife who's chief, money must be rolling in. He said for a mere fifty-thousand dollars he'd find a way for my *secret* to stay that way."

"What did you tell him?"

"I told him to get his crooked, blackmailing, freakin' ass off my property."

"Good. What'd he say?"

"He gave me his smarmy grin and said he'd give me a week to think about it before everyone on one small island in South Carolina learns about me."

I looked at Cindy who sat stiffly, showing no emotion, and then back at Larry. "What're you going to do?"

"First, I don't have fifty grand lying around. Second, if I did, I wouldn't be caught dead giving him a cent of it. Beyond that, we're at a loss."

Cindy leaned forward in her chair. "I told Larry what happened in Atlanta's ancient history. It's none of anyone's business and to let that slime bucket tell whatever he wants to anyone he wants to tell it to. It's probably a bluff anyway."

"You're wrong, hon," Larry said, his voice calmer and his hands more relaxed. "It could cost you your job if people learned it from Abe who would make a big deal out of it and try to imply that I'm still a crook and that you're corrupt."

Cindy patted his arm again. "Larry you know—"

Larry squeezed her hand. "Wait, I've kept it secret too long. It's time, past time, to tell everyone and take our chances. The mayor already knows and he's your boss, even promoted you to chief. Chris and Charles here know and neither of them has shunned us, at least as far as I can tell."

Cindy held Larry's hand and turned to me. "What do you think, Chris?"

"I agree with you, Cindy; it's been many years and is none of anyone's business."

Cindy nodded and started to speak. I held my hand up. "But, you know as well as I do, probably better, that there are some who would take the information, spread it, embellish it, and use it to derail any of your efforts as chief. They're good at working behind the scene. They won't directly attack you because they know it would look petty. Whether what Larry did decades ago is anyone's business or not, or that it's ancient history, won't matter. Perception is reality, and the perception of those who don't know him, can be devastating if they hear it from Abe."

Larry raised his hand like he wanted to ask his teacher a question. "Here's what I was thinking. Abe said he wouldn't do anything for a week, so I'd like to ask him to reconsider; tell him we don't have the money; and throw myself on his mercy. If he says no, I'll tell everyone before Abe can."

Cindy shook her head. "Larry, that idea's about as good as two broken crutches. Why in holy hotdogs would he show a glimmer of mercy? Maybe I could talk to him, being chief and all."

"No way," Larry said. "I've got to try."

I waved in their direction. "Let me throw in my two-cents worth."

They turned toward me.

"Larry, I don't think he would pay attention to you. He's already said what he would do, and won't believe that you don't have money." I turned to Cindy. "The police chief can't approach him. That could get you in more hot water than anything that Abe can say about Larry. You need to stay above the fray."

"You're right," Cindy said. "So what do we do?"

"I'll talk to him."

Cindy jerked her head toward me. "Hell no!"

Larry leaned toward me. "No way."

I held out both hands and pointed a palm at each of them. "Hear me out. It's a long shot, but think about it. I've met him so he knows who I am. He's heard Chester Carr and Cal Ballew say that I'm friends with the mayor and am dating a detective from Charleston. That gives me some creds. I can tell him that I know that you are in hock up to your shingles with the hardware store and this house and couldn't come up with five- hundred dollars much less fifty grand. He would have no way of knowing it's not true. And I can tell him that the mayor and other 'key officials' already know about you. Again, he has no idea who knows. And I could say that you've already planned to come clean."

Larry looked over at Cindy who said, "I need another beer. Larry? Chris?"

We each said yes, and I took a deep breath.

Cindy returned with the drinks and we stared at the marsh. My thoughts were going in circles and I couldn't imagine what was going on in their heads.

"Guys," I said, "me talking with him would give you deniability and a way to stay at arm's length from any volatile reaction. I'm not saying it'll work, but it's worth a try."

Larry said, "I don't like it. I'd rather just blow his brains out, if he had any."

Cindy put her hand on Larry's arm, again. "Now hon, it's really not that bad. You've made countless friends here. Regardless of your past, they will continue to support you, and for my job, hell, I'm police chief." She chuckled. "I'm supposed to be unpopular."

Her comment was intended to lighten the mood, but I suspect as far as Larry was concerned, it had failed. I know it had for me.

After more discussion, we agreed that my plan was weak, probably would fall on its face, and was possibly dangerous, but no one had a better idea. Larry gave me Abe's number, told me where he lived, and wished me luck.

I started to head home, stopped, and turned to Cindy. "Got a favor to ask."

"Gosh," she said, with mock astonishment, or I assumed mock. "Why in the world would I do you a favor? All you're doing for us is confronting a sleazy blackmailer." She nodded. "Okay, I'm all heart. What is it?"

"Use some of your police resources and see if Abe is licensed to sell reverse mortgages, and if he is, what's the reputation of the company, and if he's a financial advisor. I'm worried about members of the .5 group and Theo in particular."

"You've got it. And Chris, thanks."

I hoped that she would be able to say that in a few days.

CHAPTER EIGHTEEN

After a night of tossing, turning, and second, third, and fourth guessing my offer to talk to Abe, I called him and was now driving to his house. The good news during my morning call was that he was curious enough to want to meet; the bad news was that he said he would be in Charleston until nine tonight and I could meet him then. That meant that I had all day to worry and wonder, and I had used every minute of it. I had called Larry and told him the plan so in case no one ever heard from me again, they would have a starting point to begin the search for my body. Larry had said for me to stop teasing about something like that; I said I wasn't teasing. He wished me luck and asked that I call as soon as the meeting ended.

Abe lived five blocks from the center of town and across the street from the city's tennis court. The plan to talk to him made more sense when I was sitting with two good friends in the safety of the LaMond's back yard. Asinine was the only word that came to me to describe it as I parked a half block from Abe's house.

He greeted me on the porch of his attractive, post-Hugo, two-story brick house, one of the few brick homes on the island. He answered the door in a dark-gray suit and awhite shirt, with a red-and-blue rep tie loosened at the collar. I shook his hand and teased that he looked quite un-Folly-like. He gave me a salesman's, hundred-watt smile and said that he agreed but that he just got home from conducting a wealth-management seminar for a group of attorneys. His story sounded good, but I had my doubts about it, and from his breath, if he had conducted a seminar, it was held in a bar.

He invited me in and offered me a variety of alcoholic beverages. I said that water would do. He smiled and said that with the water tower fewer than a hundred yards from his door he figured that he could find a glass of it. I nearly gagged on his charm while he went to find my drink.

He returned with my water and a glass of an amber-colored liquid, probably bourbon, far from his first of the night. I sat on a soft-leather couch and he pulled a matching chair closer to me and took a sip.

He set his drink on a chrome-and-glass table beside the couch, leaned forward, and said, "Let me guess. You heard me talking to Connie and Harriet about the lucrative and lifetime- security I can offer through a reverse mortgage." He smiled and nodded. I almost had to shade my eyes from the sparkle from his capped teeth. "And, you want to learn how I can ensure your financial future." He leaned back but continued his syrupy smile.

I returned his smile with equal insincerity. "Not exactly."

"Then what brings you out on such a lovely night?" he asked, and took another sip.

"You may not know, but two of my best friends are Larry and Cindy LaMond."

His expression didn't change but I noticed a slight twitch in his cheek. "Oh, I believe—"

"Wait," I interrupted. I couldn't let him throw off my rehearsed introduction. "I was having a conversation with them last night and they shared some disturbing information. I hear that you and Larry go way back. He said that you had some, umm, less- than-legitimate dealings."

Abe leaned forward. "That's not—"

"Stop! Let me finish."

He reached for his glass but didn't lift it from the table, and then leaned back in his chair.

"Larry also shared that you had approached him with what he called an *untenable offer*. Now I don't know if you were serious or teasing your old friend, but let me tell you a few things you might not know about Larry and Cindy."

I threw in teasing to give Abe an escape hatch if he chose to take it, but I couldn't tell from his expression where he would go next, so I continued with the lesser-rehearsed portion of my pitch.

"Larry moved to Folly after serving a stint in prison. The first thing he did when he got here was approach Brian Newman, the police chief, to tell him about his past. That police chief is now mayor. And in those more than eighteen years there has not been a single accusation made against your former colleague. Not only does the mayor know about his past, Larry has told members of the city council, and the Charleston County Sheriff. What you think is a secret is old news to everyone who needs to know." I hesitated and took a drink of water. "Now in the next couple of days, he's going to tell everyone who comes in the store who doesn't already know."

Abe's faux-smile disappeared somewhere along my comments and his right arm began to fidget. "Mr. Landrum, you have no idea what you're talking about. To think that I would threaten my friend is ridiculous."

He reached for his glass, and squeezed it so hard I was afraid it would shatter. I took the break to continue and I ignored his comment. "Now to your blackmail attempt."

"Blackmail!"

I thought he was going to leap out of his chair. I resisted the urge to run and stayed seated. "I hate to break a confidence of a friend, but let me tell you about Larry and Cindy. Yes, his hardware store appears to be successful, but … crap, I hate saying this but you need to know, Larry's in hock up to his roof shingles. He owes a ton of money on the store, he owes countless vendors for inventory, and he's upside down on his house. He couldn't come up with five-hundred dollars, much less fifty thousand. I'm afraid you're fishing in an empty pond."

Abe stood and snarled. "And you want me to believe that pile of shit?"

"Believe what you want," I said as calmly as possible while my insides churned. "Larry doesn't know I'm talking to you; if he did he would have stopped me. I'm doing it because you need to know and if you have half the sense that I believe you do, you'll drop your plan."

I wanted to confront him on his reverse mortgage scheme and whatever con I suspected that he was running on Theo, but I didn't want to hit him with everything at once. I also didn't have evidence to make those accusations.

He reached out, grabbed my elbow, and tried to pull me out of the chair. I yanked my arm back and stood.

"It's time for you to leave before I do something you'll regret," he said and staggered to the front door.

I beat him to the door, grasped the handle, began to jerk it open, and then turned to him. "I hope I made myself clear, Mr. Pottinger. Believe me, it won't turn out in your best interest if you try to pursue your half-baked scheme."

I wasn't about to turn my back to him, so I opened the door the rest of the way and stepped backward.

"You're going to regret coming here." He took a step in my direction and shoved me out.

My foot missed the step and I fell backward. My back hit the small concrete porch and a sharp pain radiated down my arm. I looked up and saw Abe standing in the doorway. He glared at me with a smug look of satisfaction on his face.

He gave me another one of his high-wattage smiles. "Don't you forget—"

I never heard what I wasn't supposed to forget. What I did hear was what sounded like a firecracker exploding across the street behind me. What I saw was horrific. Abe's smile turned to abject fear. His chest exploded. The center of his white shirt turned crimson. And, he flopped backwards as if he'd been clobbered by a sledgehammer. He was dead before his body hit the highly-polished wood floor.

My first thought was total disbelief, followed by, *Am I next?* I rolled to my left and off the porch. I tried to maintain a low profile as I turned to see where the shot had come from. There were two security lights on in the small children's playground across the street but the shadow of the pavilion shaded the three- foot-high wooden picket fence from the light. I caught movement beside the tennis court but it was too dark and too far away to make out anything other than someone dressed in dark clothes walking toward the next street.

I was still afraid to stand and knew I couldn't help Abe. My phone had slipped out of my pocket when I hit the porch. I grabbed it and was relieved to see that the keypad illuminated when I tapped the phone icon. I was shaking and it took two tries to punch 911. I told the dispatcher what had happened but couldn't remember Abe's house number so I said it was across from the tennis court. The calm voice on the phone said that was all she needed and for me to stay on the line.

A large dog stirred up by the gunshot was going berserk a few houses away. The next sounds I heard were from at least two patrol cars and the distinct siren from the city's Fire/Rescue pick- up truck —all screaming my direction.

The Fire-Rescue truck arrived first and two firefighters who doubled as EMTs rushed up the steps to the unmoving con artist. Medical training wasn't necessary for them to tell there was nothing to do for the body splayed in the doorway. One of them turned to me as I stood on the porch and stared at my yellow polo shirt and asked if I had been hit. It was the first time that I'd noticed blood spatter on the shirt. I caught my breath and told him that I was okay. Officer Bishop, whom I had met only a few months earlier at the scene of another death, jumped out of the first patrol car and rushed over to Abe, assessed the situation, and then turned to me. Next to arrive was Officer Allen Spencer, whom I had met my first month on Folly, and had established a good relationship with over the years.

I described what had happened, and what I had seen across the street. Both officers looked toward the tennis court and asked if I had seen the vehicle the shooter left in. I said no and that the person had gone around the corner and I couldn't see anything. Bishop radioed to the only other patrol officer on duty to stop any vehicle moving in the general vicinity. Spencer walked to the fence to see if he could see anything. I figured it would be futile.

I was surprised to see Cindy's unmarked police car arrive next. Like Officer Bishop, she walked over to Abe, spoke to the EMT, and said something to Officer Bishop before coming over to me.

She looked at my bloody shirt. "You okay?" Her face was expressionless but she looked like she had aged ten years since last night. She turned and looked toward the tennis courts.

It was warm but I was shivering. I said I was okay and she asked me to join her in her vehicle. She offered me a bottle of water. I accepted.

"What happened? Don't leave anything out."

I began from when I arrived through when I called 911. She

asked me to repeat what Abe and I had talked about and what I saw across the street after Abe had taken his last breath. She mumbled a half-dozen profanities and then called Detective Adair. She slammed her hand on the steering wheel and stared at Abe's front door. I wished that I had a steering wheel to pound.

CHAPTER NINETEEN

I was still in the chief's car when the Coroner's van inched around us on the narrow road and stopped in front of Abe's house. Five minutes later, a white, unmarked Chevy Caprice pulled in behind the coroner's vehicle and Detective Adair stepped out, buttoned his navy blazer, and glanced around before walking up the steps and looking at the late Abe Pottinger. Adair looked as fresh and unruffled as if he had just stepped out of a clothing store ad as he talked to Officer Bishop and he looked back at us before walking to Cindy's window.

"Good evening, Chief," he said in a tone that didn't imply that there was anything good about it. He then leaned down and stared at me. "You again."

Cindy gave him a staccato, police-speak version of what had happened and Adair asked if Cindy and I could join him in his car. It was one of the last things I wanted to do, but didn't take it as a request. We followed with Cindy taking the passenger's seat and I slid in back.

"Mr. Landrum, why were you at the victim's house?"

I had hoped we would ease into that question, but Adair didn't seem able to ease into anything.

I nodded toward the house. "I met him a few days ago when I joined a walking group that a friend had started. Abe was a member of that group." *All true*, I thought, and continued, "He had been talking to the others about something called a reverse mortgage that he was selling. I wasn't knowledgeable about it and wanted to find out more." All true, but not quite—not even approximately—all the truth.

Cindy leaned up in the seat and turned toward me but didn't say anything.

"Why were you meeting with him this late?"

A marginally good question, I thought. "When I called him he said that he would be at a meeting in Charleston and wouldn't be home until nine."

"And your curiosity about reverse mortgages couldn't wait another day during normal business hours?"

"Could have, I suppose."

Adair jotted a note in a small notebook that he had taken from his inside coat pocket and turned back to me. "Hmm, okay," he said, and frowned. "Walk me through what happened."

This is where it's going to get tricky. I told him that we had finished our conversation about reverse mortgages and I was leaving when Abe was shot.

I looked at Adair and looked at Abe's front door. "I was going out the door and Abe was holding it for me, then the shot." I looked at Adair like that was it.

He stared at Abe's door. "Were you facing the street? Did you see where the shot came from?"

Careful Chris. "No. I was facing Abe." I glanced down at the blood spatter.

The detective followed my gaze, and then looked at his notebook. "Were you beside him in the doorway, in front or behind him?"

I knew where he was headed. "I was sort of in front of him, almost on the front porch, sort of turned sideways, I guess."

He looked at the front door and then across the street at the fence and the tennis court. "Mr. Landrum, is there anyone who would have wanted you dead?"

Other than Abe Pottinger, I thought. "No, why?"

Adair rubbed his chin, glanced at Cindy, and back at me. "From how you described what happened, it looks like you could have been the intended victim and the shooter missed. You were between Pottinger and the shooter. Why would someone have taken a shot at him with you in the way?"

"Good point," I said, knowing that if the forensic services techs were as good as I thought they were, the pattern of blood spatter on my shirt would tell a different version, would tell that I was flat on the porch when the shot was taken. How would I explain that?

Adair squeezed the bridge of his nose and stared at me. "You're certain you don't know anyone who had it in for you?"

"Not to my knowledge."

He jotted another note. "Okay, now when you were in there," Adair nodded toward Abe's house, "did he seem nervous, say anything about being in danger, or anything out of the ordinary?"

"Not really. I'd only talked to him briefly before tonight, so I couldn't tell if he was acting strange. He seemed fine."

"Did you notice anyone in the area when you arrived?"

Like someone with a rifle lurking around the house, I thought. "No."

Adair turned to Cindy. "Chief, did you know the victim?" And I thought my answers were touchy.

"Umm," Cindy said, and then she paused. "I never met him."

"Okay," Adair said. "Back to you Mr. Landrum. You told Officer …"

"Bishop," Cindy said.

"Right. You told Officer Bishop you saw someone running away by the fence." Adair looked toward the two officers who were waving flashlights back and forth lighting the ground beside tennis court fence.

"Not running, it was more like a confident walk. All I could tell was that the person was dressed in dark clothes."

"Man or woman?" Adair asked.

"Couldn't tell." The person was too far away and it was dark."

He jotted another note and then looked me in the eyes. "Tell me one more time where were you were when he was hit?"

I repeated my fictionalized version. Adair looked skeptical, but he always did, so I couldn't tell if he believed me or not. He asked if there was anything that I wanted to add. I said no and he closed his notebook.

He asked Cindy to stay behind and told me that he didn't have anything else—for now.

Detective Adair hollered as I walked away, "Mr. Landrum, please give your shirt to one of the techs standing by the Forensic Services SUV."

I said, "Sure," as if there was a choice.

Five minutes later I was pulling into my drive, shirtless, sweating and still trembling from what had happened. I was thinking how things couldn't get worse, when my phone's ringtone startled me.

"Chris, this is Sean. Thought you'd want to know. The police arrested Mel Evans for murder."

I nearly dropped the phone. "When?"

"An hour ago. He called from jail. I'd told him that I wasn't the person he needed if he was arrested; I reminded him of that, hung up, and called my buddy, Martin Camp, he's one of the best criminal defense attorneys around. I caught him at a fund-raiser for a gubernatorial candidate. He griped about having to visit the jail in a tux, but said he would head over and see what he could do."

"What evidence do they have?"

"No clue. Mel didn't know."

Will I ever learn not to say that things can't get worse?

CHAPTER TWENTY

I called Charles first thing in the morning to see if he wanted to meet for breakfast. I realized that I hadn't eaten since lunch yesterday, was starved, and needed someone to talk to about what had happened. More importantly, Charles would be on my case for weeks if I let much time pass before I told him everything. If he heard it from someone else, he'd make me regret not telling him not only for weeks, but for months, possibly years. Charles's memory would make an elephant look senile.

As usual, he was sitting on the front patio of the Dog and was quick to remind me that he had been there for a half hour, and that I was late because I had the audacity to arrive at the time we had agreed upon. After the last twenty-four hours, I was in no mood to banter, and ignored the comment.

"Did you fall off the wrong side of the bed this morning?" he asked as I lowered myself into the chair.

"If you only knew."

Amber stopped at the table after delivering breakfast to two couples at the next table.

"Coffee?" she asked.

I nodded and she headed inside. Amber and I had dated for a couple of years and we had still remained good friends.

"Then you'd better tell me what I should know," Charles said.

The patio was full and I leaned closer to the table so I wouldn't have to talk loud. "Mel was arrested last night for killing the student."

Charles reacted like he'd been hit by a Taser. "You're kidding."

"Sean Aker called me late to tell me."

I didn't want to say it was before eleven o-clock or Charles would have chided me for not calling him last night. I didn't look forward to sharing what else had happened.

"Why? What do they have on him?"

His questions were familiar since they were the same ones I'd asked Sean. I told him everything that I had learned, which wasn't much, and he asked what we could do. I said there wasn't anything until we knew more.

Charles took a deep breath, looked around to see if anyone was eavesdropping, and leaned closer to the table. "Could he have done it?"

Good question, I thought. "He has a temper; his military training probably taught him a dozen ways to kill; and, he has little sympathy for, as he puts it, 'the sniveling, spoiled, college brats,' that he ferries through the marsh."

"Christ, Chris, I hope you're not his defense attorney." I shook my head. "Hold on."

Charles gestured for me to continue.

"With that said, I haven't seen anything to make me to believe he's guilty. He came to me as soon as he heard that someone may not have made it back from the party. He asked me to go with him to Boneyard Beach to see if we could find out anything about a missing student. Would he have done that if he killed the kid?"

"Not unless he was trying to deflect blame."

"What motive would he have for killing a sniveling, spoiled, college brat?" I asked.

"You said William told you that the kid was gay. Maybe he made a pass at Mel, or vice versa, and something went wrong."

I shook my head. "Can you picture Mel killing a kid over that?"

Charles looked down at the table and back at me. "No, but it doesn't matter a fig what I think. What do the cops think? They must have something more than a hunch or Mel wouldn't be in jail."

"We need to wait and see."

Amber returned with my coffee and apologized for taking so long. I ordered oatmeal and bacon.

"Got it." she said. "And what's this I hear about you being with that guy who got murdered last night?"

Charles jerked his head toward me so quickly that I feared that he'd sustained whiplash.

I looked at Amber. "I'll tell you later."

She started to object, but instead said she'd get breakfast started.

Charles had both hands on the table and looked like he was ready to leapfrog over it to get to me. "Spit it out."

I motioned for him to sit back and I began with my conversation with Larry and Cindy and regurgitated everything from that meeting to handing my shirt to the Forensic Services tech. Charles had asked me to repeat so much of it that my breakfast had arrived and was getting cold before I had to tell him for the second time what color shirt I had been wearing.

Charles let the information percolate. "So, if you hadn't stumbled, I'd be eating breakfast by myself."

"True, but only if I was the target."

"Other than me at this moment, who'd want to shoot you?"

"You're beginning to sound like Detective Adair, without the good clothes and starched-on frown." I shook my head. "I don't know anyone who would want me dead."

"Then who'd want Abe coffined, besides, I can't believe I'm saying this, Larry?"

I pushed the oatmeal around the bowl. "Larry thought that Abe was up to no good when he joined the walking group. Chester said the same thing. If that's true, any of the walkers could have a motive."

"You said you saw someone rushing away."

I nodded.

"Then scratch Theo."

I smiled. "True."

Charles turned serious. "Who knew you'd be there?"

I looked toward the street and the small group of people waiting for a table, and back at Charles. "Only Larry and Cindy." I hesitated. "Unless Abe told someone."

"And according to my source who waited hours, many hours, to tell me about the murder, Cindy was one of the first there after it happened."

I wondered what had taken him so long to "remind" me about waiting until this morning to tell him. Wondered, but didn't acknowledge it. "She was there almost immediately."

"So unless Larry was doing something like hosting a prayer meeting, he doesn't have an alibi."

"Odds are he was alone," I said.

"And he had one humongous clump of motive."

"Yes."

Charles leaned back in his chair and looked at me. "And it slipped your mind to tell Detective Adair about the real reason you were at Abe's?"

"I wouldn't say slipped, but I didn't tell him."

Charles's head bobbed up and down. "Because if you told him, Larry'd be sharing a cell with Mel."

"Adair would need more than that, but that's a valid point."

"Let's say that Larry did it, why would he shoot him when you were there?"

"Don't know, but Larry was mighty angry at Abe. Cindy was working so he was alone, and he knew when I'd be there, and could have figured that Abe would be at the door to meet me, or see me off."

Charles rubbed his left temple and gazed at a car parking in the small lot in front of the restaurant. "It would've taken a good shot from someone across the street to hit Abe. Does Larry even know how to shoot a rifle?"

"Don't recall him saying anything. But that's not something that comes up in many conversations."

"So, we don't know if Larry was a good shot, but we do know that it doesn't take a whole hell of a lot of training for someone to take a piece of wood and smack a college student on the noggin'."

My head began to hurt. In fewer than twenty-four hours one friend was arrested for murder and another good friend became, to me, the prime suspect in another killing. And, if I told the police what I knew, Larry would go to the top of the cop's suspect list. Could both Larry and Mel be guilty? They're head-strong, neither has an alibi, and if pressed under the right circumstance, they were capable of violence.

"Are you listening?" Charles said, jolting me out of my depressing thoughts.

"Sorry, what?"

"I said what are we going to do about it?"

Take three ibuprofen, get in bed and pull the covers up over my head, and wish it would all go away, I wished. "Find out what's going on."

"Right answer."

While Charles said it was the right answer, he also said he didn't have time to talk about it because he had to deliver some surf-stuff for Dude. Before he headed out, he said that he and Heather wanted to go to Crosby's Dock Party tonight and asked if Karen and I wanted to go with them. That was Charles-speak for could I drive. I reminded him that Karen was out of town, but that I'd go. He said great and asked for a ride. I said sure.

CHAPTER TWENTY-ONE

I picked up Charles and then Heather at her tiny apartment in a former bed and breakfast that had been converted into apartments. Charles's aunt had lived there for the all-too-brief time that she had been with us on the island. Her death still hurt each time I saw the building and I knew it affected Charles, although having Heather there brought enough cheer to his life to neutralize some of his pain.

Crosby's Fish & Shrimp Co. was a family-owned seafood market by day, rented its dock and facilities for weddings and other special events, and, most every Friday evening, hosted a party featuring, to no one's surprise, fresh fish, beer, wine, and live music. The event had been a favorite for locals and enlightened vacationers for years, and garnered large crowds to enjoy the food, drink, and fantastic views of the sun sinking behind the water and marsh. I had attended a few times with Karen, and was surprised that Charles had wanted to venture this far off-island. On the mile- long drive over, I learned that attending was Heather's idea. She said that Charles needed to expand his horizons, and besides, she wanted to hear who her musical competition was. I thought, but didn't say, that no one could compete with Heather's vocal skills, although chalk scraping a blackboard would come close.

We arrived at five forty-five to find the gravel lot full even though the party didn't begin until six. I had to park along the road. Charles was quick to point out that if I wasn't late, we could have parked in Crosby's lot. I was equally quick to point out that he had said what time for me to pick him up. "Harrumph," was his articulate, clarifying response.

Not only was the lot full, but the dock was already packed and we had to stand in line to get drinks, and stand in a longer line to order supper. Charles sent Heather in search of a table, saying that she could use her charm and convince someone to move over and share the limited number of tables with us.

A thin, long-haired vocalist was under a covered portion of the dock singing "Sittin' on the Dock of the Bay" and accompanying himself on guitar. All the tables were full but by the time Charles and I had our food and drink, Heather had charmed two couples into sharing their table. Listening to the musician who had transitioned into "Leaving on a Jet Plane," hearing the sounds of the festive, Friday-night crowd, and watching the fishing boats bobbing in the water had the calming effect that I'd hoped for. The terror of the shooting and my worry about Larry and Mel were drifting away and I began to enjoy my shrimp, coleslaw, and hush puppies. A plastic cup of wine didn't hurt either.

The sounds of "Rainbow Connection" had ended and Heather noticed that the musician had taken a break and was talking to a young girl. Heather hopped up and said she needed to ask him something. She stood behind the curly-haired girl talking to the singer and Charles leaned close to me. "So, how're we going to figure out who killed the con guy and the student?"

There went my calm evening.

I looked at Heather who was now talking to the entertainer and laughing at something that he'd said. I turned back to Charles. "I'll call Sean Monday and see if he knows what Mel's attorney has learned."

"Why not talk to Mel's new lawyer?"

"He doesn't know me and wouldn't be able to tell me anything anyway. Mel's the client."

Charles thought a second. "What about Abe?"

"That's a tough one."

Before I could elaborate, Heather returned sporting a huge grin.

"That's Jerry." She pointed at the vocalist. "Jerry Crosby, nice guy. I told him I was a singer and asked if he'd ever shared the stage with guest musicians."

If Jerry only knew, I thought, but kept my mouth shut. Charles didn't. "What'd he say?"

"He said no, but he had a list of people who could sub for him if he couldn't make the weekly gig." She pantomimed writing on a large piece of paper and smiled even broader. "He said he would add me to the list. He was really nice." Heather air- strummed a guitar and returned to her seat and meal.

I prayed that Jerry had a long list as he started singing "**Margaritaville**."

If Charles's question hadn't put enough of a damper in my calming evening, a bucket of damper poured on my head when I saw Chief LaMond walking across the deck followed by two of her officers. I breathed a sigh of relief as she passed our table. She gave me a slight nod, and proceeded to the far end of the dock where some people were yelling and waving for her.

Charles dropped his fork on the plate and pushed away from the table. "Let's see what's going on."

I'd had enough police contact for the week, for that matter, for a lifetime, and declined, but that didn't stop my friend who followed Cindy and her colleagues to whatever was happening. I took a bite of shrimp but noticed that it didn't taste as good as it did before

Cindy arrived. I felt bad about not telling Detective Adair the reason that I had been to see Abe and still had the nagging feeling that Larry could be connected to his murder. Heather was telling one of the couples who had given up part of their table to us that her new friend Jerry was going to call her when he needed a fill-in. She must have forgotten the definition of list.

Charles returned more quickly than I had anticipated. "No biggie. Some drunk was seeing double and walked off the second dock that was only in his pickled mind. He's soused and doused."

Heather laughed and I was relieved that Cindy hadn't been looking for me.

"Oh yeah," Charles said after he winked at Heather. "Chief LaMond wants to talk to you before she leaves."

There went my relief, as Jerry strummed the first notes of "Bye Bye Love."

The police "event" had ended and Cindy's two officers casually walked the drunk off the property; as casually as possible with a soaked, staggering, middle-aged, bald-headed gentleman being aided by two Folly Beach police officers as they inched their way through the crowd. Cindy moved to a more isolated section of the dock behind a small storage building and waved me over. I saw her motioning and she knew I saw her, so pretending that she didn't exist wasn't an option. Charles asked if he should go with me and I said no.

I smiled as I approached the unsmiling chief. "Have fun out there?" I pointed to where the drunk had been pulled out of the drink.

Cindy shook her head. "It's the beginning of the weekend. It'll only get worse."

She took me by the elbow and moved us farther away from the crowd and music.

"Chris," She glanced at the wood deck, "we've known each other since when?"

"Since the day you got here. What, seven years or so?"

"About right. You came to my wedding; you've had faith in me even when I didn't; hell, you were even a big supporter and encouraged Brian Newman to appoint me chief despite the griping of a bunch of Folly-freaks."

I nodded and wondered where she was going with the trip down memory lane.

"It's hard to be mad at a good friend." She continued to look down. "But Chris, you've done it." She looked up at my face and shook her head. "What in holy-hell were you thinking when you lied to Detective Adair?"

I had asked myself the same thing several times. I hesitated before answering, but said, "Technically I didn't lie. I did want to know more about reverse mortgages."

Cindy tapped her polished shoes on the deck and took a deep breath. "Did you talk to him about the mortgages?"

"No."

She smacked her fist on the side of the building. "Have you talked to Detective Adair since we were in his car?"

"No."

"You never told him that Larry had asked you to talk to Abe, or that Larry knew the con artist."

"No. I didn't lie about it. I just didn't bring it up." I knew it was a pathetic argument as I said it.

She gritted her teeth, her fists were clinched. "Damn it. Why not?"

I glanced at our table and Charles was motioning for me to "invite" him over. I ignored his gyrations. Cindy was angry and I didn't need Charles to either defend me or take Cindy's side.

I turned back to the chief. "Because it would have implicated your husband."

Cindy blinked, started to speak, and then looked away from me and toward the water. I waited and she turned back toward me. "Are you serious? Do you think Larry killed Pottinger?"

"Do you?"

"No." Her fists were still clinched and she shook her head. "You think he did, don't you?"

"Cindy, I don't think so. I've known him longer than I've known you. He's been up front with me about everything, and we've been together in tight situations. He's helped me out of a jam or two, and has even used his pre-going-straight skills to help me catch a killer. I also know he was awfully mad at Abe and worried that your career and reputation would be hurt if Abe carried through with his threat."

"I thought I knew you better than that, Chris. There's no way. No way."

"You do know me that well, Cindy, but leave me out of it for a minute. Look at it like this. Does Larry have an alibi? You were working when Abe was shot."

"Yes, but—"

"Hold it," I interrupted. "Would he have known how to use a rifle? Could he have hit Abe from across the street?"

Cindy looked down at the pier and mumbled, "He used to hunt deer, but ... but you know he wouldn't—"

I put my palm up to her face. "Cindy, I may know that he wouldn't have done it, but I still have doubts. How would this sound to a detective who doesn't know either of you? Larry had motive, a good one. He has no alibi. And as a hunter, he knew his way around guns, so he would have means."

"He didn't do it."

"I'm not saying he did, but think about it. You're a cop. What would you do if faced with a situation like this?"

"I don't have to think about anything." She glared at me. "Larry had nothing to do with the murder, and I damned well don't appreciate it that you even think that he might have. Thanks a hell of a lot, *friend*."

She turned and jogged off the deck.

I gazed out over the water and listened to Jerry Crosby sing "Help Me Make It Through the Night."

I took a minute to calm down before returning to the table. I'd had a few minor disagreements with Cindy over the years, but nothing approached tonight's outburst. She saw it as an attack on Larry, and to be honest, it may have been. I had doubts about his innocence, and if Cindy looked at it objectively, she would have questions. I leaned over the railing and looked at the black water below and then closed my eyes and tried to visualize the person hurrying away from the fence at the tennis court. Could it have been Larry? I had nothing to help me judge the person's height, but my first reaction was the person wasn't tall, so yes, it could have been him, then again it could also have been countless other people.

Heather was mouthing the lyrics to "Me and Bobby McGee" as Jerry sang it from the bandstand, Charles's arm was draped over her shoulder, and the others at the table were enjoying the fine weather, friends, and music. I was miserable.

I returned to the table but instead of sitting, I said, "Ready to go?"

Heather looked at Charles and he looked up at me then at his wrist. "There's an hour to go. Why—"

I interrupted, "I'll walk home and get the car from your apartment in the morning." The last place I wanted to be was around a bunch of people having a good time. I grabbed my keys and tossed them to Charles, then headed for the road and home.

I hadn't walked more than a few hundred yards when my car pulled off the road in front of me.

Charles opened the driver's door and yelled, "Old people shouldn't be walking that far. Get in."

I started to argue and tell him to go back to the party, but decided that it would have been to no avail and instead climbed in the back seat.

Charles said that it was getting too cold to stay at the party. It wasn't. He said that Heather was getting tired of the music. Impossible. And as he pulled up in front of her apartment, he said that it was looking like rain and they decided to leave before a downpour arrived. There wasn't a cloud in the sky.

"So, what in the pluff-mud's going on?" Charles had returned to the car after walking Heather to the door. I had moved to the seat that Heather had vacated.

I told him about my discussion—argument—with Cindy. "What did you expect? You were accusing her hubby of murder. That'd piss anyone off."

"I understand, but I wanted her to look at it from an outsider's perspective."

"Did you miss the part about Larry being her hubby?" We were still in the gravel lot in front of Heather's building.

I hated it when Charles was right. "Probably."

Charles looked at the building and then at me. "You think he could've done it, don't you?"

"Don't you?"

"Yeah," Charles mumbled.

"I don't want to believe it. My heart says he didn't. I know Larry fairly well, but I know that if given enough motivation people are capable of things that would never enter their mind. Larry's protective of Cindy and he saw Abe's threats as an attack on her."

I looked over at Charles. Miraculously, he remained silent. "There's more," I said. "I know why I didn't tell Detective Adair about my reason for meeting with Abe, but now what do I do?"

"You wanted to protect your friends. I would have done the same."

"But now what? Cindy was angry because I didn't tell him. But if I tell him, it'll put Larry at the top of the suspect list."

"What if he did it?"

A sharp pain developed behind my eyes, my legs felt heavy, and I wondered why I had moved to Folly. "Then he should be arrested," I whispered.

"Even if Abe was a con artist, blackmailing son-of-a-scorpion?"

"Yeah."

"Okay," Charles said. "Let's don't get the caboose before the engine. Let's say Larry was sitting in his house figuring how many toilet seats to order when the blackmailer became dead. Who pulled the trigger?"

"If Larry's right about Abe not changing his spots, there could be several people he's either ripped-off or tried to rip off before he ever crossed the Folly River. Even members of .5 could have motive. We don't know if any of them have already fallen for his reverse mortgage scheme or if Theo has invested his significant wealth in something that Abe was pushing. In addition to club members, there could be others here who feel that he took advantage of them."

"Wouldn't we have heard if any of the .5 group felt that he ripped them off?" Charles said.

"Probably. Those folks don't hesitate to gripe."

"And gripe, and gripe, and gripe."

I smiled, for the first time in hours.

"But," Charles continued, "would that be enough reason for one of them to shoot him?"

I nodded. "What are the two most common reasons people are murdered?"

"Love or money," Charles said without hesitation. I nodded again.

"Same reasons people get married," Charles added. "Doubt Abe would have been killed for love; who could love that viper?" He hesitated and then tapped the steering wheel. "Hmm, money, yeah.

But doesn't that bring us back to Larry. Fifty-thousand smackers is a hefty amount of motive."

"And he'd be protecting the love of his life—love and money."

"Chris, you know how to ruin a perfectly nice evening." We left the parking lot and drove the short distance to Charles's apartment. I realized that tomorrow the—our—walking group would be making another mini-excursion, and told him that instead of opening the gallery, I'd meet him at the pier.

"Good. Then we can ask which one shot Abe."

On my way home, I decided that Charles's direct approach would be unwise, and unproductive, but did start thinking about the possibility that one of the .5 members did it. Was it wishful thinking to get Larry off the hook? And what should I do about telling Detective Adair the truth about my fateful trip to Abe's house? My head continued to hurt and sleep waited until three o'clock to arrive.

CHAPTER TWENTY-TWO

I met Charles at the foot of the Folly Pier. The morning was cool and there were already a dozen cars in the lot, and four men nodded to us as they pulled their fishing carts to the pier's ramp. Charles was decked out in a long-sleeve, UNLV scarlet and gray T-shirt, gray cargo shorts, gray tennis shoes, canvas Tilley, and his cane.

"A gray day?" I said.

"Semi-mourning for Abe. Thought the group would appreciate it, but couldn't quite go for black since he was a lying, cheating, blackmailing sleazeball."

I must have thought even less of Abe since I had on an orange polo shirt, unadorned with any marketing logos, my usual tan shorts, and Tilley; nothing gray except my mood.

"So," said Charles, "now that you won't let me ask the group who wiped out one of their members, what's our plan?"

"Charles, you claim to be the detective, what do you think we should do?"

"Other than asking who did it?"

I nodded.

"Hmm," He rubbed his chin. "Got it. A friend of mine, who happens to be standing in front of me, had been known to say, 'You learn more from listening than you do by talking.' I think he meant that we already know everything we say, but can learn from the other person."

I nodded again. "Good. You do listen at times."

"What?"

Charles had managed to get me to smile; the first of the day. I hoped not the last.

"What are we listening for?" he asked.

"Anything out of the norm."

He turned and watched Chester's Grand Marquis inch its way into the lot followed by Cal's classic 1971 Cadillac Eldorado. "With that group, we need to listen for something that sounds normal."

Harriet hopped out of the land yacht followed by David Darnell, Connie, and Theo. Chester slowly pulled himself out of the driver's seat by holding on to the door.

Chester watched Cal and William exit the Cadillac. "Those two beansprouts said there weren't enough cubic feet left in my car so they caravanned with us."

Cal tipped his sweat-stained Stetson toward Charles and me. In addition to a Stetson, Cal wore bright-red, shiny jogging shorts, a black T-shirt with *Amarillo by Morning* in silver script on the front, and his cowboy boots that had to be as old as his Stetson, which dated to the 1970s. I smiled and thought about Charles' comment about normal.

He also had a black ribbon tied around his upper arm, a ribbon identical to those worn by the other recent arrivals. Normal? Chester held out two ribbons. "Let me tie these on you. I thought since we lost Abe, we should honor his memory and mourn the loss. He was a valued member of .5 and the first of our close-knit group to leave us."

"Crap," Connie said. "We didn't lose him; he's dead. Besides, we hardly knew the man. I, for one, don't plan to miss him much."

David put a hand on Connie's arm. "Now Connie, a loss of one is a loss for all."

"What the hell does that mean?" Harriet blurted.

Charles leaned over to me and whispered, "Normal must be taking a later bus."

William, who does better at avoiding the mundane and pettiness around him, said, "What will be our destination this fine morning?"

"After some debate on the ride over, we decided we would get adventurous and stroll west on Arctic Avenue to where it intersects with Third Street and then up Third to Cooper, over to Center, and back to the house. It will be our longest walk yet, another step in preparation for our goal of reaching Boneyard Beach."

Chester's "adventurous" and "longest walk yet" consisted of four normal-length blocks with two short blocks thrown in. It may be another step toward the goal, but only a baby step.

"Let's get going," Harriet said. "It'll take us all day at this pace." Theo said, "Huh?"

Harriet put her arm around his bony shoulder and yelled into his ear. "This way, Theo."

Connie walked with Theo and Harriet toward Arctic Avenue. Harriet moved close to Theo and kept her arm around his waist.

The rest of us followed Theo and his escorts. Chester hung back with Charles and me.

"We're all bummed about Abe. I had trouble herding them in the car; they wanted to stand around and mope. Who would have wanted him dead?"

"Don't know," Charles said. "You have any idea?" It was better than asking Chester if he killed him.

Chester looked ahead to the group that had Theo picking up the rear, still aided by Connie and Harriet. Chester leaned closer to

Charles and me. "Between you, me, and the lamppost, I say good riddance."

There wasn't a lamppost within a hundred yards. "Didn't trust him?" I asked.

"I could be wrong," Chester said, "but I've been around the block a few times, and like I told you the other day, I had the feeling that he had a con or two in him."

"Anything specific?" I asked.

"*Too good to be true*, popped in my head when he started talking about those backward mortgages."

Always-correct Charles interrupted. "Reverse mortgages."

"Whatever," Chester said. "If they were so good, why didn't other companies pay as much as his? Think he had the gals snowed." He hesitated and pointed toward Theo's escorts. "David was also asking him a bunch of questions like he was interested. Seems that since he's an insurance agent, he'd know all about that stuff. Maybe he was just curious. Oh well, just seemed strange."

"Anything else?" Charles asked.

Chester looked at the group that was already past the Oceanfront Villas, a half block ahead of us. "We need to step it up," Chester said. "Don't want them to think their leader is a slacker."

We picked up the pace and Charles picked up the questions. "Anything else?"

"Nothing in particular," Chester said. "Didn't like the way he was sucking up to Theo."

"How?" Charles asked.

"On the way over, Theo said something about investing in a good deal that Abe showed him. That's all I know. You could ask him, he seemed to want to talk but the only person who seemed to understand what he was saying was David."

We had caught up with Theo, Harriet, and Connie—not too difficult since they were barely moving.

Connie leaned close to Theo and yelled, "That's too bad. We'll miss him."

Theo lowered his head. "We were meeting today."

Charles moved beside Connie and walked laboriously slow with the trio. "Hey, Theo, who'd you say you were meeting?"

Connie stepped back so Charles could get closer.

"Had an appointment with Abe after today's walk. I had a check ready to give him so he could put me in a special stock offering he told me about."

Charles had to yell for Theo to hear him, and Theo shouted everything he said. The rest of the group was well ahead of us, but seemed to slow, almost stop, when Theo started talking about a check and meeting Abe.

Chester said, "That's what he was talking about in the car."

I moved closer to Theo. "What kind of investment?"

Theo looked over to see who was talking. "Hush, hush," he said. "New company, going public next week. Abe said it'd make Microsoft look like a lemonade stand. Said he'd triple my million dollars overnight. Showed me a prospectus and letters from big-wigs in the industry saying it'd be the biggest thing since the iPhone."

Harriet was still holding on to Theo's arm. "Now Theo, remember I told you to check it out before giving him the money."

He huffed. "I did. Read the prospectus and called one of the experts Abe told me about. Guy out in Silicon Valley. He was real knowledgeable about the stock. Said it was a sure thing."

Having a second person involved reminded me of how Abe had used Larry as his security specialist when he was conning businesses in Atlanta.

I asked, "Could I see the prospectus?" That was the first thing that Abe was hawking that could be verified.

Theo shook his head. "No way. It was so confidential that Abe took it right back. Said if it got in the wrong hands, it could squelch the deal."

That made no sense, but I didn't see an upside of telling him so. "How about the expert's phone number in California?"

"Abe let me use his phone and he punched in the number. Sorry." He looked back down at the roadway and shook his head. "And then someone went and killed him. Such a shame."

"Now, Theo," Connie said, "you don't need the money the stock would have made you. You'll be fine."

"I know, I know. Just hate to pass on a golden opportunity."

The leaders of the group had passed the public restrooms and were stopped at the corner of West Ashley Avenue waiting for a break in the traffic so they could cross one of Folly's main streets. Chester yelled, "Wait for us!"

David waved for us to hurry. "Then speed it up, ET."

Theo, aka ET, said, "What?"

"They're waiting for us," Connie said.

A rather generous translation, I thought.

"Have we learned anything useful yet?" Charles whispered as we caught up with the frontrunners—frontcrawlers.

"No prospectus, no one to contact about the 'sure thing,' and Theo ready to hand Abe a check for a million dollars. That adds up to a con, regardless how you spin it."

Charles nodded. "Then who killed him?"

The entire group, excluding the late Abe Pottinger, was now standing beside West Ashley Avenue waiting for the traffic to thin enough for us to make it across the street, when the conversation took a troubling turn.

David said, "Anybody know the guy who owns the hardware store?"

"Sure," Chester said. "Larry."

"Why?" Charles asked.

David took off his black NRA ball cap, wiped sweat from his

forehead, and looked at Charles. "Since I'm the newbie, I was just wondering."

Just wondering would never cut it with Charles. "Why wondering?"

Chester yelled, "Go!" before David answered.

We made it safely across the street and the group gathered around David.

"Don't know if I should say anything." David then hesitated and looked at each of us.

"Sure you should," Charles said, afraid that David would clam up.

"Well, I was in Pewter the day before Abe, umm, passed away. With the house we bought, I'm afraid I've become a regular at the hardware store. Anyway, I was picking up some caulk for the shower and to see if they had .22 caliber cartridges and Larry and Abe were in the back. They didn't see me."

"And?" Charles said.

"And, they were in the middle of, how shall I say this, a heated discussion."

"Like a fight?" Chester said.

David had become the center of attention. "More like an argument, no blows were thrown."

"What were they jawin' about?" Cal asked.

"I feel bad saying all this, seeing that Abe's no longer with us." He glanced down at the black ribbon on his arm.

Charles tapped David with his cane. "It's okay."

"I didn't catch all of it, but Larry said something about Atlanta. And, Abe said prison, but I didn't catch what he meant. He said that Larry had better watch out."

I felt a knot tighten in my stomach. This was a topic I would prefer to have stayed buried.

Cal stepped closer to David. "What'd he mean?"

"Don't know. He could've been warning Larry about something." He hesitated and looked at the road. "Or I guess it's possible that he was threatening him."

Charles asked, "Was that all they said?"

"That's all I caught. That's why I was wondering if any of you knew Larry."

Harriet said, "You think Larry shot Abe?"

William looked at Harriet and then around to the rest of us and broke his silence. "Perhaps I am speaking out of turn, but I've known Mr. LaMond, Larry, for perhaps more years than anyone here, other than possibly Charles. I find him to be an upstanding, honorable, honest, and quite pleasant individual. I cannot even find it in my imagination to picture him assassinating Mr. Pottinger."

I could only imagine what William and the rest of the group would think if they knew what I knew about Larry. They wouldn't hear it from me.

Cal said, "I agree with William," Chester chimed in, "Me too."

"I'm not accusing him of anything," David said. "I don't know anything about the man other than he's been pleasant and helpful when I've been in the store. I simply found their disagreement odd in light of what's happened."

"David," Chester said, "I think you should tell the police. It might help their investigation."

"I don't know. I don't want to get someone in trouble for nothing. I really didn't hear enough to say much."

Connie had remained quiet throughout the conversation, and I was surprised when she said, "I think you need to go to the cops. They were on the radio this morning asking for information. What you heard may not mean anything to you but you never know where it might tell the police."

"Connie's right," Harriet said. "We owe it to Abe. Anything that'll help find his killer."

Theo looked at Connie and then over at Harriet. "Y'all talking about that dead kid who was killed by the queer boat captain?"

None of us were, but that got everyone's attention.

Harriet moved closer to Theo and said, "What boat captain?"

"Melville, or something like that. Don't hear good sometimes, so I could have the name wrong. He's the que—, umm, homosexual who takes drunken kids out into the marsh to do who knows what."

Charles moved closer to Theo. "The captain's name is Mel not Melville. His name is Mel Evans. What makes you think he killed the student?"

"Everyone knows he did," Theo said as he looked around the group.

"That's what I heard," Connie said. "Didn't you hear it, Harriet?"

"Yeah, but I didn't pay no mind to it. Rumors are as thick as gnats around here."

Cal stepped closer. "Gall darn it," he took off his Stetson and waved it toward the others. "Let's don't go off believing everything we hear. Let me tell you something, I know Mel and he's a fine man. He's rough around the edges. Some of you already know that. He saved my life a while back with the help of these youngsters here; almost got himself killed in the process." He pointed his Stetson at Charles and me. "He's a good man, yes he is."

"But he is gay," Chester said.

"A big freakin' so what?" Cal said. "Live and let live, that's what I say."

Charles looked at Theo and then at Harriet and Connie. "Any reason to think he killed the student other than both of them may—I repeat—may be gay?"

A large beer-delivery truck rounded the corner and drowned out Harriet's words.

The truck moved away and Theo said, "What?"

"He speaks for all of us this time," Charles said. "Harriet, what'd you say?"

"Said that Connie's brother told her that he knew Mel killed him." She turned to Connie. "Didn't you?"

Connie gave Harriet a look that could by no stretch of the imagination be considered positive, and then turned to me. "Yeah, Robbie told me that he knew, but wasn't going to say anything. Said he couldn't prove it and sure didn't want 'Mad Mel,' that's what he called him, to know that he snitched him out. He's called *Mad* for a reason, you know." She turned to Harriet. "I didn't tell you so you'd broadcast it to everyone."

Harriet returned her glare, and yanked her shoulders back. "Up yours, Connie! It's not everyone, only our group, and we were talking about it."

Everyone tried to ignore her but she was so loud that even Theo heard her.

"Okay, okay," Chester said and leaned in the direction we were supposed to be heading. "We've rested long enough. Let's get moving, we're only halfway through our walk."

William had stepped out of the fray. "A superb suggestion."

David, who had started the discussion, said, "I agree with Chester. Besides, it doesn't matter what we think, the police have that man in jail so they must know he did it."

The knot in my stomach continued to tighten as we resumed our hike. David and Cal took the lead, Theo, along with Harriet, who was helping to guide and encourage him, fell to the back of the group, and the rest of us bunched together in the middle.

"Connie," I said. "Did your brother say that he knew that Mel had killed the student?" I had moved up beside Connie and Charles leaned in from the other side to hear what I was saying.

"Big mouth Harriet," she mumbled, but then looked at me. "That's what he said, but I don't know if it's true."

"I'd like to ask him. Know where he is?"

Charles was on the other side of Connie and gave me a thumbs-up.

"Not really, but I know that he and the other tour-boat guys are meeting tonight at the Surf Bar. They meet once a month, but I think tonight's get-together is something different. They're trying to figure out how they can distance themselves from the murder. Robbie said that it sure will be good to have one less boat captain out there, but the murder will hurt business in the short haul. Let me give you his cell number."

She took her phone out of her fanny pack showed me his number. I plugged it in my phone and she excused herself saying that she needed to slow down enough for Harriet and Theo to catch us. "Think she's trying to get her hooks into old ET," she said and chuckled. "I think he's sweet on me, but I need to remind him that he is. His memory." She shrugged.

Twenty minutes later, the group gathered on Chester's porch. Harriet griped about how her feet hurt from the walk; Chester went around high-fiving everyone for completing the long walk; David said that he needed to buy more life insurance on himself if Chester "made" him walk more; and Connie brought Theo a glass of lemonade. William had a grin on his face and said that it was a "refreshing experience," and Cal strummed an air guitar and sang, "Six days on the road and I'm gonna make it home tonight."

Charles and I inched away from the group and conspired about how we were going to just happen to be at the Surf Bar tonight, and to be surprised when we saw the captains. Then we were going to invite ourselves to join them. Not a great plan, but the best we could come up with after the exhaustion from .5's longest walk ever.

CHAPTER TWENTY-THREE

Our plan to meet at the Surf Bar was thwarted by an early-spring thunderstorm, so I picked Charles up at his apartment and found a parking spot a block from the popular watering hole. We entered, shook water off our hats, and looked around for the captains. They were nowhere to be seen, so we ventured to the patio where they were huddled around a table in the corner. The table closest to them was vacant so we sat with our backs facing the group. They were in animated conversation and wouldn't have noticed if a rhinoceros had parked its ample rear in a chair beside them. There were three captains, three times that many empty beer bottles on the table, and each man had a grip on another bottle. They had arrived long before the rain.

Loud splats of rain hitting the roof and the din of happy diners at four nearby tables made it difficult to hear what they were saying, but Timothy was the loudest and I caught bits of conversation.

He was fuming and didn't try to hide it. I turned to watch the group and caught "Hell yes, he did it," and "Can you believe that macho queer making a pass at a college student forty years younger than him?"

Nemo pounded his hand on the table. "I don't give a rat's posterior who he was hitting on. He's given us a bad name."

Robbie took off his FB cap and rubbed his bald head. "All we have to do is weather the storm, and we'll make more money with him gone. Hope he fries."

Robbie finished his beer, held the bottle in the air to get the waitresses attention, and spotted us. He put his arm down and leaned closer to his two table mates. Out of the corner of my eye, I saw him put his forefinger to his mouth and say "Shhh," and something about "… friends … Mel."

Charles was closer to their table and heard the rest of what Robbie had said. That was all it took. Charles leaned his chair back and almost touched Nemo's arm. "Oh, hi guys. Didn't see you there until I heard you talking about Mel." He turned his chair toward the captains and scooted it closer to their table. "Mind if we join you?"

It was a moot question since his chair was now closer to their table than to ours.

Nemo had on the same *Hard Rock Café, Toronto* T-shirt that he'd worn the first time we'd met him here and his hair was still pulled in a ponytail. He glanced over at Robbie and then Timothy. Neither of them said yes or no, and Nemo said, "Why not. It's raining old ladies and sticks out there. We're not going anywhere."

Charles pulled his chair closer to their table. "Doing what?"

Nemo scooted his chair to the left so Charles could get closer to the table. "It's a Welsh idiom. It means the same thing as raining cats and dogs."

"Damned PhD talk," Robbie said.

I suspected the other two would have given Nemo several reasons why we shouldn't join them if Charles and I hadn't been listening.

Before Nemo had finished his Welsh idiom lesson and his feeble okay, Charles pointed to their empty bottles. "Next round's on me."

I knew who *round's on me* referred to, but it appeared to mitigate our invasion.

Robbie's hand holding the beer bottle went back in the air and the waitress returned for the additional drink orders.

"Terrible about what happened to Mel, wasn't it?" Charles said like he hadn't heard what they had been saying.

Once again, Nemo glanced at his fellow captains and turned to Charles. "Never good when something bad happens to someone in your group."

Timothy said to no one in particular, "If Mel killed that kid, he needs to be thrown in jail."

I leaned closer to the table and to Robbie. "Glad we ran into you, Robbie. I was talking to your sister and she said that you knew for certain that Mel did it."

Robbie looked at the beer bottles and then up at me. "I may have said it, but if I had to swear on a stack of Bibles, I'd say I don't know."

"Why'd you tell her that you knew?" Charles asked.

Timothy interrupted. "I'll tell you why, because it's true. It doesn't take a genius to see that if Mel had put the make on that kid while they were at that deserted beach, the kid would have been repulsed. Mel had to shut him up, plain and simple."

Nemo pointed his empty beer bottle at Timothy. "You don't know that for a fact. Just because Mel's gay, doesn't mean he did anything wrong."

"Queer and living with a nig . . . an African man, you mean," snarled Timothy.

"Timothy, don't be such an ass," Robbie said. He turned to Charles and then to me. "Sorry guys, we're all shook about this. Timothy doesn't mean anything bad about it. Mel's okay."

Didn't mean anything bad, right, I thought.

Nemo glared at Robbie. "You think he did it too? Don't get all apologetic and saccharine because Mel's buddies are here."

Robbie shook his head. "All I said was if Mel wasn't taking so much of our business, we would have enough to survive. To your question Charles, I don't know if Mel killed him."

Nemo pointed to the empty bottles in front of Robbie. "Not what you said two beers back."

Timothy reached toward Nemo and accidentally knocked over an empty bottle. "It's such a mess," Timothy said. "My wedding's going down the crapper." He waved his hand around toward Robbie and Nemo. "Our business sucks. This murder has everybody nervous. Crap, it's a mess."

"George W. Bush said, 'It will take time to restore chaos and order.'"

It was only a matter of time before Charles tried to top Nemo's Welsh idiom.

Robbie took off his FB cap and pointed it at Charles. "You're worse than Nemo with weird talk."

Nemo ignored Robbie. "Chaos is already here." It didn't take Nemo's PhD to figure that out.

The waitress returned with the drinks and cleared the empties off the table.

Charles took a sip and looked at Nemo. "So you think that Mel killed the student?"

Nemo said, "You bet." The other two nodded.

For the next twenty minutes, the captains shared a lot of bantering, mild arguments, countless reasons why business was down, and somehow how it was all Mel's fault. Their speech began to slur, and I realized that we had learned all we were going to.

Rain, old ladies and sticks, and cats and dogs continued to pound the roof, and I wondered if there was a Welsh idiom for throwing Mad Mel under the bus, or in this case, boat.

CHAPTER TWENTY-FOUR

Charles and I hadn't had as much to drink as the other three guys, but the next morning my head felt like it had a balloon inflating in it. I had drifted in and out of sleep and was nowhere near rested when I pulled myself out of bed. I kept thinking of Mel on Boneyard Beach with the students and not being able to come up with any scenario for him to harm one of them. It also bothered me that a group of his colleagues would have jumped to the conclusion that he was guilty based on his sexual orientation. It seemed more like wishful thinking to eliminate a competitor. They were homophobic, but were they so petty to want him out of the way because of his competition? Or was I that wrong about Mel?

Then there was Abe's murder. I knew Larry better than I knew Mel, but realized that there were dark corners of his past that he'd never shared. He and Cindy had a whirlwind romance and were married after knowing each other a few months. Did she know what he was capable of? And finally, why did I open myself to serious problems by not telling Detective Adair the reason that I was at Abe's? Was friendship worth going to jail over?

I didn't have ready answers, but I knew one thing. I had to mend fences with Cindy. We had been good friends for a long time and I hated how our conversation at Crosby's had ended. Instead of sulking around the house, I called to see if she was available for lunch. At first she hesitated and started making excuses, but then said she could find an hour for me. We agreed to meet at Rita's for an early meal.

I arrived ahead of Cindy and opted for an outdoor table. Last night's heavy rain had cleared out the humidity and it was turning out to be a nice day. I hoped that after my lunch with Cindy that I felt the same way.

Since I'd arrived on Folly, Rita's Seaside Grille was the third iteration of a restaurant on one of the island's prime restaurant locations. The outdoor patio faced the Folly Pier, the Tides Hotel, and the Sand Dollar, Folly's iconic bar. Early lunch arrivals wore everything from bathing-suit cover ups, to dress shirts, and one table of diners had already started happy hour. My head throbbed when I saw five beer bottles on their table.

Cindy parked her unmarked car in front of the Pier, saw me, and smiled. A good sign, I hoped.

"So what's with the lunch invitation?" she asked as she sat across from me. Her smile was intact but didn't seem as sincere as it did when she was crossing the street.

No reason to beat around the bush. "I want to apologize."

She nodded. "I admire a man who starts a conversation that way. But since I'm not great at catching nuances, you'll have to explain what you're apologizing for."

The waitress arrived before I told her. I'd noticed over the years that police chiefs get quicker service than us common folks.

Cindy ordered a Pepsi and the "biggest, baddest" burger the chef could "fry up," and I stuck with a burger and told the waitress that it didn't have to be that big or bad.

The waitress headed to the kitchen. "Smartass," Cindy said, and wasn't referring to the waitress.

I didn't deny it. "I apologize for not telling Detective Adair why I was at Abe's." I hesitated but Cindy didn't say anything. "I was afraid that if I told Adair, he'd start looking at Larry for the murder."

Cindy stared at me and then said, "Of course he would, Chris. Any decent cop would, but because Larry had a gripe with Abe, didn't mean he killed him."

Gripe was an understatement. I took a deep breath, and said what I really wanted to tell her. "Cindy, it tears me up to say this, but part of me thinks that Larry may be guilty."

I waited for her to explode.

She continued to glare and then looked toward Center Street before turning back to me. "You've known Larry longer than I have, but I think I know him better than you do. I hope I do. He hadn't even mentioned Abe to me until he moseyed into town to stomp on Larry's happiness. Even now, I feel that there's a lot of their shared past that Larry's not talking about, and that's okay. We all have stuff hidden in caves and crannies that we don't want brought into the light of day." She grinned. "Some of the stuff I did back home when I was a youngin' would've given my parents reason to adopt me out if they found out; my preacher would've had to add extra sermons; and the local cops would've been shopping for more handcuffs. But I digress. To be honest, I've given a lot of thought about what happened. As a cop, I know he doesn't have an alibi and has more reasons to want Abe dead than he did for him to live. And …."

She broke eye contact and looked down at her water; a tear ran down her cheek. I wanted to walk around the table and comfort her, but I knew that she would break my arm before she'd let me hug her in front of a dozen people.

She looked up, wiped the tears from her cheek with the back of her hand. "Do I think Larry killed him?" she said in a low voice, and moved her thumb and forefinger about an inch apart. "Part of me does, but I want with all my heart to believe that he didn't. I have to believe that, I do."

I resisted reaching across the table for her hand. "I know."

She blinked back another tear and wiped her nose with her napkin, and said, "I won't tell you what to do, and I'll still love you —in a sisterly sort of way, of course." She tried to smile but failed. "I'll love you regardless of what you choose to do."

I took a deep breath. "I'm going to tell Adair why I was there. I know it might get you in trouble; I suppose I'll be in trouble too; and worst of all, it will put Larry in Adair's crosshairs."

"Do what you have to."

"Cindy, last year when members of First Light church were getting killed, I underestimated another one of the detectives, Michael Callahan. Other than Karen, I had little faith in the detectives from the sheriff's office."

"With good reason," she said.

"True. Regardless, Callahan came through, and from what I hear, Adair is as good. I need to trust him. If Larry's innocent, and my gut tells me that he is, Adair will find the killer."

"Do you think he didn't do it?"

"Yes, the more I think about it, it wouldn't have made sense for him to shoot Abe that night."

"Because you were at Abe's house and Larry wouldn't have risked hitting you?"

"That, and because Larry had no idea what Abe and I had discussed and what we may have agreed to. If he'd bought my story about Larry not having any money and your hubby's plan to tell everyone about his past, there wouldn't have been a reason to shoot him."

"True, but—"

Her cell phone interrupted. She looked at the screen, said she had to take the call, and walked to the back of the patio.

Our food arrived while Cindy was on the phone.

I watched as she said a few words, listened for what seemed like an eternity, said a few more words, and listened more. She took the phone from her ear, muttered a profanity, and returned to the table.

"Everything okay?"

She plopped back down in her chair. "You're not going to like it."

I motioned for her to continue. "That was Detective Cox."

The name wasn't familiar. "Who?"

"He's one of the detectives working with Adair on the Drew Casey case. I met him last year; seems like an okay guy. He used to surf over here so he's familiar with Folly."

"And why won't I like what he said?"

"I called him the other night and he said he'd let me know what they had on Mel. He was vague and said that he wasn't sure he could get into it until Mel's attorney got all the information. They've got it now." She took a bite of burger.

I still didn't hear an answer in what she had said, but, unlike Charles, I was going to let Cindy tell me when she felt like it.

She looked around the patio and leaned closer. "When they searched Mel's house, they found a bloodstained rag in an old tool box in the garage."

My heart sank. "The kid's blood?" She nodded.

I looked at a young mother carrying her crying toddler to the side exit and then toward the ocean. "Mel's not stupid," I said. "Why would he keep something as obvious as a rag with the kid's blood in his garage? He's being framed."

"There's more. One of the students who was on the boat swears that he saw Mel near where they found the body."

I tried to remember everything Mel had said about that night. Hadn't Mel said that he stayed with his boat except to go to the bathroom and then he went in the opposite direction of the group and from where Casey was killed?

"How did the witness recognize Mel in the dark? And, from what Mel had said, most everyone was almost drunk when they got to the beach and all were when they left. How credible is the witness?"

"I'm just repeating what Cox said." She tilted her head and lowered her voice even more. "Chris, even if it's almost dark, Mel's easy to recognize. It'd take a mighty high blood-alcohol content for someone to confuse him for a twenty-year-old college student. Cox is confident about their case."

Cindy had a valid point about recognizing Mel, but why would the ex-marine lie about staying with his craft if a dozen people—drunk or not—could have said otherwise?

"I think you're wrong about this one," Cindy said.

I had lost my appetite and pushed the fries around on my plate; the burger remained untouched.

I wondered if I was the only person who believed Mel was telling the truth, and more importantly, wondered how I could prove it. The weather was still beautiful, but my head was filled with storm clouds and fog.

Cindy had to get to the office for a meeting with one of her officers and thanked me for the apology and the food she had barely touched. She left through the side exit and I took a couple of bites of cold burger and realized that I was no longer hungry. There would never be a good time to call Detective Adair, so I called the cell number listed on the card he'd given me. Part of me wanted it to go to voicemail, but instead he answered and I told him that I had some information about the Pottinger shooting and thought he might be interested. He was quite interested and said that he'd be at my house in a half hour.

Detective Adair was more rumpled than he had the last time we'd met. He still wore his like-new blazer, but his tan and blue striped tie had what looked like a mustard stain on it, and his white shirt had lost its starch. I invited him in and offered him my chair. He looked around for options; seeing none, he unbuttoned his blazer and sat. I offered him something to drink, and like during his previous visit, he declined.

He took the small notebook out of his pocket. "So what do you have?"

"I was shook and not thinking straight when we talked in Chief LaMond's car at Pottinger's house. I realized later that I forgot to mention something that you should know."

I gave him a summary of Larry's involvement with Abe and how Abe had attempted to blackmail him. I also shared how Larry had asked me to talk with Abe to see if I could get him to back off his blackmail plot.

Adair listened without interrupting and while he had a pen in his hand, he hadn't written anything. His face didn't give anything away. Maybe it wasn't going to be as bad as I had anticipated.

He started to speak and his facial features turned rigid. "Mr. Landrum, are you aware of what obstruction of justice means?"

"Vaguely."

"I'm certain that if I arrested you this second, your attorney would be glad to give you the legal definition. I can assure you that there's not a court in South Carolina that you wouldn't be convicted based on the cockamamie story you just told me." He sighed. "Do you expect me to believe that you were so shaken that you 'forgot' to tell me the reason you were there, and now several days later, it just popped into your head? How big a fool do you take me for? Wait, don't answer that, it'd just add more charges to the increasing list of crimes you've committed."

"Detective, I—"

He smacked his thigh with the notebook. "Silence. I'm not

going to slap cuffs on you—now. But don't think I won't in the next five minutes unless. . ." He paused and glared at me.

If there had been a glass of water between us on the table, it would've turned to ice.

"Unless what?"

He took a deep breath, paused for what seemed like an eternity, and said. "I'm going to ask you to repeat your story, every detail, regardless how miniscule, and once you're finished, I'll decide what to do. Is that clear?"

"Perfectly."

He flipped open his notebook and readied his pen. "Begin." Detective Adair wasn't kidding when he said every detail.

For the next thirty minutes I shared everything from Larry's first comments about Abe Pottinger coming to town to when I looked across the street from Abe's house and saw the shooter walking away. And then throwing my two cents' worth in on why I didn't think it was Larry. Many details I shared multiple times.

"Does Chief LaMond know this?"

I hadn't mentioned while I was telling and retelling the story that Cindy had been present during the discussion about me approaching Abe, so I regressed to telling the truth, simply not the whole truth.

"I don't know how much Larry's told her."

He didn't push me on it and his glare lessened, but ever so slightly. "Mr. Landrum, you know more about the people here than I do. If Larry didn't shoot Pottinger, who did?"

"I wish I knew. Considering what Larry's told me about Abe, it could be anyone from his sordid past."

"Isn't it unlikely that someone from out-of-state followed him?"

"Yes."

"So who here?"

I'd already withheld information from Adair that might end up getting me thrown in jail. Should I tell him about my thoughts that

Abe was pulling a con on members of the .5? Thinking about the composition of the group, I couldn't imagine anyone being able to handle a rifle well enough to hit Abe from across the street.

"I don't know anyone. Sorry."

He gave me a skeptical look and shook his head.

"Mr. Landrum, you're not off the hook. I don't believe that you forgot to tell me about Larry. I'm not arresting you, and you can thank Karen, Detective Lawson, for that, but you're walking on paper-thin ice. One more thing." He gave a sly grin. "Here's a line I love to throw at suspects. Don't leave town."

I assured him that I wasn't and he stood to leave and I should have walked him to the door, but instead asked, "Learn anything from the bullet?"

He looked back at me. "The things I've heard about your meddling are true."

I shrugged.

"It's no secret. The damned reporters already have it and will be blabbing it to everyone. The bullet was .270 caliber. It's been around for decades; it's popular and easy to get; good for deer and elk hunting. There's nothing to be learned there, unless we have a rifle to test it against." He smiled, slightly more sincere this time. "If you come across one, please don't *forget* to let me know."

I told him I would and asked, if that caliber bullet would have been accurate from the fence across the street from Abe's.

"Why, afraid you were the target and the shooter missed and hit Pottinger?"

"Just wondering."

"Yeah, it's accurate from longer distances than that, but it still took someone who's done a lot of shooting, or the luckiest person on the island."

CHAPTER TWENTY-FIVE

April showers may bring May flowers, but May showers are prone to bring flooding and areas of standing water to the Lowcountry. Overnight rains left a small lake in the front yard, flooded several streets, and gave early-morning kayakers a couple of new temporary streams, one through the middle of the historic market in Charleston. The storm had moved out and it looked like another nice day for the group's walk.

As was becoming habit, Charles and I met at the foot of the pier before the rest of the group arrived. I shared my conversation with Detective Adair. Charles asked what flavor of cake to bake a saw in. I told him that I failed to see the humor and he said that was because I was looking at it through my obstructing-justice eyes. He also asked if Adair had any leads and I said he didn't mention any, and that since I had become an obstructer of justice, I doubted that he would have been forthcoming with confidential information.

Chester's entourage arrived, followed by Cal's car, and everyone piled out excited about today's hike. More accurately, most of them moaned and groaned as they struggled to get out of the car, and Harriet complained about the cramped quarters and her aching back. After Chester acknowledged Charles and my presence and Cal joined us and said that William had to go to school for a meeting and wouldn't be walking today, Chester assumed his self-anointed leadership role.

He raised his hand in the air. "Okay walkers, here's the plan. If we're going to achieve our lofty goal, we must push harder, so we're heading up Center Street to the Folly River Park. That's about twice as far as we went the other day and more than half as far as our trek to Boneyard Beach."

I was pleased that Chester didn't open today's route for debate. That cut five minutes off the time we usually wasted arguing.

Harriet shook her head and reminded all of us about her aching back. "Probably'll take us two or three days to make it."

"We can do it," David said.

Cal took two steps toward the street. "Let's head out."

Harriet looped her arm around Theo's and nudged him toward Center Street and the group's longest walk in recorded history.

Cal was already twenty yards in front of David and Connie. Theo, with the aid of Harriet, came next, and Chester, Charles and I lagged behind.

The black ribbons from the previous walk were absent. I looked at Chester. "No ribbons?"

"Nope, we talked about it and decided the official mourning period's over. We didn't like him that much anyway."

Charles and I had made the walk from the pier to the Folly River Park many times. Unless Charles stopped to talk to everyone on the sidewalk, talk to each canine along the way, and stop for ice cream at Sugar Time, the trip took ten minutes. Today, after the first twenty-five minutes, I was beginning to believe Harriet's prediction that it may take three days. Charles, David, Cal and I had moved a block ahead of the rest of the group. Fifteen minutes later my group was at the small park and spread out on the picnic table under the gazebo. Cal and David were talking about some of the cities in which Cal had played his distinct form of traditional country music when he toured the south, and Chester leaned against the table and rested.

Charles and I were nearby when Charles's ears perked up when David said, "Did you hear about Abe?"

The others had arrived and looked like they had walked across the Sahara desert. Cal gave his seat to Theo, and Harriet, who had been limping, squeezed in beside him. Chester leaned against the gazebo and Connie brought up the rear.

Chester looked at Harriet who was massaging her ankle. "What happened?"

"Twisted it on the sidewalk over there." She turned, winced, and pointed to the steps into the park.

"What about Abe?" Charles added. He wouldn't let a twisted ankle stand in the way of finding out what David was talking about.

David looked down at Harriet's ankle and then at Charles. "They were talking about his death, and—"

"Who was?" the information-bloodhound asked.

"The radio. Last night on the news. Something about him being suspected in a stock fraud case in Georgia a few years back and running a Ponzi scheme somewhere else."

"What's a Ponzi scheme?" Connie asked.

David looked around to see if anyone was going to answer. Seeing blank stares, he continued, "Where a crook takes your money and says he'll invest it and promises you great returns."

"What's wrong with that?" Connie asked.

Again, David looked around and failed to see any takers. "The crook only pretends to invest the money."

"So how does he pay the investors?" Connie asked.

"He pays the first few who bought in with money he gets from the next suckers. That way he tells others about how great the first group did, even gives them as references."

Chester had been taking in what David had been saying, and he interjected, "Then the crook skips town with all the money leaving everyone but the first people he brought in with an empty bank account and busted dreams?"

David nodded. "Exactly."

"Are you sure it's our Abe?" Connie asked.

David said, "Guess so. The news guy said Abe wasn't convicted but some others involved were in jail."

That was consistent with what Larry had said and I wondered if Detective Adair had known it when I was talking to him.

"What else did they say?" Charles added. "That's all."

Cal asked, "Could that Ponzi thingee work with reverse mortgages?"

David looked around the group. "Suppose so, but I don't know how he'd get his money. He'd have the title on the houses but how could he convert that to cash if someone still lived in them?"

I wasn't an expert but had owned two rental properties before moving to Folly and had some experience with companies that bought large numbers of rentals. Most were legitimate, but some were sharks with big smiles and little consciences.

"Someone with deep pockets or investment companies could buy the paid-for houses from Abe at rock-bottom prices," I said. "They would have time on their side and wait until the person living in the house either died or moved because the reverse mortgage check would stop coming, and then the investors sell the houses for market value."

Charles said, "So the investors were crooks too?"

I nodded. "They would have had to know what was going on. And, Abe would have his money and would have skipped town before the scheme started tumbling down."

"So wouldn't they get arrested?" Cal asked.

"Not necessarily," I said. "They would have legitimate titles to the houses they bought from Abe and could claim that they didn't know anything about his activities and how he got the houses."

Cal said, "All so danged confusing."

"Yep," Charles agreed. "Harry Truman said, 'If you can't convince them, confuse them.'"

"Wonder if his murder had something to do with all that?" Cal asked, sharing the question that most of the rest of the group probably felt.

"What?" Theo asked.

Harriet leaned to about an inch from his ear, and repeated what David had said about the radio report. Theo's faced dropped. "Oh my. It can't be our Abe."

I knew it was and suspected everyone else did as well.

David stepped forward. "Here's what I think. One of the swindlers from Georgia who isn't in jail shot Abe so he wouldn't testify against him or maybe one of the Ponzi financers wanted him eliminated. I bet Abe moved here to hide."

Harriet kept her arm around Theo's neck and turned to the rest of us. "Doesn't surprise me. I didn't think much of it at the time, but after we walked the other day I was talking to him about the reverse mortgage plan. He was acting skittish so I asked him what was wrong." She paused and looked around the park.

Charles asked, "What'd he say?"

"He hemmed and hawed but finally confided that he was afraid that someone from where he used to live had followed him. He said he was worried."

"Worried about what?" Charles asked.

Harriet looked at each of us and then focused on Charles. "He wouldn't say. I thought it was strange and asked him, but he laughed it off and said that he was just being paranoid. There was more to it than he was saying, but it was like he snapped out of it and continued talking about reverse mortgages."

"Did anybody else hear him mention being worried?" I asked.

David and William shook their heads.

Cal turned to me. "Tell you what pard, I may have. We were talking about stocks, bonds, and money-market stuff. Actually, he was doing all the talking; most of it went in one ear and out the other and the rest of it flew over my head like a jet plane. He said something about Atlanta and a friend who brought him into the business and how well he had done with it."

Charles said, "What's that have to do with someone following him?"

"He didn't say someone was here," Cal said. "But when he was talking about the other guy, he got more nervous."

I leaned close to Theo so he could hear. "Theo, you said that you'd seen Abe's prospectus about the stock he was wanting you to buy." Theo nodded. "You said he took it back." Theo nodded again. I looked at the others. "Anybody have a brochure or other material from the stock or the reverse mortgage company that Abe said he was working for?"

Chester shook his head and looked at Connie and David. Connie shook her head and David shrugged. Harriet said, "He told me that the product was so new that they hadn't had time to print anything about it. I remember he called it a jumbo reverse mortgage, if that means anything."

Other than sounding better than a regular, run-of-the-mill reverse mortgage, I doubted it meant much, and said, "So nobody got marketing materials?"

"He gave me a three-page application," Connie said and turned to Chester. "Hard to believe, but it was longer than your stupid application to get in this group."

Chester smiled.

Connie looked around the group. "You all got applications, didn't you?"

"Sure," David said. "It was a standard application. Looked like the ones I use for insurance."

"Did it have the name of the company on it?"

"Of course, but I don't remember what it was."

"Alexander Lifetime Security Inc." Harriet said. "Knew that because it was the same name that was on the paper that Theo filled out for the stock. Remember Theo?" She put her arm around his shoulder.

"Yes." Theo squeezed her arm and looked at me. "Are you saying that Abe wasn't on the up-and-up?"

The group didn't have benefit of what I had learned from Larry, and I wasn't going to get into it with them. It wouldn't take much of a leap to see that Abe's reverse mortgage, jumbo or otherwise, deal and the yet-to-go-public stock were scams.

"That's how it looks."

"Well, how's that for a kicker," Cal said.

"And I was ready to give him a million dollars," Theo said. "Am I stupid or what?"

"Of course you're not stupid, Theo," Cal said. "Thievin', egg-sucking, con artists are good at what they do. Anybody can be taken by them."

Harriet moved her arm from Theo's shoulder and put it around his waist. "It's lucky someone shot him when they did."

Chester stood and waved his hands. "Enough gruesome stuff. Sounds like we all got off lucky. I didn't give him any money, did any of you?"

No one responded.

"Good," Chester said. "Now I've got an important announcement." We all stopped and stared at our leader. "It came to me after watching some of us huffing-and-puffing, some of us wheezing, some of us limping, and some of us taking about a week to walk from the pier to here. I realized that the river over there will freeze over before we can walk to Boneyard Beach." He stopped and pointed in the general direction of the Lighthouse Inlet and Boneyard Beach.

I wanted to shout, "Duh!" Chester was serious so instead I frowned and nodded.

"Anyway," he continued, "don't fret. We're going to get to Boneyard Beach. After we get done today, I'm going to look for one of those marsh guides who can take us there without charging an arm and a leg. Seeing that our legs aren't working too well nowadays, that's important." He smiled at his weak joke. "Now," he turned serious, "don't try to protest and get all upset, I've made my decision and it's final."

I looked around the group and didn't see a glimmer of protest; thrilled would have been how I would have described the reactions. Theo said that he thought it was the best idea he'd heard since, well, "Since I don't know when." And Connie said that she was speaking for everyone else when she told him that he'd made a wise decision, and "probably prevented a heart attack or two."

We stayed at the park for another fifteen minutes until everyone's heart rate lowered to a pre-stroke level, and then we headed back. Along the way, Connie told Chester that if it was okay with him, she'd ask her brother if he'd take us to Boneyard Beach. Chester grinned. "Sure, but he'd better be cheap."

Mel would have been the perfect person to ferry the group, but since he was restricted to a jail cell, he wasn't an option.

Harriet mumbled something about Chester being a tightwad and griped about her sore ankle the entire walk back, and I decided that Chester should win the Noble Peace Prize for calling off the .5 walk to Boneyard Beach.

CHAPTER TWENTY-SIX

Morning began with sounds of a delivery-truck driver unloading cartons of produce at Bert's and a call from Cindy asking if I can meet her at her house. I asked when and she said the sooner the better; Larry was at work and she wanted to talk to me without him around. I said to give me fifteen minutes.

Ten minutes later, Cindy poured me a cup of coffee, and we moved to the back patio and she thanked me for coming.

Sun was rippling off the gently-rolling waves on the Folly River and a small fishing boat was beginning its morning quest for a bountiful catch. I sat back in a chair, sipped coffee, and waited for her to get to the reason for calling. She sat, looked around, started to speak, hesitated, and then shook her head. She was the picture of discomfort.

"Last night, Detective Adair and three deputies showed up with scowls and a search warrant for here, Larry's truck, and the store." She paused and I waited. "They were here two hours and then escorted Larry to the store and spent two more hours there.

It was after midnight before he dragged his exhausted tush to bed."

I mumbled something about being sorry and asked what they were searching for.

"Adair, of course, wasn't specific; the warrant talked about pertaining to, knowledge of, blah, blah, blah about Abraham Pottinger. It's obvious that Larry and Pottinger had a prior relationship, and anything that would tie him to being at the scene of the crime was fair game."

All I could think was that none of this would have happened if I hadn't told Adair about Larry's conversation about Abe. "I'm sorry. What can I do?"

"You're the only person I can talk to about it. Larry said that he didn't do anything wrong so there wasn't anything to be concerned about. I tried to explain that from the detective's perspective, Larry was the most likely suspect."

"What'd he say?"

"He said he knew that but for me not to worry." She shook her head. "I can't talk to anyone at city hall; crap, I'm the police chief, for God's sake. I don't have any other close friends to yell and scream to about it. The way he's acting, I can't even have a sensible conversation with Larry. Chris. I know I can trust you, and you'll level with me about what you think."

"I appreciate that, but I don't know how I can help." She looked at the river. "Talking helps."

"Did Adair find anything?"

"They sure as hell didn't find a rifle, but they took our computer, Larry's cell phone, and two pairs of his shoes."

I said, "The soil where the shooter stood is sandy and so is the path beside the tennis court. I suppose they're trying to trace samples from his shoes back to the park."

Cindy shook her head. "You've been in Pewter's side lot, it's covered with sand. Larry's there all the time fiddling with the pipes and lumber. I'm sure there's sand in his shoes. That doesn't prove anything."

I agreed. "Did Abe send Larry e-mails?"

"Don't know. The times I knew about them communicating, it was by phone or in person." She lowered her head. "Chris, I'm scared."

And had good reason to be, I thought, but said, "Larry's right, if he didn't have anything to do with it, they can't find convincing evidence that he did."

"I guess."

"Cindy, don't shoot me for asking this, but—"

"Bad choice of words."

"True, so don't get mad, but is there a chance that he did it?"

We'd covered this ground before, but I needed to keep going back to it. I wanted to push her to be as objective as possible. I was expecting a blow-up or at least a nasty look. Instead, she whispered, "A powerful case could be put together that he did. But, I don't think so, I really don't." She looked up and shook her head. "Let me ask you something."

I nodded.

"You've known him for eight years, gone through a few tense times together, and spend a bunch of time with him. Has he ever lied to you?"

"Not that I know of."

"Me either," she said, and smiled. "He's the most honest crook I've ever known."

I knew what she'd meant and returned the smile. "I really don't think he did it, Chris."

"So, if Larry didn't, who did?"

"One whale of a good question."

I remembered yesterday's conversation with members of the .5 group and how Harriet and Cal had hinted that Abe had been worried that someone from Georgia may have followed him. I mentioned it to Cindy.

My distraught friend looked at the river and turned back to me. "Abe was a con artist, a blasted good one according to Larry."

"Did Larry ever mention anyone who might have followed Abe to Folly, someone from his past who may have killed him?"

Cindy looked at the floor and then back at me. "He never mentioned anyone, but sure, someone could have. As they say back home, where's there's a big pile of manure, there's sure to be a large critter nearby and a flock of flies. A con artist leaves a string of unhappy campers in his wake and has a bunch of acquaintances on the wrong side of the law. I suspect some of them would have been pleased to have the opportunity to deposit a bullet in him."

"Why don't you ask a couple of officers you trust to ask around and see if they hear of any strangers in town or any vehicles with Georgia plates from the counties near Atlanta? Other than sand in his shoes, Detective Adair probably doesn't have any evidence. I'm sure he's checking with the police in Georgia and getting what, if anything, they have on Abe. I suspect he'd appreciate anything your officers turn up that may help with his investigation."

"Won't it look like I'm only trying to help Larry?"

"I wouldn't worry about that. Again, if Larry didn't do it, someone did, and Adair could use the extra eyes. Besides, you can say that one of your folks uncovered the evidence, not you.

Isn't that what the police are supposed to do?"

"Yes, but. . ."

"No but. You're the chief doing your job."

"Even if there is someone, there's no reason to think he's staying on Folly. Could be anywhere and now that the scumbag is dead, whoever shot him could be long gone."

"True," I said. "But it's all you can do.

"I reckon," she said, with little conviction.

I pulled out of the drive, and repeated to myself, *if not Larry, who?* I also had the nagging feeling that something said on the group's walk yesterday was bothering me, but what?

I stopped at Charles's apartment and caught him as he was heading out the door. He said that he had been cooped up in the apartment all morning and needed fresh air. We walked around the side of his building to the front that had housed the Sandbar Seafood and Steak Restaurant, and sat on a bench overlooking the Folly River and the Mariner's Cay marina and condo complex on the other side of the waterway.

"Why the visit?" Charles said. He removed his Tilley and set it on the bench.

I shared my conversation with Cindy. He asked if I thought it was possible that Larry could have shot Abe. I rehashed what I'd told him before when I said I didn't think so. He said that he wouldn't bet the farm that Larry was innocent, although he'd be surprised if he did it.

I didn't ask him what farm he wouldn't bet, but instead asked, "Why?"

"Larry's past is a sore spot with him. We talked about it several years ago, probably before you arrived. He didn't want everyone here to know about it, but if it had to come out, he'd have mixed feelings. Said he would be relieved and would find a way to weather whatever storm followed."

"He'd also said that to me."

"But it was BC."

"Before Cindy," I said.

Charles nodded and said, "He's protective of her—overly protective."

I agreed.

"Now that she's chief, it'd kill him of something from his past caused her any hurt or threatened her job. The boy may be short, but he's got a spine of steel. I wouldn't want to mess with him if I said anything bad about his woman."

"So you think he may have done it?" I said.

"No," Charles said. "But if I carried a badge and a gun, I'd be on him like spit on a cowlick."

I hoped he was right about the first part.

We sat in silence watching absolutely nothing happening on the river.

Charles looked across the stream at the marina. "I'm glad Chester decided a boat's the best way to get to Boneyard Beach. Think if I had to hear Harriet gripe about one more thing and Theo walk at the speed of the Washington Monument, I'd be searching for a gun to send them chasing after Abe. Those two are made for each other."

"What do you mean?"

"You see the way Harriet's been doting on Theo? If they were younger, she'd be accused of stalking."

I had noticed how she had helped him yesterday and spent most of the time serving as his human hearing aid. "Think she's after his money?"

"According to Chester, she's sweet on him. Don't know if she's after his money or his winning smile and sex appeal." He snapped his fingers. "Oh wait, he doesn't have a smile, winning or other- wise, and if he ever had sex appeal he used it all up around the time Truman was camping out in the White House." He leaned back on the bench and gazed over at me. "It's the money."

My analysis would have been a bit different, but I couldn't argue with his conclusion. It also reminded me what was bothering me about yesterday's walk.

"Remember yesterday when Cal and Harriet were talking about what Abe had said about someone following him?"

"Yeah, so?"

"Cindy and Larry are crystal clear that Abe was a con artist, a good one."

"So?" Charles repeated.

"If he was working a con on Harriet and Cal, why would he tell them anything about someone following him unless it would help him with the con?"

"And telling them about someone following him wouldn't benefit him."

"Not that I can figure."

"I didn't hear everything Cal and Harriet were talking about," Charles said, "but they weren't clear about what Abe had told them. Now with them knowing he was murdered, it might have clouded their recollections and made them read more into it than Abe had meant."

"True, but look at it this way. What if one of them had killed Abe and made up the story about someone following him to deflect attention away and pass the blame on someone else?"

"You're kidding!" Charles picked up his cane from the ground and pointed it toward town. "You think little ole' scrawny, complaining Harriet or our bud Cal shot Abe with a hunting rifle from across the street?"

"Why not? Isn't just as likely as Larry doing it?"

"Don't think so," Charles said. "Larry had a motive. What motive would Harriet or Cal have?"

"You just told me Harriet's motive."

"I did?"

"Didn't Theo tell us that he was going to hand Abe a million dollars? Didn't you imply that Harriet was after Theo's money?"

"That little gal can't weigh a hundred pounds. How could she handle the size gun used to take out Abe?"

"She grew up on a ranch in Montana," I said. "I'd be surprised if she didn't spend time hunting, and if not, she probably would've been around guns most of her life."

Charles rubbed his chin. "Think she said they took care of each other back there. Bet that included killing any predator that threatened their livestock."

I nodded.

Charles returned his cane to the ground. "If Harriet pulled the trigger, why would Cal have said what he did about Abe seeming afraid?"

"Let's ask him."

Charles slapped his Tilley back on his head, grabbed his cane again, and stood. "You're sounding more like me every day. There's hope for you yet."

CHAPTER TWENTY-SEVEN

I t was noon but Cal didn't open his bar for lunch unless the mood struck him. The front door was locked so I assumed the aging country crooner wasn't in the mood to entertain diners or early drinkers. Charles and I went to the unlocked side door and were greeted by the smell of stale beer. George Jones belted out "The Race Is On" from an antique Wurlitzer jukebox, and Cal, live and in person, sang harmony as he swept under the tables. He saw us and went to the jukebox, reached behind it, and turned the volume down. "Welcome to the George and Cal show, one performance only, standing room only."

Chairs were on top of the tables so he could clean the floor, and I smiled at his joke and he tipped his Stetson in my direction. Charles said, "What's for lunch?"

Cal looked toward the tiny kitchen and back at Charles. "Cold hot dogs, frozen french fries, and cold beer. The grille ain't fired up, and I'm not turning it on for you."

"Cold beer sounds good," Charles said. "Got any chardonnay for my wine-snob friend?" He pointed to me although Cal probably knew who Charles was talking about. "He's too good for beer."

"Think I can find some." He walked behind the bar and turned on the neon Corona Extra beer sign a movie crew left behind last year after they filmed a movie using Cal's as one of the sets. They'd renamed Cal's The Bar and thought the Corona sign looked better than his Bud Light sign. The movie turned out to be a disaster, both during shooting, and in the box office. Removing the Bud Light sign was not the reason.

"You're about nine hours early for my set and from the piss-poor crowds I've attracted lately, I don't think you needed to get here just yet to claim a table." He waved toward the bandstand and the tables. "Reckon there's another reason for the visit."

Charles took a sip of Budweiser and said, "You reckon right. Lay it out, Chris."

Cal lifted three chairs off the nearest table. "Park your butts."

We did and I told him that we had been rehashing the conversation concerning Abe from the other day on the walk, and that we were confused about something Cal had said.

Cal looked at Charles and back at me. "What'd I say?"

Not a good sign, I thought. "Harriet was saying that Abe told her that he was worried about someone following him to Folly, someone from his past that he was afraid of."

Cal removed his Stetson, laid it on the table beside his beer, rubbed his hand through his long, gray hair, and nodded. "I remember. Believe she said Abe was antsy about someone."

"Yes. After that, didn't you say he told you something like that?"

Cal took a long drag on his beer and looked at the water-stained ceiling tiles. "Sort of."

Charles leaned closer to the bar owner. "Sort of said it or you sort of remember what he said?"

"Abe was jabbering about the greatest stock deal since Apple and using all sorts of words that I'd need nine years of college to figure out, so I was only half paying attention. He mentioned being from A-Town. I remembered that because I played a few shows there in the seventies and got stiffed by a scumbag promoter. Atlanta may be high in the alphabet, but it's at the bottom of my list of places to entertain. You see—"

Charles interrupted. "What'd Abe say?"

Cal looked at Charles like he would at a drunk heckling his singing, but returned to the track. "He said he'd sold stock there and his clients did real good."

If there was anything in there about being afraid of someone I missed it.

"And?" Charles asked.

"And all I remember was that he seemed nervous when he was talking about it."

"He didn't say anything about someone following him?" I said.

Cal Smith sang "County Bumpkin" in the background, Cal Ballew stared at the jukebox, and said, "Not that I heard. Why?"

Cal had rented an apartment ever since he'd been here, so I knew he wasn't a mark for Abe's reverse mortgages, excuse me, jumbo reverse mortgages, so I asked, "Did Abe convince you to buy stock he was peddling?"

Cal chuckled. "Even if I wanted to, which I didn't, I would've had to sell my car, bar, and guitar to scrape together seventy-three dollars. Doubt the late Abe would've considered my wealth a big chunk of his retirement nest egg."

If there wasn't a country song in there somewhere, I'd eat Cal's Stetson. I also couldn't think of a reason Cal would have for killing Abe. He didn't have a story about Abe being followed so he wasn't trying to misdirect blame. He hadn't given Abe any money; didn't have any to give. There wasn't a financial reason to kill him. And besides, I had always known Cal to be honest, honest to the point of harming himself on occasion. To be sure, I tried one more question.

"Cal, you were here when Abe was killed, weren't you?" I hoped it didn't sound too much like I was fishing for an alibi.

"Sure was, pard. I was standing right over there when old Roger stormed in and said there'd been a killing. He didn't know who but said there were a slew of cop cars and an ambulance out by the tennis court."

Cal got us another drink and plopped back down in his chair. "Fellas, if I was the suspicious type, I'd think you're looking for Abe's killer and that I was near the top of the chart with a bullet."

So much for subtlety. I looked at Charles, he gave me a slight nod, and I turned back to Cal. "Not really, Cal. The other day it sounded like you thought Abe was saying that he was worried about someone from back home. That didn't make sense. If a con artist was trying to screw you, he'd show confidence in whatever he was selling so you'd fall for it. He'd be good enough not to let his feelings muddle up the conversation."

"Guys," Cal said, "in my fifty-something years traveling the country, I've seen more con artists than the Better Business Bureau. Abraham Pottinger was one of the best." He raised an empty bottle in the air. "I wouldn't let him invest this bottle, much less any of my hard-earned petty cash."

Charles raised his near-full beer bottle and tapped Cal's. "You're a wise man, Cal."

"Tell us what you know about Harriet Grindstone," I said, as the bottle-clinking ended, and Randy Travis sang "On the Other Hand."

"Wow," Cal said. He twisted his head to the left. "That's a whiplash transition. Where'd that come from?"

"We're curious," Charles said.

Cal chuckled. "Yeah, right. Suppose you'll tell me when you get good and ready."

I nodded which seemed to satisfy Cal.

Cal leaned one elbow on the table and put his hand under his chin. "She's a tough old bird."

Interesting choice of words since she and Cal were the same age.

"What do you mean?" I asked.

"She's come in here a few times and threw back more than her share of brews. Told me that she reared three kids and kicked them and her husband out of the house about twenty years back. Said she's now, 'living happily ever after.'"

"What about her and Theo?" Charles asked.

Cal grinned and pointed his bottle at Charles. "Can't slip anything by you. She'd like to be on him like a mosquito on a baby's butt."

"Have they been in together?" I asked.

"Nah, don't think Theo gets out much other than his every-other-day crawl. If cancer spread as quick as Theo walks, we'd all die of boredom at 153."

Charles said, "How do you know she's out to reel him in?"

Cal pointed to the raised bandstand. "I've stood up there and on stages, truck beds, hay bales, and anything else I can stand on and performed for way too many decades and behind that bar for going on three years." He hesitated and pointed to the bar. "Know what I've learned after all those years?"

"What?" Charles asked.

"Learned a thousand country songs, about as many ways men can look stupid trying to dance, how beer kills brain cells, and a few hundred pick-up lines and flirtin' looks."

"So?" Charles said.

"So, Harriet's used most of those looks on Theo while she's trying to catch him in her web. Heck, when we're on our .5 shuffles, she can't walk down the street with him without him tripping over her flirts."

"Think she shot Abe?" Charles asked.

Cal stared at Charles, started to speak, hesitated, and finally said, "Didn't see that coming. Why would she?"

"Abe was after Theo's money," Charles said. "Harriet was after Theo. She could have been after him for love, you've said how she doted over him; but the biggest reason was for his money."

"I can see that. So you think she shot Abe to keep him from getting the dough."

"Just a thought," I said. "The problem I have with it is why she would shoot him from across the street. She's strong for her size and could have handled the rifle, but it seems like it would have been much easier and less risky to do it from close-up."

Johnny Cash was singing "Ring of Fire" and Cal looked at the jukebox, turned to Charles, and back to me. "I'm from Texas."

I nodded.

"There're more guns per-square-foot there than in Cabela's. You know what state stomps Texas in percentage of gun-owners?"

"Nary a clue," Charles said.

"Montana," I said.

"Really?" my trivia-collecting friend said.

Cal said, "You can bet your Remington on it."

Charles looked at me. "How'd you know?"

"Guessed. That's where Harriet's from, so I figured Cal was making the point that she'd know how to handle a rifle."

"You figured right," Cal said. "And she was raised on a ranch. Shooting would've been as normal to her as teasing her hair. What do the cops think?"

"They're focused on Larry," I said.

Cal shook his head. "You're pulling my spurs."

"He's serious," Charles said.

"I'd heard rumors, but why?"

Cal was one of the few on Folly who knew about Larry's checkered past, so I shared a little about what Larry had told me and the chain of events leading to the murder.

"You don't think he did it, do you?"

"If I did, I wouldn't be trying to figure out why Harriet said what she did."

"Then you've got to talk to that detective and get him straightened out," Cal said.

Easier said than done, I thought. I didn't tell Cal about my last conversation with Detective Adair, but did say that he was right and that I'd tell Adair what I was thinking.

"Good," Cal said. "Larry's my little bud, can't have anything bad happening to him. And speaking of detectives, heard anything else about Mel? I can't believe they think he killed that kid."

I told Cal that I hadn't heard anything new other than Mel was still in jail.

"They must think they've got a heaping-good case against him," Cal said.

I told him about the bloody rag in Mel's garage, Mel being at the gay bar in Charleston that the student frequented, and the other student who claimed to be an eyewitness to Mel being near where the kid was killed while the others were getting drunk at another part of Boneyard Beach.

"That's one saddlebag full of coincidences. Someone's framing my Magical Marsh Machine's man."

"I agree," I said, and thought, *how can I prove it?*

And Ricky Van Shelton was singing "Somebody Lied" as I left Cal's.

CHAPTER TWENTY-EIGHT

Cal had persuaded Charles to stay and help clean before Cal's opened for the late-afternoon drinkers, so I left him and walked down Center Street looking for reasons to not call Detective Adair and share my suspicions about Harriet. I had come up with five extraordinarily inane excuses for not calling before realizing that I might as well get it over with. I was closer to the gallery than home so I went in, left the front lights off, moved to the back room, and called the detective's cell.

"Yes, Mr. Landrum, what can I do for you," came the steel-cold voice.

I would have preferred hello or good afternoon, but forwent telling him that and said I'd like to talk about Abe's murder. He said that he would be on Folly in an hour and offered to meet me at the gallery. I took a deep breath and lied. "Sounds good."

My five inane excuses had begun to sound better, but it was too late.

As I sat and waited for Adair, the musty smell in the room coupled with the cold air blowing out of the air conditioner, brought back memories from years in this space. Most of the memories were good and the more I thought about them, the more I wondered if I should reconsider closing.

Adair's arrival interrupted whether I should remain open. "So what's so all-out important?" he asked as I greeted him at the door.

I offered him water or a soft drink, figuring I wouldn't make a friend by offering him a beer or a glass of wine. He brusquely declined and repeated, "What's so important?"

I pointed him to a chair at the table. He looked around and sat and I took one on the opposite side of the table.

He folded his arms and stared at me. I took a deep breath and shared my observation that Harriet had been paying more than a friendly interest in Theo, a member of the walking group, and that Theo had agreed to give Abe a significant amount of money to invest in a stock that he had been touting. Adair interrupted and asked more about Theo. To the detective's credit, he took notes.

I shared that I believed that Harriet didn't want Abe to get to Theo's money and that she shot him to prevent it from happening.

Adair asked for a physical description of Harriet, and I told him about her age and petite size. He didn't say anything, but from his skeptical look, I figured that hadn't helped my argument. I added that she had lived on a ranch in Montana, and my belief that marksmanship would probably have been a part of her past. I doubted that he was convinced.

The detective shut his notebook, returned it to his coat pocket, sighed, and gave me a police glare. "Mr. Landrum, what evidence do you have that Ms. Grindstone had anything to do with Mr. Pottinger's death?"

I wanted to slap him with his notebook and scream, *Isn't that your job?* Instead, I said that what I had told him was only speculation, but that it made sense. *More sense than accusing my friend Larry*, remained unsaid. To bolster my case, I told him that Charles Fowler and Chester Carr also felt the same way.

He appeared unimpressed and glared at me. "That's it?"

I nodded.

"Let me throw my speculation at you," He leaned both elbows on the table. "Larry LaMond is a friend of yours. I've heard it from several people—"

"Yes, but."

"But nothing. Let me finish." I closed my mouth.

"He's your friend, I get that, but, he's your friend who had a lengthy criminal past. He's a friend who never hesitated to break into houses and steal valuables from innocent homeowners, often while they were asleep in the same room. He's a friend whose past came back to haunt him when Mr. Pottinger showed up. How am I doing so far?"

I wanted to argue that Larry had been a model citizen for way more years than he had lived outside the law, and how he had established a stellar reputation on Folly Beach. Instead, I said, "Go ahead."

"Not only did Pottinger come to Folly, but I learned, from you, I might add, that he had threatened Mr. LaMond. He threatened to tell everyone about Larry's past which not only could have ruined Larry's reputation and business, but would have made a laughing-stock out of his wife, your police chief."

"Larry had already planned to tell everyone about his past," I said, realizing it sounded defensive.

"So you say."

"Didn't Larry tell you the same thing?"

Adair balled his hand into a fist. "What else would he have said?"

I leaned back in the chair, doing my best to not let him intimidate me. "I also said that I had volunteered to tell Abe that Larry was going to tell everyone about his past, and that he had no way to pay the extortion money, even if he wanted to. I told you that I had met with Pottinger with that message."

"Yes." He shook his head. "I believe that's the story you *forgot* to tell me the night of the shooting."

I didn't have a good response, so I continued, "I was leaving Pottinger's house after talking to him about Larry."

"That we agree on."

I held my hand up, palm facing him. "And that was when he was shot." Adair nodded. "Would Larry have murdered Pottinger before hearing the outcome of the meeting? Why would he have shot Pottinger when in your words, Larry's *friend* was only inches from a deadly bullet?" I leaned forward and stared at the detective. "Why?"

He met my stare and upped it. "Let me tell you two things I do know, Mr. Landrum. I've been a cop for a long time, much of it investigating what seems like countless murders. First, I know that logic, *making sense*, and intelligence seldom prevail when people are killed. And second, I know that your *friend* has no alibi for when Pottinger was gunned down; your *friend* has one heck of a good motive for shutting Pottinger up. Not a thing you've said has convinced me otherwise."

Nothing like an open mind, I thought. "You don't know him, but Larry's one of the most honest, aboveboard, and trustworthy people I've ever known. He may not have an alibi, but I doubt that most people over here who know Pottinger have one, and I've given you a motive for Harriet Grindstone. Why don't you check it out? And now that I think about it, you searched Larry's home, truck, and hardware store, did you find anything to indicate that he was the shooter?"

Since Larry was still free and since I was convinced that he was innocent, I knew what the answer had to be.

"Anything?" I repeated.

I was surprised when he grinned.

"Mr. Landrum, you know I'm not going to answer that. What I

can tell you is that I know that Larry LaMond shot Abe Pottinger. It's only a matter of time before I prove it."

Adair didn't storm out of the gallery, but didn't waste any time letting me know that our meeting was over and exited before I could respond.

I was convinced of two things: Larry was in more trouble than I had anticipated, and I hadn't helped him any. And, while I was still convinced that my friend had nothing to do with Pottinger's death, I knew where the detective was coming from. He had far more reason to suspect Larry than I had to accuse Harriet.

It was also clear that Adair wasn't going to be doing anything but focus on Larry. If anyone was going to pursue other possible suspects, it had to be me. Theo had said that he didn't have any paperwork on the stock he was going to fork over a million dollars on so that was a dead end. He wasn't a candidate for a reverse mortgage, but Alexander Lifetime Security Inc. was the company selling the product. I did a Google search and turned up two companies named Alexander Security, but both provided private security services for companies, and there were no listings for Alexander Lifetime Security, Inc. While I was on the computer, I looked for references about Harriet Grindstone and found only four people with that name. Unfortunately, none of them had been arrested for shooting someone, and none had lived in Montana. Wishful thinking was simply that. I knew Harriet had been married and wasn't sure if Grindstone was her maiden name or her husband's name.

What I was certain about was that if Abe was as good a con artist as Larry had portrayed him to be, he wouldn't have let anyone, much less someone he was conning, see that he was afraid of anything. Harriet had been lying. I was certain that she had grown up in Montana, and almost as certain that she'd know her way around rifles. From what Cal had said, she was protective of Theo and probably was out to "hook" him, which would have put

Abe in her sights if she felt he was trying to rip him off; in her sights only hours before Theo was going to hand Abe a million dollars.

How was I going to prove it? A simple question, but one with no simple answer.

CHAPTER TWENTY-NINE

The next .5 walk started almost identical to previous outings. Charles and I were at the pier early. Chester pulled his station wagon into the lot at the starting time, followed by Cal in his Caddy with William by his side. Harriet complained about everything else, including, her ankle, the weather, the bugs, and Chester's erratic driving. David Darnell defended Chester saying that it wasn't his fault that the "hippie on the bicycle" pulled in front of Chester so he had no choice but to drive up the sidewalk.

What was different was that there was less debate about the route. Chester made it clear that he was in charge and that the path to be taken was his to choose. Even Harriet, the consummate complainer, seemed to acquiesce to Chester's leadership. Chester began by offering a silent prayer in memory of Abe Pottinger, and then said we were going to "head up Center Street, hang a left at West Erie, and rest our weary legs while we sip Joe at Black Magic Café."

It was only three short blocks to West Erie, and the locally-owned café was fewer than fifty Theo-paces from the corner of Center Street. From what I had heard, and from the walks Charles and I had been on with the group, this would be one of the shortest walks; I doubted that Theo would have objected, even if he'd heard where we were going.

If there had been any question about Harriet's intentions for Theo, it was answered before the group hiked a block. She had her arm around his sleeveless T-shirt and kept whispering,

"You can make it, sweetie." Of course, for Theo to hear, Harriet's whisper was heard by everyone.

After what seemed like three months later, but closer to a half hour, we gathered around two round tables on the café's outdoor deck, and William and Cal went inside to get coffee for all of us except William who'd requested hot tea. Harriet still had her arm around Theo and fanned his face with his USS Yorktown ball cap. Chester told David that he had a special announcement to make when Cal and William returned with the drinks. Charles and I sat at the second table and watched the others acting like they had just completed a mini-marathon, or in Chester's parlance, a 12.1.

"See what we have to look forward to?" Charles said. I reluctantly agreed.

Cal and William began distributing drinks to the rightful owners. Considering the several thousand coffee and ingredient combinations available, I was impressed that it only took a few minutes to get the drinks sorted out. Charles said it was because Cal ran a bar and had figured out how to get the right drink to the right customer—something that had taken him three years to master.

Chester took a sip and tapped the side of his mug with a spoon. "Listen up."

Everyone quieted except Theo before Harriet nudged him and put her index finger to her lips and then pointed to Chester. Theo smiled and turned to face the leader.

"I have great news," Chester said. "Some of you know

Connie's brother, Robbie. He owns a marsh tour business. Well, Connie talked to him and he agreed to take us to Boneyard Beach."

Theo said, "In a bus?"

"No," Chester shouted, "in his boat. It'll hold all of us and he's giving us a real good deal." Chester turned to Connie. "Thank you, Connie."

"When'll we float out there?" Cal asked.

"Day after tomorrow," said Chester.

"How much?" Theo asked, the person who had more money than the rest of us combined.

Chester held up his hands and wiggled his fingers. "Only ten bucks a head. That's a great deal. Thanks again, Connie."

She smiled.

"I hear that the police know that Larry from the hardware store killed Abe," Theo said, like it was the most logical comment to make after Connie was praised for getting a good deal on the trip to Boneyard Beach.

"I don't believe it," said Cal, who turned to me. "Larry's a friend of ours."

Instead of wondering how we had transitioned from the boat ride to Larry, I said, "Yes, he has been for years."

"From my limited contact with the store's proprietor," William added, "he appears to be a fine, upstanding gentleman."

Cal was now fanning his face with his Stetson. "Well I can tell you this, my friend here will find out who the killer is." He sat his hat in front of him and pointed at me.

All eyes turned my direction.

Before I could say that ten dollars sounded like a good deal, Cal continued, "Yes sir, my friend, with the occasional help from Charles, has solved several murders that stumped the cops. A couple of you know how he saved me from getting killed by that deranged guy who owned the bar before I got it. " He gave a stage nod. "Yes sir, Chris will figure out who killed Abe." Cal picked up his hat and waved it in a semi-circle. "Right, Chris?"

"It's in good hands with the police." I hoped that Cal would let it go.

"I believe my friend, Chris, is correct," William said. "It's a matter for the proper law enforcement authorities. Shall we offer a round of applause for Chester and Connie for collaboratively finding a solution to achieve our goal of reaching Boneyard Beach?"

Thanks, William, I thought and raised my coffee mug to Chester and Connie. Everyone else offered polite applause.

We stayed on the patio for as long it would take to recuperate from open-heart surgery, before Chester said it was time to head back. David was in deep conversation with William about long-term care insurance as they led the group off the patio. The rest of us followed Chester, the unlikely leader of a band of walkers.

"Chris, Charles," William said after we had walked turned off Center Street toward Chester's cottage. "Could I perhaps commandeer a few moments of your time in private at the conclusion of our excursion?"

I translated that to mean that he wanted to talk to us without the nosy ears of the others, and said, "Of course."

Charles said, "Okay by me."

We had in Chester's words our "traditional post-walk refreshments" at his house before going different ways. Connie had cornered me to ask what Cal had been talking about when he said that Charles and I had caught some killers. I skimmed over the incidents and she didn't press for details. Theo, with the aid of Harriet, had moved over to my side of the porch and asked me what we were talking about. Fortunately Harriet yelled for him not to worry about it and he dropped the subject. Since we had overloaded our bladders with coffee, little time was spent drinking lemonade and chit-chatting.

Cal asked William if he was ready to leave and the professor told him that it was such a pretty day that he'd walk home. Cal said his ado's, tipped his Stetson at his fellow walkers, and moseyed out.

William looked over at me and tilted his head toward the door. I told the group that I was leaving, Charles said he was as well, and William said that he would walk us out. I felt like I was in the middle of a spy movie and William was going to pass us coded messages in fortune cookies. And I thought how unlikely William would be at espionage; and then again, perhaps that would make him the perfect spy.

We walked back toward town and William asked, "Shall we take a brief walk on the pier; perhaps find a venue with more privacy?"

I said that was fine, and Charles repeated, "Okay by me."

It was noon and the pier was more crowded than usual so we walked to the far end to find a bench that was both in the shade and isolated. Along the way, William never hinted at what he wanted to talk about but talked about the panoramic view of the beach from the pier, and how he planned to try his hand at fishing when he was fortunate enough to retire.

We settled on a wooden bench in the shade overlooking the east end of the island, and William looked around to see if anyone was within earshot. We were alone.

He looked at Charles and then at me. "May I be perfectly candid?"

I said of course, and Charles sounded like a broken record when he said, "Okay by me."

William grinned, looked toward the shore, then at me. "You don't believe that your friend Mel Evans killed Mr. Casey?"

"No," I said, "but to be honest, it's easy to see why the police think he did. They have a rag from Mel's garage with Casey's blood on it; Mel hadn't been forthcoming about how many times he's gone to that bar in Charleston; and most damning, the police have a witness who can place Mel in the area where the body was found, Mel had said that he only left the boat to urinate, and he had gone in the opposite direction from where the body was found."

William said, "Ah, the witness. That's what I wish to confer with you about. For you see, I am aware of who he is. The gentleman's name is Darnell Embley, and like the late Drew Casey, Mr. Embley is one of my students." William paused.

He was hesitant to talk about others, and I hoped that Charles wouldn't push him. The stars must have been aligned because Charles remained silent.

William continued, "As you can imagine, the death, especially by such despicable circumstances, of someone known by many of our students, has become a major topic on campus. Since Mr. Embley was part of the ill-fated party, and has gained extraordinary notoriety from being the individual who saw the killer, he is prone to expound upon the experiences at every opportunity." William hesitated.

I was beginning to wish we were listening to Dude. "Notwithstanding," William said, "I believe there are a couple of things Mr. Embley has said that detract from his credibility; things I must confess, I overheard at a time I shouldn't have been listening."

I said that it was okay.

William took a deep breath, and slowly exhaled. "Mr. Embley was speaking to two students who were present at the party. They were standing in the corridor outside my classroom, and I couldn't help but overhear." He took another breath.

Once again, I was surprised by Charles's silence.

William continued, "Mr. Embley was laughing and said, and these were his words, 'Were we soused or what?' And one of the others said that he couldn't remember because he was so drunk that he couldn't tell if he was on the beach or in the library. The third student said that everyone was so sick the next day that they never wanted to see another beer." William shook his head. "Mr. Embley said he quickly overcame that aversion."

William hadn't said anything that I hadn't suspected, but was surprised that the only witness admitted to being "soused" and wondered if detectives were aware of it.

Charles couldn't hold his silence. "So that's it?"

William shook his head. "Perhaps another item that one might call a clue. A young lady, someone who hasn't had the privilege of being in one of my classes, so I don't know her name, approached the gathered gentlemen. I didn't hear her salutation, but she laughed and said something to Mr. Embley to the effect that he was the hero who helped the police catch the perpetrator. Mr. Embley laughed and said that he didn't exactly recognize Mel near the scene, but, and again these are his words, 'It was an old bald guy in dark clothes. Who else could it have been?' To my untrained law-enforcement ears, that sounded inadequate as a positive identification of Mr. Evans."

I told him that I agreed. William then said that he knew we would want that information and agreed to tell the same thing to the police if they talked to him. I thanked him for sharing, and he said he was uncomfortable listening in on his students' private conversation, but was glad he could tell us what he had heard.

William headed home, and I asked Charles if he was up to a beer on the outdoor deck at the bar at the Tides.

The record was still stuck. "Okay by me."

The weather was nice and the bar crowded. We ran into Jay, the omnipresent and personable bellhop, greeter, and all-around nice guy, who told us that an accountants' convention had invaded the hotel, and for some strange reason, the participants appeared more interested in the bar, the view of the ocean, and sunshine than being in a seminar about how to depreciate heavy equipment under the new tax laws. "Go figure," Jay said, with a smile.

We ordered drinks and waited in the shade of the nine-story hotel until two bar-height chairs became available at the long, elevated bar that overlooked the beach and the pier. Finally, two men finished their beers, gazed at the ocean, and headed inside. I said that they probably felt guilty about missing the "highly stimu-lating" seminar and were returning to the meeting room. Charles said that he could tell from the sweat rolling down their faces that they were hot in their sport coats and ties and were headed to the inside bar to continue "networking." Either scenario, we grabbed their chairs.

"I've still got mixed feelings about Mel," Charles said, as he set his Tilley on the bar. "We don't know him that well; he's got a lot of past that we've never heard about. Besides, the police seem to have a strong case. Got a witness; got a bloody rag; got a motive, sort of; and got Mad Mel locked up."

"Until a day ago, I might have agreed," I placed my hat next to Charles's. "We don't know everything about Mel, but look at what we do know. He's devoted to Caldwell. I can see him frequenting the bar, he's never shied away from throwing back a few beers, but I can't see him there to pick-up college kids."

"I guess," Charles said.

"He's also smart; maybe not book-smart, but I would match his common sense against anyone. Do you think he'd be stupid enough to leave the bloodstained rag in his garage?"

"That bothered me too. But what about the witness?"

"You mean the *soused* one?"

"Yeah, but he was pretty sure the person he saw was old and bald; that wouldn't fit anyone on the trip but Mel."

"Look at the timeline. First, Mel said he asked if everyone was onboard when they were leaving the beach. No one said someone was missing. You had a boatload of drunks; some probably didn't even know they were on a boat. Then no one noticed anyone missing until the next day when the trip's organizer contacted Mel. Finally, my understanding is that the witness didn't come forward until a few days after the trip."

I paused, too long for Charles. "So?"

I looked at the waves rolling in then over to Charles. "Let's say the *soused* witness saw someone. I suspect that after the time he'd learned that Drew Casey was killed there had been many conversations with others from the trip and the witness started thinking all sorts of things. They were trying to figure out what had happened. They probably accused each other of killing him; then talked about him being gay; and then, no telling what else. In other words, days went by before the *soused* student remembered seeing an old bald guy near where the student was killed."

Charles started to interrupt but I stopped him. "I'm not saying he didn't see what he says he saw, all I'm saying is that considering the delay between the killing and him coming forward, it leaves a lot of room for doubt about credibility."

Charles said for me to hold that thought as he jumped up and headed to get more drinks. I spent the time watching a couple with three small children putting their feet in the puddles of water left on the beach as the tide receded, and a teenager walking under the pier. I thought about how many people's worlds were intersecting day in and day out with each being oblivious to each other. Charles returned before I was able to discover the secret of life and our role in it.

Charles set wine in front of me. "So Mel's being framed."

"Yes," I said and took a sip of the cold drink.

"Who and why?"

"Don't know. The first possible *who* would be one or more of the others on the boat, but that seems unlikely. Only the group leader knew who Mel was; and according to Mel, the leader contacted him by phone. Mel only uses his cell and his home address is unlisted, so how would one of them know where he lived to put the bloody rag in his garage?"

"Doesn't rule them out, though. With everything on the Internet —maps, addresses, and stuff I don't have a clue about— someone could find where he lives."

"Possibly."

"But if it wasn't one of the students, the killer had to know that Mel was taking the group out and where they were going; and had to be someone who knew where Mel lived."

"Yes."

Charles looked at the surf and back at me. "If that's true, how likely would it be for that person to know Drew Casey and to want him dead?"

"I don't think he did."

"Huh?"

"I think Drew Casey was killed to frame Mel, not because Casey meant anything to the killer."

"If it wasn't someone from the boat, how would he or she know that Casey was gay?"

"He wouldn't. Mel could still have been framed for killing a student. It turned out that he was gay and that helped the frame, but the gay angle wasn't necessary."

"If that's true, what did someone have against Mel; something that was worth killing over and going to a lot of trouble framing him?"

"That's the real question," I said and looked at a group of accountants competing for bar space, oblivious to what we were talking about.

"So what's the answer?"

The most common reasons for murder, I thought, and said, "Love or money?"

"Unless someone's out to get Mel to break up with Caldwell and put the moves on him, love seems unlikely."

"I'd eliminated that one," I said.

Charles's head bobbed and then tilted. "Money doesn't make any more sense. Mel doesn't have anything more than a pile of debt on his boat and his Camaro. How could money be the motive?"

"Charles, if I knew the answer to that, I'd be talking to the detective instead of to you."

"That's what I thought. Guess we don't know much of anything." He finished his beer and looked at the door to the hotel. "Want to learn how to depreciate heavy equipment under the new tax laws?"

I quickly declined.

"All this talk gave me a headache," Charles said. "I need a nap."

I agreed.

CHAPTER THIRTY

The next morning began with another thunderstorm pounding the metal roof, a parade of work trucks roaring past the house on the way to job sites, and me sitting in the kitchen, drinking scalding coffee from a Lost Dog Café mug, staring at a three-year- old calendar magnet stuck on the side of the refrigerator, and thinking about friends. Friendships are strange. They're often forged by things we have in common: children, hobbies, work. The emotional bonds created survive the differences friends have. After the bonds are cemented, and one of the friends does something that the other person doesn't agree with, or that happens to bend the law, the friendship generally prevails. Why? Psychologists and sociologists have pondered this question for decades and are often divided on the answer. Do we recognize and choose to overlook the differences and actions of our friends, or does friendship cloud our perceptions of the actions of others?

The friendships that I have made since arriving on Folly would confound anyone attempting deep analysis. I consider my closest friends to be Charles, Bob Howard, Cal, Amber, Chief Cindy

LaMond, William, and word-challenged Dude. I don't have children, so that it would be out as a cause for friendships. I could say that Charles and I share photography as a hobby, although before I arrived, he didn't know what end of a camera to look through. And forget work as a common thread.

There are two things my friends and I do have in common. First is a deep love for Folly Beach, its character and characters. Yes, even Bob falls into that group although it'd take a court order and an orthodontist pulling his teeth with no anesthesia to get him to admit it. And second, we all share a handful of dreadful experiences, often in chase of a murderer, or being on the barrel end of a firearm. One way or another, my friends have saved my life and I theirs. Beyond that, we share dissimilar backgrounds, dissimilar careers, if we even have or had any, dissimilar tastes in clothing, food, housing, and most likely, if we ever got into a discussion about it, politics, religion and the hereafter. With that said, I would give my life for each of them, and I suspected, and I hope never again tested, that they would do the same for me.

I also considered Larry and Mel among my friends. I haven't known them as long as some of the others and both have dark holes in their past. Larry has been more open about his years on the wrong side of the law but they were a long time ago. Since he's been here, he's been a model citizen and unless he chose to share what he'd done, no one would have suspected anything undesirable about him. Mel has never revealed anything other than a bullet-point resume of his life, but I've suspected that there's more than he'd told; more that is best not revealed to the police.

Do I believe that either was capable of murder? Good question. Larry had a powerful motive, no doubt, but I can't see him pulling the trigger, regardless how evil Abe might have been. Then again, has friendship clouded my thinking?

Mel provided me with another dilemma. Yes, I could see him killing someone; and he possibly has during his stint in the military, and maybe as a civilian. But, I can't see him having a motive strong enough to kill the college student. Again, is my belief fogged by friendship?

Friendships have given me more pleasure, more warmth, more comradery, and more depth to my life on Folly than I experienced my first six decades. I owed it to myself and my friends Mel and Larry to do everything I could to prove that they were innocent. If they didn't do it, someone else did. Abe's choices in life would have created any number of enemies; enemies from as far away as Georgia and as close as the .5 group. I had no idea who the outsiders might be, but had a strong hunch about Harriet. I would have her much higher on my list if she was twenty years younger, a hundred pounds heavier, and went by Harriet "Annie Oakley" Grindstone. But, she had grown up on a ranch, was probably familiar with firearms, and from how she doted on Theo, would have gone to great lengths to protect him.

Harriet had motive, opportunity, and possibly means; and that brought me to Mel. He had opportunity and means, but to me he had zilch motive. So if that's true, what about the witness? Sure, the student who said he had seen Mel near where the kid was killed, could be discredited in court. He was "soused," didn't come forward until days after the death, and said he was sure the person was Mel because the person he saw was bald and old, so who else could it be? Any defense attorney worth his fee could convince a jury that there were countless *bald and old* potential suspects within fifty miles of the crime scene. Would they have had motive? Of course not, but all the attorney had to do was cast reasonable doubt.

The more I thought about it, the more I was convinced that Mel was set-up. It didn't appear to be for love, so that left money. Who would benefit financially if Mel was convicted? Mel was upside down on his boat and his car. A few years ago, he'd shared that he didn't believe in life insurance; said he came into the world with nothing, planned to go out that way, and was "damned sure" he wasn't going to let anyone benefit from his demise.

And I remembered a comment made in an earlier conversation; a comment that meant little at the time, but that indicated that there was someone who would benefit from Mel's arrest and probable conviction. But how could I prove it? I'd be laughed out of the police station if I shared my theory with the detectives.

If I thought my mental gyrations would give me the answer, I was a colossal failure. The rain continued, the vehicles continued to roll by the house, and I did the most productive things I could think of to do: I poured more coffee, hoped that the weather would clear for tomorrow's boat trip to Boneyard Beach, yanked the outdated calendar off the refrigerator, and dropped it in the trash.

CHAPTER THIRTY-ONE

With Charles in tow, I showed up at the entrance to Mariner's Cay condos and its marina where Robbie's boat was docked and punched in the gate code that he'd given us. Mariner's Cay Marina was more up-scale than the Folly View Marina where Mel's Magical Marsh Machine spent its free time. Since we were operating on Charles Standard Time, I doubted that Robbie would be at the boat so we waited in the car.

The captain's Nissan pulled in beside us as I started to tell Charles my suspicion about who might have killed the student. Robbie looked around, smiled, and walked over to the car. He looked captainly in navy shorts, a tan safari shirt, and a FB ball cap.

He chuckled. "No worms here."

"Huh?" Charles said as he got out and shook Robbie's hand.

"You're early birds. Catching worms, get it?"

"This is Charles's version of on-time," I said.

We spent the next ten minutes talking about a new gift shop in town, how slow gallery and tour businesses were, and how Connie had conned her brother into taking us on the trip for such a low price. I told him how much the trip meant to Chester and how we appreciated his generosity, although it didn't appear that he had anything else to be doing.

The awkward what-next silence was broken when Chester's Buick and Cal's convertible pulled in beside us. Cal and

William hopped out, while Chester, Harriet, Theo, Connie, and David exited the Buick at the speed of an earthworm. I stifled a laugh when I saw that each of them wore a bright red cap with *.5 OR BUST* on the crown. Even Cal had replaced his Stetson with one. Chester handed Charles and me identical hats and beamed with pride as he said that he had them made for today's "historic" adventure. Crediting myself for wisdom that came with age, I didn't mention that our "historic" adventure was being accomplished by way of boat rather than the walk that was the goal of the group and the reason for .5 on the caps. Instead I replaced my Tilley with Chester's thoughtful, inaccurate gift.

Cal pulled his much-travelled guitar case out of his back seat and announced that Chester had suggested that since we were riding, Cal could share a few travelling, boat-riding, and beach tunes with the group. It didn't take much to encourage the country crooner to break into song, and I was glad that Chester had asked. Cal whispered to me that he had iced his *strummin'* hand all morning to keep his arthritis in check. David lugged a medium-sized cooler and said that all he knew about it was that Chester said it was a surprise. I'd had enough surprises recently and wasn't as enthused as David appeared to me.

Connie hugged Robbie and thanked him for taking the group; Chester echoed her sentiments without the hug, and Robbie led us to the entrance to the marina. Unlike Mel's boat that had numerous battle scars from years on the marsh and heavy partying, Robbie's Carolina Skiff was spotless and looked like it had come straight from the factory. I glanced at the bottom of my shoes to make sure I didn't track dirt aboard. Robbie managed to get everyone seated, a wise move since I suspected that some of the passengers would topple over once we began.

We moved out of the no-wake zone close to the marina and Robbie gunned the powerful Suzuki engine as we moved under the new bridge connecting Folly with the rest of the continental United States. Chester was trying to say something but the roar of the engine drowned him out. Robbie was in a hurry to get the trip over with, but pulled back on the throttle after Chester pantomimed for him to slow down.

The Folly River was sandwiched by marsh and ran behind the island. Larry and Cindy's house was to the right, and I gave a brief thought to the trouble that Larry could be in and how the person I believed killed Abe was ten feet from me.

My thoughts were interrupted when Theo pointed at a large house along the marsh. "That's mine!" he screamed as if he had to talk over the Suzuki. The engine was idling so Theo could probably be heard by his fellow passengers, and also by people miles away walking along the Battery in Charleston. Harriet leaned over and put her arm around his waist and kissed him on the cheek. Robbie must have figured that we'd had enough quiet time and gunned the engine as we continued to where the river narrowed and snaked a path through the increasingly dense marsh grasses. He had slowed to avoid running aground in the pluff mud, oyster beds, and other obstacles lurking beneath the surface. The putrid smell of decaying plants and animals assaulted my nose.

Robbie tried to point out some of the ecological features but only David listened. Connie and William were huddled together talking about how much she hated boat rides and William was countering by how much more enjoyable the ride was than trying to make the trip on foot. Theo, who couldn't have heard anything anyone was saying even if the engine had been turned off, looked off to the left and appeared deep in thought.

Harriet leaned toward Charles and me and put her finger to her lips, and whispered, "Theo and I are getting married."

She said something else that I didn't catch, and I leaned closer and said, "Congratulations. When's the big event?"

Harriet glanced at Theo who continued to stare at the marsh. "We, umm, haven't set a date."

Filtered through my belief that she had killed Abe, I wondered if Theo knew about their marital plans. Either way, it made me even more confident that she was the reason Abe wasn't making the historic trip with us.

It was low tide so Robbie couldn't take the more direct route to Lighthouse Inlet and the four mile trip was taking longer than usual as we weaved through the circuitous stream avoiding the shallower tidal creeks. We were moving at a snail's pace, and Chester was walking from person to person sharing his excitement about reaching Boneyard Beach.

William moved to my side of the skiff. "Have you learned more about the precarious position Larry finds himself in?"

"Not really," I said. "Don't think the police have talked to him again."

William grinned. "Perhaps the police will not be able to figure it out, but history would indicate that you will find a way to clear his name."

David moved closer to us. "You don't think he killed Abe?"

"No," I said.

"Interesting," David said.

"Chris is positive he didn't," William added. "He'll catch the perpetrator."

I appreciated his confidence, but wasn't as positive and said so.

"I do know that you are looking," he said.

I shrugged. "All I know is that Larry's innocent."

"And you will find a way to extricate Mr. LaMond from his dilemma," William added.

"What's that all about?" Theo asked.

"Nothing," Harriet said. "Enjoy your big day."

A small fishing boat passed us as it headed toward the dock. To its three occupants we looked like a meeting of a redneck chapter of the Red Hat Society with our red caps bathed in sunlight. Connie was standing at the helm beside her brother. I couldn't catch all of their conversation but heard bits and pieces about Timothy's wedding and how he still needed money. Connie said she felt for him, but didn't have any to loan; Robbie said he didn't and was afraid that the wedding may be off.

Cal stood behind Connie and Robbie and started strumming "Redneck Yacht Club." The song was many years newer than Cal's preferred play list, but he sang a passable version of Craig Morgan's hit; besides, with the engine revving loudly, few of the travelers could hear him.

The narrow waterway intersected the wider Lighthouse Inlet and Robbie steered the boat right toward the Morris Island Lighthouse and our destination. Cal was on much more comfortable musical ground as he transitioned into "On the Road Again," and the termination of Chester's dream trip was in sight.

Robbie inched the bow of his craft onto the sand; the opposite as Mel had when he had nearly thrown me overboard when he rammed the Magical Marsh Machine on the beach. I suspected Robbie was more concerned about his new fiberglass hull than for the aging bones that could have been broken on some of his passengers if he'd hit harder.

Chester was first off. If he had an American flag, he would have planted it in the sand before announcing, *one small step for .5 kind.* Charles and I were the next on shore and we gave a hand to the others as they exited the craft. Theo remained seated as everyone else got off. Harriet stood in front of him and leaned down and asked if he was okay. He said he was a little queasy and wanted to stay on the boat a few minutes. Robbie said he was going to stay close, and would watch after Theo. Harriet reluctantly agreed and Charles helped her to shore.

Ten minutes later, Cal had moved to the nearby graffiti- covered foundation ruins left from the Coast Guard property, had taken his guitar from its case, and began an impromptu concert. With the lighthouse and Lighthouse Inlet as a backdrop, he waded into his more-familiar songbook with a medley of Hank Williams Sr. heart-break songs. Connie and William had walked to a small grove of dead, bleached trees, and David, Harriet, and Chester moved closer to Cal as he sang, "Your Cheatin' Heart." I was thrilled that Chester's group had made it to their destination, regardless if by foot or float.

Cal finished strumming and Chester raised his hands and clapped them together over his head. "Group, gather round." He waved for us to move closer. Theo was still on the boat with Robbie but Chester didn't seem to notice. Chester motioned for David to set the cooler on the top of the foundation and Chester pulled out two bottles of cheap champagne and a stack of clear plastic cups. "I propose a toast to the best damn walking group this side of the Folly River."

A safe statement since it was the only walking group on Folly, and Charles yelled "Here, here!" as Chester fiddled with the foil on the top of the first bottle. Charles saw him struggling and grabbed the second bottle and started opening it. And, for reasons that I didn't understand, Cal started singing "Auld Lang Syne." Chester, with a grin as large as a Frisbee, sang along, followed by Connie, David, and William. As I listened to the group fumbling through the words that only seem coherent to a room full of drunks on New Year's Eve, I realized the true meaning of "it's the thought that counts."

I also realized that Theo, the primary reason we had taken a boat to Boneyard Beach, was still on the boat, and Harriet seemed engrossed in singing and drinking champagne. Robbie and Theo were in deep conversation, but since Theo was missing the festivities, I wanted to break him free and help him hobble over to the group.

Robbie's back was to me and Theo faced me as I approached. He assumed that everyone heard as poor as he did, so quiet was not in his vocal range. He said, "How do you know?"

Robbie's response was drowned out by the water lapping against the side of his boat and Cal singing, "How Can I Miss You When You Won't Go Away?"

Theo shook his head and pointed his finger at Robbie. "Okay." He saw me and waved me over to the boat. "Hey, Chris, give me a hand. I need to get to the fun."

Robbie leaned against the throttle and watched as Theo, with a great deal of my aid, managed to get off the skiff. Harriet noticed us and rushed to help her "fiancé." The three of us walked toward the foundation/bandstand/bar and Robbie followed closely behind.

The first bottle of champagne was empty but the second was hardly touched. Cal had returned his guitar to the case and the group began pairing up and walking around the deserted beach. William and Cal walked down one of the handful of paths leading from the beach to the marsh, with Cal pointing to something along the side of the path and laughing. Chester, Connie, and David explored a clump of trees the beach had been named after. Connie laughed when Chester tried to pull himself up on one of the trees. He would have had better luck if he'd been a minnow. Harriet and Theo seemed satisfied to remain at the foundation while Theo made up lost time imbibing. Charles and I stayed with them since we had explored the area several times over the years and I had been here a few days ago with Mel. And Robbie had returned to the boat, spread out on one of the bench seats, and appeared to take a late-morning nap.

I smiled to myself and thought how wonderful and cathartic the trip was for each member of the group. I smiled until I realized that Mel was in jail for killing someone within a couple of hundred yards of where we were, and that Larry was the prime suspect for killing a member of this group.

CHAPTER THIRTY-TWO

L ike most return trips, the ride to the marina seemed shorter than the trip over. The excitement of reaching their goal, combined with champagne, sunshine, and a combined lifespan approaching the age of coal, had taken its toll. Charles and I were the only members who weren't dozing. I was sitting beside Chester who was snoring louder than the roar of the Suzuki. The others were quieter, but still asleep.

We were near the bridge when we were bounced by the wake of a larger boat heading the other direction, and most of the group were jarred awake. Chester removed the red cap that had been covering his eyes and clapped for everyone to pay attention. All but Theo responded and Harriet had to shake him awake. Chester said that he was proud of everyone for their incredible accomplishment and that Robbie deserved a hand for taking the group at a reduced rate. I was slow to applaud because I was trying to figure out how the boat ride was such an incredible accomplishment. I didn't waste much brainpower on it and joined the rest of the group as we applauded while Robbie docked his pride and joy.

Chester laughed and patted each member on the back and hugged the two ladies as we stepped on the wooden dock. It was good seeing him this happy. His smile disappeared when Harriet missed the step and fell hard. William, ever the gentleman, rushed to her, asked if she was okay, and tried to help her up. She said she had reinjured her ankle and to give her a minute. David carried the cooler to Chester's car and Cal took his guitar case to his Cadillac while the rest of us gathered around Harriet.

"I'm fine," she said to Chester. "Could you drop me at my house instead of back to yours?"

William helped her up and acted as a human crutch as she gingerly hobbled to the car. They were so slow that Theo beat them to the vehicle and moved to the back seat instead of his customary spot in the passenger's seat so Harriet could have easy access.

Charles and I beat Cal and William to Chester's house and it was another half hour before the group leader pulled up and only he and Connie climbed out.

"Did Theo and David fall out?" Charles asked.

"Theo said he was a wee-bit exhausted from the trip and wanted me to drop him at his house," Chester said. "David said he had an appointment and would get his car later."

"I'm only here to get my car," Connie said. "Sorry, Chester."

Chester's smile faded. "Our biggest adventure, and look who's left to celebrate it."

I had planned to sneak out early, but seeing that his post- adventure party only consisted of Cal, William, Charles, Chester, and me, I knew I was in for at least an hour of lemonade, stale cookies, and reliving our big adventure. I hinted for Cal to get his guitar, but he either didn't catch the hint or was crooned out.

Chester had been rejuvenated from his nap and was ready to party. Charles and I hadn't had the advantage of a nap and I wondered how many more times I could hear Chester say how exciting today had been before I dumped the pitcher of lemonade over his head. Cal saved Chester when he said that he'd had "about as much fun as an inebriated hyena could have," and excused himself. William didn't put it that way but said he'd better call it a day, and Charles and I jumped on the bandwagon, or the mass exodus, and followed Cal and William off the porch.

"Hold up a sec," Chester said as I reached the car. "I nearly forgot. Theo asked me to give you this." He handed me a folded piece of paper, thanked us for being part of the "really big day," and headed in the house.

I got behind the wheel, turned up the air conditioner, tossed my red cap in the back seat, and opened the folded paper.

I caught myself holding my breath as I read: *Need to talk about the killer.*

I read it a second time and handed it to Charles who had been leaning over trying to make out Theo's words. Charles read the note and looked at me. "What're you waiting for?"

On the way to Theo's, Charles asked if I thought that Harriet had confessed to killing Abe and Theo wanted to tell us. I didn't respond but thought it had to do with something more recent, something that reinforced my hunch about who'd murdered the student.

I pulled in Theo's drive and looked up at the massive two- story elevated structure and was once again impressed by its size and view of the marsh. Theo came out the front door and waved us up the stairs.

He smiled and motioned us in. "Thought that'd get you here."

I had never been in the house, but wasn't surprised by the interior. From the entry, there a clear view through the kitchen to large windows overlooking the marsh and the river. I envied him and his sunset view. He led us to the great room filled with substantial light-colored, wood furniture and offered us seats on a latte-colored couch. There were original oil paintings of coastal lowlands on three of the walls and expensive looking knickknacks on the tables. I recognized the names of two of the artists. Either Theo had a sophisticated eye for design or the home was professionally decorated. I told him it was stunning; he said he supposed so, and that it cost him a mint to have someone get it that way.

That answered my first question, so I led into my second. I pulled his note out of my back pocket and said, "Killer?"

"First, thanks for coming. I didn't know who else to go to. I figured the cops would laugh at me and I knew you're a detective."

I started to protest, but Charles jumped in. "Go ahead."

Theo looked at Charles and back to me. "Let me ask you something," he said.

I nodded.

"Did the police tell anyone where the kid's body was found?"

"Sure," Charles said, again before I could speak. "Boneyard Beach."

Theo sighed, "I know that. That's a big place. I mean exactly where they found him?"

I thought about what I had heard both around town and from Cindy about who knew the exact location. "Don't think so." I glanced at Charles who shook his head. "Why?"

"I'm being rude," Theo said. "Want something to drink?" I wanted to scream "No! Get on with your story!"

Instead, I said "No thanks."

Theo looked at Charles who shook his head, and then he turned to me. "I'm old, ancient according to some; I know my memory's not what it used to be. I'm slow afoot, ask anyone in the group; and, I'm almost deaf." He shook his head. "There's one thing I'm not. I'm not stupid."

"You're definitely not stupid," I said.

"Remember this morning when I stayed on the boat?"

"Sure," Charles said.

"Captain Robbie was with me. I'd talked to him about everything I could think of to pass the time. I'd run out of things to say, so since we were in the vicinity, I asked him if he knew where they found the body."

I thought I knew where he was going but wanted him to get there.

Theo looked at Charles, and at me, and out the large bay window toward the marsh. "Well, the captain stood up and pointed out past the foundation where you all were partying and said, 'About a hundred feet to the left and back a small trail to the marsh.'" He cocked his head, looked out the window, and turned back to us. "Fellas, how would he know that unless he was there?"

"Good question, Theo," I said. "Was that what you were talking about when I came to get you off the boat?"

"Youngsters like the captain, think that because someone's old that he can't figure things out. Can't wonder about things that seem off. Yeah, I had asked him how he knew where the body was when you showed up."

Charles leaned toward Theo. "What'd he say?"

Theo frowned. "I was getting there. The captain stumbled through his words and mumbled something about hearing it around town. Sounded like a crock. That's when I asked for Chris's help off the boat."

"Is that all he said?" I asked.

"Yes, I know that's not anything that means that he killed the kid, but it sounded wrong, just plain wrong. And I'll tell you one other thing, that fellow sure was antsy after I asked him how he knew. That's why I figured you were the best person." He glanced at Charles. "Best *people* to tell. I know you're good at catching killers."

"You sure that's all he said?" Charles asked. "Huh?"

Charles repeated the question.

"Did you forget the part about me not being stupid? Yes, that's all. Now you fellows get busy and figure out how you can prove he did it." He yawned, hesitated, and said, "I'm going to call my buddy

Chester and thank him again for pulling the trip together, and then take a nap."

We were almost out the door when he added, "Don't tell anyone in the group, but I also know the real reason they call me ET." He then grinned and saluted us.

On the way down the steps, Charles asked, "What do you think?"

"Robbie killed Drew Casey."

"Whoa, you're that sure because Theo said Robbie knew where the body was?"

"Mel didn't kill the kid so someone else did."

"Profound."

"There's more."

"I'm all ears."

"Motive," I said. "Remember when we first met Mel's buddies, the captains?"

Charles nodded.

"One of their big complaints was that there wasn't enough business to go around, and I think one of them even said that there were too many captains doing the same thing. Robbie has a new, expensive boat, and a bunch of kayaks and he told his sister that he didn't have any money to lend his friend Timothy for his wedding. He's probably in financial straits and eliminating competition is one way to get out of the hole."

"What about the gay tie in? That's what the police are pinning their case against Mel on."

"True, but I don't buy it. There's no way Mel would have made a pass at that kid. Because they frequented the same bar doesn't prove anything. I haven't heard that the police have even put them there at the same time. I think both being gay was an unfortunate coincidence. And there are way too many people who want to think the worst about someone because of sexual orientation. Mel's an easy target."

"What about the witness who saw him?"

"The witness admitted to being drunk and didn't come forward for several days. For the sake of argument, let's say the witness did see someone near where the murder took place. The witness admitted that it was dark and he couldn't get a good look. He said it was Mel because Mel was the only *old bald* guy on the boat." I looked out the window and turned back to Charles. "What do Robbie and Mel have in common?"

Charles closed his eyes and nodded left and right. "The same height, same build, and both ... bald. But Robbie's younger."

"To a college student in the dark and through alcohol-infused eyes, he would still be an *old bald* guy."

"So he saw Robbie and thought it was Mel."

"Exactly."

"How would Robbie have known they were going to be at Boneyard Beach? Why kill Drew?"

I grinned, "Remember what Mel told us the captains talked about during their monthly gatherings?"

Charles put his forefinger to his cheek. "Bitched and moaned about cheap vacationers, stupid things that happen on their trips, and fixing prices."

"Yes, I said, "Plus, what trips they had scheduled."

Charles nodded. "So he could have known about the Boneyard Beach excursion and been there when they arrived. Wouldn't Mel have noticed Robbie's boat?"

"No doubt, and that's why I think Robbie walked from the end of Ashley Avenue to Boneyard Beach."

".5 miles," Charles added.

I nodded. "I think he killed the college student to frame Mel. Drew Casey's only crime was being in the wrong place at the wrong time."

"And Robbie put the bloody rag in Mel's garage?"

"Yes."

Charles shook his head. "So what are we going to do about it?"

"I'm going to drop you at your apartment, and then call Detective Cox and lay out my thoughts and hope he doesn't laugh his head off. All I have is speculation, and Cox thinks he already has the killer. I hope he is as good a person as Cindy says he is. I hope he listens."

Instead of getting Detective Cox, I got a metallic sounding voice mail message asking me to leave a message. I told the cold machine who I was and requested that Cox call me as soon as possible. I was exhausted but needed to run to the grocery, and hopefully could slip in a nap while waiting for the call.

CHAPTER THIRTY-THREE

I was carrying two bags of what I call groceries, or what nutritionists deride as junk food, up my front steps, and wondering if I had the energy to get them put away before falling into bed for a nap. It was an hour since I had called and I wondered why the detective hadn't called back. I stepped through the door and my focus abruptly changed.

"About time," said the strident voice of Harriet Grindstone.

She stepped out of the kitchen to meet me.

I'm not the detective some have accused me of being, but it didn't take one to know this wasn't a social call. A black, semiautomatic Beretta pointed at my head gave it away. I also realized that my bag of Oreo cookies may raise her cholesterol, but would be no match for the handgun.

I looked at the groceries, and tilted my head toward the kitchen table. She waved the gun in that direction and I set the bags on the table.

"What do you want Harriet?"

Her cackle reminded me of the Wicked Witch of the West.

She motioned for me to sit. I obliged.

She lowered her thin frame in the chair opposite me at the table, and kept the gun pointed at my head. "Let me tell you a story."

I nodded as if I had a choice.

"When I was seven, we lived on a ranch. I went to school like all the other little boys and girls and learned the same kind of things that I bet you learned. English, math, reading, and even some history helped me get to where I am today. But the real learning came from my Pop." She hesitated and looked toward the window, but the Beretta's aim never wavered. "Montana ranch life was tough, but Pop loved every second of it. One day I was playing out behind the barn when a gray wolf peeked its head around the corner. I'd never seen one that close and thought it was as cute as could be and figured it would be a mighty-fine pet. I inched a little closer and it wasn't as skittish as I thought it'd be. I was wondering how to catch it, when all of a sudden, the cute thing's head went and exploded. Boom! I was stunned. I looked around and there stood Pop, his big-ole Winchester in his hand and a wicked frown on his face. I was so mad at him that I ran to the house crying."

I stared at Harriet and waited. She stood and walked to the sink and looked out the window. Her limp had disappeared and I realized that she had faked the injury so she could be here when I got home.

She returned to the chair. "Now the lesson. Pop let me get in a good cry, and then made me sit in front of him. He said that that lovely creature he shot was put on this earth for one purpose, and that was to kill and eat—to kill and eat our livestock, my chickens, and even little girls if enough wolves were in the pack. He said they may be beautiful, but that I shouldn't be deceived. We had to over-look their appeal and kill them every chance we got. They were no good, he said. Know what else he taught me?"

I shook my head.

"Pop didn't have the benefit of a good education, had to cheat to finish high school he said, with a little embarrassment in his voice, but he told me there was one lesson he learned early on. Said that if you set your mind to doing or getting something, you need to use all the wherewithal in your power to do it."

The phone rang.

Great, now the detective calls.

Harriet gave it a dirty look. "Let it ring."

We both stared at it until it stopped and she continued, "Pop said it wouldn't always be easy but if I wanted it, I shouldn't let anything stand in my way."

"Like Abe?"

She grinned but her eyes were cold. "I've had several relationships in my life, some of them were good." She grinned again. "Most of them sucked. Then Theo came along. He's a sweet man, you know."

And a wealthy one, I thought.

"Sure he's got a few problems, but who doesn't. Speed walking's not his thing, his memory's not quite all there, and when it comes to the bedroom … never mind. The point is he likes me, and I think I'm falling for him."

And his money. "Abe stood in your way?"

"Let me put it as delicately as I can." She shook her head. "That sneaky, conniving, conning, son of a bitch, was a damned gray wolf. He was after Theo's money and would've taken him for every penny if I'd have let him. The million that Abe had already talked Theo out of was only the beginning. He had more 'great deals' he was talking to poor Theo about." She glared at me. "You see, I couldn't let that happen."

"So you did what your dad did to the wolf?"

"You bet your ass I did. Another thing Pop taught me was how to shoot a tin can off a fencepost at fifty yards. Sorry you had to be there. If you hadn't fallen out of the way, I would have waited for another time to exterminate the damned wolf. Sooner or later, I would have got him. You know, we do what we have to do to protect our self-interests. I. . ."

The phone's shrill ring interrupted a second time.

I thought she was going to shoot the phone, but instead slid it out of my reach and scowled at it until it stopped. I took the interruption to look around for something I could use as a weapon. All that came close was the Mr. Coffee machine; no competition for a semiautomatic.

"I get why you killed Abe, but why are you here?"

She sighed. "The police are after your buddy, Larry. I wasn't on their radar and never would have been, and then a detective knocks on my door and starts asking questions and fishing for connections to Abe. He finished his questions and I asked why he was talking to me. He said it was routine." She frowned. "I hate it when people think because I'm getting older that I'm stupid."

I thought how similar that was to Theo's comment about Robbie.

She continued. "I knew that was BS and asked him who gave him my name. He gave me a polite smile and said he couldn't say. He didn't have to; I knew it was you and your damned nosiness. Everybody tells me how you butt into murders and keep asking questions until you get the goods on someone. I looked you up on-line and saw they were right. You're a good friend of Larry." She shook her head. "Sorry, but you need to go." She leaned back but still held the gun on me. "We're going to sit here until dark and I'm going to escort you to my car and then we're going to head off-island so I can give you a proper *adios* where you won't be found for a while." She grinned. "If ever. Then I'm going to be back in my house moaning and groaning about my sprained ankle. I couldn't have been out-and-about killing anyone; couldn't even get off the couch."

Dark was an hour away so I had some time to come up with a plan. I didn't have to wait that long. Pounding on the front door startled both of us. Would Detective Cox have come to the house after I didn't answer? No, that wouldn't make sense.

Harriet started to push away from the table, and was momentarily distracted. This was my chance. Before she could stand, I rammed the table into her midsection. She tripped over her chair but regained her balance before hitting the floor. The Baretta was still in her hand.

Three things happened almost instantaneously. I shoved the overturned table out of the way and lunged for the gun. I had suspected that Harriet was stronger than she looked. I was right. She scooted back and kicked my shin. I grabbed the pistol's barrel and tried to twist it out of her hand.

The barrel blast was six inches from my head. The sound was deafening and the high pressure muzzle flash blinded me. I barely noticed the sting on my temple.

Then, Charles's size nine shoe kicked in the front door.

I ignored the stream of warm liquid running down my cheek and twisted the weapon away from her. Harriet screamed as her trigger finger yanked backwards. I wrenched the weapon from her grasp and hurled it across the room. I jerked her left arm behind her back. She screamed a second time and fell on her stomach. Blood from my head dripped on the back of her blouse as I grabbed her other arm and twisted it behind her.

Charles moved closer. I yelled for him to get duct tape from the drawer by the sink.

Harriet kicked, let out a bloodcurdling scream, and rolled from side to side. It took both of us to hold her still enough to tape her hands together and then tape her feet together for insurance. Once she was disabled, I sat on the floor and touched my head. Charles grabbed a towel and I pressed it to the wound while he called 911, Cindy's cell phone, and left a message for Detective Adair.

Between the time Charles called the cavalry and when the house filling with police, I must have passed out. The next thing I remembered was lying on the stretcher with an IV in my arm and an EMT smiling and saying "Welcome back."

I knew I was going to be alright when Officer Allen Spencer leaned over the stretcher. "Didn't I say that you needed a better lock?" He was referring to an incident last year when the police had broken into the house to catch someone suspected of murdering members of a film crew. I smiled when I realized that Larry would now be around to install it instead of being behind bars.

I argued that I didn't have to go to the hospital but the EMTs politely, but firmly, disagreed and I finally gave in. I gave Officer Spencer a quick rundown of what had happened as the medics wheeled me out the door. He assured me that Harriet would be leaving with him, and Charles said he would follow the ambulance in my car.

CHAPTER THIRTY-FOUR

An hour later, I was in an exam room in the ER at Charleston's Roper Hospital. I had spent so much time in the emergency room the last few years either as a patient or visiting friends that I asked the nurse if I could get the employee discount at the cafe. She faked a smile and said something about a shot in the head makes people say weird things. I didn't know about that, but knew that I had a terrible, pulsating headache and the side of my face felt like it had been held over Larry's grille.

I had been X-rayed and the first doctor to check on me had a nurse put salve on the facial burn that had been caused by high pressure gas and unburned gunpowder from Harriet's gun. The bullet had only grazed my skull and the wound was minor, no stitches necessary. Before rushing to more serious emergencies, the doc said he didn't think there was any serious damage, but he wanted to keep me overnight to be safe. I was lucky, he said, and I agreed. Did I ever!

Charles waited with me until they moved me to a room and had the need to say weird things without benefit of being shot in the head. I didn't realize how many stupid jokes could be made about my hard head and how the best way to grab a gun was the grip instead of the barrel. My head hurt too much to appreciate his stand-up comedy routine, so I changed the subject.

"Why were you at the house?"

"You said you were going home and taking a nap, so where else would you be? I called and you ignored the call. I called again and you ignored me a second time, so I thought I'd head over and pound the door until you got your lazybones out of bed."

I didn't think it was necessary to tell him that I didn't answer because I had a deadly weapon pointed at me. Besides, I owed my life to his impatience, something else that I wasn't about to acknowledge.

It kept running through my lucky head what Harriet had said about us having to do whatever necessary to protect our self- interests and despite my aching head, I began to focus on Mel. Once I eliminated him as a killer, all signs pointed to Robbie. And Robbie knew that Theo was getting suspicious. Was Theo in danger?

I asked Charles to get my cell out of my slacks.

"If you're calling for a pizza, get pineapple on it," he said.

If my head hadn't hurt, I would have uttered a smart remark, but instead I closed my eyes and held my hand out for the phone. He handed it to me, huffed, and plopped down in the only chair in the room. I saw where I'd missed a call from Chester and that he'd left a voicemail. It could wait, and I called Theo, only to get a recording. I left a message for him to call me as soon as he could.

After I disconnected, Charles said, "Theo doesn't deliver pizzas. What's up?"

I shared my fear that Theo wasn't good at hiding his surprise that Robbie knew where the body had been, and that the captain might go after him. My head hurt but everything else appeared to be working properly so I scooted my legs off the side of the bed and sat. After a minute, the room stopped spinning, and I asked Charles to get my clothes. He shook his head and asked if the bullet in my head made me forget what the doctor had said about me spending the night in Hotel Roper.

"The bullet isn't in my head. I'm leaving."

Charles response was to hand me the bundle of clothes. I had lied about feeling fine; my head pounded and the side of my face still felt like I'd laid it on an electric stove's red-hot burner. I dressed before anyone in a white coat returned and tried to tie me down.

"Don't suppose you'll let me push you out in a wheelchair?" Charles said.

I smiled even though it made my face sting more, and waved for him to follow me. We managed to avoid anyone who would want to keep me and I conceded to my condition by letting Charles drive.

I closed my eyes as soon as he pulled out of the parking lot.

I finally got my nap.

Charles nudged my arm. "Now where?"

I opened my eyes and realized we were on Folly. "Theo's." Theo's new, black Mercedes was in the drive but no one answered the door. I suggested that we check the back door and Charles and I walked around the house and up the steps. The door to the screened-in porch was unlatched and we could see that the mahogany door into the house was standing open. From our higher vantage point, Charles looked around the back yard and out Theo's private pier that ended at the river. I pushed the door the rest of the way open and called for Theo. Charles said he wasn't outside and no one answered inside.

I had a clear view of the kitchen and nothing looked out of place.

"Think we need to call reinforcements?" Charles asked as we stepped into the kitchen.

"Not time. Theo may be hurt."

Charles whispered, "And Robbie could be here waiting to kill us."

I shrugged and moved to the great room. Things appearing normal ended there. A lamp from an end table was on the floor, its bulb shattered, its shade twisted. A porcelain seahorse that had been on the table was in hundreds of pieces strewn across the floor. And, what looked like drops of blood were in a serpentine pattern leading toward the master bedroom.

Charles whispered, "Now can we call the cops?"

I put my finger to my lips, followed the stream of blood, and inched my way toward the bedroom. The only sounds I heard were my heart beating against my ribcage and a couple of creaks from the floor as Charles and I moved toward the bedroom.

The bed was as neat as it would have been if it had been made by a five-star hotel housekeeper; nothing seemed out of place except the drops of blood leading to the master bath. I moved toward the bath, and I dreaded what I might find. I could picture Theo's frail body, broken, bloody, and stuffed in the tub.

Relief spread over me when there was no one in the room— dead or alive. What was there was a white, blood-soaked, *TS* monogrammed hand towel. The blood was still tacky so I knew whatever happened wasn't too far in the past.

I looked back at Charles. "Now we call the police." Instead of dialing 911, I called Chief LaMond.

She answered on the second ring. "Where the hell are you? I'm at the hospital with a freakin' vase of flowers in my hand and there ain't no Chris to give them to."

I told her where we were and gave her quick rundown on what we had found. Thankfully, she didn't bombard me with questions and said she was on her way. I told Charles I wanted to check the rest of the house to make sure Theo wasn't bleeding to death in another room. Charles said I must have a death wish, but followed me as I canvassed the rest of the rooms. Again, no body. No killer.

Cindy didn't come alone. Two patrol cars converged, sirens blaring, as the chief pulled her unmarked car in front of the house. I met her at the door.

She shoved the vase of flowers in my stomach and walked past me into the great room. "Why aren't you in the hospital?" Her eyes darted around the room and her hand rested on her firearm's grip.

"I thought…"

"Crap," she interrupted. "Never mind, whatever you say, it means you're too stubborn for your own good. What happened?" She waved her hand around the room.

I told her my suspicions about Robbie and why I was worried about Theo. She nodded when she came to the bedroom and face-to-face with Charles.

"Don't suppose you could've hogtied him and hitched him to the hospital bed?"

Charles shook his head. "What do you think?"

"The boy's good at getting in the middle of trouble, isn't he?" she said and walked around the room taking in everything.

Charles watched Cindy check out the room and then walk into the bathroom and stare at the bloody towel. "Abe Lincoln said, 'Whatever you are, be a good one.' Chris's the best trouble sniffer I've ever known."

Officer Spencer was next to arrive. He said, "We meet again," and asked how I was without making any cutting remarks and asked Cindy what he could do.

The chief looked at me. "Any idea what Robbie drives?"

"Old, silver Nissan Maxima."

She turned to Spencer and told him to have dispatch get the license, put out an APB, and if anyone spotted it, to approach cautiously because he may have a hostage.

"Looks like someone took Mr. Stoll," Cindy said. "Hopefully alive. If it was Robbie, any idea where he may have gone?"

"Off the top of my head, no," I said. "I would guess somewhere far away, although he wouldn't know that we found this as quickly as we did. He could still be on the island."

"Don't suppose you know where he lives?" she said.

Charles stepped close to Cindy. "I heard he has a small apartment somewhere around East Seventh Street, but not sure where."

Cindy turned to Officer Bishop, the second patrol officer in the house, and told her to have someone get her the address and to take another officer with her and check his apartment. Cindy asked Charles and me to sit on the patio so we wouldn't mess up the crime scene any more than we already had, while she called the crime scene techs in Charleston and then Detective Adair and filled him in. My head still throbbed and she didn't get an argument from me.

CHAPTER THIRTY-FIVE

I sat on Theo's patio with my head resting on my hands while Charles prowled around the patio like a lion trying to figure out which unsuspecting zebra to have for supper. Patience was not in his arsenal.

"The crime scene guys are stuck behind a wreck in Charleston," Cindy said. She had been inside the house and surprised me when she was standing in front of me on the patio. I must have dozed. "It'll be a while before they get here. Why don't you go back to the hospital?" She grinned. "Maybe they won't notice that you skipped out on them."

I looked up at her and frowned.

"Didn't think you'd take my sage advice. So go home. I'll know where you are if we need you."

Charles had stopped pacing and told Cindy that was a great idea and that the Charles Taxi Service would be leaving in five minutes. My head still throbbed but I knew when I was outnumbered, so I walked to the car and once again took the passenger's seat, something that I wasn't accustomed to. Besides, the mid-eighties temperature combined with direct sun, was beginning to add to my discomfort.

We pulled to the stop sign at Center Street. Charles started to turn left toward the house. I said, "Turn right."

"Why?"

"To see if his boat's at Mariner's Cay Marina."

He huffed. "You're going to be the death of me yet."

The dock at Mariner's Cay was visible from the bridge but several larger boats blocked my view and I couldn't tell if Robbie's skiff was there. A minute later, Charles punched in the access code and we weaved around the development to the parking area.

"You okay?" he asked.

I skirted the truth and said that I was fine.

Robbie's boat was where he had docked it after our trip to Bone-yard Beach and appeared unoccupied. Charles suggested that since we were this close, we should see if there was anything unusual on the craft. I knew he was trying to delicately say signs of a struggle, blood, or Theo.

The floating dock bobbed up and down, and the fear of finding something gruesome on the boat, intensified my headache. Charles, trying to be inconspicuous, leaned close to me to keep me from staggering off the side of the dock. I appreciated how considerate he was being; perhaps I'll thank him—someday.

I blinked twice and looked over the craft's fiberglass gunwale. My fears and anxieties were unfounded. Nothing seemed amiss and the closest thing to a body was a large fly resting on the pilot's seat. I realized that I had been holding my breath.

"Now what?" Charles asked.

I suggested getting back in the air-conditioned car while I called Cindy to let her know there was no need to send anyone here.

Charles smiled. "I look forward to hearing her tell you that you are a nosy, stubborn cuss. Then she'll ask if you forgot where you lived."

I returned his Cheshire grin. "I'll tell her you were driving." The air conditioner kicked in full-blast and the sweat from under my Tilley had begun to dry. I called Cindy and had to yell so she could hear me over the roar of the air conditioner. I said where we were and what we had found. I was the recipient of an East Tennessee rant about the only difference between me and a jackass was the number of legs. To make it worse, I had to endure Charles sitting beside me muttering, "Un huh, un huh," and nodding his head although he couldn't hear everything the chief had been saying.

Cindy finished her comparative anatomy lesson and told me that her officers had found Robbie's apartment but not his car, nor had anyone answered the door. His neighbor told Officer Bishop that she had been working in the yard the last two hours and that she hadn't seen anyone come or go from the apartment. Cindy added that Detective Adair had arrived and would want to talk to me later. And finally, she asked if I needed her to send one of her officers to the marina to give us a police escort to my house, because she knew that I was getting old, senile, and couldn't find my way. I thanked her, but said that I would leave it in the able hands of Charles to get me there. She mumbled something about the "bald leading the bald" and hung up.

I remembered the voicemail that Chester had left when I was trying to get Theo. I clicked on voicemail and then the icon putting the phone on speakerphone; no sense in repeating whatever Chester had to say to Charles.

"Chris, Chester here. Theo told me what he told you about thinking Robbie killed that kid. Something about Robbie knowing some detail that only the killer would know. He was talking so fast that I couldn't follow all of it." I heard a chuckle. "The poor man was talking a lot faster than he walks. He was mighty hopped up about it. Do you think it could be true? God, I find it hard to believe; he took us to Boneyard Beach; seemed like a nice man. Have you told the police? Should I call them? Umm, that's enough questions. I was just worried and knew you'd know what to do. Sorry I missed you. Call when you get a chance."

I pinched the bridge of my nose and closed my eyes; the headache continued. I tapped in Chester's number and listened as the phone rang five times before the answering machine kicked in. I hit *End Call.*

"Why didn't you leave a message?" Charles asked.

I glanced at Charles and down at my phone. "Go to Chester's."

Charles kept both hands on the wheel and made no effort to put the car in reverse. "I suppose that I could overlook it since you just got shot in the head, but didn't you figure from Chester's answering machine that he ain't there?"

I started to scream, "Drive!" but I owed Charles an explanation. "Robbie's trying to tie-up loose ends. I think he has Theo. If I was Robbie, the first thing I'd ask Theo was who he told about his suspicions."

"True, and you'd be at the top of that list." He hesitated and looked in the direction of town. "But since you've been doing your rolling-stone-gathers-no-moss imitation the last few hours, he doesn't know where you are."

"How long do you think Theo could go without blurting out that he had talked to Chester?"

"Seconds."

"How many hours ago was it when you called my house twice, got no answer, and still came over?"

"And showed up and saved your butt," Charles added as he rammed the gear shift into reverse and almost hit a mini-van that was parked behind us.

Chester's house was less than a mile from the marina and with little traffic we could have made the trip in three minutes tops. No such luck. A Chevy pick-up had chosen the wrong time to pull out of Indian Avenue and was broadsided by a Jeep Wrangler that had two surfboards perched on top. There didn't appear to be serious injuries but the road leading on-island was blocked by two patrol cars, one fire engine, one badly damaged Jeep Wrangler, and two surfboards that had caught their last wave. I considered having Charles pull off the road and us walking the rest of the way, but my head still throbbed and I didn't know if I could make it on foot.

I tried Chester's number twice more while we waited. Still no answer. Both vehicles involved in the wreck were moveable and were pushed out of the roadway quicker than I had anticipated.

Chester's Buick was parked in front of his house but I didn't see Robbie's Nissan. I asked Charles to circle the block and see if Robbie's car was nearby. An alley separated Chester's house from the St. James Gate restaurant and a row of shrubs separated the house from the alley. The lot behind Chester's was reserved for residents of a small apartment building and two large trash dumpsters blocked the view of Chester's back door. What the dumpsters didn't block was Robbie's Nissan backed into the lot and not more than thirty feet from Chester's porch.

Charles looked over at Robbie's vehicle. "Crap."

"Park around the corner," I said as we rolled passed the lot.

Charles ignored three *No Parking* signs placed along the alley and stopped forty feet from the side of Chester's residence. I was out of the car as soon as he shifted it in park and strode along the shrub row and out of sight of the two windows on the side of the small house. The air conditioner in the living room window closest to the front of the house was working at its peak. It was so loud that I suspected I could have broken the window and crawled in before anyone would have heard me. Instead, I stood on my tiptoes and when I tilted my head just right, could see part of the room through the half-inch gap between the air conditioner's steel frame and the plywood spacer closing the foot-wide area between the unit and the windowsill. I had to stand at an awkward angle and was having trouble adjusting my line of sight to see anything. The blinds above the air conditioner were open and there was enough sun streaming in for me to see part of the room. Charles had moved to the side of the window closest to the street but didn't have the benefit of a gap. He reached around the air conditioner, tapped me on the arm, pointed at the window, held his hands out, and shrugged. I mouthed, "Patience," and turned my attention back to the window.

Theo was splayed out on one of the recliners. He wasn't moving and had a yellow towel wrapped around his head. One corner of the towel had what appeared to be a large patch of blood on it. Chester startled me when he moved into my line of sight. He waved his hands around like he was trying to make a point; he darted around the room like he was on something stronger than lemonade. He pointed at Theo. Chester was talking, but the roar of the air conditioner obliterated his words. I couldn't see Robbie, but

I saw a hand holding a baseball bat in the direction Chester kept glancing. I assumed it was connected to Robbie.

I didn't think anyone in the house could see us, but to err on the side of caution, instead of telling Charles what was going on over the noise from the air conditioner, I waved for him to follow me to the back corner of the yard. I told him what little I knew and he said we needed to call the police.

He was probably right, but I said, "Not yet. We don't need a hostage situation. Theo looks in bad shape and no telling what would happen if a bunch of cops showed up. Chester seems so agitated that he could do something that'd get one or both of them killed."

"But, they—"

I put my hand in front of his face. "I've got an idea. I'm going to call Chester."

"You've already called. He didn't answer. Why think he will now?"

"I hope he doesn't."

CHAPTER THIRTY-SIX

I reached for my phone and realized that it was in the car. I looked back at the window and then at Charles. "Go see what happens when I call."

He didn't demand a detailed explanation. He moved around the shrub and back to the window. The air conditioner continued to roar and I doubted that Robbie would've heard a helicopter land in the side yard much less Charles sneaking up to the window. I grabbed my phone from the console, thought about what I wanted to say, prayed that I wasn't making a huge—possibly fatal— mistake, and hit redial.

Five rings later, Chester's voice mail message kicked in. I glanced at Charles standing on his toes as he peeked through the slot beside the air conditioner. I took a deep breath and said, "Chester, this is Chris. Listen, I just got off the phone with Detective Adair. He knows Robbie killed the student. I told him that Theo had said the same thing. I figured that Theo told you. The police are at Theo's and it looks like Robbie may have killed him; there's blood all over the place. I told Adair that you figured it was

Robbie and Adair said he was afraid that Robbie may come after you next." I paused and wondered what else to say. "I'm rambling, but you're in danger. Get out of the house before Robbie gets there. Go to the police station. The police are pulling together the SWAT team and would be headed to your house and should be there soon. They're worried that Robbie may get there first. Anyway, get out."

I punched *End Call*, closed my eyes, calculated the odds on my spur of the moment plan succeeding, and left the steaming-hot car and headed to Charles who had stepped back from the window and pointed to the back of the house.

My ears still rang from the gunshot and the air conditioner's roar didn't help, so we moved toward the back yard and away from the distracting noise. Charles leaned close and said, "Theo's alive. Chester's trying to get him out of the recliner. He looks wobbly, but he's moving, moving at Theo speed. What'd you say to the machine?"

"Later. They'll be going to Robbie's car."

Chester's back door opened to a small, wood deck and two steps leading to the path to the Nissan. There was a large oleander shrub on our side of the deck that blocked the view of the industrial-sized dumpsters, and a four-by-eight foot, lattice privacy panel on the other side of the deck.

I pointed for Charles to hide behind the panel and said that I'd be behind the shrub. With luck, Robbie will be too distracted to notice us in the rush to get out with his hostages before SWAT arrives and also by trying to wrangle Chester and the injured Theo. He had been waving a ball bat, so I figured that he didn't have a gun. A lot rested on me being right.

The screen door squeaked open and Chester backed out while supporting his injured friend. Theo wasn't moving fast enough and Robbie gave him a shove. Chester stumbled backwards but caught himself on the rail and tumbled down the steps. His Coke-bottle glasses flew off his head. Robbie grabbed Theo's belt and stopped him from landing on Chester.

Charles inched toward the front of the lattice and within striking distance and I peeked around the shrub at the six-foot two, muscle-bound killer who looked even taller standing on the elevated porch. I had had more ridiculous ideas over the years, but none came to mind as I watched Robbie effortlessly holding Theo up with one hand while brandishing a baseball bat with the other. My feeble plan to tackle him and hold him down until the cops arrived seemed more doable when I was in the car. I moved closer to the edge of the shrubs.

Robbie was larger, much younger, and stronger than either Charles or me; but he was occupied with his elderly captives so we should have the element of surprise on our side. That may even the odds on taking him. I continued to move closer to the edge.

Our advantage evaporated when Charles stumbled on a metal trash can lid that had been propped against the porch.

Robbie jerked toward the noise. "What the—" He saw Charles move around the lattice.

Robbie let go of Theo's belt and shoved him to his right. Theo stumbled into Chester who was fishing around the yard for his glasses. Chester and Theo hit the ground like bags of rocks.

Charles lunged at the captain and Robbie moved the bat behind his back ready to swing at my friend. Charles's cover had been blown, but Robbie hadn't seen me. I took three steps toward him and grabbed the bat's barrel as he started to swing.

Robbie was startled. He twisted around to see who had grabbed the bat, and quickly recovered and tried to yank the weapon out of my hands. I held tight. He pulled again and jerked the bat from my grip. Charles moved in and grabbed him around the waist. I stepped out of the bat's range and Charles tried to twist Robbie to the ground. He was no match for the killer. Robbie clutched Charles's arm, pried it off his waist, and hurled him to the ground. I put both hands on the bat while Robbie was busy with Charles. Robbie was distracted and I managed enough leverage to jerk the weapon out of his hand.

The outnumbered captain flailed around, not making contact with anything. He took a step toward the car and tripped over Theo who hadn't moved since he'd landed. The killer jumped to his feet, glanced at Charles who was pushing up from the yard, and then looked to me. I grabbed the bat and started after him. He turned and took a step toward his car.

Chester was still on the ground to Robbie's left. Even without his glasses, he saw Robbie trying to escape. Chester stuck his leg in the killer's path and caught him by surprise. Robbie stumbled once and all six-foot-two of him hit the walkway like a giant redwood felled by a lumberjack. Chester flung his body over the prone killer while Charles and I regained our balance and hustled to his aid. The three of us piled on Robbie.

The captain may have been bigger, much bigger, than either Charles or me, but with both of us holding him down, he couldn't get enough leverage to push himself up. I asked Chester, who had rolled off Robbie and was sitting beside us on the walkway, if he had any rope.

"Or duct tape," Charles added, as he gasped for breath.

Chester, still breathing hard, found his glasses, and staggered into the house. He returned with a roll of duct tape and handed it to me. I told him to take my phone from my side pocket and call 911.

"Aren't the police on the way?" he asked.

"No."

"But your message said—"

Charles shouted, "Call the cops!"

Chester still looked confused, but nodded, stepped back on the porch and dialed 911.

Robbie continued to kick but we stayed out of range of his feet and Charles held him down while I wound the all-purpose silver fabric around his hands.

Charles said, "Didn't we just do this?"

If my head didn't ache, if my face didn't sting, and if my hands didn't hurt from Robbie yanking the bat from them, I would have smiled.

CHAPTER THIRTY-SEVEN

It had been a week since Detective Adair and a gaggle of sheriff's deputies had relieved Charles and me from our struggle with Robbie. It had been five days since the captain had been charged with a multitude of crimes, the most serious being the murder of Drew Casey, the student whose only crime had been going to Boneyard Beach with a group of fellow students for a night of relaxation, fun, and drinking. He had been in the wrong place at the wrong time.

Theo had spent three nights in the hospital. The wounds inflicted by Robbie to force him to tell who else knew of his suspicions were superficial and the main reason for the hospital stay was so he could regain strength.

The gunshot graze to my head was beginning to heal and the burn on the side of my face only bothered me when I smiled. It burned a lot the next few days. Two killers had been taken off the streets, two of my friends had been cleared, and I was alive to savor it. My main regret was that Karen was still at her training program;

I had missed being able to bounce my ideas off her and benefit from her years of experience. My face stung one more time when I smiled knowing she would be home tonight.

I was sitting in my comfortable chair in the living room, enjoying the aroma and flavor of a cup of coffee, reflecting on the activities of the last few days, and since it was only nine in the morning, wondering what I should do with the rest of the day.

I didn't wonder long. The all too familiar sound of someone pounding on the door told me that whatever I had planned would change.

Mel Evans pushed past me as he headed through the living room to the coffee pot. "Yo Chris, got a question."

I felt like I had stepped into the 1990's movie *Groundhog Day*.

"What's there to eat?" he yelled from the kitchen.

I followed the bellowing voice and was surprised to see a smile on my dour friend's face. "You should know that I—"

"Kidding," he interrupted. "There's not a damn thing here that's not stale or that doesn't taste like wet cardboard." He took a gulp of coffee and grinned. He had on the same woodland camo field pants and leather bomber jacket that he wore on his last visit when he interrupted my morning coffee got me into the mess that had dominated most every waking moment since then.

"What's your question?"

He took a smaller gulp, set the cup on the counter, and led me back into the living room. "I lied. There's no question. Move it. We're leaving."

A normal person would ask the simple question: Where are we going? A normal person would have been surprised by Mel's command.

If I had learned one thing since I'd arrived on Folly, it was that among my friends normalcy was looked down on, and a trip down Normal Street led nowhere. I grabbed my Tilley, slid my feet into my deck shoes stationed by the front door, and said, "Lead on."

Mel's Camaro was sideways in my front yard, Cal's Cadillac was in the drive, and Chester's Buick inched close behind Cal's car. Now I was surprised.

The windows in all three cars were down and I did a double take when Charles, William, Chester, David, and Theo waved at me.

Mel said, "Don't stand there drooling, get in. I'm throwing a sprung-from-the-hoosegow party. You're holding us up."

Fifteen minutes later, the occupants of the three vehicles, two large coolers, a picnic basket that looked like it had spent a decade in Alaska before being run over by a team of huskies, and Cal's guitar case were all loaded on *Mad Mel's Magical Marsh Machine* and headed to Boneyard Beach. On the ride to the boat, Charles had explained that Mel had called him last evening and asked him to put together "the clump of civvies who helped spring him, and hell, might as well invite that damned .5 group too." Mel wanted to thank everyone for what they had done and the only way he knew to do it was throw a party. He also had told Charles that it had to be early in the day because it would be a group of "old farts" and they couldn't stay awake after suppertime.

An hour later, the coolers were almost empty, we were gathered around the graffiti covered foundation where we had celebrated the walking group's successful trip a few days earlier, and Cal was strumming and singing a medley of the greatest country hits of the 1950s. Theo was still weak, and began the day depressed over the loss of someone whom he thought had loved him. But, he had not become successful in the business world by letting the past drag him down, and by the time he'd finished three beers, he was singing a duet with Cal.

Toasts were offered. Mel was the first when he jumped up on the concrete foundation, and held his Budweiser can in the air. "I'm not good at mushy stuff, so bear with me. I'm gay and always have been. Don't know if it's right or wrong. I'm not a big follower of that God guy, but if he's everything folks say he is, then there must not be anything wrong with me being queer or he wouldn't have made me that way. So, I'm thankful that everyone knows that the death of that student wasn't because he was gay or because it was anything that I had done, just the warped mind of that damned Robbie." He shook his head. "He killed an innocent kid just to frame me. All because of money. Now ain't that the shits? Well anyway, thanks for believing in me."

Mel was right, he wasn't good at mushy, but everyone knew he was sincere and was trying to thank them.

Mel hopped off the foundation and Chester waved his hand in the air like he either had a question or had to go to the bathroom. "Okay fellow .5 members and Mel, when Charles called last night to see if I wanted to come today, I wanted to say 'no way, Jose.' A load a bad stuff has happened to our little group. Abe Pottinger got himself killed, deserved to have it happen, but I suppose it was sad anyway. And misguided Harriet had to go and kill Abe. And Connie's brother not only killed the student, but beat up on our good friend Theo and was going to kill him and me. I think .5 is cursed and we should all throw our hats into the sea." Chester pointed toward the open sea, bowed his head, and then walked back to the coolers.

David, who hadn't said anything, moved to the foundation. "I've not been on Folly as long as all of you. In my brief time on your island, I've experienced firsthand more friendship, caring, and outright friendliness than anywhere I've ever been. Chester, you starting the .5 group is a perfect example of what's right. Sure, you can be a bit dictatorial at times, and that's okay." He hesitated and chuckled. "We need that occasionally. I think it would be a big mistake to disband the group. You're a great leader, and I plan to be at your house tomorrow morning raring to go wherever you tell us to go."

"Me too," Theo shouted. He'd been fitted with hearing aids the day after he got out of the hospital, and had heard everything that David had said.

"I will be in attendance as well," William said.

Charles nodded and I said so would I, and then I told Chester that he was the true hero. He caught—tripped—a killer and was critical in saving Theo's life, and probably mine.

Chester blushed. "Okay, bright and early tomorrow." He looked at Mel. "Would you like to join us?"

Mel gave one of his patented frowns. "Hell no. You won't catch me dead around you fossils."

Now that's the Mel I'd learned to love.

I looked around and figured that several of the 'fossils' were getting tired and we needed to head back. "One more thing,"

I said and pointed to the spot where Drew Casey had taken his last breath. "Could we gather over there for a moment?"

No one spoke as the group moved to the path leading to the marsh. I didn't know the exact spot where the body was, so I chose a small clearing for the group to stand in. "William, could I impose on you to offer a hymn to the memory of Drew Casey?"

William nodded, and began an a cappella version of "Amazing Grace." It brought goose bumps to my arms and took me back to first hearing him sing the haunting hymn a few years ago at a funeral while we were standing ankle deep in snow in the middle of the Great Smoky Mountains. After the first verse, William gestured toward Cal's guitar; Cal took the hint and played along.

I had no doubt that if Drew Casey was in Heaven, God had called him to his side, and they were listening.

William and Cal finished the last notes and the only sounds heard were a high-pitched squeak of an Oystercatcher sitting on one of the nearby wind-swept trees and the low roar of the water as it lapped against the shore.

Charles did what Charles does best. He lightened the mood when he said, "Last one to the boat is a Theo!"

Everyone glanced at Theo who laughed and slapped Charles on the arm.

Actually, Theo wasn't the last one to the boat. I was. My phone rang as I was heading to the boat. It was Karen.

"Just got home," she said. "Did I miss anything?"

SILENT NIGHT

A Folly Beach Christmas Mystery

CHAPTER 1

Silent Night, Holy Night! All is calm, all is bright, I sang as I took the early-morning, five-block walk from my house to the Lost Dog Cafe. Before you proclaim me certifiable because of my song selection, it's two weeks before Christmas and pitch dark. The cloudless, predawn sky was speckled with stars that went on forever, and for mid- December in South Carolina, the temperature was cool although not unbearable. Yes, all is calm, and I'm thankful.

The Lost Dog Cafe was a block off Center Street, the center of commerce and figurative center of the small, barrier island located in the shadows of Charleston. The Dog had been my favorite breakfast spot since I retired to the beach nearly a decade ago, and I was not alone in favoring the canine-centric, colorful restaurant. In season, the wait for tables could approach an hour, since it was not only the favorite breakfast locale for thousands of vacationers who arrived like swarms of locust, but also for locals who were hard-pressed to find a better alternative. The locusts, umm, vacationers, left as quickly as they had come and between Labor Day and spring, the island moved on laid-back, Folly time.

Two other things could be counted on during the winter months in the restaurant: extended, daily visits by Jim Sloan, better known as Dude, and city council members Marc Salmon and Houston Bass. Today, Dude was seated at his usual table along the wall, but neither of the people with him answered to Houston or Marc.

He saw me and waved his ever-present copy of *Astronomy Magazine* in the air and pointed to the vacant seat beside him. I took his less-than-subtle hint and headed over. Dude could have been mistaken for folk singer Arlo Guthrie with his long, stringy, graying, sun-bleached hair. Complimenting his nineteen sixties look was one of his many tie-dyed T-shirts with a psychedelic peace symbol adorning the front.

Dude said, "Yo, Chrisster, Ho, ho, ho."

Dude owned Folly's largest surf shop, had been a resident since I don't know when, and was famous for mangling the simplest sentence. People who didn't know him well had sworn it would take a cryptographer to understand what he was saying. Those who knew him better had gone through a steep learning curve, or had access to a translator, but I had gotten the drift of his "unique verbal styling."

"Ho, ho, ho, back at you," I said, in the spirit in which it was divvied out.

Dude, at sixty-three, was three years younger than me, and at least three decades older than his table mates.

"Chrisster, amigos be Finley and Teddye."

The *amigos* looked up from their eggs and gave me a bored grin.

I held out my hand to the female. "I'm Chris Landrum, and I assume you're Teddye."

It was a slight gamble on my part since their names could have been attached to either gender.

The attractive young woman nodded. Her long, blond hair contrasted with her black jeans, black turtleneck, and black boots. "Pleased," she said.

I paused waiting for more, but she must have learned verbal parsimony from Dude. I turned to the other stranger. "And you must be Finley."

He was also dressed in black, but his hair was bleached blond and as long as Teddye's. He shook my hand, shrugged, and said, "Duh."

"Chrisster, these be surfin' buds." He pointed to Teddye and Finley like I wouldn't know whom he was referring to. "We be jabbering about posers invadin', and skimpy, hot dog budget wallets they be haulin'."

Posers were non-surfers acting like they could surf and I guessed hot dog budgets translated as short on cash. Regardless, I had little to add to the conversation. I didn't have to when Dude said, "They be askin' Dude how to rid surf of posers."

I glanced at Dude's friends who stared at me like they would at a pile of pooch poop they'd stepped in. "What'd you suggest?" I asked to put the conversation back in Dude's court.

"Said be season of peace on Gaia—sharing, goody- good will, yada, yada, yada. Said to chill, let be."

"Gaia?"

Dude pointed to the floor. "Gaia, third planet from Sun."

Teddye leaned forward. "He means Peace on Earth."

She rolled her eyes like she had to explain what a tree was to a forest ranger.

My phone rang as I was wondering how I could step out of this alternative universe, skip breakfast, and get out of the restaurant as fast as my aging legs could carry me.

I moved the phone away from my ear when it was assaulted by

the ear-piercing voice of Burl Costello. "Brother Chris, my God. I'm glad I got you. Sorry for calling so early. Could you come to our crèche?"

Burl, more-formally known as Preacher Burl Ives Costello, started First Light, Folly's fourth and newest church, a couple of years ago. In good weather, its services were held on the beach near the Folly Pier, but when the weather didn't cooperate, which Burl said was the Devil interceding, services were conducted in a small storefront building on Center Street.

"When?"

"Now!"

I started to ask why, when he yelled, "Somebody stole Jesus!"

First Light's crèche, or Nativity scene, was located on a small grassy plot adjacent to Pewter Hardware and next to the Folly Beach Post Office. The slice of green space was owned by my friend Larry LaMond, a former cat burglar, current owner of the tiny hardware store, and for the last six years, husband to Cindy, Folly's police chief.

Preacher Burl referred to First Light's attendees as his flock instead of members, but either way, Larry and Cindy were neither. When the preacher realized it would be impractical for the crèche to be on the beach and there wasn't enough space on the sidewalk in front of the storefront location, Larry volunteered the plot of land. The spot wasn't perfect since it wasn't visible to most visitors to the island, but as Preacher Burl had pointed out, the setting for the event some two thousand years ago, which had inspired decades of Nativity scenes was far from visible or popular. He also had pointed out First Light's scene was within a short walk from Folly's three traditional churches, and using a little imagination, Mary, Joseph,

Jesus, and the assorted bit players could see the houses of worship from the crèche.

The Nativity was fewer than two blocks from the restaurant, and I made the trip in a couple of minutes. I noticed what normally was festive Christmas red and blue colors flashing and reflecting off the Nativity's makeshift wooden barn and the hardware store. This morning, the colors weren't nearly as festive since they were coming from light bars on two Folly Beach patrol cars.

Preacher Burl was as easy to recognize as Dude. He was five-foot-five, shaped like a football, portly in polite terms, had a milk chocolate colored mustache, and a balding head inadequately covered by a sad-looking comb over. Today, his hair was even sadder. He appeared to have been awakened and had rushed to the scene without glancing in a mirror. The preacher was standing close to Chief LaMond and his arms flailed around like he was describing an attack by a flock of seagulls.

He saw me, stopped flailing, put his hand on Cindy's arm, and pointed in my direction. "Brother Chris, I am so pleased to see you. This is the darkest of morns for First Light. The Devil has reached up and with his evil talons, yanked our sacred symbol from yon manger. It's thrown our ministry into darkness." He pointed at the empty, rustic, wooden feeding trough.

Cindy turned and faced me. "He means someone stole the replica of Jesus."

Burl's conversations often slipped into preacher-speak.

I said, "Thanks, Chief LaMond."

Cindy nodded toward Burl. "I was telling the preacher it was most likely kids playing a prank and we'd find, umm, Jesus some-where around town. I'll have my guys nose around for it."

Burl shook his head. "Who would steal Jesus?"

Cindy was a couple of inches shorter than the preacher, but better built. She pulled her shoulders back, ran a hand through her dark curly hair, and frowned. "Stealing the baby from nativities is so common, it has its own name: Baby Jesus Theft. Puts them at the top of Santa's naughty list, if you ask me."

Burl didn't appreciate the chief's humor. He mumbled, "A sad day indeed."

Two officers had been photographing the manger and the other parts of the set, but I couldn't imagine them finding anything helpful. One of them came over and told the chief they had done all they could at the "scene of the crime." Cindy told him to tell everyone else to "scour the city" for the figurine. The chief asked if I could walk her to her vehicle and said she had something to tell me. I told Burl I'd be back and followed her to her unmarked GMC Yukon. Cindy slipped behind the steering wheel and I leaned against the door. "Chris, for some reason the preacher is way too upset about someone absconding with a wooden statue. He tried to tell me why it was, in his words, priceless, but he was so upset I couldn't follow the story. He insisted on calling you—heck if I know why—I suppose he trusts you. He needs reassuring. This is not a big deal; happens everywhere manger scenes are. The youngin' will turn up."

"I'll do my best."

"Could you do me another favor?"

"Depends."

She put her hand on my arm. "I'm saying this as your good buddy. Could you for once, not get in the middle of police business; for once, keep your weird friends from nosing in our job?"

Since retiring to Folly after spending what seemed forever in a boring bureaucratic job with a huge healthcare company, I had been involved in several horrific events, including multiple murders. A few friends and I had stumbled, bumbled, and through tons of luck and a little skill, brought some bad guys to justice. Chief LaMond was more than familiar with the escapades and whether she would admit it or not had helped us with a few of them.

"I can't promise—"

She interrupted, "I know, I know, but please try. Remember, in the words of Haven Gillespie, *He knows when you are good or bad.*

"Who's Haven Gillespie?"

"Look it up."

My friend Charles Fowler had a habit of quoting U.S. Presidents and I had never looked any of them up to distinguish Charles's fact from fantasy, so I wasn't about to research Gillespie. "What brings you out this early anyway? Looks like your guys had things under control."

"Holy moly, Chris," Cindy said in her East Tennessee twang, "Somebody stole Jesus."

CHAPTER 2

Chief LaMond and her officers had departed—the officers to scour the city and Cindy to the office to wade through "Smoky Mountains-high piles of paperwork." I returned to Burl, who was pacing in front of the manger and shaking his head.

I put my arm around his shoulder. "Bad morning."

I was surprised to see him wipe a tear from the corner of his eye. What was so important about the replica of the Baby Jesus? I understood the importance of the Nativity, but Burl seemed more concerned than should be normal.

"Terrible." He shook his head. "Terrible."

I waited for him to elaborate. The temperature was mild, although the wind had increased and the wind chill made it feel colder. To get out of the breeze, I nudged him toward the open side of the three-sided, nine-foot wide, six- foot high, wooden barn.

He pointed to the figure of Mary. "Brother Chris, as you see, the figures are fiberglass. Through generous donations by those in our flock, we were able to buy them from a supply house I found on the Internet."

I wasn't a regular at First Light although I had attended several services. I motioned for him to continue.

"The structure was built from scrap wood donated by contractors and fashioned into a barn replica by me and others in the group. All this could easily be replaced."

Burl had been a carpenter before joining the ministry. "You did a great job."

For a moment, he didn't say anything and then he pointed to the crib. "Baby Jesus is another story. Do you know Brother Robert Daniel?"

"Don't believe so."

"You probably don't. Brother Robert had attended services a couple of times before falling ill to pancreatic cancer. After that, I took my ministry to his hospital bed. He is … was ninety-three years of age. He passed three weeks ago, two days after his birthday."

"I'm sorry."

Burl's shoulders slumped. "As am I. Brother Robert's son, Robert Jr. was in the military and sustained serious wounds in the Vietnam conflict. He was sent to a hospital in Germany to recuperate, and while there, was befriended by a local family, a family of quality woodworkers as only the Germans can be. Robert Jr.'s friend, whose name I can't remember, bequeathed upon him a hand-carved, painted replica of the Baby Jesus that had been handed down through three generations." Burl gave a slight smile. "Of course, it was not an exact replica since no one knows what the Christ Child looked like."

"Why did they give Robert Jr. something that had been in their family for so long?"

"I was never clear on the details of the political situation in their hamlet, but during World War II the family did not adhere to the radical views of Hitler, and when the Americans entered the community, our soldiers did not condemn the family and provided them with much-needed food and supplies. They told Robert Jr. they were forever indebted to the Americans, and the carved gift was a token of their appreciation."

"That's touching."

"Robert said his son tried to decline such a significant gift, but his German friend insisted."

"Was Robert Jr. with his father when he died?"

Burl stepped close to the manger and slowly rubbed his hands on the side of the wooden crib. "Robert Jr. had secured a position in finance when he returned from Germany. His dad said he was quite good at his trade and had earned a significant amount of money. He was to return to Germany to share additional thanks to his friend and his family for befriending him and honoring him with the statue. He planned to return the icon to its rightful owners."

"Planned to?"

"Robert Jr. was in a meeting on the forty-third floor of the South Tower of the World Trade Center on September 11, 2001." Burl bowed his head and whispered, "His remains have yet to be identified."

Once again, I put my arm around the preacher. Burl said, "May I offer a prayer?"

He did, and we stood in silence. The wind whistled through the gaps in the walls. Typical morning life was beginning on Folly and a few cars passed in front of us.

"What do you want me to do?"

"Brother Chris, I know Chief LaMond and her officers will do what they can to find the priceless statue. They are good at their jobs. I am also wise enough to know a missing piece of carved wood can't take as much priority as crimes against people. It will be natural for them to lose sight of their quest for Jesus."

"You want me to find it?"

He nodded. "I have faith you will be able to achieve doing what others may find impossible. Your track record is such that it gives me confidence."

During my sixty-six years, I had been told by preachers I needed to find Jesus, but until this morning, two weeks before Christmas, never a wooden one.

"I'll do my best."

Burl smiled. "I know you will. And Brother Chris, I wish this not to be an undue burden, but Baby Jesus must be found in time for our Christmas Eve service. It must."

Holy infant so tender and mild. And gone.

CHAPTER 3

Burl had moved to the heated confines of his car, and I continued to stare at the manger. Other than search the backstreets and alleys and root through trash containers, what could I do the police couldn't do to find the icon? There was a good chance the chief was right about it being taken as a prank and it would turn up. Burl had good intentions, something he was never short on, but why place the burden on me to find it?

I was wondering what to do next when I heard heavy breathing behind me and a cane tapping pavement. The familiar voice of my best friend Charles Fowler said, "Are you delivering gold, frankincense, and myrrh? Couldn't three wise men make the trip?"

Charles was a few years younger than me, had lived on Folly thirty years, and for reasons no rational person could explain, we had become friends. We were as similar as a penguin was to a banana split, but there was no explaining the mysteries of the universe. I had labored most of my life in a bureaucratic office environment while Charles treated work like it was a strain of malaria. I was shy and reticent; Charles would talk to and befriend everyone he came in contact with, along with their pets. He was a voracious reader; I liked books as much as I liked ingrown toenails. Regardless, he would do anything for me, including risk his life. I knew because he had done it. I would do the same for him.

Charles was staring at me. He had his hands on his hips. His heavy, red jacket was zipped to his neck with the logo of the University of Alaska on its front. I started to explain why I was there and ask what myrrh was when he turned and pointed his ever-present cane at the manger and shouted, "Where's Jesus?"

"Gone."

"I may be old, not as old as you, thank God, and my eyesight's not what it used to be, but that fact didn't escape me. Did someone take him to change his swaddling clothes?"

I must also point out that Charles's sense of humor and approach to life has been considered a tad off center. Because of his disheveled appearance, unshaven face, and thinning hair that flowed to the beat of a different eclectic style, combined with his never failing to befriend the most downtrodden individual, others often assumed he wasn't among the, how shall I say it, intellectually elite. In reality, he was a textbook example of you can't judge a book by its cover. And speaking of books, he owned and claimed to have read, more books than are shelved in many small-town libraries.

"It was stolen."

Charles stared at the manger. "Burl will be heartbroken."

"He already is."

I explained about the preacher and the police already being here and that Cindy's guys had started canvassing the city for the statue.

Charles moved closer to the manger. He removed his Tilley hat and held it over his heart. "The statue's priceless. He must be devastated."

"Do you know its history?"

"Sure," he said, like who didn't. "He told me when I was helping build this." He waved his cane around the barn. Charles had become a regular at the First Light services after Melinda Beale, his elderly aunt and last living relative, passed away. Before that, he had avoided churches for most of his life.

He appeared lost in thought, so I didn't say anything until he returned his hat to its rightful spot on his head. "He asked me to find it."

Charles grinned and waved his cane toward the center of town. "What are we waiting for?"

At some point in Charles's reality-challenged life, he'd decided he was a private detective. His total experience receiving a payroll check had consisted of landscaping and an assembly line job at a Ford plant in his native Michigan. Those jobs had ended during Ronald Reagan's presidency. Since then, he had picked up a few cash-only jobs helping restaurants clean during their busy season, provided a couple of extra hands for local contractors, and delivered on-island packages for the surf shop. He was also the unofficial executive sales manager for Landrum Gallery, a photo gallery I had opened, and after losing thousands of dollars a year, was closing. Regardless of plus or minus zero experience in the field of detecting, he had decided after watching countless whodunit television shows and reading more than countless detective novels, there was nothing he didn't know about his chosen field of work.

For the next five hours, Charles and I got a month's worth of exercise, walking each street within a mile of the manger. Most of our walk was east and west since we were limited on the south by the Atlantic Ocean and on the north by the Folly River and the marsh separating the island from the contiguous United States. The statue could have been taken off island, but there was little we could do about it. And, if Cindy was correct about it being a prank, Baby Jesus was probably on our seven-mile long, half-mile wide piece of land.

All that resulted from our efforts were four sore feet and two red faces from the increasingly brisk winter winds blowing off the ocean. We ended our search at Charles's small apartment, and I limped the remaining seven blocks to my cottage beside Bert's Market. I was exhausted, and it was only three-thirty. A nap was next on my agenda until I was interrupted by a knock on the door, and found two teen-agers on the porch, hands in their pockets, their coat collars pulled up around their necks.

"Good afternoon, Mr. Landrum," said the taller of the two. He was my height at five-foot-ten, sixteen years old, trim but muscular, and answered to Samuel Perkins. I had met the long haired, young man my first week on Folly Beach. We had become reacquainted a year ago when he had come to me after he had seen a woman being abducted. Because he'd witnessed the crime, his life had been put in danger, but through luck and the help of friends, I was able to save him.

"Hi, Samuel. Hi, Jason." Even in their heavy James Island Charter High School jackets, they were shivering.

Jason Lewis was the other visitor. He was a couple of inches shorter than Samuel and wasn't as skinny and didn't appear as athletic. I had known Jason nearly as long as I had known Samuel, although for different reasons. I had dated Jason's mom, Amber, for a couple of years, until she broke off our dating after I had exposed Jason to a murder victim. Amber felt it was too dangerous for her son to be associated with me, but despite that, she and I had remained friends. Amber was also the best waitress the Lost Dog Café had ever had and was ground central when anyone wanted to know the latest rumors.

Jason said, "Hello, Mr. Landrum."

"Come in." I waved them toward the living room. "What brings you out?"

Jason looked at Samuel, who said, "Mr. Landrum, we heard stories in school today that somebody sort of took Jesus."

I nodded and wondered how the word was already around. "How did you hear it?"

Samuel turned to Jason, who looked at the floor, and said, "My friend Hector's mom texted him during lunch. He told us."

Samuel interrupted, "She told him some kids sort of took it."

I looked at Samuel and turned to Jason. "Do you know anything about it?"

"Us?" Jason inhaled. "No, Mr. Landrum. That's why we came to see you."

Jacob, Jason's father, had told me his son had a tendency to exaggerate. While it may have been true, during my talks with Jason a year ago, the young man had been honest and accurate in whatever he had said.

They kept looking down at the floor and failed to make eye contact with me. I offered them a drink to calm them down.

Each declined, and I said, "I'm confused, why did you come to see me?"

Samuel looked at me. "Mr. Landrum, we want to help find the kid, umm, the Jesus statue. If a teenager took it, he could sort of go to our school. Jason said maybe we should go to the police and offer to look around for them. I told him the cop'd say something like, 'Now son, we'll take care of it. You all go back to your studies.'" He rolled his eyes. "I knew how you caught the killer, you know, the one the cops didn't think was real. You were a stand-up adult, and are good at finding bad guys, so I told him we should come see you and sort of offer our help at school." He smiled. "Here we are."

I returned his smile and waved for them to follow me to the kitchen and pointed at the chairs. They sat, and I again offered them a drink. They unzipped their coats and were warming up; warming up enough to say a Pepsi would be nice. I was pleased with their decision since water, wine, beer, and Pepsi were the only choices.

"The first you learned about the missing statue was after Hector's mom texted'?"

Samuel said, "That's sort of what we said." He turned to Jason for confirmation.

Jason nodded. "You don't think we did it?"

I shook my head. "Not for a second. I asked because if someone at school knew it before you said Hector did, that person might have known it before the police were called."

Samuel pointed a finger at me. "Oh, I get it. That person could've swiped it."

"Yes. What can you do to help?"

Jason and Samuel alternated telling me their plan which amounted to "sort of casually" talking to classmates and see if they knew anything, and to "snoop around" to see if anybody in the other grades had any information.

They were right about what the police would have told them, but I also didn't want them snooping. If one of their classmates took the statue or knows who did, Jason and Samuel could end up in danger.

"It's great you want to find the thief, and it could be helpful if you kept your eyes open. But guys, it could be more than a prank and if the person who took it finds out you're looking, you could get in trouble."

Jason leaned forward. "Oh no, Mr. Landrum, we'll be careful. All we'll do is keep our eyes open. Our history teacher says we need to be more, what's the word, Samuel?"

"Vigilant."

"Yeah, vigilant. He said good citizens need to do that in these dangerous times."

"Your teacher's wise. If that's all you do, it could help. The statue means a lot to many people, and it would be terrible if anything happened to it."

"I knew you'd know what we should do," Samuel said. "Vigilant, that'll be it."

I looked at each of them. "Promise me one thing. If you learn anything, call the police. If they don't take you seriously, call me. Think you can do it?"

Jason said. "Yes sir, Mr. Landrum." Samuel nodded.

"And you won't confront the person who took it or try to get the statue back?"

They nodded.

CHAPTER 4

I grew up in Middle America where Christmas was wrapped in traditions galore. Mistletoe was prevalent in nearby oak trees, and dad made the most of it by taping pieces to each doorway, and a double dose over the door to my parents' bedroom. Mom took advantage of his strategic placing of the kiss motivator. We lived where stockings were actually hung from the chimney with care, although we didn't have a chimney, so our stockings were hung on a knickknack shelf over the television—with care.

Unlike most families, a fact I learned years later, Santa not only left presents under our tree, but he decorated the large, live fir that sat unadorned in the living room until the jolly one made his overnight visit. He earned the chocolate-chip cookies mom had baked for him. Santa had enough time to decorate the tree because he didn't wrap my presents, but staged them in their ready-to-play state for when I first laid my sleepy eyes on them.

It wasn't as often as I would like to remember, but a glance outside a few Christmas mornings revealed the ground covered with the white stuff depicted in many popular Christmas songs. Sleds had an immediate playground to slide across. Bicycles came with promises to be ridden once the snow melted. And, although there weren't any in our small, three-person family, little girls could begin playing with their dolls and easy-bake ovens as soon as the lights came on.

The birth of Jesus was never far from my parents' thoughts, although to my young eyes, Christmas was the tree, the presents, candy that was seldom available the rest of the year, and smiles of joy on mom and dad's face. We had a tabletop, ceramic Nativity and on Christmas Eve, dad read the Christmas story and mom tried to lead dad and me in singing hymns. Between my thoughts drifting to what might appear under the tree the next morning, and thinking our singing sounded more like a harmonizing trio made up of a screech owl, an alley cat, and a toad, the true meaning of Christmas was lost on me.

In the following years, Christmas ebbed and flowed in my thoughts. When I was living at home, I attended church with my parents. Santa stopped coming in the back door of our chimneyless house. Mistletoe appeared in fewer and fewer places, although dad and mom didn't need the seasonal incentive to kiss. For that we were thankful. The live trees that had enveloped much of the living room were replaced by a slim, artificial one which didn't need to be large, since underwear and socks didn't take up as much room under it as had bicycles and an electric train.

During the twenty years I was married to my high school sweet-heart, Christmas was a time for a few days off work, a time for us to spend Christmas Eve with my parents and one cousin, and for visiting my wife's family Christmas day. We remained childless and never experienced the joy of helping Santa agonize over the *some assembly required* gifts that included instructions written in thirty-seven languages, none of which were English.

My wife and I attended Christmas Eve midnight service a few years but felt guilty because with the exception of funerals, those were the only times we stepped in a house of worship. After the divorce, I failed to see anything positive about church and organized religion. I was a spiritual person and believed in a higher power, but the trappings of the church did nothing for me. I expressed my need to help those who weren't as lucky as I by donating to organizations that helped feed, clothe, and bring hope to those without the means to survive. I spent several evenings each holiday season serving food to the needy, and being thankful I was fortunate enough to have a good job, and a safe, comfortable home.

Over the last year, I had spent numerous hours with Preacher Burl. Some of the time I thought he could be a killer and wondered how I would prove it. Thankfully—and in his words, thank God—he wasn't guilty. The rest of the time with him, I saw the hope, joy, and happiness he brought to his flock and most everyone else with whom he came in contact. He didn't smack people in the head with the Bible, but taught by example, combined with weekly lessons from the Good Book he translated into terms, which could be understood by all.

As he stood over the manger this morning, I had seen hurt in his eyes and defeat in his slumped shoulders. His hands had trembled as he caressed the side of the wooden crib, and his eyes watered for what was no longer there.

Was the theft of Baby Jesus simply the work of bored pranksters and the missing statue would turn up soon? And, if it was pranksters, they had little or no idea how the loss would affect others.

What if it was more? What if the statue not only had spiritual significance, but a significant amount of worldly worth, and was taken to be sold, or to go in the collection of someone who needed a valuable centerpiece for his or her Nativity? Or, was someone trying to make a negative statement about Christianity?

What could I do beyond what the police were doing to bring Baby Jesus home to be enjoyed as a symbol of all that is Christian?

I fell asleep wondering.

I awoke to a weather report indicating today's temperature would reach seventy, only four degrees shy of the record high set a century ago. It would be a good day to join the search for the statue, but before I headed out, I wondered if the police had already found it or if someone had turned it in. A call to the chief was in order.

She answered. "No, Chris. We haven't found it." I hated caller ID.

"Why do you think that's what I wanted? Couldn't I be calling a good friend to see how her day was going?"

"No. First it's seven thirty, so my day hasn't been going long enough for me to know how it's going. Second, you're the second nosiest person I know, and it'd give you an ulcer if you had to wait longer to find out if the swaddling- clothed youngin's turned up."

"Guilty."

Cindy chuckled. "Shame I can't throw you in the hoosegow for that confession."

"Well?"

"Okay, okay. I repeat we haven't found it. Sorry."

"Hate to hear it. I know how much it means to Burl."

"I do too," Cindy said. "He told me each time he called last night. I had to tell him if we found it, I would come to his door, regardless of the time, and let him know. Then my wonderful hubby got on my case. Said the manger was on his store's property, so he felt responsible, and if I knew what was good for me, I'd better find the kid."

I told her I was going to look for the statue and asked if there was anywhere her officers hadn't had time to search. She reminded me the island covered more than a few zillion square miles of water surrounded by three square miles of land, and that off-island the rest of the United States covered "more square miles than there were words to count them."

I thanked her for the geography lesson and with an overabundance of sarcasm she thanked me for pestering her.

"One question, Chris."

"Anything for you."

"If the little statue is so valuable, according to the preacher, priceless, why in "Blue Christmas" blazes did he leave it in the manger, in a deserted area, and guarded by a passel of plastic people and a herd of fake animals?"

"I wondered the same thing, Cindy, but seeing what condition Burl was in yesterday, I didn't ask."

Cindy said, "Hmm," and was gone.

The temperature may reach seventy, but it had a way to go, so I put on a light jacket and my Tilley to keep my balding head warm. I figured the police would have done a good job covering the downtown area, so I walked closer to the beach and headed away from town. I had made it a block when I saw Dude and his puppy skipping along the side of the road. Dude was skipping; his Australian terrier, Pluto, was running as fast as his little legs could carry him. Dude had told me a while back he had read that skipping had the health advantages of jogging, but at a slower pace. I didn't know where he had read it, although I doubted it was in *Astronomy Magazine*.

They pulled up beside me and I stooped to greet Pluto, named after the dwarf planet. He licked my hand, more in appreciation for me slowing his master rather than for being glad to see me.

Dude waited for me to finish my bonding moment with his dog, and said, "Surfer buds say you be cool for a geezer."

That surprised me since the number of words in my conversation with his young friends could be counted on two hands. "Really?"

"Yep, the Finleyster and Teddyetress be quick deciders about peeps. Say you be okeydokey."

I couldn't think of much to say, so I limited it to, "Good to know." I also realized Dude wasn't as nosy as some of my friends so he might not know about the missing statue. "Did you hear about the missing Baby Jesus?"

He said he hadn't, so I told him what I knew. "Terrible. Preacher man be devastated. Dude be riled."

He kicked the gravel, Pluto jumped, and I was surprised how angry my friend was. He had been involved in the problems with First Light earlier in the year, and had attended several services. He had told Burl he worshiped the sun god, but enjoyed Burl's services because they were outside and he could see the sun while hearing the words of wisdom from Burl. Of course Dude didn't use that many words, but I think it's what he'd meant.

I explained the police were looking and that was what I was heading out to do.

Dude continued to kick gravel. "Me tag along. Triple number of eyes lookin'. Me be pissed. Whoa. Is it okeydokey to say pissed about Baby Jesus?"

I said in this case it was and I'd be glad to have him along. Pluto wagged his tail in agreement.

I continued walking away from town, now with four additional eyes to help with the search. Dude didn't say anything—not much different from when he did say something—but I could tell he was troubled about the theft. Every other stride he kicked the sand along the side of the road.

Dude stopped, Pluto came to a more abrupt stop when Dude yanked the rhinestone-covered leash. Dude said, "Direction change 180."

I thought he meant to go back, so I turned.

Dude put up his hand, palm facing me. "Word direction."

"What?"

"Almost forgot. Boss crime wave on Folly." He looked at me.

"Meaning?"

He blinked a couple of times. "Vernon ordered two custom boards from *moi*. Shipped U Pee S to casa. Vernon excited and boogied to door for boards. Be gone. Boards gone, not door." He held out both arms. "Boss crime wave."

Charles wasn't around to translate. I guessed Dude had two surfboards shipped to a customer.

"Stolen?" I said.

"There minute." Dude snapped his fingers. "Gone next. Crime wave."

"Did the customer see who took them?"

"Negatory. Man in brown say dropped on porch.

Vernon find empty porch."

"When?"

"Now minus eighteen hours. Day youngin' swiped from crib."

I couldn't imagine a connection, but asked, "Do you think the thefts are related?"

He looked down at Pluto like he expected him to answer. Pluto was more interested in sniffing a discarded drink cup. "Me be surfer. Think in waves. Folly small. Two humongous crimes same day. Boss crime wave."

I didn't think the theft of two surfboards would qualify as a humongous crime, but nodded. "Could be."

"See."

I didn't, but smiled as the image of a surfing Baby Jesus crossed my mind.

Dude said, "You be needin' to figure it out. Dude be pained to see preacher man sufferin'. He be helping everyone else. Now he needs help. Figure it out."

I started to say it's what the police were for, but Dude knew that. Besides, I agreed with him. Burl was a Godsend to Folly. If there was anything I could do to lessen his pain, I would.

CHAPTER 5

Groundhog Day must have come late this year. I opened the door to the same sight I had witnessed the same time yesterday. Jason and Samuel were staring at me with their hands in their coat pockets

"We meet again," I said.

Samuel smiled, and Jason said, "Good afternoon, Mr. Landrum." He looked past me into the living room. "Got more Pepsis?"

I motioned them to the kitchen, and they took the same seats they had occupied yesterday. I handed each a Pepsi and grabbed one for myself.

"Mr. Landrum," Samuel said, "since you're sort of in charge of our espionage—"

"Don't think it's espionage," Jason interrupted. "We're looking to see if anyone knows about the missing kid, umm, Jesus."

Samuel rolled his eyes. "Whatever. We're reporting in."

"Reporting in," Jason added, "and to see if you heard about the surfboard heist?"

Samuel said, "We think the baby theft and the surfboard one are connected."

I told them I was aware of the missing surfboards but didn't think it had anything to do with the statue.

Samuel shook his head. "Mighty big ass, umm, I mean, mighty big coincidence. Everyone who watches TV mysteries knows cops say there ain't no such thing as coincidence."

Jason shoved Samuel's arm. "Sure there is. Otherwise *coincidence* wouldn't be in the dictionary. Isn't that right, Mr. Landrum?"

I was amazed how quickly the conversation had headed downhill. "Yes Jason, there are coincidences, but the police look for connections before they write off two or more events as unrelated."

Jason turned to Samuel. "See." Samuel repeated, "Whatever."

Time to get the train back on the track. "Anything to report?"

"Jason and I walked all over town after we left here yesterday. I know it wasn't right, but we sneaked through some yards." He tilted his head toward Jason. "He dug through those big dumpster things behind two restaurants." He paused and grinned. "He fell in one."

"I didn't fall in, Samuel. I caught myself."

"Didn't look like it. The point, Mr. Landrum, is we didn't find Jesus."

Jason said, "Tell him about school."

"Well, we sort of asked everyone we knew if they'd heard anything about the statue. We acted like we just heard about it and wanted to hear if they knew anything more than we did. Didn't want it to sound like we were interrogating them, if you know what I mean."

I cringed thinking about how the questioning may have sounded to their friends. "Don't suppose you learned anything?"

Jason looked at Samuel and then at me. "Not a thing, Mr. Landrum. Most of the students didn't know that the baby was gone."

It appeared the price of two Pepsis bought me nothing other than a discussion about coincidences.

Jason said, "Don't worry, we're not giving up. There are a few kids we didn't see today. We're still on the case."

I again cautioned them not to do anything that could put them in danger. Again, they said they wouldn't. I walked them to the door and wondered if they would know what danger was and how it could sneak up on them.

Samuel turned as they reached the porch. "One more thing, Mr. Landrum. About the coincidence stuff, I sort of feel like the boards being taken has something to do with the missing baby."

I smiled and told them to be careful. As they headed out, I wondered what the odds were on them following my advice.

———

I moved to the recliner in the living room and allowed my mind to wander back to some of my most memorable childhood Christmases, when another knock disturbed my sleigh ride down memory lane. Charles was standing on the porch, sporting his Tilley, wearing a jacket he bought in Gatlinburg when we'd been there a few years back, and pointing his cane toward the kitchen.

"Cooking supper?"

I laughed. The last time I'd cooked supper in my kitchen was—well, I'd never cooked supper there. Charles knew that, and I wrote off his comment as a joke rather than a symptom of early-onset Alzheimer's.

"Sorry, I was heading to the grocery to pick up some fresh fruit, vegetables, and tilapia, but got sidetracked by a total lack of desire and ability to cook it."

"So, are you coming with me to Rita's?" I smiled and grabbed my jacket.

Rita's Seaside Grill was two blocks from the house and situated on a prime piece of real estate. The property had been the site of a bowling alley, and several restaurants before it morphed into Rita's a few years ago. It had one of Folly's nicest outdoor seating areas although that feature was seldom occupied in December. We chose a booth inside and along the window overlooking the Sand Dollar Social Club, Folly's iconic private bar, open to anyone with a dollar and who could wait a day to become a member.

Ashley, who had waited on me several times, was quick to the table. She pointed to me and said, "Cabernet," and to Charles and said, "Budweiser."

We nodded, and she headed to the bar. Charles threw his jacket on the seat beside him. He wore a long-sleeve, green University of North Dakota Hockey sweatshirt. I glanced at the shirt and looked out the window at two customized Harleys parked in front of the Sand Dollar. Charles had three more sweatshirts than a Dick's Sporting Goods store, and I had been trying for years not to ask about them. I had more to do with my time than to hear protracted stories about the schools represented, their mascots, student population, number of faculty members holding PhDs in Pan American Studies, and other trivia. Ignoring him didn't always prevent him from sharing.

He pointed to his chest. "Get it? Winter, hockey." I stifled a whoop-de-doo. "Nice."

Ashley had returned with drinks before I heard more about the University of North Dakota than anyone outside Grand Forks would want to know. We ordered burgers.

Charles sipped his beer and glanced at me. "Has the APB on Baby Jesus captured him?"

An all-points bulletin was a slight exaggeration but said I didn't know.

"What did Cindy say?"

I shrugged. "Haven't talked to her lately."

Charles reached across the table, grabbed my phone, punched in a number, and handed it to me.

"What did I tell you I'd do if I found Jesus?" Chief LaMond shouted.

I said, "Fall on your knees and pray for forgiveness."

"Not funny, you sacrilegious senior citizen."

"Couldn't resist."

"Ha, ha. Now back to what I told you. Didn't I say the first thing I'd do was call you if I found the statue? Even if the person who absconded with it was shooting at me or trying to hurl me off the end of the pier, I'll say, hang on a sec. I've got to call Chris."

"You did, chief." I sighed. "I'm here with Charles and—"

"No need to say more. Two nosies don't make a right."

"I suppose it means two concerned citizens asking the finest law enforcement official on the island for an update on a criminal investigation."

Cindy giggled. "More like camel crap."

"You said it, not me. So, have you found it?"

She cleared her throat, Ashley set our burgers in front of us, the comforting smell filled the air, and Cindy said, "No, and it's not from lack of trying. Don't tell the mayor, but I added another patrol officer to the ones already on duty. They've checked everywhere. No Jesus." She sighed. "I know how much it means. Wish I could do more."

Despite a smart ass gene she and I had in common, and her irreverent take on most things, Cindy was sensitive, sentimental, and concerned about how others were treated. She hid most of it, but the more I got to know her, the more I admired her.

"I know you do, Cindy."

"I wish we had more time to look, but things are heating up around here."

Charles leaned across the table to try to hear her side of the conversation. The nearby tables were vacant, so I tapped the speaker icon. No need for Charles to dip his hockey sweatshirt in his burger while bending over to hear.

I asked. "Heating up, how?"

"Damned porch pirates. Two more deliveries have been stolen."

Charles said, "Surfboards?"

There was a hesitation before the chief said, "Chris, your voice has changed."

Charles said, "It's not Chris, chief. It's the smart one."

"Oh, hi, William."

William Hansel was one of our friends who was a professor at the College of Charleston. "Funny," Charles said. "Surfboards?"

"Nope. A woman's best friend." Charles said, "Dogs?"

"No wonder you're both single. Diamonds, dummies. Yellow and white diamond pendant from Tiffany. Cost more than I take home in months. Snatched off the porch at one of the McMansions out West Ashley."

Charles said, "Wow."

Cindy said, "You can say that again—but don't. The other one was a bracelet from Saks Fifth Avenue. Cheap, only cost a thousand bucks. Grabbed off the porch of a house on East Arctic."

"Leads?" I asked.

"Nope. The homeowners looked for the packages within an hour after they were delivered. The thief must've been following the delivery truck. Big-ole brown trucks ain't hard to follow."

"A crime spree," I said, channeling Dude.

"Wouldn't go that far," the chief said. "It's part of the dark side of Christmas in the Internet world."

Charles tapped on the side of the phone. "From Jesus, to surfboards, to jewelry. Seems strange."

Cindy said, "The surfboards and the jewelry thefts were the same MO. I don't see a connection to the statue snatch."

I looked at Charles staring at the phone and said, "The surfboards could be pawned along the coast, and the jewelry anywhere.

Unless the thief already has a buyer, the statue would be harder to unload."

Cindy said, "That's why I don't think they're connected."

"It doesn't mean they ain't," Charles added.

"No, it doesn't. I wish we could do more, especially about the statue. A couple of my guys have volunteered to spend off-duty hours driving around in their own cars following UPS and FedEx trucks. They're also looking for the Baby Jesus. The folks who could afford the jewelry will have a decent holiday even without the baubles although I suspect they will spend a bunch of it arguing with insurance companies. Preacher Burl won't have a decent Christmas. I feel like crap about it."

I thanked her for the update and asked her to let us know if she learned anything.

"Not a second will pass." She hung up.

Charles stared at the silent phone, took a large drag on his Bud, and looked at me. "Okay, what's our plan?"

I was afraid I knew what he meant, "Plan for what?"

"You heard the chief. She said she wished she could do more to catch the spirit of Christmas thief. She was begging for our help. So what's our plan beyond walking around like we already did?"

"Begging?"

"Begging," Charles said. "Plan?"

"I've got to sleep on it. Let's talk tomorrow."

"It'll have to do. See you at the Dog. Is seven too late?"

I shook my head and headed home. I didn't think I'd sleep in heavenly peace.

CHAPTER 6

I was wrong. I got a good night's sleep and slipped out of bed at five-thirty, an hour earlier than usual. Rather than visions of sugarplums, Charles's question danced in my head. What could we do that the police weren't doing to find the statue? It was worrisome that it hadn't turned up. The longer it was missing, the greater the chance it wasn't a prank, and if it was taken for more sinister reasons, I thought about Jason and Samuel nosing around and about how slim the odds were that they would stumble across the thief. Slim still left the door open.

Was it possible the grab-and-go thefts were related to the missing statue? Cindy didn't think so. Other than stealing something, there were no similarities in the crimes. Again, a slim possibility beat no possibility. Regardless, I couldn't think of anything to do.

Charles had said seven o'clock, which meant he'd be at the Dog when the door opened at six-thirty. In his parallel universe, on time meant thirty minutes early, and he wouldn't let anyone forget he or she was late when arriving at the designated hour. I was not disappointed; I stepped in the near-empty restaurant at six thirty-five and spotted my friend at my favorite booth. He pulled up the sleeve of his burnt-orange, long-sleeve Virginia Tech sweatshirt and glanced at his wrist where normal people wore a watch. He didn't own one, but the meaning wasn't lost on me.

Before I had time to take off my jacket, he asked, "Got it figured out?"

I started to say no when Amber appeared at the table with my mug of coffee. She had worked at the Dog since I had arrived on Folly. The waitress was approaching her fiftieth birthday and was attractive with her long auburn hair tied in a ponytail, but her usual welcoming smile seemed strained as she set the coffee down.

She leaned close. "I need a word when you're alone."

I was confused. Not only did she appear angry, but also in the past she'd never hesitated to say whatever was on her mind in front of Charles.

I smiled. "Sure."

She gave a quick nod. "Want breakfast?"

In the hundreds of times she'd waited on me, she had never been this abrupt.

I said, "French toast."

She headed to the kitchen.

For years, she had been on a one-person crusade to get me to eat better, and would chide me for ordering my favorite artery-clogging breakfast.

Charles watched her go. "What've you done now?"

"I don't know."

Marc Salmon was the next person to enter and distracted Charles from questioning me further.

Charles said, "Yo, Marc, join us?"

Charles was not prone to ask anyone to join us unless he had an ulterior motive.

Marc looked around the near-empty room and sat next to

Charles. "Suppose I can spare a moment until Houston gets here. City business never ceases, you know."

I didn't know that, but did know Marc's daily meeting with Houston centered more around gossip and sharing stories, some true, with his fellow council member than with city business.

Amber was quick with Marc's coffee but didn't make eye contact with me. He took a sip, looked at me, turned to Charles, and smiled. "Anything this elected official needs to know this morning? Always looking for ways to make your city better."

Anyone who knew Marc would have known it was his way of asking for gossip. Charles wasn't going to let Marc's agenda get in the way of his. "Marc, I know you have your finger on the pulse of the community," Charles said in his best suck-up voice, "Any word on the crime spree?"

Marc jerked his head toward Charles. "Crime spree?" Charles seemed to forget about his quest for information and grinned knowing he may know something the inquisitive councilmember didn't. "You know, the theft of Baby Jesus, and the surfboards and jewelry heist."

Marc leaned back and sighed. "Oh, that." He sounded disappointed. "I wouldn't call it a spree. It's terrible about the things being taken off porches, and the theft of the infant was horrible."

I wouldn't call thousands of dollars' worth of jewelry *things being taken off porches*, but he wanted to minimize the impact. I did agree Baby Jesus being stolen was horrible.

Charles repeated, "Any word?" Nothing will keep him from his quest.

"I'm certain our Department of Public Safety is leaving no stone unturned."

"So, nothing?"

"Not yet." He shook his head. "I'm appalled anyone would desecrate the Nativity scene." He surprised me when he grinned. "I'm Jewish, but my kids love Christmas. After they were born,

Mrs. B. insisted we put up a small tree. We have it to celebrate the season, but each year more and more presents appear under it."

Charles patted him on the shoulder, "Calvin Coolidge said, 'Christmas is not a time nor a season, but a state of mind.'"

Add a worthless fount of presidential quotes to Charles's long-sleeve T-shirt and sweatshirt assemblage, his library-sized collection of books, and the handmade wooden cane he carried for no visible reason. If *Jeopardy!* limited questions to presidents' quotes, Charles would be a TV star. It doesn't, and he isn't, but he still managed to impress those around him.

Amber clunked my breakfast plate down on the table and left without speaking. Houston rushed in before Charles could share more words of wisdom from Calvin Coolidge.

Houston moved to the table where he and Marc often sat and waved to Marc, and said, "Sorry I'm late."

Marc told us he'd better join his friend and said to Houston. "That's okay."

Marc didn't share Charles's obsession with promptness.

Charles watched him go and said, "That was worthless."

"Not completely, now you know you can give him a Christmas present."

Charles watched me take my first bite and said, "Did you know Saint Francis of Assisi created the first Nativity scene in Greccio, Italy, in 1223. It was a live one."

I stared at him. "Should have told Marc, although he prefers more recent gossip."

"Going to, but he left. In a cave, if you can believe that."

"Marc?"

Charles gave an exasperated sigh. "The first Nativity."

"Interesting," I said, although I'd already forgotten where it had been.

"So what's our plan?" he asked, making a sharp turn in the conversation.

"Don't have one. Remember, the Department of Public Safety is leaving no stone unturned."

"Good, we won't have to look under rocks."

Charles said he had to make a delivery for the surf shop. Dude had Charles make local deliveries rather than using the more traditional shippers. Charles's deliveries were nearby and limited to small packages since his only moving vehicle was a Schwinn bicycle. I told him not to leave whatever he was delivering on the front porch. He said no way and excused himself.

Amber must have been watching because she was at the table before Charles was out of sight. She glared down at me. "Meet me outside in ten. I'll be on break." She moved across the room to clear a table.

She didn't seem interested in wishing me an early Merry Christmas. I'd better enjoy the rest of my coffee and the next nine minutes.

The Dog had two outdoor seating areas; one in front of the building and the other on the side closest to the city's combination library and community center. Amber was sitting at a table at the back of the side patio and out of view of customers entering the restaurant. The penetrating glare she'd used on me inside hadn't softened. She motioned for me to sit and made no effort to stand to greet me. It was cold in the corner. I pulled my jacket tight and waited.

"Chris, what in the hell are you thinking?"

I didn't suppose she meant what I was thinking about what she wanted me out here for, so I waited.

"Have you forgotten why we stopped dating?"

I will never forget. It was because she felt my amateurish attempt to catch a killer had put Jason in danger. He had told me about loud television sounds coming from the apartment of someone I had wanted to talk to about a murder. The television was loud, but its owner didn't care. She was dead. Jason had sneaked in the room while I was checking on the noise and saw the gruesome sight. Right or wrong, Amber felt the need to protect her son from the events surrounding the body and put an end to our dating.

I looked at her and frowned. "I remember."

Her hands were balled into fists; her glare hardened. "Then what in all that's holy were you thinking by asking him to try to find the missing Baby Jesus? My God, the boy's sixteen."

Her level of anger shocked me. I reached out to put my hand over her fist. She yanked it back and stomped her foot on the wooden deck. "What?" she repeated.

I pulled my hand back and leaned closer. "Amber, I'm sorry, but I didn't ask Jason to do anything," I explained how Jason and Samuel had come to the house wanting to help find the statue; how they said they wanted to snoop around the school.

She flexed her hand. "Why did they go to you?"

"Samuel said it was because I had helped catch the guy he had seen abducting that woman. Said he could trust me."

"Did you insist they stop? To not get involved? To leave it to the cops?"

"I told them what they wanted to do could be dangerous; but to be honest, I doubt there was anything I could have said that would've stopped them. They're two headstrong, smart kids."

"You could've tried."

"Amber, I told them if they learned anything to tell the police and not to try anything to get the statue back. It's the best I could do seeing how determined they were."

She closed her eyes, shook her head, and whispered, "They respect you. They trust you. You could've stopped them."

She pushed up from the table and rushed inside. I remained seated and stared at her empty chair.

I thought about going inside and saying…saying what? I was

sorry. But, sorry for what? Opening the door to the two teens, listening to their concerns. I knew they were determined to keep their eyes open and see if they learned anything about the statue and if they did, they said they'd contact the police. What was there to apologize for? Could I tell her I would have them stop whatever they were doing? I knew it wouldn't work. So what could I say? Nothing.

My phone rang as I continued running lose-lose options in my head.

"Dude here."

I sighed and grinned. "Chris here."

"Be having meeting at surf shop, sun duck behind marsh plus thirty."

I went out on a limb and decided since sunset was around five o'clock, he was having a meeting at thirty minutes past that time.

"Five thirty?"

"That's what me said."

Not exactly. "Meeting about what?"

"Surfer buds. Chrisster and Chuckster not be surfers, but invited —my place, my invite list."

Did I miss the purpose of the meeting somewhere in that? "What's it about?"

"Spirit of Christmas stealer. Be here?"

I figured all I would get from continuing this conversation would be a headache. "Yep," I said and hit end call.

CHAPTER 7

As anyone who knew Charles could have predicted, we arrived at the surf shop thirty minutes before the time Dude had almost said. We would have been earlier if Charles hadn't stopped me three times to ask what the meeting was about. I had thought the *spirit of Christmas stealer* had summed it up, but it wasn't detailed enough for my friend. He would have to wait.

The surf shop, written without upper-case letters for reasons known only to Dude, faced Center Street and was in the heart of Folly's six-block retail district. He had owned the shop for a quarter of a century and had stocked it with everything an aspiring or a life-long surfer would need except for the ocean. To say it was cluttered would be like saying a few revelers gathered in Times Square on New Year's Eve. I was surprised after Charles and I had made it up the steps to see the space inside the front door void of its usual racks packed with wetsuits, enough surfboards to outfit half the island, and colorful swimwear.

Stephon, one of Dude's two full-time employees who were

listed in Wikipedia under *Horrid Customer Service*, was shoving the last rack of wetsuits toward the back of the room while cussing the entire way. Dude was waving his arm and yelling, "There be go." I assumed he was telling Stephon where to park the display.

The shop owner saw us and turned from his employee and pointed to the space vacated by the displays. "Surf shop official meeting room."

I had never seen this much open space in the shop and it could hold a dozen people. Charles offered to help do whatever needed to be done. Dude said words that meant everything was taken care of. He added, "No be servin' munchies and champagne."

He had finished sharing the un-menu when three men and a woman arrived. They were less than half Dude's age and looked like a white rap group. Each wore black pants and dark gray hoodies.

The tallest member of the quartet looked around the open area. "Cool."

"I'm stoked, Dude," the second man said as he pushed the hood off his shaven head.

The woman pointed to the floor that had held a selection of surfboards. "Sick."

Charles leaned close and said, "Means good." I nodded thanks.

The fourth person didn't say anything.

Dude waved them in. "Welcome to el meeting."

Charles, whose goal in life was to meet every human on earth, walked to the group and held out his hand. "I'm Charles, the boring looking guy over there is my bud Chris." The newcomers looked at Charles's hand and glanced at me. The tall one who had spoken first shook the outstretched hand, and said, "Roscoe." He looked at the guy standing next to him who said, "Todd." The female stepped in front of Roscoe, shook Charles's hand and said, "Deb."

The fourth person remained in the back of the group, and muttered, "Ryan." He didn't shake anyone's hand.

The door opened before I could say something like it was nice to meet them, and I had already forgotten their names. Two more people entered and gawked at the empty space. I recognized them from when they were having breakfast with Dude. Charles and I hadn't gotten the memo about tonight's dress code. The newest arrivals, like their predecessors, wore black jeans and gray hoodies. I thought their names were Teddye and Finley but waited until they introduced themselves to Charles in case I was wrong— something I often was when it came to names. They seemed to know the first group and nodded in their direction. Stephon had finished doing whatever he had been doing and joined the expanding assemblage.

"When're we starting?" Stephon groused. "I want to get out of here."

Dude shook his head. "Be waitin' on two more. Cool it. You be getting paid."

Stephon mumbled something I couldn't understand, and the door swung open.

Dude looked at the two men who were entering. "Me be psychic. Here they be."

The two looked at him like "What's he talking about?" A common response to much of what Dude says.

Dude didn't explain and pointed to the latest arrivers. "Mustache face be Truman. Skinny, youngin' be Slick Surfin' Sal."

I assumed it wasn't the name on his birth certificate, but the *youngin'* nodded, and one from the first group to arrive, mumbled, "We know."

Dude moved to the corner of the empty space and waved his arms toward the center of the room. "Gather."

The *official meeting room's* furniture must not have arrived, so we stood facing our host. The space was near capacity, and we stood closer than I was comfortable with.

Dude shook his head. "Surfin' buds Teddye and Finley wanted gatherin'. Said wanted to—never mind, Finley, be your meetin'."

Finley had been behind us. I turned and saw him look at Teddye, shrug, and knifed his way through the group and moved beside Dude.

He held his arms to his side and then moved them behind his back. He clasped them in front of him like he was saying a prayer. Speaking to a group wasn't one of his regular activities.

Dude nudged him. "Words."

"Okay, umm, we all know some sorry ass thefted the statue of Jesus from the manger by the hardware store." He paused and most of us nodded. "We're surfers." He paused again and looked toward Charles and me. "Most of us. Where I grew up, Baby Jesus in the manger was sacred. Most times it was plastic, but to my folks and others in the town, it was the, what's the word, symbol, yeah, symbol, of Christ coming down here and saving our sorry-ass souls from evil." Not quite how Preacher Burl would have put it, although accurate.

One of the first arrivers said, "Me too."

"Anyway," Finley continued, "we're surfers and often get a bad rap. Folks think we're bad and scuzzy. Me and Teddye decided we needed to do something. We can't have someone stealin' the spirit of Christmas from our island."

Teddye was standing behind me, and said, "Tell them the rest, Fin."

"Oh yeah, we heard someone had the nerve to steal two boards right off the front porch up the street. Now I'm not saying the boards are as important as little Jesus, but it takes a lowlife to steal them."

I wondered if Finley knew about the jewelry, but this wasn't the time to ask. There was mumbling from the group. I assumed they agreed with Finley.

Finley nodded. "Anyway, me and Teddye decided to organize a group and call it Surfers Against Spirit of Christmas Thieves." He turned and patted Dude on the arm. "We told Dude, and he thought it was a boss idea and offered this space for us to get together and invited the rest of you to come out tonight. That's it."

Slick Surfin' Sal, a name I could remember said, "It's horrible someone took the baby and the boards. What are we supposed to do about it?"

"Don't know," Finley said. "That's what we're here to talk about." He pointed at the group. "Ideas?"

The person who entered with Sal, the one with the mustache whose name I didn't remember said, "Other people may think it was, but do any of you know it was a surfer who stole the stuff?"

Finley looked at Dude and at mustache man. "No, Truman, we don't, but I was thinking since he," Finley glanced at Teddye, one of the two females in the room, "or she, stole two boards, it could be. Who else would want a surfboard?"

Stephon had been standing outside the group and leaning against a rack of T-shirts, said, "Someone wanting to hock them. Could've been one of the bums who hang around, or one of those hoity-toity guys who look down their designer-sunglasses-holding noses at us."

"Stephon's right," Finley said. "Could be anyone.

What can we do?"

One of the first folks to arrive said, "Catch them and cut off their hands. Stealing Jesus. Cripes, it's as bad as it gets."

Dude stepped in front of Finley. "No to cuttin' off hands. Season of peace. Other ideas?"

"Hand for a hand," one of the others said. Dude said, "Not be hand for a board." Teddye said, "How about a reward?"

Dude gave an exaggerated nod. "Boss idea. Me be donatin' five C notes."

"Five hundred dollars," Charles whispered. I told him I knew what C notes were.

Finley looked at Dude and said, "Let's pass a hat?"

Truman said, "Doubt many of us are carrying cash." Dude smiled. "Me be puttin' hat on counter *manana*.

Drop dough in."

Deb raised her hand, and Dude pointed at her. "I thought there are a lot of homeless people around here and others who don't have food. Dude, do you think we could take some of the money and give it to somebody who helps those people?"

Truman raised his hand. "That's a good idea. Lots of people slip through the cracks even with the organizations out there. Anything we can do would help."

Dude smiled. "Boss idea two. Bring big bucks and I'll figure where they can do good."

I was touched. I could be wrong, but it didn't appear there would have been many spare dollars among the group. I would contribute, although not five C notes.

Multiple discussions broke out, and Finley shrugged at Dude who raised his hands over his head and clapped. The talking stopped, and all eyes turned to Dude. "More ideas?"

The other female, Deb, I believe, said, "We could take turns and watch the Nativity scene from in the park across the street. Maybe the thief will come back to steal more of the stuff."

Finley said, "Good idea, Deb." He paused and pointed to each person in the room, except for Dude, Charles and me. "We could take, umm, let's see, three-hour shifts that'd cover all the time."

I thought it was a nice, generous offer, although from what Preacher Burl had said, only the Baby Jesus had significant value. I doubted the thief would return.

Dude said, "Cool. Sign up with Stephon for your shift."

Stephon rolled his eyes and muttered a profanity. Finley said, "More suggestions?"

No one said anything and Finley thanked everyone for coming and suggested since the group was called Surfers

Against Spirit of Christmas Thieves the meeting should end

with a prayer, and asked if anyone would like to offer one. No one did, and Dude said, "Lip-sealed prayer, be boss." The room remained silent until Stephon said to hurry and sign up because he was going home.

Charles and I stayed after the group had left and Stephon handed Dude the sign-up sheet that had the next forty-eight hours covered before mumbling another profanity and slamming the door on the way out.

Dude watched him go. "He not be playing wise man in Christmas pageant."

Charles and I agreed.

Dude shook his head. "Think meetin' be good?"

I told him I was impressed by how compassionate the group was and how seriously they had taken the thefts.

"Be good peeps," Dude said. "But they—thanks for comin'."

Charles said, "But they what?"

Dude looked at the floor. "They be fearin' surfer be guilty."

"What do you think?" I asked.

Dude looked up from the floor and at the door. "Want not to be."

CHAPTER 8

Like most kids, my early years were spent listening to my parents' music. Most of it was from a 1950s Magnavox record player where the sounds of Bing Crosby, Perry Como, and Frank Sinatra filled our modest home along with the smells of homemade spaghetti and chili. Being an only child, I had plenty of time to play by myself or listen to the music and my parents arguing who was the better singer: Frank or Perry. The rock-and-roll tsunami hit about the same time I was stretching my musical wings, and I fell hard for the rough, brash sounds that blared from seven-inch wide, thin, black, 45 rpm records; sounds dominated by Elvis Presley and Jerry Lee Lewis.

Then something happened. My friends were rocking along with Elvis, and I started enjoying the more mellow sounds of artists like Patsy Cline, Jim Reeves, and the piano of Floyd Cramer. Their songs were played on the rock-and- roll stations, so I didn't realize they were country. A year or two later, I would rather listen to Bill Anderson than to Dion; Roger Miller than to the Rolling Stones. I didn't want to be completely ostracized, so I did enjoy the Beach

Boys and the Four Seasons, but country music either touched my feelings, my outlook, or simply sounded better.

When I learned someone on Folly was a country music singer and had charted a hit record, I made a point of getting to know him. True, his hit was pressed when I was fourteen, and the most fame he'd experienced since then was from several appearances on the Grand Ole Opry, all long before I was old enough to drive. Regardless, getting acquainted with Calvin Ballew, better known as Country Cal, had been a trip, and not only down memory lane.

Four years ago, through a chain of events that would be fodder for a country song, and a story that's way too long to tell here, Cal became the owner of a run-down, rock-and- roll bar a block off Center Street and renamed it Cal's Country Bar and Burgers. Little positive could be said about the burgers, but as a country music bar, Cal's had it all: an old Wurlitzer jukebox stocked with traditional country songs, an open-mic night catering to area-wide wannabees, and the "country legend," Cal Ballew, performing on weekends. To quench his patrons' thirst, Cal featured a wide-ranging selection of beers as long as they wanted Bud or Miller, and a wine selection that included everything from red to white, with vintages dating back twelve months.

Crowds, using the term loosely, were thin in the middle of the week in December. Tonight, they were anorexic. Of the six people there, I recognized all but one, a woman who appeared to be in her late fifties who was sitting at the bar. What Cal's lacked in customer count, it made up for in Christmas decorations. Three—yes three—artificial Christmas trees were situated around the room. Their multiple strands of colorful lights matched the strands Cal had placed on each non-moving vertical surface. More were hanging from the ceiling.

The six-foot-three, seventy-year-old owner stepped out from behind the bar and greeted me with "Merry Christmas." He looked like a living version of Hank Williams Sr. Cal's long, gray hair inched out from around a Stetson that had traveled with him for forty plus years and

hundreds of thousands of miles around the South as he went from venue to venue singing his extensive list of traditional country tunes. In the spirit of Folly and the season, a strand of battery-operated LED lights was strung around the crown of his hat; he wore the rhinestone covered coat which had traveled as many miles as the Stetson; but, he had on bright red slacks and red tennis shoes. "Ho, ho, ho," came to mind as I gave him a holiday hug.

"I was getting us more drinks," Cal said and nodded to a table with one occupant. "Go on over. Wine?"

I succumbed to his high-pressure sales pitch and walked to the table occupied by Preacher Burl Ives Costello. Burl stood and pointed to an empty chair.

"Welcome."

Burl was the only person at the table so I pulled out the chair and now the *us* became Burl, Cal, and me. The preacher had told me before he'd moved to Folly he'd tended bar to make ends meet, so I wasn't surprised to see him in Cal's. Instead of beer, he had a can of Diet Coke in front of him. Cal returned and handed me red wine, my choice during the winter months, set another Coke in front of Burl, and flopped down in the chair. A slight mumbling from the other occupied table could be heard over the jukebox playing Skeeter Davis's "The End of the World."

I recognized the people at the table as employees of one of the town's small retail stores. From their colorful paper hats, I guessed it was their Christmas party.

I turned to Burl. "Heard anything about the missing statue?"

Burl shook his head. "No, Brother Chris. My heart is heavy and I feel such a tragic loss."

"The police are doing what they can. If it was taken as a cruel prank, it'll be found," I said.

Burl took a sip and set the can on the table. "Brother Chris, we are not going to be deterred. A kind, compassionate soul from the Methodist Church has offered the use of the Baby Jesus statue from his life-sized Nativity he displays in front of his home on Shadow Race Lane. He said it would be more visible in our setting and would tell whoever was overtaken by the Devil and absconded with our Jesus that good shall prevail."

Cal said, "Cool."

Burl looked at his drink. "Of course, his plastic statue is not as meaningful as the one taken, but I accepted his kind offer."

Eddy Arnold'sversion of "WhiteChristmas" replaced "The End of the World."

Cal pointed to the jukebox. "My favorite Christmas song."

Burl said, "A pleasant one, to be sure."

"I have three versions on there: Eddy, Bing Crosby, and Loretta Lynn."

Each December, he added several Christmas songs to his musical selections. Believe it or not, he'd even added some recorded in the last two decades.

Burl was more interested in the statue than Cal's jukebox. "My heart is heavy about the theft, but my spirits have been bolstered. Several people who attend First Light have banded together and will be taking turns watching over the Nativity. And, in our common spiritual quest, members from the Baptist, Methodist, and the Catholic Church have volunteered to stand hand-in-hand with our flock overseeing the security of the Nativity." Burl smiled. "They will not be literally standing hand-in-hand, but will join our flock in watching over the manger and covering all hours of day and night. Praise the Lord."

"Burl," I said, "let me ask you something and I hope you don't take offense."

The preacher set his drink down. "You have my full attention and curiosity."

"I know how much the carved statue means to you, and was wondering why you left it unattended at the Nativity."

Burl looked at the jukebox, down in his drink, and at me. "Brother Chris, faith is the short answer. I had faith our fine residents would have cherished the icon as much as I did. I trusted the good in all of us would protect from anything untowardly from happening."

"Preacher," I interrupted, "you know—"

Burl raised his hand and stopped me. "No need to say it, Brother Chris, I once again misjudged the good in people."

"Preacher, it took only one misguided soul to take the statue. Your faith is admirable, and has served as an example for many of us."

I chose not to say it was naïve to believe the statue would have been safe where he had left it. I changed the subject and told Burl about the surfers and how they are keeping watch. If I hadn't, I could picture church members calling the police on the surfers, or the surfers trying to capture members of the Methodist Church, or combinations thereof. I also thought that while the plastic Baby Jesus would be safe, the hand-carved replica was still missing.

Cal leaned back and pushed his Stetson to the back of his head. I finished telling Burl about the surfers, and Cal said, "All will be well. I have faith." He turned to me. "Christmas, as Chris knows," he turned to Burl, "is my favorite time of year. All those years on the road, I spent most Christmas days in my car, eating the meager offerings from vending machines at the few service stations that were open, and looking around realizing there was no one to celebrate the holy day with. I heard stories from other men and women who were in the same sad fix—not only singers going from town to town, but homeless, or truck drivers, or folk between meaningful relationships."

"Sad, Brother Cal."

Cal shrugged. "It's what this is about." He pointed at each of the

Christmas trees. "When the bar fell into my possession, the first thing I told myself, and all who would listen, was when the calendar page flipped to December 25, I was going to throw a—excuse my salty language Preacher—big-ass Christmas party and invite everyone who didn't have anywhere to spend the day."

"And he did," I added. "Country Cal's Christmas Celebration was a hit and it was packed."

Cal pulled his shoulders back and said, "Free food, free drinks, and free friendship. Nearly broke me. But it was damn—danged well worth it."

"That's wonderful, Brother Cal." Burl smiled. "I'm sure God was smiling over it."

Cal held up his beer. "Know what else I'm sure of, Preacher?"

Burl held up his Coke to toast Cal. "No sir, can't say I do."

"I'm sure this Christmas Day, if it's not too sacrilegious, you'll carry your priceless replica of the Baby Jesus in here, and I'll lead the group in singing whatever Christmas songs you request that'd best celebrate his birth. I promise."

I toasted the two, and prayed Cal's prophecy would come true.

The woman who had been seated at the bar had left, and the employees' Christmas party had broken up, and Cal twisted around in his chair and wished them a Merry Christmas as they left. Ned Miller was singing "From a Jack to a King," and we were the only three people left in Cal's when the door opened.

A man looked in the door and put one foot in like he was testing the water. He finally came in and closed the door. He was my height, had stringy, dark brown hair, a week-old beard, wore a faded army jacket, and gray dress slacks that were too large.

"Come in, Bernard," Cal said. "Come in."

"Where's everybody?" the man asked in a Southern drawl.

"Slow night," Cal said, stating the obvious. "Get you a beer?"

"Much obliged, sir," Bernard said, as Cal headed to the cooler.

Bernard stood in the middle of the room and looked around like he didn't know where to go when there were so many choices. Cal handed him a Budweiser and said, "Join us."

Bernard glanced at our table, over at the bar stools, and started to say something when Cal put his arm around him and ushered him our way.

Burl stood and reached out his hand to the stranger who looked like he would rather wrestle an alligator than join us. Burl introduced himself and pointed to me and told him who I was. I stood and shook Bernard's calloused hand.

"I'm Bernard M. Prine. Pleased to meet you, sir." Cal pushed him in the vacant chair. Bernard sat, wiggled, and took a long draw of beer.

Cal gave Bernard a brief bio on Burl and me. He told us Bernard "lived around town" and stopped in occasionally for a drink.

Bernard waited for Cal to finish, and offered a weak smile, "It's warmer in here than out there." He pointed at the door.

It seemed clear Bernard was one of the growing legions of homeless in the Charleston area.

"Can be pretty cold," Burl said.

Bernard ran his fingers through his beard stubble, looked at Burl, and snapped his fingers. "Your church's manger had Jesus stole, didn't it?"

"I'm afraid so, Brother Bernard."

"Do the police know who took it?"

"I don't believe so."

Bernard was peeling the label off his beer bottle. "Have you heard anything about it?" I asked.

Bernard's eyes darted from Burl to me. "Rumors."

"Rumors?" I said.

"Not that I believe them," Bernard said and glanced at Burl. "Heard it was a Devil worshipping cult, and one old drunk said it was a surfer." He shrugged. "That's it."

"Hear anything about someone stealing surfboards and packages off porches?" I asked.

Bernard gulped the last of his beer, and Cal asked if he wanted another before he could answer. Bernard nodded toward the bar, and Cal went to get another beer. The newcomer turned back to me. "No sir."

It seemed strange he knew about the statue theft but not the others. I told him what I knew, and Cal handed him his drink.

"News to me."

Cal waited to see if I was going to ask anything else, before he said, "Whatcha doing Christmas Day, Bernard."

Bernard coughed and laughed. "Let's see. Thought about flying to New York City and checking out the big Christmas tree, or maybe headin' to the Holy Land and seein' where the first manger was." He hesitated and held out his hands, palms up. "Instead, think I'll hang out around here and peek in windows at colorful trees and smiling kids. Why?"

Cal invited him to his Christmas celebration, Bernard gulped down his second beer, and Loretta Lynn sang "White Christmas."

"Might do that. I'll check my social calendar and see if I can work it in. Gotta be going."

"Beers are on me," Cal said.

Bernard reached in his pocket and pulled out a twenty-dollar bill and handed it to Cal. "Not this time, my friend. Got it covered."

Cal started to hand the money back, but Bernard waved his hand away and followed Cal to the cash register. I heard Cal say, "Win the lottery?" I couldn't hear Bernard's answer as Cal gave him change. Bernard waved our direction, and said "Merry Christmas" as he headed out.

Cal returned to the table, and Burl asked, "What's Brother Bernard's story?"

Cal stared at the door as it closed behind Bernard. "Funny, it's the first time he's had money. Sorry, Preacher. What's the question again?"

"What's his story?"

"A sad one. Bernard's been in this area going on a year. I don't know about before, but he's been in and out of homeless shelters. The boy's got a quick temper and manages to get in fights in the shelters. Gets kicked out and after so many fisticuffs, not let back in." Cal lowered his voice and shook his head. "He's one I call ghost homeless. I hear there's more than a hundred of them in the area. There're a handful over here. They can't stay in shelters; they, honest to God, have nowhere to go. They bum food, sleep in the parks or behind vacation rentals when no one's renting them. Damned sad—excuse me, preacher."

"No excuse needed, Brother Cal. I know of a few of the people to whom you refer. One's a regular at First Light. I'm taking up a collection in Sunday's service to give to them. I won't give the money to the well-known shelters or organizations that care for the homeless, but to a man in my flock who knows places where it can do the best for the unknowns." Burl shook his head. "I'm not naive enough to fail to understand some of the money will go straight to alcohol or things worse. I only pray some of it will touch these folks in a good way."

Cal touched Burl's arm. "It will, Preacher. It will." Johnny Cash sang "Sunday Mornin' Comin' Down." And Cal's front door flew open.

CHAPTER 9

Samuel took three steps in and slammed on the brakes like he was about to step on a rattlesnake. His hair stuck out from under a South Carolina Gamecocks ball cap. He glanced around the room and headed to our table.

"Mr. Landrum, Mr. Landrum, knew I'd find you here," he said and stopped and looked at Burl and Cal.

"How'd you know?"

He removed his cap and held it to his side. Static electricity wreaked havoc with his hair. "Everybody sort of knows this is where you hang out."

I needed to work on my image. I was here with a preacher, so that should count for something.

Cal said, "Getcha a Coke or bottle of water?"

"Umm, no, thank you, Mr. Cal. I'm okay."

"What can I do for you?" I asked. I watched as Samuel squeezed his cap and pushed his hair out of his face with the other hand.

"Could we talk to you?"

"We?"

"Jason and I."

"Where's Jason?"

Samuel looked down at the foot-worn thin, beer-stained carpet. "He's outside. He said his mom would sort of kill him if she found out he was in a bar. Could you come out and talk to us?"

I was in enough trouble with Amber and didn't want to incur more grief if she learned I was meeting with her son in Cal's sin-den. "Sure."

I grabbed my coat and followed the teen.

"Merry Christmas, Brother Samuel," Burl hollered as we walked away.

Samuel turned and smiled. "Thank you, Preacher Burl, sir."

Samuel led me a half-block up the street to the boys' bikes. Jason was sitting on his, and his eyes darted around like he was selling dope and hoped the police wouldn't see him. It was windy and cold, and he had his dark green, quilted jacket zipped to his neck. He wore gloves and a navy and gold Charleston RiverDogs cap.

"Thank goodness Samuel found you. We went to your house, and your car was there, but you didn't answer."

"What's going on?"

Samuel moved beside Jason and looked at him. "You tell him."

"I thought you," Jason said. "Never mind. Mr. Landrum, Samuel and I were riding by the Nativity a half hour ago and—"

Samuel interrupted. "Sort of like an hour ago."

"Okay," Jason said. "We were riding by, and Samuel saw a person—"

Samuel interrupted—again. "Suspicious character."

Jason jerked his head toward Samuel. "You going to tell it?"

"Sorry, go on."

Jason continued, "Anyway, the person, the suspicious character, was in the barn-like thing, and Samuel said he looked like he was going to steal something. We rode on by like we didn't see anything and parked our bikes and sneaked back to the barn."

"We weren't going to try to catch him, Mr. Landrum," Samuel added. "Honest. All we wanted to do was take his picture with the camera on my phone and tell the police."

"Humph," Jason interrupted. "Right when we were beside the barn, the person must have seen us. He took out running that way on Indian Avenue." He waved his hand toward the east. "We didn't get the picture so we started running after him."

Samuel said, "He had a big head start, Mr. Landrum. Our bikes were the other direction so we didn't have time to get them and ride after him. He was pretty swift but we were catching up."

"Until Samuel fell in a hole."

I glanced down and saw mud caked on Samuel's knee. "You okay?"

"Sure, nothing bad." Samuel looked at Jason. "Don't forget to tell him about what the stop sign did."

Jason gave Samuel a dirty look. "Bigmouth. Well, Mr. Landrum, after Samuel got up we started running again. It's mighty dark out there. I, umm, ran into a stop sign. Didn't see it."

Samuel laughed. "It honest to God meant stop."

"Are you okay?" I was beginning to sound like their mother.

Jason took off his cap, and I saw the red mark on his forehead. "Just a bruise. Mom'll kill me if she finds out."

"Then what happened?"

Samuel looked at Jason and said, "Sort of nothing."

"By the time we stopped and started twice, the thief was gone. It was dark."

"Did you get a good look at him?"

Samuel shrugged. "No. Don't even know if it was a guy."

"If it was a lady," Jason said, "she was tall, maybe as tall as Samuel. He, or she, had on an overcoat kind of coat."

"And one of those stretchy hats that pulls over the ears," Samuel said.

"Anything else?" I asked. "Fast," Jason said.

Samuel looked off into space like he was trying to picture the person. "And old, maybe even forty."

I considered giving Samuel another bruise. Jason said, "That's about it, Mr. Landrum."

"What made you think the person was going to steal something rather than looking at the Nativity? Could he have come from looking at the city's Christmas light display in the park across the street?"

Samuel looked at Jason, and at me. "He sort of looked sneaky. Didn't look like he was admiring the stuff, he wanted to steal it."

"But you only got a glance when you rode by?" Samuel said, "Yeah."

"Could you have thought he looked suspicious because someone had taken the statue and you thought the person would return to steal something else?"

"Umm, maybe," Jason said.

"And you were just riding by the Nativity?"

"Sort of," Samuel said.

Jason nodded.

And they expect me to believe that, I thought. I remembered what the surfers had said during their meeting. "Did you see anyone else?"

"Yeah," Samuel said. "The first, or maybe it was the second, time we rode by there was one of those surfer dudes sleeping in the park across the street. He was curled up in a sleeping bag on the side of the path with the bright Christmas displays, so we didn't figure he was going to steal anything." So much for the surfers' twenty-four-seven security.

"And that's it?"

"Yeah," Samuel said.

Jason said, "Yes sir."

Other than learning someone was looking at the Nativity, and he, or she, ran when two teenagers started chasing, a reaction that didn't seem abnormal considering the circumstances; and, learning the surfer patrol appeared less than effective; and, learning my two young friends were more clumsy than I would have thought; I hadn't heard anything to tie what happened to the theft of the statue, the surfboards, or the jewelry. Oh yeah, I was reminded Jason and Samuel had overactive imaginations.

Jason rubbed his shoe in the sand beside the sidewalk. "Mr. Landrum, you're not going to tell mom about this are you?"

I gave him a stern look. "Not this time. But listen, you said you were just riding by the Nativity, yet you told me you rode by two or maybe three times. Looks like you were riding by and hoping to catch the thief. Is that close?"

Samuel mumbled, "Sort of." Jason didn't say anything.

"That's what I thought. Now, what if the person you saw was the thief. He could have pulled a gun instead of running. Then what would have happened?"

Samuel took a step back. "Didn't think of that." A typical teenager's response: *I'm indestructible.*

"I want both of you to go home and spend time thinking about what might have happened. I know you want the thief caught. I admire you for that. I want it too, and so do the police. They're doing everything possible to find the statue." I stared at Jason and at Samuel. "Leave it to them." Jason hung his head, and Samuel stared at my feet.

Jason whispered, "Yes sir."

"Good," I said and pulled them close and gave them a hug. "Thanks for coming to tell me. Now get home."

CHAPTER 10

I woke up hungry and started to go to the Dog for a hearty breakfast, but the more I thought about last night and the potential danger Amber's son and his friend could have gotten into, I wasn't ready to face her. If Jason had told his mom what he had done yesterday and let it slip he came to talk to me, she'd meet me at the door with a rolling pin, if those things still existed, rather than with her warm smile. I wasn't ready for that fate this cold, crisp December morning.

I searched my kitchen, a task that couldn't have taken more than thirty seconds, since my food supply would be hard-pressed to feed a family of four—mice. Hidden behind an empty cereal box I had saved for unknown reasons, I found a muffin I had bought at Bert's a week ago. It wasn't quite hard enough to pound a nail through hardwood, so I stuck it in the microwave and softened it enough so it wouldn't shatter my teeth.

It tasted better than eating the cereal box and gave me enough energy to sit and worry about what Jason and Samuel were doing.

They were well intended, although had no idea what they were dealing with. None of us did. Was the statue taken as a prank by someone harmless who will abandon it and get a laugh out of it? Did someone who made a habit of stealing take it; someone, if confronted, might resort to violence rather than being caught? Considering how valuable Burl had said the icon was, could it have been taken by someone who realized its value and planned to sell it to a collector; someone who if confronted would stop at nothing to get away with it? Was the person Jason and Samuel chased running because he, or she, planned to steal something or simply was startled by two teens wearing dark clothes?

I took the last bite, stared at the empty paper plate, and wondered if there was a connection between the theft of the icon, the surfboards, and the jewelry. All I realized after finishing the muffin and asking myself several questions was that I didn't have answers, but had a kitchen devoid of anything edible.

Most of my grocery shopping was restricted to Bert's Market, my iconic next-door neighbor, but I made at least one trip to the nearest big-box grocery every six months, whether I needed to or not. I spent the next hour driving off-island, stumbling dazed-and-confused through the aisles of Harris Teeter while pretending like I knew what I was doing. Christmas was around the corner, so I felt obligated to buy two boxes of Christmas cookies; holiday fruitcakes had a shelf life of three hundred years, so I grabbed one, and I selected a colorful box of Cheez-It crackers. I was more at home when I reached the wine department, and selected three bottles of the finest, screw top Cabernets. I headed to the checkout line feeling like a true grocery shopper.

On the drive home, I swung by the Nativity. Everything looked like it should and the borrowed Baby Jesus fit with the rest of the pieces. I didn't notice surfers or church members guarding the display but didn't stop to check. I was sure someone was nearby, and maybe awake. I pulled in the drive and was unloading grocery bags when I saw Jason and Samuel peddling up the street. My cottage faced one of Folly's busiest roads, and I hoped the teens realized bikes versus cars wouldn't be a fair match. I noticed a UPS truck a block ahead of my young friends. The truck turned left two blocks up, and Jason and Samuel did the same.

Oh great. I may as well have been lecturing to their bikes last night. I threw the bags back in the car and followed the mini-parade. The brown delivery truck had stopped in the street ahead of me, but I lost sight of Jason and Samuel. I was wondering where they were when Jason's head peeked over a shrub row a half block behind the truck.

The driver returned to his truck and moved on. I pulled off the side of the road ten feet behind the bicycles. Samuel was getting back on his when he heard me opening the car door. He jumped, and his bike clanked to the driveway where it had been hidden.

He grabbed his chest. "Geez, Mr. Landrum, you scared the shi— umm, crap out of me."

Jason was beside Samuel and chuckled at Samuel's reaction. "Didn't scare me. I knew it was you."

Samuel righted his bike and glared at Jason.

I slammed the door and stared at the boys. "What do you think you're doing?"

Samuel leaned against his handlebars and glanced at Jason. "Mr. Landrum, we're just out for a ride. The weather's not cold, and we're out of school. Peddling's good exercise, you know."

I pointed my thumb over my shoulder in the direction the UPS truck had gone. "And your ride had nothing to do with that truck?"

Samuel looked toward where I had been pointing. "Well—"

Jason interrupted, "It did."

Samuel said, "We were sort of following it."

"To catch the person who's stealing packages," I added and shook my head. "And what were you going to do if you saw him?"

Each boy reached for his phone.

Jason said, "We were going to take his picture and call the cops."

"That's all?"

Jason said, "Yes sir."

"When I pulled up, did you know who it was?" Jason nodded; Samuel shook his head.

"What if it was the thief? You might think you were sneaky, but you were about as conspicuous as two Hershey Kisses in a pile of M&Ms." They both looked at their feet. "I'm serious fellas. Leave it to the police."

They mumbled, groused, stood with slumped shoulders, and said they understood. I'm sure they meant it—for the moment.

Charles stopped by the house mid-afternoon. He threw his jacket on the table by the door and his Tilley on top of it. He wore heavy corduroy slacks and a blue, long-sleeve Widener University sweatshirt with a gold lion's head on the front.

"I've been thinking," he said.

Always dangerous, I thought. I motioned for him to continue.

"Surfboards, diamonds and gold, all things that could be sold."

I hoped that wasn't the result of his thinking. "So?"

"Cindy tells us every year thefts increase around

Christmas. Munchkin mouths to feed, gifts to buy, other stuff. Stealing the boards and the jewelry makes sense." He stared at me like I was supposed to say something profound. I didn't, so he continued, "But what's with stealing Jesus? I know it's valuable, but isn't most of the value sentimental? The other things could easily be pawned, except what pawn shop would give more than a few dollars for a wooden statue, even if it's Jesus?"

"Charles, we don't know the thefts are related."

"So true, oh wise one. Let's say they aren't, although I think they are. And, let's say whoever stole Jesus isn't building a hand-carved Nativity and needed a baby to stick in it and instead wants to turn the Christ Child into cash. Where would he be able to sell it for near what it's worth?" Since Charles had been thinking about it, I figured

I'd better give him the first crack at an answer. "Where?" He shrugged. "Heck if I know."

I wondered how much thought he'd given to come up with that.

"There's still a chance it was a prank," I said. "Don't that seem less likely every day that goes by?"

"True."

"Yep, it's what Cindy said this morning in the Dog. Said she's about given up on finding Jesus hanging around on the streets or lounging by the pool at the Tides Hotel. Dude was there and said if it was still around, his surfer group would find it. To tell the truth, he didn't seem more hopeful than the chief." Charles looked at the ceiling and out the window. "So back to my first question, where could the spirit of Christmas thief sell it?"

"Not a pawn shop," I said. Charles nodded.

"This was the first year for Burl's Nativity scene so no one knew about the statue from other years and planned to take it this season. If it wasn't spontaneous, it couldn't have been planned long. The thief probably wouldn't have taken it unless he knew there was a good chance he had a buyer."

"What's that tell us?" Charles asked. "Not much, just trying to talk it through."

"John Kennedy said, 'You know nothing for sure except the fact that you know nothing for sure.'"

I rolled my eyes.

Charles shrugged, "Thought it fit." He rubbed his five-day-old beard. "Anyway, the statue was old."

"According to Burl, a hundred years old and could have been more."

"From Germany," Charles added. "Antique dealer?"

Charles said, "Could be."

"A crooked one."

"Why crooked?" Charles asked. "Don't antique dealers buy old stuff?"

"Yes, but there's been one newspaper story about the theft, and it was on television and radio. No reputable dealer'd touch it."

"So all we have to do is find the crooked antique dealer, beat him in the head with thy rod and thy staff until he coughs up Baby Jesus."

"And how do you plan to do that?"

"Don't suppose any of the antique dealers' yellow page ads say anything about specializing in stolen Baby Jesus statues?"

It didn't deserve a response, and I was ready to suggest we talk to Chief LaMond, when the phone rang.

A high-pitched voice said, "Is this Chris Landrum?"

"Yes."

"This is Finley. You may not remember, but I met you in the Dog when I was with Dude. I also saw you at the surfers' meeting at the surf shop."

In fact, I did remember, mainly from the Dog. "Sure, I remember."

"Oh." He seemed surprised. "Well, I got your number from Dude. We're having a meeting tonight and wanted you to come."

"Who's meeting?"

"The group from the surf shop."

"Meeting where?"

"My house."

I said, "Why me?"

"Dude told me how good you were at catching bad guys and told me to invite you. We want to catch whoever's giving us a bad rap by stealing boards, and we're bummed about the statue. Could you come?"

I told him yes. He gave me directions and time, and I asked if Charles could come. He said, "Whatever."

I told Charles about the meeting. "Now we're getting somewhere." We were?

CHAPTER 11

Finley's house was on East Erie Avenue near 3rd Street, and four blocks from the ocean. The large, two-story, elevated structure's wood siding was black from weather and age with a second-floor balcony that spanned the front. A wide set of stairs led to the front door, and there was a newer set of stairs on the side of the house that led to the top floor. A tarp-covered vehicle and two motorcycles were parked under the house along with two sawhorses supporting sheets of plywood, and a Datsun pick-up truck missing its front two wheels was beside the house. Two cars were parked in the front yard, and another vehicle was off the side of the road with a newer model Ford pickup parked behind it with *Landscaping R Us* stenciled on the door. Two of the cars had surfboard racks. The house on each side of Finley's had fading *For Rent* signs in the front yards, while the houses across the street were newer and one was well landscaped and maintained, and probably occupied by permanent residents.

Rock music blared from the house, and the faint smell of marijuana greeted us at the door. Finley, wearing season-inappropriate cut-off jeans, and a sleeveless, Surfin' U.S.A. shirt that could have been as old as the Beach Boys song, also greeted us. He was more formal than during our previous meeting as he shook our hands and introduced himself as Finley Livers, which explained the mildew-covered sign over the door that said *Livers*. Under it was a newer wooden sign that read: *LIVErs TO SURF*.

Finley waved us in. "Welcome to my humble abode." Charles looked around. "Nice house."

Finley grinned. "Thanks, my granny left it to me. She owned it since the beginning of time. My parents are in California and didn't want it and my sister got a bunch of money from granny and lives in Houston."

Nosy Charles asked, "Live by yourself?"

"First floor," he said and nodded toward the ceiling. "Rent the upstairs to Ryan and Truman. We're all surfers." He yelled for us to hear him over the rock music blasting from deep in the house.

Charles looked toward the direction of the music and put his hands over his ears. "Neighbors ever comment on how much they like the music?"

Finley laughed. "Nah. Rentals on each side and in back. Seldom anyone's there." He lowered his voice. "Squatters sneak in, but they're in no position to complain. You the noise police?"

Charles made a faux gasp. "No way."

"Good," Finley said. "I didn't ask you here to talk about loud music. Come on back with the rest of the gang."

We followed Finley to a large sunroom that looked like a back porch that had been enclosed. There were ten mismatched chairs with seven of them occupied. Finley moved to the corner of the room and yanked the plug on a large, industrial-strength sound system. The smell of marijuana was stronger than it had been in the entry, but I didn't see the source.

The room turned silent, and most of the heads turned toward Charles and me. Someone mumbled, "The geezers have arrived." A couple of the others chuckled, and Finley moved to the center of the room.

"Folks, some of you know Chris, umm—"

"Landrum," I prompted.

Finley nodded. "And his friend Charles Fowler. They were at the meeting at the surf shop. Yell out who you are."

Two or three of them started talking, and Finley waved his arm. "One at a time."

"Teddye," said the young lady seated closest to me. I remembered her from the Dog and from the previous meeting.

Then the names flowed as smoothly as a choppy sea: Roscoe, Deb, Truman, Ryan, Todd, and the one face I was more familiar with, but still surprised to see, Dude's employee, Stephon.

After the introductions and my once again forgetting most of the names, Finley said, "Chris and Charles are here because of Dude. He said these two have caught more bad guys than all the police departments put together. Dude said if there's a crime, they'll solve it. He said, and I quote, 'They be best dee-tectives in galaxy.'"

Teddye giggled, and Stephon said, "Yep, it's what boss man said."

"Guys," Finley continued, "we're good surfers; we're good people. I've talked to each of you enough in the last few days to know you're bummed by the missing Baby Jesus. Some folks over here may not like us, heck, some think we're the scum of the earth. We love Folly and most of the time we love everyone's, well, most everyone's, tolerance and understanding. But, we don't know a pisspot full of, well, piss, about catching crooks. Stealing Jesus and the surfboards is a call to arms. It's why Chris and Charles are here."

He turned to the two of us. "We want to ask you what we can do to catch the scoundrel."

I wanted to duck behind one of the chairs. What did we have to offer? I glanced at Charles and waited for him to say something helpful. It was not to be.

"Gentlemen, and ladies," I said to fill the void. "We appreciate your concern and the invitation." Now, what do I say? "I don't have all the answers." I should have said I didn't have any of them. "I know a couple of things. You're taking turns watching the Nativity scene. That's great and will deter the thief from taking anything else."

"It don't get Jesus back," said the surfer to my right.

I believe it was Todd.

"True, but it helps protect the Nativity. That's important."

One of the others said, "Do you have any idea who it was? Are there witnesses to any of it?"

"No, umm …"

"Truman," the questioner offered.

"No, Truman, as far as I know there were no witnesses."

Finley said, "Dude told me you'd catch him." I smiled. "I wish I had his confidence."

"What else can we do?" Finley asked.

Charles stepped in front of me. "Abe Lincoln said, 'It's not me who can't keep a secret, it's the people I tell that can't.'"

A couple of them chuckled. Truman said, "Funny." I resisted rolling my eyes, and said, "What Charles means is people, even the worst crooks, tend to run their mouths. They get satisfaction from what they did and feel the need to tell someone." Jason and Samuel came to mind. "The main thing you can do is remain vigilant. You can keep your ears open. Somebody may be bragging about stealing the statue or the other things. Don't do anything stupid. If you hear something, call the police. It's their job; let them do it."

Finley repeated, "Anything else?"

I knew it was a stretch but figured I didn't have anything to lose by asking. "Do any of you know any less than honorable people who might buy the statue, possibly an antique dealer?"

Roscoe said, "Because we're surfers you assume we know crooks—thanks."

Finley leaned forward. "I don't think it's what he meant."

"Absolutely not, Roscoe," I said. "If we're going to find out what's going on, we have to look at everything. We figured the thief wants money, and if so, he would have to find someone to pay top dollar for the Baby Jesus. A pawnshop or your average low life may buy the surfboards and jewelry, but not the statue. I figured you're smart people and might know or have heard about shady antique dealers. I'm sorry if I offended you."

Roscoe sighed. "Yeah, right."

Deb waved her hand in the air like she had a question or had to go to the restroom. Finley nodded her direction, and she said, "My uncle owns Winslow's Antiques on King Street in Charleston. If you want, I'll call him and see if he knows anyone who might buy stolen stuff."

Charles said, "That'd be great, Deb. I'll give you Chris's number. You can also tell your Uncle Chris, and I may come a callin'."

"Anything else?" Finley said for the third time. I shook my head, and Charles said, "Nope."

"That's all, Charles and Chris."

We were dismissed. Charles gave Deb my number, and he told her to call, day or night. Thanks, Charles.

Finley escorted us to the door and thanked us for coming. Inside, the sound system had been jacked up to the volume of a runaway freight train. On the way to the car, I noticed a light in the house next door. I hoped whoever it was had earplugs, but if it was a squatter, he probably couldn't afford them.

CHAPTER 12

The gods of winter had blessed Folly with a mild Friday so I walked to Cal's for a heart-unhealthy cheeseburger and to enjoy a few hours of country music. The temperature was mild, although I still needed a heavy jacket and winter Tilley. Two of the houses along the way were wrapped in Christmas lights. The sight reminded me of my dad driving mom and me around nearby subdivisions the week before Christmas and looking for the most colorful displays. A few of the years there was snow on the yards and roofs, and the colorful lights and wooden Santas and snowmen waved to us from the white lawns. I realized how old-fashioned I was since I preferred the low-tech displays with their large, colorful light bulbs rather than the LED displays that are common today. And, don't get me started on the ubiquitous blow-up decorations that may be attractive at night but during the day, when their inflating fans are off, look like Santa got run over by a steamroller.

I approached Cal's, smiled, and admitted most of my problems with today's decorations were because I was getting old and stuck in my ways. I smiled because I refused to get depressed over my rapid journey to Geezerland.

Friday nights in Cal's were festive. Locals and many vacationers stopped by to enjoy the retro atmosphere, the retro country hits, and the retro owner who entertained. No one would count the weekend before Christmas as crowded, but most of the tables were full, and Cal was on stage in his retro-rhinestone coat, his Stetson, cowboy boots, and strumming his Martin acoustic guitar.

Cal was on the last notes of "Oh, Lonesome Me" as I moved to the only vacant seat at the bar. His spine curved toward the antique microphone. "Ladies and Gents, I'm a goin' to finish the set with one of my favorite songs from my dear friend, God rest his soul, Hank Williams Sr. Hope you like my version of "Hey, Good Lookin'." He winked at two white-haired ladies sitting at the table closest to the stage and began the song he had sung three thousand times. Kristin, who typically waited tables, was behind the bar while Cal put a glass of Cabernet in front of me before I could take off my coat and decide what I wanted. She, of course, got the drink right, and I told her I'd take a cheeseburger and fries. She said she could probably find them somewhere in the kitchen.

Cal finished the song. "Now, before I take a pause for the cause, I've got a request." He waved his hand at the crowd. "All of us are lucky. We have somewhere to hang our hats." He hesitated and touched the brim of his Stetson. "We have food, and many of us have our health and someone to share life with." He paused and shook his head. "But not everyone on Folly is that fortunate. Sad as it might be, we have our share of homeless. Yes, people who have to depend on the kindness of others to make it through these cold nights and keep food in their bellies. With Christmas rolling around next week, I'm taking up a special collection with the donated dough going to the homeless."

I looked around and with the exception of one table where a couple was more interested in texting, or whatever they were doing with their phones, everyone focused on Cal. "Now open your wallets. Open them wide. When I'm on my way to take a pis— umm, to powder my nose, I'm going to walk by your table and hold out my hat. Folks less fortunate than you'll appreciate your kindness. And I'm aging a bit and coins are heavy, so make sure you drop in lightweight paper money. Appreciate it."

Cal removed his Stetson, smoothed down his hair, and headed to the table where the white-haired ladies were rooting in their purses searching for lightweight paper money.

I sipped wine and looked to see who was here. I didn't notice them when I came in, but Charles and Preacher Burl were huddled at the table in the back corner. I told Kristin where I would be and maneuvered around two tables to visit my friends.

I tapped the preacher on the shoulder, and Charles said, "Wondering when you were going to stop ignoring us."

"Didn't see you. Hi, Preacher."

"Join us, Brother Chris," Burl said and pulled out the chair beside him.

I said, "Working on your sermon?"

Burl laughed. "Yes, Brother Chris. I'm thinking about adding some of Cal's tunes to my hymn selections."

"May attract more sinners," I said. "No shortage already, Brother Chris."

Charles ignored us and had turned to the table behind ours and was talking to Finley, the surfer whose house we'd been to last night. The man with Finley was also at the meeting, but I didn't remember his name. The third person at the table was someone I didn't recognize. Charles held up his hand for Finley to stop whatever he was saying. Charles waved toward me. "Chris, you remember Finley and Truman don't you?"

I was getting older, but not senile, and said, "Hi, guys."

Finley waved at me. "Hey, Chris, meet Mary Ewing, a friend of ours."

Mary was in her early twenties, anorexic thin, with dirty blond hair, and a sad smile. She avoided my eyes and mumbled, "Pleased to meet you."

I said hi to Mary, and Finley and Truman resumed their conversation.

Charles leaned closer to their table. "Pull up a chair."

Finley looked at his friends and shrugged. "Sure." He slid their table close to ours. Burl moved his chair so the tables could touch. Mary scooted her chair closer but looked like she would rather not move.

Kristin arrived with my food, and Charles asked if the three newcomers wanted anything and said I was buying. Each said another drink would be nice.

Kristen headed to the bar at the same time Cal waved his Stetson in our faces. Burl, Truman, and I reached for our wallets. Charles didn't carry a driver's license and didn't have credit cards, so he had no use for a wallet, but pulled a twenty out of his pocket and dropped it in the hat. Burl and I did the same, and Finley started to add a five to the mix, hesitated, and said, "Where did you say the money was going?"

Cal hesitated, and said, "The needy." Finley said, "Who decides?"

"That's a good question, my friend. I'm turning it over to Preacher Burl."

Burl put his arm on Finley's shoulder. "Brother, umm—"

The surfer said, "Finley Livers."

"Brother Finley, I'm Burl Ives Costello and preach at First Light Church. In good weather, we meet on the beach. In winter, our services are on Center Street."

Finley interrupted, "I've been a couple times. You're doing a fine job."

Burl looked closer at him like he was trying to remember. "Sorry, didn't recognize you. Anyway, at Sunday's service I'll be taking up a collection to provide food and warm clothing to needy families identified by my flock. Brother Cal has agreed to donate tonight's offering— collection—to what we get."

I interrupted and told the preacher that Finley and Truman were part of a group of surfers who're trying to find out who stole the Baby Jesus.

"Ah," Burl said. "So I've heard. God bless you. Please tell me if there is anything I can do to aid in your quest. I will be praying of course, but it may take more than that."

"Heard who did it?" Truman asked.

"Afraid not," Burl said. "I'm still hopeful it was a malicious prank, and the Baby Jesus will turn up."

Finley leaned closer to Burl. "I heard a rumor someone knew and told someone else a coven of witches took it. Wanted to ruin Christmas."

Burl looked at him. "I'm sure there are people with those inclinations, Brother Finley, but I don't put much credence in a rumor about someone telling someone who told someone—think I have it right."

Mary kept glancing around the room but smiled at Burl. "Reverend Costello, what time does church start?"

Burl returned her smile. "Sister Mary, call me Preacher Burl. We gather a few minutes before eleven and have fellowship around a container of lemonade, and as a concession to winter, coffee. The service begins at eleven. Shall you be joining us?"

She lowered her head again. "Are youngsters welcome?"

"Sister Mary, all are welcome. Do you have a child?" She smiled. "Two, Preacher Burl. Jewel's six and

Joanie just turned two."

"I'd love to see the three of you there."

Cal stood and leaned close to Burl. "My fans are getting antsy. Gotta start another set. Got something you can put this in?" He pulled the paper money out of his hat, turned each bill going the same direction, and handed it to Burl.

"Think it'll fit in my pocket. Thank you, Brother Cal." Burl looked down at the money. "This'll make some people mighty happy."

Finley leaned closer to Burl and pointed at the wad of cash. "Preacher, I sure hope you don't give the money to the places that always get it. I drive a truck for Quality Auto Parts and deliver stuff to repair shops. I'm always driving in alleys and behind stores and see people, homeless, I suppose, who don't have anywhere to go and stay in the shadows. My dad worked for a welfare agency back home and was always telling us about those forgotten folks—he called them the invisible ones.

Burl nodded. "Brother Finley, throughout my years in the ministry, I have seen, and gotten to know some of those to whom you refer. A few had too much pride to ask for help; others are so socially inept that they can't adjust to being around others; and, there are other reasons I can't think of now."

"That's who I'm talking about, Preacher Burl."

Burl held the cash in front of him. "Brother Finley, I assure you these generous donations will go to those in dire need."

Cal opened the set with Freddie Hart's "Trip to Heaven," and the noise in the bar increased as customers talked over the music. Kristin returned with the drinks, and Mary looked at her watch.

"The Lord Knows I'm Drinking," was next on Cal's play list and we ran out of things to talk about. The surfers and Mary sipped their beers, and Charles tapped his bottle on the table in time with the music. Mary leaned forward. "I've got to get back to my gals."

Finley said he'd drop her off on his way to take the next shift at the Nativity. Truman stood and said he'd go to the Nativity with Finley.

Burl said, "I look forward to seeing you at our service Sunday."

Only Mary had said anything about attending.

Mary smiled, Finley shrugged, and Truman reminded Burl to not forget the needy.

"Nice folks," Charles said as they headed to the door. And Cal, saying it was in the spirit of the Christmas season, started singing "Grandma Got Run Over By a Reindeer."

CHAPTER 13

The temperature on the last Saturday before Christmas was expected to struggle to reach the mid-forties with a light drizzle darkening the already gray day. I would have preferred to stay home, but realized even though I had made my semi-annual trek to Harris Teeter, I had little food in the house, and as the old saying goes, or should go, man can't live on fruitcake alone. I called Charles and asked if he wanted to meet for lunch at the Grill and Island Bar, a large restaurant that overlooked Center Street and was close to my friend's apartment. He said he could work it in his busy schedule and would meet me there.

The manager met me at the door. "Charles told me to tell you you're late and as usual he's waiting for you out there." He pointed to the patio.

Charles waved his watch-less wrist as I approached the booth located near a portable heater.

I got his meaning. "What'd you do, jog?"

"Jog," Charles laughed. "You're quite a jokester—a tardy jokester."

Dillon, a waiter whom I'd met on several other visits, was quick to the table and put me out of the misery of having to listen to Charles complain. I ordered a Coke, and Charles said, "Beer, any kind as long as it starts with Bud."

Charles watched Dillon leave and said, "It was nice of Cal to take up a collection. It'll help folks have a Christmas."

I agreed and asked, "Are you going to First Light tomorrow?"

"You bet."

Until Preacher Burl started First Light, Charles and I had probably attended church services about as often as a sea otter recites the Pledge of Allegiance. In the last few months, he has attended almost every week. Preacher Burl has a knack for reaching a wide range of people and making everyone feel welcome, regardless of social status or level of religious commitment.

Charles waited for Dillon to leave our drinks and continued, "Probably'll be a full house being close to Christmas and Burl's been telling everyone about the special offering."

As he was talking, I looked across the street and saw Jason and Samuel peddle up the sidewalk and turn on Indian Avenue. I hadn't realized I'd said anything when Charles said, "What's with *huh*?"

I pointed across the street. "Samuel and Jason. They're on their way to stake out the Nativity. They're determined to catch the thief and I'm afraid they may get in trouble." I told him about them following the UPS truck.

Charles took a sip of beer and chuckled. "Sounds like something we'd do."

We hadn't ridden around on bikes, but we had staked out a few spots, and had stumbled on some things we shouldn't have.

"True, although we're a tad older than those two, and more mature."

"Does tad mean a half century?" I nodded.

"That's what I thought. Folks'd give you a powerful argument against us being more mature."

"Either way, I worry about them."

Charles looked in the direction of the crèche. "What do you think the odds are on the thief trying to take something else?"

I looked across the street. "Low to nonexistent." Charles nodded. "Church members, surfer group, and now Jason and Samuel. Mother and substitute child may be sleeping in heavenly peace, but they're being guarded more closely than Colonel Sanders' secret fried chicken recipe."

"It makes them feel like they're doing something to help."

Charles returned to his beer, took another sip, and looked at me. "So how're we going to catch him?"

I shrugged and looked up and saw Chief Cindy LaMond standing beside the booth and pointing at Charles's beer.

She wore a down jacket and jeans, so I figured she was off duty. "Want to join us?"

"If you'll scoot your lard ass over so I can fit in the booth."

Cindy had a way of making everyone around her feel good. I moved over, she sat, and Charles said, "Find Jesus?"

"Golly, Charles, I never knew you were interested in my salvation."

Charles huffed. "You know what I mean."

Cindy smiled. "Of course I do. The answer's no."

"Looking less like a prank," I said.

Cindy said, "You're right." She looked around to see if anyone was close enough to hear. No one was. "That's not the worst of it."

Charles leaned closer to the chief. "What?"

"At seventeen hundred hours, yesterday, a delivery truck left a package about the size of a shoebox on the porch at a house in the five hundred block of East Arctic, and—"

Charles interrupted—one of his better-honed talents, "What's with the seventeen hundred hours jabber? You forget how to talk English?"

"Practicing. Our mayor told me I needed to start speaking like a professional law enforcement official. Figured translating big and little hand time to military gobbledygook would confuse the citizenry enough to sound professional. You want to waste time talking about my vocabulary or listen to what I was saying?"

Brian Newman was the mayor and had been chief for many years before he was talked into running for his current position. He had appointed Cindy chief over a few officers with more seniority. He had said he wanted to shake things up in the force and Cindy was the person to do it. Brian was right. He also was a friend and father of Karen Lawson, the lady I had been dating.

Charles tilted his head to the left and to the right. "Continue."

"At eighteen hundred hours—six hours past noon to you citizen folk—the homeowner got home and went to the porch to get the package."

"And it was gone," Charles interrupted.

"Shut your pie hole. I'm telling the story."

He made a zipping his lips motion.

"Good," Cindy said. "And it was gone."

I stifled a chuckle. "What was it?"

"Don't suppose it was what the thief had hoped for. It was a box of printer ink cartridges, total retail value ninety- eight bucks. And it's worth that much only if you have a highfalutin color printer to stick them in. The point is, the thievin' continues."

Charles said, "No one saw the thief?"

"Sort of."

Charles rubbed his chin. "Sort of saw him, sort of didn't see him? Sort of what?"

Cindy gave an exaggerated nod. "Yep. Now where's my beer." She turned and watched Dillon head our way.

We ordered more drinks and after a brief discussion, decided that since it was almost Christmas, our lunch could consist of sharing slices of Southern Pecan Pie, and Chocolate Lava Cake. Cindy was right to call me lard ass.

"Chief, did someone see the thief?" I asked to follow up on her less than illuminating comment.

"See, no; record, yes—sort of. A paranoid couple two houses down have security cameras all over their property. When the husband saw the police lights at the house with a printer and no ink, he came strolling up the street and announced he may have caught, in his words, 'the perp on camera.' To answer your question Charles, he sort of did. His camera wasn't close enough to catch much. All we could tell from the digital file—that's professional talk for what in your day was called tape—was that the thief was a male because of his height. We judged him to be five nine or ten."

Charles said, "Could have been a tall woman."

"It's possible, sir, although he lumbered away from the scene of the crime like a guy rather than like a graceful lady." She glared at Charles. "Now, back to my description, he wore a dark hoodie with the hood pulled up over his head. He appeared to be on foot since he ran out of the yard and away from the camera instead of hopping in a car."

"That's it?" Charles said. "Affirmative, sir."

Dillon returned with our lunch and interrupted Cindy's professional cop-speak. Charles had a mouth-full of pecan pie, but it didn't stop him from asking, "Know any crooked antique dealers?"

Another of Charles's areas of expertise was changing verbal directions without giving a turn signal or concern for what others had been saying.

Cindy, being the lady in the group, swallowed a bite of lava cake, wiped a napkin across her lips, and squinted at

Charles. "Why? You steal a Roman pissing pot and want to turn it into cash."

"Umm, no," Charles said. "Just—"

Cindy snapped her fingers. "Don't tell me. You think whoever stole Baby Jesus will try to sell it, and no pawn shop will give him much, and no reputable antique dealer will want to put his white glove-covered pinkie on it."

Cindy wasn't chief only because of her pretty face and uncanny ability to shake-up the establishment.

Charles said, "Yes."

Cindy took another bite and said, "And you think you're smarter than the police and figured that out all by yourself while the cops are sitting around counting our toes?"

"Never."

Cindy said, "Mongoose manure."

"Mongoose?" Charles said.

"Charles, for your personal edification—how's that for professional?"

Charles said, "Move on, Chief."

Cindy smiled. "For your edification, at thirteen hundred hours yesterday—hell, I'm confusing myself. One o'clock yesterday, one of my guys contacted the sheriff's office to see if they were aware of antique dealers who may lean toward the wrong side of the law." Cindy took another bite of cake.

I waited, knowing she would tell us what she had learned. Charles, who counted patience as one of the deadly sins, said, "And?"

"And this is good cake. Stuff your mouth with some, Charles, so I can finish talking."

Charles stared at the chief.

"And the detective who specializes in that sort of thing is on a Christmas vacation with his family somewhere where Christmas trees look like cactuses. The guy my officer spoke to, said he wasn't aware of any crooked dealers, but would call the cactus man and ask him to call us."

Once again, Charles looked at his wrist. "He hasn't called you yet?"

"Charles, I'm off today and don't know."

"You've got to find out, so—"

Cindy waved her hand in Charles's face, sighed, and grabbed her phone.

"Is Officer Spencer around?" she asked after a long delay before someone answered. There was another delay and she said, "Have him call me ASAP, stat, or whatever our cop code number is for *now*." She hit end call and rubbed her forehead. "This pro-cop crap is giving me a headache."

I said, "Cindy, if the thief's trying to sell the statue, crooked antique dealers would be only one source. There're collectors who'd have an interest. How would we find them?"

Cindy moved her hand from her head. "We?"

"Meaning you."

"Right. Anyway, I asked Spencer to ask the detective that when he calls from vacationland. It's a long shot. I'm afraid it'll take a heap of luck for us to find Baby Jesus. I hate it for Preacher Burl, and to be honest, everyone here. A lot of folks who don't know the preacher or who don't attend his, or any church, but they look at the stealing of the statue as a personal affront to all who love Folly." She shook her head. "Gotta run some errands for hubby. He hasn't managed to get out of the store since I don't know when. It's revolting how many toilet plungers he sells this time of year."

It was more than I wanted to know. Charles said, "But—"

Once again, Cindy stuck her hand in his face. "Charles, as soon as I learn anything from the vacationing detective, I will not take another breath without calling to give you the scoop. Of course, you won't be home and since you're too cheap to buy an answering machine or one of these new inventions called a cell phone, I'll call Chris."

"That'll do."

Cindy put on her coat. "Good, because that's all you'll get." She headed to the exit.

Charles and I accomplished two things. First, we gained seventy pounds from stuffing ourselves with the rest of the holiday season entrees. Second, Charles decided we should go to Charleston and stop at antique shops and see if we could learn if they knew of any crooked ones. I had learned years ago once Charles was on a mission, little, if anything, could stop him. Instead of asking how he had planned to get this information, or what he planned to do with it if he was able to learn anything, I said I'd pick him up Monday morning. We did know one antique dealer to talk to.

CHAPTER 14

First Light's foul weather sanctuary was on Center Street in a storefront next to my gallery. Christmas was the prime selling season for most retailers, but with so few vacationers here, and the apparent shortage of residents who couldn't live without having my photographs adorning their walls, I hadn't bothered to open the last two weekends and had taped a note on the door saying: *Open by Appointment*, along with my phone number. I hadn't received any calls, so at least I wasn't stuck in the gallery waiting for desperate buyers. I would miss having the gallery, but was looking forward to not having to consistently write checks that far exceeded its revenue.

A generous benefactor had donated money for the church to rent the space and remodel and members of Burl's flock had spent hours converting the long-vacant retail shop into a place to hold services. Before they had the storefront, Burl was forced to cancel services during inclement weather. I arrived fifteen minutes before the service was scheduled to begin, and was surprised by the large number of people already there. The room only held fifty, and it was full. Preacher Burl was near the door and talking to Mel and Caldwell, two friends of mine. He saw me and patted Mel on the back and pointed him toward the coffee urn at the front of the sanctuary. Mel and Caldwell headed to the liquid refreshments, and Burl welcomed me.

"Great turnout," I said.

"God has been good to us this morning. I have spread the word all week about taking a special collection and," he hesitated and waved his hand around the room, "several have come for that reason." He grinned. "Of course, they also desire to hear the word of the Lord, and, to be honest, the last Sunday before the day celebrating the birth of Jesus Christ, brings out the twice a year church goers."

Lottie, who had attended since the beginning and who had put in hours of manual labor fixing up the building, tapped the preacher's arm. "Preacher Burl, the coffee pot needs your delicate touch. Sorry, Brother Chris, I must borrow our leader."

I told her it was fine and looked around. Charles was in front of the room talking to Dude, Finley, Truman, and Deb. Roscoe was off to the side looking uncomfortable. I hadn't seen any of them here before. I barely recognized Bernard, the homeless man to whom Cal had introduced me. He had slicked back his hair, and had on a clean dress shirt, but the same slacks he had worn when he was in Cal's. He was talking to the tall, lanky singer who attended as seldom as Finley and his crew. Stephon, from the surf shop, was by himself and seated in the back pew, and there were several couples I recognized from other services but didn't know their names. A few others I didn't know were milling around.

Preacher Burl fiddled with the coffee pot and looked at his watch. He walked to an old lectern that had spent its better years in a high school gymnasium and cleared his throat. He didn't get the results he'd wanted, so he cleared it again; this time much louder, and said, "Please repose thyselves." He pointed to the pews.

Several of his flock moved toward the pews; a few, probably those here for the first time, looked at him like "Repose thyselves?" Everyone moved to a seat. By habit, I headed to the back pew, but before I was seated, the door opened, and Mary looked in. She spotted me and I waved for her to enter. She stepped outside and seconds later she tiptoed in followed by two children. I slid to the center of the pew so there was room for them. The children's clothes fit poorly and had been mended in multiple places.

Preacher Burl raised both hands over his head. "Please silence thy portable communication devices."

To say he religiously began each service with those words, would be sacrilegious, but regardless, he had. To make sure newcomers understood his meaning, he waved his cell phone over his head.

Burl led us in the first hymn, and because of a shortage of vocal talents, he stopped after two verses. William Hansel, a close friend and regular at First Light, was out of town and unable to lend his incredible singing voice to the congregation. Burl shared what led up to the birth of the baby Jesus that I suppose is a ministerial requirement this close to Christmas. The children began to wiggle in their seats and look around but weren't talking. Each time one of them started to stand, Mary touched the child's arm and nodded at the seat. I was impressed how well behaved they were.

After another failed attempt for the group to carry a tune, Burl reached under the pulpit—lectern—and pulled out a wicker basket. "Brothers and sisters, as many of you know, we are privileged to be able to come out on such a chilly morn, healthy enough to get here on our own, and from the looks of some of us, have no shortage of nourishment." Burl patted his ample stomach and chuckled. "For many, some here on Folly, food and shelter are luxury items and outside their reach. Can we feed, clothe, and shelter all of God's

creatures who are less fortunate? No, but what we can do is to identify the most needy and give them some light on their Christmas
morning, a toy for the most innocent of children, and food to
nourish their stomach and spirit."

Burl bowed his head and gave us a moment for his message to
sink in. He raised the basket. "Now is time for us to do our share.
Please reach deep in your pockets and help brighten someone's
Christmas. While Sister Lottie walks among you so you can
contribute, I will tell you how we have selected the recipients of this
love offering." He handed Lottie the basket. "I've named a small
group from our flock, headed by Brother Dennis Richardson, a
social worker with ties to local charities, to determine where our
contributions will go. He's identified two such charities and with
agreement from the other members of the group, will be dividing
your givings between the two."

I glanced at Mary and her two children and wondered if she
would receive some of the money or the food it would buy. I also
saw her open a small purse with a broken zipper and pull out a
wadded dollar bill and three coins. She handed the dollar to the
oldest child, and the change to the youngest and whispered something to each of them. Lottie reached our pew and each child smiled
and dropped the money in the basket. I turned my head to keep from
tearing up.

Lottie returned to the front of the room and handed the basket to
Burl, and he looked in and smiled. "Praise the Lord. You have made
Christmas a time to rejoice for those in need. I thank you." He led
the flock in singing "Joy to the World."

Maybe the spirit of the Lord was present. Our singing sounded
decent.

Charles, Lottie, and I stayed after the service to help Burl clean the sanctuary. Lottie was in her forties and had been beautiful in her younger days, but life's trials and tribulations had taken its toll. She was still attractive, but wore baggy clothes to disguise her trim figure, and her dark-brown hair had seldom met a brush. We'd met the first time I'd met Burl when she and a couple of other volunteers were renovating the space. Today she wore newer clothes than usual and had made an effort with her hair.

She was in good spirits as she cleaned up around the coffee pot. "How'd we do, Preacher?"

Burl rested the basket on his lectern and had counted the donations. "Sister Lottie, we have 275 reasons for which to be thankful."

"Wonderful, Preacher Burl," Lottie said and hugged him.

There had been speculation Lottie was "sweet on"

Burl, but if it was true, no one had offered proof. She had credited him with turning her life around, and she never missed a service, but it was all anyone knew.

"Yes," Burl said. "Add the $150 donated Friday evening by the fine patrons of Cal's, and we can give $425 to Brother Dennis to distribute."

Charles had been folding chairs, which had been added to the room to accommodate the crowd. He finished and said, "Preacher Burl, Lottie, could Chris and I take you to lunch to celebrate?"

Translated, it meant could we take you and Chris will pick up the check.

Burl looked at Lottie and at Charles. "Brother Charles, have you known me to turn down a meal?"

Charles smiled.

"And where shall we break bread for our celebratory meal?"

"The Dog," Charles said. "Lottie, join us?"

She shook her head. "I need to finish, there's still cleaning to do."

Burl said, "You can do it later. Why don't you come?"

She grinned. "That sounds nice."

Burl put the money in a small lock box and put it in the bottom drawer of the old metal desk. Lottie and Burl walked side-by-side with Charles and me following. The Dog was packed; members of Folly's other churches occupied most of the tables. We took a table that had just been vacated, and Amber was there with menus as soon as we were seated. Burl said water when asked for our drink order; the rest of us followed suit. Amber didn't make eye contact with me the entire time.

"Preacher, that was a fine message this morning," Lottie said. "Christmas is such a wonderful time, especially for youngsters."

"Thank you, Sister Lottie. I hope the offering will bring smiles to some children and food to their stomachs."

She smiled and twisted her hair around a finger. I was beginning to think Charles and I should move to another table. Maybe she was sweet on the preacher.

Charles didn't take kindly to being left out. "Preacher, what was Christmas like for you as a child?"

Burl looked at Lottie and turned to Charles. "I once told you I grew up on a cattle farm in Illinois. I confess church wasn't big on my parents' agenda and we seldom attended." He stopped and smiled. "The Christian Church in town had a grand Nativity scene, one of those living ones where real people played characters from the Bible. There were animals in the scene, and one of the deacons came to dad and asked if he could furnish a couple of cows. There weren't a lot of donkeys around and finding a camel in our neighborhood was out of the question." He laughed. "Dad didn't want to. He grumbled and said his cows had more important things to do than be actors."

Lottie must have been taking lessons in impatience from Charles. "What happened?"

Burl smiled. "Mom wasn't having any of it, and she told dad Christmas only came once a year, and she figured we could do without the cows for five nights. Dad gave in but said someone had to be with his animals at the Nativity.

I remember him stomping his foot on the floor and saying he wasn't going to be the one so mom said I could do it and it'd be good for me. I wasn't certain how it would be good."

Lottie put her hand on Burl's arm. "That's sweet. Did you do it?"

"It wasn't how I would have chosen to spend those long, cold, pitch-black nights, but if mom said it was what I was doing, it was what I was doing. It turned out I was glad I did and continued the tradition the next two Christmas seasons. Each night, dad would truck us to the Nativity but wouldn't get out, so I had to get the animals over to the scene. Most of the time the cows seemed bored by it all, but I watched the people from all over town as they inched close to the Nativity. They treated it with so much reverence that I was amazed." He shook his head. "To me, it just seemed like a bunch of people dressed up like they did in the old days and stood around the manger. To see the kids holding their parents' hands and tiptoeing closer to see Baby Jesus was something else. Some adults fell to their knees in prayer. It was life altering."

Charles asked, "Was it a real baby?"

"No one thought it would be a good idea to place a live child in the manger, but the baby was the only thing that wasn't real. I was fifteen the first time and didn't understand the impact the dressed-up people and animals had on people who came to see it. Heck, I'd been around cows my entire life and didn't see anything special about them other than giving us milk and stepping on my foot when I wasn't careful."

I asked, "Is that why you wanted to have First Light's Nativity, and were so upset when the Baby Jesus was taken?"

"Brother Chris, watching those people left a lifelong impression on me. I almost cried long ago when Christmas Eve arrived, and we stopped doing the Nativity. When I found my way to God years later, I told myself if I was able to help facilitate such a symbolic representation of what happened all those hundreds of years ago, I would." He pointed to the door. "There aren't a lot of cows on Folly, and sheep are in short supply, so I bought the plastic ones so we could have the Nativity. When Brother Robert offered us the Baby Jesus and told me its story, I'm not ashamed to say, I was ecstatic."

Charles said, "You'd also be hard-pressed to find three wise men around here. Present company excluded."

Burl laughed, accomplishing Charles's intent. The preacher turned serious. "I suppose it answers why it is so important." He lowered his head. "And now I feel like someone stuck a dagger through my heart. I know a carved piece of wood is only wood, but it means much more."

Amber arrived with our drinks and took our food order. She only looked my way when she asked what I wanted. I couldn't understand how she could be so angry about whatever she thought I told Jason and encouraged him to do.

Amber left to put in our order, and Lottie said, "Preacher Burl, the Baby Jesus you were given may be missing, but there's the one the kind man from the Methodist Church lent us, and look at all the good you've done this Christmas. Look at today's collection and the money from Cal's. Look at all the people you've touched over the year. You've done good."

"Thank you, Lottie." He asked each of us what we were doing Christmas.

We shared our plans, as meager as they were. Amber arrived with lunch and all conversation stopped. Burl told us how much preaching increased his appetite and patted his stomach as if we wouldn't figure out where the food was headed. Lottie shared that before Burl and his ministry had come into her life, she had gone days wondering where her next meal was coming from. She said he had given her faith and miraculously a bounty of food had followed.

Burl was quick to point out it wasn't he but was the Lord who had provided. Again, she gently touched his arm.

Burl reminded us about the Christmas Eve service. "I'd prefer to hold it at midnight, but am in touch with my flock enough to know if I waited that late, I'd be talking to myself, and maybe a couple of our loveable intoxicated citizens." He smiled. "It's why I told everyone seven would be a good time." From the pulpit—lectern— he had said seven and if the weather was decent, the service would be on the beach. He nodded and looked at Charles and at me. "You will be joining me in sharing the blessed word of the birth of our Savior, won't you?"

"Of course," I said as if there could have been any other answer. Charles nodded, and Lottie said, "You know I will, Preacher Burl."

We spent a few minutes trying to remember what the weather gurus had said would be the temperature Christmas Eve. None of us knew, and Burl said God would be in control and hoped he blessed us with warmth.

Lottie was the first to finish and said she wanted to get back and finish straightening up the church. We thanked her for taking time to share a meal with us and she said it was her pleasure. She hugged Preacher Burl, and said she would see us Christmas Eve.

People who had just met him often underestimated Charles. Some people laugh at his ever-changing college T- shirt and sweat-shirt wardrobe. Some find it curious that he constantly carries a handmade cane, while no one had been able to get an explanation why—me included. Strangers who saw him walking around town often thought he was one of the area's homeless. And, many of his conversations drifted south of normal. I must admit, when I first met him, I would have agreed. Okay, I admit, he's still quirky, although he's one of the most perceptive and sensitive people I've ever met.

Charles watched Lottie leave and turned to Burl.

"You two an item?"

Burl looked at Charles like he had accused him of being a warlock. "Brother Charles." The preacher's eyes opened wide, and he leaned back in the chair. "Why would you say that?"

"Preacher, even one of your dad's cows could see Sister Lottie's hankering to become a preacher's wife."

"Brother Charles, don't you think Sister Lottie is being appreciative for all First Light has done for her? It's nothing more than that."

Charles shook his head. "Preacher, I believe I can sum up my answer in two letters: NO."

Burl started to interrupt, and Charles stopped him. "Preacher, there's no doubt she's appreciative." Charles glanced at Burl's arm where Lottie had placed her hand more than once. "Get your nose out of your Bible and look around. Those touches and the look in her eyes say a heap more than appreciation."

Burl looked at his arm and back at Charles. "Heavens, I'm her preacher."

Charles said, "Preacher, I haven't spent a lot of time researching the mating habits of clergy, but it seems unless you're a Catholic priest—which I'm fairly certain you ain't—and maybe some other religions I'm not aware of, courtin', kissin', and marryin' are fairly common."

Burl leaned closer to the table and glanced around to see if anyone else was listening. "I must confess, Brother Charles, I find Sister Lottie, Miss Lottie, attractive and I know we share similar beliefs on many things, but—"

Charles leaned closer to Burl. "Preacher, unless the *but* you're going to say is *but* you don't know what preacher you could get to perform your wedding, I don't want to hear it. I would advise you to give serious thought to talking to Lottie about your feelings." Charles nodded. "I think a June wedding would be nice."

And that was marriage advice from someone who had never

been married; someone who had asked Heather to marry him; and from someone who had called it off.

Burl didn't get a chance to respond. Lottie charged in the restaurant, her face red, and tears in her eyes.

"It's gone!"

CHAPTER 15

All eyes turned to Lottie, who stumbled and tripped over a table near the door. The room got quiet as she regained her balance and approached us. Burl stood and wrapped his arms around her and eased her in the chair she had vacated minutes earlier.

"What's gone?" Burl asked, although I suspected he knew.

Lottie's shoulders sagged, she rested her elbows on the table, and put her head between her hands. "Christmas is gone. Hope for the needy, gone. Oh, Preacher, it's all gone." Amber had returned and squatted down beside Lottie. "Can I get you water?"

Lottie mumbled, "Please." I said, "What happened?"

Burl put his arm around Lottie who looked up with tears in her eyes. "Back door's open. Drawer smashed. The money's gone —it's gone."

Amber was quick with the water, and Lottie took a sip. I asked Amber for the check, paid, and said we should go to the church. It was cold outside, but I felt colder inside as we rushed to First Light. We entered the sanctuary, and I suggested Lottie may be more comfortable waiting on the back pew while Burl, Charles, and I continued to the office. The lock box was on the floor, open, and empty. The back door looked like someone had used a crowbar on it. I told Charles and Burl not to touch anything and called Chief LaMond.

Five minutes later, the chief entered followed by Officer Allen Spencer, whom I'd known for several years. Cindy wore jeans, a paint-stained sweatshirt, and an old leather jacket. Spencer's six-foot frame was decked out in a crisp Folly Beach Department of Public Safety uniform with a matching coat.

"Thanks for coming," I said and pointed to the back room.

Cindy nodded and walked to the office door and looked around before turning to Spencer. "Start processing everything." He nodded and left the building.

"He'll get a print kit," Cindy said, and sat in the pew in front of us and turned to Burl. "What happened, Preacher?"

Burl told her about the special collection, how much was in it plus the money from Cal's, and about Lottie coming to the Dog to tell us. He said it was all he knew. Cindy turned to Lottie and in a softer voice asked what had happened. Lottie added little since all she had done was return to the sanctuary, saw the empty lock box, and ran to the restaurant. Spencer returned and headed to the office.

Burl had his arm around Lottie and was reassuring her it wasn't her fault, and everything would be okay. A few minutes later, the officer rejoined us and was shaking his head. "There're some prints, probably yours Preacher, but most of them are smudged over. Looks like he wore gloves." He looked around. "Security cameras?"

Burl shook his head.

"Lottie," Cindy said, "I know the thief came in the back door but did you see anyone when you were coming here or after you found the box? There could have been more than one of them."

Lottie blinked. "An older couple was walking on the sidewalk when I got here. When I ran to the restaurant, I was so shook that I was lucky not to get run down crossing the street. I didn't see anyone. Sorry."

Spencer took Burl and Lottie's prints to compare to the ones on the box and Cindy asked him if anyone had been acting suspicious or curious about the collection. He shook his head. Cindy asked who would have known the money was there.

Burl hesitated and said, "Lord help me for saying this, but I would think everyone who attended the service would have known. They wouldn't know how much other than it was a decent amount considering the size of the flock."

Cindy asked if he would make a list of everyone he remembered being at the service. Burl said he would and asked Lottie and me to help with the list. Cindy told him to take his time and to call when it was finished, and she'd send someone to pick it up. She also said there wasn't anything else she and Officer Spencer could do but did offer to send Larry to repair the door.

"Sorry about this, Preacher," Cindy said and headed out.

I asked Burl if there was anything Charles and I could do. He said no, he wanted to be alone. I told him to call if he thought of anything or needed help with the names. He said he would. Charles and I left; Lottie stayed. Burl didn't want to be completely alone.

I closed the sanctuary door and realized I was fuming. It wasn't a huge sum of money, but I could still picture Mary's girls smiling as they contributed. The money represented the generosity of many, and several had given more than they could afford. This was now personal, and I had to do something.

I wasn't the least surprised when Charles stopped in the middle of the sidewalk. "We've got to find the thief, got to get the money back, and got to find Baby Jesus."

Saying it was easier than doing it. We went in the gallery to get out of the cold and decided all we could do was to do what we'd already decided: talk to Deb's uncle, to see if he knew any crooked antique dealers.

I was becoming as impatient as Charles. I was sitting at my kitchen table, and it was only six thirty, Monday morning. I stared at the clock annoyed that it would be more than three hours before Winslow's Antiques opened. Charles had insisted I pick him up at nine so we could be at the store at ten. As usual, it was lost on him that with normal traffic, the trip would take twenty minutes.

Not able to make the time go quicker by staring at the clock, I walked to Bert's to grab a Danish and cup of complimentary coffee. Not only was the coffee free, so was a pleasant conversation with Eric, the store's well-known employee, conversationalist on topics both large and small, and wearer of one of the most distinct beards to be found in the Low country.

Eric waited for me to get coffee before he said, "Chris, hear about the theft at First Light?"

Eric wasn't as well-versed in the town's gossip as Amber or Charles, but since Bert's never closes, word of most everything that happens on the island walks through its doors. The affable employee never hesitated to listen to the ramblings of his customers.

"Afraid so, I was with Preacher Burl when he heard about it."

"Sorry," he said. "Lisa and I were talking about it last night. Stealing stuff off porches, absconding with the Baby Jesus, and now taking money for the homeless. It seems someone is trying to suck the spirit of Christmas out of our community."

Lisa was Eric's wife and another of Bert's employees.

"Hear rumors about who might be responsible?"

Eric ran his hand over his beard. "Bum, Satanist, surfer, drug addict, run of the mill thief, ghost of Christmas past, jealous preacher from another church—I've heard them all. Ask me if I believe any of them." Eric didn't wait for my answer. "Not a one. If you ask me, it's someone who's needing quick cash for the holidays. Someone with a mess of youngins wantin' to give them a decent Christmas." He hesitated and looked at the double doors leading outside. "Chris, I feel horrible for First Light and especially Preacher Burl. He's a wonderful man doing great things for folks who don't fit in at other churches. I'm not condoning the thieving, but I also feel bad for the person doing it. If I'm right about the children, I feel worse for them."

"I agree, and Eric, could you do me a favor?" He smiled. "As long as it doesn't get me killed."

"It won't. Could you give me a call if you hear anything that seems more credible than a ghost?"

Eric cocked his head to the side. "You meddling in police business again?"

I grinned. "Yes."

"Good. You're the most interesting neighbor this store's ever had. Good luck, and try not to get yourself dead."

I paid for the Danish, said I'd try not to get *dead*, and headed out as a man being dragged by two Dalmatians entered the store. And it was still before seven o'clock.

It was a mild morning, so instead of heading home and staring at the clock, I walked three blocks to the Folly Pier, sat on one of the wooden benches in front of Locklear's Restaurant, and ate breakfast. The pier was deserted, and the walkway was illuminated with amber lights set at intervals along the railings. The lights reminded me of Christmas and the deserted pier made me think of how empty the holiday would be for so many without the happiness the donated money could bring.

Three hardy surfers were trying to catch an early- morning wave, and two couples walking their dogs on the beach. The sun had peeked over the horizon and there wasn't a cloud to be seen. I saw a few stars before the light from the sun overpowered them. My mind wandered back to my childhood and the most memorable of all the church services I attended. And, although I had trouble remembering what I had for supper last night, the words to "Silent Night" were as clear as the breaking morning light.

Silent night, holy night,

    Son of God, love's pure light; Radiant beams from Thy holy face. With the dawn of redeeming grace, Jesus, Lord at Thy birth.

"Yes, Eric", I said out loud. "I am butting in. I must."

CHAPTER 16

Charles paced the crushed gravel and shell parking lot in front of his apartment. He glanced at his wrist and announced I was late. It was lost on him I was there when he told me to be. He hopped in the car and unzipped his jacket so I could see his long-sleeve sweatshirt. The green shirt had the head of a ram in the center with Colorado State above it.

He patted his chest and said, "Reminded me of the animals in the Nativity. Thought it'd round up enough psychic energy to find the slime bucket who bought Baby Jesus."

He'd said it with a straight face, so I suspected it was spoken with a kernel of sincerity. Charles had been spending too much time around his girlfriend Heather, who prided herself on being psychic and a country music singer. Her psychic powers exceeded her singing ability, but if you'd heard her sing, you would know that didn't mean squat.

"It looks as much like the sheep in the Nativity as you look like a porpoise."

"Symbolism, my literal friend, symbolism. Did you know the

Magi, those three wise dudes who brought gifts, didn't show up until days, maybe months, after Jesus was in the manger?"

"Interesting," I said, which was often enough to get him to move to another topic.

"My point, ye of lesser biblical knowledge, is that the sheep could have been rams. You're old, although not old enough to have been hanging out at the stable, so you don't know what was there."

I rolled my eyes. "Yes, your shirt will help." Charles grinned like he'd won a major victory.

King Street was home to some of Charleston's finest shops, ranging from well-known clothiers, to gift shops, to high-end jewelry stores. It also had the city's highest concentration of antique stores, with the most well-known being George C. Birlant & Co. Deb's uncle's store, Winslow's Antiques, was across the street and a half block south of Birlant. As predicted, we were standing in front of the historic building with Winslow's Antiques painted in script on the window when a man unlocked the door. He was in his seventies, five foot six, and better dressed than his visitors. He wore a dark-brown, three-piece wool suit, a starched white shirt, and a green and blue rep tie. He recovered from the surprise of seeing two men standing at his door, and looked us over like he was trying to decide if we were there to rob him. I would have done the same if a stranger looking like Charles had appeared at my door.

I stepped in front of Charles and extended my hand to the leery shopkeeper. "I'm Chris Landrum, and this is my friend Charles Fowler. We're from Folly Beach and your niece, Deb." I paused, realizing I didn't know her last name and had also assumed the man standing in front of us was Mr. Winslow. "She said you may be able to help us."

"Ah," he said. "Yes, she's a sweet girl, albeit a bit misguided. She called the other night and said there was a chance you might be stopping by. I apologize for my rudeness. I'm Saul, please come in."

The smell of dust, wood polish, and antiques assailed me as we moved past a row of dressers and tables halfway through the store to a desk that served more than an item for sale. It was covered by invoices and handwritten notes. There was a laptop on the back corner, but its top was closed and covered with a layer of dust. On the laptop was a cordless phone and a coffee mug with *When Did I Become an Antique?* printed on it. Perhaps there was a sense of humor inside the starched shirt.

Saul pulled up two frail looking chairs from a dining room set behind us and motioned for us to sit.

He waited for us to be seated before saying, "Could I interest you gentlemen in a cup of hot tea?"

We said no.

"Misguided how?" Charles asked.

Charles wasn't about to let the comment about Saul's niece go unexplained.

"Her parents are not as traditional as the rest of our family. They live on a small farm outside Summerville and raise miniature horses —sell some, show some. Their goal is to live, umm, how do they describe it, off the grid with few connections with the outside world. As is the case with most people in contemporary America, they are not always successful. I'll leave it as they march to the beat of a different drummer." He paused and fiddled with a sheet of paper on the desk. "Are either of you fond of antiques?"

"I'm fond of Chris. Does that count?"

Saul chuckled. "I reached that vaulted status years earlier than your friend."

"How again is Deb misguided?" Charles said, although I didn't recall Saul saying how the first time.

"She came along later in my brother's life. He had already raised a family, and poor Deb received much less attention than her three siblings. I suppose it contributed to her drifting."

"Drifting?"

"Shall I say a more nomadic life? She doesn't appear amenable to settling down and from what I've seen, her friends share her alternative lifestyle."

"Like what?" Charles persisted.

"Perhaps drugs, perhaps not following the more defined mores of marriage and family. Don't get me wrong, she's a sweet lass, and I haven't had enough contact with Deb to understand her motivations. How well do you know her?"

"Hardly at all," I said. "We've met her twice and only talked to her once. She does seem nice."

"She's generous to a fault, always for the underdog and every lost cause. She has little, but would give whatever she has to anyone in need, and if possible, she'd take in any stray animal and any stray person. I can't tell you how many times she's requested I donate to one cause or another. I love her for it, and have given to some of them. I think her friends share her sensitivity to underdogs." He hesitated and held up his hand, palm facing Charles. "I know it's not why you're here. Deb told me about the purloined antique, a hand-carved statue of the Christ Child. A terrible situation. She said your theory was the person who walked away with it may try to sell it to a dealer of questionable repute. Is that correct?"

"It is," I said and explained about its value and why we didn't think it could be sold to a pawnshop.

"Logical," Saul said. "And you are asking me if I'm aware of unethical dealers."

I nodded.

"It puts me in an awkward conundrum. As you can imagine, I don't want to get anyone in trouble, and anything I say is based on hearsay."

I glanced at Charles and said, "Anything you tell us will be kept in confidence. All we are interested in is getting the antique back."

Saul looked at the paper he had been fiddling with. "As you may, or may not know, this stretch of King Street is known as the

Antique District of Charleston. There are ten or more established dealers within a few hundred yards of us. Of course, not all dealers are located on King Street. Some are on East Bay, Savannah Highway, and others dot the county. The premiere dealers are no further from here than you could mallet an antebellum croquet ball."

"Crooked dealers?" Charles said.

"Now I'm not saying they're crooked per se, although there are two individuals you might want to take a closer look at." He sighed. "Are you sure this will go no further?"

I couldn't make that promise, but hedged by saying, "Your information is safe with us."

"I gave the question some thought after Deb's call. If I were looking for an antique of questionable provenance— which of course I am not, nor will I ever—I would consider shopping at Harold Lee's Antiques or possibly Arnold's Antique Barn. Mind you, I have no proof. I hope that helps."

I thanked him and got directions to the two stores. "Be sure to tell Deb I asked about her. She's such a sweet young lady."

I told him I would as he walked us out.

Harold Lee's Antiques was off Savannah Highway in a strip center that was in dramatic contrast from the historic structures along King Street. It was built in the 1970s and from the worn lettering on the side of the building, it had been home to multiple tenants. From the outside, Harold Lee's Antiques looked more like a flea market than a reputable antique store. What it did share with Winslow's Antiques was the smell of dust and furniture polish. Also like Winslow's, this Monday in December was not a busy time for antique shoppers. Charles and I were greeted by the only other person in the building, a man in his mid- forties with the smile of a used-car salesman. He wore jeans and a white dress shirt and said he was Harold Lee, owner, as if we wouldn't know Harold Lee owned Harold Lee's Antiques.

"Welcome. It's nice to see customers so bright and early. As the saying goes, the early bird may get the worm, but it's the second mouse that gets the cheese." He laughed like it was the funniest thing he'd ever said. It may have been, but I wasn't amused. Charles and I smiled.

"Anyway," he continued after the moment of hilarity, "What may I interest you in this morning?"

It wouldn't be wise to say we wondered if he bought a stolen Baby Jesus, so I began a story we had crafted on the way to the store. "My friend and I inherited a collection of wooden statues my grandmother had said were hand carved a century ago in Germany. We have fallen in love with their intricate details and were looking to expand our collection."

Charles added, "There are several life-size pieces in the collection. Amazing, simply amazing. Would you by chance have similar items we could consider procuring?"

I wondered if we sounded sincere, or just gay.

Harold gave another car-salesmen smile. "I might have the perfect piece for your collection. It came in late last week, and I haven't had time to inventory it and to put it in the showroom. Pardon me a moment and I'll get it."

"Yes," Charles said as soon as Harold was out of hearing range.

No, I thought moments later when Harold returned with a giant smile and an equally giant carved eagle. It was life size, and no doubt valuable, but by no stretch of the imagination could it be confused with Baby Jesus. Charles made an audible sigh and I faked a smile as Harold held the eagle up for us to admire.

Harold quoted a price and said, "I'm sure this one- of-a-kind replica of our nation's symbol, would make a perfect addition to your collection."

"Excellent," I lied. "It's lovely." I ran my hand over its

outstretched wing. "Do you have any other pieces we could combine with the eagle to possibly get a better price?"

Larger dollar signs may move him along. "I wish I did," he said. "This is all I have."

"Too bad," Charles said. "Oh, by the way, the other day I ran into another collector. He said he had bought a statue of Jesus out of an antique Nativity scene. He had to leave before I got his name." Charles turned to me. "We wanted to see who he is so we could see his collection. Did you, by chance, sell him the piece?"

Excellent question, Charles.

"Sorry, no. I don't know who you were speaking to. But I'll tell you what, because it's Monday, a slow day in the store," he waved his hand around the empty store. "I'll give you a twenty-percent discount on this impeccable carving."

Charles said, "My friend and I will discuss it and get back with you."

Harold's smile seemed forced. "Of course, the discount will end at closing today."

Charles smiled. "We'll get back with you this afternoon."

Now, he'd lied.

We left Harold smiling at the possibility of selling the eagle as we crossed Wappoo Creek and turned on Maybank Highway on our way to the second store Saul had mentioned.

"Well, that was unproductive," Charles said.

"Unless you want to buy a hand-carved eagle," I said as I pulled in a small parking lot in front of a two-story building with plate-glass windows across the front. It could have been a furniture store in earlier times. Today the large sign over the door indicated it was the home of *Arnold's Antique Barn. Where the past will bring a smile to you today.*

Charles looked at the sign and mumbled, "The only thing that will bring a smile to me today is if Baby Jesus is in there."

I opened the oversized front door and was struck by the smell of mold and mildew rather than furniture polish.

As was the case in Harold Lee's store, we were the only customers and were greeted by a man who was ten years older than Charles and me. He wasn't as cheery as the last dealer and looked like he'd be more comfortable selling caskets. He wore a black suit that'd been worn so often the lining was visible at his elbows. It could be an antique. The man's smile was somber, but hard to focus on because of his distracting comb over.

"Gentlemen," he said by way of greeting and proof he didn't know us. "May I be of assistance?"

We introduced ourselves, and he said he was Arnold Tunny. We gave the same fictional account for our visit we had shared with Harold. Arnold listened and gave a somber nod like he was racking his brain to identify something we couldn't live without.

"Your collection sounds interesting," he said. "I admire anyone who appreciates the quality of inherited items and finds it in his or her heart to add to the collection. And, antique wooden items from Germany are held at a premium. Were there any particular items you were seeking?"

You bet there is, I thought, but said, "My grandmother had a fondness for religious icons, cherubs, angels, even animals. Anything along those lines would interest us."

"What price point were you looking for?"

It was a question I hadn't anticipated and off the top of my head said, "Four hundred tops."

"Oh."

It may have been my imagination, but it appeared his smile, as weak as it had been to start, had now weakened more.

"Where did you say you were from?" he added. I hadn't, but told him Folly Beach.

"I hear it's interesting, although I prefer Isle of Palms. Neither here nor there. To answer your question, I don't believe I have anything that would meet your criteria. If you could leave your contact information, I will be glad to notify you if I come across something in which you might have an interest."

We thanked him for his time, avoided his request for our contact information, and pulled out of the parking lot.

"Another wasted stop," Charles said. "Not even an eagle."

"I'm not sure."

"Huh?"

"A couple of things bothered me." I turned on Folly Road and slammed on the brakes to avoid hitting a pick-up truck that had pulled in front of us. We skidded to a stop and glared at the man in the truck.

Charles braced himself on the dash. "Do I get to hear them?"

"Soon as I keep us from getting killed."

"I'll wait."

No vehicle body parts were exchanged, and we continued.

"First," I said, "he lost interest as soon as I said we had only a limited amount to spend."

"So," Charles said. "Maybe he only sells high-end stuff."

"Don't think so. The price tags on a few of the items near the front door were less than three hundred dollars, a couple less than a hundred. Besides, if he knew he didn't have the kind of German items we were asking about, why didn't he say it at first, rather than asking how much we were willing to pay."

Charles tapped on the console. "So you think he had the Baby Jesus, and either has a buyer who would pay more than you said, or knew it was worth more and didn't want to sell it to us?"

"That was my first thought."

Charles held up two fingers. "You said two things."

"Didn't you think it strange he asked where we were from?"

"Didn't think about it."

"I can see him asking, but at the beginning of our conversation. Clerks ask if they don't know the customer and want to have something to get them talking, but he asked after we told our story and he told us he didn't have anything. It struck me as odd."

"It's the kind of thing he might ask if he had the statue and knew where it had come from and was suspicious of why we were there."

I nodded. "I could be paranoid, but yes."

"Should we stop at Pewter Hardware and buy a crowbar and go back tonight and break in Arnold's and grab the statue?"

I hoped he was teasing, but at this point, I didn't have a better idea.

"Don't think so."

"How are we going to find out if he has it?"

I asked Charles to punch Chief LaMond's number in my phone and hand it to me.

Cindy said, "What are you pestering me about now?"

I continued to bemoan the fact the words *hi* and *hello* were dropped from the vocabulary. "A pleasant morning, chief."

"Yeah, yeah. What?"

"Have you heard from the detective who was on vacation?"

"No, why?"

"I wanted to ask him about a certain antique dealer who might not be on the up and up."

"Meddling again?"

"Asking questions."

"Chris, if it wasn't so close to Christmas, and I knew the big guy at the North Pole and the other one in Heaven weren't watching to see if I've been naughty or nice, I'd lay a string of profanities on you and tell you you're going to be the death of me yet. Instead, I'll tell you to butt out, and you'll say you will, and you won't. Crap, excuse me big guys, never mind. I'll call and see if they can track him down."

"You're an angel," I said.

"Of course, I am." The line went dead.

"No luck?" Charles said. "Why don't you call Karen? She could ask around to see if anyone knows anything about Arnold."

Karen worked major crimes and had been a detective with the Charleston County Sheriff's Office for several years. She was aware of my tendency to get involved in things I had no business getting involved with. When we had started dating she tolerated my involvement, but lately she had become increasingly irritated when she found out about my adventures. I didn't blame her.

"She's been tied up with a couple of murders and has been working around the clock. I don't want to bother her."

He looked at me like I had just fed him a crock, but un-Charles like, he let it go. I pulled in his parking lot. "I'll call you when I figure out how to get Jesus back," he said, and got out of the car.

"Short of crowbarring his door?"

"Maybe."

CHAPTER 17

Samuel and Jason stared at me from my front step as I pulled in the drive. They were wrapped in their high school jackets, and shivering like they had spent the day on an iceberg.

"Mr. Landrum." Samuel hopped up and jogged to the car door. "We thought you were never coming home."

"How long have you been here?"

Samuel looked at Jason, who said, "Hour or so."

Figured you couldn't be gone too long."

"We were sort of wrong," Samuel said.

"Let's get in where it's warm," I headed to the door and noticed a box on the step. It was the size of a shoebox and had the Amazon logo on the side. The top was ripped, and there were cyan-colored stains on the bottom.

I motioned them in, and Jason picked up the box and followed me. I asked if they wanted anything to drink, and Samuel asked if I had hot chocolate. I said no, and they settled for a Pepsi. They followed me into the kitchen and after I had handed them their drinks, Samuel held the box in front of him like he was holding a gold bar.

"Mr. Landrum, we found the stolen package. It's not the valuable stuff, it's ink. It was already torn open when we found it. We didn't do it, honest."

He handed me the container. "Where was it?"

Samuel rubbed his hands together to warm them. "Sort of in a big ole' trash dumpster behind Planet Follywood."

"Why were you looking in a dumpster?"

Samuel started to say something but hesitated and turned to Jason, who said, "We figured the cops were looking all over town and didn't think they'd want to get their hands dirty and stinky from looking in the trash. We've been looking where people throw stuff away. Thought the thief may get scared with all the cops running around trying to catch him and would dump the statue. We didn't find Jesus, but this was stolen too. It's evidence so maybe the police can dust it for prints, or get DNA, or something."

"Fellas, other than the large dumpsters, have you been rooting around in trash containers around houses again?"

Samuel glanced at Jason and turned back to me. "Sort of."

I frowned. "Did it enter your mind the person who stole it could live in one of those houses and could have seen you digging through the trash? Do you know the trouble you could have gotten in?"

"But Mr. Landrum, we—"

I glared at my young friends. "I'm not finished, Jason. You know your mother blames me for what happened a few years ago, and now she thinks I've encouraged you to get involved in this mess. And Samuel, remember what happened last year when you came close to getting killed? Both of you are wonderful, and I admire your enthusiasm and desire to help, but you must leave it to the police. How many times do I have to say it?"

Jason bowed his head. Samuel held out the mangled box. "What about this? It's a clue."

I didn't think it was much of one. "I'll get it to Chief
LaMond. I'll tell her how great it was you found it and I'm sure
she'll see if there are prints on it."

Jason looked up. "Thanks, Mr. Landrum."

Samuel said, "We heard a rumor a bunch of money was stolen
from First Light. Is it true?"

I told them it was.

"Jason and I were talking before you got here. We want to help
get money to replace what was taken."

"That's kind."

Samuel smiled. "Yeah, we thought we could ride our bikes up
Folly Road and rob a bank and give the money to Preacher Burl."

"He's teasing, Mr. Landrum," Jason added. "We were saying
instead of giving each other Christmas gifts we could take what we
already got back to the store and give the money we got for them to
the preacher. Think it'd be okay?"

I was touched. I smiled and said, "It's a wonderful idea."

Samuel said, "We'd get more from the bank." Jason smacked
him on the arm.

A week ago, I'd told Charles I would take him Christmas shopping in Charleston. He hadn't gotten Heather anything and said he
could use my help in selecting the "perfect" gift. I didn't know what
I was getting Karen so I doubted I would be the person to find a
perfect gift and told him so. He said it was true, but he needed
someone to drive. It reminded me of why Rudolph was selected to
lead Santa's sleigh. He had a shiny nose, and I had a car. With
everything going on, I had forgotten Charles's request until the boys
told me about getting gifts, or, not getting gifts.

I called and reminded Charles of our task, and he asked why I
didn't think of it this morning when we were in downtown Charleston. I pleaded a senior moment, and he agreed—way too quickly. A
half-hour later, I had dropped the torn box at the police station and
Charles and I were back in the car. We took a slight detour and

cruised past First Light's Nativity. Dude's employee Stephon was sitting on a bench in the Folly River Park across from the scene with his coat pulled tight around his trim body and a pea hat covering his ears. I waved at the sentinel and he gave a feeble half-wave in return.

Charles looked at Stephon and across the street at the display. "Closing the gate after the horse has skedaddled."

I headed to Charleston and listened to Bing Crosby singing "White Christmas" on satellite radio. The sun was shining, and the temperatures were mild, and for a moment, I thought about my childhood and how much fun it had been to see snow on the ground a few days before Christmas. I also recalled I was too young to drive, and the snow was more fun with dad behind the wheel.

"What are you getting Heather?"

"That's why you're along," Charles said.

"I thought it was to drive."

"The Christmas Song" played in the background. "That too."

"How about a carved eagle?"

"Too big," he said with a straight face.

"How about a car so I wouldn't have to drive you everywhere?"

"Wouldn't fit under the tree. I was thinking jewelry she could wear when she's performing."

"I like the car idea better, although jewelry would work."

Charles tilted his Tilley down over his eyes and said,

"To the Market, James."

We parked in a surface pay lot at the east end of the historic Charleston City Market, and Charles, the master trivia collector, reminded me it was one of the oldest public markets in the country. He said there were more than three hundred vendors, and products ranging from pralines to purses, so he was certain he could find something for Heather. Karen was harder to shop for, and I had put off thinking about it until the last minute—not many minutes away.

A volunteer bell ringer manning a Salvation Army red kettle

greeted us with "Merry Christmas" and a hopeful look as we crossed the street to the market's entry. Charles returned the greeting, and we dropped money in the kettle. We entered the crowded market, and I began thinking about someone's comment in the last few days about the "forgotten folks," the homeless who, for whatever reason, hadn't taken advantage of the charitable organizations, which provide services for the needy year-round, but more this time of year. I wondered how many of those people that organizations like the Salvation Army either are unable to assist or don't know about. Who had been talking about the forgotten folks?

Charles interrupted my thoughts when he held up a silver chain with an onyx palmetto tree dangling from it. "The perfect gift?"

"Nice," I said, not thinking it would qualify for the perfect gift category.

He shrugged, "Not Heather, is it?"

"Let's keep looking," I nudged him further down the aisle.

We stopped twice to sample the benne wafers and once for Charles to drool over, and exchange kisses with, a black and white Newfie the size of a Mini Cooper. We were blocking foot traffic, and I managed to separate man from dog. We weren't halfway through the market when Charles reminded me we hadn't eaten. I suggested the benne wafers were lunch and he suggested I was wrong, and pointed across the street and said he thought he heard Bubba Gump calling. I doubted it, but took the hint, and we walked over to Bubba Gump Shrimp Company and were seated at a table near the front of the chain restaurant.

"Shopping makes me hungry," Charles said as he scanned the menu. A waitress was quick to the table, and we each ordered a fish sandwich, a Dixie Fishwish in Gumpspeak, and Charles told the waitress he needed a beer because this was his busiest shopping day of the year. He was serious. I told her I needed wine because I was putting up with Charles. She headed to the kitchen and mumbled something that sounded a lot like, "Old farts."

"What are you getting Karen?"

"I hope I'll figure it out by the time we reach the end of the Market."

Charles looked out the front window where strands of colorful Christmas lights could be seen strung along the Market's roof line. "Did I ever tell you what Christmas meant when I was growing up?"

He had never told me much about his childhood except the basics about his parents dying when he was young and being raised by his grandmother. "Not much."

He continued to stare out the window. "I was eight or nine and all I wanted for Christmas was a bicycle. I was the only kid on the block who had to run beside my friends while they were riding bikes. All that running kept me in shape, but it was embarrassing. Each Christmas it seemed like one of my buddies got a shiny two-wheeler."

Our drinks arrived, and Charles took a long draw of beer.

"What happened?"

"To make sure granny got the message to Santa, I wrote her a note and printed *BICYCLE* in big red letters so if the jolly old man didn't have his glasses on, he could still read it. Even wrote a reminder note and gave it to her Christmas Eve."

"I'm thinking you didn't get a bike."

"I got up Christmas morning, put on my tennis shoes so I could ride the bike out the front door, scampered down the steps, and couldn't find anything with two wheels on it—not under the tree, not in the kitchen, even looked outside. Being a selfish little brat, I decided it was the worst Christmas ever."

"I'm sorry."

Charles smiled. "I'm not. Know what I got?"

"A Corvette?"

Charles rolled his eyes but continued to smile. "Granny gave me a first edition of Agatha Christie's *The Hollow*."

I figured it must have been something special. "Wow."

"I didn't know what to make of it. Never heard of it. Granny explained it was a popular mystery written five years after I was born. She, being a librarian, was an expert on things bookish. She said the story was a great example of a 'country house mystery,' and she didn't think I would be interested in Tolstoy, Joyce, Eliot, or a bunch of other writers I'd never heard of. She thought a mystery might pique my interest in reading." He chuckled. "She said she'd paid $2.50 for it, and I'd better treat it like it was priceless."

"Did you ever get the bike?"

Food came before he answered. The sound system was playing "The Chipmunk Song," and Charles stuffed a fry in his mouth.

"Not for a few more years," he mumbled. "Know what I did get?"

I shook my head.

"An appreciation for books. Something about *The Hollow* grabbed me; hasn't let go yet. It was the first mystery I read. Didn't understand much of the British stuff in it, but something about it was exhilarating. Think it's why I tend to stick my nose in when someone gets killed over here. Anyway, for the next three years, she gave me a first edition of a popular novel. The next one was James A. Michener's *Tales of the South Pacific*. My favorites were mysteries. Reading grew on me."

"It explains the library in your apartment," I said, and thought the trauma of him not receiving a bike was why Charles's most prized possession to this day was his pristine 1961 Schwinn.

"Granny wasn't a barrel of laughs and seemed to always be wearing her scrunched up, librarian's face, but she taught me a lot about serious stuff. There was an old Bible in the house, and after I got hooked on reading, I read it from crinkly cover to cover. Like the British mysteries, I didn't understand a lot of it, although I got the strong feeling it wanted me to be a better person than I thought I could be. It made me not want to hurt anyone and be nice to everyone. I'm not always good at it, but I keep trying."

Charles was one of the nicest, although strangest, people I'd ever met. If it can be attributed to his stern grandmother or the Bible, I was thankful. Chuck Berry was rocking through the sound system with "Run Rudolph Run," and our plates were empty.

Charles pulled on his lightweight red jacket. "Let's get this shopping done."

The Market was more crowded than when we broke for lunch, so we spent more time avoiding running into people or being run over than we did shopping, but Charles found the perfect gift, a necklace with a silver guitar charm. He said it would complement her normal stage attire of a wide-brim hat and bright-colored blouse.

Finding a gift for Karen proved to be more difficult, but twenty minutes later, I settled on a sweet grass basket. Fifty artists weaving baskets were spread throughout the Market, and there were hundreds of baskets to choose from, so the problem wasn't finding the baskets; selecting the right one was the challenge. I took the lazy way out and purchased one from the vendor with the fewest people blocking my way. We made it back to the car without stopping—actually not true, Charles managed to find two more dogs to converse with before I had the heater blowing full blast and we were weaving through the narrow streets on our way out of downtown.

We were tired after shopping and didn't say much most of the way home. I was listening to Roy Orbison singing "Pretty Paper," when Charles turned down the volume, and said, "I was thinking. Instead of you and me getting presents for each other, we could donate whatever we would've spent to Preacher Burl to help make up for what was stolen?"

I had already decided to reach into my savings and give the

preacher whatever he needed. I thought it was touching that Charles had the idea.

"That's a great idea," I said, and told him Samuel and Jason were doing the same thing.

"Wonderful, some other people told me they were going to do that too. Nobody is going to get away with stealing the spirit of Christmas from Folly." He glanced over at me and smiled. "I think Preacher Burl will be able to use the lump of coal I was getting you."

"Ho, Ho, Ho," I said.

On the radio, Ray Stevens was singing "Santa Claus is Watching You."

CHAPTER 18

We had passed Harris Teeter when I spotted a familiar person walking along the road and struggling to carry three plastic grocery bags. I pulled over and waited for the man to get beside the car.

"Bernard," I said. "Hop in, we'll give you a ride."

He panted, and between labored breaths, said, "Don't mind if I do."

He put his groceries on the back seat and slipped in. He was more clean-shaven than the last time I'd seen him, but his hair looked like it hadn't made contact with a comb in days. He had on a heavy Carhartt jacket, a vast improvement over the tattered army coat he'd worn in Cal's.

Charles said, "Grocery shopping?"

He exhaled. "Yes, sir. Never been in there before. It sure is big."

"A long walk from Folly, too," Charles said, leaning on the obvious.

"Yep." Bernard chuckled. "My Rolls is in the shop."

Charles laughed. "Hate it when that happens. That a new coat? Looks good."

I couldn't see Bernard's reaction, but heard him wiggling around in the seat. "Thanks, sir. Hitched into town yesterday and got it. It's good and warm. Christmas season's been good to me."

"That's great," I said. New coat, first time to Harris Teeter, three bags of food. Curious.

"What made it so good? I could use some of that luck." Charles asked.

He had a knack for asking personal questions without raising the ire of the recipient.

"Umm, came into a bit of money. Got a question, any—"

Charles interrupted, "Where'd it come from?" Charles wouldn't let go. If I was Bernard, I'd be flinging a banana from the grocery bag at him.

Bernard ignored Charles. "Ya'll heard if they caught the guy who stole Baby Jesus?"

I remembered how interested he'd appeared in the theft the first time we'd met.

"Not yet," I said.

"Hear more rumors about who it might be?"

"One, sir. The early talk about witches seems to be bad intel. Surfers are still the word around town."

"Where'd you say the money came from?" Charles "Persistent" Fowler asked.

Bernard laughed. "Charles, I don't recall saying." I thought, *Good for you, Bernard.*

Charles said, "Oh."

Bernard surprised me. "Might as well tell you. It was pretty exciting. I woke up the other morning and stepped out of my sleeping bag. Stumbled over a big ole rock in front of it and reached down to throw it away. Know what I found under the rock?"

Charles said, "A worm."

My admiration for the stranger increased when once again Bernard ignored Charles, and said, "Under the rock were six fifty-dollar bills. Not a soul around. It was like the bills crawled under the rock and were waiting for me to find them."

"Incredible," Charles said, and again asked, "Where'd it come from?"

"Can't say I've believed in Santa since—well, I don't know when. Yesterday morning all those visions of sugarplums dancing in my head rushed back. Nearly peed in my jeans, I was so excited."

Charles again said, "Where did—"

"I'm getting there. The funny thing is I don't know her."

Charles said, "Who?"

"The person who left the money, some woman named Tabatha."

"How do you know?" I asked.

"She left a note with the money. It said, *Merry Christmas from Tabatha*."

I asked, "Still have the note?"

"No, sir. I stuck it in my pocket but it must have fallen out. I'll tell you one thing. Whoever she is, she sure made my Christmas."

Charles repeated, "Incredible," and threw out another question from the *none of your business* file, "Where are you staying?"

"Charles, you sure are a nosy one. Ain't anyone ever told you curiosity killed the cat?"

Three zillion times, I thought.

Charles laughed. "A time or two." It was one of the few times Charles understated something. "So where are you staying?"

"Nowhere in particular. You ain't going to tell the cops?"

"My lips are sealed," Charles said.

That would be a Christmas miracle, but instead of saying it, I kept *my* lips sealed.

"I've been spending nights under some of those elevated houses out past the dentist's office. Don't stay in one place too long. The cops frown on it if they start getting calls from people complaining about me hanging around."

"Ever stayed in one of those shelters over there,"

Charles asked and pointed toward Charleston.

"Used to, except some of those do-gooders who run them said I was prone to get in fights with their other guests. Told me not to come back."

Charles said, "That's too bad."

"Nah," Bernard said, "Didn't fancy being there anyway. Crazy people everywhere. Smelly. Danged drunks. Besides, the people in charge got it right about me. I have what you call a quick temper. Better being alone."

We were crossing the new bridge to Folly and I said, "Where do you want us to take you?"

"You can let me out anywhere. Won't be far to my mansion."

"Sure we can't take you closer?"

"Yes. I'll be fine anywhere, sir."

Clearly, Bernard didn't want us to know the location of his sleeping-bag mansion.

I pulled to the curb in front of the library and Charles turned to the back seat. "Don't forget Cal's invitation to his Christmas party. He's got a big day planned."

"I'll check my calendar," Bernard said. "While we're talking about Christmas stuff, think preacher, umm whatever his name is—"

"Preacher Burl Costello."

"Yeah, that's it. Think Preacher Burl would mind me dropping in on his Christmas Eve preaching?"

"He'd be pleased if you did," I said.

Bernard stepped out of the car, set his grocery bags on the sidewalk, and rubbed his mustache. "I'll try to be there. Will it be in the store?"

"The preacher is hoping for good weather so he can hold it on the beach," Charles said. "The storefront church may be too small to hold everyone."

"Reckon I can find it, fellas. Thanks for the lift."

We watched him walk in the direction of what I assumed to be the house he'd been staying under, and I pulled back in the line of traffic.

Elvis was singing his version of "Blue Christmas," Charles sang along with the last verse, and turned the radio's volume down. "Believe his story?"

"That Elvis'll have a blue Christmas?" Teasing Charles was one of my true pleasures.

"Bernard?"

"I'd like to. It's heartwarming, a Hallmark moment. Money left for a homeless person a few days before Christmas. But, I have trouble with it. It sounds unrealistic, and remember the other night at Cal's?"

"I need more information."

"Cal was surprised when Bernard came in and had a couple of beers."

"No surprise there," Charles said. "Didn't he say Bernard had come in several times?"

"Yes, but the other times he never had money. Cal footed the bill."

"Yeah." Charles rubbed his chin. "He seemed interested if the cops had leads on the Baby Jesus thief."

"Like he did a few minutes ago."

"Think he stole everything?"

"I hate to say it, although I wouldn't be surprised. If he did, he'd have had to have access to a vehicle or someone helping him. I can't see him walking around lugging two surfboards or the statue."

We sat in his parking lot debating Bernard's guilt, and realized while we may think he was guilty, we couldn't prove it. Charles asked if I thought we should tell Chief LaMond. I said we didn't have anything concrete to tell her.

"Let me throw out another thought," I said.

"Throw away."

"Say he's telling the truth and he did get the money with a note. Who's Tabatha?"

Charles tilted his head my direction. "I don't know any Tabathas. Do you?"

"No."

"She pays better than the tooth fairy," Charles said as he got out of the car.

I pulled out of Charles's lot and realized that while I wasn't hungry, I knew I would have as good a chance finding something to eat at the house as I would finding a Tyrannosaurus Rex in my front yard. I parked and walked across Center Street to Planet Follywood. Food might help me think.

Planet Follywood was one of the town's most popular restaurants and hosted live entertainment weekend nights, karaoke every Thursday, and a wide selection of beach grub all the time. Tonight it also featured Mayor Brian Newman at a table near the jukebox. He was alone, had a serving of fried okra in front of him, and was sipping a Corona. Brian waved me over and asked if I wanted to join him. He was mayor, father of the woman I was dating, and an all-around good guy, so I couldn't see why not. Camille, one of the waitresses, was quick to the table and asked if I wanted Cabernet. I said yes, and wondered if it was bad that I was known at most restaurants in town by my drink preference.

The mayor was a handful of years older than me, but unlike me, he had spent thirty years in the military as an MP and in Special Services. Also unlike me, he was tall, trim, confident and though he had been out for years, oozed military. He had been Folly's police chief for twenty years before becoming mayor.

"What trouble have you been getting in today?" Brian asked.

"None."

"Not how I hear it."

I gave him my most innocent look. "What have you heard?"

"Rumor is you and your sidekick Charles have been asking around about our recent rash of thefts."

On Folly, rumors spread as quickly as norovirus on a cruise ship, so I wasn't surprised he'd heard. "We're worried about Preacher Burl and how the theft of Baby Jesus has affected him and First Light."

Camille returned with my wine and asked if I wanted anything to eat. I asked Brian if he was getting anything else; he said a chef salad with grilled chicken. I refrained from saying "yuck" to his healthy choices, and ordered a patty melt.

Brian said, "Chris, I'm not encouraging you to meddle in police business." He hesitated and chuckled. "History says I couldn't stop you if I tried, but I'm as frustrated over it as I've been about anything since I've been mayor. The theft of a little wooden carving has done more to suck the life of Christmas out of this tight-knit community than anything I can imagine. Do you know how many people have come to me asking if it's been found?" I figured it was rhetorical, shook my head, and waited for him to continue. "I tell them no and they, to a person, tell me how much seeing First Light's Nativity had meant to them, and how devastated they are by the theft. The Nativity scene at the Catholic Church has always meant a lot, but something about First Light having one touches so many, especially so many who wouldn't set foot in other churches."

"I'm sure Chief LaMond is doing everything possible."

A reggae song blared from the jukebox. Brian stared at the machine, at the Christmas tree sitting beside it, and at me. "I told her to do whatever she needed to do. Forget our overtime restrictions and find the statue." He nodded and smiled. "When I was a kid, my two brothers and I got to play the three wise men in a living Nativity our Sunday school had." Brian smiled. "We got dressed up like the wise men you see in most scenes. We set up in front of our church and the two Sundays before Christmas we stood out in the cold while people came to the morning worship service. We looked silly in our fake beards and all, but I was amazed how many people stood and looked at us like they were looking at the real thing. I can't explain it. It was wonderful— spiritual, you could say."

I nodded. "That's what I've heard people say about the Nativity at the Catholic Church and First Light's scene."

"It's why the mindless theft of that small statue has torn a hole out of the heart of so many people."

Our food arrived, Stevie Wonder's version of "What Christmas Means to Me" played on the jukebox, and Brian drifted into thought. I wondered if he was reliving those memorable Sundays.

Our conversation turned to more cheerful topics and he asked if I had seen Karen lately. He seemed surprised when I said it had been a couple of weeks, but understood considering her workload had increased during the holiday season. Good tidings and great joy, mixed with excessive amounts of liquid spirits, sometimes disintegrated into tension, anger, and murder. As Karen had often said, "When bad things happen, I go to work." She'd worked a lot this holiday season.

Our food was gone as were two bottles of beer and two glasses of wine. Brian thanked me for joining him and letting him share his wise man story and bemoan the effect the loss of the statue was having on his city. I told him it was always a pleasure to talk with him and headed home.

I had turned on the light when the phone rang. "Dude be here."

"Chris be here."

"Intros be done. Message. Be having meeting of surfer crime stoppers."

"Surfers Against Spirit of Christmas Thieves."

"That's what me say."

Don't think so, I thought. "When and where?"

"Here. *Manana*. Two hours past sun disappearing."

"At the surf shop?"

He repeated, "That's what me say."

"Seven o'clock tomorrow?"

"You got it."

The phone went dead.

I stared at the phone, smiled, and figured he was inviting me to the meeting. That's what me say.

CHAPTER 19

I called Charles the next morning and extended an invitation to what I understood to be a meeting of the surfer group. He pouted and asked why I hadn't asked him last night. I said I waited until this morning to irritate him; he said I had succeeded. He then told me he'd meet me in front of the surf shop at six-thirty. I said I hoped he didn't freeze waiting for me that early.

True to his word, Charles was standing in front of the surf shop at six-thirty. Untrue to my word, I was there as well. He smiled and said he was glad I'd learned to tell time.

Dude, Finley, and Stephon were the only people in the shop. The rest of the surfer group didn't follow Charles Standard Time. Finley seemed surprised to see us, Stephon gave his normal reaction and snarled in our direction, and Dude said, "Aloha."

Dude picked up Pluto, who had been leaning against his leg, kissed the Australian Terrier on the mouth, and turned to Finley and Stephon. "They be special guests."

Finley seemed less than thrilled, but thanked us for coming while Stephon continued to snarl. The awkward moment was broken when three more members of the group arrived. I recognized Deb, and Truman, but didn't know the third person. Dude continued to hold Pluto and pointed at the newcomers with his free hand and said, "Be Deb, Truman, and Andy."

Charles and I nodded to the three. Deb smiled and said, "Uncle Saul told me you came to see him. He's a little stuffy, so I hope he was friendly. He told me he was uncomfortable talking about dealers, but did anyway since I had asked him to help. Did he help you figure out who stole Jesus?"

Truman, Andy, and Finley stopped talking and stared at Charles and me.

I said, "Afraid not."

"Boards and bling?" Dude asked.

Charles said, "Nope."

Dude tapped the floor with his florescent-green tennis shoe. "Bummer."

Four more surfers arrived, and Finley looked at his watch. "Let's start."

The newcomers ignored the rest of us and were in deep conversation about parking tickets. Finley raised his voice and repeated it was time to start. It took and everyone moved to the center of the room. The display racks hadn't been moved as much as they had been for the first meeting and we were crammed together.

Finley pushed his long, sun-bleached blond hair out of his eyes and pulled his shoulders back. "It's almost Christmas, so let's begin by singing a Christmas carol. I was thinking "Jingle Bell Rock.""

I wondered in what carol book he'd found "Jingle Bell Rock," but was impressed he was trying to honor the Christmas spirit. Finley raised his arms like a choir director, lowered them and we began singing. The group's effort was spirited, although it became clear the first seven words were the only words any of us knew in the "carol." After repeating them twice, Finley waved for us to stop. The phrase *it's the thought that counts* popped to mind.

Deb and Teddye laughed. Truman said, "Good job."

"Okay, enough," Finley said. "This is important. Christmas Day is around the corner and I wanted to get together and talk about anything new we know about the stealing. Has anybody called about the reward?" Finley looked around the room.

Dude set Pluto on the floor and said, "That be *grande* N-O."

Finley looked at Pluto who had run to Deb and whimpered for her to pick him up. She did and Finley said, "That's what I thought. We've been watching the Nativity ever since we met here. I haven't heard anything, but has anyone seen anybody suspicious, something you may not have thought important at the time?"

Andy, the surfer I hadn't seen before, said, "Don't know how important it is. Two kids keep riding by. Saw them three or four days."

"Yeah," Teddye said. "They never stopped while I was watching. I saw them ride past a few times."

"Finley," I said. "That's Jason and Samuel. They're a couple of high school kids who are concerned about the thefts. The other day, they found one of the stolen packages and turned it over to the police. They're okay."

Deb said, "The jewelry?"

"The ink cartridges."

Stephon said, "A big whoop."

Deb said, "May not have been Jesus, the boards, or the jewels, but it's better than we've done."

Finley waited for Deb to finish. "Good, it explains the kids. Anybody see anything else suspicious?"

"A bunch of old folks sitting across from the Nativity in geezer cars, Buicks and Mercurys." Truman said. "Half the time they were asleep. They couldn't catch a cold on a germ farm."

Finley shook his head. "Truman, you know they're from the churches doing the same thing we are by keeping watch over the Nativity. We should appreciate them." He turned away from

Truman. "What about you guys?" He stared at Charles and me. "You're the bad guy catchers. Who did it?"

I looked at Finley and at the others. "I wish we knew.

What I will tell you is we're not done."

Finley shook his head and looked at the group. "Anything else?"

Andy said, "Yeah, well maybe." He hesitated and looked around. "A man who lives in my building lost his job a couple of months ago. He has some strange disease and kept missing work. He didn't want anybody at work to know about his illness and didn't tell his boss what was wrong. They fired him. He's squeaking by and about to lose the apartment. I've seen him going through the trash along the street trying to find something to hock or to eat. Poor guy. He'd told me he didn't want to get any help from the groups, which help people like him. Too much pride, and—"

Stephon interrupted. "What's your point?"

Andy glared at Stephon and turned to Finley. "I ran into him yesterday. He was getting out of his rusted-out Chevy pick-up truck. He had on a new winter coat. The tag was still sewn on the sleeve, but I didn't want to embarrass him by saying anything. I said, 'Nice coat.' His face turned red, and he mumbled thanks. I noticed he had spanking new tires on his truck. They stood out like an army tank rollin' down Center Street. He saw me looking at them and said, 'You won't believe what happened.'" Andy paused.

Paused too long for Charles. "What?"

Andy said, "Now I'm reporting what he said, you understand? He went into this unbelievable story. Said he came out of his apartment the day before yesterday and there was an envelope taped to his door. Guess what he said was in it?" No one guessed, so Andy continued, "Ten, fifty-dollar bills—yep, five hundred bucks stuck on his door."

"Sure there were," Stephon said and rolled his eyes.

Finley asked, "Who were they from?"

"Claims he didn't know. Can you believe it?"

"Wow," said Truman. "It's great, since he wouldn't ask for help from anyone. It's nice somebody wanted to help. I wonder how many more people around here can't get help when they need it? I think I know who you're talking about. Isn't it—"

Andy waved his hand in Truman's face. "We shouldn't say his name."

Truman started to say something, but hesitated. "Okay."

"You think he's lying and he's the person who took the baby and the other stuff?" Deb asked.

Andy said, "I don't want to say that. I feel sorry for the man. He seems like a nice guy, but doesn't it sound fishy? Someone stuck money on his door and he doesn't know who."

Stephon said, "I think he's the thief."

I thought of Bernard's windfall and the note from Tabatha. "Was there a note with his money?"

Andy seemed surprised I had spoken. "He didn't mention one. He was all excited about the cash. Why?"

"Curious," I said. "If you would, ask him the next time you see him."

"Okay, I guess."

A couple of the other surfers started talking.

I stepped close to Finley and looked at the group. "I don't know if the man you're talking about stole the statue, or for that matter, stole anything." I pointed at Andy. "You need to tell the police, and if there was a note, please let me know." He wrote my number on his palm and said he would.

"What have the cops done so far?" Stephon grumbled. "Why do you think they'll do anything?" Charles, who had been silent, stepped beside me.

"Chris and I know Chief LaMond better than any of you know her. She's as concerned about finding the statue as you are. I'd trust her with my life and Chris is right. You need to talk to her."

Andy looked for support from his fellow surfers and turned to Charles. "Okay, but it won't do any good."

Dude took three steps and took Pluto from Deb's arms and pointed a finger at Andy. "You be seein' chieftress."

Andy nodded. "Soon," Dude said.

Andy nodded a second time.

Finley asked if there was anything else to be shared and when no one answered he asked if we wanted to end the meeting with another Christmas song.

Unlike the group's rendition of "Jingle Bell Rock,"

"No!" was shouted in perfect harmony.

Each of the surfers patted Pluto's head before heading out, most to local bars to get more in the holiday spirit. Charles and I stood on the sidewalk.

Charles looked up the steps to the door of Dude's shop. "The five hundred dollars stuck on the door sounds like another story we heard."

"Bernard's three hundred dollars under a rock."

"Yep. It's why you asked about a note."

"Both men down on their luck," I said. "Both, for whatever reason, unable or unwilling to get assistance."

"If they're telling the truth, it seems we have a secret Santa handing out big bucks."

"Secret Santa named Tabatha. I still see more questions than answers. Are Andy's neighbor and Bernard telling the truth? If they are, is there a connection between the thefts and the gifts? If so, why would someone commit crimes and give the money away?"

Charles said. "I think the person who stole the stuff is doing it. It's Robin Hood in our hood." He pulled his jacket closed. "Tell you what else I know. I'm freezing my keister off. Let's figure this out tomorrow."

CHAPTER 20

I had a hard time sleeping. I tossed, turned, and replayed the meeting in my head. Christmas Eve was two days away, and it didn't seem I was closer to honoring Burl's request to find Baby Jesus than I was the morning I had learned it was missing. What I did know was the theft of the statue wasn't a prank, and the surfer group, the church members, and the police were doing what they could to find it. Since the surfer meeting had ended, something was tickling the far reaches of my memory, something important. But what? It was tied to the surfer meeting, or something said at the meeting that reminded me of something else. The only thing that struck me as important was Andy's neighbor finding the money, if, in fact, he had. Did the neighbor have anything in common with Bernard, the alleged recipient of another gift? There was no doubt both were down on their luck, although so were many others. Is Tabatha the link?

What else did I know about the missing items? Chief LaMond assured me she was working with the police in Charleston to check the city's pawnshops to see if the jewelry showed up, but I wasn't optimistic. Years ago, Brian Newman had told me pawn shops were good about record keeping and identifying people who left items with them, but no shortage of other less-savory individuals would buy and fence items. The no-questions-asked crowd could have purchased the jewelry, and the police wouldn't have a way to trace it.

What about the statue? I thought about Charles and my conversation with Deb's uncle and the antique dealers he'd referred us to. What was it that bothered me about the last dealer we talked to? Oh yeah, Arnold at Arnold's Antique Barn, and how we'd told him we were looking for German antiques and he didn't say he didn't have any until we told him how much we wanted to spend, and how unusual it was when he asked us where we were from. When we said Folly, he rushed us out of the store. It was as if he knew what we were looking for. Granted, there was nothing in what he had said that could implicate him, but it felt off.

There was still something bothering me from the meeting in the surf shop.

Sleep must have come, because the next thing I remembered was waking up, glancing out the window, and seeing daylight. What I didn't see was an answer to what had bothered me.

I was headed to Bert's for coffee when I saw Mary Ewing leaving the store. She had a paper bag in one hand and held her two-year-old's hand with the other. Her older girl was on the other side of the young one and was holding her hand as they crossed the street and headed toward the beach. Three cars stopped for them to cross.

There were half dozen customers in the store. Three were standing at the coffee urn in back, two were fawning over a Lab near the beer coolers, and, Lisa, the clerk, was adjusting the volume on an old-fashioned boom box behind the counter. It was playing "Little Drummer Boy."

I waited for one of Bert's regulars to put sugar in his coffee, and I drew a cup. Lisa had finished with the boom box and waved at me. "Merry almost Christmas."

I smiled and thanked her. She asked if I was doing anything special for the holiday, and I said I was going to First Light's Christmas Eve service and planned to be at Cal's Christmas Day. She said she had to work Christmas Eve but was off Christmas and would try to "meander over to Cal's." She asked if Karen was coming and I said I didn't know.

"I know what you mean," Lisa said. "Seems killings are almost as common around Christmastime as sales at the mall."

I looked at the door. "Lisa, what do you know about the lady and the two kids who just left?"

"Mary, Jewel, and Joanie?"

I wasn't surprised Lisa knew their names. "Yes."

"Don't know a lot. They come in a couple of times a week. Jewel's six and Joanie's two. Mary usually buys milk and packaged food. She pays with a handful of change; counts it out like it's precious diamonds." Lisa hesitated and lowered her voice. "She doesn't always have enough. We kick in the difference. It's only a dollar or two. Figure most of the food's for the kids."

"Know where she lives?"

Lisa shook her head. "She doesn't say much, sort of shy, I think. I don't like to ask many questions. Ever once and a while, when she has a few extra dollars, she hires one of our young clerks to babysit for a few hours. Mary takes the kids to the sitter's apartment so the sitter doesn't know where they live. Why?"

"Curious. I met her with a couple of surfers at Cal's the other night."

Two more customers entered and Lisa said she'd better get to work. I thanked her, paid and grabbed my coffee. "Have a Merry

Little Christmas" was playing in the background. From the way things were going, I began to doubt I would.

Instead of going home, I zipped my jacket, pulled my Tilley down low on my head, and headed in the direction Mary had gone. The temperature was mild although the breeze off the ocean was chilling, and the sky was clear and the bright sunshine tempered the chill, but only a little.

I crossed East Arctic Avenue, looked each way, but didn't see Mary. I reached the wooden walkway that crossed over the dunes line separating the small parking area from the beach, and saw Mary sitting on the other side. A child was on each side of her, huddled close to their mother, and eating powdered mini-donuts. Mary had coffee in one hand and a plastic orange juice container in the other. She also had on what appeared to be a new, mid-length cloth coat.

I pretended to be surprised to see them and Mary looked at me like she recognized me from somewhere but didn't know where. I told her we had met in Cal's and at church. She smiled and apologized for not recognizing me, and said she had been distracted. The kids looked over their shoulder at me and smiled. Each had on new clothes.

Mary pulled one of the children closer so I could pass. I did and pointed to the oldest child's fire engine red, mud boots. "Pretty boots."

She gave a wide smile and Mary turned to her. "Jewel, thank the nice man."

"Thank you," Jewel said, much more polite than most of my friends would have been. "They're new." She stood and pirouetted. "So's my coat and dress."

"They're lovely," I said and returned her smile.

Joanie looked at her mom and raised her hand. Mary put her arm around her and said, "Joanie's boots, coat, and dress are new too." Joanie tried to pirouette like Jewel had and tripped and landed on the ramp. Jewel giggled, and fortunately, so did Joanie.

Mary pulled the girls close. "We don't live far from here, but the girls don't get to see the ocean often."

I kneeled and looked at the little girls. Powdered sugar was sprinkled on the front of their coats. "The ocean's neat, isn't it?"

Jewel answered. "It sure is. Momma said she's going to bring us here every day until Christmas and even on Christmas Day. She got us these new clothes, but said seeing the ocean is our Christmas present. She said kids everywhere could get clothes, but only special ones could see the ocean for real and not just in books or on TV."

"Your mom's a smart lady." Jewel nodded. "Me, too."

I smiled. "You sure are."

Joanie raised her hand again, and I patted her on the knee. "You are, too."

Mary slid over to the edge of the ramp. "I'm being rude. Would you like to sit?"

I wouldn't have wanted to interfere with her kids Christmas present, but was curious about where she could have gotten the money for new clothes, after what Lisa had said about Mary not having money for food.

"If you don't mind."

Jewel patted the space beside her.

A woman with two boys about the girls' ages approached us as they walked down the beach. They were following two German shepherds.

"Mom," Jewel said. "Can we pet the dogs?"

"You don't know them," Mary said. "I don't think—"

Joanie squealed, "Pleeeze."

The woman with the dogs looked over and smiled. "They're friendly."

Mary sighed, shook her head. "Okay, but don't pester the sweet lady, and be sure to thank her when you're done." Jewel and Joanie were halfway to the dogs before

Mary could caution them to be careful. "Great kids," I said.

Mary continued to watch the girls. "I'm blessed to have them."

The kids stood on each side of one of the dogs and hugged it like it was a long-lost relative.

I continued to watch the dog and the kids. "You live here long?"

She glanced over at me. "No. Just since...." She paused and looked at the pier.

"Since what?" I asked, and hoped I wasn't being too nosy.

She looked down at the sand on the step and up at me. "I had a job at a convenient store in Charleston after my husband, umm, was gone, but got laid off because of some tax trouble the owners got in. We didn't have anywhere over there to live, and I got to know some guys here and moved."

"What happened to your husband?" She again looked down at the sand.

I was afraid my Charles-like questioning had gone too far, and I didn't say anything. The German shepherds were sitting in the sand, and the girls were running around them with the boys.

The wind was picking up, and Mary whispered, "He's in prison."

"I'm sorry."

She pointed to her girls. "I'm not. He gave me Joanie, the greatest gift possible."

"She's a doll."

"Yes," Mary hesitated before saying, "My husband was selling drugs, and I didn't know a danged thing about it. I felt so stupid."

"Will he be away long?"

She glanced at the girls, and said, "He was caught in the back of a warehouse selling to an undercover cop. Instead of giving up, the idiot tried to shoot his way out." She shook her head. "He shot a police officer. Thank God it didn't kill him. I don't know when he'll ever get out. I hope he doesn't. I don't want him to see Joanie, and I don't want her to see him again— never again."

She looked back at the sand and a tear rolled down her cheek. I wanted to put my arm around her, but didn't. Laughter from the four kids and a couple of barks from the dogs were the only sounds I heard.

Mary looked up at the kids. "I'm so ashamed. I can't bear to go to a homeless shelter because the people there always want to hear what happened. I can't tell them."

"I'm sure they've heard worse, Mary. It wasn't your fault."

She looked at the girls and yelled, "Jewel, Joanie, come on back now and let the nice lady get on with her walk."

Joanie dropped her head. "Mom."

"It's fine," the lady with the dogs said. "The dogs need a rest anyway. They're okay."

I smiled at Mary. "You're outnumbered."

She wiped the tear from her cheek. "It's nice to see them happy. Doesn't happen too much. Hope her next few years aren't as rough as poor Jewel's."

I wondered how to ask what she'd meant without being pushy and regressed to what I'd learned in college psychology. "Oh."

I was afraid my rusty technique had failed until she said, "I grew up near Chicago and never finished high school." She hesitated. "Don't know why I'm telling you this; don't even know you."

"Sometimes it's easier to tell a stranger than it is to tell someone you know."

"I guess. I was in the tenth grade and started dating." She air quoted, 'the greatest guy in the world.'" She looked down at the sand. "I got pregnant and learned the second I told him he wasn't so great."

"He dumped you?"

She chuckled. "Quick as a hummingbird."

"Sorry."

"If you can believe it, that wasn't the worst of it. My parents wanted me to get rid of the baby, wanted me to get an abortion.

They insisted. I wasn't the brightest kid around, after all, I was pregnant and in the tenth grade, but I couldn't see how it was the right thing to do. I told mom I wasn't going to." She stopped and looked back at the sand.

"What happened?"

She looked up and pointed to her children. "Jewel." I patted her arm. "Perfect name."

She nodded. "They didn't kick me out of the house, but I felt unwanted. I took some of my things and the little money I had saved from babysitting and bought a bus ticket to Birmingham, Alabama."

"Why Birmingham?"

She smiled. "Have you ever been in Chicago in January?"

I shook my head.

"I figured I had to go south where it was warmer, and I didn't have enough money to get to Florida, so Birmingham was it. Found a shelter for the homeless that had a special area for kids like me. They helped me get a job at a convenient food store. Jewel was born and was the prettiest baby I'd ever seen."

I smiled. "She still is."

"Thank you. You're mighty easy to talk to."

"Sometimes it helps to talk."

"Wanna know about Joanie?"

"Only if you want to tell me."

"I met her dad in Birmingham. Vernon's his name. It was three years ago, around Christmas, in fact. He came in the store, and I thought he was the cutest guy I'd seen since I was there. He was a charmer. Kept coming in and buying chewing gum and he finally asked me out. Dumb me, I said yes. Well, to make a long story short, he proposed on our third date and we got married at the court-house two weeks later." She smiled. "I was married when I got pregnant with Joanie." Her smile faded. "I thought everything was going fine. He had a job and brought in a pretty good amount of money. Honest, Mr. Landrum, I had no idea he was getting it selling drugs."

"I believe you."

"Thank you. And then the drug bust and that's when he shot the policeman. Oh God, I was so ashamed. I had to get away and with Jewel in one hand and a child carrier with Joanie in it in the other hand, I got on another Greyhound and ended up in Charleston." She looked over at me. "So there's mystery. Hope I haven't got you all depressed about it."

I smiled and patted her arm. "All I see is a sweet young lady with two wonderful children who are spending time with their mom, playing with two big dogs, and being thrilled to have the gift of the ocean for Christmas."

She patted my hand. "I am blessed. This may be the best Christmas I've had in forever. You know what happened?"

"What?"

She pointed to her two girls. "All the new clothes, a couple more surprise gifts I'll be giving them Christmas morning, because of a gift from someone I don't know."

"Gift?"

"Two days ago there was an envelope under the door of the house…umm, the house where I'm staying. I still can't believe it, there were six, hundred dollar bills in it. At first, I thought it was a mistake, but since the house was supposed to be, umm, vacant, it had to be for me, didn't it?"

"Seems like it," I said, and thought of the money Bernard and the man in the apartment had received.

"I probably should have turned it over to the police, but what would I say? Besides, Christmas was a few days away and I wanted to take the girls to church Christmas Eve and thought how wonderful it would be if they didn't have to wear tattered clothes. Maybe us having a few days without looking poor would be good. What should I have done?"

"Do you have any idea who left it?"

She looked down at the sand and mumbled, "There was a note."

Bernard all over again, I thought. "Did it say *Merry Christmas from Tabatha*?"

She jerked her head up. "How did you know?"

I started to answer, when she said, "Did you say Tabatha?"

I nodded.

"No, it was from someone named Tiffany."

"Are you sure?"

"Yes," she said and smiled. "It reminded me of that fancy jewelry store."

Could Bernard have gotten the name wrong? Could his note have said Tiffany? If it did, it was far beyond a coincidence some of the jewelry stolen was from Tiffany and now money was being left with a note from Tiffany. Charles was right. There was a connection between the thefts and the gifts.

Mary interrupted my thoughts. "Mr. Landrum, are you okay?"

"Oh, sorry Mary. My mind was wandering. Umm, who knew where you were staying?"

"You're not going to get me in trouble, are you?"

"No."

"A few people know, I guess. People who live nearby see us coming and going. I don't think I've told anyone in town. I wanted to tell the nice folks at Bert's because they help me sometimes, but I didn't."

I remembered a light on next door to Finley's house the night Charles and I were there. Finley had said the house was a rental, and squatters occasionally found their way in. "Mary, are you staying in a house on East Eric?"

She stared at me. "Why did you say that?"

"A few nights ago I was at Finley Livers' house and—"

Mary shook her head and interrupted, "He said he wouldn't tell."

I guess that was yes. "He didn't tell me." I explained about seeing the light on and what he had said about squatters.

"It's us. Finley even gave me a ride to Wal-Mart to buy the clothes for the girls. He said we could stay at his house but he'd already rented out the upstairs. Said if the guys living there ever moved, we could have it, real cheap. He's a nice guy."

"You know you can't stay where you are long. It's a rental, and you never know when it'll be needed."

"Mr. Landrum, I know, but I don't know what to do."

"May I make a suggestion?"

"Sure."

"Preacher Burl is a good friend. He understands the bad situations people can get in, and best of all, he's not judgmental. He cares and has helped many people find housing, find jobs, and find their way through rough times. I'd suggest you talk to him, lay everything out, and trust him. He can help."

She tilted her head. "Do you think so?"

"I know so."

"Funny you say that about him. I haven't been to church for a while, umm, years, but when I heard people talking about the Christmas Eve service, something told me I should go. It's why I asked him if children were invited. I liked the way he said yes. He didn't even think about it. It's why I was so happy to get new clothes for my girls."

"He'd love to see you there tomorrow night."

The woman was calling the dogs to continue their walk. Jewel and Joanie hugged the dogs bye, and Mary hugged me.

CHAPTER 21

On the way home, I kept thinking even though the spirit of Christmas may have been sucked out of the hearts of some because of the missing statue, how Mary, despite what many would consider to be a tragic young life, was making the most of the season. She was sharing the ocean with her children and told them how lucky they were to see it firsthand. She had taken the mysterious gift and bought clothes for her children so they would look their best at church Christmas Eve. Mary was a survivor, a survivor who had valued life enough to stand up to her parents at a huge cost and had given birth to Jewel. Yes, Mary was a survivor who had stood strong when many would have given up.

I walked in the door and felt the blast of heat from the over-worked furnace and realized how fortunate I was to have my health, a roof over my head, and enough food to fill, or overfill, my stomach. I moved from room to room staring at the walls and started thinking about the money left for Mary, Bernard, and the man who lived in the apartment near Andy. I was confident the money had come from the sale of the stolen jewelry and the Baby Jesus. Mary was certain her note said the money was from Tiffany, and it wouldn't be a stretch to conclude Bernard's had as well.

Regardless how kind and generous the gifts were, I kept coming back to how they may have been the result of thefts of jewelry, surfboards, and the statue. I prayed I was wrong, although doubted it after hearing Mary. Did the recipients of the anonymous cash know about the crimes I suspect had been committed to get the money? Probably not. Did the recipients need the cash? No doubt.

I grabbed a Diet Pepsi, moved to my comfortable chair in the living room and said out loud, "Mary, Bernard, Andy's neighbor." What do they have in common? Down on their luck was a given. But so were others on Folly, as there were everywhere. Two had received a note, and I'd bet Andy's neighbor got one, but hadn't mentioned it to Andy. Did the three know each other? I wasn't certain.

It struck me that there was something else each had in common other than being needy. Bernard, according to Cal, and by his own admission, because of his quick temper, was not welcomed at the area homeless shelters. Andy's neighbor told him he had too much pride to seek help from anyone. And, Mary had said she was ashamed of what had happened to her husband, so much that she wouldn't seek help. It was tenuous, but still a connection. The phone rang before I could give it more thought.

"I've figured it out," Charles said in response to, "Hello."

I sighed. "Anything in particular?"

"Baby Jesus thief. You home?"

I said yes; he said, "Be there in ten." The line went dead.

Nine minutes later, Charles pounded on the door. He rushed past me into the house. He was rubbing his hands together. His coat was zipped up to his neck. He said, "Burrr," unzipped his coat, and threw it on the ottoman. He wore a navy sweatshirt with *UMaine* in white on the front.

"Get serious," he said and headed to the kitchen.

"I've figured it out."

I followed him as he got a Pepsi and plopped down at the kitchen table.

I sat opposite him. "Okay, who did it?"

He took a sip and leaned back in the chair. "Finley, surfer boy, Livers."

"The Finley who started the group to catch the thief?"

"Yep."

"The Finley who invited us to his house and asked us to help the surfers catch the thief?"

"The same one."

Over the years, we had become involved in murder investigations, which should have been none of our business. Through blind luck, a rare burst of skill, and stumbling on information the police were unaware of, we had solved some of the crimes. Much of our success had been because we had spent hours talking through the situation, bounced ideas, good, bad, and terrible, off each other, and somehow figured things out. It appeared we were heading down that path again.

"How do you figure?"

"Misdirection." He leaned forward. "Of everyone here, who looks the least guilty?"

"Preacher Burl, Chief LaMond, you, me, umm—"

"Finley," Charles said and nodded.

I wouldn't have put him far up on my list, but he would have been on it. "Go on."

"I was up half the night thinking about it. Finley started the surfer group so he'd look as innocent as the pope. To throw us off, he asked us to find the thief. What better way to keep us from suspecting him?"

"Preacher Burl asked me to find the person who stole the statue. By your logic, he would be as likely as Finley."

Charles shook his head. "See, that's where my all- night thinkin' paid off. Burl couldn't have done it because he was with us when the money was stolen from First Light."

"I wasn't saying Burl did it. I was pointing out that because someone asked us to help doesn't mean he's guilty."

He took another sip and tapped his forefinger on the table. "I'll give you that one. How about this: What do Bernard and Andy's neighbor have in common?" Before I could answer, he said, "Hard times," and leaned back in the chair. "Do you remember what Finley talked about two of the times we'd been with him?"

"He hoped the money collected by both Cal and Burl went to people who didn't benefit from the regular groups serving the homeless."

Charles held out both hands. "You do pay attention. And then money shows up at Bernard's sleeping bag and the neighbor's door. Chris, it's Finley. I know it."

I wasn't ready to concede he was right and remembered other surfers had said the same thing about the underserved homeless, but knew the next thing I was going to tell him would have him pulling a muscle trying to pat himself on the back and then reaching for the phone to call the police. I slipped the phone in my pocket and told him about Mary and the note. When I reached the part about her living next to Finley, I thought Charles was going to erupt.

"Wow," he said and jumped up and waved his hands in the air. "We got him. Let's call Cindy and Preacher Burl."

I motioned for him to sit. He returned to the chair and shouted another "Wow!"

"Charles, let's say you're—we're—right. What we don't have is the statue. Let's say Finley is the thief and if he doesn't still have it, he knows who he sold it to. What do you think the chances are he'll tell the police where it is?"

"None."

"I agree. I also think Finley is serious about wanting to help people who aren't served by the traditional agencies, people like

Mary, Bernard, and the other guy." I took a deep breath and couldn't believe what I was going to say next.

"We need to talk to him."

Charles stared at me, scratched his head, and stared at me some more. "Chris, if I'd said it, you'd call me a bloomin' idiot, someone with a death wish, and a bunch of other things you college-educated logical thinkers could come up with. Have we died and you came back as me?"

"If Finley took the statue, the only chance we have of getting it back is to talk to him. It's not much of a chance, but it's a chance. And, I don't have a death wish. We could call him and see if he would meet us at a public place. We could tell him we found something about the thefts and wanted him to know before we called the police. I'll offer to buy him supper."

Charles looked at his Pepsi, and at me, and shrugged. "What're you waiting for?"

Finley answered on the second ring. Music blared in the background, and I had to yell for him to hear who it was. The music stopped, and I lowered my voice and made the pitch to share information about the thefts and supper. He hesitated but agreed.

CHAPTER 22

Finley had chosen to meet us at Planet Follywood at six-thirty, and as sure as clockwork—Charles's clockwork—he and I arrived at six. There was one vacant table, the same table Mayor Newman and I had shared a few days earlier. From the jukebox, Bob Marley's distinct voice bopped through "Get Up, Stand Up."

Charles looked at the entry and at me. "Before you ask if I'm going to say, 'Hey, Finley, steal any Baby Jesus statues lately?' what's your plan to get a confession?"

"I've got an idea and still have thirty minutes to figure the rest of it out. I hope he's as concerned about the underdog as I think he is."

"Hi, guys."

I looked up, and Camille was at the table and setting a glass of Cabernet in front of me and a Bud Light beside Charles. She said, "Anything to eat?" I told her we were waiting for someone, and she said to wave when we needed her.

I took a sip and stared at the Christmas tree beside the jukebox.

The lights were much brighter and more festive than I felt. Did my plan make sense? Earlier it sounded like a good idea to talk to Finley, but now I was beginning to agree with Charles. I was a bloomin' idiot.

Charles was facing the door and cleared his throat as he nodded toward it. I looked over my shoulder and saw Finley in the entry. He looked around and spotted us. He took a step back, hesitated, appeared to take a deep breath and headed our way. I hoped we didn't look as nervous as he did.

I moved around to Charles's side of the table and pointed to the seat where I had been sitting. Finley gave a slight nod and took the seat.

Charles said, "Bad day for surfin'."

He was trying to put Finley at ease since to Charles every day was a bad day for surfing.

"You bet."

Camille was back at the table and asked if Finley wanted anything. He looked at what we were drinking and said water.

I glanced at Charles who for once was keeping his mouth shut. The ball was in my court. I turned to Finley. "We appreciate how much you've done with your surfer group to make sure nobody takes anything from the Nativity, and the collection you took at the surf shop will help the needy. It took a lot of work to organize the group."

Finley said, "Too bad it didn't work." He looked at the Christmas tree and back at me. "You said you had something about the stealing."

The Beach Boys version of "Little St. Nick" blasted from the jukebox, the savory smell of hamburgers filled the air, and it was my turn to attempt to save the spirit of Christmas for Preacher Burl, First Light Church, and all who had been hurt by the disappearance of the iconic statue.

"Yes, and I think you'll find it interesting. There might still be time to get it back," I said and received a stare from Charles and a shrug from Finley.

"Charles and I decided the only thing we were interested in was finding the statue. We don't care about the jewelry or the surf-boards. Insurance will take care of it." Charles looked at me like *we did?* "Remember the money someone left Andy's neighbor?"

Finley said, "Sure."

"I've learned someone had left money for Bernard, a homeless man, and for your friend Mary. They don't know who gave it to them. We're pretty sure we do. Have you heard about it?"

"Umm, don't think so."

Wouldn't yes or a no have been the right answer? I began the story, which sounded much better earlier than it did now.

"Do you know the guy who lives across the street and up a house from you? It's the brick one." I asked, and crossed my fingers the answer was no.

"I don't recall ever seeing anyone there. Don't know who it is."

"That makes sense," I said. "Jimmy Russell's a friend, about my age. He travels with his job; gone weeks at a time. Because he's gone so much, he has a security system that monitors the inside of his house for movement, and he has cameras inside and outside that keep watch on his property."

Thank you, Cindy, for giving me the idea about cameras from you talking the other day about someone capturing the video of someone leaving the porch after stealing the ink cartridges.

Camille returned with Finley's water. Charles and I ordered burgers and fries, and Finley said, "The same."

I took a deep breath and continued, "I don't understand how it works, but through some high-tech gadget, he can monitor the system from anywhere through his telephone. He said it records a couple of weeks of data, and he also can see what the cameras see in real time."

Finley said, "I've heard of that stuff."

Charles looked like he was afraid to break into my story since he didn't know where it was going. All I hoped was he didn't ask who Jimmy Russell was. I didn't know where I was going either, but I continued talking slower than I was thinking.

"Jimmy's been in Oklahoma all month working with a company installing a new computer system. He thought he'd be home for Christmas, but it looks like he'll be stuck there until January."

"That's too bad," Charles added. "I'll miss seeing him at Cal's."

Charles couldn't bear for me to have a friend we didn't share, even an imaginary one.

"Me too," I said to Charles, and returned to Finley. "Jimmy doesn't have family here so it won't be too bad. Anyway, it's way more than you probably want to know. The important thing is he called this morning, and after he told me he wouldn't be here Christmas, he asked what had been going on since he'd been away. I told him about the missing statue, the theft of jewelry and surf-boards, and the mysterious cash people had been receiving."

Our food arrived, and another reggae song reverberated off the walls. We each took a bite—Charles and Finley, because they were hungry, and me to stall until I figured out what to say.

I took another breath and said, "Jimmy asked a strange question. He asked if the lady with the two kids who got the money was staying in the house across from his. He said he'd seen a woman with two children coming and going. He knew the house was a rental and was surprised to see three people since there wasn't a car in the drive. Jimmy's a *live and let live* person, and said he didn't care how or why she was there. I told him it was Mary."

Finley fiddled with his fries and stared at his plate. I took a bite of the burger, and impatient Charles said, "So?"

"Here's the interesting part, Finley. Jimmy called me back later and said because of our conversation, he'd reviewed the video that had been recorded and a few days ago one of the cameras caught someone looking like he was sneaking up to Mary's back door and then running back in the direction he'd come from. Jimmy said it seemed strange and wondered if it had anything to do with her getting the money." I paused to let it sink in. "I asked him to describe the person. He said the guy was dressed in black, about your height Finley, and his head was covered with a hoodie."

Finley said, "Are you—"

I waved for him to stop, and continued, "Jimmy said the guy was running back to the house where he had come from. Funny thing Finley, it was your house."

It was my imagination, but it seemed like the world had stopped. If music was playing, I didn't hear it. If people in the crowded room were talking, I couldn't hear them. Was my bluff going to work, or was he going to laugh at me and walk out?

He looked at his burger. Charles was silent, for a change. And, my heart thumped like a bass drum.

Finley picked up his fork and pointed it at me, and started to speak. He shook his head and returned the fork to the table. Silence was deafening until he said, "Mr. Landrum, I'm not a thief. I didn't steal anything. Your friend didn't see me. He couldn't have because I never went over there."

Crap, I thought. I had begun to believe my story. I glanced at Charles, and he looked as dejected as I felt.

Then Finley said, "What if I can get the statue back?"

Charles leaned forward. "How?"

"I don't know for certain if I can, but I think I know what happened to it."

"How?" I asked.

"Are you going to turn me in to the cops?"

"Don't plan to," Charles said.

That's the truth since we didn't know any reason to—yet.

"Dude said I can trust you, so I'm taking him at his word. I honest to God didn't know anything about it until the other day. When I started the surfer group, I hoped we could catch the thief and get the Baby Jesus back to the church. I didn't know about the money for Andy's neighbor." He stopped and caught Camille's attention. "Think I need a beer." He turned back to Charles and me, lowered his voice, and said, "I saw the person take money to Mary's."

Charles interrupted, "Who?"

Finley shook his head. "Sorry, Mr. Fowler. I'm not going to tell you."

I didn't want him to stop talking. "That's okay, Finley. You said you might be able to get the statue back."

"Yeah, maybe. I didn't put two and two together until I saw, umm, the person leaving the money for Mary. I know he, or she, didn't have any to give so he, or she, had to steal the stuff. The next time I saw the person I said what I had seen and asked if he, or she, stole the Baby Jesus, the jewelry, and the other things. Then he or, never mind, I'll say he to make it easier to talk about. It don't mean it was a *he*."

I nodded. "Go on."

"He told me, yes, but if I went to the cops he'd deny it, and there wouldn't be any proof. I asked why he did it, and he said he was tired of seeing so many people in hapless straights who weren't being helped by poverty agencies. He knew agencies were doing a good job, but there were folks who for one reason or another had fallen through the cracks, the invisible ones I had talked about before."

"I remember you mentioning it in one of the meetings," I said, wanting to make him comfortable and to continue talking.

"The person who took the stuff told me he'd heard the statue was valuable. He didn't know why and confessed if he had known the story behind it, he wouldn't have taken it. He said he knew someone in Charleston who would buy it for a bunch of money, something about the person having a buyer he thought would want it. The other stuff was taken to hock. He was going to give every cent of what he got to the people he felt were in greatest need. He said he left bunches of money for people we haven't even heard about." He hesitated, glanced at Charles, and back at me. "Did you know Bernard's a war hero, has all sorts of medals, but came home from Afghanistan with a bad head injury. It knocked some of his memory out and left him with a bad temper."

I had known something was wrong but didn't know why, and it possibly explained his confusing Tiffany for Tabatha. I said, "VA would help him."

Finley shook his head. "Yeah, if he'd let them. He won't. Don't know why, but he's walked away from several VA facilities. They can't make him stay."

I said, "That's too bad."

Charles said, "So how can you get the statue back?"

"You sure you're not going to the cops?"

In twenty-four hours First Light will be holding its Christmas Eve service. Getting the statue back was more important than anything else. The thefts from the porches were another matter, one I'd deal with later.

I nodded. "Yes."

"How can you get it back?" Charles repeated.

"I'm not certain I can. A person in Charleston bought the statue, paid good money for it. He told the person who took it that the man he was going to sell it to lived out of state and was going to come to Charleston to get it in a few days. I don't know what a few days meant. He might already have it, and it's long gone."

"So it could still be in Charleston," I said. "If it is, how will you get it?"

He took a sip of beer. "I don't know."

Charles said, "Let us help."

Finley looked at the bottle and at Charles. "No. This is on me."

I didn't want to push more than we already had. "Okay, if you need anything or think of anything we can do, call me."

"Sure."

He slid his chair back, stood, and scurried out of the restaurant.

Bruce Springsteen's version of "Santa Claus is Coming to Town" filled the room and I wondered if the Baby Jesus would be coming back to town.

CHAPTER 23

Charles and I stayed in Planet Follywood and debated what to do. We could tell Cindy what we knew, or thought we knew, but we had no proof and if the police got involved, Finley's chances of getting the statue would vanish. Besides, the chief may think the three people we knew who'd received cash had been involved and could get them in trouble. I wasn't going to let that happen. Charles suggested we could follow Finley, and if he got in a tight spot, we could help. The more we talked about that idea, the worse it sounded.

We speculated who the thief was, concluded it was one of the surfers, but that only narrowed it down to a dozen or more people, and those were the people we had seen or met at the meetings. There could be others we didn't know. So, that was little help. It could also be Finley, and he made up the story to get off the hook. As much as it went against Charles's grain, we decided the best course of action was to wait and hope Finley had told us the truth and was able to get the statue back. The only good news was when

Camilla told us the temperature tomorrow was going to be warm. It may not have made the children who had hoped for a rare dusting of snow happy, but it was great news for Preacher

Burl who could hold his Christmas Eve service on the beach.

I had a hard time going to sleep. I played Finley's words over in my head. I couldn't remember everything that was said when I was around the surfers and at the meetings, but I kept thinking there were others who were concerned about people who had fallen through the social services safety net. Ryan and Truman rented the second floor from Finley so he had more contact with them than the others. Hadn't Teddye said something? I wondered why Finley had been so concerned about saying he or she. Most people would have said he, regardless of gender. Did it mean anything or was I grasping for answers?

I didn't know about the temperature, but the weather forecasters were right about Christmas Eve being cloudless. Beams of sunshine streamed through the bedroom window, and I realized I had slept a couple of hours later than usual. I also realized I was hungry, so I walked to Bert's, received a cheerful "Merry Christmas Eve," from Eric, grabbed a cup of coffee, and remembered how good the mini donuts looked that Mary's children ate. I bought a pack, and walked to the Tides Hotel where I could sit in a comfortable chair in the lobby and look at the ocean.

"Come to help us?" I turned and saw Jamie, a longtime employee of the hotel and leader of the Folly Beach Bluegrass Society. He was holding a large, clear plastic bag stuffed with ropes.

"Going to hang someone?" I said.

"Not a bad idea, but not on Christmas Eve. We're putting up a tent on the other side of the pier."

The hotel rented tents for special events although I couldn't imagine a wedding reception or any other kind of event today. "What's the event?"

"We heard Preacher Burl was having Christmas Eve service on the beach, and a few of us decided it may get cold and windy, so we pitched in and rented a tent. The hotel helped. We're putting it up now. It's terrible about the Baby Jesus; thought it would be something we could do."

I told him I'd stop by after finishing my healthy breakfast.

Jamie looked at the donuts and the powdered sugar on my shirt. "No hurry. At your age, you couldn't be much help." He chuckled and walked away.

I saw little humor in his comment, but he was right. I continued eating the donuts and wondering when, or if, I would be hearing from Finley. It wasn't ten o'clock, but I was as impatient as Charles.

It turned out to be a beautiful Christmas Eve. Reflections of the sun sparkled off the calm ocean; the temperature was in the low-sixties and several people were walking on the beach and around town in shirtsleeves. I decided not to go home because if I did, I would stare at the phone and worry about when or if Finley would call. I dropped by a couple of shops and talked with the owners about the weather, and how early they would be closing. At each store, I had to answer if there was anything new about the statue. As much as I wanted to, it was impossible to get it off my mind. I grabbed a quick lunch at the Crab Shack, walked to the small Folly River Park overlooking the river and admired the large, real, Christmas tree covered in colorful lights and ornaments as it watched over the park. It was surrounded by other decorations, which brought joy to young and old. I stared at the river, and headed back to the Folly pier. At the intersection that led to Pewter Hardware and First Light's Nativity, I saw Samuel and Jason sitting on the incline leading to the edge of the park. Their bikes were on the ground beside them, and they stared at the display.

I shook my head and walked the half block to the teens. "Merry Christmas Eve, guys."

They had watched me walking toward them, stood, and wiped the dust off the back of their jeans. Jason looked across the street at the Nativity and at me. "What's merry about it, Mr. Landrum? We failed."

"You didn't fail. You've done everything you could. You found the ink cartridges. You've asked students about the statue. And Jason, to tell you the truth, even though you got me in trouble with your mom, I'm impressed how hard you've worked to help. No, you didn't fail."

Samuel looked at Jason to see if he was going to say anything. He didn't, and Samuel turned to me. "All we wanted was to find Baby Jesus, and all we found was some stupid ink." He pointed to the manger. "Jason's right, we failed."

"You didn't find the statue, but Christmas is more than a carved piece of wood. It's a time to celebrate the birth of the real Jesus. That will happen if the statue is over there or not. It's time to think about all the good in our lives. Jason, you have a great mom," I smiled, "and she has a great son. And Samuel, I don't know your dad as well as I do Jason's mom, but from everything I know, he's a wonderful dad. Think how lucky you are."

"I guess you're sort of right," Samuel said. "But we also know how much the statue means to people."

I looked at the distraught teen. "Many of them will be at church tonight. Why don't you come and look at all the good we have and celebrate instead of the bad stuff that's happened?"

Jason looked at the ground and glanced at Samuel before saying, "Don't worry, Mr. Landrum, we'll be there. Mom'll kill me if I'm not."

Samuel giggled. "Dad will too."

"What's so funny?"

Samuel said, "Dad and Jason's mom are sort of coming to church together."

It surprised me more than him giggling. "A date?"

Samuel patted Jason's arm. "Sort of. He said they are doing it because we're friends. He said they might as well be friends too."

Jason laughed. "Ain't it a crock?"

I looked at Jason. "I think it's nice."

Jason said. "I think it's weird."

To my knowledge, Amber hadn't dated since we'd broken up. To be honest, I didn't know what to think other than I was happy for them and while I hadn't thought of them together, I had a good feeling about it.

"See you tonight," I said as they mounted their bikes and peddled away. If the rest of the teenagers growing up on Folly were half as good as those two, the island's future was in good hands.

I continued to the pier and walked about halfway to the end and looked at the large, white tent at the spot on the beach where First Light met in nice weather. Jamie and a couple of his helpers were carrying folding chairs to the tent from a trailer at the beach access point. I was touched by how the island's residents, regardless of social status, wealth, beliefs, and differences came together to help each other in the time of need. I had seen this level of community support numerous times. I also thought of the misery, demons, and helplessness Bernard must be going through, and how Mary must be having mixed thoughts about how wonderful it was to have her two girls with her, but feeling the weight of such a bleak outlook for their future. I didn't know Andy's neighbor or the other people who had received money but hoped the anonymous gifts had brought cheer and hope.

I had never been a fan of telephones, but I couldn't recall wanting one to ring more than I did at this moment. It was three o'clock, four short hours until First Light's service, and nothing from Finley. Thirty more minutes had passed before I heard the much-awaited ring. The screen showed a number I didn't recognize. I would normally have let it go to voicemail, but not today.

"Mr. Landrum, this is Finley."

I had long championed a more civil and hospitable way of answering the phone. I abandoned my crusade and blurted, "Did you get it?"

There was silence on the other end; I wondered if he had heard my question. I caught myself holding my breath.

"No."

I lowered myself on one of the benches that dotted the pier. "What happened?"

"I tried," Finley said, sounding as depressed as I felt. "Honest, I tried."

"I'm sure you did. What happened?"

"I went to the place that bought it and told the guy I was a friend of, umm, the person who took it. I made up a story and told him my friend had taken it by mistake, and the statue meant a lot to the owner. I told him I'd buy it back." Finley hesitated. "I didn't know where I'd get the money. I figured you and Charles, and maybe the preacher could help. The slimy son of a … the guy said he'd seen on television where the statue had been stolen, and he didn't think I was telling the truth. He said two old guys had come around asking about buying a wood carved statue from Germany. He said he didn't know how stupid I thought he was, or how stupid the old guys thought he was, but he knew my story was a bunch of sh —umm, crap."

"What did you say?"

"I didn't know what to say, Mr. Landrum. I didn't confess to lying to him but told him how important the Baby Jesus was to the church and even to people who don't go to church over here. I figured he wouldn't call the police after what I knew about him, but I was afraid he was going to throw me out on my ass. Anyway, he calmed down a little and said he was sorry about the missing Jesus, and he was busy and couldn't talk any longer. Busy, huh? I was the only person in his store. I didn't argue with him." Finley sighed. "What else could I have done, Mr. Landrum?"

I assured him there wasn't anything and thanked him for trying.

He said, "Sorry," and hung up.

"Me too," I said to silent air.

CHAPTER 24

The sun had set an hour and a half before I walked to the beach, head down, and feeling like I'd failed Preacher Burl. Three, duel-headed halogen lights on telescoping stands illuminated the inside of the tent. The heavy-duty work lights were in the rear of the tent, and their power cords snaked across the sand to an electric box under the pier. Solar- powered pathway lights were placed in the sand every six feet to light the way to the service.

Jamie leaned against a post at the beach access point.

He looked exhausted but was smiling. "Where'd all this come from?"

He shrugged. "Called in favors. Got everything donated. It'd take a cold-hearted person to turn down helping a church on Christmas Eve. Besides, I know a thing or two about the builder I got most of the stuff from." He chuckled. "He'd rather I don't share what I know."

Charles had been standing by the tent and came over to Jamie and me. It was a half hour before the service was to begin so we stayed with Jamie as a few other early birds arrived. Charles stared at me. I knew what he wanted, but I wasn't ready to tell him. Jamie said he had a volunteer crew from the hotel who would take everything down after the service, and he'd better check in and make sure they would be around when he needed them. I thanked him for his effort; he grinned and said he didn't do it for me, but would accept thanks anyway.

Charles leaned closer. "Okay, I was trying not to be my nosy, nervous, impatient self, being it's Christmas Eve, but we've been standing here ten minutes."

"Yes," I said.

"And I haven't pestered you about what you learned from Finley. And, you've not thought it was important enough to say anything about it."

I looked at the tent and at Charles. "Suppose I didn't want to say it. Finley talked to the man who bought the statue and offered to buy it back. He wouldn't sell. He told Finley two *old* men had been to see him, but he had known about the thefts and figured the *old* guys were trying to trick him."

"So it was one of the antique dealers. Damn."

"I heard that." We turned, and Burl was standing five feet away.

Charles took off his Tilley and bowed in Burl's direction. "Sorry, Preacher."

Burl waved the apology off. "What pray tell caused such an utterance, Brother Charles?"

Charles turned to me, and I realized Burl didn't know about Finley. This wasn't the time to get into it.

"Charles was expressing disappointment that Baby Jesus hadn't been found."

Burl frowned. "I echo his sentiment, but perhaps would have chosen another expression. As disheartening as it is, I am focusing on the positive and refuse to let whatever happened to the icon ruin such a glorious night on the eve of celebrating our Savior's birth."

Dude and Pluto were next to join us. In addition to Pluto's rhinestone covered collar and leash, he wore a red and white striped sweater. Dude wore typical Dude. Burl smiled and suggested we move to the "magnificent sanctuary provided by the good folks of Folly." We took it to mean the tent and followed him. Lottie was seated near the front as we stepped under the tent. A steady cool breeze had been coming off the ocean all afternoon, and Jamie had lowered all the sides except the back flap. Before Burl moved inside, he slipped his robe over his jacket. He moved to the portable lectern and placed his Bible and a folder on top of it.

Next to arrive was Dude's snarky employee Stephon, followed closely by Teddye, Deb, Truman, and Finley. The group looked around and mumbled something I couldn't hear. Burl was quick to reach them and gave his best pastoral smile, told them he was thrilled they were here and told them to take seats of their choice.

Others arrived in clumps. Members of other congregations appeared, I assumed to show support for First Light. Another of the surfers, Todd, arrived by himself and quickly attached himself to Truman and Finley. Samuel's dad, Jacob looked around the corner of the tent and stepped inside; Amber was at his side. I was glad their sons had told me about them coming together. They looked around and headed to the back row, left two seats vacant, and sat in the next two.

Bernard arrived next and had on his new jacket and wore a look on his face that looked like a combination of fear and confusion. I rushed to him and said, "It's good to see you."

"Thank you, sir. I almost chickened out. I'm not comfortable in crowds."

I wanted to ask if the name on the note could have been Tiffany, but figured now it didn't matter. I said, "You'll be fine. You can sit with Charles and me if you'd like."

"I might." He nodded and walked over to Finley and said something.

I spoke to George and Shelesa Brew, a couple I recognized from my gallery and knew were regulars at the Catholic Church, and they introduced me to their friends Jim and Dianne Stevens. I told them how much Preacher Burl appreciated their support, and excused myself. I then walked over to Jacob and Amber and said I was glad to see them together. Jacob blinked twice, looked at Amber, and said, "Thank you, Chris. Amber and I've shared a few meals. She's quite a lady." He patted her arm.

I smiled. "Yes she is. Where're the boys?"

Amber looked around. "They're on their way. It's irritating, they're getting more unreliable all the time." She looked at me like it was my fault and then looked at her watch.

"They're teenagers," Jacob said. "Doubt we were any better when we were their age."

Amber grinned. "You're right."

Burl tapped on the lectern—pulpit—with his Bible. "Please take thy comfortable seats provided by the good and generous folks at the Tides."

The harsh halogen lights gave Burl a deer in the headlights look. He blinked a few times before his eyes adjusted to the unflattering lighting. Even with that distraction, his smile was infectious. He began with his traditional *silence thy portable communication devices* opening and looked toward the back of the room, paused, and waved for someone to come in.

I turned and saw Mary and her girls step in the tent, and at the preacher's urging, walked to four empty seats in the next to last row. Mary was wearing her new coat and gingerly stepped through the sand in shiny shoes, which looked to be as new as the coat. She held her shoulders back, her head held high, and motioned for the girls to take the seats beside her.

Burl smiled at the latecomers. "Welcome ladies. Welcome."

At the same time, I caught someone else entering from the back. I was surprised to see Karen looking around the tent. She had called yesterday and said she didn't think she'd make it. A man was sitting beside me, but there was an empty chair on the other side of him. I asked if he would mind moving one chair over. He noticed Karen, grinned at me, and scooted to the next seat.

She took the empty seat and leaned close and whispered, "Sorry for being late. The dead don't keep good track of time."

"Thanks for coming," was all I said before Burl asked us to stand and sing "O Come, All Ye Faithful."

We stood, tried to sing, and if nothing else, sounded spirited. After our enthusiastic, although off-key effort, Burl thanked us for attending, and gave a special thanks to everyone who had helped make the service possible. He opened his folder and glanced down before continuing.

I looked around and wondered if the thief was here, and then focused on Burl.

"Tonight's not about First Light, not about me, it's about everyone. It's about faith. It's about hope. It's not about the past and whatever has been negatively tugging at our minds and bodies. We're gathered to look to the future. I know several of you are members of other congregations on our incredible island. You've been part of the dedicated group who have watched over the Nativity day and night, and have shared with me you are in attendance to show solidarity. Some of you are part of the caring surfer community who has been standing sentry at the symbol of our Lord's birth." He smiled. "Some of you do not attend church on a regular basis but feel compelled to visit a place of worship at Christmas. I say to each of you, regardless of your reason, welcome. I love you, God loves you." He squinted at the bright lights as he looked out at the assembled group. "Please stand and let's join together and blend our melodious voices into singing "The First Noel."

Once again, the group made a valiant effort to not sound like a flock of seagulls fighting over a fish. Perhaps I was in the Christmas spirit, because the singing sounded pleasant.

We finished singing, *Born is the King of Israel!* and Preacher Burl motioned for us to be seated. We did and waited for him to continue. Instead, he stared at the back of the tent, his mouth opened, but no words came out. I turned to see what he was looking at.

Samuel and Jason were at the entry. Their coats were zipped up to their neck, each had a huge smile, and they were holding a dark green blanket wrapped around something. By now, a few of the others had turned to see what had stopped the service. Jason pushed the top of the blanket to the side, and I could see a tiny head peeking through—the head of a hand carved, statue of the Baby Jesus.

Jason and Samuel's smiles were so captivating I barely heard Preacher Burl scream, "Hallelujah!" The next thing I saw was Amber and Jacob rushing to their sons. They beat Burl by a half step.

Samuel cradled the Baby Jesus in his arms and held them out to the preacher. Burl took the statue, which was still wrapped in the blanket and held it close to his chest. He whispered something to the boys; Jason said something, and Burl walked to the front of the church. The boys followed as did Amber and Jacob. There were low mumblings from some of the flock, but most of us stood and stared at the group assembled at the lectern. Burl said something to Amber and Jacob, and they moved behind their sons. The boys glanced at Burl and down at the sand. Burl motioned for us to be seated.

"Brothers and sisters," he said, his voice stronger than ever. "We have witnessed a miracle, the type of miracle that can only come from God. Please join me in silent prayer."

The only sounds that could be heard were a couple of vehicles on Arctic Avenue and the faint sounds of live music from a nearby bar.

Burl broke the silence. "Brothers Jason and Samuel have agreed to share how they came upon the miracle I am now holding to my bosom." He looked at Jason.

Jason turned to Samuel, who gave him a dirty look and said, "Thanks a lot."

Samuel started to speak to the group, hesitated and moved behind the lectern. He was five inches taller than the preacher and visible to everyone.

"Umm, hi folks." He hesitated and glanced at Burl and back at the group before him. "Hi, flock people. Preacher Burl asked us to tell how we found Baby Jesus. Well, some of you know Jason and I have been looking for the missing baby since we heard it'd been snatched." He smiled. "My friend here, Jason, got in trouble from his mom for us nosing around the island—sorry about that, Mrs. Lewis. Anyway, Mr. Landrum told us we better stop nosing around in people's trash, so we sort of did stop. We almost gave up on finding it, and we were on our way over here a little while ago when Jason said we ought to ride by the Nativity one more time. He said you surfers and church people who have been watching it would have stopped and headed to church. Isn't that right, Jason?"

Jason nodded and motioned for Samuel to continue. "Well, we sort of rode by and almost didn't see it. The Baby Jesus, the man from the Methodist Church lent the Nativity, was lying in back in the hay. And holy moly, there was another baby's head sticking out of the manger. I was so excited I nearly ran my bike into a pole before I could stop." He paused and looked at me. "I know, I know, Mr. Landrum. The bad guy could still be there and get us in trouble. We looked around all cautious like and didn't see anyone so we thought it was safe. Jason said we shouldn't be carrying a baby around on our bikes, even if it was made out of wood, so I rushed home and got this blanket while Jason stayed with Jesus." He lifted the corner of the blanket up so everyone could see it. "We came here, and that's the entire story."

Jason leaned toward Samuel and said, "The note."

Samuel reached into his jacket pocket and pulled out a small slip of paper. "Oh yeah, stuck under the baby's head was this." He held the paper in the air. "It says, *Merry Christmas*. He turned the note over and looked at the back of it and turned it back to the front. "That's all it says. Don't it beat all?"

I couldn't have said it better; differently, but not better. I looked around and saw tears in Mary's eyes, and Amber and Jacob were beaming. Preacher Burl wiped a tear from his eye, put his arms around the boys, and then took the statue and its blanket from Jason and placed it on the lectern.

Charles leaned over and said, "I suppose sometime in my many years on this earth, I have been happier, but for the life of me, I can't remember when."

Preacher Burl took a couple of deep breaths, looked at the carved statue, and motioned for us to stand. "How about singing "Away in a Manger"?" He had lost track of where he was in the service, but I doubted anyone cared. I could feel the excitement in the tent as we stood and began:

Away in a manger, no crib for a bed, The little Lord Jesus lay down His sweet head.

The stars in the bright sky looked down where He lay,

The little Lord Jesus asleep on the hay.

Some of us got several of the words right; none of us appeared to care. Pure joy filled the spaces unoccupied by the correct lyrics.

CHAPTER 25

I spent Christmas morning walking around town and enjoying the warm weather. I grabbed coffee from Bert's, received a hardy "Merry Christmas," from Eric, who was way too cheery for someone who had to work Christmas Day. I chuckled at his words, and the red Christmas hat that adorned his well-maned head. I walked to the Folly River Park, looked out at the one small boat meandering downstream, and walked over to the Nativity, the site of the crime, which had nearly stolen the spirit of Christmas from the community. No surfers or church members were looking over the empty manger. The town was silent, not quite *not a creature was stirring* quiet, but close. I smiled as I thought about the look on Preacher Burl's face when Jason and Samuel entered with the statue.

I didn't know who had taken the icon, nor who had stolen the packages or the surfboards off the porches, but I had a strong suspicion. What was I going to do about it? I couldn't prove it. If I was right, the thefts were to get money to help people who needed it the most. Admirable, but stealing was stealing. So, why was I so conflicted about what to do? Maybe it was because I had seen the look in Mary's eyes when she could do something good for her children.

Perhaps it was because I saw the glimmer of hope in Bernard's confused and distressed mind when he could buy groceries and know someone did care about him. I imagined the neighbor who had received the early, and unexpected Christmas gift as he went through a tough time, had also felt gratitude and the strength to get back on his feet. Maybe…maybe I don't know. I did know it was time to get to Cal's party.

The smell of fries met me at the door, the sounds of laughter filled the room, and the festive colors of Christmas lights twinkled from most every surface as well as from the multiple Christmas trees. It was early afternoon, and Cal's Country Christmas Celebration was in full swing. The jukebox, normally full of country classics, had been stuffed with Christmas tunes, and as unbelievable as it may have been to regulars, some of the songs weren't being performed by country artists who were either crooning for their Master or spending eternity in a much warmer climate. Harry Connick, Jr.'s version of "Jingle Bells" could be heard between bursts of laughter. Cal's Christmas day celebration had grown to be one of Folly's most popular events, especially for those who didn't have families to spend the holiday with.

Charles was the first to notice me. I almost didn't recognize him since he had abandoned his college mascot sweatshirts and had on a bright red one with a giant Santa's head on the front.

"About time you got here," he said. "Merry Christmas to you, too."

He put his arm around my shoulders. "I'll let you sugarcoat being late. It's Christmas." He looked behind me. "Where's Karen? She told me last night she'd be coming with you."

"She called this morning. Another death."

Our conversation was interrupted when Cal tapped on a vintage, baseball-sized silver microphone in the center of the tiny stage. "Let this old cowboy interrupt your celebrating for a minute."

Most of the gathered group stopped talking and turned to the stage. One group kept talking and Cal, tapped on the mike. "To paraphrase a preacher I know, please silence thy big mouths."

That got everyone's attention. Cal grinned, the twinkling lights on the crown of his Stetson matched the smile on his face. "I wanted to thank ya'll. This is the fourth year I've had this shindig, and this is the best by a Texas mile. Now some of you have asked if I'd sing a few Christmas ditties so who am I to turn down such nice requests?"

It wouldn't have taken many requests to tempt him. He took his guitar out of the case, strummed a couple of chords, and said, "I'll start with a song my good buddy, Gene Autry, made famous a few years back. Some of you may know it. It's called "Rudolph the Red-Nosed Reindeer."

Cal's *few years back* happened to be before I was born, and from the number of people in the room who started singing along with him, "Some of you may know it," was a Texas-sized understatement. Charles said he was going to spread some Christmas cheer and headed toward the bar. I looked around the room and saw many of the people who had been at the Christmas Eve service. I was surprised to see Dude's employee, Stephon. He was standing at the bar, sipping a beer, and frowning, but at least he was here. I recognized a few of the surfers I had met in the last two weeks. Teddye and Finley were huddled in discussion at one of the tables, and Roscoe, Todd, Slick Surfin' Sal, and Ryan were at the adjoining table watching Cal as he finished singing and placed his guitar back in the case.

Cal said, "Be back a little later with a couple of more of my favorite Christmas songs." He pointed his finger at me, stepped off the stage, and headed my way.

I said, "Merry Christmas. Looks like a full house."

He gave me an awkward hug and said, "Ain't it great news about the Baby Jesus coming home?"

I said it was as he reached in his back pocket. He said, "Was wondering when you'd get here. Got something for you." He pulled out a light-gray envelope and handed it to me. It was addressed *Chris and Charles.*

I shrugged and took it from him. "Where'd it come from?"

"Found it under the door when I opened up this morning."

I looked for Charles. He was talking to Mel Evans and his significant other Caldwell. I caught his eye and he said something to Mel and came over to Cal and me. I showed him the envelope and yanked it back when he tried to grab it out of my hand. I opened it and pulled out a small sheet of paper the same color as the envelope. On the paper was a neatly printed note and I read it to Charles and Cal: *Sorry I stole the stuff. Didn't mean to hurt the city or the church. You see, I had to help my forgotten friends, the invisible ones. Couldn't think of any other way to do it. Please apologize to the preacher for me. He seems like a good person. Also, say I'm sorry to the police.*

Charles glanced at the paper. "Don't suppose it's signed?"

Cal removed his Stetson and pointed it at the note. "Holy horse-radish. We've got a confession right here on Christmas Day."

Nat King Cole's version of "Frosty the Snowman" played from the jukebox and I stood silent and stared at the note.

As if on cue, Preacher Burl stepped in the door. I was surprised and pleased to see Lottie with him. They weren't walking hand in hand, but their body language said they weren't far from it. Burl saw Cal and headed our way.

"Merry Christmas, Brother Cal. Thanks for the invitation." He put his arm behind Lottie and nudged her closer to Cal. "You know my friend, Lottie, don't you?"

Cal tipped his Stetson to her. "I do. Welcome, Miss Lottie."

She smiled, thanked Cal for letting her come, and nodded to Charles and me.

"Preacher," Cal added, "I hear a herd of prayers was answered last night. Baby Jesus came home."

Burl said, "It was a Christmas miracle."

Cal looked at the note in my hand and turned to Burl. "Preacher there's something Chris wants to—"

Before Cal finished the sentence, Bernard stepped between Burl and Cal. "Please accept my apology for interrupting, Preacher Burl, sir. If I didn't say it now, I was afraid I never would."

Burl said, "That's okay. What's on your mind, Brother Bernard."

"Preacher, Mr. Landrum suggested I might be able to unload some, umm, burdens on your ears. He said you might be able to help. Do you think you could spend some time with me in the next few days? I'd appreciate it."

Burl glanced at Bernard and me. "I'd be honored, Brother Bernard. How about tomorrow morning? I'll be in our storefront sanctuary around nine."

"I'll be there, Preacher. Again, I apologize for interrupting. Merry Christmas."

Burl watched Bernard leave and turned to Cal. "You were saying."

Before Cal could mention the note, I said, "I wanted to say how wonderful I thought the service was last night."

Charles gave me a sideways glance and Cal opened his mouth and closed it. Burl thanked me and said the return of the statue made the night the best he's ever had.

Cal said, "Preacher walk up to the stage with me and help me sing a song."

"You know I'm a better preacher than a singer, but it's your party."

Cal and Burl headed to the stage and Charles said, "Why didn't you tell him about the note?'

I watched Cal and Burl on the stage and said, "It's Christmas."

Charles started to say something and I stopped him. Cal, with his duet partner, sang, *Joy to the world! The Lord is Come*.

Mary and her children were the next to arrive. She smiled when she saw me with Charles. I waved her over. "Merry Christmas, Mary," I knelt down. "Merry Christmas, Jewel and Joanie."

The girls smiled and each held up a starfish. "Look what we got for Christmas," Jewel said.

"They're lovely."

The girls smiled; Mary beamed. And Cal and Burl finished with, *And wonders of his Love*.

"Ladies," Charles said, "How about let's go get something to drink? I bet that bartender can rustle up a Coke."

Mary hugged me and followed Charles, Jewel, and Joanie to the bar. I took the opportunity to look around for someone I hadn't seen yet. Still not seeing him, I walked to the group of surfers, nodded, and received lukewarm responses.

I put my hand on Finley's back. "Finley, could I borrow you a minute?"

He looked scared but said yes. I led him to the corner of the room where there were the fewest people.

I said, "Thank you for whatever you did to get the statue back."

"Mr. Landrum, I wish I could take credit. I didn't do anything more than what I told you. It was you who figured most of it out and made me try. All I can figure is the man who bought it felt guilty and brought it back."

"Maybe," I said. "Could the person who stole it in the first place have done something to get it back?"

"Yes."

"Like I told you before, all I cared about was the church getting the statue back, so whatever happened, I'm thankful."

He sighed. "Me too, Mr. Landrum."

I looked at him for a moment and asked, "Where's Truman? He was at church last night but I don't see him here."

Finley looked down at his shoes like he'd never seen them before. I waited, listened to a verse of "Frosty the Snowman" from the jukebox, and Finley said, "Umm, Don't know. I went upstairs to his room this morning to thank…umm…to see if he wanted to come with me." He hesitated again. "He was gone. His stuff was gone."

I wasn't surprised. "That's too bad. I wanted to wish him Merry Christmas."

Finley gave me a knowing glance. "I think he's having a good one, Mr. Landrum."

Cal tapped again on the mike to get our attention. I reached in my pocket and wadded up the note and turned to the stage.

"Ya'll join in," Cal said. And the singing began:

Silent Night, Holy Night! All is calm, all is bright,

'Round yon Virgin Mother and Child Holy Infant so tender and mild

Sleep in heavenly peace, Sleep in heavenly peace.

.

DEAD CENTER

CHAPTER 1

Breakfast is the most important meal of the day, or so they say. Whoever *they* are would probably say French toast slathered with maple syrup was not their idea of what the most important meal of the day should be. *They* were not with me as I took a shortcut from the house to the Lost Dog Cafe, a path through the alley behind a couple of bars, the foul-weather sanctuary of First Light Church, and the site of my former photo gallery.

The February sun had slept in on Folly Beach, a small barrier island a handful of miles from beautiful and historic Charleston, South Carolina. Fog enveloped the island like a fluffy, gray, cotton comforter, and was so thick I imagined having to part it with my hands. It was still dark and I took advantage of the feeble illumination from three security lights on nearby poles as I made my way to the restaurant. I coveted the smell of fresh coffee greeting me as I thought about a peaceful morning enjoying breakfast while celebrating another day in my retirement paradise.

I felt a twinge of regret as I passed the back door of what used to be Landrum Gallery, my lifelong dream. As with many dreams, reality had slapped it down. I had kept the never-successful business open for eight years, but expenses exceeded income tenfold, and locking the doors had become the sane choice. Six months ago, I hauled the last framed photo to my car and felt both sadness, and also relief knowing it was something I didn't have to continue to struggle with. I had experienced my share of battles during my sixty-six years, and most I had no control over. This one I did.

I was distracted from reliving the demise of the gallery when I caught a glimmer of what at first glance looked like a large laundry bag veiled in the deep shadows of a trash dumpster between First Light and the former gallery's back doors. I hesitated and waited for my eyes to adjust to the dark and inched closer to the mass. Thoughts of a peaceful breakfast evaporated. The object on the ground was folded in a fetal position and, from appearances, dead.

I blinked to be sure I wasn't imagining the body, held my breath, and turned to see if anyone was nearby. I heard a car traveling up Center Street, Folly's main drag in front of the buildings, and a dog barking for its most important meal of the day. I didn't see anyone.

I inched closer. The body was a man in his late fifties, wearing a dark-green polo shirt, tan slacks, boat shoes, and an Atlanta Braves ball cap cocked sideways on his head, most likely knocked that way from the fall to the gravel alley. He was well-dressed for the laid-back, casual beach community and didn't look like he'd been homeless. There appeared to be a puddle of blood that had oozed from under the ball cap. I stooped and touched the left arm which was twisted at a right angle to his torso. It was cold. The man had eaten his last meal, regardless how important it may have been. His right hand had a death grip on a gun.

I stepped back and tapped 911 in my phone, something I had done more times than a former small business owner should have ever done, and told the emergency operator who I was, where I was, and why I had called. I assured her I would stay where I was, and she, in a well-modulated, professional voice, said the police had been dispatched. Folly Beach was a half-mile wide and six-miles long, and its downtown was condensed into a six block area. The combination city hall, fire, and police station was fewer than three blocks from where I was standing, so I wasn't surprised to hear the high-pitched wail of a patrol car as it left the station seconds after I'd ended the call.

The siren was followed by the distinct sound of the city's fire and rescue truck and a second patrol car coming from the other direction. I took a deep breath and lowered myself to the concrete step leading to my former business.

Officer Bishop hopped out of her patrol car and scanned the area before moving in my direction. Her hand hovered over her holstered firearm. She gave a slight nod, said, "Mr. Landrum," and continued to peruse the area before focusing on the body.

I had met the officer two years ago when she was new to the department and I was stuck in the middle of a murder investigation. She was pleasant and competent, one of the few female members of the Folly Beach police department, and half of the city's African-American cops.

"Officer Bishop," I said, and realized that although I'd known her for a while, I didn't know her first name. I also thought it was strange that that had popped in my mind as I sat, hands trembling, and traumatized by what should have been a pleasant early-morning, fog- shrouded walk.

She pointed a black Maglite at the corpse, and leaned down to touch his arm. She discovered there was nothing medics could do for him.

A second patrol car pulled in the alley behind Bishop's vehicle, an officer whose first name I could remember, rushed to the body. I had known Allen Spencer since I had arrived on Folly a decade ago. Bishop asked him to make sure there wasn't anyone in the vicinity and to secure the scene. He nodded and pointed his light at me. I shielded my eyes.

"Sorry, Mr. Landrum. Didn't recognize you. What happened?"

"I don't know, Allen. I was—"

"Officer Spencer," Bishop interrupted, "*please* make sure the area's secure."

Please was said with more force and irritation than politeness. Bishop was worried the killer might be nearby. It was possible, although with two cops here and more first responders on the way, I doubted whoever was responsible was hanging around. Officer Spencer didn't wait for the rest of my answer and began circling the area near the alley.

The city's fire and rescue vehicle was next to arrive, followed by a fire engine. Two EMTs moved to the body and Officer Bishop lowered herself onto the step beside me.

"Are you okay?"

I sighed. "Think so."

"What happened?"

I shared my morning from when I left home to finding the corpse. I left out my breakfast choice.

She pointed her flashlight at the group surrounding the body.

"Know who he is?"

"I didn't get a good look, since the only light was the one on the pole. I didn't recognize him."

Chief Cindy LaMond arrived and moved beside Officer Bishop and put her hand on the officer's shoulder. The chief was in her fifties, five-foot three inches in stature, with curly hair and a quick smile.

Bishop looked at her boss. "Morning, Chief. Mr. Landrum was telling me what he found."

Chief LaMond and I had been friends since she'd moved to the island from East Tennessee eight years ago. She'd been promoted to chief a couple of years back after the previous long-time chief, Brian Newman, had been elected mayor.

Cindy nodded at Bishop and turned to me. "Chris, don't tell me you've stumbled on another murder."

Officer Bishop stood. "If it's okay, Chief, I'll help the guys secure the scene."

LaMond nodded and Bishop left to join her colleagues. "Cindy, I was walking to breakfast, minding my own business."

She shook her head. "How do you do it, Chris?"

I knew what she meant, but still asked, "Do what?"

"Manage to stumble on every dead body within twenty miles; stumble on it before anyone else; manage to get in the middle of police investigations; manage to stay alive while surrounded by dead people and murderers." She rubbed her chin. "Oh yeah, and manage to piss off every law enforcement official from here to Timbuktu."

I smiled. "It's a gift."

Cindy, God love her, had a way of dredging up smart-aleck remarks in me while at the same time calming me even in the most serious situation. Besides, much of what she'd said was true.

She shook her head. "I suppose it's just coincidence your latest find happened to be behind the building that was your gallery for what, eight years?"

I nodded and said I was sure it had been a coincidence, and that I hadn't stepped foot in the building since shutting down the business.

Spencer moved to Cindy's side and waited for a break in our conversation. She turned to him. "What?"

Spencer glanced at me and looked at the chief. "Umm, I have something." He again looked at me.

"Want me to leave?" I asked Cindy.

"No," she said, and turned to her officer. "Go ahead Officer

Spencer. Hell, Chris'll find out soon enough. Might as well get it over with."

Spencer gave me a nod and turned to Cindy. "No ID on the body."

I wondered what was so confidential about that.

He continued, "I did find this."

He moved his hand from behind his back and showed the chief the small, matte-blue, semi-automatic pistol I'd seen in the man's hand. Spencer held it with his ballpoint pen through the trigger guard.

Cindy said, "I saw it."

"Doesn't smell like it's been fired," Spencer said.

Cindy looked at the gun, and then toward the body. "Don't suppose he shot himself in the head and cleaned the gun."

Spencer said, "Unlikely."

A colossal understatement, I thought.

"Crap," the chief said. "Don't go anywhere, Chris. Suppose I'd better call the sheriff."

Folly Beach had its own police force, although major crimes were handed to the Charleston County Sheriff's Office. Cindy had never been happy with the arrangement, but knew her department didn't have the resources to investigate serious crimes. The relationship between the two departments was cooperative, yet often strained.

Cindy walked to her unmarked SUV, leaned against the hood, and made the call. Spencer stayed with me and looked around like he was at a party, but didn't have anyone to talk to. The temperature was in the mid-forties, above average for early-February, but I was shivering and Spencer offered to let me wait in his patrol car. He didn't have to ask twice and we got into his car.

The chief returned and I rolled down my window and she said a detective would be here in a half hour. She turned her gaze to Spencer. "Bullet wound?"

Spencer nodded and amped up the patrol car's heat.

The chief rolled her eyes. "Where?"

Spencer pointed his finger at his forehead. "Dead center."

Sheriff's Office Detective Kenneth Adair stepped out of his unmarked car. He was six-foot-one, in his mid-thirties, and sported a military- style buzz cut. I had met him a year ago when he had investigated a murder and one of my friends had happened to be the prime suspect.

Adair nodded to the chief, Spencer, and me as we got out of the vehicle. He passed by us and moved to the group huddled around the corpse, so we returned to the comfort of the car. The detective looked like a high-end clothing store model in his navy blazer, light gray slacks with a sharp crease, a starched white shirt, and polished shoes. After sharing a few words with one of the EMTs and bending down to get a closer look at the deceased, Adair came over to Spencer's vehicle.

"Chief, officer, Mr. Landrum." He slipped into the back seat beside me. "Who wants to begin?"

It's satisfying to be recognized, although much of the luster is dulled when the recognition comes from a frowning police detective.

Chief LaMond twisted around from the front seat and looked at me and told Adair I had been walking to breakfast and found the body. She said there was no ID, and they found a handgun with him. She tilted her head toward Spencer who handed Adair a clear evidence bag that now held the weapon.

Adair asked Spencer to turn on the interior lights and held the bag up and inspected it like it contained a piece of fine sculpture. "Browning 1911-22," he said, more to himself than to us. "Interesting."

Cindy looked at the bag. "Why?"

"Oh," Adair said, like he hadn't meant to say *interesting* out loud. "Nothing. It's a common firearm, sold everywhere."

Nothing in that made it sound interesting. It wasn't my place to pry further.

"Anyone recognize him?" Adair asked, back on track. "No," Cindy said.

Adair turned to me and pointed to the door where Cindy and I had been sitting. "Isn't that the back of your shop?"

I hadn't seen the detective since closing the gallery. "Used to be. I closed in September."

"Oh, sorry. What's there now?"

"Used bookstore," Cindy said. "Barb's Books opened four months ago."

Adair pointed to the door on the other side of the body. "And there?"

Spencer said, "First Light Church. They hold services there when the weather's too bad on the beach."

Adair nodded. "I remember. It's been around a couple of years."

"A little more than that," Spencer said.

Adair jotted something in a small notebook. "Give me a few minutes. Don't leave."

I assumed he meant me, since I doubted either the chief or Spencer would be going anywhere.

The detective walked fifty yards down the alley and then retraced his steps and strolled behind the police and fire vehicles. He was on the phone when he returned to the car.

He ended the call and said, "Crime scene techs are on the way. Now, Mr. Landrum, let's hear your version."

It was identical to what the chief had told him. Adair jotted some notes as I recounted what I'd found.

"Why did you take the alley instead of Center Street?"

"Short cut."

"Wouldn't it have been safer along the well-lit main street?"

"I didn't think about it since I'd gone this way hundreds of times. Could do it blindfolded. In fact, with the dense fog, I felt like I was blindfolded."

"Can anyone vouch for your whereabouts before finding the body?"

I felt a knot in my stomach. "I was home."

"Alone?"

"Yes."

"You're certain you don't recognize him?"

"It was dark when I got here, but I don't think I do."

"That's it for now, Mr. Landrum. Let me have your number in case I have more questions." He jotted down my number in his book, handed me a card, and told me to call if I thought of anything else.

I was no longer hungry, but knew I needed to eat and continued my tragically-delayed walk to breakfast. This time, I took Center Street.

CHAPTER 2

The Lost Dog Cafe was a block off the main drag, within easy walking distance to anywhere near the center of town, and was my favorite breakfast spot. Fortunately for the restaurant, although not always convenient for me, I was not alone in singing the praises of the Dog. Most of the year, its dining room, with walls covered with photos of dogs of all shapes, sizes, breeds, and poses, was packed and groups gathered outside waiting for a table. The restaurant's two patios were canine hospitable, and there were often as many dogs waiting as there were children. February was not the busiest time and despite the traumatic delay, I was able to get a table.

The warm, inviting décor was complimented by a helpful, cheery wait staff. After what I had been through, a kind voice was as important as food, and I was pleased to see Amber Lewis headed my way with a mug of coffee. She was my favorite waitress, and we had been an item when I first arrived on Folly. It had been years since we had dated, yet she remained one of my best friends.

"Granola and yogurt?" she asked as she set a mug in front of me.

She knew I was as likely to order granola and yogurt as I was to ask for a chocolate-covered paper clip.

"French toast," I replied, sharper than I had intended.

Amber cocked her head, her long auburn hair tied in a ponytail flipped to the side, and her eyes narrowed. "Got up on the wrong side of the bed, did we?"

"Sorry. Bad morning."

That was all it took. She looked around, didn't see anyone demanding her attention, and slid in the other side of the booth. Amber was in her late-forties, had been on Folly for eighteen years, and had worked at the Dog since it opened fourteen years ago. The restaurant and its staff epitomized the character of the island. The Dog was also Folly's epicenter of rumors, gossip, and occasional facts, so, for obvious reasons, it was a hangout for locals as well as a destination spot for vacationers.

She gave me a few seconds to sip the coffee before saying, "Spill it?"

She hadn't meant the coffee, and I gave her the rundown on my morning walk.

She reached across the table and put her hand on mine. "You okay?"

I assured her I was getting there.

She put her finger in the air. "Hold that thought." She headed to the kitchen with my order.

I was thinking that thought wasn't something I wanted to hold when she returned and slipped her trim, well-proportioned, five-foot- five-inch frame into the booth.

"Who was it?"

She must have figured I was okay and wanted to start collecting information, although I didn't give her much to talk about when I said the man didn't look familiar.

A couple seated at a table by the window was looking around.

Amber saw them, said she needed to get to work, said my "healthy" breakfast would be up soon, and went to see what the pair needed.

I was watching Amber laughing with the diners when a woman yanked the door open and looked around. She was tall, thin, had short black hair, and was attractive in an angular sort of way. Even if the restaurant had been full, it would have been hard not to notice her attention-grabbing red leather jacket and bright-red blouse. I had seen her around town, but we had never met, so I was surprised when she headed my way.

She stopped beside the booth and looked at the seat Amber had vacated. "You're Chris Landrum?"

"I am."

"May I join you?"

Politeness and curiosity kept me from saying no, and I pointed at the open space. "You may."

She threw her jacket on the other side of the bench seat, slid into the booth, and looked around for a waitress. My first thought was she was accustomed to getting her way.

She smiled, yet her tired-looking, hazel eyes portrayed sadness. On closer inspection, I realized she was in her sixties but looked younger.

"I'm Barbara Deanelli. I own Barb's Books in a space I believe you're familiar with."

"Yes. I spent many hours there trying to make a go of it as a photo gallery. I hope you're having better luck."

She looked at me. No emotion showed. "That's what the Realtor said when he showed me the space. I think you know him. Bob Howard. He's the one who tried to tell me who you were and what you looked like."

I chuckled. "That's a scary thought."

I had known Bob since my first week on Folly. He'd helped me find a house after the one I was renting was torched with me in it. Bob had also rented me the space for the gallery. He was the antithesis of what most would expect in a realtor. His dress was slovenly at best, he was conversant in George Carlin's seven dirty words plus a few more, and he had never fallen for Shakespeare's idiom, "Discretion is the better part of valor." Despite his shortcomings, he was a good friend.

Barbara nodded. "I was beginning to wonder when he showed me the space and said, 'Yes ma'am, I'll be glad to rent this dump to you. The last person who had it went bust.'"

"Welcome to the charming side of Bob Howard. I'd hate to hear how he described me."

She stared at me. If I didn't know better, I would think she could see directly into my brain. "Howard said you were handsome back in the day when you had hair and were a few pounds lighter. Said you'd be easy to find. All I had to do was go to the Dog and look for a guy long in the tooth wearing boring clothes and drinking coffee." She grinned.

I laughed. "I'd be insulted if it hadn't come from someone who was a decade older than I am, who could seesaw with a hippo, and thinks dressing up means tying his shoestrings."

"Yes, we're talking about the same Bob Howard."

Amber made it back to our table and asked my guest what she wanted. Barbara said she wasn't hungry and coffee would do. I nodded at my mug and Amber gave me a thumbs-up.

Barbara turned to me and still showed no emotion. "I was told you found the body."

I said yes and she continued, "I'm an early riser and walked to the store from my condo to work on inventory. I didn't know what was happening in the alley until I opened the back door to get some air. The back room was way too hot." She looked at me like the temperature was my fault. "A policeman stopped me from exiting and said it was a crime scene."

"I imagine that was a shock."

"A surprise. I went out the front door and walked around to the alley to see what was going on. A young officer was standing guard at the yellow tape; his name was Spence or Spencer. He said there was a body. I asked what happened and he said he couldn't say more than that."

I was beginning to wonder where she was going with this. I waited for it to unravel at her pace.

"One of the other cops said your name, so I asked Spence, or whatever his name is, if he knew you since you'd owned the gallery. He said not only did he know you, you found the unfortunate soul. I looked around and didn't see anyone who fit your description, and asked the officer if you were still there. He said no and thought you had headed here." She tapped the table. "So there you are, and here I am."

That explained how she arrived at the Dog, but not why. "Officer Spencer was correct. I found the body. How long were you in the gall—the bookstore before you opened the back door?"

"A little while."

Vague, I thought. Before I could get a better time line, Amber returned with Barbara's coffee and my refill. The comforting aroma of bacon coming from the table beside us filled the air. It was the only comforting thing this morning.

"Sure I can't get you something to eat?" she asked.

Barbara said no without looking at the waitress.

The lady at a nearby table leaned toward us. "Bacon's mighty good. You ought to try some."

"Thank you," my table mate said, again avoiding eye contact.

Amber smiled at the bacon connoisseur, looked at Barb, and then at me. "Let me know if you need anything."

Barbara gave a sideways glance at the next table, watched Amber move to the other side of the room, and leaned toward me. "People here are friendly."

Her tone made it sound like she said they had malaria.

"Yes, they, we, are. A great place to be. Where are you from?"

She sipped her coffee and then set the mug down. "Out of state."

I waited for her to elaborate. Nothing.

"You came looking for me," I said, hoping I wouldn't have to ask why.

She spoke in a low voice. "Did you know the deceased?"

It reminded me of a question someone would ask at a funeral visitation. I repeated what I had told the police about it being dark and that I didn't recognize him.

"Could you describe him?"

I tried. She nodded and continued not to show any reaction. The conversation, if you could call it that, was getting stranger by the sip.

"From where the body was positioned, would you speculate he was trying to enter my space?"

"I have no idea." I felt like I was testifying in court.

"Anything strike you as unusual about the circumstances of his death?"

I didn't think I needed to say everything was unusual about finding a man with a bullet hole in his head and a gun in his hand. I tried to picture the scene and the body. I also began to think if I had noticed something I shouldn't tell the person sitting across from me.

"No. Why?"

She stared in her half-empty mug and I wondered if she had heard the question.

She grinned. "Nothing. Once a lawyer, always a lawyer."

She had grinned so I hoped I could keep the mood going, and smiled. "From law to owning a bookstore."

She gave an abbreviated nod. "Yes."

Progress, I thought. "How did—"

"Have to go," she interrupted and grabbed her jacket. "Thank you for talking with me, Mr. Landrum."

She hopped up and headed to the door. I watched her leave and realized it was one of the strangest conversations I'd had in the Dog — and that was saying something.

Barbara had barely exited when Amber was back at the table. Instead of saying something like, *Would you like more coffee young, handsome gentleman?* she opened with, "Was that the woman with the bookstore in your old space?"

"Yep."

"What did she want? Something about the body you found?"

"She wanted to know if I knew who it was."

"Why?"

I shook my head. "Don't know. A little strange. What do you know about her?"

"Not much. I think this is the first time I've seen her in here. Jason's been in her store a few times and described the owner as tall, skinny, and old, so that's why I figured it might be her."

Jason was Amber's seventeen-year-old son. I'd known him since he was eight and he was the reason she and I had stopped dating. A few years ago, he had been exposed to a murder victim I was standing over. I had nothing to do with the death, nevertheless Amber thought it was too dangerous for him to be close to me. She'd called me a "murder magnet." I'd regretted her decision, and occasionally wondered how things would have turned out between us if she hadn't made it.

"Old?" I said.

Amber smiled. "Figured you caught that. He's a teenager, Chris. We're all old to him."

"Know anything about her, other than being *old*?"

"Heard she's all business, not easy to make friends with. She's also a bit snobby." Amber paused. "That's from women. A couple of the guys, older than you, if you can believe that, said she was intriguing. That's their word, and they say if they weren't married, they'd be buying lots of books."

"Where did she come from?"

Amber shrugged. "First I heard about her was when someone said a truck was unloading a bunch of shelves over there. Said some woman seemed to be in charge of the unloading. Haven't you been in her store?"

It would have been impossible for me not to know a bookstore had occupied my former space, but closing the gallery had been traumatic, and I hadn't visited the new tenant. It even hurt to see *Landrum Gallery* painted-out over the door and replaced by *Barb's Books*. I knew I was being petty, but having put my time, energy, and much of my life savings into the gallery, I felt the loss much as I would have a death in the family. Barbara Deanelli hadn't moved to Folly at the time I'd shut the door, yet I still resented her for being in the space. Yes, I was being irrational, and did I already say petty?

I said. "Not yet."

"Think she'll make it?"

"I hope so. From what I've heard, bookstores, especially small, independent ones, are almost becoming extinct. Suppose more people read books than buy photos, so she might have a chance."

"Jason said she's selling used books. Takes them in trade for other books and if you're not trading for them, she sells them for a lot less than they would cost new."

"That's what I heard, and if it's the case, she has a chance."

Amber said she'd better get back to work, patted me on the arm, and said she was sorry I'd found the body. I couldn't have agreed more.

CHAPTER 3

After talking with Amber, I realized I was more curious about the bookstore than I cared to admit. It struck me as odd how the owner had sought me out for information about the body. And, after my attempt to turn my lifelong hobby into a successful business had failed, I was curious about how successful Ms. Deanelli would be. Truth be told, not often as easy as it sounded, I was ready to move past my wounded feelings and despondency over surrendering my dream.

It was time to turn to Charles Fowler, the one person on Folly Beach who knew more about books and rumors about newcomers than all other residents combined, and that was only a slight exaggeration. I had met him during my first few days on the island, and for reasons years of psychoanalysis might take to unravel, we had become friends, best friends, if two mid-sixty-year-old guys could use such a youth- centric term. We were as opposite as two people could be. I had spent my entire professional life working in the human resources department of a large health insurance company. Charles had spent his entire professional life—never mind, he had never entered the professional work force unless you count working on the line in a Ford plant in Detroit, and that was during Richard Nixon's illustrious presidency. He—Charles, not Nixon—had *retired* to Folly thirty years ago at the ripe-young age of thirty-four.

My friend had a serious aversion to W-2 forms and paychecks, yet was addicted to books. His apartment looked like a public library, minus a librarian saying "shhh" to all who entered. He had floor-to- ceiling bookshelves made of stacked concrete blocks and irregular pine boards along three walls in the living room, four walls in the bedroom, two walls in the kitchen, and not to be neglected, one wall in the bathroom. My unlikely friend swore he had read each tome with the exception of the cookbooks. My book collection could be counted on one hand, so needless to say, I wasn't a fan of reading.

His mini-library was in a small apartment building attached to the former home of the Sandbar Seafood and Steak Restaurant, and three blocks from the Dog, so I decided to walk. I could have called first, but after everything that had happened, the walk would do me good.

Charles answered the door wearing a long-sleeve, cardinal-red T-shirt with the image of a head of an eagle dominating the front. Running second to his book collection, he had a hundred or more T-shirts, most from colleges and universities, all long-sleeve. Years ago I had made a concerted effort to stop asking about them. That didn't deter him from continuing to share comments that would be fodder for *Jeopardy!*

Charles pointed to the logo on his chest. "It's Big Stuff, Winthrop University's mascot."

I pointed to my chest, "It's Chris Landrum. You receiving company?"

"You're no fun," He waved me in and pointed to a wicker rocking chair in the corner.

I knew it had a wicker seat because I had seen it on previous visits. Today it was covered with two stacks of books, paperbacks with a few hardcovers mixed in. I moved them to the floor so they could keep three larger stacks of reading material company, and sat.

Charles pointed to the books I had moved. "Barb's Books, an answer to my prayers."

When Landrum Gallery was open, Charles had been there almost as often as I had been. He appointed himself executive sales manager and, without receiving a penny of pay, had served with pride in that position. He said it had given him purpose, something to do, and a positive identity, three things that he had been lacking. He was devastated when the gallery closed, and had taken months to get over the anger and frustration. Perhaps his comment about Barb's Books signaled the end of his funk.

"You're in good spirits," I said.

"Lincoln said, 'People are only as happy as they make up their minds to be.'"

Spouting presidential quotes came in a close third to Charles's penchant for accumulating books and T-shirts.

"Jennifer Lopez said, 'I'm Glad.'"

He cocked his head. "You made that up."

I leaned back in the chair. "Look it up. Aren't you going to ask why I'm here?"

"Why are you here?"

"To tell you about my walk to breakfast."

"Hope it was more exciting than it sounds."

"It was." I shared what had happened in the alley.

He huffed. "And when were you going to tell me?"

Charles prided himself on knowing everything that happened on his island. One of the quickest ways to exasperate him was to fail to tell him something in a timely manner. To Charles, that meant within the hour, or sooner.

I thought the answer was self-explanatory. "Now."

"And you don't know who he was?"

"No." I described how he was dressed.

"Doesn't sound like he was from these parts. Think he was walking down the alley and got in a fight?"

"No idea."

Charles looked at the ceiling and back at me. "Could he have been coming out the door from First Light or the bookstore?

"No idea," I repeated. "Add this to strange." I told him about my visit from Barbara Deanelli.

Charles looked at the stack of books on the floor and back at me. "You know she's Dude's sister—half-sister."

And I didn't think I could be more shaken than I already had been this morning.

"You're kidding."

"Who'd kid about that?"

Jim "Dude" Sloan had owned the "surf shop"—yes, without any upper-case letters in the name—for thirty years, had worn hippie garb for fifty years, and had been a surfer for all but the first three of his sixty-four years. I'd known him since I arrived on Folly, although knew little about his life before that. He had seldom talked about his past; seldom talked about anything.

"Did he tell you?"

"Nope. Got it from Rocky."

"Dude's obnoxious employee?"

"Yep. Ran into him a couple of nights ago at the Surf Bar. He'd been there a couple of hours enjoying their libations. He was so lit he almost sounded human."

Rocky and Stephon were Dude's tat-covered employees who appeared to think customers were works of the devil and should be mistreated at every opportunity. Dude had told me he kept them because he didn't have to pay them much, and they had a visceral way of communicating with fellow surfers. His actual words were: "They be hangin' on the same wave." They had treated me, and most other baby-boom-generation citizens, like we weren't from the same ocean.

"Why was he talking to you?"

He held out his hands and shrugged. "What can I say. My engaging, charming personality can win over the most obnoxious surf shop employee."

There had to be more. "And?"

"Ever since Aunt M. befriended Dude's employees, Rocky's been borderline civil."

Charles's Aunt Melinda had moved to Folly three years ago. She hadn't seen him for decades and wanted to reconnect with her last living relative. She arrived full of humor, sassiness, a love for almost everyone, and terminal cancer. She had overcome many obstacles in her life, but couldn't beat the disease and passed away two years ago. During her brief time on Folly, she had achieved the impossible when she had been befriended by Dude's employees.

"What did he say about Dude and Barbara?"

"Same pop, different mom; had seen each other only a few times in the last dozen years. Barb got divorced and Dude suggested she come to Folly."

"Did you know Dude had a sister, half or otherwise?"

Charles nodded. "Sure. Known it since way back two nights ago."

That's what I thought. "Where's she from?"

"Don't know. Rocky ran out of beer and pleasantness. Gave me a farewell growl, and left."

"Don't you think it strange she came to the Dog to ask about the body?"

"Maybe, maybe not," my definitive friend said. "Not everyone is used to hearing about a dead body out their back door. You're the only person I know who has a propensity for that. It riled up her curiosity, she heard about you finding him, and voila."

"That could be all, but it didn't strike me as normal. Something seemed off."

"How do you know what Barbara's normal is?"

"Good point," I said. "Regardless, I can't put my finger on it. Just didn't sit right."

"So, how are we going to find out who the guy was?"

His question wasn't out of mere curiosity. In addition to volunteering when I had the gallery, he had taken odd jobs for off-the-books cash from local businesses, and on a more frightening note, he prided himself on being a detective. He was unlicensed and untrained, but said he'd read enough PI mysteries that he ought to be able to figure out most crimes. The scary thing was he and I had been mired in more murders than anyone who doesn't carry a badge should be. Through luck, amateur detecting, the help of a cadre of friends, more luck, being at the wrong place at the wrong time, and a touch more luck, we had solved several of them. That reinforced Charles's self- anointed private detective status.

"I'll call the chief later and see if they've identified him," I said.

"How much later?"

"Tonight."

"And then you'll call me?"

"Yes."

"Promise?"

"Yes."

CHAPTER 4

Good to my word, I called Charles, not to tell him who the victim was, but to let him know the police hadn't learned the identity. The man's fingerprints weren't in IAFIS, the FBI's national fingerprint database, and Chief LaMond said none of her officers had recognized him. The handgun found on the body was with Detective Adair who was trying to trace it through the serial number. Charles was disappointed and said I should have done more to learn who he was. I asked how, and he suggested I figure it out. He often offers similarly helpful suggestions.

A cold wave swept through the Lowcountry overnight and I couldn't think of a good reason to leave the house. February on Folly beat being anywhere in the North, although the cold, damp air could still be uncomfortable. Besides, I had to start pulling together everything needed to prepare my taxes, which next to a trip to the dentist, was my least favorite event of the year. Chief LaMond would call if she learned more. If I called Charles, he wouldn't let me off the phone until I agreed to harass the chief; something neither I nor the chief needed.

I was halfway through going over my bank statements when the phone rang. I figured it was impatient Charles. I was wrong.

"Brother Chris, this is Preacher Burl. Is this a convenient time?"

I told him it was.

"Brother Chris, might I impose upon you to meet me at First Light? I have a delicate situation to discuss and would rather not do it over the phone or at a public dining emporium. I have to wait here for a plumber, or I'd come to your house."

I was intrigued enough to agree; intrigued and would rather do anything other than taxes.

I avoided the alley and rapped on First Light's front door. Preacher Burl opened it halfway, looked to see if anyone was with me, and waved me in. Burl Ives Costello was five-foot-five, shaped like a football, and fifty years old. He and I had become acquainted the first year his nondenominational church had been open when three of his members, or members of his flock as he referred to them, had been murdered. I had originally suspected the preacher of the deaths, but ended up helping save Burl after the killer had tried to electrocute him. The preacher locked the door and pointed to one of the pews. "Thanks for coming, Brother Chris. I'm sure it was an inconvenience."

I sat and said it wasn't.

"I hope you don't find what I'm about to say silly." He paused and smiled. His blue eyes sparkled.

I returned the smile. "Preacher Burl, you'd have a hard time competing with some of my friends when it comes to silly."

Burl knew I was referring to Charles and Dude, both semi- regulars at First Light. After I closed my gallery, which had been open on Sundays, I lost my best reason—excuse—for not attending, yet I still could count on one hand the number of times I'd been to a service.

Burl nodded. "I will grant you that."

I leaned forward in the pew. "So, what is it?"

He groaned. "If I were in your shoes, I'm afraid I would think the preacher man's paranoid. You, of all people, know how much the devil has bequeathed upon my ministry."

"You've had your share of bad luck."

"Then I hope you can understand my trepidation when I learned a gentleman's life was taken from this earth mere inches from our walled sanctuary." Burl nodded toward the back door.

Inches was a stretch. "Did you know him?"

"I don't think so. Of course, I didn't see the body. The police came by my apartment this morning and showed me a photograph. The dead don't have the spirit within them and their appearance is never as remembered as when they walked this flawed earth."

No would have sufficed.

"Do you think he had something to do with First Light or one of your flock?"

Burl stood, walked to the back of the sanctuary, opened the rear door, looked out, and returned to the pew.

"Brother Chris, I am unable to detect a connection, but as you may recall, not that long ago I was oblivious to some of the events surrounding the unspeakable murders that I hold myself responsible for causing." He pointed to the corner of the room where one of his flock had been killed after being pushed from a ladder. "That's not to mention how you and your friend Brother Bob saved me— praise the Lord—from electrocution in this very room. To reiterate, I do not see any direct connection between our church and the unfortu- nate soul who met an untimely death in yon alley." He leaned toward the back door.

I understood his anxiety, although if he didn't see any connec- tion and didn't know the deceased, why had he called and requested this secretive meeting?

I wanted to scream, *why am I here?* Instead, I said, "Preacher

Burl, you and your flock went through a terrible time, and I admire you for continuing your ministry here. You've meant so much to many people."

I hesitated and waited for him to get to the reason. Charles would have chided me for hesitating and would have demanded an explanation from Burl.

"Brother Chris, that brings me to the reason I requested your presence."

Hallelujah, I thought, followed by a pensive nod.

"You have connections with local officials. You also have a reputation for aiding the civil authorities in identifying and catching those who have given their life over to the devil. Unlike many others, you are known for keeping confidences and not spreading rumors."

"Preacher Burl, I don't—"

He held his hand up. "Please allow me to finish."

I didn't see an upside to irritating a minister, and stopped. "Thank you. To be candid, the events of the past two years have me, as they say, shell-shocked. I have had difficulty sleeping; I have had trouble eating, although you can't tell it from my girth. I'm startled by the most innocuous sounds. My mother, God rest her soul, would say I was a mess." He looked toward the front window, and back at me. "Please don't share this with anyone. I've put my fate in the hands of the Lord. He hasn't seen fit to help me successfully sail these choppy seas."

I felt his discomfort and pain, but didn't know how I could help. "What would you like me to do?"

"Brother Chris, I don't feel I am doing justice to my ministry and to my flock as long as I remain in this unsettled condition. The latest death at the church's doorstep has accentuated everything negative within me. With that in mind, I am asking that you grant me one wish—and a huge one it is."

I motioned for him to continue.

"It may be paranoia, but I feel the death is related to First Light. Would you use your connections, intellect, and unique power to unravel the most amorphous clues to see if the death does, in fact, have anything to do with my ministry?"

I exhaled, looked at the floor, then at the large neon cross on the wall that was the focal point at the front of the room, and turned my attention to the suffering preacher. "Yes."

Burl closed his eyes like he was in silent prayer. After a moment, he said, "I will be forever grateful."

"I appreciate it, although I don't know what I can do. The police have resources. Detective Adair, the detective in charge, is good, and you know Chief LaMond. She'll make sure her entire department assists the detective in finding who did it."

Burl shook his head. "I don't doubt they'll perform. Additionally, I would feel better if someone without the restraints imposed upon the authorities was looking at the situation. A different perspective is welcomed."

I didn't see hope, yet also didn't want to say no. "Preacher, I'll do my best. I can't do it alone. With your permission, I'd like to discuss it with Charles and one or two others. I can assure you confidentiality will be foremost in their minds as well as mine."

"I would prefer you didn't," Burl said, "Nevertheless, I trust your judgment. Do what you must." He started to walk me to the door, hesitated, and said, "Please allow me to offer a brief prayer for your success."

I did, he did, and we shook hands. He invited me to church Sunday, and escorted me to the door. I thanked him for the invitation, but didn't commit to attending.

I stopped on the sidewalk outside the church, and thought I would have been better off working on taxes.

CHAPTER 5

Tuesday was open-mic night at Cal's Country Bar and Burgers; known as Cal's to the locals—first, because no one wanted to say the long name, and second, because no one wanted to associate burgers, good burgers, with the bar. The country music focal point on Folly was owned by Cal Ballew, a septuagenarian Texan who had spread country charm and music to most zip codes in the southern half of the country for forty-five years. His fame had come when he hit the country charts in 1962 with "End of the Story." It was followed by a string of records with song titles that had never become worthy enough even for the most arcane trivia question. Cal took over the bar five years ago after the previous owner slithered over to the wrong side of the law and was now residing at taxpayers' expense far from the beach.

Open-mic night often attracted a handful of local wannabes, a guitar-toting vacationer or two, and each week, as regular as clockwork, Heather Lee. She was in her late forties, attractive, plied her trade as a massage therapist during the day, had the singing voice of a rooster, and was Charles's girlfriend. Most Tuesdays, Cal reserved a table for Charles, Heather, and me. Extra chairs were nearby in case some of our friends happened to drop by in need of an adult beverage, moderately-entertaining entertainment, and to, as Cal would say, *sit a spell*.

Tonight we were joined by the bar's owner. The crowd was typical for a cold, damp Tuesday evening in February: sparse, a kind way of saying the place was almost empty. Three of the twelve tables were occupied, and each had a guitar case setting close to one of the occupants.

Cal leaned his lanky, six-foot-three-inch body back in his chair, pushed his sweat-stained Stetson back on his head, and turned to Heather. "Hon, guess you're gonna get to honor us with three songs. Carla Sims, one of the other gal singers, don't look like she'll make it. Said she'd be here by now. Bad for her, good for you."

Heather beamed, Charles smiled, and I suppressed a groan. Cal, who had listened to hundreds of singers during his years on the road - and, as he seldom hesitated to point out, during his appearances on the Grand Ole Opry - tried to limit Heather to two songs and late on the program so his patrons would have had time for their ears to be desensitized by alcohol. Tonight there was more time to kill than entertainers to fill. Wisdom prevailed when he said he'd save her for last. To her, it meant she was the headliner, and none of us had the guts to tell her Cal's thinking.

"So, Kentucky," Cal said. "Hear you stumbled on another dead body."

Cal had a tendency to call people by their state of origin.

Charles and I had tried to break him of the habit and had made progress. Like many reformed addicts, he backslid. "Afraid so."

"Hear you chased the killer down the alley. That must've been scary."

I smiled. The Folly rumor machine had been at work. "It would have been if it was true. I found the body. He was dead, and no killer was nearby."

"You did see him, didn't you?"

"Not a glance. Who said I did?"

"Three or four people. They said they heard it from a guy who was hanging around after the murder. Said he heard it from the cops."

"Sorry, Cal. No truth to it."

He looked disappointed. "Then I don't suppose you found a stack of hundred dollar bills beside the body?"

"Did you hear that I did?"

"Yep. The guy who said it was about four beers south of soused so I took it with a grain of mustard seed."

Charles glanced at me then turned to Cal. "Know who he was?"

Charles was still displeased I hadn't found out the identity. "Old drunk Jim."

Charles rolled his eyes. "The dead guy."

"Not a clue, Michigan."

Okay, maybe we weren't making as much progress as I thought.

Heather asked, "What'd he look like?"

I gave her the best description I had, considering I had only seen him for a few seconds, in the dark, and in a condition that didn't show his best side.

Heather pointed at a bar stool. "Sounds like that fellow in here Friday. Hung out over there. Cal, remember?"

Cal looked at the stool Heather had pointed to. "Was I tendin'?"

Bar owner talk for tending bar, I assumed, which was scary coming from Cal. After six years, he had mastered the hang of ordering beer and wine from the distributor, as long as the wine wasn't more complicated than red, white, or pink. Cal's never had any intention of owning anything other than his classic 1971 Cadillac Eldorado that had been his home and transportation. When the bar's former owner went to grayer pastures, Cal, who had been a regular entertainer in the bar, stepped in and took over. A few friends pitched in and helped him learn the basics. No one was able to teach him the fine art of grilling burgers, fries, and onion rings, although that hadn't stopped him from trying. And to our delight, he had hired a part-time "chef," as Cal called his help. Calling his part-time help *chef* was like calling Waffle House a five-star restaurant. Regardless, the food was tolerable, and after a few drinks, tasty.

"Nope," Heather said. "You were in the middle of a set covering Ernest Tubb classics."

"How long was he here?" Charles asked.

"Don't know," Heather said. "I wasn't here long. Stopped by for a beer after giving a massage to a flabby conventioneer from Alabama. The guy was here when I left. Didn't—"

Cal snapped his fingers. "Got it. Know who you mean. Unfriendly-like character. He was here for a beer on Friday, but the night before he parked himself on that stool and took up space for an hour."

"Are you sure it was the dead guy?" Charles asked.

Cal smiled. "He wasn't when he was in here."

Charles sighed. "You know what I mean."

"Hang on," Cal said. "Gotta play MC." He scooted his chair back and tore another runner in the ancient, dark brown, indoor-outdoor carpet he inherited with the bar. Years ago, I had suggested he rip it out, but he said it was disintegrating fast all by itself and it'd be gone soon enough. He had added, "It gives off that good ole, stale beer, mushed in grease aroma of a fine country bar." He'd played most of them, so I figured he knew.

Cal mumbled something under his breath about the carpet, and waved for one of the aspiring musicians to meet him on the tiny elevated stage in front of the rectangular, tile dance floor. The future star unpacked his guitar and Cal switched off the old Wurlitzer juke box, cutting short John Anderson bemoaning coming home to count his memories. Cal tapped a microphone that was old enough to have been crooned into by Hank Williams Sr. He asked the musician's name, and in his best master of ceremonies voice, announced to the uninterested assembly who the opening act was, and that open-mic night was brought to you by "Folly's foremost country music venue."

Folly's only country music venue would have also been accurate.

Those who knew more about music than I did said many country tunes were made up of three chords and the truth. The young man on stage appeared to run out of guitar-strumming ability somewhere shy of three chords. His lyrics may have been the truth, but were hard to focus on. Heather may be the headliner after all.

Cal returned to his chair and shook his head. "That ought to drive customers to drink. Where was I?"

"The dead guy," Charles said.

Cal stared at the musician strumming two chords. "Oh yeah. Remember him now because he wasn't dressed like most folks here. He didn't come to town riding two to a mule."

"Huh?" Charles asked before I could.

"The boy had dough. His clothes were casual and expensive. Can you believe his shirt was pressed?"

"Wonder you let him in," Charles said.

Cal winked at him and looked toward the stage when the singer, whose name I forgot after Cal introduced him, began Kris Kristofferson's "Help Me Make It Through the Night."

Cal shook his head, again. "And I thought Kris couldn't sing."

Charles was undeterred. "The dead guy?"

"Hold your stallion," Cal said. "Where was I?"

"His clothes," I said.

"Out of place," Cal said.

"That boy could use some strummin' lessons," Heather said to no one in particular.

I wasn't as good a detective as Charles, but knew she wasn't referring to the well-dressed stranger with the, heaven forbid, pressed shirt.

Charles ignored Heather and looked at Cal. "Anything else?"

Cal looked at the singer and back to Charles. "I was playing in honky-tonk bars before that guy's daddy was hatched." He pointed his thumb toward the stage. "Been bartending here for a few years so I can tell what a customer's thinking before the thoughts reach his mouth." Cal chuckled. "Can tell you a couple of things about the stranger. First, he got his hackles up when anyone tried to talk to him. Two tried; two failed. The second thing is, he wasn't here to pick-up some lovin'. No he wasn't."

Charles said, "How do you know?"

"You miss the first part of what I said? Trust me on that one. I know."

I knew that wasn't good enough for Charles. In a rare fit of wisdom, he didn't pursue it.

I asked, "What's your gut tell you about him?"

He started to say something, hesitated, and instead put up his hand. "I'll be back."

He headed to the stage, encouraged everyone to give a nice round of applause for *what's his name*, and asked the second vocalist to make her way to the stage. The smell of grilling burgers came from the small kitchen by the bar and reminded me I hadn't had supper. I'd only had one glass of wine, but figured I could stomach one of Cal's burgers. The next singer was in her twenties and I'd seen her perform a couple of other times before. Her voice was pleasant, and her guitar playing about fifty times better than her predecessor, although her song selection leaned more toward 1970s soft-rock than the traditional country Cal and most of his patrons preferred.

Anita, I remembered her name from her previous performances, began her set with Carly Simon's "Haven't Got Time for the Pain," and Cal headed toward the small kitchen to "rustle up a burger." Charles added, "Make it three, and a heaping serving of fries."

Charles watched Cal say a few words to the group at the next table and head to the kitchen, then turned to Heather. "Remember anything else about the dead guy?"

"He paid more attention to his beer than Cal's singing. Something heavy was on his mind."

Anita continued on her Carly Simon track with "Anticipation," and Cal returned with our burgers and fries.

"While you're up," Charles said, "how about another round?"

Cal tipped his Stetson. "Your wish is my command."

Heather put her arm around Charles and said, "Chucky, ain't this terrific? I'm the headliner."

Charles bristled when anyone called him anything other than Charles. To him, Chuck or Charlie were overgrown four letter words. No one other than Heather could get away with an occasional Chucky; other offenders would incur the wrath of Charles, and that wasn't pretty.

Charles—Chucky—kissed her on the cheek. "Terrific, sweetie, terrific."

Cal arrived with our drinks and leaned back in his chair while Anita transitioned into Jim Croce's "Time in a Bottle."

The bar's owner shook his head. "Ain't bad; ain't country."

His review appeared to be over, so I asked, "Remember anything else about the guy?"

"Had a fondness for Bud Light. That's it."

"How'd he pay?" I asked.

"Andy Jacksons."

Charles waved his hand in Cal's face. "Don't suppose you made him show a driver's license."

Cal stared at Charles. "In case his bucks bounced?"

Charles said, "Trying to figure out who he was."

"He was a loner who liked Bud Light, had a pocket full of Jacksons, and was as cold as a cast-iron commode in Alaska."

I figured we were at the bottom of the well of information about the stranger and it was time to mosey another direction. Cal was rubbing off on me.

"Cal, what do you know about the new bookstore?"

"Been there once. Checking to see if it had songbooks—nary a one." He paused and looked at the stage. Anita was sliding her guitar back in its case. He stood to return to the stage. "Don't drift off."

Since Heather was one singer closer to being in the spotlight, he couldn't get her to drift off if the building was in flames.

Cal thanked Anita for sharing her version of country, and then said, "Our next crooner's been with us a few times and is always a favorite with the gals. Make welcome Ed Robinson."

Ed smiled at the rousing round of applause he received from the middle-aged couple and another woman at his table. Someone slamming the men's restroom door at the side of the stage was the only other noise in the room.

Cal returned to the table and Ed began Conway Twitty's "Hello Darlin'."

"Bookstore," I said, trying to rechannel Cal's thinking.

"Bunch of books, no songbooks. Gal that owns it'd be a looker if she put some meat on her bones and cracked a smile. I tried to welcome her to Folly, and all she did was nod. It was cool outside that morning, but her look was as cold as a frosted frog." He shook his head. "If she wasn't Dude's sis, I'd never go back. She—"

Charles leaned toward Cal. "How'd you know she was Dude's half-sister?"

Cal leaned away from Charles. "Don't know much about fractions, but Dude told me."

"When?" I asked.

"Been a while now. Don't recall for certain, a few weeks maybe."

Charles leaned closer once again. "How come you didn't tell us?"

He was peeved because he thought he was the only one who knew about Dude's *half*-sister.

"Figured you'd already knew, being you're such a good detective and a friend of Dude." He smiled when he said detective.

"Well, umm… sure, I knew," Charles stammered. "Wondered when you found out."

I suspected Charles's feelings were more hurt because he hadn't heard it from Dude than he was Cal knew.

Heather had pushed away from the table and stared at her guitar case. She was focused on her pending performance and had no interest in our conversation.

"Did Dude say why she was here?" I asked.

"He surfed-talked about seven words that meant she'd split from a bad marriage and needed somewhere to lick her wounds. He told her Folly was a 'boss hangout' and she had moved lock, stock, and barrel of books to our fine seaside community."

Dude had never met a sentence he couldn't butcher. He didn't believe in using ten words, when one would almost do.

Charles asked, "Moved from where?"

"Dude didn't say, or if he did, I didn't understand."

Two other couples drifted in and grabbed tables. A man I hadn't seen before came in and sat at the bar. Ed had finished the late Merle Haggard's classic "Okie from Muskogee" and was introducing his wife, Gretchen, and two of his friends "out in the audience" who'd travelled "all the way" from Summerville to hear him. It was a whopping thirty-five-mile trip. Heather applauded loud enough for the rest of the table; most likely so Ed and his wife and friends would reciprocate at the end of her set. Cal headed to the new arrivals to welcome them and take their orders.

I now knew a bit more about the body and an equal amount new about Barbara. I didn't need to know more, but I was still curious.

CHAPTER 6

Heather tapped her fingers on the table, looked at her watch, and then glared at Cal who was delivering drinks to a table of recent arrivals. Ed finished his introductions and broke into "I'd Be Better Off (In a Pine Box)." Heather frowned and agreed it was where Ed should be. He was bullying into her stage time. The first two performers had exited, taking their fan base with them, leaving the crowd sparser than when we had arrived.

Cal returned from playing bartender. Heather put her hand on his arm, gave him her best stage smile, and tilted her head toward Ed. Cal nodded.

Charles said, "Who's the newcomer?" He pointed his beer bottle in the direction of the man at the bar.

"First time I've—"

Ed strummed the last notes of the Doug Stone cover, and Heather yanked Charles away from Cal. "Let Cal go to work."

It was her turn and she wasn't about to let a stage-hogging musician play another chord. Cal pushed away from the table and headed to the stage. Heather grabbed her guitar and followed.

Cal said, "Let's have a big hand for Ed."

Three people at Ed's table and the newcomer at the bar applauded.

"Now ladies and gentlemen," Cal's spine curved toward the mike, his long, gray hair poked out of the sides of his Stetson. "Let's make welcome one of our regular girl singers, the pretty and talented Miss Heather Lee."

Charles stood and applauded, while the two tables of newcomers gave a polite acknowledgment. The man at the bar looked around the room and smiled.

Heather moved to the antique mike, tipped her wide-brimmed straw hat she wore to each appearance, gave the audience an aw-shucks smile, and broke into the country classic "Crazy." In addition to making a living as a massage therapist and singing for tips, Heather claimed to talk to ghosts, was handy with a divining rod, and, as she said, could spot a demonic apparition a mile away. Her weakness as a psychic was her voice which fell far short of channeling Patsy Cline. Regardless, nothing could stop her from trying. Her endearing smile, unending enthusiasm, and overblown desire combined to make up for her lack of vocal skills.

Charles knew better than to let Heather see him doing anything other than paying rapt attention when she was performing. Cal hadn't answered his question about the man at the bar, so Charles faced the bandstand and leaned closer to Cal.

"Who is he?" Charles said out of the corner of his mouth.

I looked at the man sipping a Budweiser. I didn't see why Charles was interested other than it was someone he didn't know. The stranger looked to be in his forties, had short-cropped hair, and one of those three-day-old beards that was too short to be intentional, yet too long to have been shaved. He wore jeans and a North

Face jacket over a plaid shirt. Nothing unusual for February on Folly.

Cal said, "Don't know."

And Charles had waited all this time for that. Charles gave him a look that screamed, "Why not?"

Cal shrugged and said he had to tend to his paying customers. He headed to the bar to see if the person Charles had been so interested in needed another beer, and Charles turned his attention back to his main-squeeze who had transitioned to "I Fall to Pieces."

Cal's closing time in winter was as predictable as a puppy. Most nights, he closed as soon as the last customer left; often before eight o'clock. On open-mic nights he stayed later. Participants brought their own fans, and the quality of the performances brought out the beer in higher quantities. It was approaching ten and Cal was moving slower by the minute. He looked at his watch and wiggled his index finger at Heather. It didn't take a degree in music management to know what it meant.

Our table, one other couple, and the man at the bar remained. Heather finished "I Fall to Pieces," put her hand over her heart, and said she was going to close with "Sweet Dreams," Patsy's most popular song and the one that was released after her death.

Heather said *Patsy* like they'd been best buds. A psychic thing, I suppose.

The couple waved at Cal for their check, the man at the bar wrote on a business card, and Heather performed a passable version of the country standard.

It had been a long day and I was anxious to get home, but knew Heather, like most performers, needed all the positive reinforcement she could get once she left the stage. She finished her set, and Cal returned to the mike. "Fine job, Heather. Fine job," and then he thanked everyone for coming. He also reminded them he was open every night and he'd be performing "a set or two," Friday and Saturday.

Heather started to the table when the man at the bar waved her over. She set her guitar case beside Charles and moved to the bar. The stranger shook her hand and pointed to the adjacent stool.

Heather and the man were in deep conversation. Charles glared, Cal cleaned tables, and I yawned.

Charles continued to glare. "He better not be flirtin'."

"She can take care of herself. Perhaps he's a new fan."

"Smarmy sleazebag'd be more like it."

Charles pushed his chair back and I was afraid he was going to save his damsel in distress—whether she was in distress or not. The man patted Heather on the shoulder and headed to the exit.

Heather returned to the table with a bigger smile than she had shared with her adoring audience from the stage and waved the business card in the air in front of her. "Guess what? Guess what?"

Something told me whatever it was wasn't as good as Heather thought.

Charles, through gritted teeth, said, "What?"

"That's Kevin. He's a music agent. Holy moly, he's from Nashville."

Heather handed the card to Charles, and I looked over his shoulder as he read: *Kevin Starr, Starr Management*. That's all that was on the front of the card—no address, no phone number. Charles turned it over and stared at a handwritten phone number beginning with 615.

Heather squealed, "That's Music City."

"What'd he want?" Charles asked, not sharing a glimmer of her excitement.

She ignored his lack of enthusiasm. "Said he liked my singing. Said if I ever get to Nashville to give him a call. Hinted he'd like to represent me. Oh, Chucky, isn't it fantastic?"

"He came to hear you?" Charles said.

"No, silly goose. He's been at the Tides since Friday meeting with record execs from New York, something about them being on a retreat, recharging their batteries, or something. He said he was sick of listening to them brag on themselves and found Cal's. He's heading out in the morning. Lucky he was here and heard me. Ain't it great?"

Charles nodded. He didn't say how great he thought it was. "Have you heard of his agency?"

"No. That don't mean a bunch. I haven't heard of most of them since I've never been to Nashville. He represents some of the biggest stars out there."

"He name any?" I asked.

"Don't think so. If he did, I was too excited to remember."

"That's great, Heather," I said. Not because I thought it was, but Charles wasn't sharing in her joy. "He say anything else?"

She rubbed her chin and looked at the bar where they had been sitting. "No, I gave him my number and got his card. He said he had to leave early in the morning and needed to get back to the hotel."

Charles sat ramrod-straight. "You gave him your number?"

"Why sure, Chucky. He said he might call if he had any news I'd need to know about." She paused and put her hand over her heart. "He said there might be some paying—yep, paying—gigs he could get for me."

I wondered what news or gigs that could be. I kept my mouth closed.

Charles looked around the room and caught Cal's eye. "Mosey over a sec."

Cal flipped the bar towel over his shoulder. It knocked his Stetson sideways. "Dang. That always works when bartenders do in the movies." He straightened his hat and walked over to us. "What'cha need?"

Charles handed the card to Cal. "Ever hear of this guy or his agency?"

Cal squinted at the information. "Can't say I have. There are more agents in Nashville than turds in a zoo." He shook his head. "Smell as good too."

During Cal's years on the road, he had been exposed to numerous corrupt and sleazy promoters, managers, and agents, and had been taken advantage of by several of them. He was not a fan of anyone who made a living off performers' talents, yet had become a good judge of people and I would trust his take on Starr.

"What do you think of him?" I nodded toward where the agent had been seated.

"Nice enough. He was polite, didn't say much, no red flags. He was a lot more pleasant than that dead guy."

I didn't take it as a ringing endorsement. At least Cal didn't label him as being anything but what he claimed to be. I hoped Heather didn't get her hopes too high. I was no judge of talent, yet suspected Heather didn't have the skills to hold a paying singing job on Folly, much less in the country music capitol of the galaxy.

Charles waved the card over his head. "What's with no address? Doesn't he have an office? How's that possible for a big-time agency?"

"Got an answer for that one," Cal said. "Many Nashville agencies don't list addresses, or they only list a PO Box. If their location got out, they'd have a stream of unwanted hopefuls flitting through their doors. Everyone's a star, or thinks so."

"See Chucky, Kevin's smart. And he's gonna call."

So much for hoping she didn't get her hopes too high. Cal headed to the back room to start turning lights off, I headed home, and Charles and Heather left for their apartments walking hand in hand.

I'm usually quick to fall asleep. Not tonight. The conversation about Heather and Nashville weighed on my mind. I had known Heather for years and thought the world of her. She may have been flighty and off-kilter in most of the country, although on Folly she fit in like the candy coating on a Skittle, and often dressed as colorfully. She was the first person Charles had dated in three decades. Their needs were minimal, they would do anything for anyone, they both loved animals, and could find good in almost anyone, a trait the rest of us could learn from.

Heather lived in a small dilapidated former bed-and-breakfast and had been across the hall from Charles's Aunt Melinda during the short time she had been with us. They had become co-conspirators in trying to get Charles to propose to the singing, psyching, massage therapist. Before Melinda left to entertain God with her charm, wit, and enthusiasm, she'd convinced Charles to pop the question. He did, and at the time, had meant it. Then reality set in. He had been a lifelong bachelor, and had one serious romantic relationship in all that time. He had told me two mice had moved out of his apartment because it was too small, so there was no way within the laws of physics for Heather to share it with him, and he was as addicted to his residence with wall-to-wall books as he was to oxygen.

After weeks of painful soul searching, and an even more lengthy discussion with Heather, the engagement was called off. Their apartments were less than a block from each other and in Charles's world they "sort of" lived together. The important thing was it worked for him, and Heather had confided she enjoyed having her own "psychic and physical space," whatever that meant. The main thing it meant was their relationship thrived, which was more than could be said for many couples.

What worried me and kept me awake was how her eyes lit up and her voice quivered when she spoke of her brief encounter with Kevin Starr, the alleged agent. She had never made any secret about her ambition to become a star. I had hoped her dreams had been couched with knowledge she might not have the talent. Charles and the rest of us had politely shared her enthusiasm and attended most every performance. The reality was, besides her regular appearance at Cal's open-mic night, and an occasional appearance with the

Folly Beach Bluegrass Society that brings together bluegrass performers from the area for its regular Thursday jam session, no one else had heard her. None of us dared share our thoughts about her shortcomings. Could the agent, alleged agent, from Heather's dream destination have heard something we'd missed?

CHAPTER 7

Mr. Coffee had gurgled the last drop of its namesake into the carafe when a knock on the door jarred me out of my half-awake state. I wet my hands in the sink, pushed my mostly-gray, receding hair back in the same direction, and went to see who had the nerve to pester me this time of day.

Dude and Pluto stood grinning on the screened-in porch. The last time they had showed up at my door was in the middle of a thunderstorm and they'd looked like they'd stepped out of the wash cycle at the Laundromat. Today the sky was clear, the temperature cool, and they looked human—human and canine. Dude's 1970 Chevrolet El Camino was parked crooked in the drive.

"You be here?" Dude asked with a straight face. Pluto continued to grin.

Dude was in his typical winter garb of a tie-dyed shirt, a multi-colored jacket that looked like it had spent decades living in a cardboard box under a bridge, faded orange slacks, and bright-white Nike tennis shoes. Pluto, a fifteen-pound Australian terrier, was dressed in a rhinestone-covered, fire-engine red collar. Dude and Pluto looked a lot alike, although there was a five-foot height discrepancy.

I didn't think I needed to answer and waved them in. Dude nodded at Pluto. "Water?"

I pointed at Dude. "Coffee?"

"Tea?"

"No."

"Coffee okeydokey."

Dude and Pluto followed me to the kitchen and two minutes later Pluto was lapping his drink of choice, and Dude was sipping his second choice.

"What brings you out this chilly morning?" I looked at Dude, since I didn't expect Pluto to answer.

"To say howdy."

There's a first for everything, although Dude showing up didn't strike me as a *howdy* visit. "I'm glad you did," I waited for him to boogie nearer to the real reason.

"Howdy done," he said and looked at his look-alike canine. "Pluto be worried. Me, too."

"About?"

"One half sis."

"Barbara?"

"Affirmente."

I didn't know if it was Dude-speak or a foreign language, and without Charles, my Dude-speak translator, I was on my own. I took it as yes.

"Why worried?"

Dude looked at the Mr. Coffee. "History lesson be comin'."

I took the hint and refilled his mug while he lifted Pluto and set him on his lap. Pluto rested his chin on the table, and I nodded for Dude to continue.

"Dudester entered world in Altoona, P A. Chug-chug town

named after Allatoona, an injun. Most peeps think named for Latin word altus, meaning high. Most be wrong."

All many of us had known about Dude's past was he arrived at Folly about a hundred years ago. I will now be able to tell Charles that, despite rumors, Dude hadn't immigrated from another planet.

"Interesting."

What else could I have said?

"Pop worked for Pennsy—that be Pennsylvania Railroad to those not from P A. Dudester hatched for twenty-four full-moons when mom died birthing a bro. Boss snowstorm, hospital slick road far away." He hesitated and looked in his mug.

"I'm sorry. Was the baby okay?"

He shook his head. "Never saw sunrise." I didn't repeat sorry. I shook my head.

Pluto licked Dude's hand.

"Pop rehitched. New momster birthed Barbara when I aged thirty-six full-moons."

After what I knew about Dude, and what little I had observed about Barbara, I suspected I knew the answer. yet asked anyway. "Were you close?"

"Close as Saturn to Jupiter."

Next to surfing and butchering sentences, astronomy was Dude's favorite hobby. My knowledge of the science was that there were a bunch of planets, stars, and other stuff up there, but took a leap and guessed Saturn and Jupiter weren't in the same hood. I motioned for him to continue. Pluto continued to lick his hand.

"Childhood, she go right, I go left. She be tall, I be Dude. She be pretty, I be Dude."

I was beginning to be glad Charles wasn't here. Otherwise he would have had to know how many pets they had, their names, breeds, and eating habits, who Dude's friends were, who Barbara dated, what posters were on their bedroom walls, what books they read. That would have been for starters.

"After childhood?"

"Me moved to Pittsburgh and hired by dumb dumbs at US Steel. Me took gig and sweated in steel mill too many full moons." He waved his hand over his head. "Got fed up to here and skedaddled to Laguna Beach, Cee A. Surfin' be more fun than steel-millin'."

This was the longest I'd heard Dude talk and didn't want to interrupt, but wished he would get to why he was worried about his fractional sister.

I said, "California to South Carolina?"

Dude pointed to my back door and then toward the front door. "Got tired of seeing sunset over ocean. Thought sunrise over boss waves be cool. Packed two bourbon boxes of stuff in Chevy Nova — that be before bought luxury wheels drivin' now—then stomped on gas, and skidded to a halt here day Sonny Bono elected mayor of Palm Springs, C A." He nodded. "You be knowin' rest."

I didn't know when Sonny had been elected mayor, but did remember hearing that Dude had bought the surf shop in 1988. That I knew, and still had no idea why he was worried about Barbara.

"What about Barbara?" I hoped to move the story along before another full moon passed.

Dude took a sip and set Pluto on the floor. "Half-sis be smarter than half-bro. Barb colleged at Penn State and became lawyer from Penn State Law. Got sheepskin and hubby named Karl, with a K. Both got low-pay, long-hours job at big law house in Harrisburg." He stopped and looked around. "Any eatins?"

Silly me, how could I have forgotten to offer my uninvited guests a full breakfast.

"Cereal, no milk. Cheetos. Maybe a stale bagel." Dude smiled. "Cheetos boss."

As unlikely as it sounded, he seemed serious so I grabbed a cereal bowl and filled it with the non-Breakfast of Champions and placed it between us on the table.

Dude grabbed two Cheetos, or as Frito-Lay described them,

"playfully mischievous cheesy crunch that add a little lighten-up moment to any day." Yes, I looked it up; remember, I'm on Folly. He offered Pluto one, but the offer was rebuffed. Pluto didn't need his day lightened.

Dude shrugged and stuffed two morsels in his mouth. I ate one and waited for the history lesson to continue.

Dude asked, "Where be in story?"

"Barb and Karl with a K working for a large law firm."

"They dumped *grande* law store, opened legal lobby shop. Two biggest hirers in H-burg be state of P A, and feds. B and K made tons of lucre sellin' large corporation BS to law writers. Me visited couple of times. Karl be slimy, said if he ever wanted to escape world, would move to Folly. Said he told all his *amigos* about here. Me be thinkin' yuck. No way Jose-Karl."

Was it possible the story was getting closer to current history? If not, Dude would next be asking what's for lunch and I'd have to say he's looking at it. He then moved the story along.

"Karl then thrown into same wave with Dick Nixon, Spiro Agnew, and innocent O. J.'s lawyer, Beetle Bailey."

"F. Lee Bailey."

"That's what me say. Pay attention."

I rolled my eyes and motioned for him to continue.

He shook his head. "Karl be disbarred."

"What happened?"

"State of P A. frowns on lobby guys giving fishing boats to state employees. Go figure."

"Was Barbara involved?"

"No proof. Guilt by wedding ring."

"What happened?"

"D-I-V-O-R-C-E. Crookster hubby wrangled a no-pokey-time sentence and moved to New Jersey. He now be scribing legal briefs and counting sixty full moons till can beg to get back in the P A. bar." He stuffed another Cheeto in his mouth.

"And Barbara?"

"He, she had major blowout. Accused her of taking his money. Decided law not her cup of oolong tea, and called Dudester. Can you believe, Barbster asking Dudester for advice? Hit me like salami."

"Tsunami?"

"What me said."

I nodded and didn't tell him it stretched the limits of my imagination as well. Instead, I asked what he told her.

"Said Folly favorite hangout of Sun God; said judging others frowned on by Folly-folks; said snow be as rare as clocks in Vegas; said good place to hide, especially from history."

"And?"

"She said last reason be boss and blah, blah, blah. Here she be: Barb and Barb's Books."

I knew we must be closer, but I still didn't know what Dude was fearful of. "Now what are you and Pluto afraid about?"

"Karl with a K."

"Why?"

Dude lifted Pluto up again, and said, "Barb's no big jabberer. She, me never dialogued much sproutin' up." He stopped and waved his hand around the room. "She got to Dude-land and say not much. Dude know she be fearing something."

"Why?"

"Half-bro intuition. She not say afraid, but that Karl being wantin' moola back, said get it one way or another. Me be fearing another." He kissed Pluto on the head and looked at the empty Cheeto bowl. "Me know she fearin' him. Don't know her good, but know she no fear fast. Chrisster, me be afraid for half-sis."

The thought flashed through my head that the man murdered outside her door could have something to do with her situation. I still wondered why Dude was here.

"Why tell me?"

"Pluto and me trust you." He pointed his forefinger at Pluto, and then at his chest. "You helped before. You be one friend I can tell puerile things to and not be cackled at. Maybe half-sis will talk to you."

He lost me at puerile.

"What do you want me to do?"

"Bod found behind half-sis's door." He held out his left hand, palm up. "Omen." He then held out his other hand. "Or related? She be in danger." He wiggled his left hand. "Or Dude's imagination gone willy-nilly?" He wiggled his right hand. "You figure it out."

"Dude, I don't—"

He waved both hands in the air, almost knocking Pluto off his lap in the process. "Whoa. Trula say copsters know nothing. Need help."

"Trula?"

"Coptress Bishop. Like faux-sugar except she be like brown sugar and older than faux-sweet."

It was interesting that Dude knew Officer Bishops first name, even though Truvia was the sugar substitute and not Trula. Regardless, he knew more than I did about the mysterious officer.

I frowned. "Did Officer Bishop—Trula—say they needed help?"

"Not same words. Hinted be clueless." He nodded. "You figure it out."

I was trying to figure out how and why I should figure it out when Dude said, "Gotta skedaddle to shop. One of clerksters won lotto and got handful of Benjys. Bought big-buck board, took day off, and surfin'. Clerkster Two need Dudester."

I hadn't heard anything about it. "Won the lottery?"

Dude shook his head. "Not zillion dollar lotto. Few hundred buckeroos."

"Oh," I said, as Dude and Pluto headed out.

First Burl and now Dude. Both friends, both asking the impossible, both asking me to do something I was unprepared to do. What now?

CHAPTER 8

After my American Heart Association disapproved breakfast, and a headache caused by hunger and Dude's visit, I headed to the Lost Dog Cafe for a substantial lunch. It was a little after the traditional lunch rush and two tables were vacant and another had a single occupant, Charles. He wasn't hard to spot. He wore a long-sleeve T-shirt with a large *C* on the front with an orange camel stepping through it.

I shook my head and slid in the other side of the booth. He had a good start on a quesadilla, and his ever-present cane was on the seat beside him, along with a stack of paperback books. A discussion about his shirt would do nothing to sooth my headache. I was saved when Amber appeared carrying a Ball jar of water, and asked if I was ready to order. I resisted asking for a dozen ibuprofen and ordered a chicken salad croissant.

Amber patted me on the shoulder. "Almost healthy."

"I'll get over it."

She chuckled and headed to the kitchen.

Charles looked up from his food. "You look like someone stepped on your pet pelican."

I translated it to mean he didn't think I looked good. "Got a headache and, I've been talking to Dude."

"Redundant."

I smiled. "True."

"What were you doing at the surf shop?"

"Wasn't. He came to the house."

Charles set his fork down, wiped a crumb off his straggly face, and stared at me. He knew a home visit by Dude was as common as a submarine surfacing at the Folly pier. "Let's hear it."

I shared Dude's concerns and that he wanted me to look into it.

Charles, the wannabe detective, perked up.

"Hard to believe, but Dude could be right."

"Why?"

"I've been in Barb's several times. Don't suppose that's a surprise."

"Hardly, besides I already knew it." Book collectors of a feather flock together.

"She doesn't know much about books. I thought it was weird for someone with a bookstore. Anyway, I traded her some of mine for some I didn't have. Two for one. It beat having to pay real money."

I was shocked that she had books Charles didn't have, and that he would trade away any of his collection. I still didn't hear anything to reinforce Dude's concern.

"Why do you think Dude's right?"

"Barb's not a big talker, not a big smiler either. Took a whole passel of Charles's charm to get much out of her. Of course, I did."

"What'd you learn?"

"Did you know she's a lawyer?"

"She'd mentioned it."

He huffed. "You didn't think it was important enough to tell me?"

"Nope."

He huffed again. "Anyway, she's articulate once she starts talk-ing. No doubt she and Dude got their talking skills from different mothers." He glanced at his lunch. "She came here to get away from her ex and for a new start on life. She said she'd talked to Dude four or five times in the past twelve years before he'd encouraged her to come here. I asked her if she was going to open a law business on Folly and she said no. She was kaput with the law. She said it better than that. It's what she meant. I innocently asked if she ever heard from her ex."

It was unlikely his question was innocent.

"The second I said it, she tensed up like a fiddle string. Our pleasant conversation, that was just getting started, skidded into a brick wall." He clapped his hands. "Smack!"

Amber arrived with my almost healthy lunch and asked if we needed anything else. We said no and she moved to the next table. I took a bite and nodded for Charles to continue.

"Was Pluto with him?" asked Charles, the master of awkward transitions.

"Yes."

"Good."

"Back to Barbara?"

"Right. She didn't say anything about the ex. She got all nervous. Her eyes shifted around the room, she stood up straighter, either it was a shadow or the veins in her neck looked like they were going to pop. She was afraid. I didn't think anything of it when—"

"Hey, Charles," interrupted a man standing in the spot Amber had vacated moments earlier.

"Hey, Russ," Charles said. The newcomer was in his mid-50s, six-foot tall, stocky, with a full head of dyed brown hair graying in the temples, and a well-groomed, full beard.

"Didn't meant to interrupt, wanted to say hi."

I'd often wondered what the phrase *didn't mean to interrupt* meant. Of course he meant to. He wasn't walking by and for some unconscious reason, his mouth started talking—interrupting.

"No problem," Charles said. "Have you met my best friend Chris?"

"Don't believe I've had the pleasure," said the interrupter. He cocked his head and snapped his fingers. "You're the one who found the body. Heard about you; seems stumbling on the dead and who made them that way is something you do."

"No. It was bad luck finding him and worse luck for him."

"The murder was all people were talking about when I got back in town."

"Where'd you go?" nosy Charles asked.

"Las Vegas."

"What's in Vegas?" continued Charles's inquisition.

"Trade show. T-shirts, other logo wear. Boring." Russ hesitated and looked at me. "Who killed him?"

"Don't know."

"I don't know either," Charles said. "I've known Chris since Justin Bieber was a babe in swaddling clothes. Chris used to have a photo gallery down the street. Now he's a bum like me."

Russ leaned down and shook my hand. He had on a *Folly Beach Forever* T-shirt, tan Dockers, and scuffed deck shoes. "Nice to meet you."

Russ pointed to Charles's T-shirt. "Story?"

"Glad you asked," Charles turned and winked at me, and looked at Russ. "Gaylord the Camel. Campbell University, up the road, Buies Creek, North Carolina."

"Cool," Russ said.

"Thanks," Charles said, and then turned to me. "Russ owns the new T-shirt stores on Center Street. Wised up and moved here from Delaware to live happily ever after."

I hadn't known who owned SML Shirts and Folly Tease, although I wondered when they opened how the small island saturated with gift shops could support another one, much less two. Charles had said there could never be enough T-shirt stores. Since he had the largest collection outside their manufacturing plants in China, I wrote off his biased proclamation. SML Shirts selection was similar to the other island gift shops. Folly Tease's slogan was "Folly's finest shirts of all colors with off-color messages." A niche, albeit a popular niche, market.

"Oh," I said.

"Again, good to meet you." He then turned to Charles. "Gaylord, that's good. Be sure and let me know." He saluted at Charles, or at Gaylord, and headed to the exit.

Charles watched Russ leave. "Nice fellow. Good to have someone to talk Ts with. Maybe he'll take me with him to the T-shirt hootenanny next year."

That would be as close to heaven on earth as Charles could get. "Let him know what?"

"Nothing," Charles said.

I didn't believe him, but knew him well enough that if he didn't want to tell me, he wouldn't. "How's his business? Seems like there were already enough shops."

Charles nodded. "I think SML Shirts is sucking wind. It has too many shirts that are like all the other stores shirts. Folly Tease's another story. Never a shortage of vacationers wanting shirts that say things like *Tell your boobs to stop staring at my eyes*."

Maybe Gaylord the Camel wasn't so bad after all. After the unintentional interruption, I wanted to get Charles back on track. "You think Barb's afraid of something?"

"Yeah. Except, I don't know what, other than she seemed nervous after talking about her ex."

"Have you seen her since the body was found?"

"You mean since you found the body?"

I sighed. "Yes."

"No." He had finished his lunch and watched me pick at mine.

"Tell you what. I'm going over there now to trade more books." He pointed at the stack beside him. "Want to go?"

I still had bad feelings about having to give up the gallery, and wasn't ready to make an appearance in its former home. I couldn't shake the feeling of loss.

"Not today," I said and took another bite.

"How was Pluto?"

I smiled and said fine. Of course, that wasn't enough information for my canine-loving friend. I had to tell him about giving the dog water, about how he hadn't shared in our breakfast Cheetos, and that he had on his red collar.

Charles must have figured he'd milked me for all the Dude and Pluto details and headed to Barb's Books.

My head had stopped hurting, my stomach was full, and I still had no idea what I was supposed to do to allay Burl and Dude's fears. So I did what I have been doing more of, I went home and took a nap. Inspiration didn't often come while sleeping, but I was determined to keep trying.

CHAPTER 9

I wasn't overwhelmed with inspiration about how to learn if the death in the alley was related to Burl or Dude. What I was inspired to do was overcome my irrational anxiety and visit Barb's Books. That inspiration came after I had reduced the contents of a box of Oreos and stared at a reality show where ten contestants were dumped in Paris and had to survive French food, hostile locals, and an irritating host who kept throwing embarrassing challenges at them. I made a mental note not to apply for future seasons. I decided visiting Barb's Books couldn't be as bad as what the dimwitted contestants had to endure when subjected to televised humiliation for a chance to win fifteen dollars after taxes, agent fees, and years of therapy.

After a decent night's sleep, I wasn't as inspired to visit my former hangout, yet willed myself to do it anyway. I grabbed a lightweight jacket, my canvas Tilley, and headed out. It was before ten o'clock, but the temperature was in the upper forties, and it should be a nice day. Bert's Market was next to the house so I stopped in for coffee and some local conversation. Bert's was as well-known on the island as the Folly Pier and the view of the Morris Island Lighthouse. It billed itself as the grocery that never closes, although I'll admit I don't frequent groceries in the middle of the night, and couldn't verify that claim. The smell of fresh coffee drew me to the back of the store where a coffee urn met the needs of even the most addicted coffee drinker. I got my morning's first caffeine fix, talked to Ted, one of the store's employees, about his latest boating misadventure, and headed to Barb's.

I took a deep breath, a sip of coffee, and entered the bookstore.

I was jolted by how different the space looked than how it did the day I carried the last box out. During its tenure as Landrum Gallery, framed photos lining three walls, a couple of aluminum and canvas photo racks stood along the back wall, and little else. The center of the gallery was open and potential customers could see the framed images from anywhere in the room.

Now, I faced a five-foot-high, four-foot-wide, pine-colored wood bookcase with six rows of shelves filled with books with their covers staring at me. It looked like a mix of new and used books. Ting into it was another bookcase, nine feet long; a walkthrough, and another nine-foot section. There were two bookcases, each fifteen feet long and six feet high lining the wall to the right. They were crammed with used paperbacks, standing at attention, spines facing out. To my left, there was a waist-high counter. On top of the counter were two shell-shaped bookends sandwiching four books, and Barbara Deanelli perched on a bar-height chair behind it. Everything in the store, other than the used books and Barbara, looked new. The fixtures alone cost more than I took in the entire time I occupied the space.

The proprietor stood and came around the front of the counter and held out her hand. I gave her soft hand a brief shake. "Welcome, Mr. Landrum. I've been wondering when you would make an appearance." She wore another bright red blouse and black slacks, her face unsmiling as she waved her hand around the room. "What do you think?"

From my new vantage point, I saw twenty more feet of shelving along the left wall and two additional sections of bookshelves that matched the ones behind the front end cap.

I hated to admit it, but I was impressed and told her so.

She smiled. "Thank you. I suppose it looks a bit different than it did when you had it."

About as different as a kayak to an aircraft carrier. I smiled. "I'd hardly recognize it."

"I never saw the gallery. How did you have it laid out?"

I walked her through an abbreviated description. If she cared, it didn't show, but she'd been kind to ask.

The door was closed to the back room and I didn't feel comfortable asking to tour the small space that had been the unofficial meeting room for my friends. Back in the good-ole-days, it featured a Mr. Coffee, a refrigerator whose contents contained a high percentage of alcohol, and an old, beat-up table and chairs that held many memories—mostly good, but with a couple of horror stories mixed in.

The front-section of the store was only nine hundred square feet so the entire tour and description of how it looked took two minutes.

"Are there any books I could interest you in?" she asked, businesslike. Her smile had disappeared.

"Afraid I'm not a big reader."

"That's too bad. To my good fortune, there are several locals who are, and from what I understand, there should be many more when vacation season arrives."

"True. There are three or four places on the island where you can buy books, but they only carry a couple of local authors."

Since Charles didn't generally sell his books, I didn't mention his collection would exceed the number of books available in many small bookstores.

She grinned. "That's my hope."

"I hear you're Dude, umm, Jim Sloan's sister."

Her grin disappeared. "Yes."

I waited for more, but after an uncomfortable silence, I decided it'd be best if I left. Where, I had no idea. I didn't see an upside to staying.

"Before you go, could you tell me how you regulated the heat? When it's comfortable out here, it's hot enough to melt plastic in back."

"Poorly." I explained that the furnace and ductwork were as old as the building and all I had figured to do was to block the vent in the back room to keep the temperature tolerable. She thanked me and I offered to answer other questions that might come up. She nodded and looked at me like it was a trick offer, yet still thanked me.

I reached for the doorknob and she said, "One more thing, Mr. Landrum."

"Call me Chris."

She nodded and pointed toward the alley. "Have you learned anything else about the body?"

"Nothing new. The detective on the case is good, so it's in capable hands."

She started to say something, but didn't; her fist was clenched, and she gave a curt nod. "Good seeing you again."

Her message couldn't have been clearer than if she'd shouted, "Go away."

I told her I hoped her business was a success and repeated my offer to share whatever I knew about the building.

She shrugged.

I closed the door behind me and shook my head. Strange, I thought. Ms. Deanelli was courteous, but not friendly, something that did not bode well for her success. Her total response to being Dude's sister was, "Yes." And, it was clear she wanted to learn more about the body. It was more than mere curiosity. Strange—strange and interesting.

CHAPTER 10

Cindy LaMond called as I walked away from the bookstore and wanted to know if I could meet her on the Folly Pier. There are a few requests I wouldn't turn down. A free meal, an invitation to attend a state dinner at the White House, and a request to meet the police chief were near the top of the list.

It was an hour before we were to meet, and I had nothing to do so I headed to the thousand-foot iconic structure to take a stroll. There were several fishermen on the wood deck and an elderly couple walked hand in hand along the rail and was gazing toward the horizon. I was approaching their age and wondered what they were thinking. Were they seeing their past in the waves rolling in as regular as the beats on a metronome? Or, could they be pondering their future, regardless how few years may be remaining? I shook my head and refused to go down that same road.

What I couldn't shake was Barb's terse acknowledgement of her brother, even if only half-brother, and her interest in the body. Did she know more than she was telling? Did she know the victim? I even wondered if she'd shot him; although, if she had, why come to the Dog to get his description?

I had often ventured to the Atlantic end of the pier where I convinced myself that I'd done my best thinking. I had also spent hours there without a significant thought, and on occasion had found myself dozing after listening to the soothing waves and looking back on the island I called home. Today was to be a day without significant thoughts, so I headed to the beach. I nodded to the older couple who was still at the railing.

The woman gave me a contented smile that only one who has been around for many years can pull off. "Have a pleasant day, young man."

I smiled. "You, too."

I don't know if it was from being called a young man, a salutation I hadn't heard in years, or because I was going to meet one of my favorite people, but I felt lighter and my step quickened. Before I started down the stairs to the parking lot, I saw the chief headed my way.

"Undercover?" I said and smiled. She was dressed in a white turtleneck sweater and jeans instead of a uniform.

"Off work."

"Good," I said.

"Get a day off every seven months whether I've earned it or not."

"Poor chief."

"Hell's bells. I asked for this rodeo. Gotta take the bad with the badder."

"How come you're not spending the day with Larry?"

Cindy was married to another of my friends, the owner of Pewter Hardware store. Both Larry and his store were small in stature; Larry was 5'1" standing on a surfboard and if he weighed in triple digits it was the day after Thanksgiving. Cindy was a couple inches taller and had her twenty-five pounds on her spouse—a fact that wasn't wise to mention in her presence.

"The boy would rather work to make enough money to eat rather than hear his adorable wife gripe about work all day. Can you believe it?"

"His loss."

She laughed. "Keep that up and I'll dump the shrimp and run off with you."

Despite their differences, the LaMonds were the happiest couple I knew. I also knew Cindy didn't ask to meet me to flirt. She suggested we find a vacant bench on the pier.

"I don't get out here as much as I'd like," she said by way of explanation. She stared at the choppy waves and didn't appear to want to get to the meat of the meeting. She told me about how she and

Officer Bishop had chased a middle-aged drunk two blocks down Erie Avenue before he decided he'd rather stop and throw-up on a kid's scooter. The hardest part of the capture was holding him, since he thought summer was just around the corner and all he had on was orange racing Speedos. She took more delight in telling the story than a police chief should.

She finished laughing about Speedo man, and asked, "How's Karen? Haven't seen her in a while."

Cindy still wasn't ready to talk.

Karen Lawson and I had dated for the last four years. She was a detective in the Charleston County sheriff's office, which was how we had met several years before we'd started seeing each other socially. She had been lead detective on a murder I'd stumbled on. To compound our relationship, her father was Brian Newman, Folly's mayor. He and I had been friends before his daughter and I had started dating. Prior to a shake-up in the sheriff's office, Karen had been assigned major crimes on the island. Nearsighted governmental minds prevailed, and she was banned from investigating criminal activity on Folly.

"I haven't seen her in a while. Something about murderers not taking vacations and continuing to kill folks in Charleston."

Cindy tilted her head and glanced at me from the corner of her eye. "Speaking of murder, I learned the identity of the vic."

Now we're getting somewhere. "Who was he?"

She leaned forward and took a small, bent notebook out of her back pocket.

She waved the book in my face. "Butt-contoured. Latest in police-chief fashion." She flipped a couple of pages. "Lawrence Panella, age fifty-eight, Caucasian, five-foot-eleven, currently deceased and residing in the coroner's office in Charleston, previous residence Myrtle Beach. Retired from various sales jobs, lives with loving wife, Elaine."

"How'd you find out? You said his prints weren't on file."

"Traced the gun. Hard to believe in this day and age, he bought it legally, registered it, and had a South Carolina concealed weapons permit. All squeaky legal. Combine that with the fact his honey reported him missing the day before yesterday."

"Why not earlier?"

"She said he was away on a part-time sales job, whatever that's supposed to mean. He'd been gone a month. If that's part-time, I'd hate to hear what his full-time job would've been. Anyway, she reported him missing. Now he ain't."

"What kind of job?"

"Here's where it gets interesting." She hesitated and looked toward the beach.

I waited.

"Wifey-pooh doesn't have a clue about the part-time gig. Said when he was working full-time he sold farm equipment, like big-ass tractors, combines, other things I haven't heard of. Made a hay bale of money doing it."

"She didn't know why he was here?"

"Didn't know he was. If you think that's the interesting part, I'm gonna scramble your shriveling brain cells." She grinned.

I motioned for her to continue.

"I'll start with the pistol he was packin'. It's a Browning 1011-22, compact rimfire semi-automatic, shoots 22 long rifle. Guess who's a big fan of that handgun."

"Gandhi, or the Dalai Lama—"

"Stop," Cindy interrupted. "Don't take the fun away by guessing it."

"Who?"

"Hit men."

I remembered when Detective Adair saw the gun and started to say something and hesitated. Did he already know it?

"Detective Adair said it was a popular gun. Don't thousands of law-abiding citizens own them?"

"No doubt. There's a tad more you haven't heard."

"That is?"

"It seems five years before our latest murder victim moved the road up to the hoppin' community of Myrtle Beach, he lived in Newark, New Jersey, where frustrated state cops spent years trying to pin a couple of hits on him. He was never arrested; seems the boy was as slick as WD-40 on ice."

"So he moved, unscathed, to Myrtle Beach, semi-retired from 'selling tractors,' and took a *part-time* job doing something his wife knew nothing about, and turns up here."

Cindy nodded, "Add dead to that and you've got it."

"Here's my question, Chief LaMond, what was Lawrence Panella doing on Folly?"

She shook her head. "Citizen Landrum, I have not a freakin' idea. I do know when he got here, at least in the area."

"Am I going to have to drag it out of you?"

"Might be fun trying." She chuckled. "Mr. Panella checked into the Holiday Inn a week before he took his perma-nap in the alley."

"Holiday Inn-Riverview?"

"That's what I said—sort of. He checked in under his name, paid with a credit card, didn't make any calls from the hotel phone, but nobody does anymore since every Tom, Dick, and Alexander Graham Bell has a cell phone. Nothing suspicious."

"What next?"

Cindy shook her head. "State and sheriff folks are wading through his things, physical and digital: bank records, electronic correspondence, phone records, other high-tech stuff. To be honest, if he managed to thwart law enforcement much smarter than our state and local guys for all those years, I can't imagine being able to pin anything on him."

"So, I repeat, Chief LaMond, what next?"

Cindy bit her lower lip, glanced at a fisherman pulling his rolling cart toward us, and nodded. "Let's see. I'm going to, umm, take an hour of my day off and go to the office, answer a couple of irate e- mails, one from one of our fine, upstanding citizens who thinks my department is playing Gestapo, and the other one from a fine, upstanding citizen who thinks we're too easy on the bad guys, and then—"

I chuckled. "Okay, okay, what will you do about the murder?"

One of Cindy's most endearing qualities, and I suspect one that helped her diffuse difficult police interventions, was her sense of humor and irreverence. It was also her way of pleading helplessness without having to say she didn't know something.

"I could go to the post office and see if the John Deere salesman slash hit man sent me a letter mentioning who hired him and who he was hired to bump off, maybe even including a signed confession by the hirer. My keen woman's intuition tells me those documents ain't there."

"So there's nothing you can do?"

"Chris, the state cops have the resources to do all the digital forensics, the fuzz in Myrtle Beach are capable of tearing the man's home and records apart, the gun's already been analyzed, and the bullet from his head is setting somewhere waiting for the tool that put it there to show up."

"But—"

She put her hand in my face. "From what I can tell, no one on our beloved island knew anything about the *hombre*. What do you suggest I do?"

I couldn't think of anything and told her so.

She started to stand. "Now I have to go start communicating with my constituency."

"Cindy, will you—"

She huffed. "Yes, Chris, I will let you know if I learn anything. You know I live and breathe so I can tell you everything that's going on, especially when it involves dead folk.

I smiled as she walked away. The smile was for my relationship with Cindy, and not for what was going on—whatever it was.

CHAPTER 11

My earliest memories of Charles were of us walking down the side streets and taking photos. I focused on Lowcountry landscapes, and rustic houses and cabins encapsulated in character and inhabited by some of the finest people on earth. Charles, to put it artistically appropriate, leaned toward the avant-garde and captured images of discarded candy wrappers, flattened soft drink and beer cans, and interesting shaped, and often tire-flattened pooch poop.

Our conversations, which I enjoyed more than the photography, were as varied as the photos. My friend was one of the island's leading experts on gossip, arcane information, the lesser- known dalliances of prominent citizens, and everything related to how to get through life without a visible means of support. I brought to the table, or more correctly, the street, my experiences from many years in a bureaucratic megacorporation, and insights into human nature gleaned from human relations training and a degree in psychology. Charles also credited me with saving his life on a couple of occasions, and I gave him kudos for doing the same related to a few hair-raising situations I'd found myself in.

Charles greeted me at the door of his apartment with a broom in his hand, and on his torso a long-sleeve, gray Bowling Green State University T-shirt with a falcon's head on the front.

I pointed at the broom. "Flying somewhere?"

"Funny. It's called house cleaning. Did it last March, but figured since there wasn't a gallery that needed me, I'd do it again."

He still hadn't forgiven me for closing the gallery, but was coming closer to accepting it was gone and never to return.

"Grab your camera. Let's walk."

He grinned, and told me to give him a minute.

Twenty seconds later, he was back. He had slipped a Lost Dog Cafe sweatshirt over his college T-shirt, drooped his Nikon camera strap over his shoulder, plopped his Tilley hat on, shrugged into a bright-yellow jacket that had somehow hid in his closet void of any college logo, and he wore a genuine smile on his face.

"Where to?" he asked.

"Your call." I was interested in talking about the recent events more than our destination.

"How about Vermont?" he said with a sly grin.

"How about somewhere closer?" I was pleased with his mood.

"Party pooper. Okay, follow me."

We left the gravel and shell parking lot he shared with a few other apartments, walked past Heather's building, and away from town on West Indian Avenue. We had gone about two hundred yards when Charles came across a treasure-trove of photo ops. An opossum or a raccoon had foraged through someone's trash, and left three, empty green beans cans, a Ritz cracker box, and five Payday wrappers along the side of the street. You would have thought Charles was a paparazzi and had stumbled on a secret meeting of Jennifer Lawrence, Brad Pitt, and the Pope. He snapped photos from all angles and treated each discarded wrapper photo like it would become a Pulitzer Prize finalist.

I stood at the side of the road and watched my friend at play. I wanted to tell him about what I'd learned from Cindy, but wasn't ready to interrupt his mission to document the trash of the world, or at least our small corner of the globe. He had exhausted the angles from which to photograph the detritus and looked around for somewhere to discard the mess. While he may wait eleven months in between house cleanings, he couldn't stand litter on *his* island. He pointed to an aluminum garbage can on the other side of the street and I dragged it over while he used his foot to scoot the trash in a pile and onto a piece of cardboard to scoop it in the can.

He finished cleaning the roadway and I lugged the can back to its rightful yard.

He tapped the camera. "Too bad *we* don't have a gallery to display these photos."

I started to respond, when he said, "Kidding."

Right, I thought as we continued away from town.

We had reached the corner where Shadow Race Lane intersects West Indian when he asked, "Any news on the killing?"

"Glad you asked." I continued walking. "I talked to Cindy."

"When?"

There was a reason Charles was one of the island's top contenders in the race to accumulate the most trivia.

"Are you ready to hear what she said?"

I told him about Lawrence Panella and his alleged career.

Charles stopped, and pushed his hat back on his head. "A hit man. A hit man like in the movies who gets paid to go around killing people?" He waved his arm around his head. "A hit man like in the movies was right here on Folly Beach?"

I wondered what other kind of hit man there was. I nodded. "Wow! And you didn't call me from the pier so I could hear what she was saying."

I looked at the pavement and shook my head. "You want to mope or hear the rest?"

"The rest."

I repeated Panella's bio and about the gun found on the body and that his wife didn't know why he was here.

"Doesn't sound like he was on vacation since he lived by the ocean at Myrtle. Don't suppose he was hired to kill himself."

"It wasn't his gun that killed him."

"Who was he here for?"

"Don't know and neither does the police. Besides, I'm not sure he was here to kill anyone."

We had reached the turnaround at the end of Shadow Race Lane and Charles had stopped to look at a small boat parked in the drive of one of the large, elevated luxury homes that dominated Folly's newer developments. He mumbled, "Who killed the killer?"

It was rhetorical and I shook my head. We walked in silence as we headed back toward Charles's apartment. I was shocked he didn't ask more questions. Something was on his mind, but something else you didn't do with Charles was to ask what was bothering him. He was obsessive about being early to everything—to Charles, on-time meant thirty minutes early—yet when it came to talking about his feelings, later, if ever, was his time line. I was the same way so I didn't push.

He was the one who couldn't stand silence, and had a comment to make regardless of its relevance. This time I was feeling uncomfortable and shared I also had visited Barb's Books.

"Oh."

"She has a nice store," I said.

"Yeah."

I had expected an avalanche of questions since it was my first visit. I decided to drop the subject and enjoy the pleasant weather and scenery.

Instead of turning on his street, Charles continued on West

Indian Avenue and headed to the pocket park behind Folly's combination community center and library. The Lost Dog Cafe shared a property line with the park and in-season there were often groups of vacationers waiting in the shade for a table. Today, the park was empty and Charles sat on a bench overlooking a wooden bridge that crossed a tiny, dry stream. He removed his hat, rubbed his hand through his hair, and moved his head around like he was working a crick out of his neck. I sat beside him and waited.

Charles turned and looked at the crepe myrtle behind the bench. "He called."

"Who?"

Charles was slumped over; he reminded me of a deflating balloon.

He glanced at me. "The Nashville sleaze ball."

"The agent called Heather?"

Charles nodded. "Why?"

Charles looked at the ground. "Told me last night. She called and was so giddy I had a hard time understanding what she was talking about." He sighed and looked up at me. "Kevin Starr wanted to know if she's a songwriter. She told him she'd written a couple, but mainly covered hits by Patsy Cline, Loretta Lynn, and other classic country greats, or something like that."

He closed his eyes and shook his head. "And?"

"He said a couple of Nashville's well-known bars had open- mic nights and with his connections, he'd get her appearances. Said bunches of singers and writers were 'discovered' there."

I wondered if Kevin Starr had been listening to the same Heather I knew.

"Why'd he want to know if she's a songwriter?"

"The open-mic nights he was talking about were for writers, not singers, but they'd still get to sing the songs they wrote."

"And he thinks someone would hear her and want to sign her to a record deal?"

"That's what Heather thinks. She told me she'd heard of a couple of people who had *made it big* after being discovered at these bars."

I'd been a longtime country music fan and when I was living in Kentucky had visited Nashville a few times and knew a little about its popular music venues.

"Remember the name of the bars?"

He looked up at a nearby palmetto tree, or was looking heaven-ward for divine inspiration. "One was Bluejay something."

"The Bluebird Cafe?"

"That's it. Heather said Garth Brooks played there before he became famous. The other one was Douglas Corner Cafe. Ever heard of it?"

"No, but that doesn't mean anything. I haven't been there in years." I hesitated and dreaded the next question. "What does Starr want Heather to do?"

"Duh. Go to Nashville. He wants to sign on as her agent and make her famous."

That was as likely as me flapping my arms and flying to Kuwait. I bit my tongue. I didn't know what Starr's game was, and suspected it couldn't turn out good for Heather. "You said open-mic nights. Can't anyone sing? Why would she need an agent to get in?"

Charles shrugged. "The open-mic nights I know about are at Cal's and showing up is his only requirement. Don't know about famous Nashville hot spots. Know Heather was babbling like a four- year old on Christmas morning."

I didn't tell him, but I would check the websites on my own to see if the venues he mentioned had other requirements for appear-ing. "Is she going?"

"I love Heather. She's a kind, funny person." I nodded at his non-answer.

He looked at the bridge and said, "She's a good masseuse; maybe good at being a psychic."

I didn't think he wanted a response.

He looked around and leaned closer. "Between you and me, her singing might not be the best in the world."

It was like saying a chipmunk *might not* win the Westminster Dog Show. I said, "You could be right."

"Heather knows her voice isn't as great as some. She also says the voice isn't all there is to be famous."

Ernest Tubb and Kris Kristofferson came to mind, and don't get me started on Bob Dylan. Compared to Heather, they would have been candidates for the Metropolitan Opera.

"Is she going?"

"Remember the other morning when you met Russ and he asked me to let him know?"

I wondered what that had to do with Heather and Nashville, but following Charles's logic was occasionally a circuitous trip, so I chose to take it with him. "And I asked you what he was talking about and you said nothing."

"Russ wants me to run one of his stores," I was stunned.

"Like a real job?"

He nodded. "He knows I'm a big fan of T-shirts and I was your sales manager at the gallery. He thinks I would be good at the SML store since its sales ain't up to snuff."

"Are you considering it?"

"The best time I've had in years was when I felt you needed me in the gallery. It gave me a reason to get up in the morning. I miss that, and doing the same for Russ might be what's best for me."

"I'm surprised, but understand. And then the Nashville thing comes up with Heather."

"So yeah to your earlier question, about her going, I don't think I can stop her. What can I do?"

"What do you think?" I asked, channeling my counseling training from the dark ages.

He looked at the urn-shaped concrete fountain and then back at me. "What kind of stupid answer's that? I thought I asked you."

So much for my rusty education.

"Let's try it this way, what'll you do if she goes?"

He whispered, "I don't know."

CHAPTER 12

I would love to say Charles and I came up with a perfect solution to his dilemma. I would love to say Heather had miraculously acquired a world-class voice and became as famous as she had dreamed of becoming and she and Charles would still never have to leave Folly Beach. I would love to say I knew what he should tell Russ. I would love to say I'd found the Fountain of Youth. I couldn't say any of these things. What I could say was Charles agreed to suggest to Heather that perhaps her voice wasn't up to country stardom, and I would search the Internet and see what I could find on Kevin Starr. Was he on the up-and-up? Had he discovered stars? Was he a con artist trying to take advantage of Heather? Or, and my guess, was he tone-deaf and delusional? What I was certain of was if Heather moved to Nashville to chase her dreams, Charles would follow. I would be devastated.

Karen called when I was on my way home and asked if I was interested in sharing a feast of chicken fried in eleven herbs and spices. I agreed and asked if she wanted to meet me at the KFC near her house. She said no and would bring box suppers to my place.

I had an hour to kill before the home-delivery accompanied by a detective, so I began an internet search for Kevin Starr. I had hoped the first reference would say something like: *Fake music agent arrested for bilking thousands out of aspiring singers*. Instead, there were five LinkedIn references to Kevin Starr; two of them referring to Nashville and music agent. I wasn't a member of LinkedIn, so those sites were useless. I found a photo of him on an on-line Nashville weekly paper over the cutline: *Agent Kevin Starr with newcomer*

Sandra Ball. The photo showed Kevin with a well-endowed woman in her twenties. Both were smiling at the lens. The photo was taken at a cocktail-party fundraiser for an animal shelter, although I couldn't tell how recently it had been taken. It didn't prove anything other than Kevin was in Nashville and had told the photographer he was an agent. More digging, but I couldn't find any websites listed for Sandra Ball, Kevin Starr, or Starr Management. I understood a newcomer might not have a site, but found it incredulous there wouldn't be one for Starr or his company. I Googled yellow-pages for a phone number and an address, for Starr Management, and found a listing with a phone number, the number he'd written on the card he'd given Heather. No address was listed.

Karen arrived before I could dig further. The familiar smell of fried chicken seeped from the large sack she handed me as she stepped into the living room. Karen was pushing fifty, runner-thin, with shoulder-length, chestnut brown hair, and, in my opinion, beautiful. Instead of her typical navy-blue pantsuit work attire, she wore a dark- green blouse and tan slacks.

I took the chicken and set it on the kitchen table, placed her leather jacket on a chair in the corner of the kitchen, and took a long, mushy kiss offered by the detective. I reciprocated.

She stepped back and looked at the refrigerator. "Happen to have beer in there? This has been one gruesome week."

I told her I thought I could find one. She said she thought I could too since about the only things in the refrigerator would be beer, wine, and ice cream. She wasn't far off, and I handed her a Budweiser. I poured a glass of Cabernet from a bottle on the counter and asked if she wanted to relax in the living room before digging into the "feast."

She smiled. "No way. I'm starved."

I took the hint. I smiled at the set of steak knives Bob Howard had given me as a housewarming gift before he knew I had zero culinary skills. The chicken wouldn't need such heavy tools, and I grabbed two of my finest paper plates and four McDonald's napkins from the silverware—in my kitchen, plastic ware—drawer.

Karen had already torn open the bag and removed two box meals and was ready to dump the coleslaw on the plates. She took a bite of chicken before I was back at the table. Gruesome weeks brought out her appetite. Karen had been blessed with a metabolism that allowed her to eat huge quantities of high calorie food without gaining an ounce. I envied it, and had learned over the years it wasn't contagious.

I said, "Want to talk about your week?"

She had finished the first breast and started on the second. She took a spoonful of mashed potatoes and shook her head. "No. Two bodies and the usual suspects: drug deals gone bad and cheap guns."

"Sorry."

"Don't be sorry, nothing else to say." She took a deep breath. "My job starts after bad things happen. It'll never change."

Karen has been a detective for several years and a beat cop for years before that. She was good at her job, and seldom let the dark side get her down. I was surprised it seemed to be getting to her more than usual.

"Anything I can do?"

"Being here helps. It feels good to be away from the blood and gore for a few hours." She grinned. "What's been happening over here?"

I wanted her take on the murdered hit man, but considering what she had said, I knew it wasn't a good time. Instead, I filled her in on Heather and Kevin Starr. She started to interrupt once, but let me finish.

"What?" I asked.

"Are you talking about the Heather Lee I've heard sing?" I nodded.

"The agent, he a con or deaf?"

"Don't know. He must be one or both."

"One of our detectives came over from the Metro Nashville Police Department. Want me to have him check with his buddies in Tennessee and see what they can find on Starr?"

"If it's no trouble."

"He's new with us and should still have friends there. I'll ask tomorrow."

"Thanks. Charles will appreciate it, though he'd appreciate it more if the cops in Nashville would arrest Starr and stick him in jail for a hundred years."

Karen smiled. "I'm sure he would."

"Unless someone proves Starr is a mass murder and bumping off all the naïve, aspiring singers he cons into moving to Nashville, I don't think anything can stop Heather for heading there to find fame and fortune."

"And if she goes, so goes Charles."

"Yeah."

"If he leaves Folly you'll lose your best friend."

"That's part of it. There's more than that. I keep thinking how traumatized Charles was when I closed the gallery. He lost his identity, his purpose, as he called it, and the gallery was only open a few years. Charles has been here more than thirty. Folly and Charles are as close as skin on your hand, and I can't imagine him in Nashville. For Heather, she'll be pinning her hopes and dreams on a man she doesn't know in a city known for chewing up and spitting out singers like mulch from a wood chipper." I shook my head. "Nothing good can come from it. They know nothing about Nashville, and don't have a way to get there."

She reached across the table and took my hand. "Don't get the cart before the horse. Let me see what I can dig up. If it's nothing bad, what's the harm in them going to Nashville for a few days? Let Heather sing, or whatever it is she does, at the open-mic nights. Can you picture someone hearing her, going gaga, and signing her to a record contract?"

I smiled at that image. "True, but I know Charles and think I have a good feel for Heather. All it takes is someone to say she has potential, or that she has a unique singing style, and she'll want to stay forever."

"As a true friend, you can't stand in Charles's way."

"I know. If he wants to go for a few days or a few years, I'll support him." I smiled. "Besides, he'll want me to take them."

She squeezed my hand. "That's what friends do. Let me see what our detective finds before getting too upset." She let go of my hand and sat back in the chair. "And speaking of friends and detectives, when were you going to tell me about finding a body?"

I wasn't ready for that transition. "Tonight." It sounded weak as I said it.

"Um, hmm. I bet." She clenched her fists.

"How did you hear?"

"Give me some credit, I am a detective." She glared at me. "Although, it didn't take much detecting. Ken, Detective Adair, told me, and then your mayor—you know, the one who happens to be the father of the lady you're eating chicken with—called to tell me. It would've been nice to tell them I knew."

"Sorry. It's that—"

"That's a sorry I accept," she interrupted. "Continue."

"I knew you were snowed under at work and I didn't want you

to worry. Besides, all I did was come across the body. I didn't know the guy or anything about him. It has nothing to do with me."

"Then why did Detective Adair ask me to tell you who the guy was and where he was staying?"

"Curious, that's all."

"Chris, if I find out you're butting in police business *again*, I won't have to worry about somebody killing you. I'll do it myself."

"I'm not getting involved."

"I've heard that before." She showed no signs of softening.

"Honest. It's in good hands with Detective Adair. It's none of my business. Period."

She made a slight nod. "So you don't want to know who he was or where he was staying?"

I didn't tell her Chief LaMond had already told me. "If Detective Adair wanted you to tell me, I guess you should. Wouldn't want him angry with you."

She gave me the hit man's name and local address, and reiterated she would kill me if I got involved.

I nodded, crossed my fingers in hopes she wouldn't explode. "Does Adair have any leads?"

Karen chuckled. "Glad you're staying out of it."

I held my hand up, palm facing Karen. "Curious."

"Yeah. Adair doesn't know anything more than the basic facts: Where the vic lived, what his wife said about what he was doing, where he was staying in Folly, and the rumors about his past."

"Nothing about why he was here?"

"Nothing." She rolled her eyes. "So, I come over and you're trying to get my mind off my terrible week by talking about murder."

I smiled. "Maybe I should try a different strategy."

Fortunately, she returned the smile. "I do know something you could do to get my mind off the week."

The next morning, she said I had succeeded. I still had a feeling something was bothering her.

CHAPTER 13

I watched Karen pull out of the drive a little after sunrise, and turned on the radio to hear a cheery meteorologist tell me today was to be the "pick of the week with enough sunshine to keep dermatologists in caviar and temperatures to tempt listeners to buy Fourth of July fireworks." Instead of going caviar and fireworks shopping, I decided time in Charleston photographing its historic churches would be a good way to spend the day. Having my photographs displayed in a gallery was a fading memory, yet I'd been a photographer for many years and still enjoyed capturing my surroundings. Besides, it would be a welcomed distraction.

I would have invited Charles, but knew he had to deliver packages for Dude. Charles didn't have a working car, so he pedaled around the island on his pride and joy, a classic 1961 Schwinn bicycle, and picked-up a few bucks in the process.

On the way to Charleston, I took a chance my friend hadn't begun his carrier route and gave him a call. He didn't have a cell phone or an answering machine, so I was pleased when he answered, and told him what my Internet search had uncovered about Kevin Starr.

"Oh great," he said, with dejection in his voice. "He's for real. Heather'll be thrilled."

He either hadn't heard, or ignored, what I'd said about it seeming strange that Starr's agency didn't have a website, and there wasn't anything about the singer in the photograph. If Cal was right about agents not listing their address, I would have thought it unusual he wouldn't have at least a post office box.

"When does he want her in Nashville?" I was hoping it wasn't soon so it would give the real detective time to dig into Starr's credibility.

"A week, give or take. Heather's going to ask around the salon to see if someone knows about a cheap car she can buy. She wants to be ready when Starr calls back. She's so excited."

"I'm happy for her." I hoped he didn't hear disappointment in my voice. "Do me a favor."

"Okay, maybe."

"The next time Heather talks with Starr see if she can get names of some of the singers he represents. He should want to brag on them, being they're stars."

"I'll try. She's mighty hopped-up about going, so I think if he said she'd be his first client, she'd still be packing."

"Try anyway."

Charles hesitated and then said, "I'm off. Surf shop customers are waiting to get their goodies from CPS."

Charles and his vibrant imagination had named his pedal-powered delivery service Charles Parcel Service. He'd said he hoped the "slightly larger" UPS wouldn't feel threatened by his moniker. I'd told him they could withstand the economic impact.

I was lucky enough to find a parking spot a block off Meeting Street and within a few hundred yards of some of the most beautiful houses of worship in the southeast. I was eleven miles from my small bohemian island, yet it didn't take much imagination to feel I had stepped into history. Seconds later, I was standing in front of St. Michael's, perhaps the most photographed church in Charleston. The crisp-white Anglican church's towering steeple was visible from numerous vantage points and left no doubt about the importance and historic significance of the building that opened in 1761, the oldest church building in the city. With more than four hundred places of worship, Charleston was dubbed "The Holy City," and St. Michael's had been the most visible symbol of religion's importance to the community. The front of the church with its impressive steeple was the subject of most photographers, though I preferred to wander through the small, brick-walled cemetery behind the sanctuary. Sunlight filtered through a large magnolia tree and illuminated the ancient tombstones with soothing light and brought to life the importance of those who had departed a century ago.

The temperature was still cool, yet I was able to shed my jacket as I walked from St. Michael's to the French Protestant Church on the appropriately named Church Street. The gothic-revival structure, better known as the Huguenot Church, was different in appearance than many of the other magnificent churches. Instead of being hidden behind a brick wall, its cemetery was surrounded by a wrought-iron fence. I took a few shots of a tombstone framed by the fence and then sat on a Charleston Battery Bench and gazed at the wide variety of foliage growing in the well-maintained area. The differences between the two churches reminded me how much their location and buildings differed from the oceanfront services at First Light. While First Light's services were held on the beach in good weather, the hope it offered its followers was no different than what Charleston's magnificent churches promised.

I understood Preacher Burl being concerned about the possibility of someone in his flock meeting an untimely demise after what had happened before with his church. What I couldn't understand was his concern over the recent death. The body was in the alley behind a row of stores along Center Street. It wasn't closer to First Light's door than it was to Barb's Books. The alley was off the beaten path, but not isolated. It was often used to get to the rear entrances of a couple of the bars, and others took the shortcut between two parallel streets. There was no evidence of anyone trying to get in First Light's rear door. Why was the preacher concerned? Paranoia? Or was there something he wasn't telling me?

There's one way to find out. On my drive home, I called the preacher and after three rings, I heard, "Good day, Brother Chris, learn anything about the poor soul?"

I detested caller ID. "Not yet, Preacher Burl, but I'd like to meet and talk about it."

"I don't." He hesitated. "But will. When's good for you?"

I told him today. He said he wasn't available and we agreed on a time and place to meet tomorrow.

It was getting warmer so I decided to park at the house, change into lighter clothes, grab a sandwich, if the bread hadn't turned blue, and walk on the beach. I needed to lose a few pounds and had been trying to get more exercise—something I'm not a fan of.

I opened the door and my day took a nosedive, I took two steps into the house when I noticed the living room looked like a tornado had touched down. A small table from the corner was on its side in the middle of the room. Photo magazines that had been on the table were scattered everywhere and one of the ceramic vases I'd bought at a yard sale to make the room look more homey had been smashed, shards everywhere. The ottoman was on its side and my flat-screen television was face down on the floor.

I took a deep breath and started to back out of the room, when I heard a rustling behind me and turned to see the second ceramic vase hurling at my head. A sharp pain registered in my brain, I saw what looked like the finale of an Independence Day fireworks show in my eyes, followed by everything turning white, and then black. I didn't feel anything as I hit the floor.

CHAPTER 14

I opened my eyes and saw the living room from ankle level. My head felt like it had been hit by a meteorite. I stared at my table lamp, bulb shattered, and cord snaked out behind it on the floor beside my leg. I didn't move, because my head hurt too much and if the intruder was still in the house, I didn't want him, or her, to know I was still among the living.

A minute later, the only sounds I heard were cars passing in front of the house and blood pulsing through my aching temple. I raised my head a few inches and looked around. I blinked back a tear and pushed up to a sitting position. Still no sounds from inside the house. I glanced at the floor and didn't see blood, a good sign. I touched my head and felt a knot the size of a basketball. Again, no blood.

I inched the phone out of my pocket and tapped 911 and told the dispatcher what had happened. She asked if the intruder was still in the house. I said I didn't think so, and prayed I was right. I ended the call and moved to my lounge chair which appeared to be the only thing unharmed in the room.

My legs stopped shaking enough for me to venture farther, so I walked in the kitchen. There was little in it so there was not much that could be disturbed. Drawers by the sink were open, but nothing was out of place. I moved to the second bedroom I used as an office and storage room for prints from the gallery. Whoever had invaded my privacy appeared to have spent the most time here. The four-drawer filing cabinet where I kept most every piece of paper I had, had been ransacked, and papers from it were strewn around the room. A taped banker's box that had held hundreds of slides dating to the pre-digital age had been ripped open and the contents flung in every direction, and my photo printer looked like the visitor had taken a sledgehammer to it. Its plastic shell was shattered and magenta ink from one of the color cartridges seeped out of the mangled machine.

A siren from a Folly Beach patrol car disturbed my dismay as I looked at the disheveled room. I wanted to check the bedroom before anyone arrived. Dismay turned to anger as I gripped the door frame for balance and looked in. One of my steak knives was plunged in the pillow and the sheets were shredded and lay useless on the floor. A piece of copy paper was on the pillow beside the knife and something was printed on the paper in red ink. I stepped closer and read: *LEAVE TOWN.*

If I had had food in my stomach, it would now be on the bedroom floor.

"Mr. Landrum, sir?" came the familiar voice of Officer Bishop from the front of the house.

"In here." I turned to meet the officer.

She looked left and right as she approached. "Are you okay?" She continued to look around.

My head throbbed, my legs were still weak. I was furious, and bile was inching its way up through my throat. "Yeah, just a bump."

The officer stepped closer and examined my head like she was trying to identify the genus of a bug. "Doesn't look okay to me.

There's an ambulance on the way. Why don't we go in the living room, so you can sit down and tell me what happened?"

I thought it was a terrific idea, especially the sitting down part. Allen Spencer was next to arrive. "Are you okay, Mr. Landrum?"

I gave him the same answer I'd given Bishop. He nodded and frowned. He knew I was lying. While Spencer went from room to room surveying the damage, Bishop asked me what had happened. I told her I came home from Charleston to find this and then someone smacked me in the head with a vase. Not insightful or detailed, but it was all I could offer.

"Did you see who?" Spencer asked from the bedroom doorway.

"Afraid not."

Bishop asked Spencer to keep an eye on me while she looked around.

He said, "The ambulance should be here soon."

I closed my eyes. My head hurt, although not as much as it had minutes earlier.

Bishop returned and Spencer asked her how the intruder had gotten in. A couple of years ago, someone had broken into the house and at the time Spencer had suggested I get stronger door locks, which I had. in."

"Broke the window in the office, opened the latch, and climbed

So much for the extra-strong locks. At least Spencer wouldn't be able to chide me for not heeding his advice.

I heard the piercing wail of an ambulance in the distance.

Spencer said, "Do you know anyone who would want to do this to you?"

It seemed like a big coincidence that within the last few days, I found the body in the alley and now this, but I said, "No."

Cindy LaMond walked through the door followed by two paramedics from the Charleston County Emergency Medical Services. Cindy stood in the background talking to Officer Bishop while one paramedic examined the knot on my head and the other one checked my pupils, reflexes, blood pressure, followed by a plethora of questions about the injury and my overall health.

The paramedic voiced what I dreaded when he said they wanted to transport me to the hospital to get a more thorough check up. I hated hospitals, and that disdain had increased tenfold since I had been on Folly. I had spent more time in medical facilities the last eight years than some surgeons. I had visited my closest friends as they fought battles with death, and had been a patient myself a handful of times. I would rather swim to Bermuda than enter the emergency room doors at the hospital, and I was a poor swimmer.

"I'll be fine."

The paramedic gave me a stern look. "Sir, there's a chance you have a concussion. You should let the docs check you over."

I shook my head. "I'll keep a close watch on it. I'll have someone stay with me a day or so. If anything happens, I'll go to the hospital."

In the background, Cindy mumbled, "Hardheaded."

"Your call, sir. I would recommend against it. If you're certain, you'll need to sign papers and we'll be on our way."

The other paramedic stuck a clipboard in front of me with forms attached. I didn't read the fine print. No need, I knew it released them of responsibility for anything horrible that happens because I had refused their kind offer of a ride. I scribbled my signature on the bottom. They grabbed their medical equipment, and on the way out, said, "Take it easy, sir."

The chief told Spencer he could go back on patrol, and asked Bishop to stay. Cindy then put her hand on my arm. "You sure you're okay?"

"Will be," I smiled—a mistake. It hurt.

Cindy glanced in the kitchen, took a brief look at the mess in the office, and went in the bedroom.

She returned and said, "Chris, I'm going to call Detective Adair to see if he can come over. It seems strange that this would happen so close to you finding the body. Besides, I'd like him to get his lab rats to take a look at the love note on your pillow. I think chocolate would have been more appropriate, but that's me. Doubt they'll find anything, but you never know. It looks like whoever wrote it was a five-year-old you've pissed off, or someone trying to disguise the handwriting with piss-poor printing."

Cindy stepped outside and made the call, I remained as still as possible in the comfortable chair, and Officer Bishop walked around the room avoiding the mess on the floor.

"So you're certain you didn't see the assailant?" she said, asking the question I had already answered three times.

"Yes." I pointed to the overturned ottoman. "Have a seat, relax." Her pacing was making me nervous.

She didn't say anything, but righted the stool. "Nice house, Mr. Landrum."

"Thanks, officer, and call me Chris."

She nodded. "I'm Trula."

"Nice name." I smiled. My head didn't hurt as much this time.

She lowered her head. "Thanks."

Cindy returned. "Okay, here's the deal. Detective Adair will be here as soon as he can get away. I have to get to city hall for a blankety-blank freakin' budget meeting." She turned and pointed a finger at Bishop. "Don't repeat that." She turned back to me. "Officer Bishop will stay with you until the detective arrives." To Bishop, she said, "Since our headstrong friend here told the EMTs someone would be with him all the time, you get first shift." She huffed. "Now Mr. Landrum, you stay there with your butt stuck in that chair. Don't get up. Don't touch anything. Try not to let anyone conk you on the noggin until you tell your story to Adair. Think you can do that?"

"I'll try."

"Good. I'll have Larry stop by and fix the window."

It was close to an hour before Detective Adair arrived. Officer

Bishop met him at the door and pointed to where I was seated, although since he was a detective, I suspected he could have found me. I stood and shook his hand.

"We meet again, Mr. Landrum." In addition to Adair's normal preppy look, he wore a forced smile. He glanced around the room. "It appears your housekeeper had the day off."

I assumed it was his paltry sense of humor, so I smiled. Trula, standing behind Adair, grinned. Adair walked from room to room taking in the sorry sights and I returned to my chair. He came back and sat on the ottoman Officer Bishop had vacated.

"Start from the beginning."

I repeated the story. He took notes and nodded as I finished each point.

"Mr. Landrum, I doubt they'll find anything, but I'm having the crime scene techs do their thing. Who has it in for you? Why does someone want you out of town?"

I wished I had taped my earlier answers so I could play them back, although if I had a tape recorder, which I didn't, it would have suffered the same fate as my printer. I told him I didn't know anyone. He looked skeptical.

"Mr. Landrum, I've known you for what, a year?"

"Yes."

"And in that time, you've been involved in two, no, three murders counting the one the other day. Now that's a lot even for a cop to deal with, and you, what, a retired pencil-pusher and former shop owner, are smack-dab involved in three." He shook his head. "And you don't know anyone who could have done this. That's hard to swallow."

My head still hurt and the last thing I wanted to do was get in a protracted conversation about the past. I appreciated his point of view, but the unfortunate events a year ago had been resolved, and I couldn't see how stumbling on a body in an alley could have anything to do with me.

"Regardless, Detective, I don't know anyone."

"Then I'll leave and let you get some rest. I don't know when the techs will get here, so please don't touch anything that's been disturbed until they're finished."

I thanked him for coming and Officer Bishop walked him to his car. Before he pulled away, I wondered why I hadn't told him about Barbara Deanelli's unusual curiosity about the victim, and Preacher Burl's free-floating anxieties about the death. I suppose it was because I couldn't see how either could be relevant. Was I right?

Two hours later, the techs from the Charleston County Forensic Services Unit arrived; two hours of awkward conversation with Trula Bishop. The techs only comment on my housekeeping was to say they'd seen worse. They went about their business, apologized for any mess they may have made, and told me to have a good evening. I couldn't see how it could go any way but up. Officer Bishop went above and beyond her assigned duty to babysit me. She helped straighten up as much as possible. The techs had taken the tattered sheets and stabbed pillow, so she helped me make up the bed and carry the printer's remains to the trash. The flat screen television had survived the fall. It took me another hour to convince the vigilant officer I was okay enough to stay by myself. I was surprised when she hugged me on the way out the door, told me she was sorry for the trouble I had been through, and said she would drive by every hour to make sure everything seemed okay. I was touched.

Winter temperatures didn't bother me as much as the early sunsets. It was a little after seven and dark. I started to fix a glass of wine, but figured if I had a concussion I'd better stick with some-thing non-alcoholic. I refiled some of the more current documents, before feeling weak and moving back to the living room chair. I thought about drifting into a peaceful nap, but decided against it, again, because of the possible concussion.

My headache began to get better until I tried to think who could have done this. I tried to convince myself that I had interrupted a burglary. The knife and note blew that wish out of the water. If someone wanted me dead, he or she had the perfect opportunity. Why leave me alive? Did the intruder think I was dead? Or, did something scare the person before he or she could finish me off? The who and why remained unanswered.

The conk on the head not only hurt and slammed me with new unanswered questions, but reminded me of things I had been giving way too much thought to; things I had avoided until the death of Charles's aunt a couple of years ago; things that had been bothering me since the beginning of this year. I was approaching my late sixties. Today my life could have ended; at best, I probably have thirty years left, and that's if I was lucky. What have I contributed? I had spent most of my work life plowing the fields of bureaucracy. My employer was in good shape when I was hired; was in good shape when I retired. My professional legacy will be a page of notes in an archived file in a storage room, never to be resuscitated.

My dwindling bank account shattered my dream of owning a photo gallery, and damaged the pride and purpose of the best friend I'd ever had. It was also the same best friend who will probably be following his significant other six hundred miles away to follow her dream. My twenty-year marriage ended a quarter of a century ago. I had become reacquainted with my ex-wife four years ago, only to see her murdered while trying to restart her life on Folly; a murder I may have been able to prevent. I'm in a relationship with Karen, yet for reasons I can't articulate, am avoiding taking it to the next level.

I had spent most of my years avoiding talking about myself. I was a much better listener and more comfortable being on that end of a conversation. Would I feel better if I shared some of my doubts and fears with someone? I considered myself spiritual, while not being big on organized religion. Maybe I could talk to Preacher Burl about some of the things that had been bothering me. Why not start at lunch tomorrow? I could ask about his concern over Panella's death and seek his guidance with my fears and anxieties. I smiled for the first time in hours when I thought by talking to the preacher I could kill two doves with one stone.

Despite my efforts not to, I drifted off. The phone jarred me awake, and jarred even more when I answered and Karen screamed, "Are you okay?"

"I'm fine." I shook my head to see if I was telling the truth. A headache, but that was all. "Detective Adair tell you?"

"I sure as hell didn't hear it from you."

"Guess I got busy cleaning up and didn't have time to call."

"Yet Kenneth Adair had time to be there, go back to the office, go out on a new homicide case, and still call me."

"I'm sorry. I should have called. I'm still shook up."

She sighed. "Are you sure you're okay?"

She had calmed. I reassured her I was okay and only had a little headache. She asked if I had any idea who did it, and she got the same story I'd shared with everyone and his or her brother over the last few hours.

"Want me to come over?"

"Thanks, but I need to get to sleep. I'm fine."

"You'll call if you need anything?"

I assured her I would. "Like you did today?"

Okay, she wasn't over it yet. I repeated that I would call.

"You better. Oh, I almost forgot. The detective who'd worked in Nashville talked to his buddy over there. His friend called back this afternoon and our guy called me. Some people do call me."

"What'd he learn?" I hurried past her snide comment.

"Good and bad news for Heather. Starr Management, owner Kevin Starr, is real. That's the good news for Heather. I know you wanted to hear something terrible about him."

"What's the bad news?"

"The cop in Nashville had to make several calls before he found someone who'd heard of it. The Music City insider told the local cop Starr Management had been around for a couple of years and Starr's relatively new to the business. The contact called him 'A minnow in an ocean of sharks.'"

Oh great, I thought. "Because he has an agency and a stack of business cards, doesn't mean he can help Heather?"

Karen's chuckle surprised me. "I've heard Heather sing. Nothing can help her." Then she said she was glad I was okay.

Karen's call had shaken me awake. It didn't do anything to make me less depressed.

CHAPTER 15

I was to meet Preacher Burl at eleven o'clock at the Folly Beach Crab Shack. Burl had said he wanted to meet early to avoid the lunch crowd. Being the middle of the week in February, I knew there wouldn't be a wait regardless when we arrived. I suspected it was so we could have a more private conversation, which was fine, since I wanted to know what he had been reluctant to share.

The popular restaurant had opened moments earlier and I was given a choice of tables. I would have preferred outside on the deck, but it was in the low-fifties so I picked the spot that offered the most privacy. Burl hadn't arrived and I spent time cracking open complimentary peanuts, tossing the empty shells in a blue plastic bucket in the center of the table, and looking around the brightly- colored interior. Whoever had chosen the colors avoided the beige section of the color wheel. Festive oranges, greens, and reds dominated most surfaces and left no doubt the Crab Shack was beach- centric, fun, and a casual-dining destination.

The hostess had been pleasant, the atmosphere cheerful, and I knew the food would be excellent, yet I still couldn't shake my feelings of despair and sadness. Were they the after-effects of yesterday's assault, or something deeper?

Burl approached and said, "What's with the long face?" He smiled.

I returned his smile. I didn't tell him what I found amusing was how his full, milk-chocolate colored mustache contrasted with a few stands of combed-over hair covering his balding head as well as a diaper could cover a rhinoceros.

"Welcome, preacher." I avoided his question, and pushed the peanuts toward him.

"Ah, my weakness." He grabbed three nuts from the cardboard container and started breaking them open.

"You could have worse weaknesses."

"I'm afraid that I do. Though none so onerous to render me inadequate as a spokesperson for the Lord."

Do I ask what they were? I wondered. I didn't want to get distracted. "Don't we all."

He nodded as the waitress approached and she asked if we were ready to order. I had been in the restaurant many times and knew what I wanted without looking at a menu. Burl had as well and we each ordered fried flounder and water.

"Preacher, the other day when you asked me to look into the death of the man in the alley, you said—"

He leaned forward. "Have you learned something?"

"No."

Burl leaned back, his shoulders sagged.

His reaction reinforced my thought that he knew something he hadn't shared. "You said you didn't know the man, and didn't know how he might be connected to First Light."

"That is correct, Brother Chris." Now the delicate part.

"Preacher, the body was in the alley. He wasn't any closer to First Light's door than to Barb's Books or from the parking lot on the other side of the alley. People walk through there all the time. There wasn't any indication he had tried to break in the buildings, and he could have been going anywhere. What makes you think he had something to do with the church?"

Burl frowned and looked at a mural featuring the Ferris wheel that had towered over the beach years ago. "Brother Chris," he mumbled as he turned back to me, "you know better than most about the various trials, tribulations, and challenges God has bestowed upon me dating back to the first church He led me to establish in Mississippi."

I nodded. Burl had an unbelievably poor record of starting churches before he had crossed the Folly River two years ago. One burned, one was run out of business by other local churches, and one closed after Burl was accused of killing a member of his flock to inherit a substantial sum of money. After arriving here, three of his followers were murdered and suspicion fell on their preacher. Some friends and I found the real killer and First Light survived the rumors and innuendoes.

"Preacher, help me understand why you believe the death may be related?"

"As you have heard me espouse, the Lord works in mysterious ways. I have also said, albeit on not as many occasions, the Devil follows a parallel path. He weasels into our lives, plants seeds of sin, and can appear at the most inopportune time and place."

Burl paused and stared at me. Was the answer to my question in there somewhere? Did Burl believe the hit man was at his doorstep at the behest of the Devil?

"I'm dense this morning. Tell me again why you believe the death was related to First Light."

Lunch arrived before he could clarify, and Burl asked if he could offer a prayer. I said, "Of course." He thanked God for the food, our friendship, and asked him to offer solace to those who were in pain. He said "Amen," and pounced on his fish like he hadn't eaten in a week. Was he hungry, or avoiding answering?

He gulped down his drink and coughed as he swallowed. "Brother Chris, there are only so many times one can be pricked by a pin before believing he is a pincushion."

"You think since you've had horrific experiences with your churches there could be a connection with this recent death?"

"Possibly." He didn't make eye contact.

I didn't have to be an expert on body language to know he wasn't telling me everything. If he wanted my help, whatever that might be, he had to level with me.

"Preacher, please don't take this wrong. There's more than you're telling me."

He looked at me and grinned. "Heavens Brother Chris, how could I take offense from you calling me a liar?"

"That's not what—"

"Brother Chris" he interrupted, "no need to explain. I was teasing. The reason I asked you in the first place was because you have a gift of sorting through the, shall I say, excrement, most others slip and slide in and never get past. I know you have no law enforcement training, but returning to my belief about the mysterious ways God works, He has allowed you to see what others fail to get a glimmer of."

Those were some of the best suck-up lines I'd heard. "Preacher."

He waved a peanut in my face. "Brother Chris, allow me to finish."

I closed my mouth and stared at him.

"I have lied to you." He tilted his head to one side and the other. "Not a lie, but more of a failure to share additional information that may be helpful in your quest for answers." He cracked open a peanut and continued, "I'm conflicted. You see, one of my flock confided something I believe is tied to the incident in the alley."

"What?"

He sighed. "I take seriously my duties as a minister for the Lord. People of all ilk share with me their darkest secrets. To serve both the Lord and my flock, I must hold their words tight to my bosom. You understand, don't you?"

I did, and thought he could use a lesson in brevity from Dude. "Hence my conflict," Burl said looking at his plate. "The individual who shared his secret did so while he was under the influence of the devil's juice. Now don't get me wrong, on occasion I will consume an adult beverage and once upon a time made ends meet by tending bar. Excess is a tool of the devil. Plastered, you might say, was the condition of the gentleman to whom I am referring." He looked up. "Under soberer circumstances, there is no question what my actions would be. His words would not be shared with anyone." Burl hesitated and looked around the nearly empty room and back at me. "I believe the gentleman is in danger; his life may lie in the balance. I feel I have to tell you."

"If that's true, you need to tell the police."

"That was my first reaction. I have no more than suspicions. The man didn't indicate there was an immediate threat. And, to be honest, I promised him I wouldn't tell the authorities. That word I can keep by telling you."

I wasn't up on the ethical or legal constraints between a preacher and a drunk, and still thought Burl should tell the police. I was curious enough to not let it go with what he'd said, or hasn't said. "I understand." I waved for him to continue.

Burl closed his eyes. "Lord, please reassure me that this is the right thing to do."

I couldn't help with that and remained silent.

He sighed. "I received a call from a bartender on James Island with whom I have been counseling on issues I will not divulge. He said one of my flock was in his establishment and had consumed an inordinate quantity of alcoholic beverages. Unbeknownst to the bartender, someone had been buying the man drinks, and if the bartender had known, he would have cut him off. Regardless, I was asked if I could collect the gentleman. I, of course, said I would."

"That was kind of you."

"It is my duty as his spiritual leader. I rushed over and with aid of the bartender, was able to load him in my car. I knew where he lived and was headed there when he said." Burl stopped and put his hands on the table. "Lord, should I continue?"

I waited and Preacher Burl must have received an affirmative answer.

"The gentleman said his name wasn't Douglas Garfield, the name I know him by, and that he was Harlan Powers. Said he had been placed in the 'wit pro pro,' which I looked up and learned was the US Witness Security Program. He didn't confide what he had done to be assigned to the program or where he had come from. I didn't ask." Burl looked at me for a response.

I had known someone else on Folly who had been in the witness protection program. Someone once joked Folly wasn't dubbed the Edge of America for nothing.

"When was this, Preacher?"

"The night you found the body at our door."

"Go ahead."

"Brother Douglas, or Harlan, was both fragile and piano-wire strung at the same time. He kept looking around like someone was following us, and when I got to his apartment it took me a long time to get him inside. I tried to assist him to the bedroom. He flopped on the couch and I didn't possess the strength to move him. One second he was cursing and saying things like 'the nerve of them,' and 'I'm a dead man,' and then he passed out. I'm not naïve to the ways of the world or to those under the influence, yet to be honest, I didn't know what to do. I left him on the couch."

"Did he say anything else?"

"Nothing coherent."

"Are you thinking he thought someone from his past found out where he was and hired the man in the alley to kill him?"

"Yes."

"Have you seen him since that night?"

"Two days later. I stopped by his apartment to see if he had, umm, recuperated."

"Had he?"

"He was sober, although I wouldn't say he was okay. We were in front of his building. His head flicked back and forth like a sparrow at a large bird feeder."

"He say anything about the body?"

"No. I felt so sorry for him and told him I wasn't going to the police, but I had a friend who might be able to find out what was going on."

"What'd he say?"

"Funny thing is I thought he'd be relieved seeing he was so upset before. Instead he stared at me and shook his head, and made some excuse about needing to get back to doing something in the apartment."

Great, I thought. "Did you tell him who I was?"

"I may have mentioned your name. I didn't tell him anything else. Will you please help?"

I nodded that I would.

Burl returned the nod. "It might be helpful to know Brother Douglas might come across as a bit obnoxious."

"Might?"

Burl smiled. "In the spirit of candor, Brother Douglas is obnoxious. He's rude, only interested in himself, and is hard to converse with in a positive nature."

Who wouldn't want to meet Douglas, I thought. I also wondered if it had entered Burl's mind Douglas Garfield could be the person who killed Lawrence Panella if the man thought Panella was on Folly to kill him? I also wondered if it had entered

Burl's mind that he told the potential killer I was looking into the murder. My head began to ache again. This time, it wasn't from contact with a vase, a vase Douglas may have shattered on my skull.

Burl asked the waitress for a water refill, took a sip, and tilted his head. "Brother Chris, I'm not prone to meddle. I can't help but observe that something seems to be bothering you. Care to share?"

Let's see, I find a body; and then someone ransacks my house, before the ransacker uses my head as a vase catcher; and with good intentions, a local minister fingers me to the possible murderer as the person who will try to find out who murdered the man in the alley. Add to that, my best friend may be leaving Folly; my business goes bust; and I'm on the downward side of my life. Why would it appear something's bothering me?

"I'm tired, Preacher." Why not compound everything with lying to a man of the cloth?

"You sure, Brother Chris?"

I needed to work on my lying. This wasn't the time to seek pastoral counseling. It was time to change the subject. "Yes. By the way, what do you know about Barbara Deanelli?"

Burl tilted his head down and his eyes rolled up to stare at me. "You saved my life last year and I owe you big time. I'm here if you ever need to talk." He paused and took another sip of water. "Sister Barbara, the lady with the bookstore?"

I told him yes.

"Not much, I'm afraid. She attended our seaside service three consecutive weeks, and then stopped coming."

"When was this?"

"About the time she opened the store. I may be underestimating the lady's spiritual quest, although I had the impression she was there to promote her new business. As far as I know, she may have visited each church on the island on weeks thereafter to get better known. Marketing, you know."

"Did she spend more time with anyone more than with others before or after your services?"

"Good question. To be honest, as preachers are prone to be." He hesitated and smiled and I returned his smile, more to keep him talking rather than seeing humor or truth in his statement.

"I said I suspected she was there to promote her store, yet she didn't appear good at it. You've partaken in our pre-service sharing of fellowship, lemonade, and coffee, so you know it's an opportune time to catch up on what's happening with the others."

"That it is."

"Well, Sister Barbara was in physical attendance, and shared what I perceived to be a forced smile with those nearby. From what I could tell, she never spoke to anyone to say more than hello. Granted, I was often enveloped in conversation and didn't observe all of Sister Barbara's interactions, yet it struck me that she wanted to market her store, and perhaps herself, but because of shyness, distrust, or not enjoying communicating with others, she was not successful. Chris, I observed her three times at the most, so please don't take this as gospel. I could be off base."

Burl's observations were consistent with my impressions of the store owner and I told him so.

"One more question. The other day you told me you didn't think you knew the man who was killed."

Burl nodded. "Correct. I've given additional thought to it and I still hold to that conclusion. If he was looking to find Brother Douglas, or whatever his birth name was, he didn't seek him out at a First Light service. Of that I am certain."

My phone rang before I could respond. I would have let it go to voicemail and not interrupt our conversation, but I didn't recognize the number and thought I'd better answer.

A familiar female voice said, "Mr. Landrum, this is Barbara Deanelli. I hate to bother you. Is it possible for you to stop by the store in the next day or so? It's about this confounded thermostat."

I looked at Burl and said, "I'm nearby and could be there shortly."

"Perfect, thank you." The phone went dead.

"I appreciate you breaking bread with me," Burl said. "I'll get the check if you need to go."

I almost asked the waitress to take a photo of this historic moment: someone offering to buy my lunch. God does work in mysterious ways.

CHAPTER 16

Barb's Books was fewer than a hundred feet from the Crab
Shack so including a sidewalk conversation with Jamie
about this week's performance of the Folly Beach Bluegrass Society, I was at the bookstore five minutes after leaving
Preacher Burl gobbling down peanuts for dessert.

Barb was the only person in the store. She wore black slacks
and the third red blouse I'd seen her in. She smiled and asked if I
could follow her to the backroom where I could explain the fickle
thermostat. When Landrum Gallery had occupied the space, the
backroom was a hodgepodge of mismatched yard-sale and clearance items. The refrigerator had been discarded from a nearby
house being remodeled; Mr. Coffee had come from the clearance
shelf at Walmart; and the distressed table that had been the center of
social, and occasional work, activities had been surrounded by four
chairs that would have looked at home in a condemned trailer park.

Night-and-day popped in mind as I looked around. The sole
similarity between then and now was the four-foot-long fluorescent
light fixture in the ceiling. My refrigerator had been replaced by an

apartment size, shiny black model. The space where my battered table and chairs had resided now held a glass-top rectangular desk with black, steel legs. On the desk was what I assumed to be the latest iSomething laptop, and a portable Bose sound-system was playing an orchestral arrangement being broadcast from satellite radio's Classical Snob channel. An expensive oriental rug was centered on the foot- worn wooden floor.

Despite feeling like I was in a parallel universe, I was impressed and shared the feeling with Barb.

Her smile widened. "Thank you." She pointed at the thermostat.

Having spent countless hours in the space, I knew what the problem was and had previously told her my solution was to block the vents in the office. She didn't think that was the best plan and said she wanted to make sure the "gadget on the wall" was operating as it was designed to before she blocked the vents. I stared at it like a mystical cure would appear, and wiggled the toggle that set the temperature, before saying, "It's doing the best it can."

"That's what I feared. Can you recommend a reputable repairman?"

She said it like finding someone reputable would be a rarity. I offered her two company names I had heard good things about. She entered them in her laptop, looked at the thermostat, and then at me. "Would you like some water?"

"That would be nice."

"Tap or sparkling?"

Many things had been said by my friends and even a foe during the years I'd occupied the room, yet I was certain that was one question that had never been voiced.

"Tap, please."

She got two glasses—another first for the space—out of the cabinet, the distinct green bottle of Perrier Mineral Water from the refrigerator, filled each glass with ice and poured the Perrier in one and pedestrian tap water in the other. She set both glasses on the table and moved to the door leading to the gallery, whoops, book-store, to see if potential customers had wandered in. Like the hundreds of times I had made a similar move, the store was quiet.

I took one of the seats and after she realized she was customer-free, lowered herself in the chair on the opposite side of the table.

"How do you like Folly?" I asked.

She sipped her Perrier and tilted her head left and then right. "Seems pleasant. I like the mild winter compared to what I'm used to."

Ah, a door into her life had opened. "Where was that?"

"Pennsylvania."

Okay, that's a slight crack in the door.

"Always live there?"

She looked at her glass. "Yes."

The history lesson was over. "Like anything else about Folly other than the mild winter?"

She looked at me like I had asked her bra size. Had I pushed my questioning to its limits?

She paused, and said, "I find Charleston fascinating. Its history, architecture, waterways, thriving art community, all outstanding."

I couldn't disagree, although she still hadn't said anything about Folly. "I've been here going on nine years. I think the people are wonderful and I love the laid-back atmosphere on the island."

Priming the pump might help get her talking about where we were.

"My brother, biological half-brother, told me the same thing before I moved."

"Dude?"

She glared at me. "How do you know that?"

"Small island, few secrets," I said and was surprised because she'd acknowledged being his relative during my first visit. "I think it's great. Dude's a friend and I think the world of him. I didn't know he had any relatives until I heard about you."

"You may have noticed we have little in common."

I'd been thinking nothing in common. "I have."

She smiled—the crack widened. "I hear you have a strange way of helping the police."

"An exaggeration, I'm sure. Rumors are never in short supply."

"Rumors and friendliness." She continued to smile. "Folly folks could friendly a body to death."

"Over the top is an alien concept to some residents. Folly is chock full of passionate people: passionate about their independence, passionate about keeping Folly Folly, and passionate about their friends." I stopped and looked at Barb, hoping she would comment. She gave a slight nod, nothing more. "Anyway," I said, "newcomers tend to either love it or hate it, not many in-between."

"You've been here a long time. I assume you're in the love it category. I know Jimmy does."

It took me a second to realize Jimmy was Dude. I nodded, and didn't want to interrupt her first extended comment. She looked at me like it was my turn to speak.

"Dude's one of the people I think everyone would hold up as a perfect example of what Folly is."

"I hope his two employees aren't good examples. I don't know what Jimmy, Dude, sees in them."

I grinned. "You mean other than being insolent, obnoxious, and rude?"

"That describes the two. The taller one, Rocky I believe, tried to be nice, but fell short. When I met him he said something like, 'Oh, chick, you're Dude's snooty sister. He's stoked you're here.'"

I laughed. "Rocky's a charmer."

Barb chuckled. "Steven, the other one, turned his back on me."

"Stephon," I said. Charles's propensity for correcting others' mistakes was rubbing off. "His ignoring you could be a blessing. It's neck-and-neck to who's the rudest. Back to your question about what your brother sees in them, it's loyalty, and many of his customers identify with them. They're protective of Dude. They'd do anything for him, well maybe not anything, I doubt they'd be polite if he asked them to. Anything else, probably."

"Yes, I noticed how Stephon hovered on each of Dude's truncated words. I'd as soon stay far away from him." She closed her eyes. "I ran into him in Bert's Market, and he was trying to be polite by asking me how I was doing, if everything was okay." She looked at me. "It was like he'd never spoken the words before. He's weird."

I told her each had a kinder side and I shared the story of them participating in Charles's aunt's funeral. Barb said she was surprised; I told her I would have been shocked if she wasn't.

"You live in that house next to Bert's."

"Yes." I tried to hide my surprise she knew. "How'd you know?"

She hesitated and then said, "I saw you coming from there one day as I was leaving the store."

"Yeah, I've been there most of my time here."

"Cute house." She walked to the sink and refilled my water glass.

The front door squeaked open as she set the glass on the desk.

"I'll be back."

I took a sip, stared at the door leading to the store, and thought maybe Barb wasn't as bad as I had thought. We were having a pleasant conversation and she seemed more comfortable. Then another thought struck me. Was she the person who'd broken in my house and smacked me in the head with the vase? Did I think that because she knew where I lived? That didn't make sense; it was no secret and many people knew about it. And, what possible reason could she have? I barely knew her and couldn't imagine a motive. Then why had it occurred to me?

She returned before I overanalyzed it further.

She sighed and pulled another Perrier out of the refrigerator. "I hate romance novels."

"Oh," I said, not knowing a better response.

"Doesn't matter what I like. They outsell every other fiction genre two to one, especially in used books."

I wasn't much of a reader and doubted I'd ever touched a romance novel, much less read one. I moved to more familiar territory and shared how some of my least favorite photos were my best sellers and I had to keep reprinting them. She seemed interested and added that mystery novels were her second best seller.

"Speaking of mystery," she said. "Have you learned more about the man in the alley?"

Why did she keep coming back to that? I told her what the police had learned about his background, his alleged career, and that they didn't know why he was here.

"Think the killer's the person who broke in your house and conked you in the head?"

Now it was my turn to be surprised. "How'd you hear about that?"

She smiled. "As someone told me a few moments ago, it's a small town."

"Who told you?"

"Someone. Are you okay?"

"Only a headache left." I grinned. "You didn't do it, did you?"

She tilted her head, started to say something, paused, and said, "Why, Mr. Landrum, would I do that?" She gave me another smile. "Did you have the secret to operating the thermostat hidden there?"

"Is that a no?"

"What do you think?" She continued to smile.

So far she sounded like an attorney with a sense of humor not giving a direct answer.

I returned her smile. "I think you're avoiding the question."

She looked at the door to the shop and then at me. "Sorry. I've spent too many years deflecting questions both at work and well, elsewhere. Of course I didn't break into your house. Why would I? I am sorry you were hurt."

To believe or not to believe? That was the question; one I couldn't get a handle on. I doubted she was going to help. More than anything, I wanted to see her reaction.

"I can't think why you would." I said, although there was one huge reason she may have. She killed the hit man.

"Are you working with the police on finding the killer?"

"No, all I did was stumble on his body."

"You've helped in the past." She glanced at me and then at the door, either a nervous habit, or wishful thinking someone would come in and end our conversation.

I shrugged. "Ancient history." Once again it popped in my mind about the possibility that she had been the person in my house. I wasn't about to tell her Preacher Burl had asked me to look into the murder.

"Interesting. I'd better get back to running a bookstore. Thank you for your assistance with the thermostat."

She stood and motioned to the door. I was being dismissed.

Why interesting? I wondered as I closed the door on the way out.

CHAPTER 17

I was on my way to bed when the phone rang. It was a little after ten and I couldn't recall ever receiving a call that late bringing good news. I was pleased to see the caller ID indicated it was Karen.

"I'm a couple of miles off-island wrapping up an interview. Have a few minutes for me to swing by?"

I said of course. There had been nothing in her voice to indicate my streak of bad evening calls was about to be broken.

"I hope it's not too late to bother you," she said as she came in.

Her eyes were red and her usual confident gait was absent.

I said it was fine and asked if she wanted something to drink.

She said beer as we moved to the kitchen.

I handed her a Budweiser and sat beside her at the table. "Rough night?"

"Yeah," she said and took a long swallow. "Tracking down a suspect in that high-profile murder on East Bay the other night."

"The tourist from Arizona?"

She nodded. "It was a wasted trip. The guy has an alibi. I'll verify it tomorrow, and if it holds, I'm back to square one." She took a deep breath and shook her head. "That's not why I wanted to come by."

She took another drink and I waited for what was coming. I feared it nevertheless.

"I wanted to talk about it the other night, but ... to be honest, I didn't have the nerve. Then you started about Charles and Heather leaving, and I chickened out." She exhaled. "I've been a cop my entire adult life, and I'm pretty good at it. I rose through the ranks quicker than most, and with an exception of one or two, I have the respect of my colleagues."

I agreed.

She stared out the window and said, "I'm thinking of quitting."

I was shocked, and as calmly as I could asked, "Why?"

She shrugged. "A mid-life crisis, or maybe I'm sick of seeing society's underbelly. Crap, I could be worn out." She looked at the ceiling and back at me. "Or, a combination."

Karen thrived on her work. According to her colleagues, she was one of the best, and from what I could tell, seldom let it get to her.

"What would you do?"

"That's a great question. If I had the answer I wouldn't be struggling with this as much."

"Options?"

She smiled; her eyes screamed anything but happiness. "I could live off my savings, tap out my 401k, pay a bunch of penalties and taxes. That'd carry me a year."

"Not the best option."

She looked down at the table and then at me, yet didn't make direct eye contact. "There are two possibilities." She paused. "I've been approached by a large company that has two corporate security openings. I met one of their big-wigs in November, after he and his wife were witnesses in a fatal hit-and-run I was investigating. One of the jobs is in Charleston. It doesn't pay near what I'm making, but it's convenient." She rubbed her hand through her shoulder-length hair and bit her upper lip.

"The other one?"

"It's at the corporate headquarters. A VP position and I'd be over security at seventeen locations, looking into corporate espionage, theft management, and other stuff I know enough about to get by." She grinned. "The pay's twice my salary."

"It sounds great." I tried to appear enthusiastic, although felt there was a but coming.

"It is." She paused. "But, it's in Charlotte."

More than two hundred miles from Charleston. "Oh."

She glanced at me. "Yeah, oh."

"What company?"

"They asked me not to divulge their name unless I take it."

"They've made an offer?"

She nodded.

"Is it what you want?"

She looked at the floor. "I'm leaning that way."

"The job in Charlotte?"

"Yeah," She mumbled and continued looking down.

After spending umpteen years in human resources with much of that time conducting exit interviews and negotiating contracts with employees who were being hired or promoted. I'd learned to ask one telling question when someone was talking about changing jobs.

"Are you considering it because you're running to something you want, or away from something you're tired of or frustrated with?"

"When I was lying in the hospital bed, gosh, two years ago now, I gave a lot of thought to why I was a cop. I've suppressed a lot of fear since then. I can't shake the feeling I'm not ready to get killed for a paycheck."

Karen almost died from two gunshot wounds sustained while trying to stop a restaurant robbery. It was touch-and-go and the doctors had all but given up on her. She was young and in excellent shape, both things contributing to her recovery. She was off-duty at the time and stopping at the restaurant to get supper.

I thought about reminding her that since she wasn't working when she was shot, it could have happened to her regardless what her job was. I kept those thoughts to myself. "I suppose it would be safer chasing corporate crooks."

She nodded.

"When do you have to let them know?"

"They want to know now, but I bought a few days." She scooted back from the table and went for another beer.

I stared off in space. She returned and I said, "Have you talked to your dad about it?"

She smiled. "Sort of."

Before becoming mayor, Brian Newman had been Folly's chief law enforcement official, and before that had been a military cop.

"What'd he say?"

"Before or after the steam stopped rolling out his ears?"

"After."

"He said he didn't like it; said I wasn't cut out to be a paper-pushing, pseudo-cop; said I'd be bored out of my gourd. He then said he knew where I was coming from and he'd support me either way. He wasn't happy. After grousing about it, he put on a smiley-face and hugged me."

"Back to my question, running from or to something?"

"I wish you didn't have such a good memory. It's both. I'm tired and frustrated with the job, tired of the sadness, tired of the increasing politics that are seeping in, tired of being tired. Then again, the thought of new challenges is appealing and I feel young enough to take them on with enthusiasm."

That was more of a non-answer than I was hoping for, although it led to the real issue for me. It wasn't many hours ago when Karen was telling me if Charles was Heather's true friend, he wouldn't stand in her way of chasing her dream in Nashville. Was I more selfish? Could I leave Folly and move to Charlotte? Could I give up my dream home, at my dream location? Was I too old to make the drastic change?

"That brings up the big question: you and me?" I said. "Charlotte's hours away."

"I've given it a lot of thought, Chris, and I don't know if you'll like what I have to say." She looked me in the eye. "If I take the job, I don't want you to leave Folly. I know how much it means to you."

"Karen."

She held up her hand. "Wait, please. We've dated what, five years? Our relationship isn't much different than it was in the beginning. Doesn't that tell us something?"

I started to interrupt. Instead, I bit my lip and remained silent. "Would I like us to be married?" She nodded. "I think so, yet after this long, I'm not certain. You don't have to say anything. I believe it's the same with you. Besides, if we're destined to be together, whatever that means, we'll find a way to make it work. The good thing about the position is it has regular hours, five days a week. After what I'm used to, it'll be like a part-time job."

She was right. You would think after dating that long, I would have been ready to settle down. There was no one else in my life, and as much as I hated to admit it, I wasn't getting younger. We had a relationship based on love and convenience. There was a good chance of that changing—changing dramatically.

"Separating the new job out of the equation, if that's possible, do you want to give up your job? Is it that bad?"

She sipped her beer. "If I had to make a decision tonight, I'd say yes. Have I thought about it enough to feel I'd be making the right choice? Maybe not, I don't know. That's why I asked for a few more days."

"Is there anything I can do to help?"

"Listening helps. I've still got to think about it, and," she chuckled. "I need to get some sleep and look at it with a clearer head."

I said she could stay the night. She said she'd feel better at home. I walked her to the door, gave her a lingering hug, and tried to hide the tears that were beginning to roll down my cheek. She left the porch and didn't look back.

CHAPTER 18

I had never fallen victim to migraines, but knew they were debilitating. Perhaps it was from the blow to my head but if this wasn't a migraine it was its evil cousin. The pain, feeling like a chainsaw ripping off the top of my skull, kept me awake three hours. I stared at my bedside clock for forty-five minutes after Karen had left. That was after I'd spent the first fifteen minutes trying to wrap my mind around what she'd said. I'd spent the next fifteen minutes feeling sorry for myself, a condition I detest, but one that slips in more as I get older. In the last few days, my best friend was considering moving away, my significant other, or whatever others would refer to Karen as, may be leaving, and I, out of everyone on Folly, had to be the one who stumbled on a body. Had it only been ten minutes since I looked at the clock? Sleep, where are you?

Is there anything I can do to stop any of these things from happening? The simple answer was no when it came to the body. It gets more complicated from there. Charles will make up his own mind. As a good friend, and if he asks, I'll do whatever I can to help him make the best decision, and if it's to follow Heather, I'll step out of his way and support his decision. That would be much easier if I felt Heather had a snowball's chance in a microwave of becoming the star she so dearly covets.

Then there's Karen. She's a good cop; she loves Charleston; she loves her work; and she may, or may not, love me. Is the job in Charlotte something she wants? Is she running to it, or is there something more? Could that something be me?

Love was a four letter word we'd seldom mentioned. On a few occasions she had said she loved me; I'd done the same. But, we had never talked about taking our relationship to the alter. I suppose I knew before tonight it was something she would have wanted.

Five more minutes. Come on clock, either speed up or let me go to sleep. Do I have anything to take for a headache? No. I could go next door to Bert's, the headache cure headquarters on Folly. Never mind. Try to fall asleep—again.

I closed my eyes, but instead of sleep I realized I was the problem. I've been single for a quarter of a century. My marriage ended poorly and while on occasion I appeared to be a glutton for punishment, I wasn't ready to give the sacred institution another chance. Why not? I'm more mature, or think I am. I've learned many lessons about relationships over the last few decades; most were positive. What am I afraid of? I'm set in my ways and look askance at change. Does that make me selfish? Possibly—okay, probably. Could I find anyone I could like more than Karen? Therein lays the problem; why did I think *like* instead of love? Was it poor word choice or intentional? I confess, I'm not certain what love means. Am I trying to overanalyze it? And even if I said I wanted to get married and Karen took the job out of state, was I willing to leave the one place where I feel more at home than anywhere ever; the place where I had more friends than I had accumulated in my first six decades?

The answer didn't come, but sleep had.

The chainsaw in my head was out of gas. The excruciating pain had mellowed to a dull ache. Two things popped into my mind. I hadn't solved a thing during the three hours of pre-sleep misery, and I was starved. Did I feel good enough to walk to the Dog? Would food calm my head and help me find answers to the questions that had seemed so acute in the middle of the night?

I concluded no to both questions, so I ran water over my face, and drove to the Lost Dog Café instead of walking. The restaurant had just opened, but Dude was already at a table sipping on a mug of tea. He was dressed in his ever-present Day-Glo, tie-dyed T-shirt with a peace symbol on the front.

He pointed to the chair facing him. "Yo, Christer, two for tea."

I had hoped to have a quiet breakfast and not have to talk to anyone, and decided eating with Dude would be the next best thing to silence. Besides, I didn't want to be rude being that we were the only two customers. I smiled—yes, it hurt—and joined him. He waved a current copy of *Astronomy Magazine* in front of me.

"Wanna gander?"

The cover had something that looked like a zillion stars, or planets, or space gnats on it. I declined.

He set the magazine on the chair beside him. "Your loss."

During the winter, Dude spent most mornings in the Dog, and by most mornings, I meant five or six days a week in two or three hour blocks. Much of that time was spent with him pondering the solar system, and why the surf shop wasn't as busy as it was in the summer. Years ago I had stopped reminding him about the definition of *off- season*, and now when he asked, I limited my answer to *don't know*. He made enough money the rest of the year to support his tea-drinking habit. You couldn't tell it looking at him, but Dude was one of the most successful business owners on the island.

"Be out early." he said.

I nodded and didn't burden him with the reason. "Business be slow last sunshine," he said and shrugged.

"Oh," I said, my common comment either when I had no idea what a person was talking about, or didn't care to get in a discussion about it.

"No board bidness today. Rocky be back after spendin' lotto fortune. He plus Stephon be handlin' no customers."

"Oh," I repeated, as Amber delivered coffee, water, and a smile. She asked if I wanted to order and I said not yet.

"Didn't think so. Could tell since you look like you've been run over by a shrimp boat." Her smile faded. "You okay?"

I thanked her for her kind comment and said I was tired.

She looked at me like I had told her the sun wasn't coming up today, but nodded and didn't push about my condition.

Amber went to greet another tired looking couple, and Dude said, "Hear you be visitin' fractional-sis."

"She tell you?"

Dude grinned. "No. Have bookshop bugged."

He had the ability to bug the bookstore as much as I could calculate the square root of seventy-three. It was safe to ask the next question.

"You seeing much of each other?"

"More than since she surfed off to grade thirteen."

"How does she like it here?" I'd heard her version and was curious about what she'd told her *fractional* brother.

"She be adjustin' slow, but not warmin' to Dudester."

"Why not?"

"She don't appreciate smarts, charm, and wit of fifty-percent bro."

I smiled. "That explains it."

"That, plus she not accustomed to small berg. She be hanging with lawyersters too long. She be pleasanter with Stephon than be with bro."

"Your employee?" I tried not to show disbelief.

"Employee be like people who want train cats—no can do, but he and Rocky be on job each day."

"Showing up's half the job nowadays. Haven't they been with you for years?"

"Who else be hirin' them? Yes, been around many moons. Some days, want to blast them with my AK-47. Other days, man hug them."

I didn't know Dude had an AK-47 and cringed at the image of him hugging anyone, man hug or not.

"Where'd they come from?"

"Earth moms," Dude said with a straight face.

"You sure?" I said with an equally straight face.

"No."

"They have a past?"

"Odds and biology say yes. Be at tat-shop being inked, but that be all. Me don't know it—don't ask; they don't tell. Both take fondness for part-sis, like they did for Aunt M. Look like puppies around Barb. Tat-covered pit bull pups, but pups."

Dude was spouting more words than usual, and I was trying to figure them out when Russ Vick arrived. I waited for him to say he hated to interrupt. He didn't have to, because Dude invited him to join us.

"You know Russter?" Dude asked as he moved his magazine for the newcomer to sit.

I said I'd met him a few days ago.

Russ shook my hand and said he hoped he wasn't interrupting anything important. With Dude I never knew what was important and told him no.

Russ turned to Dude. "Question, Dude."

"Answer, Russter."

Russ gave me a *huh?* glance and turned to Dude. "You've run a business here for a long time—"

Dude waved his finger above his head. "Many a moon."

This time Russ shared his *huh* look with Dude. "Anyway, I'm trying to do things right. I've joined the business-owners group. I've kept my prices competitive with other stores. I've participated in city events, even gave away T-shirts for that auction the women's group had in December. I've not badmouthed anyone—tempted once or twice. Never did." He paused and looked at me and back at Dude.

Dude said, "What be question?"

I was on the same wave with Dude.

"It seems like others in the business community are treating me like a piranha. They're not saying anything, and when I ask a question, I get one-word answers. I hear grumbling behind my back. I feel I'm not wanted."

I was amused he complained to Dude about one-word answers. It wasn't the time to point out the irony.

Dude rubbed his straggly beard and nodded. "Stealin' money from other businesses be frowned on."

Russ jerked his head back like he'd been punched by an invisible fist. "Stealing?"

"Old saying *competition be good* be wipeout bad. Two-bucks-in-wallet vacationster spend at place already here, store get two bucks. If two places, store get one buckaroo. Store one be pissed. You be store two, the piss-causer."

That's a lesson you won't find in marketing textbooks. The frightening thing was I understood what he meant. Dude was making my headache disappear. I glanced at Russ.

"Are you saying they're afraid of competition?" Russ asked. The *piss-causer* was quicker than I'd given him credit for.

Dude gave a thumbs-up.

"Your sister's new to town. How's she doing? Is she being snubbed?"

"She be selling *libros*. Who else doing that?" Dude asked as he looked around the restaurant like he expected to find someone selling books, umm, *libros*, in the corner.

"Point taken," Russ said. "So there's nothing I can do?"

Marketing 101 by Professor Dude was sinking in.

"Stop hawking T-shirts. Sell penguin suits or totem poles," Dude said. "Be only one in town—be a mono polly."

Russ looked at me. "Monopoly," I said.

To his credit, Russ laughed. "Good suggestion. I'll pass. You're nothing like your sister."

"She be log taller, times two smarter, and chick."

Russ nodded.

I started to say a store named Tuxes and Totems had a nice ring to it, but knew Russ was serious. I said, "Newcomers to Folly, especially if they're opening a business similar to one already here, go through a period feeling like they're being snubbed, or worse, ignored. It's the nature of most businesses. It sounds like you're doing what you can. After a while, you'll be accepted as another business struggling to make it. It takes time to overcome rejection."

Russ frowned. "I hope you're right." He turned to Dude. "Sorry to take up so much time. I'd better get back to not selling T- shirts." He stood, looked around the restaurant, and headed for the door.

Dude watched him go. "Okeydokey *hombre*. FB need new T-shirt bidness like need nuclear power plant."

I agreed and told Amber I was ready to order. She looked at me and said, "French toast?"

I grinned.

"Barb be okay," Dude said.

I told him I had visited her store and had a pleasant conversation.

"Fractional sis say be afearin' ex?"

"No. Is she?"

"Yes sir."

"Why?"

"You know she be art major?"

I didn't and wondered what that had to do with her being afraid. "I didn't know that."

"Yes sir. She be makin' clay sculpture thingees before headin' to legal school. Me never grasped vector change."

"Dude, what does that have to do with her being afraid of her ex-husband?"

"*Nada.* Be trivia."

I wondered if Dude was taking Spanish lessons during the off season.

"Why is she afraid of her husband?"

"Ex. Don't know. Think has to do with him crossing legal lines and bribin' bureau-krats. Be frowned on by fuzz."

"Is that why they got a divorce?"

Dude shrugged. "Hope so."

"Does she think he would harm her?" He nodded. "Would it help if I shared this with Chief LaMond? She could talk to Barb and keep a closer eye on her."

"Barb would kill if you do. Not real kill, figure-like kill. Wants no one to know her bidness. What happen in Harrisburg stay in Harrisburg."

"It's your call, Dude."

"I be watchin' over her. You no worry." Dude grabbed his magazine and started to stand. "Thanks for offerin'. You be good *amigo*."

Dude headed for the door. I hadn't thought about it for a while, but realized my head hurt again. I took a deep breath and wondered what the Spanish word was for headache.

CHAPTER 19

French toast and a half-hour without talking or listening had worked wonders for my head. Its ache was reduced to a dull thud and stayed that way until I tried to make sense out of the death in the alley. I wanted to push it aside, yet, regardless of how hard I tried, it lingered. The more I thought about, the more questions and scenarios came to mind.

If Lawrence Panella was on Folly to ply his trade, was Barbara the subject of his attention? Did her ex hire Panella to kill her? Did she find out and kill him instead? Were Burl's fears about Douglas Garfield valid? Was Panella here for Garfield? If so, did Garfield find out and get to him first?

Did the break-in at my house have something to do with Panella's death, or was it simply a burglary I had interrupted? The note on the bed all but eliminated burglary. On the other hand, I couldn't imagine anyone would think I had something there related to the murder, nor would anyone have any reason to leave the note.

Was the alleged hit man walking through the alley and found himself in an argument with someone who settled it with a bullet; a senseless killing that had nothing to do with Barb, Garfield, Burl, or me? Was I thinking about it to avoid thinking about Karen and Charles's possible moves?

I looked around the near-full restaurant, and, as incredulous as it may seem, not a diner had ventured over and answered my questions. It was up to me, and so I did what many wise people on Folly did when they had difficult questions or wanted to hear the latest rumor. I waved for Amber.

She returned with a coffee pot and a smile. "And how may I be of assistance, Chris?"

Her smile was infectious and I've never stopped looking forward to seeing her. "Ms. Amber, I have a question?"

She continued to smile. "Make it easy."

"I'll try. Do you know Douglas Garfield?" I realized with that question I had told her everything I knew about him except what Burl had confided to me.

"Chemically-induced thin, six-foot-three, long black, greasy hair, with evil-looking, dark-brown eyes?"

"Don't know, never met him. How do you know him?"

Amber shrugged. "We're engaged."

"You're kidding."

"Yep. Seeing if you were paying attention."

I breathed a sigh of relief. "I always pay attention to you."

She batted her eyes. "That's why I've always loved you."

"Am I blushing?" I teased.

"Not enough. What else do you want to know about Douglas?"

"Everything you know."

"That's about it. He's been in a few times. His breath smelled like bad habits and beer, and it was eight in the morning. He's familiar with the brew. He's a hundred pounds shy of a beer belly, so I figure drugs are a staple in his diet. He's tried to be hospitable. My gut tells me it doesn't come easy. He could be as mean as a snake without working up a sweat."

"Does he work over here?"

"He never said and from his clothes he could work in any store, or sit at home and watch soaps all day. He's been in at different times, so I don't think he works off-island. That help?"

I smiled. "Not much. Know where he lives?"

"No, but if you wanted to find him, I'd start at the bars. A dollar to a donut, I bet you'd catch him at one of them."

"Thanks."

"Now, I've got one for you. Why the interest?"

I skirted the question and said I was talking to Burl who said Douglas was one of his flock and he was concerned about him and thought I might talk to him.

Amber stared at me and her eyes narrowed, but didn't pursue it. Instead, she said, "I lied about asking one question. Think Charles will leave with Heather?"

"You want to know what I want to happen or what I think will happen?"

Her smile faded. "Crap."

Two men at a nearby table waved for Amber so she patted my arm and left to see how she could be of assistance.

It was almost lunchtime and since I had nothing else to do, I decided to peek in on some of Folly's bars in hopes of finding someone who fit the sketchy description of Douglas Garfield. There were at least a dozen bars and restaurants with bars so finding him was a long shot, although the odds were better than waiting at home in hopes Mr. Garfield stopped by selling Girl Scout cookies.

After twenty minutes of looking in doors and saying, "No thanks. Looking for someone," I hadn't found Douglas, but knew seven of the town's watering holes where he wasn't. Luck, and the law of averages, smiled at me when I stuck my head in Logger-head's Beach Grill. If the weather was warmer, its elevated deck would have been packed, but it was cool and a crisp wind rolled in off the ocean a block away, so the deck was deserted. The inside bar was near the door and I spotted a man who fit Garfield's description.

A half-dozen customers were seated along the bar on the right side of the restaurant. Sitting alone, with three seats separating him from the others, sat a tall gentleman, wearing a black T-shirt, black jeans, and black work boots. To compliment his attire, he had shoulder-length black hair that looked like it'd been dipped in motor oil. He was in his late forties and was studying the bottle of Miller he held in a death grip. I had the impression it wasn't his first beer of the day.

I took a deep breath and sat in the stool beside him. He glanced over and gave a dismissive look like he would if a fly had perched on the stool. I ordered a glass of Cabernet and waited for it to arrive before speaking.

"Are you Douglas Garfield?"

He was staring at a car commercial on a flat-screen television behind the bar. "Why?" He didn't turn from the TV.

This was going to be fun, I thought. "I'm Chris Landrum, I—"

"Who gives a rip," he mumbled, still without taking his eye off what must be a mesmerizing commercial.

He hadn't denied it, so I assumed he was the right person. "Your preacher is a friend of mine and he asked me to talk to you."

"Buttin'-in Burl, excuse me, Preacher Burl," he slurred and finished off the beer. He waved for the bartender and pointed at his empty bottle.

She said nothing and headed to the cooler. I waited to see if he had anything to say.

"The man gives me one ride home and thinks he's my guardian angel—preachers, guess we need them." He took a sip of his replacement beer and turned toward me. "I know who you are. Hear you stick your mug into as much of other people's business as the preacher does. Seen you walking from your house to Bert's. So why *pray* tell are you supposed to talk to me?" He smiled at his pathetic attempt at humor.

"Preacher Burl is worried. He shared a little about your, umm, situation and was afraid the man who was killed may have something to do with your past. Thought he may have been here to cause you harm."

He took a drag on his beer, slammed the bottle down on the bar, and twisted on the barstool to face me. His beer breath assaulted my face. "I didn't ask the preacher for help. I didn't give him permission to tell anyone what I told him. And, I freakin' don't need help from some damn do-gooder stickin' his nose where it don't belong. I can take care of myself." He pivoted back to facing his beer and stared at the bottle.

It didn't take my degree in psychology to grasp that Douglas Garfield didn't share Preacher Burl's concern he may need help. I finished my drink, slipped off the barstool, and started to leave and let Douglas stew in his brew, when he twisted back to me.

"Who did you blab to?"

I stared at him. "No one."

"Keep it that way," he growled, and returned to his drink.

Not only was that my plan, I was trying to think of a way to erase him from my memory. I learned nothing from the brief encounter other than I wouldn't want to share a meal with Douglas and knew no matter what he had done in his pre-witness protection life, it had nothing to do with running a charm school. What I did begin wondering was whether he was the person who ended Panella's life. It was a short hop to think the answer was yes.

The headache began to return when I realized if I was right about him, he could consider me a threat and could have already left a love note on my bed. Scary, I thought and headed home.

CHAPTER 20

Despite seeing Douglas Garfield's frightening scowl and penetrating dark-brown eyes whenever I closed mine, I managed a good night's sleep. As has almost become a regular event, knocking on the door jolted me out of what should have been the peaceful period between sleep and my first sip of coffee.

Charles stood in the doorway in a navy blue sweatshirt, with Belmont Bruins in red on the front, jeans with a hole in the right knee, his canvas Tilley cocked at an angle on his head, and carrying his handmade cane. "Let's walk."

"Where and why?"

"Bert's for caffeine, anywhere for exercise, somewhere quiet to talk."

For years I had tried to avoid asking him about his massive collection of logo-wear, but knew Belmont University was in Nashville. I hoped his shirt wasn't an omen. The way to find out was to go with him.

Our stop at Bert's coffee urn was followed by a brief conversation with one of the employees. We left the grocery and Charles pointed toward the beach. The temperature was in the low fifties, so the coffee was a pleasant walking companion; so far, better than Charles. Something was on his mind and he wasn't ready to talk. I wasn't ready to ask.

There weren't more than ten people on the beach. Three surfers in their black wetsuits sat on surfboards waiting for the perfect wave that seldom appeared. Two couples were walking dogs, and a lady with a young child was throwing a stick in the surf and watching her enthusiastic Golden Retriever scamper into the water to fetch the priceless piece of driftwood.

Charles stopped to watch the retriever do what retrievers do, and turned and walked away from the pier. He slid the tip of his cane in the wet sand and walked for a couple of hundred yards. I kept pace beside him and realized this was the only time since I had known him that he had gone that long without talking.

Silence was broken when he said, "I spent yesterday and last night with Heather." I remained silent, and we continued walking. "We talked about Nashville."

Duh!

He pointed his cane toward the horizon. "She's got a stubborn streak as long as from here to Wales." He shook his head. "Come hell or high-tide she's set on following her dream to Tennessee."

"You try to talk her out of it?" I bumped into him as he stopped to watch a colony of seagulls perched on the beach resting after a morning hunting breakfast.

He stepped away from me and continued to look at the birds. "Chris, you know how, umm, how shall I say it, vocally challenged my sweetie is. What do you think her chances are of becoming a successful singer?"

I wanted to say nonexistent, but I was walking a tightrope. They were a couple—a strange couple—and I didn't want to insult his *sweetie.* "There's a lot of competition and much of it's in Nashville. I suspect her chances are slim."

Charles surprised me when he chuckled. "How about I'd have a better chance of being crowned Queen of England?" Charles started walking again.

So much for insulting her, I thought. "That may be true. Have you said that to her?"

He glanced at me. "Every time I start thinking you have half a brain, you say something stupid like that."

Charles took an abrupt left turn and headed toward the beach access crossover at Sixth Street. We walked two blocks to East Cooper, and without saying a word, turned toward town. Christmas decorations adorned a house on our right and being February, that would normally have brought a smile to my face. Not today. The ominous feeling I was getting from Charles's discussion and more-telling, his silence, dimmed my view of anything humorous.

We had walked two more blocks. "She wants me to go." I nodded. "My life is here," He waved his cane around and pointed it toward town. "It's my home … it's my … Chris, it's my everything. I'm in my sixties, and after all those years, God, for some reason, sent Heather my way. She says that same God's calling her to Nashville."

I doubted God had anything to do with Heather being called to Nashville.

"You feel you need to go with her."

He took three more steps, stopped, and turned toward the ocean and away from me. "Yeah."

Perhaps it would be best. Heather could make the rounds of open-mic venues, realize stardom might not be in the cards, and return to the island where her quirkiness was normal.

"When are you going?"

"Starr said open-mic night at the Bluebird Cafe is on Mondays so we'll have to leave in the next couple of days. Chris, I've got a favor to ask."

I had been waiting for this. They didn't have a drivable car and whenever Charles and I had to make a road trip, I was the designated driver. A few days in Nashville could be fun.

"What?"

"Would you go with us to buy a car?"

I wasn't expecting that. "How long are you planning to stay in Nashville?" I was prepared to offer to drive them.

"Forever. We're moving."

After spending hundreds of hours with Charles, I didn't think he could say anything that would shock me. I was wrong. I was stunned.

"Moving," I said, trying to hide my reaction.

He stopped and moved to the side of the road. "Heather says nobody hits it big the first day. Says it takes years of making the rounds of free appearances, knocking on studio doors, and working with her agent before *the sky opens up and the sun shines in*, whatever the heck that means. She's talking like that since she started trying to write more songs."

"Where will you live? What will you do?"

"I've got dough left from the inheritance."

Charles and I had shared in the estate of an elderly lady we helped save from a horrific hurricane that destroyed her house a few years back. She had no family and left her estate to us. I had spent most of my share on the failed gallery, while Charles had hardly spent any of his.

I said, "True."

"We can find a cheap place to live and what do I do here? Nothing. It shouldn't be harder doing nothing there. She said she planned to take singing lessons; said they'd help tune up her voice. She has her massage skills so she could get a job anywhere."

I couldn't think of a kind comment about her taking singing lessons, and said, "What if she doesn't find what she's looking for?"

"Suppose it'll be no different than her not finding it here, except without an ocean in the backyard."

While I had to support my friend, I felt like someone had rammed a knife in my back. I put my arm around his shoulder, pulled him close, wiped a tear from my eye with my other arm, and stepped back.

"So when do you want to go car shopping?"

Charles looked at the sandy berm and mumbled, "Today."

A good chunk of Charleston's car dealers were west of town on or near Savannah Highway, so that's where I headed with Charles in the front seat and Heather, along with her guitar that was as ever-present as Charles's cane, in the back. When she got in the car carrying the guitar case she said she wanted it to be as happy with the car they bought as she and Charles would be. I thought she was kidding, although I wouldn't have bet on it.

Charles's previous car buying experience had taken place twenty years ago with a used Saab 900 convertible. I knew because the Swedish vehicle was still sitting in his parking lot in a spot it hasn't moved from in the last five years. As a piece of yard or parking lot art, it was attractive, but as transportation it had as good a chance of moving on its own as did the Folly water tower. I wondered who would inherit the Saab after they moved, but didn't ask; more out of fear it would be bequeathed to the person who was driving them car shopping.

After a back-and-forth discussion between Charles and Heather, they decided they wanted to find something large enough to carry Heather's worldly belongings and Charles's clothes. Charles's apartment was rented for three more months, so he would have time to come back for his books. Unless they bought an eighteen-wheeler today, he would have to rent a U-Haul to move the collection to Nashville. Heather said she wanted them to get a Toyota because she had a dream last night where she was driving one through a field of sunflowers and a quartet of rabbits were propped up on their hind legs singing "You Are My Sunshine."

I was proud of myself for not laughing. I said, "Okay." After all, she was a psychic.

Charles felt he was being ignored and added, "George W. Bush said, 'More and more of our imports come from overseas.'"

I was beginning to feel I was in that sunflower field. Instead of laughing or crying, I pulled in the parking lot of a Honda dealership. Heather asked me to drive through the used car area so she could see if the car *of her dreams* was there. It wasn't and she said to keep going. Charles gazed at four long rows of used vehicles and shook his head.

After the same results at three more dealers, Heather yelled for me to stop. We were in the second row of used cars at the Fred Anderson Toyota of Charleston. She hopped out of the car and made a beeline for a red metallic Toyota Venza crossover, and a middle-aged man wearing a Toyota logoed jacket made a beeline toward Heather.

In the next five minutes, the helpful salesman, who told us his name was Thom, with an *h*, shared that the three-year-old "almost new" vehicle had thirty-nine thousand "easy" miles, had one owner, was accident free, packed with everything Toyota put on a car, and the color was called Barcelona Red. He said since it was February, he could offer a fantastic deal on the "pristine" vehicle. I was almost convinced he was going to give the car to Charles and Heather.

Instead, he said it was a steal at a hair under twenty thousand. That probably was more than Charles had earned during his thirty-plus years on Folly, and he gasped when the salesman threw out the number. I didn't think it sounded bad, and when the salesman learned Charles would be paying cash, he said he would twist the manager's arm and might do better.

To Thom's delight, Heather was jumping up and down and had a huge grin on her face, so Charles agreed to a test drive. The four of us climbed in, and if the salesman was surprised when Heather insisted on taking her guitar, he didn't show it. I was pleased how well the vehicle drove and was impressed by how low-key Thom had been. He pointed out each feature, but didn't apply high-pressure sales tactics. Charles appeared to get more in the swing of things, and when we returned to the lot, told the salesman to give us a few minutes, and if we were interested we would join him in the building.

Our discussion didn't take long.

"That's it, that's it," Heather said and giggled. "That's what I was driving in the field. It's meant to be."

And it was. It took fewer than twenty minutes for us to negotiate another thousand off the price, for Charles's trembling hand to write the check, for the title and registration paperwork to be filled out, and for Thom to say they could pick the car up in the morning.

Our ride back to Folly consisted of Charles mumbling over and over again, "What have I done?" and of Heather singing "You Are My Sunshine" over and over again.

CHAPTER 21

I was exhausted after ferrying Charles and Heather around and watched the local news, something I did to see if there had been any murders in Charleston that Karen might be investigating. Fortunately for the citizens of Charleston and for Karen, no suspicious deaths had been reported. I wanted to call and see if she had decided about the job, but I wasn't ready to know. I had told Charles I'd meet him at his apartment in the morning, help him pack whatever he would be taking, and take him to pick up their chariot. He said with luck, and Heather's ability to get her stuff together, they would leave by mid-afternoon. Realizing Charles and Heather would be leaving tomorrow was enough for me to assimilate. I wasn't a big reader, so reading materials were in as short supply in the house as was food, and nothing of any interest was on television. It was still early, but maybe I could go to sleep and not dream about sunflowers and rabbits.

I was awakened by a strange sound and glanced at the bedside clock that glowed nine-thirty. I shook my head and had to think which nine-thirty. It was dark outside, so it was still night and I had only been asleep a couple of hours. I remained still and waited to see if I heard the noise again. Had I dreamed it?

No dream—there it was. The distinct clink of breaking glass came from somewhere in the house. I sat up and reached for my cell phone on the bedside table. The only light in the room was from the illuminated numbers on the clock and I fished around for the phone before remembering I had left it in the living room.

Nothing nearby could be used as a weapon. I didn't know if the intruder was armed or why he or she was here. I wasn't certain what to do, but figured staying in bed wasn't it.

The floor creaked as I took my first two steps. To me, it sounded as loud as a jet, but in reality, the noise wasn't enough to carry outside the bedroom. I was at the door when I heard a sharp crack of breaking glass coming from the spare room. Someone was removing glass from the window frame.

The sound gave me hope. Whoever it was may not be inside. The person didn't worry about masking noise since it was only nine- thirty and he must've thought I wasn't home. The only weapon in my arsenal was surprise. Would it be enough to scare off the intruder?

I tiptoed to the door to the spare room and reached around the corner for the light switch. I gave a second, and third thought to running for the back door, rather than doing what I was about to do. Instead, I held my breath and flicked the switch.

White light bathed the spare room and blinded me. More glass from the window shattered and I blinked a couple of times for my eyes to adjust. I saw the silhouette of someone's back falling away from the window frame. A gloved hand appeared on the ledge. One leg had been inside and caught on the sill as the body tried to pull it out. I moved toward the window. If I couldn't catch the intruder, I had to see who it was. A sliver of glass slashed into my foot and changed my priorities.

I stumbled. My foot felt like it was walking on burning coals.

My knees hit the floor and I grabbed my foot. My eyes watered from pain and from the abrupt switch from pitch black to bright white light. I pulled the shard out and looked at the window. He was gone.

I hobbled to the window and stuck my head out, looked both ways, and saw the headlights of a truck was barreling down the street from the direction of the Washout. Nothing else. All I was left with was the second broken window pane in two weeks and a painful cut on the foot.

I pogo-sticked myself to the bathroom using the walls as a crutch to lean against on the way. My foot felt like it had a samurai sword stuck through it, but under the harsh bathroom light, I saw there was little bleeding and the cut was minor. I rinsed it in the tub and put some anti-bacterial cream on the wound before applying a bandage I found under the sink.

I hobbled to the living room and plopped down in my chair. I looked at the door to the spare room and despite a foot that still felt like it was on fire, realized how lucky I was, and how foolish I had been to burst in on the intruder without anything with which to defend myself. I looked at my phone on the table beside the chair. Do I dial 911 and have a fire truck, an ambulance, and several patrol cars in front of my house for a minor injury? Instead of 911, do I call Chief LaMond?

I continued to stare at the phone and wondered what calling anyone would accomplish. The intruder had worn gloves so there wouldn't be prints. He didn't get in the house so nothing had been stolen. And why would I want police, EMTs, and no telling who else, traipsing around the house and telling me there was nothing they could do. Besides, adrenaline had taken me from the bed to the spare room and now here, but I realized I was exhausted and tomorrow would be worse. I wondered what could be in my house to cause someone to break in once and now try again, and to have left the not-so-subtle hint for me to *LEAVE TOWN*. Did the intruder try a second time because I scared him off the first time before he found what he was looking for? Again, what could it be? And, could it have been a female breaking in? The question was bouncing around in my head when I fell asleep.

Another noise woke me. It was the phone that jolted me out of sleep rather than the sound of breaking glass.

"Where are you?" Charles yelled. "It's almost sunrise and you're not here."

I wanted to yell, "I'm not there because it's almost sunrise." Instead, I said, "Give me a half hour."

"Hurry. I've been helping Heather get her stuff together, and we need to get moving. The car's going to be ready in three hours."

My brain wasn't awake enough to do the higher math, but at first thought, we could get Charles's stuff together in thirty minutes and be at the Toyota dealer staring at Thom nearly two hours before he told Charles the car would be available. I didn't share any of that with my anxious friend.

I hobbled to the bedroom to get dressed and decided there was one other thing I wasn't going to share with Charles: last night's break in. He didn't need to worry about me. His mind was made up about going with Heather and as a good friend, I needed to respect his decision; respect it even though it hurt more than the gash in my foot.

CHAPTER 22

C harles and I had finished packing and had his stuff by the door awaiting the arrival of his car. We had driven to Charleston, and were now sitting in front of Thom's desk an hour before the time we were to be there as he told us for the third time the features of Charles's purchase. Charles didn't appear to be paying attention and kept looking at his wrist where most people wore a watch. My friend didn't own one, but it didn't stop him from the visual reminder to Thom.

I'm sure Thom was relieved, and I know I was, when a service rep called to say the Venza was out front and ready to go. Charles beamed as Thom handed him the keys. I asked Charles if he wanted to stop at a liquor store so I could buy a bottle of champagne to break over the front fender to christen his new craft. His frown indicated he didn't see humor in my suggestion. I didn't either.

I followed him to his apartment and helped him load three copy paper boxes in the hatch. He borrowed my phone and called Heather to see if she was ready to load. After saying, "Yes, sweetie," twice and kissing the phone's screen, he asked if I could help them load the car. In a moment of weakness, he said once they got to Nashville he was going to buy a cell phone. He had never had one, nor had he ever had an answering machine or a computer, so I had to tell him how to find a store that sold phones. He promised to call with the number.

I'm not a sappy person, and was embarrassed that I had to wipe tears away on the short ride to Heather's apartment. It was finally hitting me that my best friend was leaving. I also reconsidered my decision not to tell him about last night's excitement. No, nothing good would be accomplished by raining on his parade out of town.

Heather was on the front step when we pulled up in front of her building. Her guitar case rested on her lap and a huge smile adorned her face. She jumped up and down—actually, she jumped up and gravity brought her down—when Charles opened the hatch from the driver's seat. She threw her arms around him like he'd arrived home from three years in the Sudan after serving in the Peace Corp.

I stood back and watched. I wanted to be happy for the couple and Heather's success in the music world, I truly did, but all I managed was a fake smile.

It took a half hour to haul Heather's belongings to the car. Searching for something to be thankful for, I was reminded her apartment had come furnished, so none of the furniture had to be crammed in the Venza. We did have to find room for a large, black and silver karaoke machine, a music stand, and her "favorite" chrome picture frame with crystals attached by a thin thread dangling from the top edge.

She placed her guitar case and wide-brimmed, straw hat she wore when performing on top of her possessions, and announced she was ready to *meet her destiny*.

I hated to see them go, but I was happy for Heather. On the other hand, I was sure her elation would be short lived, though it wasn't my place to tell her. I asked them if they wanted to go to the Dog for a farewell meal.

Charles glanced at Heather. "Nah," he said. "Better hit the road. Hope to get to Knoxville and spend the night before going the rest of the way in the morning."

"Mr. Starr wants me to call as soon as we get there," Heather said, and hugged me. "Thanks, Chris. You're the best thing that ever happened to Chucky—other than me. I love you."

I returned her hug and didn't say anything. I wasn't able to.

She headed to the passenger seat and Charles scuffed his foot in the shell and gravel parking lot. I noticed he wore a black, long-sleeve T-shirt unadorned with any college identification; the same shirt he had worn at his aunt's funeral, and one that was out of character from his logoed T-shirt collection. I wondered if it was intentional or the next shirt in line.

He looked at his foot that was still pushing gravel around.

"Guess this is *adios*. You know I'm bummed about leaving." He looked at me. "She's special. Don't find gals like her every day."

You can say that again, I thought.

His eyes began to water. "Now," he paused, sniffed, and said, "danged allergies. Chris, I think I've done a good job of training you to carry on my reputation. You still need to practice being nosy, and lazy, and you need to concentrate on being dumber. You've learned from the best, but you still have a way to go." He stepped back and looked at my navy blue polo shirt and lightweight tan jacket. "As Andy Jackson said, 'There goes a man made by the Lord Almighty and not by his tailor.' I never did learn you how to dress."

He was right, thank goodness. I told him I would try harder to be like him, but he could never be replaced. He said he would be back in a few weeks to get the rest of his valuables, which meant a hundred or so T-shirts and three zillion books.

"Chucky," Heather squealed. "Music City's awaitin'."

"Yes, sweetie."

He tipped his Tilley to me, winked, told me to take care of his island, and slid into the driver's seat.

Heather was ecstatic. Charles was happy. And I felt a void growing in my stomach, heart, and head.

There were a few people on the street and sidewalks, yet all I could see on my short drive home was a small town that hadn't yet realized it had lost one of its most endearing characters. The colorful exteriors of The Grill, Woody's Pizza, Planet Follywood, the Crab Shack, Taco Boy, and Snapper Jacks looked duller. Even the red signal on Folly's stoplight looked pale.

I walked in the house and tried to tell myself to cheer up. One glance at the broken window deepened my depression. Was my world falling apart, or did it just seem that way? It had been fifteen minutes since he had pulled off-island, and I was already missing Charles. I didn't know her as well as Charles did, but I also missed Heather's unique outlook, her quirky hobbies, and her ability to make him happy. I wouldn't miss her singing.

My mind switched to Karen. Would she be next to leave? I shouldn't—couldn't—stand in her way when it came to the job opportunity. She'd had a long and stressful career. She deserved to be happy, and if taking the new job met that need, I would support it. Then again, am I part of the reason for her considering it? She wanted more from our relationship; at least she did at some point. Would that have made a difference in her career decision? I moved to the kitchen, grabbed a Diet Pepsi, sat at the table, took a long sip, and flipped through a copy of a new photo magazine that arrived yesterday. Neither the Pepsi nor the magazine offered solace.

My mind switched to Preacher Burl and his concern for Douglas Garfield. After meeting with the obnoxious member of his flock, I had no interest in honoring Burl's request to help him. I wondered if Garfield was responsible for the two break-ins. He had said he could take care of himself; that's all I needed to know. So why did I feel guilty?

Now to Dude. I had known him for years and while we had little in common, I considered him a friend. If I'd learned anything since moving here, it was that friends looked out for each other, watched each other's back, and I could cite several examples of where they put their lives on the line for each other. Dude was worried about his sister and therefore, so was I. But what could I do? Was she in danger, or was she a murderer?

I moved to the spare room and stared at the broken window. Cold February air rushed through the opening, bringing a chill, but no answers. I closed my eyes and pictured Douglas Garfield smashing the glass; I could also see Barbara doing it. Or it may not have anything to do with the death in the alley and was someone high on drugs looking for the money to feed his habit.

I shut the spare room door to keep the cold from infiltrating the rest of the house, took a walk on the pier, wondered if Charles and Heather had made it to Knoxville, watched the sunset behind the Tides hotel, and tried to cheer myself up by watching a sitcom. The artificial laugh-track failed to convince me anything was worth laughing about. I prayed tomorrow would be better.

CHAPTER 23

For the second time in the last few days, I called Larry to repair my window. He wasn't at the hardware store and Brandon, Larry's only full-time employee, said the owner was taking the day off and spending it with his "cutie-pie." I asked if that was any way to refer to the chief of police. He said "yep," and added if I wanted to incur the wrath of Larry, I could call his cell. Why not, I thought, and punched in the number. Larry said he was having a "delightful" day with his lovely spouse watching her select onions at Harris Teeter. I told him the problem and he said, "Thank God. A reason to get out of this frickin' grocery." For Larry, shopping ranked up there with barreling over Niagara Falls. He said he'd be here as soon as he convinced Cindy they didn't need asparagus and okra.

Fifty minutes later, Larry pulled up in his yellow Pewter Hardware pick-up truck. Instead of asparagus and okra, he carried a red toolbox and a pane of window glass wrapped in brown cardboard. He also had a police escort in the form of Chief Cindy LaMond.

Cindy said, "No way am I going to let the boy get away from me that easy on our day off."

I assumed it was her explanation of why she was with him on the emergency hardware store run. I also had a hunch she wanted to find out how the window got broken. I welcomed them and offered coffee, water, Pepsi, beer, or wine. They chose coffee. Larry said if he wasn't working with sharp glass, he would have taken beer. They grabbed their drinks and followed me to the spare room.

Cindy looked at the window and squinted. "Hmm, rock? Kid throw a baseball through it? Meteorite?" She gave me her best police stare. "Wait, I've got it. Somebody broke in. Again."

I smiled. "Don't suppose you'd buy a seagull strike?"

Larry, showing wisdom, ignored our conversation and began scraping away the caulk around the broken pane.

Cindy sat in the chair in front of my computer and leaned back. "Who and when?" She wore jeans and a denim work shirt, but had morphed to on-duty.

"Night before last," I said and took a deep breath. "Don't know who."

"Night before last," Cindy growled. "When were you planning to report it? Christmas?"

"Now."

Larry hummed "Jingle Bells," and continued his work as if we weren't there. I wished I wasn't.

"Did you think someone was taking a shortcut through your house to Bert's?" She shook her head. "Lay the details on me."

I told her what little I knew. She asked why I was asleep at nine-thirty and if I was positive I didn't see who it was. I said I didn't get a decent look and added I didn't see any reason to call the police. What I did see was an intruder wearing gloves so there wouldn't be prints, and I scared him off before he—"

"Or she," Cindy interrupted.

"Or she, got in."

Larry's cell rang and he listened for a minute and said, "Okay, I'll be there in fifteen." He put the phone back in his pocket, sighed, and said he had to go to the store and bail Brandon out. "The credit card machine—on its own, without any assistance from my computer- illiterate assistant—added three extra zeroes to a thirteen-dollar charge and the peeved customer won't leave until the problem's corrected."

Larry put the finishing touches on the new window and asked Cindy if she was ready to go. She said she had things to discuss and Larry could pick her up when he finished battling Brandon and MasterCard. He tried to plant a kiss on her mouth on his way to the door. She turned her head and he got her cheek.

"Remind me to never, never, not ever take that boy to the grocery," Cindy said, as that boy drove away.

I smiled. "Thought you two were having a fun day together."

"Yeah, right."

We moved to the kitchen and she asked if the offer of a beer was still good. I said yes and she accepted and plopped down in a kitchen chair. There was something on her mind, so I remained silent.

She took a sip and put the bottle on the table and held it with both hands like it was trying to escape. "Got a strange call last night."

I remained silent.

"Detective Adair called around ten and apologized for calling so late. That got my attention."

She took another sip and I nodded.

"He said he had been talking with a detective with the Pennsylvania State Police. They were calling about Barbara Deanelli. Seems there's an investigation going on up there and they knew she was living here and wanted to know if the sheriff's office had her on its radar. They had contacted the great detective agency in the cloud, Google, and saw where her name popped up in a Charleston TV station's report about a body found behind Barb's Books, owned by you-know-who." She paused and took a draw of beer. "Detective Adair told the Penn police person that if he knew that, he knew as much as Adair knew. He told the detective he would contact me since I was closer to what happened here and would get back with him if he learned anything. As you can imagine, he learned zero from me."

"Why's she being investigated?"

"Chris, haven't you learned by now that hoity-toity state cops look at sheriff offices like you'd look at a rabid opossum; sheriff-office fuzz look at us local yokels like you'd look at the rat bit by the rabid opossum. State cops tell county cops squat; county cops tell local yokels half squat."

"Adair doesn't know why Barbara's being investigated."

"You missed your calling. He learned a bit more than I thought he would. The Penn police said it had to do with Barbara's husband, now ex-husband."

"She's not the subject of the investigation?"

"He didn't say, but my take is no. That'd depend on what they turn up."

"Think our murder could be connected?"

"Our murder?" She frowned at me, and continued, "Doubt it, remember, my half-squat status doesn't get me invited to many meetings about what's going on."

"Has Adair learned anything else about Lawrence Panella's death?"

"Now that you ask, Adair did share a sliver of information with Chief Half-Squat." She pointed to her face. "Seems Mr. Panella was living, as we say back home, high on the hog in Myrtle Beach; had a nice fancy house, wife belongs to an exclusive country club."

"You said he was a successful equipment salesman. Wouldn't they make good money?"

"No argument with that. Except a forensic audit of his finances showed there wasn't a legitimate source of income to keep them in the lifestyle to which they had been accustomed."

"If he was retired, there wouldn't be as large an income as when he was working."

"There you go," Cindy said. "I agree with you again, that is until he said the audit went back the last six years he had allegedly been selling those big-ass machines."

"Is this where you tell me his W-2s didn't add up to the money he was spending?"

"Lordy, Chris." She put her hand over her heart. "We've never been on the same surfboard together like we are now. You've smacked the dilemma right on its bald spot."

"If Charles were here, he'd quote a US President who said something about cash being king. People who hire hit men don't pay with a payroll check."

"Right again. The bank records show a bunch of cash deposits under the ten-thousand-buck limit that has to be reported. The cops up there would love to question him about them. Unfortunately, as you know, he's unavailable."

"Any deposits in the last few weeks?"

"You're pushing the limit on what the big-wig cops shared. If I was guessing, I'd say no."

"Why?"

"Because the Pennsylvania cops asked Adair if he found a large quantity of cash on Panella or in his hotel room."

"Cash for the hit?"

"That's my take."

"And none was found."

"Five hundred bucks rolled up in a shoe in his hotel room, and he'd paid for the room with a credit card."

"Learn anything else?"

"Cripes, Chris. Thought I did pretty good to charm that much out of Adair."

"You did."

"Speaking of Charles, do you think he and Heather are serious about heading to Nashville?"

It was a stretch to say I'd been speaking of Charles. "Not thinking about it, they left yesterday."

Cindy leaned back like I'd slapped her. "You're kidding."

"Wish I were."

"Details?"

I proceeded to tell her about their decision, Charles buying a car, their packing, and leaving.

"How long do you think they'll be there?"

I shook my head. "The way Charles talked, it could be forever."

"Damn, double damn."

An hour later, the phone rang and an unfamiliar out-of-state area code popped up on the screen. Great, all I need is a telemarketer trying to sell me a condo, offer a free cruise, give me an opportunity to donate to an incredibly worthy cause, or to buy a coffin at a discount. Larry had picked Cindy up after our cheerful discussion about death and Charles leaving, so I thought *what the heck*, and rehearsed all the ways I was going to say no.

"Mr. Landrum, I'm glad I caught you. This is Barbara Deanelli. Is this a bad time?"

I was surprised. "It's fine, how are you?"

It beat having to say no, but I realized how dumb it was to ask her how she was. I doubted she called to share her condition.

"I've got a favor to ask," She hesitated. "A couple more questions. Could you stop by tomorrow?"

"Sure. Any particular time?"

"I'll be here from nine on."

I told her I'd see her in the morning. I didn't tell her it would be close to her opening because I had acquired a couple of nosy genes from Charles.

CHAPTER 24

If Charles was here, he would have me standing in front of Barb's Books thirty minutes before she unlocked the door. He was hundreds of miles away, so I exerted a dollop of patience, and opened the door to the bookstore five minutes after it opened; not quite fashionably late, but the best my curiosity would allow.

"Good morning, Mr. Landrum. What took you so long to get here?"

A lighthearted comment, more progress. Barbara stepped from behind the counter and greeted me with a handshake. She wore the same red blouse she had on the first time I'd met her. She had switched from black to gray slacks.

"Please call me Chris. Would've been here sooner, but my flight was late."

Instead of looking at me like I was an idiot, she smiled. "Call me Barb. Tap water or coffee?"

I started to ask if *Barb Tap Water or Coffee* was her Indian name, but decided not to push my luck with humor—attempt at humor.

"Coffee would be great."

She waved for me to follow her to the back room. "Good, I got a new coffeemaker and wanted to try it out on someone."

She pointed at a black and polished-chrome Keurig machine that looked like it should be in a science lab rather than a bookstore. I was informed it made one cup of coffee at a time, a feature I didn't think was efficient, as I watched her insert a cartridge in the machine, pull a lever, and push a button. My Mr. Coffee machine that had lived on the same counter for years would have been humiliated sitting next to the high-tech gadget.

We watched one cup brew and she repeated the steps and prepared one for herself. She said she should get back to the front of the store and motioned for me to follow. We sipped our high-tech coffee and talked about how nice the winter weather was as compared to the part of Pennsylvania where she'd been, and about how business had picked up. I didn't figure either topic was why she had called, and waited for her to feel comfortable enough to share.

After an awkward pause, she said, "The reason I called is I was wondering if you had a problem with rats?" She pointed to the corner of the room.

And I worried half the night about that?

"No. There are a lot of them on the island. I've had a few in my house, never in the store. Do you have some?"

She looked at the floor like one was going to step out from under one of the bookcases so she could introduce us.

"There were a few, umm, droppings in the back room," She wrinkled up her nose.

I thought it was cute, and said, "It must have scooted in when the door was open. I don't think there're any openings; none large enough for a mouse, much less a rat."

"I'll get a trap."

And that was important enough for her to call. To offer a bad, although timely, pun, I smell a rat.

"While you're here, I have another question." Barb looked around the empty store. "Let me show you."

She led me back to the office and to the back door. She unlocked the door and twisted the deadbolt.

"I'm having trouble with the lock." She gave it another twist. "It gets stuck and I wondered if there was a trick to working it."

She stepped aside and I pulled the door to and twisted the knob. It was tight, but it wasn't any different than what I had remembered.

"I'm worried about it not being locked. I'm here alone so much and worry about safety after what happened …" She stopped, looked at the door, and at me.

The squeaky front door opened before she could continue and I followed her to the front. A man had entered and walked to the mystery section. He was my height, a few years younger, wore a black polo shirt, khaki slacks, and a red Chicago Bulls ball cap.

I leaned on the counter and Barb sat in the chair. I said, "Back to your question, the locks may be a little more difficult to turn. If you're concerned, you may want to call Pewter Hardware and ask for Larry. He'd be glad to come over and replace the mechanism. He's a good guy and will treat you right."

Barb watched the customer as he came around the shelves and down the next aisle. "Is there anything in particular you're looking for?"

"Just browsing."

Barb continued to focus on the browser, and said to me, "That's a good idea. I'll call." She jotted down Larry's name on a note card.

The man pulled a couple of books off the shelf, flipped through them, seemed to tire of browsing and left. He was gone, and Barb continued to stare at the door.

"Do you know him?" Her fingers tapped on the counter.

"I don't recall seeing him before. Could be a vacationer killing time while his wife's in Charleston shopping. Why?"

"This is the third time he's been in since yesterday morning. He gives me the willies."

Three times in that short a time was unusual, but why the willies?

"Has he bought anything?"

Her fingers continued to tap on the counter. "No."

"What bothers you about him?"

She turned away from the door and back to me. "Want more coffee?"

I declined and wondered if she'd heard my question.

"I haven't had the store long, although long enough to learn to tell the difference between buyer and browser. I may be paranoid. It seems more like he's casing the store rather than browsing. Does that make sense?"

"Elaborate?"

She looked toward the bookcases. "I hate to admit it, and it wouldn't hold up in court, but I ran into a lot of men like him when I was practicing law. I didn't do criminal law, but some of the white collar crooks had that look in their face. There's an arrogance about them." She pointed to the door. "That guy took a few books from the shelves, like that was what he was supposed to do and each time he looked around like he was taking everything in. I can't explain it. Seemed creepy."

From other things she'd said, the man killed behind her store had bothered her, bothered her more than the tragedy of someone being killed there.

"The police chief's a friend. If you want, I'll ask her to check around and see if her people—"

"No," she interrupted. "No big deal; I'm being melodramatic. Sorry I said anything. Besides, I can handle any trouble that comes this way." She leaned down and touched something under the counter.

"You sure? I'd be glad to."

She shook her head. "I'm sure. I know the chief's your friend. Has she said anything else about the guy who was killed?"

"No." Not the whole truth, but all I was willing to share. She sighed and asked again if I wanted more coffee.

She wanted to talk so I said yes and we headed back to the latest-greatest way to brew coffee. I still had the feeling she had called for another reason other than to ask about rats and a sticking lock.

Barb brewed two more cups, pointed to the desk, and moved her chair to where she had a view to the front door.

"Rumor is on this isle of gossip, you're someone who keeps your mouth shut when you learn something rather than spreading it around." She cocked her head to the left.

I smiled. "Where'd you hear that?"

She returned my smile. "If I told you, I'd be spreading gossip."

"If it's true, it isn't gossip."

She shrugged. "I was in Jimmy's—Dude's—surf shop yesterday; had gone over to ask him if he was having trouble with his phone system. Mine's been dropping calls and I wondered if it was a system problem or mine."

I waited.

"Anyway, he'd run out to pick up lunch and I was stuck talking to Stephon and Rocky." She giggled. "It was more like me listening to the surly employees complaining about stupid customers, wimpy waves, cold weather, and how some people like to tell tall-tales about Dude being retarded."

I smiled. "Customer service isn't their forte."

"True. I'll tell you one thing, those guys are more loyal than a hound dog would be to my brother. In another canine reference, they're like two pit bulls protecting him from what, I don't know. That makes me like them despite their attitude."

"They grow on you."

"If I'd had people around me as loyal as those two, I wouldn't be here. Anyway, my brother returned with a sack of food, and gave Stephon and Rocky lunch and took me to his cluttered office."

I may have imagined it, but I thought she cringed when she said office. I wouldn't have been surprised since hers was 180 degrees opposite of Dude's clutter-filled, disorganized work space.

I waved my hand around the room. "Looks like this one."

Barb laughed. Her hazel eyes sparkled and this was the first time I'd seen her relax. "I bet the city dump's neater." She turned serious. "After we figured out the phone problem was in the system, I was telling Dude you came in the store for the first time the other day, and he started telling me about the escapades you had been involved in and how he helped you catch a murderer a few years back. He also said if you learned anything that was none of anyone else's business, it stopped with you. That's what I meant about gossip." Her smile returned. "He also told me about giving you surfing lessons."

"One lesson, and *he be talkin'* too much," I said in my best Dude voice.

She laughed again. "Dad used to tease that I got all the words and Dude got all the trouble."

"Don't know about trouble, although he was right about words. Dude doesn't waste many."

Someone came in the door. Barb said she'd be back. I once again looked around and continued to be amazed how different the room looked. I also wondered where she was going with her stories. I didn't wait long. She returned to her seat and lukewarm coffee.

"Two books lighter."

"Two more than I ever sold this early."

She turned her coffee cup around a couple of times and stared in it like she expected to see something more interesting than coffee. "My husband, ex-husband, and I started our law firm in Harrisburg."

I already knew this from Dude who wasn't as good at keeping secrets as I was. I nodded.

"I did most of the legal work, mainly defending executives accused of white-collar crimes, and Karl, my husband, carved out a niche lobbying for corporations that dealt with state government. To be honest, we were successful beyond our wildest dreams, especially Karl's area. Don't know if you know much about it, but influencing the right legislators could mean millions, crap, hundreds of millions of dollars to companies that either deal directly with the government, or can use their government connections to get jobs or make sales outside the public realm."

"Made more than from selling two books?" I may be good at keeping secrets, but I wasn't as good at not being a smart aleck.

She giggled. "Slightly."

"So, you two were tearing up the world." I motioned for her to continue.

"Then the proverbial shit hit the fan." She frowned and gazed in her coffee cup. "A dozen law enforcement officials from every agency known to man stormed in our exquisitely-appointed offices, threw search warrants around like confetti, escorted Karl, our receptionist, our befuddled paralegal, and me into the corridor, and proceeded to turn the place upside down. It would have made my brother's office look like an ad in a design magazine. They hauled out computers, files, and my self-esteem."

Barb blinked and closed her eyes. I remained silent and hoped no customers would come in and distract her.

"Chris, I was my high school valedictorian; I was in the top five in my law school class; my IQ's in the top quartile, or so the records say. I'm not stupid. You have to believe me. I had no clue about what was going on with Karl. None."

I took her cup, poured out the cold coffee, and fixed her another one. She sat and stared at the wall.

"What was going on?"

"Long story short." She took a sip. "Karl was bribing legislators and regulatory officials, bureaucrats in charge of projects affecting his clients. He was bribing them to switch votes, bribing them to sweep reports under the rug that reflected negatively on actions his clients wanted, or to overlook roadblocks to the client getting their way. All that time, I was going about my business of defending crooks, doing the time-honored, within the law, job of helping clients." She shook her head. "No clue, Chris. I had no clue."

"I'm sorry."

"That makes two of us." She looked up from her coffee. "Before it hit the fan, our marriage was, shall I say rocky, but when everything broke, my only option was to leave." She forced a smile. "And now I'm here."

"What happened with the…the legal problems?"

"I was interviewed—interrogated—by numerous cops, my bank records received more scrutiny than the Affordable Care act, and despite their best efforts, they found nothing which would indicate I knew about his activities. Of course there are those who think I know more than I do. When it hit, some of the corporate officials who were involved scattered like cockroaches when the lights turn on. One was caught trying to sneak over the border to Canada in the trunk of his Mercedes." She smiled, more sincerely this time. "I've heard a couple are hiding in Florida under assumed names and a couple more are still on pins and needles thinking I could send them to prison if I told what I know—which is nothing."

I'd heard Dude's version and asked, "What happened to Karl?"

"It's remarkable what high-powered lawyers can do. Karl had a few 'bucks' stashed away the feds didn't get their hands on, and hired the best of the best. Instead of spending time playing Scrabble with other white-collar crooks in a country-club prison, he got off with disbarment and time served, a whopping three months. He moved to New Jersey and if you can believe tax records is making minimum- wage. He's not practicing law, but writing briefs for large law firms."

"Why tell me?" I shouldn't have said it. I had to admit some of Charles had rubbed off on me.

She smiled and nodded. "To be honest, I don't know. I had to, no, wanted to tell someone. Telling Dude would have been like telling that Keurig machine. I don't know anyone else enough to confide in. I don't want it spread around. And, Lawrence Panella." She hesitated and looked at the back door.

"What about him?"

"He was here to kill me."

Barb's declaration was followed by two families arriving in search of beach reads. There may have been a worse time to end a conversation, but I couldn't think of any. While she played the part of shop owner, I waited at her desk and ran several scenarios through my head. Was she right? If she was, how could she have known? Why was she telling me instead of going to the police? And, the most intriguing question, who hit the hit man?

Fifteen minutes later, I heard another customer enter. I was thinking there were more visitors than were ever in my gallery at any one time when Barb stuck her head in the doorway.

She was in customer mode and smiling. I was impressed how she could go from talking about a hit man out to kill her to helpful owner. She shrugged and pointed toward the group of customers. "Sorry, Chris, I'll get back to you."

CHAPTER 25

I left Barb with her customers and my stomach growled a reminder I hadn't eaten. I walked to the Dog and was almost run down by a pick- up truck while my body was in the middle of Center Street and my mind was in the alley behind Barb's Books rehashing my introduction to Lawrence Panella. A horn blast stunned me back to reality. I waved an apology and continued to the restaurant. It was chilly and no one sat outside so I hoped I wouldn't have a long wait for a table.

The restaurant was full and after what Barb had said, I was too nervous to stand and wait for someone to leave. I turned to go back outside where I could walk around the nearby community park and wait for a table.

I started to push the door open when I heard, "Brother Chris."

Preacher Burl was seated at the table behind the hostess stand and waved me over. If I had known who was with him, I would have pretended not to hear him. Douglas Garfield, or whatever his real name was, glared at me. He had no interest in seeing me and didn't hide it.

Burl said, "Join us, Brother Chris."

If he was aware of Douglas's glower, he ignored it.

"Thanks, Preacher," I said while Garfield's glare lasered through me. "I don't want to interrupt. I'll wait for a table."

"No interruption. We'd love for you to join us."

Douglas didn't say anything. His scowl said he was not part of *we*. I took the chair beside Douglas so I wouldn't have to make eye contact with him.

Amber was at the table before I was settled. "Yogurt?" She knew I had never ordered it, nor ever would.

I smiled. "Not today. How about French toast?"

"What a surprise," she said and started to leave, but instead stopped behind Douglas, tapped me on the shoulder, pointed at him, and mouthed, "Douglas Garfield."

She'd remembered I had asked about him and I nodded. Preacher Burl looked to see if anyone was within earshot and leaned closer to Douglas and me. "Brother Douglas and I were talking about what I shared with you the other day."

"Preacher," Douglas interrupted, "I was drunk and never should have told you. If I wanted people to know, I would have told them." He pointed his thumb at me. "I don't know this guy from Adam. It's none of his damn business. We're talking about my life."

"Brother Douglas, Brother Chris is a friend and can be trusted. God has worked through him to help solve several difficult situations. He's on our side."

I'd never considered God had a hand in me stumbling into bad situations, although have had several occasions to thank him for helping me survive them. Plus, I had no idea what their side was.

Douglas exhaled, looked at his half-eaten pancakes, then at Preacher Burl. "I don't like it. I don't like him." He pointed his thumb at me once more. "Your big mouth could get me killed."

"Douglas," I said. "I don't know what you and Preacher Burl were talking about and I don't know why you're in such a precarious situation. I assure you I understand the delicate nature of the, umm, program, and would never do anything to endanger someone in it."

"And I'm supposed to believe that crock because a complete stranger said it?"

"Yes," Burl said. "You've shared some thoughts with me and I don't have either the wherewithal or influence to provide assistance. Brother Chris does and I would recommend you give him a chance."

I regretted not leaving when Burl first called my name. Douglas Garfield was obnoxious, rude, and had said nothing to make me want to even talk to him, much less help. Instead of excusing myself and walking as far as I could away from him, I took a page out of Charles's playbook.

"Douglas, what were you and Preacher Burl talking about?"

Douglas was gripping his fork like he was afraid it would jump out of his hand and stick him in the eye. He glowered at Preacher Burl. "You tell him."

One of Burl's talents, and one I suspected had helped him through some of the bad times that had plagued his life, was his ability to look past insults and attacks on his church and find the good in everyone. If he couldn't sleep at night, it wasn't because he harbored resentment or took mean-spirited attacks personally.

Burl gave Douglas a calming smile and turned to me. "Brother Douglas believes Mr. Panella, the gentleman murdered behind First Light's foul-weather sanctuary, was sent to Folly Beach to end his life."

"The damned piece of...never mind. He was scum and here to kill me."

"How do you know?" I asked.

He stared at me like I'd asked him how he knew the ocean had water in it. "The people the damned Marshals Service are hiding me from found out where I was and want me dead."

"How would they have found you, and again, why think that's why Panella was here?"

"Can't you see?" Douglas growled.

Burl gestured toward Douglas's face. "Allow me to contribute."

Douglas looked like he was going to slap Burl's hand away. Instead, he took another deep breath, and went back to stabbing his pancakes.

"Chris," Burl said, "Brother Douglas has long had a fear the federal protection program was susceptible to leaks—"

"Like a damned sieve," Douglas interrupted.

"He believes," Burl continued as if Douglas hadn't said anything, "word has reached those for whom he was responsible for, shall we say, having their freedom removed, are now seeking retaliation by contracting with the late Panella to murder him."

I understood, but still hadn't heard anything to substantiate his claim.

"Did you see Panella?"

"No," Douglas said.

"Had you heard someone might be out to get you?"

"No."

"Has anyone from the witness protection program contacted you about a leak?"

"No," he said, continuing Dude-like responses.

I was beginning to understand why someone would want him dead, and I didn't know anything about his background.

"Help me understand. I get how the people you helped the government convict would want revenge, but I still wonder how you know he was sent for you."

He looked up from his food, his eyes squinted. "Preacher Burl said you were a bright fellow and someone who could help me out of this situation. All I see you doing is asking stupid questions and sounding like you don't think I know what I'm talking about. It was a foolish mistake telling the preacher about my past. It'll get me killed. And you're as idiotic as he is." He pushed away from the table and stood. "Forget it, and forget you ever saw me. I've taken care of myself pretty damn well."

He stormed out of the restaurant and nearly barreled over a toddler at the door.

Burl watched him go and cringed when Douglas grazed past the kid. "That went well, don't you think?"

"Couldn't have said it better," I smiled at the preacher. I appreciated his humor and composure during the difficult conversation.

Burl looked toward the door and down at his empty plate. "He's scared."

"Has a funny way of showing it."

Burl shrugged. "He's all plugged up with the past, the life he had to leave, fear that his secrets will follow him here, and a bit of paranoia thinking everyone is out to get him. He uses anger and obnoxiousness as a wall to keep people out."

"He's good at it. Did he tell you he was afraid?"

"Didn't have to. Despite his attitude, he's got a sensitive side."

"He hides it well."

Burl smiled. "That he does. He acts like he hates everyone, yet he's at our service most Sundays. He doesn't say much. He sings the hymns, and nods his head when I say something profound. Yes, Chris, on occasion I say something important. Anyway, he knows what's going on and seems to benefit from church."

"I'm glad to hear it. What do you think I can do if he doesn't want to talk?"

"I don't know. I have faith you'll figure something out."

If only I was that confident. I opened the door to something that was going through my mind the entire time Douglas was talking.

"Got a question, Preacher." I hesitated, and continued, "Do you think he could've killed Panella?"

Burl looked at me and gave an almost imperceptible nod. "Chris, I've got to tell you, my calling is to find the good in people;

to help lead them down the path toward salvation; to give benefit of the doubt when no one else will. I must confess, Brother Douglas has caused me to reevaluate my position." He hesitated, took a sip of tea, and continued, "I would not be shocked to learn he's responsible."

That wasn't what I'd expected.

"Preacher, I don't know Douglas. He does seem capable of taking a life. If he found out about Panella, it wouldn't take much imagination to see him killing him before it was the other way around."

"I don't disagree, yet I still want to think he's not guilty. Please do whatever you can to determine for sure."

I said I'd try, and Burl said he had to go.

He left the Dog and I picked at my French toast and realized in a matter of a few short hours, both Barbara Deanelli and Douglas Garfield said they were convinced Lawrence Panella had been contracted to kill them. One or both were wrong. If either were correct, did he or she kill Panella? During times like this I would get with Charles, discuss it, come to some horrible conclusions, say something that made sense, and decide what, if anything, there was we could do. I missed him.

CHAPTER 26

I left the restaurant and stuck my head in Barb's Books hoping to hear why she thought Panella had been on Folly to kill her. To her benefit, and with a tinge of jealousy on my part as former owner of a failed shop in the same space, she had her hands full with customers browsing, asking about books, buying books, and fighting for Barb's attention. Instead of waiting, I decided to visit her half-brother.

The surf shop wasn't as busy as Barb's, nonetheless, I still had to get past Dude's gatekeepers to get to his tiny office. Stephon frowned at me before the front door had even closed. "What?" he asked.

"Want to see Dude."

"Don't know if he's here. Yo, Rocky, boss man here?"

Rocky was in the middle of the store fiddling with surf-board stuff, their names and purposes alien to me. "Who wants to know?"

"Old man Chris," said Stephon, taking customer un-service to new heights and throwing it off the roof.

"I'll see if he's taking *unexpected* visitors," said Rocky, who apparently had gone to the same school of customer service as Stephon.

Stephon proceeded to ignore me while I waited for the verdict from Rocky.

"Chrisster!" Dude yelled from the office.

I looked toward the back and Dude waved for me. Rocky didn't growl when I passed him, it just felt that way. Dude's surf- product, decal-covered door was another sign that the owner believed in using every square inch of wall and floor space to stick ads and logos of surf paraphernalia, or fill with items the ads promoted.

Dude slid a stack of wetsuits off the extra chair in the room and motioned for me to sit.

"I was lucky to make it past your bodyguards."

"They be protective. Charmers be not."

Be understatement, I thought. "That's a good thing. And, they're so good with customers." I smiled.

Dude waved his left hand and then his right. "Keep um, kill um, be daily dilemma. Hear Chuckster and main-squeezette boogied to surfless music town."

"Yes."

"Wipeout. Be sad for Folly and canines."

"You're right."

"Bummer." Dude looked out the door. "You be here to visit my peeps?"

"Stopped by to see you. Seeing them was an added treat."

"Lucky you." Dude smiled. "Here me be."

"I was talking to your sister a little while ago and she mentioned you so I thought I'd stop to see how you were."

"Fractional-sis." I nodded.

Dude walked around me, stepped over the wetsuits, and closed the door. "She share worry about killer man?"

"Why do you ask?"

Dude held up his thumb. "Dead guy be carrying gun," stuck out his index finger, "reputation as never-caught hit man," and added his middle finger to the count, "fractional-sis knowing stuff shouldn't know."

Dude's lengthy—lengthy for Dude—multi-media presentation threw me. He didn't extend another finger, so I said, "She did share the thought that Panella was on Folly to kill her. What do you know about it?"

"She don't tell me more than ripple. Me be seeing fear in frac-tional-sis face. When we were home as tiny pup and puppette, she fearin' nothing. Scary strong."

"Do you think she has something to be afraid of?"

Dude looked at the closed door and fiddled with a ring of keys on the desk. He nodded. "Someone sent never-caught hit man, hitter be hit, bad guy be sending more." He frowned. "Fractional-sis be good gal, me do anything to keep her safe."

I changed the subject. "Why do you think the hit man was killed?"

Dude waved his arms around the room. "Folly folks fight with each other—yell, scream, give finger, bite finger. Outsider mess with us, be enemy of us all. Fractional-sis now be Folly gal."

I knew what Dude had meant. It didn't answer the most impor-tant questions.

"Dude, if Panella was supposed to kill Barb, how would someone here have known?"

Dude opened a desk drawer, pulled out a wrinkled five-dollar bill, and waved it at me. "Dude pay o-pressive taxes to fuzz to figure out killing."

I couldn't disagree. Dude is often underestimated because of his clipped and nonsensical speech pattern, but he's brighter than many give him credit for, and sees things in a much different light, a perspective that is missed by more, shall I say, traditional observers. I still wanted his take.

"True, so what's your opinion?"

"Me no detective, be store owner on way to geezerhood. Someone from her history wants her extinct; someone from her current wants her alive. Hit man stand in way of current want and got bullet. There it be."

It was a summary I couldn't find fault with, although still shy of answers. "Who?"

"How be easy, who be hard. Hit man ready to break in fractional-sis's store. Hit man hitter strolled up and put lead in head."

Two thoughts came to me. First, the most logical candidate would be Barb. Second, the other most logical suspect was talking to me.

"Who here would know her well enough to have learned about her past to know what's happening, much less find out about a contract killer and kill him?"

"Barb say she talked to you about history." He hesitated and looked at the ceiling. "Me be knowin' most of it." He slid the five-dollar bill back in the drawer and looked at me. "That be it."

A pounding on the door interrupted us. "Boss, get your ass out here," yelled the *pleasant* voice of Stephon. "Some bill collector says he needs to talk to you. Talk to you now."

Dude rolled his eyes. "Fans beck in."

I followed him to the front of the store, patted him on the back, and left him with his fan.

I thought about going home and trying to forget everything. Instead, I weathered the cold breeze, pulled my jacket tight, yanked my Tilley down as far as I could over my balding head, and walked to the end of the pier where I did my best thinking.

If Barb was Panella's intended victim, both she and Dude were the most-likely suspects. From what she had told me, Dude could be right. I doubted she had told anyone other than me enough to figure it out. She would have had the most to gain from his death. It would make sense that she would have known what had transpired to make someone want her out of the way. I watched a flock of seagulls circle a section of beach, and kept coming back to my initial reason for thinking she wasn't the killer. Why would she have approached me the morning I found the body to ask what he looked like? It didn't make sense, and then it struck me. What if she had been fishing to see if I saw anyone else on my ill-fated walk? Her, for example. It still didn't feel right, but it was a reason that made sense.

That left Dude. Their relationship didn't appear to be close, but it seemed he would have been the one other person on the island who would have known her well enough to know she was in trouble. He could have learned about Panella and killed him before he could harm her. I had never heard Dude talking about guns, but remembered he had kidded—or I thought he was kidding—about blasting his two employees with his AK-47. If he owned that powerful weapon, it would be nothing for him to have a handgun. Dude was protective of Barb, and I didn't doubt he would do whatever he could to shield her. But hadn't Dude asked me from the beginning if I could help Barb? Why would he have done that if he was guilty?

The seagulls flew to another dining spot on the beach and a young couple walked a large Greyhound under the pier. My mind wandered to my earlier conversation with Preacher Burl about Douglas

Garfield who was convinced the hit man was on Folly for him. While I suppose it was human nature, I wanted Garfield to be the intended victim. I was beginning to like Barbara and didn't want her to be involved in Panella's reason for being here, or his death. I couldn't find anything likable about Douglas and felt sorry for Preacher Burl who had become involved in the surly man's problem.

I wished Charles was still here so we could talk about the situation. The fact was, he's gone. Someone broke in my house twice and I suspected it was related to Panella's death and me finding the body. And most importantly, two people I consider to be friends had asked me to help solve the crime. At this point in my life, friends are the most important thing I have.

CHAPTER 27

I answered the phone after the third ring. "Did I wake you?" Barb asked.

She had. It was a little after ten o'clock and I was already asleep after an exhausting day meeting with potential killers and bemoaning Charles's departure. She didn't know me well enough to know that unless it was a major emergency, along the lines of a nuclear attack, my phone and door were disturbance-free zones when the evening hours reached double digits.

Of course I lied. "No, I was awake."

"Good. I felt bad about how I left this morning's discussion. I apologize for not finishing our conversation."

"Never apologize for too many customers," I said, describing a condition I had seldom experienced.

"Thanks. Anyway, I'd like to make it up to you. Could I buy you breakfast tomorrow?"

I was often the one doing the buying when it came to my friends. I said sure and we agreed to meet at the Dog at seven-thirty to beat the church crowd and other Sunday regulars.

I turned over in bed and wondered how it would feel having breakfast with a possible killer. I smiled when I realized it wouldn't be my first time. I didn't wonder or smile long, sleep returned.

We had been wise to meet early. When I greeted Barb at the door, the Dog was almost full. Once again, she was wearing a red blouse, this time under a heavy, pleated, black, Patagonia jacket. I wondered if she had as many red blouses as Charles had college T-shirts. She also wore black, "skinny" stretch jeans and black-leather calf-high boots. It was in the forties, but she was dressed for Pennsylvania winters.

My favorite booth was taken and we were seated at a table against the wall. I took the chair facing the room and Barb sat facing a kennel-full of canine photos. She was quick to shed her jacket and Amber was as quick to welcome us to the Dog and ask what we wanted to drink. We said coffee and Amber started to the kitchen and stopped behind Barb and gave me the kind of look that only women could muster. It was a cross between "shame on you," and "you sly dog." Men's facial muscles weren't sophisticated enough to send mixed messages with a single glance.

Nearby tables were full and Barb leaned closer. "I left you yesterday with a strong, albeit unsubstantiated, accusation."

Strong was an understatement if she was referring to her accusation that Lawrence Panella was there to kill her.

"About Panella?" She nodded. "Why do you think you were the target?"

"I can't prove it, but I believe it as much as I believe anything. After my divorce and before I decided to leave Pennsylvania, I received several calls. Anonymous, disguised voice, *unknown* number. Each with the variation on the theme: *We know you know about us. Tell anyone and you're dead. Don't think about running. We'll find you and we don't have to tell you what'll happen then."*

"Do you know what they were talking about?"

"It had to be about Karl. Like I told you, the magnitude of corruption he was involved in was never revealed. Millions were never recovered. There were enough skeletons left in closets to equip every anatomy lab in the country."

"Did you go to the police?"

"And tell them what?" She paused when Amber returned to take our order. Amber smiled. From years of observing her many customer expressions, I knew it was forced.

"Tell them about the calls," I said after Amber had moved on.

"Calls from unknown numbers. Calls cryptically implying I knew something. And calls telling me not to run. What would the police have done with that?"

"Good point."

Barb looked at her coffee. "Besides," she was barely audible, "I didn't know anything about what was going on. I wish I did so I could have told the cops. Truly, I don't know anything."

I didn't want to argue, but pointed out, "You said the magnitude of the corruption was much greater than known and there were millions never recovered, and something about skeletons."

"I figured out most of it from Karl's court proceedings and from the little I knew about who he had dealt with before getting caught. I have no proof, and not enough information to help the police put together a case against anyone."

"Yet if you're right about Panella, someone thinks you do. Someone thinks you have enough to put him away, and enough that he wants you dead."

"I wish I did know something," she repeated. "Honest to God, I do." sighed.

Our food arrived and Barb took a bite. She closed her eyes and "Who do you think killed him?"

"If I were the police and knew about Karl's troubles in Pennsylvania, I know I'd have a suspect." I pointed to my table mate.

"Yes," she said.

"Have they talked to you?"

"Not yet. It's a matter of time before they learn about Karl and come knocking."

"What'll you tell them?"

"The truth."

I assumed *the truth* wouldn't be a confession. "Could it have been one of your friends who didn't want you hurt, someone trying to protect you?"

She chuckled. "Let's see. In Pennsylvania I had two friends, both women, both attorneys, both happily married with kids, and who wouldn't be able to find Folly Beach, much less a gun and shoot someone in the head."

"And here?"

"If you don't count Jim, umm, Dude, my extended friends list would include Stephon and Rocky at the surf shop who almost speak civilly to me because I'm related to their boss, and you."

"Oh," I said, sounding more like Dude each day. "I hate to ask, but should get it on the table. Could it have been Dude?"

She sat her mug down with a clunk and scowled at me. "I thought he was your friend. How could you say that?"

I was afraid she'd react that way. I sipped my coffee, glanced around the room, and turned back to her. "Put on your attorney's hat and look at the situation like you would if someone accused of a crime came to you and asked you to defend him. Wouldn't it be prudent to look at the crime from all angles, look at all possible suspects, and look for any connection to the crime to be able to defend your client?"

She continued to stare, but nodded.

"Wouldn't Dude have motive to kill the alleged assassin?"

"I don't know the adult Dude. Why would he?"

I refrained from pointing out I had never heard adult and Dude mentioned in the same breath. "He's protective."

"He was that way as a kid. I don't know about now."

"I do, and heard someone say he would do anything to protect you."

"Really?"

"Yes, and Dude is my friend. I can't imagine him putting a gun to Panella's head and pulling the trigger unless he was provoked or Panella pulled a gun on him and Dude had to defend himself. That doesn't mean he didn't. He told me the other day his employees irritated him so much at times he'd like to shoot them with his AK-47. He was teasing, but until he said it, I didn't know he owned a gun, much less an AK. The point being, he's a man of few words, and I suspect, many secrets."

"If what you're hinting at is true, how would he have known that guy was here for me?"

"Good question. How would anyone have known? The fact is, unless the killing was a robbery gone bad or the result of a disagreement, someone found out and didn't want him to succeed."

"I still can't see Dude doing it. And before you ask by sounding like you weren't trying to ask, I didn't do it."

"I know."

She reached across the table and patted my hand. "Thank you. How do you know? I have the strongest motive, and I knew someone was out to get me."

"True, yet remember the morning I found the body."

"Like I could forget."

I pointed to the next table. "You went right over there where I was sitting."

She glanced at the table where we had met.

"And what did you ask me?"

"Several things. I have a tendency to ask multiple questions."

"You did ask a few. The two that stuck with me were: Did I think the body was closer to your back door or to the door to First Light, and would I describe him."

"From that, I assume you think if I killed him I would have known where he was?"

"And what he looked like."

"I still have my lawyer's hat on, and to be honest, those two things wouldn't carry much weight if the prosecutor had a preponderance of evidence, albeit circumstantial, against me. They would argue that I was asking to see if you saw anything, possibly the killer—me."

"Maybe, but when you came in here that morning, you'd just learned about the death, and those were two emotionally-charged questions. They weren't you setting up a defense."

She smiled, the first time this morning. "Thanks for thinking I'm not that devious. I'm going to take it as a compliment, although they would have thrown me out of law school for that character flaw." Her smile faded and she looked around the room. "That doesn't let Dude off the hook."

"No."

I returned her smile and then turned serious. "Let me throw out another scenario. What if you weren't the intended victim?"

Russ Vick interrupted. "Hi." He was wearing one of his off-color T-shirts and a denim coat, and standing behind Barb. "Don't mean to interrupt, Chris. It is Chris, isn't it?"

I had seen the back of the burly T-shirt maven on the other side of the room with two men when we came in. I started to tell him he should put *Don't mean to interrupt* on one of his T-shirts, since he'd perfected the technique. Instead, I said, "Hi, Russ. Good to see you."

Barb's head was twisted around to see who I was talking to.

"Russ,' I said, "have you met my friend Barbara Deanelli? She owns Barb's Books."

Russ looked toward the door and glanced at Barb. She craned her neck to see him and smiled.

"Don't believe I've had the pleasure."

One of the men at the door yelled, "Come on, Russ."

Russ smiled and said, "Would stay and talk, but got to catch up with my friends. Wanted to say hi. And, oh yeah, Chris, if you see Charles tell him I need an answer. He'll know what it's about."

I hadn't recalled inviting him to stay and talk, so wasn't that distraught he had to go, nor did I feel the need to tell him about Charles.

"Nice meeting you," Barb said as Russ headed to the exit.

I doubted he heard her as I watched him leave the restaurant with his friends.

I said, "Russ owns SML Shirts and Folly Tease, the two new T-shirt stores on Center Street."

"I've seen him around. I've not been in his stores, but have seen some of his T-shirts on my customers. I imagine the Folly Beach city fathers are thrilled Folly Tease is bringing near-obscenity to the wholesome families vacationing here."

I smiled. "We all contribute to society."

"Yes," Barb said. "I also suspect his stores are far more successful than the new bookstore on Folly."

"And that bookstore is far more successful than the photo gallery before it."

She grinned. "And now you can sit around and drink coffee while I'm slaving away selling books."

I shrugged. "Before we were interrupted, I started to—"

"Hey, Chris." Interruption number two. "Hi, Barbara."

Marc Salmon, one of Folly's city council members and one of the island's leading gossip spreaders, was standing where Russ had been. Barb."

"Am I interrupting?"

Of course. I didn't point out the obvious. "I see you know Barb"

"My wife is one of her best customers."

Marc and his fellow council member, Houston, spent an hour or more each weekday in the Dog. It was unusual to see him here on Sunday, yet not surprising. Rumors don't take the weekend off, so he had to make an appearance.

"True," Barb said. "Mr. Salmon's wife devours romance novels like a bat gobbles mosquitos."

"Please call me Marc. I'm glad your store's here. Miss B. was driving me to the poorhouse with the new books she was buying. Used's the way to go. It's also great we have a new, positive business on the island."

I wondered if it was a cut at Folly Tease.

"Gotta get to the grocery and home," Marc said. "Good to see you. Oh, Chris, before I go, rumor has it Charles Fowler and his gal friend might be moving."

You're slipping, Marc, I thought. Charles and Heather leaving wasn't a conversation I wanted to have this morning with the council member. "I'll check."

"You do that, Chris," he said and was gone.

Barb asked, "What's the deal with Charles and Heather? He's not saying one of my best customers is leaving Folly?"

I told her that her customer was not leaving, he was gone already. I gave her a five-minute version of a story about Charles and me that would take days to tell. She listened and interrupted with a couple of good questions. I didn't tell her about Russ's job offer for Charles, now a moot point.

"I'm sorry to hear it. I wish I could have a friend as good as Charles has been to you."

I blinked a tear out of my eye, wiped it away, and made a joke about how the sun was in my eye. Barb pretended to believe me and asked, "What's a possible scenario where I'm not the target?"

I looked around expecting another interruption. None appeared. "What if Lawrence Panella intended to kill someone from the church? The body wasn't any closer to your door than it was to First Light. Have you met Preacher Burl Ives Costello?"

"I went to a few of his services and he's been in the store looking for used bibles. We've not talked beyond a polite greeting. Why?"

"He's a good man and is doing a great job with his non- traditional church."

"Meeting on the beach was refreshing."

"Preacher Burl has come to me to ask if I could check into a delicate situation."

"By delicate, I suppose that means you aren't going to tell me about it."

I smiled. "If I ever get in legal trouble, I want you as my lawyer."

"I hope that day never comes."

"Me too. No details, but the situation involves one of his members whose past is not available for public consumption."

"Witness protection program?"

"I didn't say that. His member has reason to think Lawrence Panella was here to revenge something he may have said or done that got the person who hired him in a heap of trouble."

Barb looked out the window, down at the rest of her food, and at me. "And my hippie brother's main selling point for Folly was it was a laid back, happy place; not his exact words, but that was the gist. He forgot to mention the murder per-square-foot ratio."

"Not be chamber of commerce friendly," I said, channeling Dude.

Barb laughed and her hazel eyes glowed in the sunlight that had allegedly caused my eyes to water.

I glanced at my watch and realized it was a half hour until First Light's morning service.

"Want to go to church?" I said, and wondered where that had come from.

"Think book buyers will wait until this afternoon for me to open the store?"

"Don't know about them. Photo buyers never kicked in the door to buy anything when I was away."

CHAPTER 28

I had attended church on a regular basis until I was in my twenties. I stopped going one Sunday and forgot to go back— for four decades. My introduction to First Light came after I nearly got killed when someone ran down one of the church's followers, killing him within inches from where he and I had been standing.

It was chilly, so I glanced in the First Light foul weather sanctuary to make sure the morning's service had not been moved indoors. It was empty and Barb and I continued down Center Street and past the Folly Pier to the opening of the beach where I saw Preacher Burl. He would've been hard to miss in his white robe made from a bed sheet. His arms were outspread and from the rear looked like a kite readying itself to be pulled skyward by the breeze. He was standing behind a repurposed school lectern and facing fifteen or so people who were moving toward the folding chairs in the sand.

Charles wasn't there to point out I was late, while Barb and I took seats in the back row. I knew, either by name or face, most of the others. When everyone was seated, Preacher Burl asked us to "silence thy portable communication devices," and to join in singing a hymn out of a photocopied songbook. The group warbled through the hymn and Preacher Burl said, "What a joyful noise to the Lord."

I grinned as I remembered when he had told me the definition of joyful didn't contain the words pretty, pleasant, or good. Burl's flock showed an overabundance of joy, and a dearth of singing ability. It was the thought that counted.

Burl was a master at preaching to the common man. He was down to earth, translated the complex parts of the Bible into language everyone from an illiterate street person to a college professor could understand and relate to. That talent, combined with the uniqueness of meeting in the midst of people walking dogs, playing Bocce ball, building sandcastles, and sunbathing, helped First Light meet the religious needs of many whose shadows would never darken the doors of traditional houses of worship. In addition to his sermons touching all comers, they tended to be long-winded and redundant, which gave me time to focus less on what he was saying, but on who was there. An advantage of being on the back row was being able to see everyone. Today, that consisted of regulars and for the first time I noticed Douglas Garfield. He wore his scowl, but was focused on each word out of the preacher's mouth. Dude was on the other end of the back row and nodded toward Barb and me, and his two employees sat in the sand behind him. I didn't know if they were his bodyguards or were church goers, which, if so, would surprise, no, would shock me.

I also did a double take when I caught the profile of the man who had been in Barb's store several times. I wouldn't have noticed him if he hadn't kept glancing our way.

The service ended with the last verse of a horrific rendition of "Onward Christian Soldiers," and Dude was quick to welcome his sister—half-sister, fractional sis, whatever—to First Light and ask her why she was here.

She explained she and I were having breakfast and I invited her.

"Woe, Chrisster be marketing for God."

Rocky and Stephon had been trailing Dude and moved beside him. Stephon looked at Barb and said, "Good to see you." He looked at me and snarled. We continued to bond. Stephon told Dude they were headed to the surf shop and the two of them left. Burl joined the group and said he remembered Barb from his earlier visits and said he was thrilled she joined the group this morning. Douglas Garfield had started our way, kicked the sand, turned, and slinked away.

Dude asked Barb if she wanted to walk with him to the surf shop. She looked over at me and gave an almost imperceptible shrug, I nodded, and she said, "That would be nice."

I was glad to see she and Dude were spending time together. From what she'd said, it was clear she needed more friends, and Dude, in addition to being her half-brother, could be a good one.

My gladness ended when Burl said, "Is it true Brother Charles and the darling Sister Heather are no longer among the residents of Folly?"

I told him it was.

"Folly will never be the same."

"You're right, Preacher." I looked around to see if the stranger who had been in Barb's was nearby. He wasn't. "Burl, do you know the man who sat in the row in front of us on the other side? He had a brown coat and a black scarf."

Burl looked toward the seat where the man had been seated. "Don't recall his name. I'm bad about those, you know. He arrived a few weeks ago. I try to meet each newcomer at the end of the service. He was here three weeks ago and told me his name, which I forgot as soon as he walked away. He said he'd come from somewhere up North and was looking forward to our warmer weather."

"Did he say where up North and what he was doing here?"

"No to both questions, and I didn't feel it was my place to ask. If, or when, the gentleman wishes to disclose details of his life, I will listen. If he seeks spiritual guidance, I will oblige."

"I understand." Understood, yet wished Burl had picked up some of the inquisitive habits of my friends.

"He seems like a pleasant sort," Burl added. "I doubt he has anything to hide and would be glad to disclose the answers to your questions upon your inquiring."

My phone rang and I pulled it out of my pocket. It was fortunate whoever was calling hadn't tried fifteen minutes earlier since I hadn't *silenced my portable communications device.*

"Guess what I got?" came the distant, tinny voice of Charles. I could barely hear him with the ocean's roar in the background.

"Diphtheria," I said, both in the spirit of my friend, and to combat the irritating habit of most everyone who calls me skipping courteous greetings.

"Huh?"

"Never mind. Hi, Charles, what did you get?"

"I'm now in the twenty-first century. I've got a handy-dandy cell phone, with a camera, and a texting thing, and can tweet, whatever that is."

I had pestered Charles for nine years to join nine out of ten Americans who owned cell phones, and now he moves away and gets one. Progress, although irritating and belated, is still progress.

"Glad to hear it." I covered my other ear to block some of the ocean sounds that were making it hard to hear. "Did you make it to Nashville?"

"I am standing smack dab in front of the Country Music Hall of Fame and Museum right here on 5th Avenue in downtown Music City, USA."

"Okay. Did Heather make it?"

"She said I could stand out here and talk all day if I wanted to.

She already went in, said she'd waited all her life to be this close to country music fame and couldn't wait another piddlin' second."

"Found somewhere to live?"

I waved bye to Burl and walked away from the beach. It was still hard hearing Charles and I wanted a private spot to talk.

"We're in a motel. Got two appointments to look at apartments this afternoon after Heather sniffs around every square inch of the Hall of Fame. Both apartments are in walking distance of downtown."

"That's great," I said, although my heart wasn't in it. I was happy for Heather and therefore happy for Charles.

"Guess what else? No diseases this time."

"Heather's signed with Sony Records, is appearing on the Grand Ole Opry, and you've opened a private detective agency."

"And people think I live in a fantasy world. You're not far off, though. We met with Kevin Starr last night at Starbucks. He was excited to see her and gave her the name of the man to contact at the Bluebird about singing open-mic night. She tried calling last night, but he won't be in until tomorrow."

A couple of things didn't sound right. "Why didn't you meet Starr at his office?"

"He said he meets all his artists near where they are, rather than the inconvenience of having them come to his office."

I didn't like the sound of it, but let it go. Who was I to step on Heather's boundless enthusiasm?

"If Starr is representing Heather, why didn't he contact the Bluebird?"

"That felt funny to me. He said since he wasn't contractually tied to Heather yet, it'd be better for her to do it."

"Has he asked for money?"

"Not a dime."

He said something else, but the roar of a diesel engine from a large truck or bus on his end drowned out what he was saying.

"Can't hear you," I said.

"Tour bus. We're meeting Starr Tuesday."

"At his office?"

"Starbucks."

"Oh."

"You think that sounds fishy?"

"Do you?" I asked, the best non-answer I could come up with.

He mumbled, "Yeah."

"Be careful, I wouldn't want to see Heather hurt."

"If she fell off the cloud she's been on since we crossed the Cumberland River, it'd break every bone in her body, along with her heart."

Another country song, I predicted.

Charles continued, "Speaking of breaking things, have you broke that killer case yet?"

"Nope." I filled him in on what I'd learned since he left. I made the mistake of mentioning Dude as a suspect. If he wasn't so far away, Charles would have smacked me.

"No, no, no, to Dude killing anyone. Whoops, Heather's at the door waving for me. No to Dude. Bye."

I left the beach and headed home, missing Charles every step of the way.

CHAPTER 29

I was a block from the house when Rocky jogged up beside me. I was shocked. First, because I had never seen Dude's employee move faster than a slug, and second, because he'd stopped when we were shoulder to shoulder.

"Got a minute?" the sharp-featured, tat-covered, frowning man asked.

It was the most civil thing he'd said to me. "Sure."

We moved off the roadway.

"You're a damned meddler." His frown deepened.

I didn't have a quick retort so I waited. Besides, I didn't think he had gone out of his way to tell me that.

"I like that about you, especially being you're an old guy." His facial expression remained unchanged. "You're not a damned poser like some old farts. Geezers trying to be hip."

I knew poser was a non-surfer who acted like one—thank you Charles for that bit of trivia. I still didn't know what to say.

"Dude's like pop to me." Rocky almost broke a smile. "Maybe like grandpa."

"He's a good guy."

Rocky looked around, kicked the weed-covered, sandy soil, and faced Bert's Market, fifty yards away. "I'd do anything for him. Subsequently, I'd do anything for his sis. Blood's thick."

Rocky's saying *subsequently* threw me momentarily. What didn't throw me was his loyalty to Dude. I still had no idea why he had stopped me; stopped me after spending years treating me like I was a splinter in his toe.

"Dude's lucky to have you and Stephon with him."

"Dude said you were going to figure out who Panella, that malevolent, was out to off."

"He asked me to—"

Rocky waved his tat-covered arm in my face. "Save you the trouble. It was Barb."

"How do you know?"

Rocky cocked his head and smiled. "Old dudes like Panella and you, underestimate guys like me. They—you—see tats, hear surfer talk, watch us ignore geezers, and jump to conclusions. Think we're stupid, the lowlifes of society."

I wasn't sure of all that, but was impressed by his vocabulary. He was a cross between Dude and William Hansel, a professor pal of mine.

"You're right. What do you know about Panella?"

"He was a strange one. He came in the shop near dark." Rocky stared off in space like he was picturing the visit. "Dude was in the office with his sis. Stephon was in back tagging boards. I ignored Panella like I do most old guys. Don't think he saw me. He started looking at our boards, so I figured he may know what he's looking at and I caved and asked if he needed help. The old guy said he was a surfer and asked what I thought was the best wax. I said Mr. Zogs Sex Wax. He asked why and I started to tell him when Barb came out of Dude's hangout." Rocky reared back his shoulders and his head jerked toward the sky. "The old guy almost, umm, defecated a brick. He turned away from Barb and slithered over behind a rack of T-shirts. He tried to be inconspicuous." Rocky paused and shook his head. "Geezers figure scum like me don't see things."

This was by far the longest, and strangest, conversation I'd had with him, but I still wasn't sure why he'd stopped me.

"You said you know he was here to kill Barb."

He looked at me. His lips turned up almost in a snarl. That was more like the Rocky I had learned to detest.

"The old guy did everything he could to keep Barb from seeing him. Was like he didn't want anyone to know he recognized her. Barb headed out the door and the old guy still pretended he hadn't seen her. I asked him again if I could help and explain why I thought Mr. Zogs was the best. Dude calls that customer service. He says I need to get better at it." Rocky shook his head. "The geezer fiddled around some more. He was killing time. I gave it one more customer-service try. He looked at his watch and said he didn't have time to talk because he had to meet someone at their house."

"Did he say anything about Barb?"

"Don't you get it? The old man pretended he didn't know her since he was going to kill her. He didn't want someone to tell the cops they were seen together in the shop."

"Is that why you thought she was his intended victim?"

"Sure, but it didn't come to me until he turned up dead. That's when I knew he was the hit man and Barb was the target. That's why I'm telling you. You're nosy. You're known to figure out who killed people. Dude trusts you, and I figured if you knew who the old guy wanted to bump off, it'd help you figure out what's going on. The hit man was dead. It didn't mean the guy who hired him wouldn't send someone else to finish the job." He drilled a stare at me. "Barb's kin to Dude and that's good enough for me. You've got to save her."

Rocky was trying to be helpful, so I didn't want to sluff it off. "Did you tell the police? They'd be interested in hearing about Panella's activities."

"No freakin' way." Rocky was more animated than before. "The cops and I have a compound, complex relationship. We don't see eye-to-eye. Our interactions are like eye-to-ass."

The wind off the ocean had picked up and it was getting colder. I resumed my walk toward the house and to my surprise, Rocky tagged along. Something Rocky had said struck me as strange and I was trying to recall what it was when he stopped and pointed at my house.

"Is somebody staying with you?"

"What do you mean?" I looked in the direction his index finger was pointing.

"What's to mean?" He looked over at me like it was a stupid question. "Is someone at your house?"

"No," I continued to look, and didn't see anything unusual. "Somebody looked out your front window. Whoever it was saw us and went poof."

"Crap, not again," I said to the space where Rocky had been standing.

Instead of waiting to hear my succinct analysis of what was going on, he was jogging toward the house. A Honda slammed on its brakes and skidded to a halt, and another vehicle blew its horn as Rocky darted into the stream of traffic, and charged into my front yard. I stopped at the street, waved for the Honda to continue, waited for several more vehicles to pass, and crossed to the yard. Rocky had kicked in the front door and was in the house by the time I reached the yard. The thirty-five-year difference in our ages was made clear seeing how much quicker he had made it there.

I wasn't anxious to follow him in. I grabbed a three-foot-long, broken limb from the yard and inched the door open. If the intruder was the same person who had already invaded my space twice and clobbered me during one of those times, he wouldn't hesitate to do whatever he had to do to escape. I looked from side to side as I entered.

The rear screen door slammed and I heard a string of profanities coming from the kitchen. I gripped the branch tighter and moved toward the sounds. Rocky was on the floor, leaning against the cabinet by the sink. He had a gun in one hand, and held the back of his head with the other hand. He said damn and a couple of surfer-speak profanities I didn't know. I caught the drift.

I scanned the room and rushed to my new friend. He was trying to stand, so I helped him to his feet and nudged him into a chair.

"What happened?" I continued looking around.

"Kook slammed me upside the head. I charged in here after him and he must have been behind the door." He pointed to the door leading into the kitchen. "Didn't see him. Damned sure felt whatever he hit me with."

I saw the Teflon skillet Bob Howard had given me as a gag gift for my birthday. My realtor friend knew I couldn't, and had no desire to, cook, fry, or whatever you do with a skillet. I now knew one of its uses. Bob will find it amusing.

"Let me call an ambulance?"

"Nah, I've been hit worse."

I reached for my phone. "I'll call the police."

Rocky shot up out of the chair and grabbed for the phone. "Whoa," I said. "I don't have to call them."

"Don't." He sat back down, and whispered, "Please."

I nodded, realized it was the most polite thing I'd heard him utter, and returned the phone to my pocket. I doubted the police would learn anything anyway. They might get a print off the skillet, but if the intruder had been as careful as he had been the other two times, he had worn gloves. I noticed that the back door had been pried open, wood splintered around the lock. If the police came, they would now tell me in addition to better locks, I needed a security system, twenty-four- seven armed guards, a Rottweiler, and a moat with famished alligators.

Rocky said, "Give me a minute. I'll be fine."

He focused on being fine and I went from room to room to see if anything had been disturbed. The mattress on my bed was turned sideways and the top two drawers of the dresser were pulled open. From what I could tell, nothing had been taken.

I returned to the kitchen. "You sure you're okay?"

"Will be." Rocky rubbed the back of his head. "Why would someone break in here?"

He made it sound like he was shocked anyone would think I had anything of value. More than likely it was his rude gene kicking in. I didn't tell him this was the third intrusion in ten days.

"Don't know. Could have been a drifter looking for money or something to hock."

"In here?"

He'd saved me from a concussion, or worse, so I refrained from smacking him on his sore head.

I shrugged and offered him a soft drink.

"Yeah, thanks," he said in a second burst of courtesy, probably a result of the blow to the head.

"Did you see who it was?"

He shook his aching head. "No. Couldn't tell from across the street. There was a reflection of the sun on the window and I couldn't get a good look. When I came in here he hit me from behind and boogied while I was wiped out on the floor."

He sipped his drink, stood, and looked around the room, then walked to the living room.

"Anything else I can get you?" I asked.

"Nah. Hey man, what the hell you have in here that dude was looking for?"

An excellent question, and one I had no answer for. After one dead body, two friends concerned enough to ask me to try to figure out what was going on, and three blatant invasions of my personal space and my little slice of heaven, nothing short of death was going to stop me from finding out.

CHAPTER 30

Rocky left after assuring me he was fine, and once again, I called Larry and told him I needed his hardware store expertise and carpentry skills. Once again he said he'd be right over. And, once again, he arrived with his spouse in tow.

Larry carried his tool box, gave a cursory look at the splintered wood by the front door's locking mechanism, and walked through the house and focused his energy and talents on the seriously-damaged back door. Cindy glanced at the door and pointed to the kitchen table.

She sat across from me, looked over her shoulder at the back door, put both elbows on the table, and stared at me. "Let me guess. Your door stuck when you were opening it and you kicked it with your bionic foot, and the back door was struck by one of those mini-earthquakes that erupt beneath homes of walking, talking, disaster magnets?"

"Quick, analytical mind, succinct summation, it's easy to see why you're chief," I said, to inspire a smile. I came close. I proceeded to give her a blow-by-blow description of what had happened. She patiently, patiently for Cindy, waited for me to finish.

"The same Rocky who works for Dude? The Rocky who thinks kicking canes out from under senior citizens is Nobel Peace Prize winning behavior? You sure you weren't the one hit on the head?"

I explained why Rocky had approached me, about his loyalty to Dude, and because of that, why he had been worried about Barb. She started to get huffy about why he didn't go to the cops with that information and I shared his reluctance.

She leaned back and said, "Well-founded."

"Have you learned anything new about the murder?"

She pointed to the back door. "You think that has something to do with it?"

"Yes, but before you ask what, save your breath. I don't know. Back to my question, news?"

She shook her head. "The mayor, the mayor pro-tem, the head of the merchant's association, and everyone else who has a stake in the economy of the island, has been on my case. Something about a shot- in-the-head visitor puts the kibosh on vacationers clambering to spend their hard-earned dollars on our island paradise. I don't give a cockroach about that, but I do have more than a hankering to catch the son-of-a-skunk who killed someone on my watch."

Cindy had given a broad interpretation to my question, so I tried to limit its scope. "Leads?"

"No, faux-detective Chris." She frowned. "Detective Adair told me yesterday they were at the end of the line. Ballistics gave them nothing. Their forensic auditor guru said there was nothing in his records to lead them anywhere, other than he managed to live quite well off a piddling amount of taxed income. His wife seems as clueless as their pet dachshund. And if the wonderful, loving husband was in fact a gun for hire, there appears to be no way to trace who hired him."

"So, there's nothing?"

Cindy rolled her eyes and waved both hands in the air. "Dang, can't slip anything by you."

"What's next?"

"Adair says unless we find out who Panella was after, there's not much he can do."

"So until whoever hired him hires someone else and that person kills someone here, nothing's going to happen."

"Freakin' frustrating, isn't it?"

Frustrating and unacceptable, I thought. "If I'm right and this is related to his death," I said and pointed to the door Larry was working on, "help me see the connection."

"You're the one who said it's connected."

"I found the body."

"So?"

"So, someone, I'd guess the person who killed him, thinks I found something on the body that could lead me to him."

Cindy looked at the table and back at me. "What?"

"Money," Larry said, without turning away from his project.

"That makes sense," I said, remembering the rumor Cal had heard about me finding a pile of cash beside the body.

"Everything you know about Panella indicates he paid for most things with cash, he had little legitimate income, and you said there was five hundred dollars in his hotel room and none in his car." I hesitated and said, "So, if that's the case, whoever broke in here wouldn't have been who killed him, but could have been the person who hired him."

Cindy said, "Or he would have found the money on the body after he shot him. There would have been no need to break in."

"Whoever did this is taking a big risk. It could be anyone who knew I found the body, but only the person who hired Panella would know about the money. Wouldn't he want to stay as far away as possible? Why risk getting caught breaking in?"

Larry put his tools down and moved to a vacant chair at the table and looked at Cindy. "Hon, cover your ears."

She rolled her eyes for the second time and looked at me. "He says stupid things like that when he wants to say something he thinks I shouldn't hear." She turned back to Larry. "Consider them covered."

"From my contacts years ago with folks who, umm, didn't follow the letter of the law, I heard the going rate for top-notch hit men could hit thirty-thousand bucks, and much higher for high profile or hard to get to targets. That was a quarter of a century ago. I can't imagine that high a profile target here. I wouldn't be surprised if it wasn't around forty or fifty grand."

"Breaking in here would be worth it if the person who hired Panella wasn't busting out with money," Cindy said. "Would the hirer think Panella had the money with him? He could have left it at Myrtle Beach."

"Not if he didn't get paid until he got here," I said.

"That would mean whoever hired him was here before you found the body and may still be here," Cindy said. "I'll have my guys check hotel and rental agencies to see if someone who checked in a day or two before you found the body is still around."

"The person could be anywhere in the area," I said. "You can't check them all."

"True," Cindy said. "I'll call Adair tomorrow. That'll give his folks something to do. They can't canvass each nook and cranny, but maybe they'll get lucky."

I debated telling her about Preacher Burl's concern about Douglas Garfield. Just because Rocky thought Panella was here to hit Barb, didn't make it so. Douglas was still a strong possibility, but I had told the preacher I would keep his worries away from the police. Larry helped make my decision when he said he had done all he could for the back door and had put a piece of wood over the damaged section of the front. He told me he and Cindy had better be going. Besides, I had experienced enough excitement for the day and needed to think more about Douglas before breaking my promise to Burl. I asked Cindy to suggest to Adair that he might want to talk to Barb. If Rocky was right, she could shed light on a motive. Cindy said it was on her to-do list.

I apologized for calling and thanked them for coming out on a Sunday night. Cindy said she was glad I did because it was more fun than watching Larry lay on the couch and snore while the television blared some kissy-faced movie on the Hallmark Channel.

I was exhausted after Cindy and Larry left, and slumped down in my recliner. My body may have been tired, but my mind continued to wander. Was Rocky right about Barb being the target? What other reason would someone have for breaking in the house unless it was related to Panella's murder? Was someone trying to scare me into leaving Folly with the note, or was that a smokescreen to keep me from thinking he was looking for something? And, if it was something, was Larry right about it being the money Panella had been paid for the hit?

Did Preacher Burl have a legitimate concern about Douglas? Other than Douglas being the target because of something from his earlier life, I could see how someone would want him dead because he was so obnoxious.

Where was Charles when I needed him? We had occasionally proven the whole was, in fact, greater than the sum of its parts, and found answers. Of course, more often than not, we had proven two wrongs don't make a right. I groaned at my bad clichés, and reached for the phone to make my first long-distance call to Nashville, Tennessee.

Instead of hearing the familiar voice of my best friend, I got a mechanized voice-mail message saying the person I was calling was unavailable and to leave a message. I paraphrased another cliché, and mumbled you can lead a Charles to a cell phone, but you can't make him turn it on.

CHAPTER 31

In addition to being frustrated by the lack of answers, angry about my house becoming break-in-central, and my friends feeling threatened, I woke up hungry. There was little I could do about the first two problems, but a trip to the Lost Dog Cafe would solve my hunger.

Several tables were vacant, but before I could choose one, Dude waved for me from the far side of the room. His table mate was Russ Vick and with only water in front of them, I suspected they hadn't been there long. I wasn't in the mood for conversation. Dude pointed at the chair beside him with such enthusiasm that I didn't have the heart to decline.

Dude wore his ever-present, tie-dyed, peace-symbol-adorned T-shirt and Russ had on ratty jeans and a black T-shirt with PORN STAR in fluorescent yellow on the front. They looked like two aging hippies reliving their old bad-trip days.

Dude said, "Chrisster, welcome."

"Hi, Chris," Russ said with less enthusiasm. "Good to see you."

"We be flapping lips about business," Dude said as if I had asked. "T-shirt sales sucking."

Russ looked at Dude and smiled. "Don't believe we need to share our conversation with Chris. I'm sure he's not interested."

"He be nosy, but lips be sealed." Dude mimed closing a zipper on his mouth. "Okeydokey to share."

Russ turned to me. "I suppose you know how difficult it is to break in a successful business."

I smiled, but didn't mean it. "Do I ever. Winter's a terrible time for business anyway."

Dude waved his hand around the Dog. "Be Dude's winter office."

"I see why," Russ said. "Nobody's in the stores."

Dude jerked his head away from looking at Russ and turned to me. "Speakin' about broke and brakin', hear *su casa* be boss break-in spot."

Russ, a relative newcomer to Dudespeak, said, "Huh?" I knew what he'd meant. "Where'd you hear that?"

Dude put his hand to his ear and imitated a telephone. "Stephon thought big news since you and me be big buds. He interrupted quality time with Pluto."

"Stephon?" I said.

"He be learnin' it from Rocky Horror surf-stuff seller." Russ repeated, "Huh?"

The waitress approached and asked if we were ready to order, before he could say more. We each ordered and Russ watched the college-age waitress walk to the kitchen.

I thought I'd better translate for Russ who already seemed confused. "Dude's two employees are Rocky and Stephon. Rocky told Stephon about the break in, and then Stephon called Dude who was playing with his dog, Pluto."

Russ looked at Dude then me. "You got all that from what he said?"

I smiled. "Clear as day."

"Ah, thanks," Russ said. He didn't look convinced.

Dude nodded. "The Rock man boogied in Chrisster's *casa* and got skilleted. Good deed, bad ending."

"Is he okay?" Russ asked, grasping the salient points of Dudespeak.

"I think so," I said. "Someone was breaking in my house and Rocky was trying to catch the guy when he got hit."

Russ looked at Dude and at me. "Why was someone breaking in your house?"

Dude said, "New popular Folly event."

"This is the third time," I said to the confused T-shirt shop owner. "I don't know why."

"Note say for Chrisster to boogie-board off island," Dude said.

"The person left me a note saying I needed to leave, or else."

Russ said, "Sounds like you've got an enemy."

"Chrisster be catching dude who kilt kill-man. Somebody pissed about that. Trying to run my bud off." Dude shook his head. "No be workin'."

"It had to be terrible finding the guy," Russ said. "I can't imagine it."

"I've had better mornings."

"I'm glad I wasn't here," Russ said. "I'm often in that alley since my store is less than a block from where you found him. It could have been me who stumbled on him."

"Doubt it," Dude said. "Chrisster be early bird. He caught dead bod instead of worm. He be out before most creatures be stirrin'."

"What do the police say?" Russ asked.

Dude said, "They be befuddled."

I figured Russ caught Dude's drift and didn't say anything. I had also heard enough about yesterday. "Have you always owned T-shirt shops?"

"Nope."

"What'd you do before moving here?"

"VP of a global import business."

"Flip side of T-shirt sellin'," Dude said.

Russ smiled. "That's an understatement."

"Why'd you leave?" I asked.

Dude interrupted, "Said he be nosy."

Russ laughed. "I noticed. I got tired of the red tape and crap I had to deal with. I knew it'd do me in if I stayed. Took retirement and got the hell out of there. Selling T-shirts doesn't pay as well and I'm not wealthy, but if I stayed, I'd be dead long before my time."

"I know what you mean," I said. "My story's not much different."

"That's what I hear. At least, I think it's what Dude's been saying. I've been taking some getting-along-with-the-locals lessons. Being the newcomer is a hard nut to crack."

I chuckled. "Learn anything helpful?"

Russ looked at Dude and tilted his head. "Me be patient."

I smiled. "Good lesson."

"I was going to open one shop. The rent was so good on the second location I figured two shops would be twice as good as one."

Food arrived and feeding our curiosity took a back seat to feeding our faces. Russ asked a few questions about the other gift shops and if we knew how well they were doing. I didn't want to be too direct, but tried to hint the small island was over saturated with similar items. Russ agreed he may have made a mistake by opening two stores and said if he kept one open, it would be Folly Tease because its shirts were different than the hundreds of others and its sales were double those at SML Shirts.

"Not be easy, being at two shops same time," Dude said.

Russ chucked. "Good point, Dude. And paying someone to work in the other store is draining. Chris, that's what I'd been talking to Charles about. With his local knowledge and appreciation for T- shirts, he would've been a natural to run SML Shirts. Now I hear he's moved. I didn't know him well, but that came as a surprise."

"A bummer," Dude said.

I agreed, more than he knew.

I wanted to move away from talking about Charles. "Have you talked to Barbara Deanelli about her experiences of opening a store? The two of you might have a lot in common, with both moving here and opening a business. I think she's having a hard time adjusting to the beach life and lifestyle."

"I haven't, but that's a good idea."

"She be my fractional-sis," added Dude. "She be lawyertress turned queen of books."

"Wise move," Russ said, and laughed. "I avoid lawyers."

"You plus everyone else," Dude said.

I nodded to that, and my phone rang.

"Chris," said the familiar voice of Preacher Burl, "did I catch you at a bad time?"

"No. I was finishing breakfast."

"Good. I don't usually call anyone this early. I knew you're an early riser and took a chance."

It sounded better than calling me a bird catching a body.

"What can I do for you, Preacher?"

"Can you meet me at the church? I promise not to put you to work.

"When?"

Dude began waving his hand in the air and pointing to the phone.

"Just a sec, Preacher. I'm with Dude and he wants to say something." I handed the phone to Dude.

"Boss sermon, yesterday. Inspired to the gills."

He handed the phone back to me before the preacher had a chance to respond.

"I'm back, Preacher."

He laughed. "Don't often inspire to the gills. Tell Dude I appreciate his endorsement."

I said I'd pass the message along and asked when he wanted to meet. He replied soon; I suggested how about now and he invited me to come on over.

I had left Dude and Russ continuing their bemoaning about the poor business climate on Center Street. Both had given lip-service to it being the middle of winter and off-season, yet continued to wonder why the full-time residents and handful of vacationers weren't clamoring to buy surf gear and T-shirts.

First Light's front door squeaked open and I was greeted with, "Thanks for coming, Brother Chris. All I have to offer is water."

"I'm fine."

Burl pointed to a pew near the front and followed me as I took a seat.

"I had a disturbing visit last night from Brother Douglas."

"Oh."

Burl shook his head. "I smelled Devil juice on his breath. I wouldn't call him inebriated, but wouldn't want him driving. He said his fear had exceeded his desire to remain on Folly." Burl hesitated. "Sure you don't want water?"

"No thanks."

He fiddled with the button on his shirt, wiped a cobweb off the back of the pew, and finally said, "Even though the first man sent to kill him had been taken care of, Douglas was certain there'd be others. He decided to leave the Lowcountry and despite his rude and loathsome demeanor wanted me to know he appreciated my efforts to ensure he had a better life."

I doubted those were Douglas's words. "When's he leaving?"

"He didn't say. I had the impression it was soon. He could have been heading off-island when he left my apartment. I had asked you to assist in finding out if Brother Douglas was in danger, so I felt it incumbent to share this with you."

"Preacher, someone broke into my house yesterday. One of Dude's employees, Rocky, saw him and was rewarded with a skillet to the head for trying to catch the intruder."

"Oh, I'm so sorry. Is Brother Rocky okay? He was at yesterday's service with his associate, Brother Stephon."

"He's fine."

"Why did someone break in? It's happened before, hasn't it?"

I told him about the other two times, and he asked if I knew why. I shared what I had told everyone else who had asked, and I asked if he thought it could have been Douglas.

"I would feel better if I could say no. To be honest, it wouldn't surprise me."

"That's what I thought. Let's get back to what he said last night."

Burl nodded.

"I believe you said he told you the first man who had been sent to kill him had been 'taken care of.'" The preacher nodded again.

"Are you certain those were his words?"

Burl looked to the door, swiped another cobweb off the pew, and turned back to me. "I can't be certain. It was late, and I was trying to figure out what he was talking about, instead of paying attention to each word. Why?"

"Is it possible he could have said he took care of it rather than it had been taken care of?"

Burl squeezed his hands together and took a deep breath. "Are you saying Brother Douglas killed the gentleman sent to kill him?"

"It's possible. I don't know what he did to get in the witness protection program. From his actions and attitude toward me, it's not a big leap to picture a violent past. He'd told me he could handle his own problems and didn't need me, or you, to butt in."

Burl looked at the floor and shook his head. "To answer your question, Brother Chris, yes, it's possible he said he had taken care of the problem. In fact, the more I think about it, the more I believe you may be right." He sighed. "As we discussed the other day, I acknowledged the possibility of his guilt, but I didn't want to believe it."

Burl would feel I was breaking a confidence, and I might lose a friend because of it, but I also knew the police were getting nowhere with the case.

I walked to the large plate glass window overlooking Center Street and glanced across the street at the combination city hall, police and fire station, and turned to Burl. "Preacher, I need to tell Chief LaMond. I know you'd prefer I didn't. The police need to find Douglas before he gets too far away."

"I suppose I knew that when I told you about Brother Douglas leaving. I prayed about it last night. God chose not to give me a clear answer. He left it up to me, and I chose to call you. Perhaps it's his will, Brother Chris." He hesitated, and said, "Do what you must."

Burl needed alone time to pray about the situation, and said he'd be there if the police wanted to talk to him. I walked home and called Chief LaMond who said she was in her office playing Angry Birds on her laptop, but figured she could break away a few minutes to catch a killer. An hour later, I met her at First Light and listened to Burl tell everything he knew about Douglas Garfield—Harlan Powers. Cindy took notes, gave Burl and me dirty looks, and told us how irresponsible we were to not tell her sooner.

She said, "Yeah, yeah, yeah," twice when Burl started talking about his role as pastor with Douglas and why he didn't feel comfortable telling the authorities. She came close to forgiving him when he told her what kind of car Douglas drove, where he lived, and where he may be going.

I felt some progress had been made on learning who had killed the hit man. And I felt better knowing Barb wasn't in danger.

CHAPTER 32

The phone rang at five forty-five the next morning.

"Guess what I've got?" came the familiar question from Charles.

I knew not to guess cell phone since that train had already left the station.

"Insomnia? It's not even six o'clock."

"Not five here, but that's not it. Want to guess again?"

"No," I growled.

"You've turned crankier since I left. Okay, I doubt you'd be able to guess. Got myself a picture on this phone to send you as soon as I figure out how."

"Picture of what?"

"Not only what, but where, Mr. Crank."

I sighed. "Where?"

"The Bluebird Cafe and guess who I got to listen to?"

A six a.m. phone call, a picture, the Bluebird Cafe, and excitement in his voice; I knew the answer, although for the life of me, I couldn't imagine how it could be true.

"The Rolling Stones?"

If he woke me up, the least I could do was give him grief. "Close, but no cappuccino. Heather got to sing at the galaxy-famous Bluebird Cafe. Can you believe it?"

No, I thought. "Wasn't she going to call them yesterday to see about scheduling a date?"

"She was, she did, and low-and-behold, they told her they didn't take open-mic singing reservations over the phone, and because of the yucky weather yesterday they told her if she was there by sign-up time at five-thirty she had a good shot at slipping in. We were there at two-fifteen, shivering, starving, and so excited about playing she made five pit stops at McDonald's down the street while I held her place in line."

"That's great," I said. "How'd she do?"

"By the time she went on at eight-thirty, a half hour before open-mic night ended, the place was two-thirds full. I was surprised how small it is; holds about ninety people. Anyway, she did the song she wrote and a few people applauded when she was finished."

A few applauding didn't sound like a rousing debut. I moved to the kitchen and fired-up Mr. Coffee while trying to comprehend Heather performing at the Bluebird. It seemed like a dream, but I knew I was awake because I stubbed my toe on the counter.

"What'd she think?"

"She was peein'-in-her-pants excited. Said it was the happiest day of her life. She left there flying higher than the space shuttle."

"Glad to hear it," I said, not as happy as I should have been. "Was Kevin Starr there?"

"Nah," Charles said. "She called him after they said she may be able to sing. He said he had to take a meeting with one of his famous recording artists last night and couldn't make it. *Take a meeting* is what big time music peeps call gabbin' with someone."

"That's too bad. What's next?"

"She has a meeting—whoops, is *takin' a meeting*—with him tomorrow."

I still didn't like the way it was going with Starr. Hadn't he told her to call the Bluebird to make an appointment? Now Charles said that wasn't the way to sign up for open-mic night. And, I didn't trust him after what Cal had said and because I knew how little singing talent was crammed into Heather's adorable body. Charles was sharp enough to know this, so there was no need to remind him.

"You're going with her, aren't you?"

"I want to. It's up to her."

"It'd be best if you went. She could use the moral support and you'd get to hear what he has to say."

"I know." He told me how excited she was in case I'd forgotten, and said, "Caught the killer?"

I told him about Preacher Burl's suspicions about Douglas Garfield, and about Douglas leaving town and Cindy putting an APB out on him.

Charles didn't respond immediately. He finally said, "When were you going to tell me?"

He was miffed. I told him Burl had told me in confidence and I wasn't comfortable telling anyone. Charles pointed out he wasn't anyone. I agreed and halfheartedly apologized.

"I know Douglas," Charles said after letting me sulk in my apology.

"I didn't know that," I refrained from asking when he was going to tell me.

"You would if you told me earlier. The boy's bitter, he's rude, he doesn't have anything approaching a friend on Folly. Overall, he's unbearable."

That's Douglas Garfield. "True."

"Chris, there's one thing he's not."

"What?"

"The person who shot Panella."

"How do you know?"

"In addition to all those things about Douglas, you can add addicted to hops."

"He's a drunk."

"Crude translation, but true. Woodrow Wilson said, 'Never murder a man when he's busy committing suicide.' Douglas is busy drinking himself to death. I had a civil, not quite so rude, conversation with him a month ago when he was semi-soused. He told me some things about his childhood. Did you know he had a baby sister named Gail?"

"No, so?"

"Let me finish. When he was seven and Gail was five she found one of their daddy's guns. She thought it was a toy and started slinging it around like a Roy Rogers toy cap gun that Douglas had. It went off and shot Gail in the arm. The wound wouldn't have been so bad, but Douglas didn't know what to do and there wasn't anyone around. Gail bled to death."

"That's terrible."

"Yeah, for both of them. Douglas said he was sent to all sorts of doctors to help get over what had happened and the guilt he felt. Therapy helped him some, yet he never got over seeing her laughing and playing with the gun, and then dying while he held her hand and not knowing what to do to save her." Charles paused and whispered, "Chris, Douglas told me he had done many bad things in his life. The one thing he never did after that was touch another gun, and he never would."

"That doesn't mean he didn't—"

"I know. It's still possible he shot the guy, but I'd bet my car he didn't."

"So, wonderful detective from afar, who killed him? Who was Panella here to kill? Who thinks my house is a stepping stone to bigger and better burglaries? And—"

"Slow down. Too many questions. It's five o'clock."

"You called me."

"To spread Heather's glee, not to solve a murder, a puzzle, and whatever else you asked."

"Fair enough. I'm happy for Heather. Bye."

"Whoa, slam on the brakes. I'm awake now. Let's take one question at a time."

Leaving unanswered questions dangling in front of Charles was like waving a Starbucks' mocha latte in front of a yuppie.

"Question one," I said. "If Douglas didn't kill Panella, who did?"

"The person he was here—there—to kill."

"Or someone else," I said.

"Gee, that helps."

"Hear me out. At first, I thought it had to be the person he was hired to kill, but if he was good at his trade, and since he had been on the radar of cops in New Jersey for years and they couldn't get anything on him, he was good, he wouldn't have tipped his hat to whoever he was after."

"You made my argument it wasn't Douglas."

I agreed, although it didn't eliminate him from being the target. "So, who shot him?" Charles asked.

"That's my question."

"Okay, how about this. What if it doesn't have anything to do with why he was there? He was strolling through the alley humming a tune and someone came up behind him—maybe to rob him, or to say howdy. It was dark and foggy and considering Panella's career, he would've grabbed his gun. The robber or howdy person saw Panella's gun and pulled out one of his own and shot the hit man before the hit man shot him?"

I took a sip of coffee that had brewed quicker than I had awakened. "What are the odds on that happening?"

"Better chance of me getting elected president. You have a better idea?"

"Let's skip the random act of stupidity theory. If it wasn't the person he was here to kill, that leaves someone who found out who Panella was and why he was here."

"And that person is, who, or whom, whatever?"

"You said Douglas didn't have friends, so I don't see anyone killing Panella to save him."

"True."

I said, "I suppose Panella could have been here to kill most anyone, although I don't think so."

"Was who or whom in there somewhere?"

For reasons I would have a hard time explaining, these were the kind of conversations I missed the most. I hated we were having it via phone.

"Not yet," I said. "I think the intended victim was Barbara Deanelli."

"Why?"

"The first time I met her was the morning I found the body. If I had learned moments earlier a body was found behind my store, I'd be shocked. It was in a public alley, a shortcut between two streets, near the back door to the bookstore, yet just as close to First Light. I wouldn't know what to think."

"Me either, so?"

"So, she heard I'd found the body; she asked the police about me; was told where I might be, and came to the Dog to find me. We'd never met. She comes in, shares a couple of pleasantries and insults about Bob Howard, and asked if I knew the dead guy."

"Did I miss why she was the intended hitee?"

"Not yet. Then, of all the things she could have said, she asked me to describe him. Doesn't that seem odd? It was almost like she had expected someone and wanted to know if Panella was that person."

"Following your dusty, wiggly path, why would Panella have wanted to kill Barb?"

I realized I hadn't told Charles about my recent conversations with her.

"Barb told me her husband had been part of illegal activities that involved bribes to politicians and bureaucrats in state government. It involved millions of dollars. She claims she didn't know details, but it was the main reason for her divorce and move to Folly."

"I suppose you forgot to tell me all of that."

I told him it happened when he was in the process of moving and had other things on his mind. He groused, blew out his breath, and said, "You think she either is lying to you and knows more than she's saying, or she doesn't know anything but someone thinks she does."

"Yeah, I don't think she's lying about everything. I also think she knows more than she told me. Someone's afraid of what Barb may know and sent Panella."

"I don't suppose you've told Chief LaMond, Detective Adair, or Karen your theory."

"What's to tell? I don't know anything for certain."

And, I didn't want to get into the situation with Karen. I wasn't ready to discuss it, and I didn't know how Charles would react on the heels of his leaving.

"Do you think Barb killed him?"

"No. If she had, she wouldn't have asked me to describe him."

"Do you think someone knew about the hit and came to Folly to stop it?"

"Could be. I hope that's the case, otherwise it would be someone here, and that leaves one suspect. It could—"

Charles interrupted, "I told you it wasn't Dude."

I heard Heather in the background ask who Charles was talking to. It sounded like a chair being dragged across the floor and Charles told her it was me. Heather squealed, and said, "Is he excited for me?"

Charles told her of course I was. She said something about needing to celebrate her resounding success. Charles said, "Time to go. I'll leave you with four words: It *was not* Dude."

CHAPTER 33

I stared at the phone and reheated my coffee in the microwave. Panella's death may not have anything to do with Barb. He could have been here for someone else. What I was certain of was he wasn't here selling heavy farm machinery. I had taken the first sip when the phone rang—again. I expected to hear Charles calling with more reasons Dude couldn't be the killer.

"He was in again." Barb said.

She may be new to Folly, but had caught on to the nontraditional conversation starters.

"Morning, Barb. How are you?" I was trying to bring civility to phone conversations.

"Fine."

"Good. Who was in again?"

"The man who came in when you were here."

"The one who gives you the willies?"

"The same. Listen, I feel like a fish out of water. Back home I could do this myself, but ... well, you're the one person I know, other than Dude, I trust enough to ask, and I don't think it'd be good to ask him."

"What do you need?"

"He bought three books this time; two on Early American history and a mystery by Robert B. Parker. He paid by credit card, and his name's Sylvester Lopp."

"Did he say anything?"

"He asked if I had read Parker's books. I told him I didn't read mysteries. He hemmed-and-hawed like he wanted to say something else, but gave me his credit card and left."

"What can I do?"

"I thought you could ask the chief if she could find anything about him. I had enough contacts back home to get it done, yet here, well, you know. I Googled him and didn't find anything. He could be in a police data base. I know it's not normal procedure. I'm afraid of the guy and maybe since the chief is your friend, she could check. There's been one person sent to kill me. What if that's why Lopp's here?"

I doubted a hit man would come in the store four or five times, buy books, and give a credit card, nevertheless, she was afraid. I said I'd call Cindy.

"Thank you, and please don't tell Dude. He worries too much about me and I don't want him to do anything stupid."

I prayed he hadn't already. "I won't." I wished it had been Charles calling.

It was before eight o'clock, but I knew Cindy was out and about, so I might as well get the lecture over about butting in police business. She answered with, "What trouble are you going to cause me now?"

"No trouble, Chief. Good morning."

"No matter how you try to sugarcoat it, you're going to ruin my morning."

Not the good mood I had hoped for. I told her I had a favor to ask and it was police business, and I didn't see how it could ruin her morning.

"You underestimate yourself. What now?"

I told her and she said I'd asked for worse. She also said she liked Barb because she brought a strong, female presence to Cindy's male-dominated world, and the island needed an estrogen fix. I remained silent and let her continue giving me grief. It was less than I'd expected, and it's the price I pay to get anything from her. She said she would see what she could find and told me to try to stay out of trouble and not invite any uninvited guests into my house until she got back to me.

I re-reheated the coffee and was determined to enjoy a full cup before another distraction. Twenty minutes later, and thinking about the events of the last few days, I realized the main reason I was having trouble getting a handle on what was going on was because there were two distinct, but related, mysteries: the murder of Panella, and the reason the hit man was on Folly Beach. If Barb was correct, it solved part of the second one, but was she right? Charles had made a reasonable case why Douglas Garfield hadn't killed Panella. He could still have been the target. If he was, who had killed Panella and why?

As much as Preacher Burl had tried to convince me Douglas Garfield was the intended victim, my gut said it was Barb. And, I could only think of three people who would have been concerned about her enough to kill Panella. It was time to talk to one of them.

The surf shop wouldn't be open for another fifteen minutes, so I walked around downtown. I passed the bookstore and wondered how things would be different if my photo gallery had succeeded. I suppose Barb's Books would have opened somewhere else. I peeked in the window of First Light and revisited my thought that Douglas Garfield wasn't in danger, at least not from a hit man. Then I remembered something Rocky said Panella had told him during his visit to the surf shop. If it was true, it gave me a different view of Panella and who may have hired him. Dude almost ran into me when I stopped in the middle of the sidewalk to think through Rocky's conversation.

"Yo, Chrisster, be imitating light pole?" said the articulate hippie.

"Sorry, Dude. I was thinking."

"Heavy thinking?"

"Believe it or not, I was thinking about asking you something and had a question for Rocky."

"Rude Rocky?"

"Yes."

"That be first." I smiled. Dude said, "Q and A here?" He pointed to the sidewalk, and at the surf shop. "In shop?"

"Inside."

"Boogie with me." He walked, skipped, toward the store.

My boogieing could better be called a slow walk, and Dude had unlocked the door and turned on the lights before I got there.

Stephon and Rocky followed me up the steps. If I didn't know who they were, I would have taken one look at their all-black attire, matching black watch caps, tattered leather jackets and scowls which would intimidate most anyone, and would have feared for my life. I didn't waste time talking to them and followed Dude to his office.

"Rocky?" Dude said.

"Let's talk first."

"Your party. Talk on."

I charged on. "How long have they worked for you?" I nodded in the direction of his employees.

Dude followed my head nod. "That be question not expectin'. Stephon, plus-minus sixty full moons. Rocky, ninety-seven fms. Why?"

For those who don't know Dudespeak, and it took me three years to learn to translate his full-moon calendar, that's about five years for Stephon and seven for Rocky. In either language, it was a long time for retail store employees.

I ignored his question. "Suppose you know them pretty well."

"Better than know Adele. Not as good as know Pluto—pupster Pluto, not the faux-planet. Why?"

"Know much about their background?"

"Had okay drivers' license, tax paperwork not flagged by CIA, FBI, or ASPCA. Okay by me. Why, times three?"

"One more question and I'll answer you."

"Getting old waitin'."

"Could you see either of them killing Panella?"

"Whoa! You be flingin' from left field."

The door was open and I heard surfboards being moved around in the store. I got up and pushed the door closed.

"Could you?" I repeated.

Dude looked at a colorful PREY FOR SURF poster taped on the back of the door and then at the floor, before turning to me. "Not be friendliest clerks." He squinted and nervously stroked his long, gray hair. "They suck at spelling. Pray to Sun God, pupster Pluto be as loyal as they be."

I waited, but Dude had finished talking. "Could you see them killing him?"

Dude glanced at the poster and held up three fingers. "Chrisster, chill. Be asked you one, plus one, plus one time why you askin'. Answer ain't cookin' at me yet. I be getting there."

I smiled. "Fair enough."

He blinked twice and tapped his fingers on the cluttered desk. "Here be answer. If swearin' on Bible-book and asked question." He mimed putting his hand on a Bible and raised his other hand like he was testifying in court. "I'd say yep. Sorry, yep."

I wasn't surprised, but asked why.

Dude shook his head. "Don't know why. They be loyal rude. If thought Dudester in trouble, they'd help. If thought Dudester's fractional-sis be in trouble, they do same. Blood be thicker than surf."

"Dude, this is an unfair question since they're your employees, and, I agree, they're loyal to a fault, has either one said anything that would lead you to believe he was guilty?"

He closed his eyes, his head gyrated left and right and then up and down, and he bit his lip. "No."

I was at the end of the line talking to Dude. I thanked him, told him I appreciated his candor, and asked him not to say anything to them.

He patted his lips with his forefinger. "Be Super Glued."

CHAPTER 34

Instead of talking to Rocky as I'd planned, I left through the back door. I was close to figuring out part of the mystery, and had to think it through and what to do with it.

I got home and took a pad of lined paper and wrote down what I knew, and what I felt I was almost certain of. I was convinced Barb was the person Panella was hired to kill. If she'd killed him she wouldn't have sought me out to ask what he looked like. She knew more than she was saying; she knew she was in danger. She acted frightened, both to me and to Dude. I was almost certain Dude hadn't shot him. So that left the two people who would do anything for their boss, and for Barb as an extension of Dude: Rocky, Stephon, or both.

I didn't know if Stephon had talked to Panella, but I knew Rocky had. Like many others, Panella didn't take Dude's employee seriously, and figured Rocky, who looked like a burned out junkie, wouldn't remember anything he'd seen. I smiled to myself. If there was one thing I'd learned during my years here, it was not to make assumptions about anyone.

I missed being able to bounce this off Charles. And, in addition to not having Charles, I didn't have proof.

I added three question marks after Rocky's name, skipped two lines, and wrote: Who hired Panella?

If I was right about Barb being the target, more likely it was someone from Pennsylvania, but something Rocky had said nagged at me. I added two more question marks to the bottom of the page when someone rapped on the back door. Rocky was on the small porch. He was in the same black outfit he had worn in the store, and looked behind him as I opened the door.

"Got something to tell you, Mr. Landrum. Could I come in?"

To say I was torn was the understatement of the year, perhaps the decade. I could now ask him what had bothered me about his conversation with Panella, but I could also be facing the man who sent Panella to hit-man hell.

"Umm, sure."

He stepped inside and I took a couple of steps back. I wasn't ready to offer him a drink or a seat. I also didn't want him to see how nervous I was so I leaned against the counter. I turned the pad over and smiled.

His eyes darted around the room and he focused on the door to the living room. We were standing facing each other when he pushed his coat out of the way and reached behind his back. The next thing I knew, I was staring at the business end of a handgun.

"Sit." he said with nonnegotiable force. I sat.

With his other hand, he removed two plastic self-locking cable ties from his pocket, pointed for me to put my hands behind my back, and said not to do anything foolish. I had already done one foolish thing by letting him in and wasn't about to compound that mistake. He slipped one restraint over my wrists and yanked it tight. It stung as it tore into my wrists. He looped the other tie over the one securing my wrists and weaved it though the rail in the middle of the backrest. He was silent as he went about the task, scary silent.

"What do you want?" I asked, to get him talking rather than expecting to get a reasonable answer.

"Wait." He stepped in front of me, and pulled out a third, and longer, restraint. "Cross your legs and move them against the chair leg."

He stared at me until I nodded and set the gun on the counter out of my range and wrapped the tie around my legs and the chair. It had hurt when he tightened the tie around my wrists, but it was a tingle compared to how my ankles felt when he jerked the tie tight around my legs. I grimaced.

Rocky retrieved the gun and walked from room to room; he appeared to be doing it out of nerves. He came back in the kitchen and looked out the window. He then bolted the back door and stood three feet in front of me.

"I don't want to hurt you," he said.

Too late, I thought.

"You're Dude's friend. You saved his life a while back and he thinks the world of you. Honest, I don't want to hurt you." He glared at me. "If I have to." He shrugged. "You understand?"

I nodded.

He looked at the pistol he held to his side, and said, "I killed him."

His calm voiced frightened me more than if he had screamed it. I swallowed hard. "Why?"

"He was going to hurt Dude's sis. I couldn't let that happen."

Rocky had come in from the cold, and it was cool in the kitchen, but a bead of sweat formed on his forehead. "You know what I mean?"

He paced, looked around one more time, and grabbed one of the chairs and set it in front of me. He walked to the back door and opened it a crack, looked out, and returned to the chair. I squeezed my wrists apart and tried to twist them enough to restore circulation or loosen them enough to get free. All I achieved was pain.

"Tell me about it?"

It seemed an eternity before he spoke.

"Remember how strange I told you he acted when he came in the shop?"

"Yes."

"Nothing good was hiding up his sleeve, so I remembered him."

"Good."

Rocky stared at my bound feet. "I was headed to catch a wave before work that horrible morning. My apartment—not much more than a closet—is in that old building on Huron. I was taking a shortcut to the surf shop where I keep my board. It was dark—dark and foggy. Wow, was it ever foggy. I saw nothing more than a shadow of someone fiddling with the lock on the bookstore door. I was ten feet away before I got a good look at him. That stopped me in my tracks, I can tell you." He shook his head as he relived the moment. "He must have heard me because he turned. I stopped and said, 'Shit man, I'm only walking by.'"

Rocky paused. "What happened?"

"My eyes were adjusted to the dark and I saw it was the dude who'd been hiding from Barb in the store. I took a step back and he pulled a gun out of his jacket. Aikona. She's not going to get hurt; not if I can help it."

Thanks to my Dude-speak translator, Charles, I had learned *aikona* meant *not going to happen*.

Rocky hesitated and looked at the gun. "I had this and pulled it out. The guy raised his arm like he pointed his gun at people all the time. Swear to God, he was going to shoot me. All I was doing was walking down the alley." He sighed. "I don't know how I was quicker than him. I didn't aim. I pointed my gun in his direction and yanked the trigger."

The sweat was now running down his face. His gun hand was shaking, and I thought he was going to break into tears. I held my breath.

"He flopped back like I'd smacked him with my board. I didn't know what to do. I looked around and no one came running so I went over to him. He wasn't moving. And ... and, there was a hole right in the middle of his head. He was deader than a week-old beached grouper."

"What'd you do?"

"I wanted to know his name. Don't know why, but I did. Sure as hell wasn't going to tell anybody. He was on his back, and his coat was open. I wasn't about to roll him over. Then I saw two of those money bags like Dude has when he gets cash from the bank. They were sticking out the inside pockets of his coat. Puffed him out so much it looked like he had on a bulletproof vest. Crap Landrum, they held stacks of cash, hundred-dollar bills, thirty-seven thousand bucks—more money than I'd ever seen."

"You took it?"

Rocky wiped the sweat from his forehead and nodded. "He didn't need it. Don't get me wrong, Dude treats me good, but that's more money than I take home in a year and a half. Yeah, I took it."

My hands were tingling, and my legs ached from their awkward position.

"It was self-defense, Rocky. He was trying to kill you. Tell you what, cut these ties off and I'll forget about what's happened. We can call the police. I'm sure they'll understand."

He stood and waved his gun around the room. "Don't you think I've pondered that? It's about all I've been thinking about since that morning."

"Now'd be a good time to do it," I hoped it made more sense to him than it did to me.

"Can't."

"Why not?"

"I know how people look at me. I'm that worthless surfer at the surf shop who scares off customers. If I went to the cops, I'd be in jail before sunset, and wouldn't get out while geezers like you are still alive."

"Rocky, the police will understand, and—"

"Enough. There's more. Before I moved here, I'd spent some years locked up. I was deep in drugs—using, not selling. One night in Louisiana I was high and ran over an old dude; never saw him in the street. Convicted of vehicular homicide; spent seven years behind bars. Deserved every minute of it. I'd still be there if I didn't get clean—as if I had a choice in jail. I traversed the straight and narrow. They called me a model prisoner, can you believe that? Even got some college credits while I was l locked up. They let me out before my time was up."

"That's great."

"Yeah. Moved here and Dude hired me without asking anything about my past. Best thing that's ever happened to me. I owe that man my life."

"The police will—"

"The police won't ignore my past like Dude did. They'll say I killed before and now killed that dude in the alley to rob him. If I was on the jury, I'd convict my ass and ship me away forever." He pointed the gun at my feet. "That's why you're hogtied. I want you to know what happened. You're buds with the cops and'll tell them my side. They will believe what you tell them I said. You'll also tell Dude and he'll tell Stephon. They'll believe me."

I shook my head. "I'll go with you to the police. Detective Adair and Chief LaMond are good at what they do. They'll give you a fair shake. If you run, it'll look like you're guilty and they'll catch you."

"Good try. No way. Besides, I figure I can get mighty far away from here on the dead guy's cash. You're an old fart, so I figure it'll take you a while to get out of that." He pointed to my legs. "You'll call the cops and tell them what happened, and none of you'll have any idea where I went."

He started to the door and turned back to me. "Sorry for tying you up."

It struck me he wasn't going to kill me. "Can I ask you one thing?"

He grinned. "You ain't in a position to ask much. To show you I'm not as bad as you think, go for it."

"When we were talking the other day and you were telling me about your conversation with Panella, didn't you say something about him having to leave to meet someone at his house?"

He shook his head. "That's one stupid-ass question to ask while you're sitting there like that."

I shrugged, or as much of a shrug as I could muster with my hands bound behind my back. "It's important."

"Yeah, that's what he said. He'd looked at his watch like he was late."

"And you're sure he said he had to meet at someone's house, not hotel room, in a car, or anywhere else?"

"How many times do I have to say it?"

"Thanks. Good luck."

He closed the back door on his way out. I realized he wasn't the only person with perspiration running down the face.

CHAPTER 35

I was alive, thank God and I suppose, thank Rocky. Now what? I was strapped to a chair in the middle of the kitchen. I couldn't use my hands or legs. The phone was in the other room and even if I could get to it, I doubted I was dexterous enough to nose dial. Frustration stuck me from all directions, yet again, I was alive, and I wouldn't have put money on my chances a few minutes ago.

I could scoot the chair a few feet. What would that accomplish? In movies, when the good guy's tied to a chair, he'd tip it over and manage to twist himself like a pretzel and miraculously escape the bonds. In the real world, I pictured myself tipping the chair over, smacking the floor, cracking my skull, and don't even think about the pretzel thing. I needed to come up with Plan B, Lord knows, I had time.

I could think of many things I couldn't do, but the one thing I could do was to scoot the chair across the floor. To what end? The steak knives Bob had given me were in the top drawer by the sink. They had remained in the drawer unused since Bob had given them to me. Unused, unless I count the one that had attached the note to my pillow. I could use my teeth to open the drawer; get my mouth around the handle of one of the knives. Then what? A knife in mouth is better than two where? *Enough foolishness, focus.* What I was certain of was there was no hope parked in the center of the room.

I inched the chair to the counter, careful not to tip over. Now what? I pulled the drawer open enough to get part of my head in and put my teeth around the plastic handle of one of the knives. My mouth slipped and I was afraid I'd slit my tongue. That would have been a poor introduction of the never-used blade to its intended use. On the second try, I got the knife out without drawing blood. I leaned up and dropped the knife on the edge of the counter. Well done, but worthless. Even if I got the chair turned around, the knife was still a foot and a half higher than I could reach. *Think, Chris, think.* I could use my Uri Geller-psychic powers and will the knife to float through the air and land in my hands so I could cut the binding. *Stop it. Get serious.*

I stared at the drawers and realized the next to bottom drawer opened at hand level. If I could get my knee close enough, I might be able to nudge it open.

I inched the chair closer to the counter, leaned as far as I could, and moved my knee to the side of the drawer. The tie around my ankles was digging into my skin and it stung more when I tried to get leverage to pull the drawer open. I failed.

I caught my breath and tried again. No better luck. I leaned back in the chair to conjure up another solution. None appeared. I had to keep trying.

The third time was more painful, but it was a charm. The drawer opened an inch. I hesitated to compose myself, and repeated the action until the drawer was open enough to have a chance to catch the knife. The knife was on the counter directly above the drawer. All I had to do was reach it with my mouth and slide it off the edge of the counter, watch it land in the open drawer, turn the chair around, grab the knife without cutting a finger off, and maneuver it around to cut the tie. Nothing to it. *Yeah, right.*

Problem. With the drawer open, I couldn't get to the knife without performing a circus act of balancing the chair on two legs while leaning over the counter to reach Bob's gift. If the chair slipped, I'd be screwed. If I slid the knife too quickly, it'd miss the drawer and land on the floor and out of reach.

Careful, Chris, I told myself as I leaned the chair to one side. It began slipping, and I quickly leaned the other direction to set it back on all four legs. I took a deep breath and inched nearer to the open drawer. Time to try again. My chin touched the knife and I nudged it closer to the edge. I said a silent prayer, and gave it another push. The knife not only landed in the drawer, its handle faced me. Proof that prayer, even a strange one about knocking a knife off a counter, worked. It also could have been pure, dumb luck. Either way, I'd take it.

After rejoicing over my knife-dropping act, I scooted the chair to the front of the drawer, turned it around, reached in the drawer, and put my tingling hand around the knife's handle. A minute later, I had cut through the tie. My hands were free. To think, Charles had said I'd never use the knives.

I rubbed my hands to restore circulation, and bent over to cut the strap that held my feet. I stood and almost fell when my legs gave way. I sat—fell—back down, caught my breath, and looked at the clock. I figured my ordeal had lasted a week or so. It had been less than an hour. I gave my legs a couple more minutes to recuperate and stumbled to the bedroom and grabbed the phone.

I tapped 9, another 9, then moved my finger off the keyboard. Rocky was rude, obnoxious, and guilty of killing Panella—in self-defense. He had stolen close to forty thousand dollars off the corpse, not to mention binding me to a chair. Still, he'd saved Barb's life, had been devoted to Dude, and had taken a risk by telling me what had happened. He'd had an hour to escape, but I figured if he had another hour, his chances of getting caught would drastically decrease. I owed it to Dude and Barb to give him the extra time. I grabbed a Diet Pepsi, moved to my recliner, and thought about how lucky I was to be alive.

———

"Lordy, lordy, what now, Mr. Landrum?"Officer Bishop said, as I greeted her at the door.

I rubbed my wrists and welcomed the way too familiar first responder.

"Good afternoon, come in please," I said, trying to allay any fear there was any immediate danger.

She stepped past me and looked around the living room. "Anyone else here?"

I shook my head. "Just us, Officer Bishop."

"Might as well go with Trula. I'm seeing you more than I'm seeing my husband. What's up?"

I began telling her about being tied up when the door flung open and Chief LaMond stormed in.

She did the same police gaze around the living room Officer Bishop had performed. "You okay?"

"Fine, now."

The chief glanced at Bishop and down at the red welts on my wrists. "Holy recipient of bad luck, do I need to post *Warning! Hazardous to your Health* signs in your yard?"

"It might not be a bad idea."

"Okay," the chief said, "What now?"

Officer Bishop interjected, "We were getting to that."

Cindy said, "Go ahead, Chris. I'm sure this will be a doozy."

I waved for them to follow me to the kitchen and offered them a chair.

"Would you like me to start with having a gun pointed at me, being tied up, escaping using my extraordinarily creative skills, or learning who killed Lawrence Panella?"

Cindy looked at Trula. "You did hear me say it'd be a doozy, didn't you?"

Bishop nodded at her boss and turned to me. "Who killed Panella?"

I was hurt she didn't want to hear about my trials and tribulations. I "entertained" the ladies by sharing everything that had happened, up to, but not including, giving Rocky the extra hour to get the hell out of Dodge, or Folly Beach.

Bishop reached for her notebook. "What does Rocky drive?"

"No idea. Don't know if he has a car?"

"What's his last name?" she asked.

I was embarrassed to say I didn't know.

"Did he say anything to indicate where he was going?" the chief asked.

"No."

Cindy turned to her officer. "Call Jim Sloan and get Rocky's name, address, and what he drives."

Trula said, "Jim Sloan?"

"Dude at the surf shop," Cindy said.

"Sorry," Bishop said. "Didn't know that was Dude's name." She went to the living room to call.

Cindy turned to me. "And he left you tied up, and alive, so you'd tell us he killed the hit man?"

"Yes."

"Why say anything? Why risk getting caught? You know we don't have any leads and saw the case getting colder by the day. It's now a popsicle."

"I think he overheard me talking to Dude. I had begun to suspect Rocky, Stephon, or both because of their loyalty to their boss. He figured I was getting close and wanted someone to hear his side. That someone was me."

"If what he said's accurate, it's self-defense."

"I agree. He felt his past would've clouded your version of what happened."

"Didn't give us cops much credit."

Officer Bishop returned to the room. "Got an APB out on Rocky."

"Good," Cindy said. "Now call Detective Adair and tell him he may want to mosey over. Chris, the walking, talking, disaster magnet, has an enthralling tale to share."

Bishop smiled and headed back to the living room.

Cindy shook her head and looked over at the drawer that was still open. "Want to show me your knife throwing trick before the hot-shot detective from the big city comes a callin'?"

"No."

Cindy chuckled. "Didn't think so." She put her hand on my arm. "You sure you're okay?"

"Better than I was."

The next two hours were spent with me repeating my ordeal to Detective Adair. I regaled him with my circus-like escape, although he didn't appear as impressed with my creativity and dexterity as I had been. I told him for what it was worth, I believed Rocky's story that he had killed Panella to save himself, and Adair told me my opinion wasn't worth much. I lied to him when on his way out I said I hoped they'd catch him.

My wrists were still red and stung from my escape attempt. My ankles hurt, but not as badly as my wrists, and I bounced between euphoria for being alive and learning who had killed Panella, and sadness that Rocky, trying to do a good deed, one of the few in his life, was wanted for murder, and when caught would face prison time unless he could convince the cops he was acting to save his own life.

And, there was still one huge unanswered question. Who hired Panella to kill Barb and had he or she hired someone else to finish the job? I gave it more thought before my body told me I didn't have a future as a contortionist. It was my last thought before falling asleep in the recliner.

CHAPTER 36

hree hours later, the phone rang. Had the police found
Rocky? The answer was not forthcoming, when I heard
the excited voice of my best friend blaring out a usual,
non-socially preferred, Folly greeting.

"Heather and I met Starr. She's going to cut a demo."

"Whoa. Hello Charles, how are you?"

"Huh? Oh, fine, gee. Listen, this is exciting."

I started to interrupt and share what had happened to me. I
wasn't certain, but thought it would beat whatever he had to say. I
knew not to waste words until he'd wound down.

"Start over. Demo?"

"It's great." Enthusiasm spewed from the speaker. "Heather and
I met Kevin Starr. He's excited and said she needs to get her voice
out to record execs—that's how he talks. He said she needs to cut a
demo record, tape, digital thingee, whatever they do now."

"That's great," I lied—the second bigee of the day.

"Yeah, except it'll cost $2,900. She's got $735 unless she sells her guitar, which'd defeat the plan. I can make up the difference, but it'd lop a big chunk off my estate."

"Did she sign a contract with Kevin Starr?"

"Yeah. He's officially her agent."

I knew little about the music industry and wondered what Starr's responsibilities were. It seemed strange Heather would have to pay for everything.

"Why does she have to pay for the demo? If Starr's representing her, shouldn't he cover it?"

"You're asking the wrong person. I know as much about this stuff as I know how to teach a camel to sing. What I do know is Heather's on cloud thirty-seven. She zoomed past cloud nine, as soon as she stepped in Starbucks and saw Starr sipping a latte."

That's what I was afraid of.

"When's the demo going to be cut? When does she need the money?"

"Day after tomorrow. Something about needing to reserve the studio and stuff. Starr says he can pull strings and slip her in ahead of some of the famous singers booking the studio."

Had Charles realized how ridiculous that sounded, or was he getting caught in Heather's draft?

"Does it make sense Starr could move her ahead of popular artists?"

"Chris, even if I wanted to, I couldn't stop her with a ten-foot-high concrete wall topped with barbed wire. It's her dream."

I felt uneasy, yet told him I understood. I added I had a story to share and proceeded to tell him about my day and Rocky's confession. "When were you going to tell me? Was I going to have to read it in the *Tennessean* or hear it on CNN? Was—"

"Charles, it just happened and what part of your story were you going to let me interrupt?"

"Picky, picky, picky," he said as if it he was trying to make some illogical point. "Tell me again how you flipped the knife and didn't slit your wrists?"

"Never mind. Don't you wish you were here to share the excitement?"

He didn't say anything for a minute and then whispered, "Yes." There was another pause before he said, "Gotta go. Heather wants to go to Walmart to get a new outfit to wear for her demo session. Try not to get killed and stay away from sharp objects." The phone went dead.

Now there were two things bothering me in addition to a cut foot, sore wrists, and ankles. While I doubted Cal could do anything for my sore body parts, he was the closest person I knew to the music industry. I walked three blocks to his bar. To say Cal's midweek crowd in February was light would be like saying a candle might not illuminate Times Square. There were two of the town's better-known drunks at a table in the corner discussing the economic advantages of Budweiser over Miller; and a young couple at another table who appeared more intent on caressing each other's arms, back, and lower extremities than listening to Waylon Jennings regretting something on the jukebox.

Cal stood behind the empty bar and was nodding his head in time with the music.

"Howdy," he said and tipped his hat in my direction. "A glass of California's finest?" he asked as he reached for a bottle of red wine.

If what Cal served was California's finest, the Golden State better gear up production of walnuts and Napa Valley better rip out its grapevines and start planting marijuana. Regardless, I nodded as he set a glass of wine in front of me.

Cal leaned on the bar and cocked his Stetson back on his head. "What brings you out? Doubt it's to peek at my packed house or listen to Hank Snow."

I shared what Charles had said and asked for his thoughts on Kevin Starr and the demo session.

"Be back," he said, grabbed a couple of Budweisers and took them to the drunks. He returned with four empty bottles. "Sorry. When they finish those, I'm shooing their soused selves out of here. They ain't driving so all they can hurt is each other on the walk home. If they weren't here, they'd be in another bar."

That was more than I wanted to know. I could tell Cal had mixed feelings about how to deal with them.

Cal gazed at the men and turned back to me. "Know how many star-struck, dreaming, country-music-star-wannabees plane, train, bus, drive, or thumb to Nashville each year?"

"How many?"

"Don't have the foggiest, but it'd fill cattle cars seven miles long. Know how many vulturin' fake agents, record producers, and talent scouts are waitin' for the wide-eyed, narrow-brained wannabees?"

I wasn't going to let him trick me again. "Seventeen thousand."

"You made that up," my astute friend said.

"Yep. How many?"

"Hell if I know, but you could be close. Without getting too numbery, it's a feed trough full of them."

"Do you think Starr is trying to rip Heather off?"

"Let me put it this way." Cal looked at the ceiling, over at the lovers, then at me. "Charles moseyed over to Music City with Heather. Heather's got herself an agent. The agent wants to make her famous."

He paused and waited for me to nod. I accommodated him, and he continued. "It's the same Heather who's performed a bunch of times on that stage."

I nodded again.

"And you've heard her. You heard her doing what she calls singing?"

I gave one more nod.

"Did Agent Starr strike you as tone deaf?" My head went the other way this time. "That answer your question?"

I was afraid it did. I tried one more possibility. "Could Starr hear something in her voice that shows potential?"

Cal shook his head and put his fist to his forehead. "Yes. He hears her song of desperation, her dream, and the sweet ka-ching of his cash register."

I told him about her appearing at the Bluebird for open-mic night and asked if anything good could come from it.

"Depends."

"On what?"

"The Bluebird's open-mic nights are for songwriters. They're hawking songs, not their singing. A good singing voice ain't a gift God bestowed on many writers. If Heather was there to plug her ditties, and someone liked them, she could sell a song or two. Songwriters have used the Bluebird's tiny stage to leapfrog successful writing careers. It's possible one in a zillion kicked off a singing career there."

To my knowledge, Heather had written two songs, and they weren't anything to kick her to a higher tax bracket. Her sole reason for going was to find fame as a performer. Cal also said Starr should be fronting the demo fee, and even if he didn't, for what Heather needed, it shouldn't cost more than half of what he was charging. Cal said there were millions to be made in Music City, although newcomers were often on the spending end. Regardless how we tried to spin it, we decided Heather's chance of achieving anything beyond emptying her bank account was no better than Cal being elected into the Rock and Roll Hall of Fame. We also concluded there was little, if anything, we could do to dissuade her from moving full-speed ahead. I told him I would let Charles know what Cal said about the cost of the demo. After that, it was up to Charles and Heather.

"Another question?" We had exhausted our fame for Heather discussion.

"That'll cost you another glass of vino." Cal filled my empty glass. The couple of lovers had taken their laying on of hands to another venue and the town drunks had staggered out. From the jukebox, Tom T. Hall was telling us how much he loved beer, and Cal and I were the only occupants of the tired bar.

"Do you know a man named Sylvester Lopp?"

"Takes a mighty strung out woman named Lopp to name a kid Sylvester, don't it?"

I nodded. "You know him?"

Brenda Lee was singing "Big Four Poster Bed," Cal was pushing his Stetson farther back on his head, and taking his time answering. "Sure."

"You do?"

"Yep."

"Tell me about him."

"He's a salesman. Sells those imitation Tupperware containers you see at groceries and dollar stores. Or, that's what he says. The boy does have a strange way about him. Sometimes it looks like he should be talking and he's not. A little shy, I think."

"Known him long?"

"No. Started sipping a brew or two the last couple of months, maybe not that long. Why?"

"He'd been in Barb's Books a few times and she thought he seemed strange."

The room got silent and Cal smiled. "Makes sense." Cal went to the jukebox and punched in a few numbers.

Jim Reeves began "He'll Have to Go," and Cal moved to one of the tables and pointed for me to join him.

"These old clodhoppers don't keep the feet from painin' like they used to."

I waited to hear why Lopp's visits to Barb's Books made sense, and motioned for Cal to continue.

"Sylvester's single, divorced, been that way for three years. Born in Missouri. I'm not a good judge of age, but I'd say he's in his late fifties, early sixties. Anyway, I think he's got a crush, or whatever you call it when someone that old's likin' someone." Cal smiled. "Think the boy's besotted with Barb."

"Why do you say that?"

"Let's see." Cal said, as he took off his Stetson and looked in it like it was full of tea leaves waiting to be read. "His first time in he asked if I'd been in the bookstore. I said no, reading ain't my thing. Second time he asked me if the bookstore lady was hitched. I told him I didn't think so. Next time I saw him, he was right over there." Cal pointed to the stool at the end of the bar. "Heard him ask Chester the same things about Barb. I didn't hear all they said, but remember Chester saying, 'Go for it.'"

That would explain Lopp's visits to the bookstore. Could he have been working up the nerve to ask her out? It had never made sense if he was hired to kill her he would be that conspicuous.

"Know where he lives?"

"Must be around here. This ain't the neighborhood bar for folks in Idaho."

"Anything else about him?"

"Good tipper."

"While we're alone, let me ask another question?"

He rolled his eyes. "Charles may be in Music City, but a hefty bunch of his nosiness has rubbed off on you."

"Someone's got to do it. What do you know about Rocky, the guy who works for Dude?"

"As much as I want to know, and that ain't much. He's been in here twice I know of. Seems like a hateful little prick. Demanding and gave my regulars the dirty eye like he thought they were covered with jellyfish. If he has friends, which I doubt, they weren't with him. Why?"

"Wondering," I sipped my drink and looked down in the glass. "He pointed a gun at me today, tied me to a chair, and told me he shot the hit man who came to town."

I peeked at Cal who was staring at me like I had recited the Declaration of Independence in Hungarian.

"Holy heifer. When were you going to fess up about that?"

I smiled, and felt good I still could after my day. I gave him an abridged version of Rocky's visit and what he had told me.

"He telling the truth?"

"Think so."

"So Bookstore Barb was the hit man's target?"

"Yes."

"So who hired the hit man?"

"Don't know, but I'm going to find out."

"How?"

"No idea."

CHAPTER 37

Overnight, the bottom dropped out of the thermometer. I awoke after a fitful sleep, with the temperature hovered around freezing, several degrees below average. I was surprised when Karen called and said she had to go in to work late and wanted to come over and walk on the beach. I was more surprised when she said she'd be at the house in a couple of minutes, and less than a minute later she was at the door.

She looked more like she was heading to the North Pole than to the beach. She wore a black barn coat, a wool, red and black plaid, Tilley Aviator hat I'd given her a couple of years ago, black jeans, and old boots, the kind that'd be more at home on a ranch rather than a fashion magazine. I asked if she wanted coffee and she looked at her watch and said she didn't have time. I grabbed my heaviest coat and my hat and followed her. I tried not to venture out when it was this cold and didn't have appropriate outerwear.

We walked to the beach and limited our conversation to the weather and how deserted the streets were. My fellow residents had more sense than the two of us. The palmetto trees were shivering in the wind along with me. Other than a lone walker, we had the beach to ourselves and Karen turned left when we reached the shoreline. We nodded to the walker as we crossed paths. Karen started to say something and hesitated.

We walked a few more yards and she said, "I've decided."

I couldn't imagine her wanting to be out here in this weather if her decision was to stay. The icy breeze off the ocean felt like daggers of ice blowing right through me. A deeper freeze grabbed my heart.

"You're taking it," I said and looked toward the ocean.

I didn't want to look at her when she answered. "Yes."

I mumbled, "Congratulations."

She reached over and grabbed my arm. We stopped.

"Chris, I can't pass it up. I don't know how much longer I could keep doing what I'm doing. It's a young person's game and I'm… well, I'm not getting younger. I'm good at catching bad guys, although it's getting more difficult and frustrating. I'm not only battling criminals, I'm fighting with the courts, attorneys, the bureaucracy, and infighting among the various outside departments, crap, even my own office." She pulled her coat tighter and leaned closer to me. All I felt was her pulling away.

"It's too good to turn down. You deserve it."

"If it was nearby, I would've accepted in a heartbeat." She sniffled.

Maybe it was the cold.

"Leaving Dad and … you … never mind. It was the hardest thing I've had to do."

"Hey," I said with little enthusiasm, "it's not like you're moving to France. It's just a couple hundred miles away."

She smiled, with equally little enthusiasm, and said, "A little ways up the road."

I looked at the frigid, breaking waves, and back at her. She had wiped the tears from her cheek and put her arm in mine.

"I'd love to say I'd move to Charlotte." I hesitated, then continued. "I can't, my life is here. This is what I dreamed about forever. My friends are here." I hesitated and cringed thinking about Charles being gone. "I'm sorry."

She squeezed my arm. "I love you. Like I told you before, you wouldn't be happy and that would kill everything. Besides, the company has seventeen locations, one's here in Charleston and another in Savannah. I'll be traveling with the job and some of those trips will be nearby. We'd be able to see each other. That way—"

She put her head against my shoulder and her arms around my waist. Her body shook and I thought I heard sobs through the icy wind. We stood for several minutes, neither of us wanting to move. We had seen less and less of each other the last six months and she had talked more about our age difference. I had known it was a problem from day one, and had hoped, possibly unrealistically, that it was a minor issue. If I was fifteen years younger, I would look at moving. I would look at a long life ahead of me with options. Now, I knew I won't be around for many more years and change becomes more difficult. Karen needs to move on with her life, and the new job will provide her the financial stability a single woman on a governmental salary can only dream about.

"Charlotte's not that far away," I said. We were both mature enough to know I was lying.

She pushed away from me. "I have to go to work. Let's get back."

When she called, I had hoped to be able to share what had happened yesterday and talk through the situation and see if the detectives had more leads on who may have hired Panella. That was until I saw the look on her face as she stood in the door. Now wasn't the time to bring it up. Besides, I was freezing.

Karen kissed me on the cheek as she walked me to my door and headed to her car. The temperature in the house was forty degrees warmer than outside, but the chill from the walk and her announcement stayed with me the rest of the morning.

CHAPTER 38

Avoidance had long been one of my go-to defense mechanisms. After spending the best part of the morning thinking about how I felt about Karen leaving, the prospect of moving to Charlotte to be near her, or proposing, and her possible reactions, I had to switch gears else I'd go crazy or ram my fist through the wall. I began running through everything I knew about the threat to Barb. It didn't take long once I realized I knew almost nothing about why someone was out to get her, or who it might be. It seemed obvious that it was about her life before moving here. Her husband was involved in crimes that involved millions of dollars. Barb said she didn't know what was going on; the police believed her or she would have been indicted. Yet it seemed someone didn't buy her story and felt she was a threat.

I fixed more coffee and moved on to something that had bothered me for days. Who had broken into in my house and why? Then, while replaying the conversation with Rocky, I began to feel more confident about what I had speculated about the other day. The person who hired Panella must think I have the money he'd paid the hit man. The police hadn't found it on the body, nothing was found in his car, not much in his hotel room, and no one knew Rocky had pulled the trigger. I would have been the logical person to have killed Panella and taken the cash.

If true, the person who hired Panella would have been in the area, at least the three times my house was violated. And, according to Rocky, Panella said he had to meet at someone's house. The person who wanted Barb dead was not in Pennsylvania, but here.

My cupboard was bare so I headed to the Dog for a late lunch.

The restaurant wasn't as empty as the beach had been, but it was close. Three tables were occupied; two with regulars and the third by Jane Campbell, a lady who owned several rental properties but whom I had seldom seen in the Dog. Her arm was in a sling and her head buried in the morning's *Post and Courier*. Amber saw me and waved for me to sit wherever I wanted, so I headed to my favorite booth.

She delivered meals to a nearby table and brought me coffee. "Afternoon." She frowned. "You look like someone ran over your Corkie. You okay?"

"Rough morning."

She grinned. "Someone break in your house again?"

I smiled. "Not this time."

She took my order, brought it to the kitchen, returned to the table, and looked around the restaurant and didn't see anyone needing her attention. She slid in the booth.

"Give." she said.

Despite being friends, I was uncomfortable talking with her about my personal life. My friends didn't have that reservation and kept her updated on everything that went on with me. I'd often kidded she knew more about what was happening to me than I did. I had only been half kidding.

"Karen is taking a job in Charlotte."

"Oh."

For once, I shared something that someone hadn't already told her.

"You going with her?"

I shook my head. "No."

"Oh."

That was as close as Amber comes to speechless.

"We'll see each other from time to time. The company has an office here and she'll be back."

Amber waited for me to continue. I didn't, and she said, "They say absence makes the heart grow fonder. From what I've seen, it makes it hell on relationships. If you don't mind me saying, I don't see it working. Maybe it will at first, but not for long." She shrugged. "I'm being honest."

"I know, and don't disagree. Folly is my home and I can't see leaving."

"I don't know about the new job and why she's taking it, but I'll tell you what I do know. I'm butting in. If you want to hear it, I'll tell you."

"Amber, I've known you longer than anyone here. I always want to know what you think. I don't always agree, but ..." I smiled.

"Here it is. You're one of the most regular regulars in here. You're in a couple of times a week or more and you're my favorite by far, and that's not because you're that great a tipper. Anyway, I hear bits and pieces of your conversation with folks and I've got to tell you, you've talked less and less about Karen, and I honestly can't remember the last time she was here with you."

"Okay."

"That tells me there's drifting going on. Could be you drifting away from her or her from you; either way, something's coming on, and it hasn't been wedding bells."

I hated to admit she was right. Regardless, I didn't want to talk about it. I glanced over at Jane.

"What happened to her?"

Amber leaned closer. "She fell down the stairs of a rental she owns on West Huron." She leaned even closer and whispered. "Hear she was a tad under the weather, if you get my meaning. She missed a step. Was lucky to get off with a broken arm."

There was a reason Amber was one of the island's leading contenders for top gossip collector and distributor.

I nodded and Amber stood. "Let me grab your food."

A minute later she returned with my lunch and a question. "Speaking of accidents, do you know if Russ Vick was in a bad one?"

"Is he in a cast?"

"No, I don't mean recent."

"Why?"

She pointed to her forehead at the hairline. "Most times I see customers when they're sitting at a table and I'm looking down at them. I've got a great view of your bald spot a lot of people can't see."

"Thanks, that's what I needed reminding of."

She smiled. "My point, Mr. Self-Conscious, is Russ has a scar right about here." She again pointed to her hairline. "Most people wouldn't see it unless they were looking."

"You think it's from a wreck?"

"Suppose so. Don't know what else it could be."

"Yoo-hoo, Amber," called Jane from across the room as she held her coffee mug in the air with her good arm.

Amber smiled at Jane, hopped up, and headed to the coffee pot. I watched her go and thought about what she had said about Russ's scar. I then remembered something that had been said when Russ, Dude, and I were in here right after I had met the T-shirt store owner. I didn't think about it at the time, but he'd said Dude wasn't anything like Barb. That wasn't profound for anyone who had met the siblings, half siblings, but unless I was mistaken, Russ had said he hadn't had a chance to meet Barb. How would he have known they were different?

Until now, I hadn't given Russ a second thought in relation to the dead man. Other than both being recent arrivals to Folly, there was no obvious connection between the two. And, Barb first met Russ the day she and I were in here, and after he left, she said she'd seen him around town. Had he hired Panella? Hadn't Barb said when her husband was caught some of the people her ex had been in cahoots with had gone missing—like cockroaches when the lights came on. Could Russ be one of them? Thinking back on when Barb had met Russ, he didn't stay long and she didn't get a good look at him. Could the scar have been from plastic surgery to alter his appearance, rather than from a wreck? The full beard could add to his disguise.

Amber had refilled Jane's mug and was occupied with a family of four who had braved the cold for a hot breakfast. Russ had also made a point of sharing he had been in Las Vegas when Panella had been murdered. In hindsight, his revelation seemed unusual to be sharing with someone he'd just met. Could he have been planting his alibi for the time Panella should have killed Barb?

Despite a new look, Russ could have figured that with both of them on the small island and having businesses within sight of each other, she would eventually recognize him as one of her ex-husband's partners in crime; one of the partners in hiding.

I left my lunch unfinished, left a substantial tip for the lady who might have given me the biggest tip, and left the restaurant to start an Internet search for Russell Vick, current resident of Folly Beach, formerly of locations unknown.

A crick in my neck was all I got after an hour searching websites and references for Russell Vick, Russ Vick, and variations of the spelling of the name. He had said he was from Delaware, so I started the search there. There was no shortage of Russell Vicks on the Internet, and many of the sights had images of the various Mr.

Vicks, and even if he didn't have a beard or plastic surgery, none of them came close to looking like the T-shirt shop owner. I wasn't optimistic about the search since I figured if he went to that much trouble to change his appearance, he would have changed his name. It had been worth a try though, and besides it took my mind off Karen.

I had suffered another sleepless night before semi-focusing my eyes enough to brew a pot of coffee. As cold as it had been yesterday, I half expected to see a rare layer of snow outside my window. There wasn't snow, but the bleak grayness of the sky led me to believe today wasn't going to be warmer than yesterday. In the middle of the night, I had decided to call Chief LaMond and incur her ire by telling her my theory about Russ Vick. I knew she would call me every creative name someone from East Tennessee could call a jackass. In the end, she'd listen, and if a glimmer of what I said made sense, she'd investigate.

I was reaching for the phone to call the chief when it rang. "Guess what Heather got?" Charles said.

I didn't share his enthusiasm for a daily quiz. "What?"

"No guesses today?" He sounded disappointed.

I sighed. "Okay, a pet chinchilla."

"Not a bad idea, but no. She got the prettiest little red and white gingham dress you've ever seen. Found it at Stein Mart. You wouldn't believe all the stores they have here."

I had often thought Charles would be dangerous if he had a way to get around other than by bike. Nashville's retail establishments were getting a taste of my friend.

"For her demo session?"

"She wants to look her best when she's cutting it. 'Look good, sound good,' she says."

"Has she paid for the demo?"

"Tomorrow."

"Good. I talked with Cal about it. He—"

Charles interrupted, "Do I want to hear what he said?"

Doubt it, I thought. "Let me tell you and you decide."

He didn't respond, so I told him Cal's, shall I say, less than enthusiastic, opinion of what was happening to Heather and how he felt the alleged agent was playing on her ambition and ripping her off.

Charles listened, interjected a couple of comments along the way, and when I had finished, he didn't speak for a long time, until he said, "Cal's been around the block so many times he's worn the pavement off. I trust his opinion. I sort of have a bad feeling about Starr, but you know Heather. It'd take more than a herd of buffalo to stop her once she has her mind made up."

Charles was right, yet I felt I'd be letting my friend down if I didn't share what I'd learned.

"Tell you what," Charles said. "I'll tell my honey what Cal said. I'll even, gulp, tell her I agree with him. And if she hasn't already clobbered me with her guitar, I'll try to tell her I think it's best if we *temporarily* abandoned her dream and head home, home being Folly Beach."

I smiled. "Good."

"If she tries to throw me out the window, I'm going to tell her it was all your idea."

"That's what friends are for."

"Now that you've decided what I should do, have you figured out who hired the killer man?"

"Interesting you should ask. I think so."

Charles proceeded to lambast me for not calling him in the middle of the night with my theory. I told him I would have shared it at the beginning of this conversation if he hadn't been intent on giving me a fashion update. I got down to telling him everything I'd been thinking. He asked if I had proof, the question I would have asked him when he was on one of his tangents. I said no, and he asked what I was going to do. I said I was getting ready to call Chief LaMond when he called. He said he'd step outside so he could hear the chief's scream all the way to Nashville. I said thanks.

He finished by saying, "I hope to see you soon."

I refilled my coffee and called Cindy's cell. She was in her office and said she had a meeting with the mayor in ten minutes. She added, "Of course, whatever you have to say is much more important than meeting with my boss, so take your time."

It didn't take the entire ten minutes to lay out what I suspected. I finished and she didn't yell, probably because she was in her office.

"Chris, you never cease to amaze me—not impress me, not convince me, not even make me think you're making sense." I heard her sigh. "On the other hand, it's more than the super-duper, hotshot detective Adair has come up with. I'll give him a holler and do some nosing around. And hey, when it proves to be worthless and Adair says it's the dumbest thing he's ever heard, don't worry, I'll give you credit."

Cindy had her hands full with the usual day-to-day bureaucratic and personnel issues that she had to deal with her department, and would be tied up for the next couple of hours with the mayor. Even if she got time to call Detective Adair, it wouldn't be soon, and from other things he'd said about my previous theories, he may not give credence to what she'd tell him. Barb's life was in danger, and my house was becoming a hangout for unwanted visitors, so I didn't have the luxury of waiting for something to happen. I needed to talk with Barb, so why not over a meal?

I reached for the phone, still warm from my previous two conversations, and called Barb's Books. After four rings, I had begun to wonder if she was there, but then she answered. I told her who I was and was pleased when she said she recognized my voice. I asked if she was free for supper. She hesitated, then said she needed to eat. We agreed to meet at Loggerhead's since it was across the street from her condo and close to my house. After I hung up, I wondered why I didn't go to the bookstore to talk to her. Oh well, I too had to eat.

I was standing at the steps leading to the elevated restaurant when Barb rushed across the road from her building.

"Is it always this cold in February?" she asked, as I met her in the restaurant's parking lot. "I moved here to get away from icicles hanging off my nose."

I smiled, not only because she was a pleasant sight in her black leather jacket and dark-gray wool fedora with a narrow red band around the crown, but because she'd already fallen prey to not greeting people with common courtesies.

I explained it was exceptionally cold this year and most winters she wouldn't have to worry about icicles.

"Good," She jogged up the steps.

Loggerheads, like most restaurants on the island in this weather, was nearly empty and Ed, the owner, said for us to sit anywhere. We settled in a booth along the wall and a waitress took our drink order. Barb asked for a gin and tonic with a brand of gin I'd never heard of. Neither had the waitress who said she'd see if they had it. She returned and said no and Barb ordered a Loggerhead's Draft, a step down from a gin and tonic, yet a drink the waitress was certain she could find. I stuck with the house Cabernet.

Barb took off her heavy coat to reveal another bright red blouse, her trademark color, and said, "Something tells me your invitation wasn't social."

"I confess, you're right. There is something, although I could have done it on the phone."

"Hmm." She watched the waitress return with our drinks and ask if we were ready to order.

I looked at Barb and she shook her head and I told the waitress we needed a few minutes.

I sipped wine to stall and figure out how to ease into a discussion about Russ Vick.

She took a long draw on her beer and gave me a look that would have intimidated a hostile witness in court. "What is it?"

"Have you had much contact with Russ Vick?"

She tilted her head. "Russ Vick?"

"The T-shirt store guy."

"Folly Tease and SML Shirts. Just met him once, at the Dog. You were there."

"That's the only time?"

She frowned, uncomfortable with my line of questions. "Why?"

Might as well hit it head on. "I've got a theory." I held out my palm. "It might sound ridiculous, and I'll admit, it might be, but I think he hired Panella to kill you."

She took another sip and shook her head. "It doesn't make sense. I've had one, thirty-second conversation with the man. I don't know anything about him other than he caters to kids, kids of all ages, who think suggestive comments on their T-shirts are cool. What makes you think it was him?"

The waitress returned and we each ordered flounder and I began my convoluted story of why I thought Vick instigated the hit. Barb's laser focus was on me the entire time, and I suspected if she had pad and pen, she would have taken notes. I was not accustomed to getting this far into a story without interruption, and began to wonder if I was so far off track it would take a search party to bring me back.

When I finished, I expected her to laugh and tell me how stupid my theory was. Instead, she looked around at the few other tables of diners and then at me. "I'm pretty certain my ex wasn't in bed with anyone named Vick, but he could've changed his name. I'd met most of the people he either bribed or had taken money from. Business was never discussed in my presence, thank God. I don't recall anyone who looked like Vick."

"Picture him without the beard, and with more wrinkles or with his nose looking different, anything plastic surgery could change."

She didn't respond right away so I hoped she was trying to make those adjustments. She shook her head.

"What about his voice? That's harder to change than hair or facial features."

Her eyes widened. "I didn't think about it until now. I do remember thinking when I heard him in the Dog that there was something familiar about it. I didn't give it a second thought, since I could have heard it around here."

"So it's possible?"

She closed her eyes and gave a slight nod. "You're saying of all the places in the world, I decided to come to the same island where one of my ex-husband's crooked colleagues moved to hide?"

I nodded. "It's a coincidence, but I've given it some thought. It's not as big a stretch as it might seem. Most likely, your ex-husband told his buddy Russ, or whatever his real name is, about Dude and Folly Beach. I remember the first time I talked to Dude about you, he mentioned he had visited you and Karl a couple of times and how your ex told him Folly would be a good place to escape the world. Russ also told me he hadn't owned a shop before moving here, but had worked for a large company in Delaware. I didn't ask, and he didn't offer the name of the company."

Our food arrived yet neither of us lifted a fork. Barb looked at the plate and back at me. "And you put all this together after a conversation with Dude?"

I smiled. "I've become decent at understanding Dudespeak. I didn't think about it at the time. It wasn't until a waitress mentioned the scars at his hairline. And when Dude's employee, Rocky, mentioned the killer had told him he was meeting someone at his house, I started thinking the person who hired him may be living here."

"Whoa. Back up. What's Rocky have to do with it?"

I realized she didn't know about my close encounter with Rocky and proceeded to tell her about my pointed contacts with him and what he had said about killing Panella.

"Holy crap," she said, unlawyerly. "And I moved here to get away from drama."

I smiled. "We have our moments."

"What are we going to do about it?"

"I've shared what I told you with Chief LaMond, and she's going to talk to Detective Adair. They have the resources to follow through and will be contacting you."

"Russ could have hired someone else to kill me," she said, more to herself than to me.

That reminded me about something. "True. Remember when you were worried about Sylvester Lopp? I was talking to Cal Ballew, a friend who owns Cal's Bar. He told me Lopp sells plastic containers and had been in the bar a few times. He'd asked Cal about you and Cal figured out Lopp had wanted to ask you out. Cal said Lopp was shy and that was why he had been in your store several times without saying anything."

Barb smiled. "Sy, that's what he likes to be called, came in yesterday afternoon. He bought three more books, stuttered a couple of times, and asked me if I was seeing anyone."

"Oh."

"Yeah." She chuckled. "I started to tell him it was none of his business, then didn't want to appear rude. I said no. He began sounding like Dude when he strung enough words together for me to figure out he was asking me to a movie. I had the feeling that if he wore a hat, he would have held it over his heart, got on his knees, before asking. He was so sweet."

"I'm glad he talked to you. Don't think you have to worry about him—being a hit man anyway."

She hesitated, twisted her napkin, and took a bite of fish. "Yeah, it's not him. Chris, I'm scared."

"I know." I put my hand on hers. She didn't pull away. "The police are good. They'll get it figured out now that they know how it could be tied to your past."

I wish I had as much confidence in the police as I told Barb. She shook her head like a dog shaking water off its back and started talking about how pleased she was with business and how much she was looking forward to the vacation season. We shared avoidance as a defense mechanism. I wondered what she had said to Sy's date request, and wondered why I had wondered.

We declined dessert and Barb said she'd had a long day and needed to get home. She halfheartedly fought for the check, but gave in and let me pay. We left the restaurant and I offered to walk her to her condo. She said it wasn't necessary, but protested less than she had about the check. Her condo was on the top floor of the four-story complex so I punched the button on the elevator. There were a handful of vehicles in the lot; a few permanent residents were the only people in the large building. As we waited for the elevator, it felt like we were in a wind tunnel as the icy ocean breeze whipped through. Barb leaned close to me until we got on the elevator and I pushed the fourth-floor button.

The elevator opened at the exterior walkway to her condo and the night went all to hell.

CHAPTER 39

Barb gave a high-pitched shriek and I took a quick step back, neither overreactions to the black, compact, Sig Sauer, semi-automatic pistol with a color-coordinated seven-inch silencer pointed at us.

"I thought you were never going to leave," said the raspy voice of Russell Vick as he nodded across the street toward Loggerhead's. "You're going to give me the death of a cold waiting out here." He smirked.

I didn't see any humor, nor did I see anyone else on the windswept walkway.

"I notice you're shivering, my dear. Shall we go in your condo?" He waved the pistol toward the door.

It took Barb three tries before her hand was steady enough to open the lock. Russ stood far enough away that I couldn't reach the gun. Still no one appeared on the walkway, and from the few cars in the lot, I doubted anyone was nearby.

Once inside, Russ ushered us down the corridor to the living area. The door closed on its own. He waved the pistol for Barb and me to stand close together and he leaned on the granite counter separating the kitchen from where we were standing.

"Mrs. Deanelli, you've caused me many sleepless nights." Russ faced Barb, yet pointed the gun at me. "I spent most everything I had getting work done on my face, growing this miserable beard, changing my name, and moving to this, as your idiotic brother Dude, says, 'Hidin' spot from *el mundo*,' to get away from your husband, and the feds." He pounded his fist on the granite counter. "Then you show up."

I didn't doubt his intentions. Barb and I would never leave here alive unless I found a way to get to the gun. To do that, I had to buy time.

I said, "So you hired someone to solve your problem, and made sure you were out of town when he was supposed to kill Barb."

Russ grinned. "Vegas is nice this time of year. Who would've thought you'd shoot the guy? Thanks a hell of a lot, Landrum."

I caught a glimpse of Barb's head jerk toward me.

"You figured I'd shot Panella and took your money. You broke into my house to find it. Nice touch, leaving the note to throw me off from thinking you were looking for money."

He glared at me. "I'm not rich. It took all I had to remodel my body and get the stinking T-shirt shops. Panella took forty grand from me. I gave it to him the day I left for Vegas and two days before he was supposed to earn it." He waved the gun toward Barb, but I was still too far away to do anything. "I heard the cops didn't find my money on the body, in his car, or his hotel. You've got it."

Here's a way to buy more time. "Panella had no use for it." Barb continued to stare at me.

"Where is it?" Russ asked.

"Sorry. Don't see an upside of telling you."

"Your call." He pointed the weapon at Barb.

I had to think quickly if we had any chance of leaving here alive. "Shoot her and kiss your money good-bye."

"Where is it?"

"If I told you, you'd still never find it."

"Try me."

"Have you heard the stories about pirates burying treasure on Folly?"

Russ nodded.

"People have looked for it for decades. No one's found it."

"You buried my money?"

I nodded. Now what?

He looked at Barb, back at me, and pointed the gun toward the hall to the door. "Why would you bury it? That doesn't make sense."

"I didn't until you broke in the first time." I remembered the recliner was the only thing that hadn't been disturbed. "I had it with a stack of magazines under my recliner."

"Shit. You're kidding."

I grinned and hoped to keep him talking. "It was still there after the first break in, so I figured whoever broke in might try again."

"So you buried it?"

"Yep."

He glanced at the floor and gave a slight nod before returning his stare at me. "Then let's dig it up." He motioned us to the door.

Yes. A glimmer of hope. I still didn't know how I was going to get his weapon.

Barb opened the door and Russ lowered his gun hand so no one would see him holding us at gunpoint. It wasn't necessary since there was no sign of life on the outside walkway and the temperature was still dropping. I couldn't imagine anyone being nearby.

Russ stopped Barb. "Don't try anything stupid."

She turned toward the elevator with me close behind.

"No!" screamed a voice behind Russ. Then someone rammed the gunman in the back.

Russ stumbled forward. He regained his balance, twisted around and fired two shots at the person who'd shoved him. The silenced handgun still sounded as loud as a jackhammer. Russ turned back to Barb and me.

At first, I was too stunned to move, but knew this may be my only time to take the offensive. I shoved Barb in the open elevator and swung around to knock the pistol away.

Russ was quicker. I deflected the gun as he pulled the trigger. The sound was deafening and the bullet couldn't have missed my head by more than an inch. Russ, who was a couple of inches taller and outweighed me by thirty pounds, lowered his shoulder and lumbered into me. I sidestepped most of the blow. He stumbled again. I wasn't in great shape, but fortunately, I was in better shape than Russ. I knocked him sideways toward the edge of the walkway. His back hit the top of the waist-high railing. The gun flipped over the side.

Russ lunged for the weapon, missed, and glanced over the railing as the weapon bounced off the pavement. He glared at me. The distraction had given me enough time to swing at his head. He was moving toward me as my fist connected with his nose, increasing the impact of the blow. I'd never hit anyone in the face, and was jarred with the understanding why boxers wore gloves. Sharp pain radiated from my hand up my arm to my shoulder and it felt like the fillings in my teeth had been shaken loose.

Russ fared worse. He staggered sideways and smashed into the railing with all his weight. His feet left the deck. His body's momentum catapulted him halfway over the side and he teetered on the railing.

For a split second, I hoped he would fall before I grabbed him around the waist and pulled with all my dwindling strength. My left arm felt like it was being separated from my body. And Russ was still precariously close to falling four stories to the concrete parking lot.

I screamed for Barb's help. No response. The elevator door had closed and she was probably on her way to the bottom floor. I continued to struggle to keep Russ from falling, but was growing weaker.

My shoulder was killing me. The pain was so severe that I was ready to let go when Barb peeked out the elevator door and saw what was happening. She was still on the fourth floor, and moved to the other side of Russ and put her arms around his legs dangling on our side of the railing. She pulled, slipped, and quickly regained her balance and continued to pull. Russ flailed his arms. All they came in contact with was air. I yelled for him to hold still so we could pull him to safety. He continued to thrash around. My left arm felt weaker and I was afraid we wouldn't be able to stop gravity from taking him over the edge.

I glanced at Barb. She had a death grip on his legs and a look of determination on her face. I gritted my teeth, tried to ignore the pain in my shoulder, and pulled. Russ had finally stopped trying to escape, yet it still took several seconds for us to slowly pull him back from the railing. He flopped toward me and hit the deck. I grabbed his arm and twisted it behind his back before he could push his body up. Barb rammed her right foot on his back, and I continued to twist his arm so he couldn't wiggle out of the grip.

The sirens of two of Folly Beach's patrol cars filled the air and their brakes squealed as they skidded to a stop at the entry gate to the complex.

Officer Bishop was the first cop to the fourth floor and without saying anything cuffed Russ.

With Russ in restraints, I rushed to the body of the person who had saved us. I recognized the tat-covered neck, and yelled for Bishop to get help and knelt beside Rocky. He was breathing, yet struggled for each breath. Blood was pooling under his chest.

"Hurry!" I yelled.

Rocky moved his trembling hand to my leg. I moved closer. He was trying to speak.

He blinked a couple of times. "No one going to kill Dude's sis … couldn't leave her …"

"You saved her."

He closed his eyes. I prayed he'd heard me. If he had, it was the last thing he heard.

Officer Bishop, with the help of an officer I didn't recognize, had hauled Russ to his feet and to a patrol car. Chief LaMond had arrived, along with three EMTs from Folly's force. There was nothing they could do for Rocky. The chief suggested we would be more comfortable in Barb's condo, also knowing we didn't need to be outside with Rocky's body. The chief came with us, asked Barb where she kept coffee, and fixed a pot while Barb and I moved to the couch to regain our composure. Fortunately for each of us, her coffeemaker wasn't as high-tech as the one in her office. One of the paramedics gently maneuvered my arm back and forth and said that it was probably sprained. To me it felt like it was torn, ripped, and shredded. I struggled not to scream as he continued to manipulate my arm. He offered me a ride to the hospital. I declined, took a deep breath, and thanked him for the offer. He mumbled something about me being stubborn and told me I should get ice on it as soon as possible. He said he'd get an icepack from the ambulance and left the condo.

I assured the chief and Barb that I was okay, I spent the next ten minutes telling the chief what had happened, including my lying about stealing the money.

Cindy took notes, and I said, "How'd your guys get here so fast?"

The chief looked back toward the door. "A retired principal and his grandkids from Kentucky were eating at Loggerheads when you got there. The guy'd been standing by the window as you came up the steps and saw, and these are his words, 'a suspicious looking, slimy, young guy sneaking around outside.' Said the guy was watching you and Barb. After you ate and headed over here, the retired vacationer saw the guy hiding behind a pole, still spying on you. He figured the tattoo-covered guy was going to rob you and had the bartender call us."

I wondered how long Rocky had been looking out for Barb, how long he'd been watching to protect a near stranger because she happened to be his boss's sis. And, had given his life out of loyalty and love for Dude.

CHAPTER 40

The next hour lasted an eternity. At times, Barb's condo and the open corridor outside were more crowded than the beach on the Fourth of July. Crime techs, cops, EMTs double checking to make sure I was okay, Detective Adair, and a few others I didn't know, came and went. Other times, Barb and I were alone and struggled with anything to say to each other.

Dude barged through the door. "Be okeydokey, sis?" he said, as he gasped for air.

Barb nodded and Dude wrapped his spindly arms around her waist.

"Praise be to Sun God."

Dude unwrapped himself from Barb's waist and the two of them sat on the couch.

"I'm sorry about Rocky," I said. "He saved us."

Dude looked at the ceiling. "Rockster now be celebrating with his personal deity. He be goodest, orneriest surfer me know."

I was exhausted and had to get home and Barb seemed in good, albeit strange, hands with Dude. The pain in my shoulder was beginning to ease slightly, and I said I was heading out and Barb said she'd walk me to the door. I said it was unnecessary. She insisted.

We reached the door, she hugged me, and said, "Thank you."

I didn't let her know how much the hug hurt my shoulder, and pretended it was no big deal. I said I saved damsels in distress on a regular basis.

"Right." She shook her head and smiled.

Instead of falling into bed as soon as I stepped out of the cold, I called Charles. If he had heard what had happened from anyone else, he would be the next person in line to wring my neck, and it would be worse if I waited until tomorrow to call.

Somewhere after the fifth interruption with "you're kidding," third "no way," and umpteenth "you did what?" Charles settled down and let me finish.

"See why I can't leave you even for a few days," he said.

"That mean you're coming home?"

"Sweetie and I are talking about it. I told her everything Cal had said and she didn't throw anything at me. That's a good sign. Not sure yet. Call me when you know about Rocky's funeral."

That sounded hopeful.

I thought I'd been asleep for only a few minutes when someone pounded on the door. Daylight leaking around my blinds indicated I was wrong about how long I'd been asleep.

"Yo, Chrisster," Dude said as I blinked my eyes open. "Skip along with us."

I realized the '*us*' included Barb who was standing behind Dude. Both were bundled in heavy coats, hats, and smiles, and were more awake than I was.

Instead of doing what normal people would have done and asking where, what, and why, I said to give me a few minutes to get dressed.

Dude looked at my pajamas. "Be boss idea."

My arm felt better than it did last night, but still hurt. I took extra time pulling on my shirt and jacket, swallowed three ibuprofens, and told Dude to lead on.

Fifteen minutes later, Dude had ushered us to the end of the Folly Pier. It was cold, but last night's brisk wind had moved elsewhere and it didn't feel as frigid as it had been. Instead of sitting on one of the wooden benches at the end of the pier, Dude led us to the railing looking back on the Tides Hotel and Barb's condo building.

Dude said, "Me share tidbit not to be heard by copsters." He looked around like he was afraid a *copster* was hiding behind the steps leading to the second deck. No one was within three hundred yards.

"Rocky be bunkin' at *mi casa*."

"After he tied me up and said he was leaving town?"

Dude shrugged. "Be rude to do to Chrisster. Yeah, he no go bye-bye."

"You were harboring a criminal?" Barb said.

"No. Be bunkin' a bud."

"Why?" I asked, figuring an extended legal discussion between an attorney and Dude would be like talking thermodynamics with a hermit crab.

Dude looked at Barb and turned to me. "Rockster afearin' harm be visitin' fractional sis. Said not be letting that happen."

Dude bowed his head, leaned against the railing, and a tear rolled down his cheek.

"Rockster said gandering-out for sis be one good thing he ever do." He looked back at the beach. "Customers no be missin' Rockster, but should."

Barb put her arm around Dude and I inched farther away from the two so they could have their moment. So many emotions were racing through my head I nearly lost my balance. Karen was leaving. Charles may never move back. And, I was grieving over a man who had been nothing but rude to me most every time we had contact, not to mention strapping me to a chair.

Barb was saying something about Rocky's funeral and wanting to pay for it, so I stepped back to the two and asked if anything had been discussed about the funeral. Dude said Rocky didn't have any family and he was going to take care of everything and he figured it'd be in two days. Of course, he didn't use those words.

My phone interrupted Barb and Dude arguing over who would pay for the funeral. Barb seemed to think she had won and would be footing the bill, yet I knew once Dude set his mind to something, his sis—fractional or otherwise—wouldn't stand a chance.

"So when's the funeral? Heather and I don't want to miss it."

I started to remind my impatient friend that poor Rocky had only met his demise hours earlier, but instead told him what Dude had said.

"Good. Bye," he said.

"Charles," I said, hopefully in time to keep from talking to dead air.

"What? Heather's ready for breakfast."

I crossed my fingers. "Back for good?"

"Don't know," he said and hung up.

It wasn't what I wanted to hear, but it left room for hope.

Dude and I were on each side of Barb as we walked down the steps and off the pier. She put her arms around our waists, squeezed, and turned to me.

"Think we can do dinner again without almost getting killed?"

"Why not."

ABOUT THE AUTHOR

Bill Noel is the award-winning author of thirteen novels in the highly- popular Folly Beach Mystery Series. In addition to being a novelist, Noel is a fine arts photographer and lives in Louisville, Kentucky, with his wife, Susan, and his off-kilter imagination.

Bill lives in Louisville, Kentucky, with his wife, Susan.